TAMED

TAMED

Book Cover by Avelley Greer

First edition 2026

For the ones still becoming.

For everyone who was handed a map and chose to draw their own instead.

For the ones who refused to be tamed.

This one's for you.

CONTENTS

CHAPTER ONE

The lock gave beneath her fingers with a soft click, smoother than she'd expected.

Cassara didn't breathe. Not yet.

A gust of wind tugged at her coat as she slid through the narrow garden door, careful not to let it creak on the hinge. Beyond the frost-rimed hedgerow, the manor grounds stretched quiet and pale under the full moon, bathed in silver light.

She moved low, swift, steps silent against the cobbled path. The outer gates would be watched, but the perimeter sensor on the western wall had a known lag—seven seconds between pulse intervals. She'd timed it. Tested it. And unless the old bastard had upgraded his security system in the last two days, she had exactly *one* shot.

There was no room for hesitation.

The pack on her shoulders bumped against her spine as she broke into a run, sharp, controlled strides as she skirted the ivy-covered wall, heartbeat thudding like a war drum behind her ribs. It wasn't the first time she'd snuck out, but it was the first time she had no intention of returning.

Not unless she won.

She dropped into a crouch as the sensor flared, silver threads slicing the air above the wall's edge. One. Two. Three. On the fourth beat, she launched herself upward, boots scraping for purchase on the stone as her gloves caught the carved edge. Six. Seven. She vaulted over as the pulse flared again, just behind her heels.

A hissed breath. A triumphant grin. And then—

"Going somewhere?"

Cassara froze.

The voice came from the shadows to her right—smooth, cool, and far too amused.

She didn't turn. Not yet. Her stomach tightened with dread, with fury, with the slow-burning certainty that she'd been played.

Of course he'd known.

Of course he was waiting.

She turned slowly, every muscle locked in silent defiance. Her father stepped into the moonlight like a judge into the chamber, hands folded behind his back, his coat pristine, his face unreadable. No accusation. No fury. Just that steady, suffocating disappointment he wore like armor. Cassara's breath caught in her throat. Not because she feared him—never that—but because of what his presence meant.

He hadn't been sleeping.

He'd been waiting.

"You always did have a flair for drama," he said, eyes flicking to the pack on her shoulders. "Was it going to be a clean break? Or were you planning to leave a note?"

Cassara clenched her jaw. "Didn't think you'd care."

A pause stretched between them, filled with the rustle of wind through frostbitten ivy. Her father studied her the way a scholar might examine a flawed artifact: cold, detached, calculating. He took a step forward, and though Cassara didn't move, her spine straightened, chin lifting instinctively.

"I care about the family name," he said. "Which you are dragging through the mud. Again."

"You mean by not marrying the boy you picked out?" Her voice sharpened, laced with heat. "Or by applying to Vallemont without your permission?"

"Both," he said, without missing a beat.

Silence again. She hated how still he could be, how unaffected. Like none of this mattered, not really—not the threat of exile, not her dreams, not the fact that he'd cornered her like a criminal in her own garden.

"I'm not Mother," Cassara said, the words cutting through the cold air between them. "I'm not going to die out there."

His expression faltered.

Just for a breath. But it was there.

A flicker of something behind his eyes—grief, worn thin by years but still buried in the lines of his face. It passed quickly, tucked back beneath iron composure, but the crack in his armor lingered.

"She thought that too," he said. "But where is she now?"

Cassara swallowed. "Then let me prove I'm not her."

His gaze held hers, steady and sharp. "You want Vallemont? Fine. You'll go. But you'll do it on my terms."

Her chest tightened. "What terms."

"If you're not top of your class by the end of the year," he said, "you come home. No protest. No excuses. You'll marry Julian and resume your duties as the heir of Allencourt."

Her mouth went dry.

It wasn't a challenge. It was a life sentence, framed in velvet and iron.

For Cassara, Vallemont wasn't just an escape. It was the only path that hadn't already been written for her in ink and blood. It was reputation, legacy, freedom, a place where power wasn't inherited, it was earned.

The academy took the best. It forged leaders. Warriors. Strategists. Field tamers who could walk with beasts no one else dared approach. Cassara didn't just want the crest. She wanted the skill, the command, the knowledge to be more than ornamental.

She wanted to train as a combat tamer—not to stand beside someone powerful, but to be the one they turned to when things fell apart. For years she'd studied the curriculum in secret, memorized the elite programs, watched the victory parades from the shadows of embassy balconies.

And if she could rise to the top at Vallemont, if she could claim that place by merit and will, then no one—not her father, not Julian, not the name she'd been born into—could decide her fate ever again.

She hadn't risked everything to chase a dream.

She'd done it to prove she deserved to shape her own future.

"And if I am top?" she asked, voice low.

"Then I'll tear up the contract myself." His voice cooled again, retreating to its usual edge. "But if you fail, Cassara—if you disgrace this house again—you don't get to run. You fulfill your obligations."

She hesitated. "So this is what it takes to make you proud of me?"

He turned without answering.

Whatever softness had surfaced, it vanished in an instant. "Don't be late. The airship departs at nine."

Then he was gone, boots crisp against the stone, coat catching in the wind as the garden door closed behind him.

Cassara didn't move.

Not as his footsteps faded down the path. Not as the garden door clicked shut behind him. The wind tugged at her sleeves, colder now, though she barely felt it. Her pack sat where she'd dropped it, one strap tangled in the roots of the hedge, a smear of dirt darkening the edge of her coat.

Twenty-one years of her life had led to this: one chance to prove she was more than a bargaining chip in her father's political games.

She'd thought she was ready.

Ready to leave, to start over, to cut herself free from this place and everything it expected of her. She hadn't imagined he'd let her go so easily. She hadn't imagined he'd twist the knife so cleanly.

Top of her class.

Not just survive, not even excel. Win. Outperform every legacy, every scholarship prodigy, every politically groomed golden child in the first-year cohort. Fail, and the bars would close around her again—smooth, gilded, and inescapable.

She swallowed hard and rubbed a hand over her face. Her gloves smelled like iron and cracked leather.

Julian.

She hadn't let herself think too much about him. Not since the last time they spoke, when he'd tried to convince her it wouldn't be so bad. As if being kept, paraded, and sealed off from the world was some kind of prize. As if her freedom were negotiable.

He still thought he was her future.

Cassara's gaze drifted to the garden wall—the same one her mother had walked past, years ago, before boarding the airship that carried her to the front lines. There had been no body. No farewell. Only a sealed letter and the scorched remains of a crest badge that didn't even look like it had been hers.

Her father never talked about her.

Not really. Not the way Cassara remembered her. He carried her memory like a locked file—opened only when it served a point. He'd loved her once, maybe. But all Cassara saw now was the aftermath. The silence. The expectations.

"I'm not her," she'd said to no one.

But maybe part of him still believed she would be.

Cassara sank onto the low stone wall beside her pack and tilted her head back toward the sky. The stars were sharp tonight, scattered like broken glass across the dark. She searched them for something—an omen, maybe. A sign.

Nothing answered.

The manor was still wrapped in shadow when Cassara descended the steps, pack slung over one shoulder, boots echoing softly against the stone. She hadn't slept, simply returned to her room and waited until the sky had begun to pale, streaks of soft gray and lavender stretching over the eastern horizon. Dawn hovered just out of reach, the world caught in that breathless moment before it turned gold.

There was no sign of her father waiting to send her off.

She hadn't expected him to be there.

Still, some small, traitorous part of her had hoped.

Instead, it was the household staff who stood waiting in the entryway—lined in quiet rows, their heads bowed slightly in respect. Old Gerren offered to carry her trunk, which she'd left by the door hours ago. A young scullery boy handed her a tin of steaming tea with trembling fingers before scuttling away again. None of them spoke beyond hushed goodbyes, but their presence said enough. They had known her since she was small, taught her how to tie her first riding harness, mended the knees of her uniforms, cleaned the shattered glass when she'd thrown a paperweight at Julian's head.

At the front of the line stood Madame Brielle, her governess since she was six. Her spine remained impossibly straight despite the soft tremor in her hands.

"Do write," Brielle said, brushing invisible lint from Cassara's collar. "Even if it's only to say you're alive."

Cassara gave a faint smile. "I'll try."

The older woman's mouth twitched, caught somewhere between fondness and sorrow. Her eyes searched Cassara's face, as if memorizing it for the last time.

"You have your mother's fire," she said. "She would've been proud."

The words struck deeper than Cassara expected. She didn't trust herself to reply.

She only nodded, stepped back, and turned toward the waiting car at the end of the drive.

It stood tall and dark, lacquered wood inlaid with etched bronze, a lean-bodied carriage resting atop broad wheels wrapped in whisper-silent runic bands. Faint sigils glowed along the axles—subtle enchantments keeping the ride steady and smooth, even on rough terrain. Two mechanical lanterns flanked the front grill, each flickering with arcane light that pulsed in time with the steady churn of the motor-stone embedded beneath the driver's platform.

It smelled faintly of heat-treated brass and oilspun charm-ink.

The door swung open with a low, hydraulic sigh, the handle marked with the Allencourt crest.

Cassara crossed the gravel path, the hem of her coat stirring frost where it brushed the ground. She moved with purpose, the hush of farewells trailing behind her like smoke.

Just before she ducked inside, something shifted at the edge of her vision.

High above, in the window of her father's study, a curtain fluttered.

She paused.

The movement stilled as the drape fell back into place, leaving only glass and silence.

Cassara's jaw tightened.

She didn't look again.

Instead, she climbed into the carriage and let the door shut with a soft clunk behind her.

The station emerged from the thinning fog like a shadowed sentinel, built into the cliffs that overlooked the lower quarter of the city. Pale stone archways framed the docking platforms, their buttresses gleaming faintly with ward sigils and riveted iron. Lanterns burned along the rails in hues of gold and violet, casting long halos in the chill morning air.

The Allencourt car pulled to a smooth halt at the outer gates. An attendant in Vallemont livery greeted her with a shallow bow and a quick inspection of her summons scroll before waving her through. Cassara stepped down without assistance, coat swaying around her knees as she adjusted the strap of her pack.

She didn't pause to take in the view.

The airship towered ahead—sleek, armored, beautiful in its menace. It gleamed like forged silver in the light of the rising sun, its runes pulsing a steady rhythm across the hull. Twin stabilizer fins arched back from the stern like folded wings, and the engine core beneath thrummed with a quiet, restrained growl. She could feel the charge in the air, magic held in tight suspension.

Dozens of students and family members milled across the platform, a sea of uniforms and embroidered coats. Some were already posing for farewell portraits. Others clung to their parents in tearful embraces or traded excited chatter over the hiss of steam lines and the barked orders of dockhands.

Cassara moved through them like smoke, expression unreadable, stride cutting clean through the crowd.Until someone slammed into her shoulder.

Cassara stumbled, caught herself, and turned on instinct.

"Sorry!" the girl said quickly. She had a narrow frame and a knot of frizzy hair piled too hastily on her head, held in place with what looked like a copper beast-pin, unusual, handmade, definitely not standard issue. Her boots didn't match. Her pack was overstuffed and slipping sideways. But it was the eyes that stood out: wide, green, and quietly observant, like she was already filing Cassara away in some private ledger.

Cassara's mouth curled. "Try not to get trampled, will you? Better yet, do us all a favor and stay behind when the ship lifts. This place doesn't need dead weight."

"Right," she murmured, voice soft, but steady. "Thanks for the welcome." She dipped her head and hurried off. As she vanished into the crowd, something dropped from her bag and hit the platform with a soft clink.

Cassara paused.

It was a carved token, no bigger than her palm. Bone, from the look of it. Old. Worn. Etched with curling script and the faint outline of a beast's snout across the center. Not jewelry. Not decorative.

A trophy.

Cassara's stomach turned before she could stop it.

She'd had one just like it once. A talon from her mother's first corrupted kill, dark and curved, strung on a braided cord. She'd worn it every day like armor. Until the day it slipped from her wrist on a trade route stop, and her father refused to go back for it.

"You'll lose more important things in life," he'd said. "Better get used to it."

She'd cried for hours after. Quiet, because he didn't tolerate loud grief. But something in her had never forgiven him for that.

And now this girl had something like it, dangling carelessly from an unraveling satchel like it meant nothing.

Cassara crouched and picked it up before she could talk herself out of it.

It was heavier than it looked. Warm from the girl's body heat.

She stood, eyes scanning the platform, but the girl was already halfway across it, disappearing into the crowd.

Cassara moved to follow.

She didn't know why. Maybe to return it. Maybe to reprimand her for being careless. Maybe to prove to herself that she hadn't turned to stone completely.

She called out and the girl glanced back. Their eyes met, just briefly. And whatever she saw in Cassara's face made her flinch and bolt.

Cassara froze. A hollow, irritated breath escaped her.

"Why do I even bother?" she muttered.

And that's when it happened.

A sharp, panicked shout rang out across the platform, and a trunk the size of a small cart barreled toward her, wheels clattering over the metal grates. She caught a flash of sigils sparking wild across the side.

She was going to be crushed to death on her first day because some idiot had overloaded the stabilization array.

Cassara didn't even have time to drop the token before someone caught her around the waist and yanked her clear.

Cassara stumbled into a solid chest and shoved herself back just as the trunk slammed into the rail where she'd been standing. Steam hissed. Runes sparked. Somewhere behind it, a red-faced student flailed apologies.

But all she saw was *him*.

Tall. Broad shoulders. First-year cuff. His coat hung open, collar turned, one hand still half-raised like he expected her to need catching again. Sun-kissed skin, dark wind-roughened hair that looked like it had never obeyed a comb, and a mouth set in something dangerously close to a smirk.

He was confident. *Too* confident.

Cassara bristled.

"Careful," he said, lips curving into a grin. "I doubt we've even finished enrollment forms yet. Would've been a rough time to get crushed."

Cassara wrenched her arm free.

"I had it under control," she said tightly.

"Looked that way," he replied, clearly amused.

She narrowed her eyes. "If I needed saving, I'd have asked for it."

"Apologies, my lady, I didn't realize helping someone avoid catastrophic injury was such a personal offense." He tilted his head, studying her like she was the confusing part of a puzzle. "You always this charming, or am I just that lucky?"

Cassara's temper flared and she could feel her cheeks growing warm.

She wasn't blushing.

Definitely not.

"I don't remember asking for your opinion, either."

He laughed under his breath, not mocking exactly, but infuriating nonetheless. "Ungrateful and combative. Good to know."

"Cass!"

Julian's voice—low, urgent, *afraid.*

Then he was in front of her—hands on her arms, pulling her in. His grip was firm, warm, too steady for how fast his chest was rising.

"Are you alright? Did it hit you?"

He was already checking, her shoulders, her ribs, her hands. His palm skimmed her jaw, tilting her face toward him to catch the light. The proximity made everything else fall away: the press of voices, the clatter of carts, even the airship's low pulse. She could smell his cologne, something clean and familiar, laced with the faint spice of ceremonial oil.

"I'm fine," she said, but it came out soft. Unconvincing.

His brows knit. "You weren't moving. I thought–" He exhaled hard, mouth flattening. "Next time, maybe don't stand in the middle of the blast zone."

Her lip curled faintly. "Wasn't exactly a plan."

Still, she hadn't pulled away. Not yet. They fit too easily like this, like a worn-in pattern, a dance they'd repeated too many times to unlearn. His hand brushed a strand of hair from her face, a touch so familiar her heart stuttered before she could stop it.

"You scared me," he said quietly.

She let out a breath she hadn't realized she'd been holding and leaned into the touch, just for a second. "You always worry too much."

"Huh," he said. "Guess the whole 'I didn't need saving' thing has a time limit."

Cassara stiffened.

She turned.

The boy who'd pulled her from the path of the trunk stood a few paces off, arms loosely crossed. His posture was casual, but the set of his mouth told another story. He was watching the two of them like a brewing storm.

A few nearby students went quiet. Someone glanced up from their trunk. The space around them, once buzzing, began to still.

Julian didn't look at him. Not even a glance. Instead, he ran his thumb over the back of Cassara's wrist like he hadn't heard a thing.

But he had, she knew it he had, She felt the shift in him, saw it in the way his mouth curved with slow, deliberate precision. Not anger. *Control.*

"Gideon," he said at last. Not surprised. Not pleased.

The boy, Gideon, gave a slow shrug. "Wasn't planning to interrupt. But I figured someone should check if she needed a leash or a pedestal."

Julian didn't flinch.

Cassara's spine straightened. She didn't look at Gideon, she didn't need to. The edge in her silence said enough: *You're not important enough to answer.*

The tension felt magnetic, pulling the attention of half the platform now. A dockhand hesitated mid-step. Two second-years pretending not to eavesdrop suddenly had a great interest in their clasps.

Julian's voice dropped, intimate only in tone. "No name. No lineage. No sense of boundaries. Vallemont really is letting anyone through the gates."

Then his gaze slid to her, not fast, not sharp. Just there. A quiet, elegant possession.

"You don't touch what's mine. Not unless you're prepared to bleed for it."

Cassara's throat tightened. The words landed with the quiet weight of ceremony: measured, deliberate, meant to be remembered.

Gideon didn't blink. Didn't raise his voice. Just looked at Julian like he was calculating the effort it would take to break him in half.

"Say it all you like," he said, voice low and even. "The thing about threats is, the wrong one tends to get tested."

Julian's mouth twitched—tight, calculated.

"I don't recall asking for your opinion, Delvanir. Must be hard, watching from the edges while the rest of us make history."

Gideon's smile didn't touch his eyes. "Is that what you call it? History?"

His gaze flicked down to where Julian's hand still hovered near Cassara's waist. "Looks more like desperation."

Julian stepped forward, just half a pace, enough to draw a breath from someone nearby. "Careful," he said, voice a shade too smooth. "Legacies matter here, Gideon. Some of us arrive to uphold them. Others... spend their lives trying to erase them."

Julian's hand drifted to the small of her back again, casual and confident. The world was watching and he was basking in it.

"Come on. You've wasted enough breath on things that don't belong here." He turned slightly toward the gangway, every inch of his posture assuming she'd follow.

Gideon tilted his head, gaze sliding to Cassara for the first time since the standoff began. Not pity. Not interest. Just the faintest thread of cold amusement.

"Leash it is, then."

Cassara exhaled sharply. The token still pressed into her palm like a reminder that kindness could still cost her. She looked at Julian, at the claim behind his words, and wanted to scream. She looked at Gideon and felt her temper coil hotter for a different reason entirely.

She'd had enough.

"I don't belong to anyone," she said, voice flat, controlled, deadly. Her eyes slid towards Gideon, sharp, burning. "And I don't need a leash."

Julian reached for her arm. "Cass–"

She yanked it out of reach.

Without a word, she turned on her heel and stalked toward the gangway, the airship's hull humming with restrained magic and heat.. Her boots rang against the metal, every step driven by pride and fury and something she didn't want to name.

Let them talk and stare all they wanted.

She was done letting anyone else speak for her.

She was here to make them listen.

CHAPTER TWO

As Cassara climbed the loading ramp, their voices followed, Gideon's mockery, Julian's claims, and her father's ultimatum, all pressing down on her at once.

This school won't make you better. It'll just reveal the ways you fall short.

You don't touch what's mine.

Leash it is.

She clenched her jaw and pushed the words aside. They weren't worth remembering. Not here. Not now.

"Cassara?"

Cassara stopped and slowly turned to see Olivette Ashton pushing through a tight knot of students, cheeks flushed, eyes wide with delight. Her thick chestnut curls, which had been pinned up in a twist, were already sagging under the damp weight of steam and magic-charged air. Her Vallemont uniform was neat but a touch snug through the middle. Evie had always favored second helpings over appearances.

She beamed and Cassara felt the tension in her chest ease just a fraction.

"It is you!" she called out, breathless. "You actually came!"

Cassara raised a brow. "You sound surprised."

Evie's grin faltered just a little. "Well, we weren't sure if your father would let you go, we all know how against the idea he was."

"It just took a bit of convincing," Cassara replied with a casual shrug.

"And?"

"Well I'm here, aren't I?" She wasn't about to discuss the terms of her enrollment in the middle of the crowded deck.

Before Evie could respond, another voice glided in, sugar-dipped and far too smooth.

"Well, well. Look who's defying expectations."

Cassara didn't need to turn, she knew the tone. Sonia de Kere, poised and perfect as always. Her braid was woven with school colors, the crimson contrasting sharply with the honey blonde. Her makeup was flawless, and her expression held just enough warmth to pass for friendly.

If you didn't look too closely.

"Sonia," Cassara said, her smile thin.

Sonia gave her a once-over. "I honestly thought we'd be reading about your failed escape in the society pages." She laughed, light and sharp. "Evie nearly bet her first-year stipend on you."

Evie rolled her eyes. "It was dessert tokens, and only because I knew she'd show."

"Mmm. You're sweet," Sonia said, her smile stiff. "Sweetness isn't often rewarded here, but... admirable."

A moment later she gasped, lifting her hand to cover her mouth.

"Oh dear, what happened to your complexion?" Sonia tilted her head, studying Cassara's face with theatrical concern. "All those freckles... Did you spend the entire summer in the stables? There are creams for that, you know."

Cassara's jaw tensed. The freckles Sonia was so pointedly noticing had multiplied over the summer due to hours spent conditioning for Vallemont rather than hiding in drawing rooms giggling over tea. Cassara started to say as much, but Sonia's attention had already shifted along with the expression on her face.

"Oh," she breathed, pushing past Cassara. "Here comes Julian."

Cassara's stomach knotted and she could already feel the shift in the air around them, the way students subtly glanced his way, how space carved itself in his wake.

Sonia straightened, adjusting her collar. "He looks positively devastating in crimson, doesn't he?"

"Has he gotten taller since your birthday gala, Cassara?" Evie asked.

Cassara's hands slipped into her pockets. Her fingers closed around the smooth edge of the carved token like it was a lifeline.

She wasn't ready for another confrontation, not after the dock, not after the way he spoke like she was already his.

"Cassara?" Evie turned to look at her when she didn't answer.

"You'll have to ask him," she said, already stepping back, "Save me a spot at the railing will you? I need to return something."

Evie blinked. "Right now?"

"Before I forget."

Sonia tilted her head. "I'll be sure to keep him entertained in your absence."

Cassara didn't answer. She turned and slipped into the crowd, boots thudding against the metal grating as the din of the platform swallowed her whole.

She made her way inside and down a set up stairs. Wood creaked beneath her boots as she descended, the hum of the engine growing stronger with each step. The air felt heavier here, warmer, infused with magic and the smell of polished brass and something vaguely sweet, like candied citrus left too long in the sun.

The common room opened before her, a mismatched sprawl of first-day anxiety. Students were already vying for space, claiming window seats, spreading jackets across lounges, bickering over luggage carts and snack trays.

A cluster of upperclassmen occupied a row of velvet-backed booths near the rear, laughing too loudly and eyeing every first year who passed like fresh meat.

Cassara slipped through without drawing attention. Her hand was still buried in her pocket and the carved token tucked in her palm grounded her more than she cared to admit.

A cursory glance and Cassara spotted the girl almost instantly.

She was seated at a narrow window table, half of her enormous satchel upended across the surface. Books, scarf bundles, an old tin lunchbox, a cracked mirror charm, and what looked suspiciously like a faded stuffed phoenix chick lay scattered across the cushions. Her brows were pinched in panic, hands rifling through layers of haphazard clutter.

Cassara stopped beside the table.

"Looking for this?"

The girl froze.

Her head snapped up and the moment her eyes landed on the token in Cassara's hand, her entire face lit like morning sun breaking through storm clouds.

"Oh my stars, yes! Yes—I—thank you! Gods, thank you,"

Before Cassara could react, the girl pulled her into a crushing hug, arms wrapped around her like they'd known each other for years.

Cassara went stiff. "What are you—"

"You found it!" the girl said into her shoulder. "I thought I lost it for good! It's my great-grandfather's! He was the first tamer in our line and my grandmother always said I had to carry it when I started at Vallemont and—gods I can't believe I dropped it,"

Cassara peeled herself free, face burning.

"Okay. You have it now. Personal space."

The girl stepped back, sheepish but still glowing with gratitude. "Sorry. I get... excited. Thank you again. Really. That thing's survived three generations, two border crossings, and one accidental plunge into a fjord."

Cassara raised a brow. "Then maybe keep it somewhere it can't fall out."

"Yeah. That's fair."

She paused, then added, almost shyly, "I'm Liri, by the way. Lirien Halvorsen. I, uh, asked around. You're Cassara Allencourt, right? I wasn't sure at first, but... well. You kinda stand out."

"Do I?" Cassara tilted her head.

"Not in a bad way," Liri rushed. "Just... you know. Famous legacy. Your mom was the Ember Songbird. No pressure or anything."

Cassara offered a tight, noncommittal smile.

Liri gestured to the opposite seat. "You wanna sit?"

She hesitated. It was the way Liri had said it, like it wasn't weird and they weren't strangers. As if offering a place at her table was the most natural thing in the world.

For a moment, Cassara considered it, though she couldn't have said why. Until she caught sight of Julian ducking as he reached the bottom of the stairs and stepped into the common area. He was scanning the room, coat open, stance casual but unmistakably looking for her.

She straightened. "Another time."

Liri blinked. "Oh. Okay. If you're sure,"

But Cassara was already moving again, deeper into the ship's twisting halls. Away from the soft invitation and from the boy whose gaze she didn't want to meet just yet.

The corridor tilted slightly under her boots as the airship began its ascent, a low rumble thrumming through the floor and into her bones. Cassara moved without urgency, letting the curve of the hallways guide her.

She passed a viewing deck with an open arch of glass showing the sky behind them. She stopped and watched, arms folded, as the last edge of Ergemont disappeared from view.

For the first time in days she didn’t feel like she was running, she felt like she was gaining altitude.

She was free.

Cassara stood a few minutes longer before she let out a soft sigh and continued down the corridor, steps slower now as the hum of the ship deepened and the magelight lanterns along the wall flickered as if adjusting to her pace.

As she rounded a bend someone stepped out of a maintenance alcove directly in front of her. She pulled up short, stepping back only to knock her elbow painfully against the railing.

“Are you blind?” she snapped.

The stranger went still, his gaze leveling on her like she was the one who'd interrupted him. He was tall and lean, the black sleeves of his shirt rolled to the forearm, a dueling harness slung low across his back. His eyes beneath a sweep of black hair were a pale blue, cool and utterly indifferent.

He didn't respond, just stepped aside with a nod so curt it barely counted as acknowledgment, and started walking away.

Cassara scowled and called after him. "Most people say 'excuse me' when they nearly run someone over."

He didn't stop, he didn't even slow.

She took a step forward, annoyed. "Or is basic courtesy not taught wherever you're from?"

Still nothing, just the sound of his boots thudding against wood, steady and unbothered.

Her jaw clenched. "Fantastic. Another charmer bound for Vallemont."

He rounded the corner and disappeared.

She stood there a moment longer than she meant to, irritation curling beneath her skin like a spark that hadn't found air.

She'd spent her life learning how to provoke a reaction—from men, from teachers, from her father. A sharp word, a well-placed insult, a challenge they couldn't ignore. It always worked. Always.

But he hadn't flinched, hadn't even cared enough to sneer.

It served as a reminder that silence could be sharper than any insult.

Worst of all?

She hated that she cared.

The halls ahead grew more opulent—wood paneling polished to a high gloss, floors covered in thick, plush carpeting that muffled her step, and gently pulsating magelights that illuminated plaques etched with names.

Morvaine. Ellesmere. Straton.

She knew them all. She'd been raised alongside many of them, or rather their children. They mingled at every society dinner, every gala where bloodlines mattered more than skill.

This was the legacy wing, she realized, reserved for families who'd sent tamers to Vallemont for generations, whose children were expected to follow in perfectly polished footsteps.

Her gaze moved from plaque to plaque, steps slowing when she found it. Allencourt. The list beneath stretched back hundreds of years. She found her Uncle Ormand's name, marked retired, and then her mother's—Katrinel Allencourt.

She reached out and brushed her fingers across the polished surface, as though touch might somehow bridge the distance between them, this woman whose legacy was easier to recall than her face, her laugh, or her smile.

Cassara let her hand drop and stepped back.

There was no time for sentimentality.

She moved on, paying little heed to the other plaques and their prestigious lists.

Around the next corner a heavy oak door stood slightly ajar. The scent of steeped tea and honeyed fruits drifted out, warm and inviting. Cassara glanced at the crest embossed in the brass handle, an older Vallemont emblem, reserved for patrons, donors, and the highborn few.

She crossed the threshold allowing the door to whisper shut behind her, sealing off the hum of the corridor.

Inside, the lounge was all polished opulence, arched windows casting morning light across velvet seating, tables of etched brass and darkwood arranged in intimate clusters. Crystal trays glinted with stacked cakes, sugared fruits, and folded tea napkins that had probably never touched a spill. A runework kettle purred softly at the center of the refreshment cart, steam rising in elegant curls.

Cassara shrugged off her coat and draped it over a velvet-backed chair in a partitioned alcove near the window. She poured herself a cup of tea, light amber, floral, not too strong, and let the warmth soak into her palms.

This, at least, was familiar. Highborn spaces always were. Controlled and curated, tasteful to the point of sterility.

She settled into the cushioned bench, stretching, her boots scuffing against the leg of the table. One of the attendants entered only long enough to replenish a platter of fruit and bow slightly before disappearing again.

Cassara took a sip of tea, letting it sit on her tongue before swallowing.

Her gaze drifted to the sky beyond the glass. The clouds were thinning now, sunlight streaking through in pale ribbons as the airship continued its ascent. Somewhere far below them, the Allencourt estate sat cloaked in silence. Her father would still be in his study.

She wasn't surprised he hadn't come to see her off, but the curtain had moved. She hadn't imagined that.

For a second, her fingers stilled around the delicate handle of her cup. Maybe he *had* watched her go and he'd said nothing because anything less than a command felt like weakness, or because silence was easier than trying to name whatever fractured thing lay between them.

A familiar ache pressed behind her ribs.

Sentimental. She was being sentimental again.

Gods, she hated that.

She glanced across the table, searching for anything to distract from the heat building behind her eyes.

That's when she saw the paper.

A copy of the Aerithian Dispatch lay folded beneath a tea tray, its edges curled from use. She tugged on the edge until she could read the headline printed across the top in bold lettering.

"Western Patrol Lost, Two Vallemont Graduates Among Dead."

Cassara froze.

A drawing beneath it showed scorched earth and the charred remnants of a crest badge. The article mentioned a rise in corrupted beast attacks, another outpost under lock down, and unconfirmed leviathan sightings near the southern ridge where repairs were still underway from the last breach.

Her stomach twisted uncomfortably.

This.

This was the future waiting at the end of Vallemont. Not polished duels and prestige, this. Obliteration. She imagined herself in that uniform, holding her ground while the world burned behind her. And for the first time since boarding the ship, doubt curled cold around her ribs.

What if she had made a mistake?

No. She scowled at the thought, but it still dug in.

But still, what if her father hadn't been entirely wrong?

Vallemont won't make you better, Cassara. It'll only show you how far you fall short.

The memory needled sharper now, like it wanted to see her flinch.

And yet... something in them caught. Not the warning, but the challenge buried beneath it. The fact that he expected her to fail. That he was already waiting to say I told you so.

Cassara's hand clenched around her teacup. The sweetness had turned sour. She set it down too fast and the porcelain clicked sharply against the tray.

She wouldn't prove him right.

She wouldn't be another crest-badge buried in ash. Another girl remembered for what she could've become.

If this was what lay ahead, so be it.

She would meet it on her terms.

Turning away from the paper, her eyes landed on a painting hung just above the door, an oil rendering of one of the school's founders astride a gleaming drake, flame trailing from its throat like a banner.

It reminded her of her mother's flame-winged kestrel. It was said the fire it breathed was so hot it could carve stone mid-flight, that its cry alone could silence a battlefield.

Cassara remembered the stories and the way other tamers' voices dropped reverent when they spoke of her mother. The Ember Songbird. The beast that followed her had been feared and worshiped in equal measure.

A slow exhale escaped her. Would she be able to catch a beast like that? What if she was paired with something docile or decorative? A status symbol and nothing more.

She didn't want impressive, she didn't want obedient, she wanted something real, something fierce and unruly.

She wanted a beast that would choose her not out of deference, but defiance.

Her forehead fell to rest against the window, her breath fogging the cool glass.

Every inch of her body ached from tension, her mind worn thin from holding itself too tightly. She'd been up all night and it was finally catching up to her, but as much as she wanted to close her eyes, she didn't let herself unwind, not fully. The quiet, the tea, the soft flicker of magelight, it was all too clean, too composed. Just like this place. Just like the role she was expected to play.

She didn't hear the door open. Didn't register the soft hush of steps behind her until a breath brushed her ear.

"That look on your face," Julian murmured, his breath warm, amused, too close. "Should I hope you're thinking of me... or worry that you're not?"

Cassara startled. Not enough to let him see it, but enough that her body went rigid.

He was already sliding into the seat beside her, arm stretched along the backrest like he belonged there.

"Do you ever knock?"

"I prefer dramatic entrances," he said, voice low. "Though I admit, I was hoping for something more welcoming. You looked almost wistful."

"Must've been the tea, it's too sweet," she muttered, straightening.

"But not sweet enough to soften that scowl," he teased. "Which is... very you."

His eyes swept her face like he was trying to memorize it, soft in the corners, brow faintly drawn. Not the polished gaze he wore at public functions. This one was quieter, hungrier, almost tender.

"I've been looking for you," he said finally, his voice barely rose above the hush of the room. "I was worried..."

"I've been avoiding you. How did you find me?"

He tilted his head slightly. "You're a highborn. I assumed you'd go where you belong."

She stared at him for a long moment, unsure if it was a compliment or a challenge. Julian's expression softened further, his voice dipping. "I didn't mean to upset you."

Cassara said nothing, but her silence wasn't cold, it was cautious.

She was watching him, measuring.

"I just didn't like the way he looked at you, the way he spoke," he continued. "Like he thought you were... available. Like he wanted to use you."

Cassara's brows lifted faintly and she turned to gaze out the window again. "So you decided to mark your territory without consulting me first?"

"I decided to remind him that you're not some token for the loudest fool to chase." He sighed. "I didn't come to fight," he continued, voice quiet now, gentler. "I just thought you might want... company."

She turned toward him, slow and steady. "I don't."

He leaned forward slightly, his expression . "I came to apologize."

"Mm. For starting a scene, or for assuming you speak for me in public?"

Her words didn't hold the bite she wanted them to. She was tired and staying angry at Julian had never been easy.

He smiled, wry this time, almost sheepish. "A little of both."

Cassara set her cup down with quiet precision. "Apology noted."

"But not accepted."

"You've known me long enough to know the difference."

His eyes searched hers for a beat too long. "You've known me long enough to know I don't give up that easily."

He leaned forward then, elbows resting on his knees, hands clasped loosely, no longer performing, not outwardly. But there was calculation behind the ease, a tension to his stillness, like a thread pulled taut waiting to snap.

Julian's voice was lower now, intimate in a way that curled beneath her skin. "You remember your birthday gala, don't you?"

She remembered. The gardens at dusk. Stolen cordial in glass flutes. The taste of plum and summer heat, the way the lanterns caught in his hair, how he looked at her like she was something rare and untouchable.

Until he'd touched her anyway.

A kiss. Slow. Certain. Too practiced to be innocent, too honest to be forgotten. And hands, his hands, exploring places that left her breathless.

She hadn't forgotten. Not even close.

Julian leaned closer, his fingers brushing the edge of her skirt just above her knee, thumb grazing where fabric met skin.

"I haven't stopped thinking about it," he murmured. "The taste of you. That night."

Cassara's breath caught. She didn't move, didn't lean in, but didn't pull back either. The room had become little more than velvet cushions, warm light, and the press of memory clouding judgment.

His other hand came up, fingers tracing a chestnut curl behind her ear. That night came flooding back and she could almost smell the cordial on his breath again, sweet and sharp.

"I've been wondering ever since... if it was just the wine that made my pulse race. Or if it was the sound you made when our lips met..."

Cassara's heart gave a traitorous skip. Gods. He remembered that, too?

She hated the way heat blossomed in her chest, half embarrassment, half something far more dangerous.

His hand moved, slow and sure, fingers brushing her jaw, curling around her chin, guiding her closer. Their faces were inches apart now. His breath mingled with hers as he leaned closer, the tension between them pulling taut,

A soft chime rang out overhead, followed by the crisp crackle of arcane amplification.

"All first-years, please report to the viewing deck for initial landing procedures. Orientation to follow."

Cassara exhaled sharply, the spell broken.

Julian's gaze didn't drop. He waited, just one second more, to see if she'd close the distance.

She didn't, not quite, but she didn't push him away either.

Instead she stood, smoothing her skirt with hands that shook, partly from restraint, partly from the echo of almost. Part of her still wanted the kiss. The rest already regretted how close she'd come.

She let him touch her. Let herself remember the garden, the way it almost felt like something real, until the warmth of it started to feel like a warning. Because none of that changed what he'd said. How he acted, like she was property to be claimed before someone else got there first.

"We should go," she said.

She didn't wait, instead grabbed her jacket from the back of the chair as she moved towards the door, pulse racing, skirt swaying just enough to remind him she'd let him almost have her.

But not quite.

Julian reached the door ahead of her and with all the pretense of gallant nobility, grasped the handle and pulled it open, motioning with a sweeping gesture for her to go first. She regarded him carefully before sweeping past.

He lingered a moment, no doubt watching her, before falling into step beside her with the kind of ease that made it look like she'd chosen him.

The viewing deck buzzed with noise and motion, steam rising in lazy curls past tall windows etched with pulsing glyphs. Students clustered near the railings, excitement thick in the air.

Cassara stepped through the archway, a breath slower than she meant. Her skin still burned in places she wished it didn't.

Evie noticed first.

"You okay, Cassara? Your face is all red... you're not feeling ill, are you?" Her concern was genuine, but it still made Cassara stiffen.

"It was warm in the lounge," she said evenly.

"Mm," Sonia hummed, all amusement. "That must've been why the lounge door was locked."

Cassara turned sharply to glare at Julian. *You locked the door?*

He only shrugged, completely unbothered.

Evie gave her a puzzled once-over but didn't push. She shifted aside with a slight frown. "You sure you're okay?"

"I'm fine," Cassara replied, too fast. She slid into the space between them, Julian trailing behind with that insufferable curl at the corner of his mouth, like he'd just won a round no one else knew they were playing.

From across the deck, Vash and Jonas made their approach, uniforms pressed, boots spotless, their confidence as casual as it was curated. Julian's lackeys. Truth be told? Cassara couldn't stand either of them. Jonas reached them first, his gaze swept over Cassara, slow and assessing in a way that made her skin crawl.

Julian lingered at her side with that infuriating curve to his mouth, like he was daring someone to ask why she looked like she'd kissed lightning.

And someone did.

"I wondered what you meant when you said you were going on a hunt," Vash said as he joined them, voice light but edged with amusement. "Guess you caught her."

Jonas snorted. "More like cornered her. Sonia said the lounge door was locked."

Cassara's head turned, slow. Julian, maddeningly, said nothing.

"We figured it was a strategy thing," Jonas added, grin widening. "Old school charm, tight quarters, no escape..."

His eyes flicked toward her, not suggestive, but curious. Calculating. Testing the water.

Julian moved. Not much. Just a step closer to Jonas, his tone even.

"Drop it."

Jonas raised his hands, palms up. "Hey, no judgment. Would've locked the door too."

Cassara stepped away from the railing and let her boot clip Julian's heel on her way past. "Next time, don't lock the door."

Julian winced, barely. But the corner of his mouth curved, not smug this time, but amused. Maybe even impressed.

She didn't look back, but she felt Julian fall into step behind her. She'd let her silence say exactly what she wanted it to.

In an effort to distract herself, Cassara's gaze lifted, scanning the crowd. It didn't take long to settle on him.

Gideon.

He was standing by the rear railing, arms folded, posture relaxed in a way that was anything but casual. Their eyes met.

And the corner of his mouth lifted, not a smile. A flicker. Crooked. Cold.

Mocking.

His gaze dropped to where Julian's hand brushed against the small of her back... and then lifted again.

The look on his face said enough.

How's that leash feel?

Cassara's entire frame stiffened.

Julian's voice came soft beside her, low enough for her alone. "You alright?"

She didn't look at him. "Fine."

The lie barely scratched her throat on the way out. Her tone was cool, effortless. The kind that sounded like she meant it.

But she could feel Gideon's stare even after she broke eye contact, could feel her pulse ticking faster than she wanted to admit.

Julian didn't press. He shifted slightly closer, a quiet shadow at her side as the instructor stepped forward.

He was tall, composed, his dark hair tousled, his long black coat clasped high at the collar and lined with faint silver thread. His presence alone straightened spines. No crest adorned his chest, but he didn't need one. Authority rolled off him in steady, unyielding waves.

Cassara's breath caught.

It was him. The man from the corridor. The one she'd snapped at hours ago without realizing, without knowing.

Mortification surged hot under her skin.

"For those who don't know, I am Auren Veth. You'll refer to me as Instructor Veth. If I need to speak with you, I will. If not, don't give me a reason to."

He scanned the deck in one long, sweeping pass, his expression as indiscernible now as it had been then.

"First-years," he said, voice low and sharp, "we are now approaching final descent. Remain in position until stabilization sigils engage. Do not tamper with any enchantments."

A few students chuckled.

"If you experience dizziness or pressure, breathe through it. The wards are tuned to accommodate discomfort. Not dramatics."

Julian's shoulder bumped hers faintly, as if to ground her, but she couldn't take her eyes off Auren.

"Touchdown will occur at the eastern landing ring. From there, orientation marshals will escort you."

The instructor's gaze passed over her again. If he recognized her, he didn't show it.

Cassara's jaw clenched. Her earlier words echoed in her head: Most people say excuse me.

Of course he hadn't apologized. He didn't have to.

She should've been embarrassed, and she was, but it curdled into something sharper. A flare of annoyance. He could've said something in the hallway. Given a name. A warning. Anything.

But he hadn't.

And now she was standing there, red-faced in front of half the cohort, trying not to look like the girl who mouthed off to an instructor on day one.

Julian leaned in slightly. "You sure you're alright?"

"I said I'm fine," she bit out.

"Welcome to Vallemont," Auren finished. "If you remember anything, remember this. The difference between a tamer and a corpse is often a single mistake. We're here to reduce that margin. Pay attention."

Cassara's gaze narrowed, a slow breath hissing between her teeth.

Of all the people in the sky...

CHAPTER THREE

The clouds were thick, stretching endlessly beneath them in churning sheets of silver. They clung to the hull like fogged glass, veiling everything beyond the viewing deck windows. Runed panels lining the curved wall thrummed low, casting soft pulses of amber light over the gathered students as the ship dipped lower. Every few seconds, a faint vibration trembled underfoot, signaling a shift in altitude.

Cassara stood near the archway, one hand braced against the doorway, the other folded tightly beneath her ribs. Her coat hung open at the collar, barely touched by the breeze slipping through the subtle vents along the ceiling, yet she felt the air press cold against her neck. Not from the chill. From instinct.

The students had begun to gather at the front of the deck, pressed against the reinforced magisteel railing, faces lit with the glow of anticipation. Liri's nose smudged the window. Sonia perched on the balls of her feet like a cat waiting to pounce. Even Evie stood breathless with her hands clasped to her chest, eyes wide with wonder.

Unlike the other students, Cassara wasn't looking up.

She was watching the clouds.

And something was wrong.

It was a flicker, no more than that. A streak of motion through the mist: dark, sinuous, impossibly fast. Gone before she could track it.

Too high for birds and far too large for anything that should be flying this close to the descent path.

Another blur rippled through the cloud bank, larger, lower, angled toward the hull.

Her breath caught.

"Did you see that?" Evie whispered. She turned slightly, half-laughing, half-afraid. "Tell me someone else saw that."

"It's a scare tactic," Sonia said, though her voice lacked its usual sharpness. "A little flash before orientation. It's probably an instructor showing off their bonded beast."

"Maybe a projection," Jonas added, leaning on the rail like nothing had changed. "You know, some weird enchantment to welcome the newbies."

Cassara didn't answer. Her fingers curled slowly against her arm.

Because she'd read the paper that morning.

She remembered the headline.

Something twisted through the haze again, closer now. A blur of segmented limbs and trailing shadow. The ship tilted slightly as the stabilizers adjusted, but the light in the room seemed to shift, dimming for the briefest moment.

Cassara didn't speak. Her pulse quickened as dread clenched in her gut. She turned, eyes sweeping the deck.

When she found who she was looking for, it confirmed her fears.

Auren had moved to the edge of the deck. One hand rested lightly on the support rail, the other raised, not in alarm, but in analysis. His head tilted just slightly. He was listening. Watching.

And that look on his face?

It wasn't the look of an instructor preparing to deliver a scare tactic, it was the look of a soldier about to enter combat.

The deck jolted.

A violent, teeth-rattling shudder as something slammed against the hull from below, hard enough to rattle the magelights overhead and pitch a few students off balance. A whoosh of displaced air followed, hot and sulfurous, sweeping through the vents like breath from a furnace.

Then came the sound.

Not a roar. Not the shriek of wind.

A screech, raw, metallic, ear-splitting, like steel dragged across stone. Cassara's hands clenched the railing on reflex as the noise vibrated through the glass, through the floor, and straight into her bones.

Around her students scattered, screams erupting near the viewing windows as another impact struck the port side, this time accompanied by the hideous scrape of claws against enchanted plating.

Something huge was circling them.

Auren was already in motion, the hem of his coat snapped as he moved, all sharp lines and sudden velocity. He began barking orders, giving commands to someone unseen, calling in positioning and stabilization. Readying for combat .

Movement drew Cassara's eyes back to the window where a creature had begun to uncoil from the clouds with unnatural grace.

It spiraled upward, impossibly long, a segmented horror with a sinuous body wrapped in charred bone plates and wings that didn't flap so much as tear through the air in great lurching pulses. Four limbs extended from its torso, mantis-like and jointed wrong, ending in bladed claws that scraped sparks against the hull. Beneath its twisted rib cage, lightning pulsed through translucent sacs, crackling with every beat of its impossible heart.

Its head—gods, its head—was wrong. Finned like a serpent's, its jaw split down the center to reveal rows of barbed teeth, and from between them, a tongue lashed like a whip, barbed and wet.

Cassara froze.

It wasn't fear that gripped her, it was awe, ugly and electric. A shiver of knowing. This was what the world could throw at her. This was what Vallemont trained for.

And she was not ready.

The creature shrieked again, closer this time, its thunder sacs glowing hotter with each pass. Sparks rained down as one of its clawed limbs scraped along the upper hull again, scoring the protective wards. A tremor rolled through the deck, and the lights flickered in their sconces.

Chaos erupted.

First-years screamed. Some dropped to the floor, others sprinted for the exits, crowding the stairwells in frantic waves. A few brave, or foolish, students hovered near the railings, eyes wide and mouths slack, too stunned to flee.

Cassara was among them, breath locked tight in her chest.

Auren's voice rose above the panic. "Crimson Talon squad. Aerial flank. Bracket left and keep it clear of the rudders. Do not engage directly if at all possible, our goal is to redirect."

And like that, they moved.

One third-year launched herself from the upper deck, wind shrieking around her as her glider-wing caught, stabilizing into a controlled dive. Her beast, an obsidian wyvern with ember-lit veins and an impossible wingspan, shrieked below, circling to meet her midair. She landed on its back with practiced ease, mana conduits flaring along her bracers as she leveled her hooked glaive. The weapon pulsed with heat as the wyvern banked hard and dove toward the creature tearing at the hull.

Another followed, this one on a beast built like a plated wasp-raptor, all blade-legs and lightning-hum wings. The rider stood braced between the creature's spines, his ACS igniting a magnetic shield just as a strike came too close. Sparks skittered across his curved blade, charged by his beast's electric pulse.

Cassara's stomach dropped as the sky exploded into motion.

A third beast thundered up from the cargo ramp: a granite-scaled charger with curved tusks and rune-scarred armor plating. Its tamer crouched low between the reinforced shoulder-straps, raising a short hammer that blazed with sigils as the beast hurled itself against the airship's side and latched on, hooves gripping like claws. A defensive pair, holding the line. Their support glyphs flared, forming protective arcs beneath the other riders.

A wall of wind swept across the deck. Cries rang out as another shriek split the air. The beast, talons clacking, tail spiked like a flail, curled tighter around one side of the hull. Its four wing-limbs cracked the air, throwing off bolts of sound and heat. Its barbed tongue struck out again, too fast for a blade to catch, too wild for spellwork to counter.

And then—

He moved.

Auren emerged from the command tier like he'd been waiting for this. There was a glimmer of silver, dual daggers flaring as he activated the core embedded in his ACS. Firelight spilled across the sigils lining his arms.

"Maintain distance! Flank on the eastern drag! Don't let it pin the hull!"

He didn't hesitate, didn't panic, he didn't even look back. He directed the chaos like it belonged to him and him alone.

The third-year circled wide on her wyvern, signaling with a spin of her glaive. Her beast dove low, drawing the creature's attention. Another rider intercepted midair, their lightning-charged raptor unleashing a thunderburst from its crest that staggered the attacker mid-coil.

Auren leapt into the fray, blades flashing as he vaulted from the deck edge, caught a support rig, and landed on one of the hull anchor points. The corrupted beast struck toward him. He lashed outward, the blade leaving a searing trail of red along the tongue that came for his throat.

Cassara's breath snagged, her heart pounding.

This wasn't the man from the corridor. This wasn't even the instructor who'd faced them moments before with clipped warnings and judgement in his eyes.

This was something else.

Auren moved like he had been born for it, as though countless battles had carved his reflexes from steel and adrenaline alone.

The creature reared back with a thunderous screech, wings snapping wide, and slammed its tail against the underside of the viewing deck. The ship lurched, the sigils along the stabilizer edge blinked red, flickering fast.

Cassara staggered, catching herself on the railing. Someone nearby screamed as another jolt tore through the hull.

And then, the ship began to tilt.

Julian grabbed her arm, tugging hard, trying to pull her towards safety. "Cassara. We need to get below deck. Now."

But she didn't move. Her eyes were fixed on the stabilizer glyph flickering near the port side, its pattern sputtering, destabilized from the hit. If it failed completely, the ship would tilt into a spiral and dozens would fall.

Julian's voice sharpened, cutting through her haze. "Cass."

"I see it," she muttered.

"See what? Cass? What are you—"

"There." She pointed and could almost feel the decision calcify in her bones before her mind had caught up.

"Don't," Julian warned, sensing it before she even shifted her weight. "Cassara—!"

But she was already moving.

She ducked out of his grip and sprinted for the side panel ladder, weaving between panicked first-years and trembling luggage bins. Her boots slammed against the metal rungs as she climbed, fingers biting into the cold rail. The wind tore at her coat the moment she reached the maintenance scaffolding, the pressure forcing her body sideways as the ship groaned beneath her.

Bracing herself against the edge, she stared down at the malfunctioning glyph. It flickered in and out of sync, throwing pulses of unstable magic into the air. Reaching it would require crossing an exposed framework—one that was already starting to crack.

She hesitated, hands clenched tight. Her breath came fast now, too fast, her vision tunneling as fear reared its head again.

What was she doing?

She wasn't a hero. Wasn't even bonded.

But there was no time to find someone else. If she didn't act now, if she didn't do something...

Below her, a student slipped, nearly falling off the deck before a third-year yanked them back.

Cassara grit her teeth, adrenaline surging hot beneath her skin.

No more hesitating.

The wind knifed against her skin as she crept low across the narrow support beam. Below, the storm-scarred clouds boiled in spirals, broken by bursts of blue magic and black shadow where third-years and beasts clashed in blinding arcs of combat. The glyph was still several feet away, stuttering in its pattern, a dull flicker where once it had glowed steady.

Cassara crouched low, hands gripping the edge of the beam. Her knees quivered. She wasn't afraid of heights, she'd scaled the edge of the Allencourt estate's watchtower more than once, but this wasn't polished stone and ornamental railing. This was jagged metal and rattling pipes, everything groaning beneath the weight of its own failing enchantment.

Her mind screamed at her to turn back. Julian had been right. This was stupid.

She wasn't trained for this.

If she slipped, if she fell—

But another screech cracked across the sky. A second stabilizer flickered behind her. The ship bucked.

Students shouted in terror. Something toppled on the deck and someone hit the floor hard. Cassara looked down at her hands, pale-knuckled on the beam.

Maybe she didn't have a bonded beast yet.

But she wasn't helpless.

She edged forward slowly, one foot after the other, boots slipping once, twice, until her fingertips snagged the next handhold welded to the hull.

The ship shifted again, throwing her sideways. Her shoulder scraped a metal ridge and pain lanced through it, warm and immediate. She hissed through her teeth and pressed on, every inch a fight against the tilt of the ship and the wind clawing to tear her loose.

Almost there.

The glyph pulsed feebly just ahead, its etched runes jittering.

Cassara gritted her teeth and pushed forward, half-crawling the last stretch until she could brace herself against the edge of the stabilizer's casing. Her fingers scrambled for purchase on the rune housing, slick with condensation, vibrating faintly with misaligned energy.

She had no idea what she was doing.

Her breath came fast.

Now or never.

She drove her palm flat against the seal and shoved the mana orb back into the slot, completing the disrupted circuit path. The glyph flared once, resisting, before snapping into alignment with a sharp clang that echoed through the struts like a gunshot. Light blazed along the carved conduits, cascading outward. The ship groaned and began to level.

Cassara had just enough time to realize it was working and not nearly enough to get out of the way.

The stabilizer surged beneath her, shifting with a violent jolt as the enchantments snapped back into balance. The entire structure lurched to one side, overcorrecting.

Her foot slipped and she lost her grip, the sudden movement ripping her from the narrow ledge. She was falling, air tearing past her in a shrieking rush as metal vanished from beneath her boots. She twisted, her arms flailing for something, anything.

An arm caught her hard around the ribs, knocking the breath from her lungs as momentum snapped taut between them.

"Got you."

The world sharpened back into focus.

Auren's face hovered inches from hers, jaw tight, eyes dark. They were falling, no, gliding, his body angled just enough to steer them downward with one arm cradling her close and the other adjusting the control glyphs etched into the glider strapped to his back.

Cassara couldn't speak, she could barely breathe.

He wasn't looking at her anymore, his gaze already scanning the deck below, calculating descent, angle, trajectory. Cool. Efficient. Entirely unbothered, as though plucking an unbonded first-year from a thirty-foot fall was routine.

They landed hard. Auren absorbed the impact with a practiced bend of his knees, one hand still braced around her. Cassara staggered when he let go, her boots skidding slightly on the deck.

Her heart hadn't quite caught up to her yet.

He took a step back. Looked her over once. "Are you hurt?"

Cassara shook her head, pulse racing.

"Next time you feel like proving something," Auren said coldly, "try not to die doing it."

She felt heat rushing to her cheeks, not from embarrassment but fury. "I wasn't proving anything."

His brow lifted a fraction. "Weren't you?"

The ship was still trembling slightly, but the tilt had stopped. Stabilizers hummed evenly now, the deck no longer at risk of pitching students into the sky.

But here, between them, the tension was quiet.

Auren exhaled slowly and turned away, his coat flaring. "Heroics make poor habits," he said over his shoulder. "Especially in first-years."

Cassara stared after him, fists clenched.

She wasn't sure if she wanted to scream, or chase him down and argue every inch of it.

But somewhere, beneath the bruises and anger and adrenaline still thudding through her veins, something inside her whispered:

You can do this.

And he'd seen it too.

What she didn't understand was why he'd seemed so angry about it.

Silence reigned on the deck with only the whispering creak of metal and the faint hum of stabilizers filled the void. Students stood scattered, gripping railings, clutching one another, blinking like they'd surfaced from a dream that had turned sideways.

The creature had been driven back into the clouds below, leaving only the memory of its scream and the faint scorch marks clawed into the hull.

A few sobs broke the quiet. Sonia sat flat on the deck, breathing fast, muttering something under her breath like a mantra. Even Julian looked uncharacteristically rattled, his eyes trained warily on the sky.

Cassara stood apart from the others, arms wrapped tight around herself.

She could still feel the pressure of Auren's arms around her, the dizzy weightlessness of the fall, the moment the world snapped sideways and she moved anyway. Not everyone had done the same. Some had frozen. Others had run. But she had climbed.

A hand brushed hers. Evie stood beside her, quiet but present.

"You okay?" she asked.

Cassara nodded. "Yeah."

Her voice cracked on the word.

Evie didn't comment, but she stayed beside her, a grounded presence she found oddly comforting after what had happened. Not that Cassara would admit it.

Nearby, Auren conferred with the third-years who leapt into the fray. Several still remained airborne, their beasts circling slowly now, casting long shadows across the deck in wingspan-shaped patches. One of them, the wyvern, let out a low, rumbling call before banking away, and Cassara watched the way its rider didn't flinch, awed at how practiced their connection was. How controlled.

They weren't just tamers, they were fighters, and, someday, she would be one too.

She pushed off from where she'd been standing and made her way to the railing, needing distance from the crowd. Wind tugged at her hair, sharp and cold, but she made no move to tuck the strands away.

Julian found her before the silence could.

"You're out of your mind," he said, his voice quiet.

She faced him slowly. His mouth was pressed into a line and a fury she had never seen before lived behind his eyes. Not just anger, but fear, or guilt, maybe even shame.

"You could've died," he said.

She didn't turn. "But I didn't."

"No," he bit out. "Because someone else caught you."

That landed harder than she wanted to admit. Her brows lifted and she turned to look at him. "So now I'm not allowed to help?"

"You risked your life," he snapped, the words sharper than she expected. "For what? For a stabilizer glyph? You think anyone would've blamed you for staying safe?"

Cassara's spine stiffened. "No. They'd just remember I stood there and watched."

"You shouldn't have been up there," he went on as though she hadn't spoken. "It was reckless and stupid. You think a stunt like that makes you brave? Did you think everyone would be impressed?"

"I didn't do it to impress anyone."

"Then why?" His voice dropped low. "To prove you don't need saving? Because the reality is—" he stepped in close, the words meant only for her, "—you did need saving. And if he hadn't been there..." He didn't finish, he didn't have to.

She looked away, heat flaring in her throat. Not shame, not exactly. She'd done what needed doing, but the truth still stung.

For a moment, neither of them spoke. Around them, the crew moved about the deck in tired motions, resetting arcane shields, sweeping wreckage, gathering shattered mana crystals like broken glass.

"I'm not sorry I did it," Cassara said at last, staring out at the horizon.

Julian's fist clenched where it rested against the railing, but he didn't argue. He just stepped back, shook his head, and left her standing there with the burn of his words curling between her ribs.

Before she could linger too long on what had remained unsaid, Auren's voice rang out, clear, clipped, impossible to ignore.

Cassara turned toward the bow just as he stepped forward, the third-years flanking him in quiet formation.

"You were lucky," he began, eyes sweeping the deck. His words were met with silence, not a soul moved. "That wasn't part of your welcome," he continued, "but it was a taste, a glimpse, of what's out there."

He let the words settle.

"If it shook you, good. It should have. There is no shame in fear. Only in denial of it. This was unfortunate, but perhaps also a blessing in disguise. Because now, you don't have the luxury of pretending."

He paced between them. "Some of you were brave. Some of you were reckless. And some of you froze."

Cassara felt the words strike like a heartbeat. He wasn't looking at her, but it felt like he could've been.

"That's not judgment. That's clarity. Out there, a moment's hesitation costs lives. Out there, glory is rare. Death is not. If you came to show off, you should go home now." The wind stirred his coat. "Because what we teach here isn't heroics. It's survival."

He stopped and let the weight of silence hang.

"Vallemont does not coddle." His voice was quieter now, but no less sharp. "You are not owed greatness. You will earn every inch of it."

His eyes swept the deck one last time. "For those who choose to stay..." A slight incline of his head, nothing more. "...welcome to Vallemont."

CHAPTER FOUR

A hush fell over the students clustered near the railing, whispers fading into anticipation. Most of them bore scrapes and bumps. One girl's arm was wrapped hastily in cloth. No one spoke of it. Not yet. They were all caught up in the moment and it was as if the attack had been a distant dream.

Cassara stepped forward, fingers tightening on the edge of the rail. This was it. This was the moment she had fought for.

Vallemont rose from the clouds like a dream carved from stone and stormlight. The Central Spire speared skyward at the heart of the floating island, built from pale, weatherworn stone veined with gleaming metal. A brilliant beacon crowned its peak, pulsing with magic, part navigational ward, part declaration.

Terraced walkways spiraled outward, linking towers, platforms, and courtyards, each rimmed in bronze and rune-lit steel. Sky bridges arced over gorges and waterfalls that plunged into open air. The main courtyard was visible even from this height, its massive compass rose glinting in the morning light. Below it, the arena sat like a yawning scar, wide and waiting.

Cassara pressed a hand against her chest, trying to steady the thud of her heart beneath her ribs. This wasn't her father's house.

This was hers.

No matter what came next, she'd made it, and no one, not Julian, not her father, not the threats he wielded like a blade, could take it from her.

The airship banked gently, leveling as it drew closer to their destination. Wind rushed past in controlled bursts as runes aligned and anchoring wards pulsed to life.

Auren's voice rose from somewhere behind them. "First-years! Prepare for disembarkation. Keep to the right. You'll be led through intake before the welcoming ceremony."

Despite the instructions, Cassara didn't move. Vallemont gleamed before her, vast and alive. She could already feel it breathing and she wanted one more second to stand at the edge of everything she'd fought for.

Nearby the gangway extended with a low hiss, steam curling around its braces as it locked into place. The runes beneath the deck pulsed, anchoring the ship to the platform, and a signal bell chimed somewhere beyond the railing.

They'd arrived.

Still, Cassara didn't move, not until a warm hand touched her elbow and another pressed lightly against the small of her back.

It was Julian.

He said nothing, just guided her forward with that quiet, entitled ease of someone who had always known how to steer her without being asked.

Cassara didn't resist, she was so caught up in the splendor of it all that she barely registered the touch. She descended the ramp one slow step at a time, a rush of wind tugging at her coat, the platform alive beneath her feet with hums of warded energy. Every breath she took felt too big for her chest.

She was here. She was finally-

An arm bumped her shoulder hard, right where she'd scraped herself raw against the metal ridge during the climb.

Pain flared hot beneath her coat, and Cassara stiffened, a sharp hiss escaping through her teeth. She caught her balance with a step, scowling as she turned her head.

"Oops, didn't see you there," Gideon called over his shoulder without bothering to look back. The movement hadn't been aggressive, but it hadn't been accidental, either.

Her arm throbbed as she watched him go.

Julian muttered under his breath beside her. Cassara didn't catch the words, but the tone was unforgiving.

She shifted, just enough to ease the pressure between them. A half-step, almost nothing, the kind you could pass off as a balance adjustment or a better view of the spire, but it wasn't either of those.

Cassara had suddenly needed distance, even if it was small. If Julian noticed, he said nothing, his hand continued to hover, claiming the space between them like it belonged to him.

There was something about that moment, the way it rewound her heartbeat and left a sour taste in her mouth, but Julian's presence, despite being familiar, suddenly felt heavier than it had a second ago. It wasn't unwelcome, not really, but she wasn't entirely sure she wanted to be steered anymore.

Her gaze trailed after Gideon despite herself, catching just enough to see him pause near the far edge of the platform. A girl stood waiting, tall, auburn-haired, her uniform crisp, her smile easy. He said something Cassara couldn't hear. The girl laughed, and he answered with a grin, warm, real, the kind he hadn't spared for anyone else all day.

The sight of it caused her breath to snag unexpectedly in her chest. She stamped down the flutter before looking away.

Focus, Cassara.

Whatever *that* was, it didn't matter. Neither did Julian's possessive touch, or Gideon's lingering smirk, or the way they both stood like storms waiting to pull her in.

Her eyes lifted again to the Central Spire, to its pale stone and dark metal. Power incarnate.

This was why she'd come.

Not for them.

For herself.

Another instructor appeared at the head of the group barking for first-years to follow. They formed something resembling a line as they moved along the path from the landing platform through a high-walled archway. It was etched in flowing script that shimmered faintly as each student passed beneath it. The ground under Cassara's boots changed, shifting from metal to smooth, white marble shot through with faint veins of copper.

The main courtyard opened before them, the massive compass rose Cassara had seen from the air lay before them, carved directly into the stone. Each directional point was inlaid with a different kind of metal: gold for North, silver for East, iron for South, and burnished bronze for West. Arcane sigils danced in and out of sight along the rim, pulsating too fast to read, like the courtyard itself was breathing.

The statue at the heart of it loomed over them, Vallemont himself, or so the plaque at its base said. The statue was carved from dark stone and weathered steel, his cloak forever billowing in a wind that no longer touched it. One arm was stretched skyward, a curved spear clenched in his fist, while the other was planted at his side with an open palm as if daring the sky to challenge him.

Cassara's steps slowed as they passed it. Every part of the space pulled at her, commanding attention and demanding reverence.

Beyond the courtyard, a series of broad steps led them toward the spire's base. Ornate stained glass doors opened into a towering hall lined with shifting banners, each one emblazoned with a stylized beast mid-flight or coiled for battle. A series of marble columns ran the length of the corridor, engraved with the names of prior graduates, years fading into centuries. Her mother's name would be somewhere on one of them.

Cassara didn't look for it. Not yet.

They were led down a side corridor, narrower, but no less grand. Wall sconces lit with pale magelight flickered as they passed, illuminating faded murals that stretched ceiling to floor: beasts and tamers mid-combat, wings and talons frozen in gold-leaf motion. The air here was cooler. Quieter. Like the academy itself had drawn a breath and was holding it.

Finally, they stopped.

A wide set of doors opened into what could only be described as a holding room. Not large, but ornate. Deep red velvet drapes framed tall, narrow windows. A long wooden bench circled the room's perimeter, polished to a shine. In the center, a sunken sigil pulsed in a steady, soft rhythm, marking time, or perhaps tempering nerves.

"Wait here," their escort said, voice clipped. "You'll be called when it's time."

The door clicking shut behind him leaving fifty-six first year students in total to wait. But for what? Some whispered amongst themselves while others postured. A small handful pretended not to care.

Cassara didn't sit, she was feeling too restless, anxious even. Instead she crossed to the window, gaze sweeping the sky beyond. Clouds churned in the distance, shot through with streaks of gold from the setting sun. The view didn't settle her like she had hoped. Even now she thought she saw shadows moving, could picture with unsettling clarity the way the creature had unfurled from the clouds...

She heard him before he reached her. Julian's footsteps didn't rush, but they carried a certain precision now, quieter than usual, more cautious.

He came to stand beside her, not quite touching. "You should sit."

Cassara didn't move. Arms folded, she stared past the glass, its reflection catching the set of her mouth, the strain that hadn't quite left her shoulders. "I'm fine."

A moment of silence. "You nearly weren't."

Her gaze didn't shift. "Is this where you scold me again? You're not my father, Julian."

Julian exhaled through his nose, not quite a sigh. "No." He hesitated, then added, quieter this time, "I was wrong. I shouldn't have grabbed you like that."

She glanced at him, her expression sharp.

He met it anyway and took her silence as permission to keep talking. "It wasn't anger. It was watching you climb into the rigging and knowing if you fell, there wouldn't be a damn thing I could do."

The sharp retort she'd been preparing died in her throat. When he spoke to her like that, in that quiet, almost desperate way, she found it difficult to stay angry with him.

"You're not invincible, Cass," he continued, his voice just above a whisper. "And I guess I'm not interested in watching you try to prove otherwise."

She didn't answer right away. Her focus drifted back to the reflection in the glass.

"I didn't do it to prove anything," she murmured. "It had to be done."

"I know," he said. And for once, it didn't sound like agreement for the sake of it. "But you don't always have to be the one to do it alone."

Silence settled over them again, more fragile than before.

"Sit with me?" He asked at last.

Cassara couldn't bring herself to look at him. But her arms uncoiled, and after a breath more, she followed him to the bench. Not for comfort or because he had asked, but because she let herself choose to.

He didn't speak again, but he sat just close enough for their sleeves to brush if either of them moved.

Cassara didn't.

She watched the pulsing seal, let it steady her breathing. This was the last moment before initiation, before her name was called and the real weight of this place settled around her shoulders.

Finally, the doors opened with a slow, resonant creak.

Cassara rose with the rest as the instructor from earlier returned.

"They're ready." That was all he said before motioning for them to follow.

They were led down a narrow corridor lit with flickering sconces, the hum of arcane currents moving through the walls. The corridor opened into a vast chamber, a sign over the entryway reading in ornate lettering: The Orientation Hall.

The ceiling soared overhead, ribbed with shimmering arches. Stained glass windows cast streaks of crimson, blue and gold across the concentric stone platforms ringed with wooden benches. At the center, a circular dais lay embedded in the floor, etched with runes that glowed faintly with dormant power.

Cassara's eyes adjusted quickly. The upper tiers were already filled with older students, fourth year apprentices who would be gone by the end of the week to begin the final leg of their training. The hush that met the first-years as they entered wasn't welcome, it was scrutiny.

They took their places, filling in the curved rows that surrounded the central platform. Cassara sat near the midpoint, Julian, again, beside her. Liri somehow to her right this time, humming softly under her breath, tapping her fingers against her knees like she might leap up and bolt if she didn't keep herself busy.

Across the dais, directly opposite, Cassara caught the glint of the auburn haired girl from earlier. Calm, composed, her hands folded neatly in her lap. And beside her sat Gideon.

He didn't smirk, not exactly, but the corner of his mouth lifted when his gaze caught hers. Like he'd already seen how the day would go and was just waiting to watch it unfold.

Cassara's spine straightened.

She didn't break eye contact. Not until Julian shifted beside her, his hand resting on her knee for the briefest moment, nothing overt, but grounding, or perhaps possessive. She couldn't tell the difference anymore.

A hush fell over the hall and the air grew heavier, as if the walls themselves were bracing for the moment.

Then she appeared, the headmistress, stepping into view from an alcove above, descending a spiral staircase that curved along the wall. She didn't look old, but time clung to her in a way that made age irrelevant. Her hair was dark, streaked silver at the temples, pulled back in a coiled braid. Her shoulders were squared, her stride sharp, her presence undeniable.

Even Julian sat straighter.

Cassara's heart gave a single hard thud.

When the headmistress reached the center, she paused beside the dais and turned, sweeping her gaze over the assembly. Her eyes passed over the first-years without softness, her silence speaking before her voice did.

"Welcome, first years, to Vallemont. As many of you already know, I am Kalisandra Alerand, Headmistress of Vallemont Academy," she began, her eyes sweeping over the assembly. "When you leave this room, you will no longer be merely first-years. You will be initiates. Tamers-in-training, bound to this academy and its traditions. You will have begun your contract with power."

She let that settle, let it breathe.

"Some of you have already experienced what that means."

A murmur stirred at the edges of the hall and Cassara felt the hairs lift at her nape.

"The skies are not safe. The world below is worse." She turned her back to them, and the runes on the dais flared to life, soft at first, then brighter, curling in a slow spiral. "What happened aboard your vessel was unfortunate and if that encounter shook you, good. Let it serve as a reminder of what awaits beyond the protection of these walls."

The silence in the Orientation Hall pressed like the calm before a storm. A large crystal suspended above the central dais flared to life, pulsing with a slow, internal light. It hovered like a star, humming with dormant power.

"The Echo Sigil," the headmistress began, her voice carrying the weight of ritual, "is one of the oldest shards collected from the Aetherheart. It remembers. It sees. It connects." She paused, letting the ancient weight of those words settle. "When you step into its light, it will read the truth of your potential, the shape of what you might become, and show you the path that lies ahead."

The headmistress's voice rang clear across the chamber.

"You will be called one by one. Step into the circle. Let the Echo speak. What it shows you is yours alone. Let the truth it reveals guide you in your journey here."

A murmur rippled through the rows of first-years. Cassara held still, hands on her knees, breath slow.

"Julian Tremaine."

He rose like he'd been waiting for the cue his entire life. Chin high, shoulders back, every movement deliberate and elegant. Cassara watched the line of his jaw as he stepped onto the dais, the Echo Sigil pulsing sharply overhead.

The illusion took him fast.

She couldn't see what he saw, but she saw how still he stood, not a flicker of doubt crossing his face. When the vision ended, the Sigil released a sound like shattering crystal, held just barely in check. A sharp tone, elegant but unsteady at the edge.

Julian returned to his seat acting like nothing had changed, but something had. Cassara could feel it in the tension beneath his skin. She wasn't sure whether it made her jealous or uneasy.

More names were called, Cassara watching as each student rose and approached the dais on unsteady legs. Some were more confident than others when it was over.

"Lirien Halvorsen."

Liri hesitated only a moment, then hurried down the steps, her ruddy curls bouncing with each step. She looked like she might trip over her own nerves, but at the last second, her shoulders straightened.

The Sigil greeted her with a flicker of brightness, almost playful. As the vision took hold, Cassara watched her gasp, then smile, then tear up all in the same breath.

She swayed slightly, like listening to a lullaby no one else could hear.

The Echo Sigil sang with a chiming tone, soft, layered, persistent, like wind chimes stirred by a breeze. Liri returned to her seat still blinking, still a little dazed, but brighter than she'd been before.

"Gideon Delvanir."

He moved without urgency, his steps were quiet, steady. There was no showmanship, no performance. He paused once, taking a deep breath, and then stepped into place beneath the crystal.

The reaction was different.

There was no sharp flare, just a slow, low shimmer of light that rolled across the dais like a tide.

He barely moved. Whatever passed through him didn't break him. But, like Julian, Cassara could see that it changed something in him, the way his posture shifted and his eyes seemed to grow distant.

When the tone came, it was almost too low to hear, but she felt it, a steady hum beneath the skin. He walked back to his seat without looking at anyone, not even his red haired companion.

"Cassara Allencourt."

Cassara's heart beat hard against her ribs and she rose before the tension could fully settle. Her legs felt unsteady as she crossed the floor, aware of every eye tracking her movement. This was it—the moment she'd fought for, schemed for, risked everything for. The dais seemed impossibly far away and then suddenly she was there, stepping onto the raised platform.

The crystal flared, and the world fell away.

She stood in a grand hall lined with polished stone and soaring banners, her crest at the center, blazing with gold. Light poured in from vaulted windows, catching the edge of her armor, her hair, her crown. She was taller here, older, stronger. A presence, not just a girl. Cheers thundered from the faceless crowd surrounding her. Dozens of them, hundreds, all eyes turned to her.

She had won.

A beast stood at her side, massive and breathtaking, its wings folded, its head bowed in deference. Its presence pulsed with power and pride. It was hers, their bond unbreakable.

Cassara turned her face toward the light, chest rising with quiet, victorious breath.

This was what she had worked for. What she had fought tooth and nail to reach. Not a prize, not a pedestal, but proof.

Proof she could become what they told her she'd never be.

But then the light dimmed. The banners began to tear, the wind silent but cruel. The beast turned. Its gaze passed over her, disappointment in the tilt of its jaw, the drop of its wings, before it walked away. Its form unraveled into mist.

The crowd stirred. Their cheers became murmurs. Not derision. Worse.

Disinterest.

They began to vanish. No dramatic exit. They simply turned their backs, one by one, and melted into shadow.

Cassara reached out, but no one took her hand.

At the far end of the hall stood a woman. Tall. Composed. Her dark hair swept in soft waves that shimmered like embers, her eyes a mirror of Cassara's.

Katrinel Allencourt.

Her mother.

She didn't smile, didn't speak at first, but when her voice finally came, it was quiet. Kind.

"You win everything," she said. "And still, you are alone."

The feeling of triumph was gone and all that remained in its wake was heavy, numbing silence. Her breath hitched, but she didn't cry, she didn't scream at the unfairness of it. She simply stood in the center of her echo, victorious and utterly, inescapably alone.

The vision shattered with a soft, mournful tone, a single, aching note that hung in the air like the memory of a name no one had spoken in years.

Cassara opened her eyes and the hall swam back into focus as the Sigil overhead dimmed to a dull glow. She descended the dais with steady steps. Julian reached out, fingertips brushing hers, but she didn't take his hand, didn't look at him. She returned to her seat without a word.

Even after the final name had been called and the last echo rung out, she sat straight-backed, eyes fixed ahead. Her mother's voice still whispered through her thoughts. The beast's retreat. The emptiness that followed.

None of it had broken her.

Across the chamber, a soft chime rang, three distinct notes.

The Echo Sigil dimmed to a steady pulse as a platform rose at the center of the ring. Upon it sat a single, obsidian-bound ledger glowing with gold-etched sigils—the Tamer's Accord.

The headmistress descended without ceremony and circled the ring, her voice calm and weighted with tradition. "By facing the Echo you have faced yourself and now you will speak your vow." She lifted the silver quill beside the ledger, its runes flickering as she moved. "One by one, you will sign your name as hundreds before you have and bind your will to this place. Not by force, but by choice."

Her gaze swept the room once, and paused on Cassara.

Not long. Barely a beat. But enough.

The headmistress's face remained unreadable, carved in elegance and poise. But her eyes held a curious spark, like a scholar watching a page write itself.

Cassara looked away first.

Julian rose when called. His signature was confident, almost theatrical. When he stepped back, a faint flare of crimson flared beneath his name, locking it into the page. He turned toward her, brushed a hand against her shoulder as he passed, but she didn't react.

Liri's signature pulsed with a gentle seafoam blue.

Gideon's flared silver, sharp-edged and steady.

And then:

"Cassara Allencourt."

She rose without hesitation.

Her boots echoed against the stone as she approached the platform. The weight of the hall pressed in again, the faculty watching from somewhere above and the rest of the first year cohort seated in tense silence.

The headmistress extended the ledger, its heavy spine bound in dark leather etched with the academy's crest. The ink shimmered faintly in the light, no doubt charmed to catch the eye, to make the moment feel larger than life.

Cassara stepped forward, her posture sharp, her expression composed. The weight of the hall pressed around her, but she didn't falter.

On the page words bled into existence and she read them aloud as the others had before her.

"I swear by wing and claw, by flame and frost, to stand as partner, not as master. To guard the bond that cannot be broken, to shield the innocent from shadow's reach. Let my heart beat in time with my companion's, let my strength serve those who cannot defend themselves. In darkness, we are light. In chaos, we are order. In unity, we stand. In service, we endure."

The ledger pulsed once beneath her hand, a quiet affirmation, and the ink flared gold, rippling like flame, before settling into permanence.

The attendant produced what looked like a bound sheet of dark crystal, etched with circuit-like patterns that glowed faintly blue. "Your Codex," he said, placing it in her hands. The moment her fingers made contact, the etchings flared brighter, syncing to her magical signature.

Cassara watched her name materialize in the crystal's depths before tucking the device away. Four years of her life would be recorded in those crystalline matrices. Every success alongside every failure.

She returned the quill, turned on her heel, and resumed her place beside Julian, her shoulders squared. A few more names were called and the ceremony ended not with applause, but with the soft toll of a suspended bell marking the binding of fifty-six names to Vallemont's legacy.

Doors groaned open at the far end of the hall, the sound echoing through the room. Around them upper year students began to file out until only one remained. It was a second year student who stood in the archway, gesturing for them to rise. Around her, benches creaked as the other first years stood.

Cassara followed in step, chin high, breathing even. The echo of her trial still hovered behind her eyes, buried beneath purpose. She had not come this far to unravel.

She should've felt triumphant, the trial was done, her oath sealed, the impossible within reach. But the vision clung to her like cold silk. She had seen everything she wanted: power, victory, reverence. And yet it had ended in silence. In abandonment. Even the beast had turned away.

You win everything. And still, you are alone.

Her mother's voice had sounded almost kind, perhaps a little apologetic. That was the worst part.

Cassara's steps didn't falter, but her thoughts did. She tried to dismiss the ache as leftover adrenaline, focusing instead on the rhythm of her heels against stone.

She'd trained for this, fought for this, faced death for this. So why did it feel like she'd glimpsed the end of a story she hadn't even begun?

Julian walked beside her, his presence looming, possessive, but also familiar. His shoulder occasionally brushed hers, just enough to remind her he was still there. She didn't move away, but she didn't lean into it either.

Her attention was focused on her future as the corridor opened ahead of her and Vallemont, opened with it.

CHAPTER FIVE

The Great Hall was a cathedral of light and shadow with vaulted windows that stretched three stories high, arched like wings poised to take flight. The sky beyond them churned with amber and violet, the last kiss of sunset catching on the edges of distant floating islands.

Between the panes, the glass rippled faintly with magic, casting ever-shifting glimmers across the polished marble floor in sweeping, spiral patterns that mimicked flight paths of beasts in motion.

Above, iron chandeliers the size of carriages hovered unsupported, enchanted crystals threaded through their frameworks. The lights pulsed not at random, but in time with the rhythm of wings beating or hearts racing.

Long banquet tables stretched across the hall, their surfaces etched with hundreds of names and crests, legacies immortalized in polished wood. Students were already filling them, grouped by year, their uniforms in perfect order, their voices a low tide of excitement and nerves. Every table shimmered with illusionary decor tailored to each year's crest: crimson for the fourth-years, deep violet for the thirds, gold for seconds, and silver for the new blood.

The first-years were guided to the nearest set of tables, new wood, unmarked. A reminder that nothing had been earned yet.

Cassara took all of it in, the ornate architecture, the fierce elegance, the whispered legacy of power built into every seam. Vallemont was built for steel and strength, and she had never wanted something more.

Julian's hand once again pressed into the small of her back as they were ushered toward their seats. She almost shrugged him off but decided against it, not wanting to ruin the moment by having him sulk the rest of the evening.

Her attention had already drifted past him anyway, passing over the other students as they settled in, the upperclassmen moving with easy confidence while first-years clutched their seats like lifelines.

A tall figure passed between them, Darius Eravian, if the excited whispers were right. Lean, sharp-featured, with a smile that promised both charm and danger. A cluster of second-year girls trailed in his wake, not quite following but clearly angling for his attention. Students parted as he strode through the hall, a plume-feathered raptor perched on his shoulder casting watchful eyes over the crowd.

Cassara's attention drifted past Darius to the high table at the far end of the hall where the instructors sat, not yet introduced. Among them, unmistakable even in formal attire, was Auren Veth.

He looked different here. Younger than she'd initially thought, almost startlingly so compared to the gray-templed veterans flanking him. His coat was impeccable now, no trace of the scorch marks or damage from the attack.Nothing in his posture revealed the man who had leapt into open air to catch her, who had taken on the corrupted beast without hesitation.

Their eyes met across the hall.

For a heartbeat, she thought she saw recognition flicker in his gaze, not warmth, certainly not approval, but awareness. Then it was gone, his attention shifting elsewhere as he leaned to speak with an instructor beside him.

She tried to ignore the heat of annoyance that prickled once more beneath her skin.

The moment the last of the first-years settled into place, the ambient murmur of conversation fell into silence. The lights above shifted hue, casting the room in a burnished amber glow, as if the Hall itself was holding its breath.

Then a single tone rang out.

Not a bell, not magic, but a whistle, sharp and commanding.

From the far end of the hall, the doors slammed outward in a rush of sound and smoke, revealing five figures standing beneath the arch.

Second-years. Clad in segmented training armor chased with crest-silver and ward-steel, their beasts beside them in perfect formation. The crowd erupted in whoops and applause, but it was the first year students who leaned forward the most, eyes wide with awe.

Cassara sat straighter.

The five second-years moved in a fluid, rehearsed arc, three darted into the open space between the tables, while two vaulted into the air with the help of their beasts. Wings snapped wide. Talons scraped sparks from the floor. A pair of razor-feathered falcons dove in tandem before pulling up at the last second, their arcane markings flaring in brilliant gold as they swooped over the crowd.

They weren't fighting. They were performing. A choreographed display of perfect control, raw magic, and precision teamwork between tamer and beast.

It was breathtaking.

At the head of it all came a man in a sleeveless coat and char-patterned bracers, moving like a flame given form. His wyvern dove low in a corkscrew of steel and scale, sweeping the field in a blazing arc. He spun with it, not leading the charge, but dancing through it, his steps perfectly timed, his voice rising above the roar without any need for magitek enhancement.

"This is synergy," he called, his words striking like drumbeats. "This is discipline. This is what it means to earn your crest. My name is Fenric Caldane, my job is to teach you how to stay alive."

At the opposite end of the makeshift arena, a broad-shouldered bear-beast barreled through a series of enchanted dummies, swatting them aside like toys. Behind it, an instructor advanced, tall and sure-footed, a multitude of dark braids swinging behind her as she twirled a gleaming halberd in her grip. She laughed as one of the constructs lunged unexpectedly and pivoted in a clean sweep, knocking it flat before saluting the crowd with a flourish and a smirk.

"Lesson one," she called. "Be bigger, or smarter, and if you can't manage either, at least be fast. I'm Nareen Rythorn, and I'll teach you which fights to pick and how to win them."

The students cheered.

And then came the silence.

The third instructor didn't announce her arrival. She didn't need to. She moved like a shadow cut free from its source, sleek, silent, wrapped in scar-patched armor. Her jaguar-beast shimmered at her side, flickering between light and shadow. They circled the edge of the performance pit without a sound, weaving between opponents as though they already knew how the fight would end. She didn't speak. Her eyes said enough, a single, sharp look toward the first-years that sliced cleaner than any blade.

A challenge. A dare.

Earn it.

Cassara's heart thundered in her chest. Not with fear but with hunger.

This was what she came for. Not the lectures, not the titles. *This.*

As the demonstration ended, the lights shifted again, now a silvery pale hue that glittered like frost, and the faculty rose from the dais one by one.

Auren stepped forward first, arms folded behind his back, expression flat as stone.

"Don't mistake theatrics for victory," he said, voice low, cool, and razor-clean. "You'll find out soon enough whether you're a performer... or prey."

A chill rippled down Cassara's spine. Julian chuckled low beside her.

Then came Darius.

He didn't walk, he prowled. Lean and golden, glowing like he'd stepped out of a painting. His coat was a vibrant blue. On his shoulder, Virex was perched, practically preening for the crowd.

"Welcome to Vallemont," Darius said, spreading his arms like he'd built the place himself. "Where you'll learn to fight, fly, and, if you're lucky, survive. Preferably with all your limbs intact." He winked. Several first-years tittered nervously.

The applause for Darius had barely faded when the chandeliers dimmed once more, casting the hall in flickering, anticipatory shadow.

Gasps rose from the tables and whispers cracked like sparks through the crowd.

At the far end of the dining hall, the floor shimmered, then split down the middle. With a low mechanical groan, a platform began to rise, seamless polished stone edged in glowing sigils. Tables shifted aside as if compelled by unseen forces, granting a clear view from every seat.

From opposite ends of the dais, Darius and Auren stepped forward—the golden showman and the ghost of the battlefield.

Cassara's pulse quickened. Hours ago, she'd watched Auren leap through open air to battle a corrupted beast. Now here he was again, this time in controlled exhibition rather than desperate combat. Would he fight differently here? Would anyone else even know the difference?

The two men didn't speak, they didn't need to.

Darius gave a sweeping bow, theatrical as ever, one brow arched in playful challenge. Auren didn't return it. He simply rolled his shoulders back, twin daggers sliding free with a hiss of steel and intent. Light caught on the mirrored etchings of the blades, one dark, one pale, glinting like twin truths about to be told.

The same blades that had cut through corrupted flesh, Cassara thought. The same hands that had caught her mid-air. She found herself studying his stance, looking for signs of fatigue or injury from the earlier battle. There were none. Either he'd recovered completely, or he'd learned to hide weakness perfectly.

Darius's weapon snapped into being with a flick of his wrist, its spear-point gleaming before unspooling in a ribbon of segmented chain. It crackled faintly with magical charge.

All around her the room seemed to hold its breath.

Then the duel began.

Auren struck first, no preamble, no warning. A blur of motion as he darted low and fast, blades singing through the air. Cassara recognized that same economy of movement from the attack, nothing wasted, nothing for show. This wasn't a performance to him. Even here, this was practice for survival.

Darius twisted away, the chain spinning out in a wide arc to keep him at bay. Sparks flew where whip met dagger, the clash of magic and metal casting flares of blue light across their faces.

Cassara leaned forward without realizing it, her scraped arm pressing against the edge of the table. The dull ache barely registered. She was too focused on Auren's technique, memorizing it, learning from it.

Auren was precision incarnate, every step measured, every strike calculated. But Darius? Darius fought like the world bent around him. Like gravity forgot him on purpose. His whip-spear snapped and coiled, shifting from spear thrusts to sweeping arcs of chain, unpredictable as a storm.

They moved like opposite forces. Control versus chaos. Ice versus fire.

A flurry of blows. Auren nearly landed a strike to Darius's side, but the instructor pivoted with impossible grace, sliding beneath the blade, grinning.

"You've slowed," Darius teased, breathless but laughing.

"You've gotten louder," Auren replied coolly, driving him back with a flurry of dagger strikes that forced Darius to shift Encore into its spear form.

This wasn't just an exhibition, there was history here, rivalry perhaps. She wondered what Auren had been like before he became the cold, efficient fighter she'd seen today. Had he ever fought with Darius's joy? Had he ever smiled during combat?

Their beasts appeared only once, projected briefly behind them like flickering echoes. Auren's emerged in near silence—a serpent of polished mirror-scale, wingless and sinuous, she moved like smoke, her coils drifting just behind his shoulders. She didn't roar or strike. She watched. Unblinking. Unseen by many until she was already passing through them. For a moment, the light seemed to bend around her, distorting the air as if reality itself was holding its breath.

The beast suits him, Cassara thought. It was silent. Lethal. Impossible to track until it was too late. So different from the corrupted horror they'd faced on the ship, yet equally deadly in its own refined way.

Darius? Virex rose in a flare of fire and feathers, soaring above him with theatrical grace, wings wide, talons gleaming, a creature born to bask in the spotlight. He circled once, twice, then perched on the opposite side of the hall, preening as if the applause already belonged to him.

Finally, with a clash of light and force, the duel ended. Darius stood with the retracted tip of the chain spear pointed toward Auren's throat, just close enough to threaten, not wound.

But Auren's blade was already at Darius's ribs.

A draw, technically. But Cassara knew which strike would have been fatal first. She wondered if that knowledge was why Auren's expression remained so carefully neutral, even in victory.

The hall exploded with applause.

Darius grinned wide, bowing again. "A draw," he said cheerfully, "as always."

Auren gave a single nod before sheathing his blades and vanishing back into the shadowed line of faculty.

The dueling platform lowered into the floor and the golden light of the chandeliers brightened once more. A hum of conversation surged through the Great Hall, brimming with a new kind of energy, excitement, awe, and the sharp crackle of expectation.

Headmistress Kalisandra stepped forward once more, her voice cutting cleanly through the noise without needing to rise. "Our gratitude to our combat instructor for that demonstration. You've set the standard our first-years will be expected to meet."

Kalisandra gestured to the faculty table where several other instructors sat.

"Here at Vallemont, knowledge is as important as your physical prowess. You will meet your professors throughout the week so I shall keep the introductions brief. Professor Marlowe Idrin will guide you through the fascinating complexities of beast classification and the dangers of the Wilds." A woman with wild silver-streaked hair and at least three pairs of spectacles perched at various angles on her head offered an enthusiastic wave.

"Professor Thendrick Donall will help you understand the bond itself, what it means to share your soul with another." A lean man with deep eyes and long, simple robes inclined his head serenely. "And Professor Wenric Valarde will ensure you know the history that brought you here, and the mistakes you'd be wise not to repeat." An older man with a scarred face and ink-stained fingers raised a glass in sardonic salute.

"But tonight," Kalisandra continued, her tone warming slightly, "we celebrate. Welcome to Vallemont."

The Great Hall erupted in applause once more, not as exuberantly as it had following the combat performance, but enthusiastic nevertheless.

Cassara turned her attention to the table and the empty plate sitting before her. She could barely remember the last time she'd felt hungry. But now, with the air still buzzing and her heart still racing, the scent of roasted meats and honey-glazed vegetables caused her stomach to growl.

The first platters arrived in a synchronized sweep, attendants gliding between tables with effortless grace. Silver domes were lifted in unison, revealing fragrant spreads: charred wildroot in honey glaze, crisped duck with candied peel, soft-baked bread spiraled with sea salt and accompanied by thinly sliced fruits and cheeses. Even the water tasted faintly sweetened, a luxury rarely granted outside the great houses.

Cassara tore into the bread, the salt and warmth of it anchoring her. She'd fought for this, had nearly died for it. She could at least taste it.

Across from her, Julian bit into a roasted thigh of boar like it owed him an apology. Sonia was still talking about the duel, the instructors, the "absolutely ridiculous" way Darius caught Auren's wrist mid-spin, but Cassara barely heard her. Her fingers were trailing lazy circles along the rim of her glass, mind drifting somewhere between exhaustion and exhilaration. The hall felt warmer now, voices blending into a comfortable hum around her.

Until the ping resonated through the air.

A sharp crystalline chime. Then another. All around the room, first-years fumbled for their Codices as the devices awakened. The dark crystal sheets lit up from within, their etched patterns blazing to life as information bloomed in the translucent depths. Text and diagrams shifted like living things beneath the surface.

Orientation Status: Complete

Echo Trial: Registered

Tri-Oath Signature: Verified

Class Schedule: Uploaded

Dorm Assignment: Updated

Her name was etched in fine script across the top of the screen. Cassara Allencourt. Below it: her weekly timetable, a list of orientation events marked in gold, and her dorm assignment.

Room 5.

She stared at it for a beat longer than necessary, heart suddenly louder than it should've been. This was it. The final shift. No longer the heir of House Allencourt. No longer a runaway or a shadow of her mother's memory.

She was a Vallemont student now, part of the first year cohort.

Julian leaned closer to peek at her Codex. "We match?" he asked, tone light.

Cassara tilted hers just enough for him to see her room number, then shut the Codex with a soft snap.

"Guess you'll find out," she said.

He laughed under his breath, amused and unbothered, as always.

Another crystalline chime of a bell cut through the chatter, and Headmistress Kalisandra rose from her seat at the high table. She didn't need to speak—her presence alone commanded silence.

"First years," she said, her voice carrying effortlessly through the hall. "Your Codices now contain everything you need. Curfew is at tenth bell. Classes begin at eight. Do not be late." A pause, her gaze sweeping across them. "You are all free to go when you've finished your meals."

The scrape of benches and burst of conversation resumed instantly as students began filing toward the exits, Codices still glowing in their hands.

Cassara didn't hesitate, pushing up from the bench, her plate barely touched. She slipped from the table and made her way through the dispersing crowd. She needed to see it, Room 5, her new beginning.

"Cass," Julian's voice carried after her.

She didn't slow and didn't look back to acknowledge the sound of approaching footsteps. It took all she had not to sigh when Julian fell into step beside her, brushing an invisible thread of lint from his sleeve. "You didn't show me your schedule."

She arched a brow. "I wanted to keep the mystery alive."

"Dangerous game," he murmured. "You know how curious I get."

Cassara gave a noncommittal hum, gaze flicking over the names etched along the walls, honor lists, crest ranks, Vallemont's legacy carved into stone. She didn't say anything else. Julian didn't take the hint.

"I could walk you to your room," he said, voice lower now. "Make sure it's livable. Finish what we started in the lounge?"

She stopped, one brow arching higher. "You're not allowed in the girls' wing."

Julian's mouth curved slowly into a smirk. "You think a rule is enough to stop me?"

Cassara shrugged and turned back toward the corridor, stepping into the side wing clearly marked for first-year girls. The moment her boot touched the runed threshold, the air shimmered around her, faint, iridescent, like sunlight refracting on glass, and then cleared. She passed through without resistance.

Julian followed, or at least he tried to.

A sharp crack split the air and he stumbled back, catching himself against the wall with a startled grunt. Light flared across the runes at his feet, locking him out with a hiss of arcane energy. His palm was red where it had hit the barrier.

Cassara turned slightly at the sound, just enough to glance over her shoulder.

"Oh," she said, in as innocent a tone as she could muster. "I guess it does stop you."

Julian's mouth pressed into a thin line. "That's different."

She offered a half-smile. "Maybe the warding system's finally catching up to your reputation."

And then she was gone, striding down the corridor with the click of boot heels on polished stone, not sparing him another glance.

She didn't have to. She could feel his glower burning holes in her back and gods it felt good.

Room 5 sat at the end of a curved stone corridor, the number carved into the wall above the doorframe and glowing a faint blue. Cassara paused for a breath, her palm still tingling from the warmth of the Aether Codex tucked under her arm. The rest of the first-years lingered somewhere behind her, still caught in dinner and conversation.

She reached out to grasp the handle and heard the door unlock with a whisper of shifting wards.

Inside, the dormitory was dimly lit, no voices, just quiet stillness and the subtle pulse of magelight threading through the blackstone walls. The room itself curved gently inward, shaped like a crescent around a sunken common space scattered with mismatched seating: a battered armchair, some floor cushions, and a crooked-legged table already scuffed with old cup rings and scratched initials.

Her gaze swept across the room.

Five small alcoves and within each a bed and a trunk at its base and a small writing desk set back into the wall. Each space was preassigned, the meager shelves neatly stacked with folded uniforms, basic supplies, all of it carrying the faint scent of fresh polish and spell-cleansed wool.

Cassara's trunk sat before the far-left alcove, the crest of House Allencourt gleaming faintly beneath a layer of transport dust.

She turned slowly, taking in the small space with more scrutiny—the cramped arc of it, the hard simplicity of the furnishings. Her own bedroom at home was larger than this entire dorm. There, she'd had silk curtains and scented oil lamps, a view of the gardens and her own private bathing chamber carved from imported jade.

Now? Five girls. One room. One bathroom.

Gods.

She was going to have to share a sink.

She set her Codex down on the desk beside her bed and let out a sharp breath through her nose.

At least it was clean.

She brushed the curtain of her bed aside, and ran a hand along the raised mattress. Firm but not uncomfortable. She noted the shelves inside, just enough space for her Codex, a journal, a book or two. It offered privacy, but not seclusion.

The scent of oak and polished iron hung in the air, mingling with the faint residual magic of climate control. It was warm here, despite the high altitude. Cozy in a rustic sort of way, if you squinted.

Still alone, she took a few moments to inspect the communal shelf, noting a crooked teapot and a trio of mismatched mugs: one with a chip, one stained, one shaped like a snarling beast's head. The faintest smile tugged at her mouth.

It wasn't exactly a palace, but it wasn't a prison either.

The quiet didn't last.

Footsteps echoed outside, multiple pairs, and the hum of conversation approached like a rising tide.

Cassara moved back to the center of the room and turned towards the door just as Sonia swept into the room, followed closely by Evie.

"Well, this is lovely," Sonia said, gaze sweeping over the walls, nose wrinkling in disgust, acting as though she'd stepped in something unpleasant. "I hope the showers are enchanted. I'd rather not catch something."

Evie dropped her bag onto her assigned bed with a thump. "At least it's clean."

Sonia scoffed. "Low bar, Olivette. Dangerously low." She set her satchel down with more force than necessary, eyes flicking from Cassara to the rest of the room. "Well, at least we know who's slumming it together."

Evie turned toward Cassara and smiled. "Honestly, I'm glad it's you. I was worried I'd end up stuck with a bunch of strangers."

Cassara offered a slight nod, though she wasn't certain Sonia was who she would have picked given the choice. "Likewise."

The door creaked again drawing all of their attention. This time it was Liri who stepped inside, her oversized bag balanced in her arms and her Codex dangling precariously between her fingers. Her eyes widened when she saw them. "Oh! This is... us?"

Cassara's expression shifted, uncertain. She hadn't expected the girl to be in her dorm, in fact, she hadn't even considered it a possibility. "Apparently."

Sonia's smile sharpened. "You again."

Liri blinked. "Me?"

"From the platform," Sonia said, voice dipped in honey and vinegar. "You nearly flattened her, didn't you? Or was it your luggage?"

Cassara stepped forward before Liri could answer. "It was neither."

Evie gave Liri a once-over, less out of judgement and more out of curiosity. "You're the one who was looking for the beast token, right?"

Liri nodded and held out her hand in greeting. "Liri Halvorsen."

Cassara tilted her head slightly taking in the girl's flushed cheeks and the rapid rise and fall of her chest. Had she been running? "You look... flustered."

"Oh, well, I got lost," Liri admitted with a sheepish grin. "Took a wrong turn near the aerial wing and ended up in an alchemy lab. Pretty sure I'm cursed now."

Before they could say more, the door opened one final time and a tall girl stepped through without a word. Her skin was deep brown, eyes dark and sharp behind a sweep of black curls tied low at the nape of her neck. She took one look around the room, noted each of them with a calm, unreadable glance, then moved to the farthest alcove.

"Name's Talia," she said flatly. "Don't snore. Don't touch my stuff. We'll get along fine."

Without another word she climbed into her bunk and pulled the curtain half-closed behind her.

Sonia rolled her eyes. "Charming."

Cassara watched her for a long moment. No flourish, no posturing, just a blunt straightforwardness that Cassara could respect.

Interesting.

Evie made a soft hmm as she settled near the central table where Liri was unpacking her satchel. "Well. I guess that makes five."

Cassara didn't respond. She let her gaze sweep the cramped space one final time. Five girls, one room, and already enough tension to last the term.

It was going to be a long year.

CHAPTER SIX

Bright morning light cut low across the floor of the Orientation Hall, washing the stone in a cool, pale sheen. Without the crowd from the night before, the space felt quieter, stripped of ceremony. The crystal relic no longer hovered at the center and whatever force had charged the air then was absent now.

All that remained was the stone and the silence as the first year cohorts filtered in with murmured guesses about what came next.

Cassara chose her seat with care—centered, but not conspicuous. She wasn't the first to arrive, and she wouldn't be the last. Her posture was relaxed, but her eyes moved constantly, mapping the room and more importantly the other students. She wasn't the only one watching, of course, but she was the best at pretending she wasn't.

Julian slid into the seat beside her, his knee bumping hers lightly. The action was deliberate but she didn't move.

"Hm." He leaned back, arms folding lazily across his chest. "Didn't see you at breakfast."

Cassara didn't look at him. "Wasn't hungry."

A lie, technically. She'd arrived at the great hall early, poured herself a cup of tea, stared at it for a solid ten minutes, then left it untouched on the table. Her body ached, her arm was still tender, and her mind had spun all night like it was still climbing the rigging of a spiraling airship.

Julian made a quiet noise of acknowledgment, the kind that said he didn't buy it but didn't care enough to call her out. "Suit yourself. The lemon scones were decent."

She shook her head, finally allowing a sideways glance toward him and caught, just briefly, the way his gaze lingered on her, studying her like she was a puzzle he was determined to figure out.

Across from them the red-haired girl lounged, back too straight to be relaxed, one ankle hooked over her knee like the room existed for her alone. Gideon sat beside her, his arms crossed and jaw set, a silent dare carved into his silhouette.

The air shifted as the last of the students settled into place. Slow, measured footsteps approached from behind the dais. The real morning was about to begin.

The headmistress stepped forward and this time, she didn't stand above them, but among them, level, poised, and no less formidable. The light caught on the pale metal of her mantle, and for a moment, the room held its breath.

"You are here," she said simply, "because each of you made the choice to commit yourselves to this path."

A few students straightened in their seats. Cassara remained still, waiting.

"Now we begin the real work."

From her sleeve, the headmistress drew a narrow rod and tapped the floor once. Arc-light surged across the stone, unfurling a projection in the air above them, row upon row of empty crests arranged in a tiered formation that pulsed faintly like a heartbeat.

“Vallemont runs on competition,” she said. “Prestige is not ceremonial. It is power. It decides your instructors, your unit invitations, your training slots. It decides which names are remembered and which are dismissed.”

A hush rippled through the first-years.

Across the row, a wiry boy with cropped black hair was hunched over his Aether Codex, fingers flying across its surface, mouth pressed in a thin, determined line. Liri looked daunted. Curious too, maybe, and eager, but not afraid.

Sonia's expression had sharpened, the bored disdain from earlier replaced with something calculating. She tilted her head slightly, gaze flicking across the room as if already sorting students into categories of threat and irrelevance.

Olivette sat straighter, hands folded neatly in her lap, but her eyes tracked the glowing tiers with quiet intensity. No excitement. No fear. Just focus.

And Gideon... Cassara couldn't read him at all. He sat perfectly still, expression neutral, gaze fixed on the projection. Nothing in his posture suggested triumph or concern. He could have been watching paint dry for all the emotion he showed.

The headmistress raised her hand once more. The projection dimmed. Magic bled from the air casting the chamber back into its more mundane form of stone and morning light.

"That will be all," the headmistress said. "You are dismissed to your classes. Good luck as you take your first true steps into the future that waits for you."

The corridor buzzed with residual tension. First-years clustered in small knots, comparing notes, trading quiet speculation about the Prestige system, already weighing who might land where. Cassara moved through them without pausing, her stride even and expression composed.

The hallway narrowed as it curved toward the central stairwell. She was nearly through when she heard it—a light, almost musical voice too smooth to be casual.

"You move fast for someone carrying that much legacy weight. Not to mention those bruises."

Cassara slowed, turned slightly. It was the red-haired girl, the one she kept seeing with Gideon. As much as she wanted to just turn and keep walking, Cassara stopped and regarded the girl with thinly veiled disdain. "Something you wanted?"

"Just a word." She fell into step beside her like they were old friends instead of strangers circling each other like predators. "You're Cassara Allencourt, right?"

Cassara didn't bother confirming. They both knew she wasn't really asking.

"I heard you almost got yourself killed during the attack. Climbing up where you didn't belong, falling like some sort of damsel in distress. Had to get rescued by Instructor Veth? Very dramatic."

Heat flushed Cassara's neck, but her expression remained cool. "And?"

"Nothing," the girl replied airily. "Must be nice, having all that confidence. Thinking you could fix that stabilizer when you've never seen combat a day in your life." She gestured vaguely toward Cassara's injured arm. "How's that working out for you?"

"I stopped the ship from tilting," Cassara said, the words out before she could stop them.

"And then needed saving anyway." The girl smiled. "Some people think their name or their attempt at heroics are enough to earn respect here. But Vallemont doesn't care who you were before, or what desperate stunts you pull. Only who survives now."

Cassara's teeth clicked lightly together, but she didn't take the bait. "Is there a point to this, or are you just bored?"

The girl shrugged, glancing down the hall where another knot of students filtered into a classroom. "Only that you might want to be careful where you throw your weight around. Especially with certain company."

Cassara's eyes narrowed. "What company?"

The girl didn't smile this time. "Gideon."

There it was. No careful circling, no pretense.

"Whatever sparks you might have felt," she added, voice calm but clipped, "don't get your hopes up. He's not interested. Especially not in legacy brats who need rescuing when they try to play hero."

Cassara nearly laughed.

"You know where Gideon was during that attack?" the redhead continued, voice dropping even lower. "He was securing the cargo hold where three first-years were trapped. No audience. No glory. Just doing what needed to be done." Her gaze slid over Cassara. "Girls like you," she said. "You think you're special because your daddy has money. You're used to being wanted, being watched, but Gideon isn't like the boys at embassy dinners."

A slow, satisfied pause. "He doesn't chase after ornaments that break if they fall."

Cassara didn't answer, not because she couldn't, but because the words that rose weren't sharp enough. Not yet. Not for a girl like this. The kind who smiled while cutting you open.

So she held her tongue, refusing to give the girl the satisfaction of a reaction.

Cassara was about to turn and leave when Gideon's voice came from behind them. "Verena."

He approached without hurry, eyes flicking between them, face unreadable as usual. Cassara didn't meet his gaze, uncertain of how much of the conversation he had heard.

Verena's entire demeanor shifted. Her smile widened, shoulders softening like she'd been mid-joke. "We were just chatting. Weren't we, Cassara?"

Once again, Cassara didn't reply, at least not with words. The look she shot Verena could've flayed stone.

Verena seemed unbothered as she turned back to Gideon, fingers brushing his arm. "Come on or we'll be late to our next class."

From the corner of her eye, Cassara saw Gideon glance her way. She kept her gaze lowered and pretended to scroll through her Codex. Seconds ticked by and Cassara could feel Gideon watching her, though he said nothing. When she'd finally had enough, she looked up only to discover that they were gone.

Cassara stood still for a moment, trying to piece together what exactly that had been. A warning? A performance? Perhaps both. It didn't matter. Whatever game Verena thought she was playing, Cassara wasn't interested in being a piece on the board.

She didn't even know Gideon, didn't care. Not like that.

And yet...

The insult wormed beneath her skin.

There was a rustle of movement behind her.

"I don't like her either," came a soft, breathless voice.

Cassara turned to see Liri standing a few paces back. Her satchel looked even more lopsided than usual and her braid had half-unraveled down her shoulder.

"She's mean," Liri added simply, wrinkling her nose.

"So am I," Cassara pointed out.

"Yeah," Liri agreed, causing Cassara to huff in amusement. "But you don't hide it. She's the fake-smile kind of mean. I hate that kind."

Cassara blinked, caught off guard by the bluntness. No flowery politeness or careful flattery. Just truth, delivered without agenda.

"Thanks, I think," she replied before she could stop herself.

Liri surprised her by offering a smile that felt genuine. "You're welcome."

Then, glancing down the hall in the direction Gideon and Verena had gone, she added, "But we should go or we're going to get stuck sitting in the back."

Cassara nodded and fell into step beside her, tension loosening, if only slightly. She didn't say anything else, but the weight of the moment, Verena's insults and insinuations, Gideon's silence, all of it lingered behind her like a shadow.

Stepping into the Beast Theory & Classification classroom was like stepping into another world. Massive glass cases lined the walls, each one housing preserved skeletons Cassara couldn't begin to name. Some were sleek and serpentine, others jagged and birdlike, all of them seemed to have too many limbs or horn structures that defied symmetry. Overhead lanterns flickered with soft magelight, casting rippling shadows that made the whole room feel more like a museum than a place of learning.

Wooden desks were paired off and set in neat rows, many already filled with anxious looking students.

The only thing missing?

The professor.

Liri slid into a seat near the center without hesitation and patted the one beside her. Cassara hesitated, scanning the room. There was no sign of Verena or Gideon, which was odd considering they'd left ahead of them. Julian was also nowhere to be seen, and for that Cassara felt relieved. Her gaze returned to Liri, who was watching her with wide-eyed anticipation, and she sighed before sitting in the seat beside her.

She was pulling out her text book when she heard the thud of boots followed by the scrape of a chair. She resisted the urge to look, tilting her head just enough that she caught sight of Julian from the corner of her eye. He dropped into the seat behind her with the kind of ease only someone supremely confident in their place could manage. Cassara didn't turn to acknowledge him, but she felt him settle in, leaning back, arms resting loosely across the back of the chair like he owned the row.

More students filtered in, Talia, alone as always, flipping through her Codex without looking up. She sat down opposite of Liri and directly behind the wiry boy Cassara recognized from that morning.

Then came Verena.

She entered with a sway to her step while Gideon followed at her side, expression neutral. They took seats toward the back, his arms folding across his chest, hers draping along the edge of the seat like she was lounging in court.

Cassara glanced their way, just for a second.

Verena's gaze snapped to hers as though sensing Cassara's shift in attention—or perhaps simply hoping for it. She smiled, then leaned into Gideon, hand coming to rest against his leg just above the knee. She said something Cassara couldn't hear and he laughed.

She turned sharply forward, pulse flickering higher, and caught sight of Julian watching her. His head tilted, brows lifted, clearly curious about what had captured her attention. He started to turn and she felt an odd sense of panic rise in her chest.

"Julian—!"

He turned back and her mind went blank. She tried to come up with something to say that didn't sound forced or stupid, but she didn't get the chance before all chaos broke loose.

A blur of motion exploded through the open classroom door, followed by a shriek from one of the students in the front row. A creature the size of a large hunting hound tore into the room, its skin black and scaled like polished volcanic glass, but riddled with jagged fissures that oozed soft, bioluminescent green light. It had too many eyes, none of them blinking, and its tail was long and barbed like a whip made for bone-breaking.

It snarled, not a sound of pain or fear, Cassara realized, but of delight.

Several students screamed. A chair toppled. Someone threw a book which bounced uselessly off the creature's plated hide, and still, no professor in sight.

The creature began prowling the aisles, tail lashing, jaw parting to reveal rows of needle-thin teeth. Students scattered in every direction, a boy tripped over his own feet and went down with a yelp. Liri clutched her Codex like it could protect her. Cassara didn't move. She was watching its pattern, the way it stalked, circled, enjoyed the fear. This wasn't a beast lashing out.

It was *playing*.

The classroom door slammed shut with a decisive clang.

Professor Idrin strolled in from a side entrance like she'd been watching the whole time, which, knowing her reputation, she had. She wore a long, patchwork duster made from mismatched beast hides, stitched together with visible threading in a dozen different metallic colors. One of her boots was thigh-high, the other stopped at her knee, both caked in mud and something that shimmered unnaturally when it caught the light.

A pair of iridescent goggles had replaced the spectacles from dinner, and her graying honey blond hair was a wild halo of curls barely contained beneath a jeweled claw pin.

"Really, Elska," she said to the creature now stalking her way. "I said *observe*, not terrorize. You're not on the field anymore. You're a guest in my classroom. Act like one."

The creature let out a guttural noise somewhere between a purr and a growl.

"Oh, don't give me that look. I've seen your feeding report, three extra haunches *and* a marrow bone. You've had a very cushy week."

Julian straightened, still wary. A few others climbed back into their seats. The creature, named Elska, apparently, turned in a slow, irritated circle, then padded obediently to the front of the room and curled beneath Marlowe's desk like a cat sulking after being told off.

Marlowe clapped her hands once. "Excellent. Now that we've established who the real threat is, me, of course, let's begin."

She turned toward the chalkboard with a flourish that sent a dozen small charms jangling from her coat sleeve.

"Welcome to Beast Theory & Classification, children. No," she paused, raising a chalk dusted finger to her chin, "I suppose you aren't children anymore are you? As you all know, I'm Professor Marlowe Idrin. If you think you're here to memorize lists of fanged horrors and their dietary habits, you're half right. But if you think knowing a beast's weight and wing span will save you in the field?" She tapped the board once with a chalk-tipped pointer. "Then you'd best start praying your partner is smarter than you are."

She spun to face them again, hands clasped behind her back, eyes gleaming.

"This year, we'll cover classification, threat assessments, origin patterns, territorial hierarchies, and the difference between a beast that kills you and a beast that judges you first."

Cassara blinked. Liri leaned closer and whispered, "I think I'm scared and excited at the same time."

"Good," Marlowe called without looking. "That means your survival instincts are intact."

The professor strode between the rows, chalk dust clinging to her fingertips. "Unlike your previous institutions, we don't have the luxury of years for theoretical discussion. You have precisely six weeks before your first excursion to the Wildes."

A ripple of murmurs spread through the classroom.

"Yes, you heard correctly." Professor Marlowe confirmed. "Six weeks from now, you'll be tracking and attempting to capture your beast for bonding. Some of you will succeed. Some will return empty-handed." Her gaze swept the room. "Some may not rcturn at all."

Cassara felt a chill trace her spine. Six weeks seemed impossibly short.

"I'm sure you're tired of hearing this, but it's important you understand just what you're facing. The attack on your airship was no accident," Marlowe continued, turning back to the board. "Corrupted beasts are drawn to power signatures, and every one of you carries potential energy like a beacon."

She began sketching a serpentine creature with too many limbs uncomfortably similar to what had attacked their ship. "This is why you're here. To learn what calls them. To know what corrupts them. And most importantly," she tapped the chalk against a particularly vicious-looking fang, "to survive them."

"So," she turned to the class. "Does anyone know what causes a beast to become corrupted?"

Silence stretched for three heartbeats.

Then a hand shot up near the front. A girl with neat braids and an eager expression. "They're evil?"

Marlowe's expression didn't change. "No. Next."

Another student, this time from the back. "They eat corrupted meat?"

"Closer, but still wrong." Marlowe gestured broadly. "Come now, surely someone paid attention during orientation materials."

Verena's hand rose with practiced elegance. "Corruption occurs when beasts are exposed to unstable mana concentrations in certain geographic regions. The raw, unfiltered magic saturates their systems and causes physiological and psychological degradation."

Marlowe's eyes gleamed. "Textbook perfect, Miss Montero. Now tell me what that actually means."

Verena blinked, clearly thrown by the follow up question.

"Anyone else want to translate?" Marlowe prompted, scanning the room.

Julian leaned forward slightly. "The magic poisons them. Too much, too fast, and they go mad."

"Better," Marlowe said, snapping her fingers. "Think of it this way: magic, raw magic, is everywhere. It's in the air, the earth, the water. Most places, it's diffuse enough that beasts live perfectly normal lives. But in certain regions, pockets of highly concentrated mana have formed over the centuries."

She sketched a quick map on the board, marking several areas with X's. "The Black Wastes. The Westernesse Peaks. The Fettenveil. These zones and others like them are saturated with unstable magic. Beasts that wander in, or worse, are born there, absorb far more than their bodies can handle."

Cassara watched as Marlowe drew a simple beast outline, then added jagged lines radiating from it.

"The magic doesn't just poison them, it rewrites them. Their instincts warp. Their bodies mutate. They become aggressive, unpredictable, and driven by something that isn't quite hunger and isn't quite rage." Marlowe's voice lost its theatrical edge, becoming quieter, more serious. "What you saw attack your airship was a mid-stage corruption. It was still beast enough to have patterns, but twisted enough to be almost unrecognizable."

Liri raised a tentative hand. "Can they be saved? Once they're corrupted?"

Marlowe's expression softened slightly. "No, Miss Halverson. Once the corruption takes hold past a certain threshold, there's no reversing it. The kindest thing you can do is end their suffering quickly."

The room went very still.

"But," Marlowe continued, her voice brightening just a fraction, "early detection can save them. If you catch the signs before deep corruption sets in, removal from the contaminated zone and careful monitoring can sometimes halt progression. It's rare, but it happens."

The wiry boy near the front spoke up, his voice precise and measured. "What's the correlation between proximity to unstable zones and corruption rates? Is there a measurable gradient?"

Marlowe grinned. "Excellent question, Mister Straton. Yes, there is. The closer a beast lives to a high-concentration zone, the higher the risk. We map these regions constantly, tracking spread patterns and identifying new danger zones as they develop."

She tapped the map again. "Which brings me to the uncomfortable truth you all need to understand: these zones are growing. Slowly, but measurably. Twenty years ago, the Thornveil was half its current size. Fifty years ago, the Blackfen barely registered as a threat."

A student near the back shifted uneasily. "Why? What's causing them to spread?"

Marlowe paused, chalk hovering over the board. "That's the question every researcher at the Academy is trying to answer. The prevailing theory is that magic, like all energy, seeks equilibrium. As we draw power from the Sundering Stone for our cities, our tech, our way of life, the balance shifts. Instability spreads."

She turned back to face them. "But theories don't keep you alive in the field. Practical knowledge does. So listen carefully."

Marlowe began listing points, ticking them off on chalk-dusted fingers. "Signs of early corruption: unusual aggression toward previously neutral stimuli. Erratic movement patterns. Physical mutations, extra eyes, asymmetrical growths, bioluminescent markings. Discoloration of hide or scales, usually toward darker, oil-slick tones."

Cassara's hand moved across her notes, capturing every detail.

"Advanced corruption," Marlowe continued, her tone darkening, "presents as complete loss of natural behavior. The creature no longer hunts for food or defends territory. It hunts for the sake of destruction. Its body warps beyond recognition. And most importantly," she fixed them with a hard stare, "it will target you specifically because you carry potential bonding energy. You are a beacon to them."

Julian's voice cut through the tension. "So we're walking targets."

"Yes," Marlowe said simply. "Which is why you learn to recognize threats, assess danger levels, and know when to fight versus when to run."

For the next hour, chalk scraped against slate as Professor Marlowe filled the board with classifications, behavioral patterns, and survival rates.

Cassara's hand cramped from taking notes, but she didn't pause. Every detail felt vital now, not just academic. The diagrams of beast anatomy suddenly weren't abstractions but practical knowledge she might need in only six weeks' time.

"The Wildes wait for no one," Professor Marlowe said, circling a particularly ominous statistic about first-year bonding success rates. "And neither will I. First assignment: field journal entries on the native fauna visible from academy grounds. I want structural observations, behavioral patterns, and potential corruption indicators. Due by the end of the week."

The class was beginning to pack up as Professor Marlowe wiped chalk dust from her hands and fixed them with a final piercing look.

"One last thing. After yesterday's incident, beast activity around Vallemont has increased, even in the safe zones. Stay within warded boundaries unless accompanied by an upper-year or instructor." She tapped her pointer against her palm. "Remember, caution is not cowardice. But cockiness? That's how you lose limbs."

Chairs scraped as students surged to their feet.

Cassara didn't rush. She gathered her notes with practiced care, letting the hum of chatter and footfalls rise around her. Liri lingered nearby, still scribbling something in her margins.

And that's when Verena passed her desk. Her voice was pitched casually, but just loud enough to carry.

"Must be exhausting, having to prove you belong every single second."

Cassara froze and the students nearest them turned slightly, some pretending not to listen, others openly curious. Julian hadn't heard; he was already halfway to the door, Jonas and Vash trailing after him. Beside her, Liri stiffened.

Cassara, however, didn't take the bait.

She finished packing her things and when she glanced back up, Verena was gone. Taking a deep breath, Cassara followed the tide of students into the corridor, her movements brisk, the echo of Verena's parting words still burning at the edge of her temper.

"She's the worst," Liri muttered, trying for a comforting tone. "I don't even think she's that clever. Just... venomous."

Cassara didn't answer, because there he was.

Gideon.

He was leaning against the far wall with no Verena in sight. Just him and that infuriating blank expression, watching the hall like he was already bored of it all.

Cassara didn't hesitate. "Wait here."

Liri faltered behind her. "Wait, where are you-?"

"Just a second."

Gideon looked up as she approached, and the way he barely straightened only sharpened her frustration.

"What is your problem?" she asked, her voice low and clipped.

He blinked once, lazily. "I assume you'll narrow that question down?"

"Your little girlfriend won't stop pestering me."

He didn't blink. "You seem like you can handle it."

"Oh, I can. I just figured if you're going to make her your attack dog, you might want to rein her in before someone kicks back."

He gave a faint scoff, stepping closer, enough that she had to tilt her chin to meet his eyes.

"Relax," he drawled. "You're not that important."

Cassara's jaw tensed but Gideon didn't wait for her to recover.

"If this is how you treat everyone who bumps your pride," he said, already turning away, "I can't wait to see midterms."

"You think this is a game?"

"I think you're predictable," he said softly. "All flare and pride and sharp little barbs until someone calls your bluff. Verena sees it. I see it. You'll break before you bend."

A hand brushed her elbow.

"Cassara?" Liri's voice was careful. "We should get going..."

Cassara didn't move. She stared at him another second longer, like she could hold the tension there, burn him with it.

“Well, isn’t this cozy.” Julian’s voice came from behind them. On the surface it sounded casual, but Cassara knew better. Her stomach sank as Gideon’s mouth curved upwards, just slightly.

Julian stepped between them, shoulders squared and every inch of him radiating cool authority. For Cassara, his presence was immediate and suffocating.

His gaze bypassed her entirely and locked on Gideon instead, measured and unblinking. "Problem?" The word cut through the tension, deceptively calm.

“Not for me,” Gideon replied. “But leash training seems like a bigger job than I thought. You might want to put in some more practice hours with her, Tremaine.”

Julian huffed a laugh.

“How dare—”

But Gideon was already walking away without sparing so much as a backward glance. Cassara stared after him, rage simmering beneath her skin. She’d been baited, toyed with, dismissed, and the worst part? She hadn’t even landed a blow in return.

She scowled and started walking.

“What was that all about? You looked like you were going to throw him off the bridge,” Julian said as he fell into step beside her, tone light, posture lazy, but his eyes flicked toward where Gideon had gone.

“That’s still on the table,” she muttered. “What the hell is his problem?”

Julian’s smile turned sharp. “Obsession. With legacy, with proving something.”

Cassara frowned. "You say that like it's personal."

"It is," he said simply. "His grandfather left mine to burn in an ACS malfunction. Walked away while the wreckage was still smoldering. Never even tried to save him."

Cassara's breath caught. She remembered the incident, vaguely. A prototype gone wrong. Julian's grandfather had spoken about it once at a dinner she barely remembered, leaning on that cane with the silver lion head. His scars were real but surface level. His bitterness? That went much deeper.

"I thought it was an equipment failure," she said, walking slower now.

"That's what they said. What they claimed." Julian's voice cooled. "But the design belonged to the Delvanirs. The oversight, too. And when it failed, they ran."

Liri's voice was small, hesitant. "That's awful. Does Gideon... does he know what happened?"

Julian turned, just slightly. His smile never slipped, but it stiffened at the corners.

"Oh, he knows," Julian said. "His family has never recovered from it. Lost their contracts, their standing, most of their holdings."

Liri looked down, clearly wishing she hadn't asked.

"His family's been clawing for relevance ever since. And now he thinks throwing weight at anyone who still has a name will even the score." He tilted his head. "He's not targeting you, Cass. You're just a convenient way to get under my skin."

Cassara didn't answer right away. Gideon's attitude, his disdain, it certainly made more sense now. Maybe Julian was right.

"Look," he continued, his tone gentling. "I'm not saying you can't handle yourself. You've made that clear."

Cassara gave him a sidelong glance, but said nothing.

He stepped closer, just slightly, as they moved down the hall. "But you don't need to waste your time with someone like him. He doesn't respect what this place is. What it means. He's bitter, Cass. Bitter people break things when they can't have them."

His hand hovered near hers, not quite touching. "I'd rather not see you dragged down just because someone can't stand seeing you rise."

She let out a heavy sigh. It would've been easier to dismiss him if he didn't actually care, at least in his own way. Julian's smile curved like he'd already won.

Ahead of them the faint thrum of arcane light grew stronger. Their next class loomed beyond the archway, its door wide, its space already filling with students.

Julian's hand moved toward the small of her back, that familiar possessive gesture.

She stepped forward before he could make contact, putting distance between them.

"Try not to fall behind," she said, not even glancing over her shoulder.

Behind her, Liri snorted.

But Julian? He said nothing and Cassara felt his gaze follow her all the way through the door.

CHAPTER SEVEN

There were no desks in the Beast Bonding classroom. No podium, no chalkboard, no benches.

Just cushions. Neatly arranged in concentric circles across the floor, each one marked with a different beast crest. The space was dim and quiet, walls of smooth dark crystal absorbing sound instead of echoing it. High overhead, magelight orbs scattered like constellations across the arched ceiling.

Cassara hesitated in the doorway. Liri hovered beside her, clutching a book to her chest like a shield.

"This feels like a trap," Liri whispered. "A soft, comfortable, mind-magic trap."

Cassara didn't answer, but she couldn't deny the unease curling under her ribs. It was too still. like the room itself was watching.

Students began to filter in, voices lowering as they entered. Julian swept past her, his stride easy and unhurried as always. He gave the space a once-over and then dropped onto a cushion with exaggerated care, stretching out like he had every intention of napping through the hour.

When he spotted her lingering, he patted the empty cushion beside him with a crooked grin.

Sighing, Cassara moved toward him, her gaze sweeping the room as she did. She regretted doing so immediately. Gideon was already seated near the center, arms crossed, looking like he wanted to be anywhere but there. To Cassara's surprise, Verena sat in the back row beside a dark-haired girl she didn't recognize, managing to look bored and elegant all at once.

She was about to turn away when Gideon's eyes found hers. She could almost see the wheels turning as he flicked his gaze toward Julian, then back to her, and mouthed a single word: *Leash*.

Heat flared in her chest. She pivoted sharply and dropped onto the cushion beside Liri instead.

"Good call," Liri muttered, glancing toward Julian. "He was going to talk the entire time, I could feel it."

Before Cassara could respond, a soft voice spoke from the front of the room.

"You all sat by trust, not instinct."

Professor Thendrick Donall stood at the center of the room as though he'd always been there and they simply hadn't noticed until now. He was barefoot, robed in star-threaded navy, his dark hair hanging loose down his back in clean, symmetrical lines. His expression was placid, the kind of calm that unsettled rather than soothed.

"As you all know, I am Professor Thendrick. This is Bonding Mechanics and Empathic Sync. You are here to learn how to listen, not with your ears, but with everything else. Your bonds will not be built with orders. They will not be won by brute force. They will begin here." He pressed a hand to his chest.

A flicker of motion near his feet caught her attention. When she looked, Cassara glimpsed part of a tail, long and faintly translucent, before it vanished behind his legs again.

Thendrick didn't acknowledge it.

Instead, he lifted his hands, and the magelights dimmed further until the room was bathed in twilight. "Many of you encountered your first corrupted beast yesterday. You felt fear and helplessness."

A murmur rippled through the students.

"What you didn't feel," he continued, "was connection."

With a fluid motion of his wrist, he cast a small crystalline orb into the center of the room. It hovered, then expanded, unfurling into a three-dimensional projection. In its depths, a corrupted beast materialized, far smaller but no less terrifying than the one that had attacked their ship. Its segmented body writhed in slow motion, lightning pulsing through translucent sacs.

Several students flinched and one girl near the back gasped.

"Corrupted beasts cannot bond," Thendrick said, circling the projection. "They have forgotten how to listen to the mana vibrations. How to connect to the magic itself and thus they are driven only by an insatiable need to consume, to seek that which they can no longer find." He passed his hand through the image, dispersing it like smoke. "But they remember. Somewhere deep, they remember what they once were."

The projection shifted, the corrupted form dissolving and reforming into something sleeker, brighter, the same creature, but uncorrupted. Beautiful in its alien way, lightning sacs now glowing with controlled, rhythmic pulses.

"Today," Thendrick said. "You will reach out."

From a hidden compartment in the floor, a second crystal rose, larger, faceted, humming with subtle energy.

"This is an Echo Stone," he explained. "It contains the empathic signature of a juvenile skywhale. Harmless, curious, and currently circling the eastern tower."

He gestured, and the stone began to pulse with soft blue light.

"Close your eyes," he instructed. "Breathe. Feel for the presence beyond your own. Don't try to control it. Don't demand its attention. Simply... acknowledge it."

Cassara did as he instructed, skeptical but intrigued. At first, there was nothing, just the darkness behind her eyelids and the awareness of bodies around her.

Then, faintly, a presence brushed against her consciousness, not a voice, not a thought, but a sensation. Curiosity. Movement. The vastness of sky and the joy of currents.

"If you are reaching correctly," Thendrick's voice sounded distant, as though he were suddenly addressing them from across a chasm, "you will feel the skywhale's response."

The presence nudged closer, gentle but insistent, and Cassara's eyes snapped open. Her shoulders tensed, breath catching as she pulled back instinctively from whatever had been reaching toward her.

Around the room, reactions varied. Liri was smiling, eyes still closed. Julian looked bored, though his fingers twitched slightly against his knee. Gideon sat perfectly still, his expression intense rather than relaxed.

Verena's eyes were open, watching Gideon instead of participating.

"Those of you who felt nothing," Thendrick said after several minutes, "do not despair. Connection takes practice. Those who felt the response, remember it. That is the foundation of bonding."

The crystal dimmed and the presence receded.

Thendrick moved between them silently. Once or twice, he murmured something too low to catch.

When he passed Cassara, he paused. His gaze lingered on her for a moment, thoughtful.

"Resistance," he said quietly, just loud enough for her to hear. "Interesting."

She met his eyes. "It's just a meditation exercise."

"Is it?" His expression didn't change, but his tone suggested he knew better. Then he moved on without waiting for an answer.

When Thendrick dismissed them, Cassara gathered her things quickly, not particularly interested in lingering. The professor had already turned his attention to a small stone basin near the wall, his beast, whatever it was, still hidden from view.

"That was weird, right?" Liri said as they headed for the door. "Like, deeply weird?"

"Extremely," Cassara agreed.

"Did you feel anything?" Liri asked, her voice dropping to a whisper. "I think I did, but I'm not sure if I actually did or if I just wanted to."

Cassara hesitated. "Something. I don't know what."

"Well, at least you're honest about it." Liri adjusted her satchel. "Half the class is probably going to claim they had some profound spiritual awakening when really they just fell asleep sitting up."

Despite herself, Cassara smiled. "Probably."

"Come on," Liri said, picking up her pace. "We've got combat class next, and I heard Instructor Nareen makes latecomers spar with third-years."

The first year training field was on the western edge of campus, a long walk that took them past massive windows overlooking the floating academy grounds. Clouds drifted by at eye level, occasionally parting to reveal dizzying glimpses of the world below. At one junction, the corridor opened to a balcony where a squad of third-years were engaged in aerial drills, their bonded beasts, mostly avians and winged reptiles, banking in tight formation.

One rider spotted them watching and directed her mount into a theatrical dive that made Liri gasp and clutch Cassara's arm.

"Show-offs," Cassara muttered, but she couldn't help feeling a pang of envy. How long before she'd have a beast of her own?

"We should hurry," Liri said, glancing at her Codex. "We still need to change, and Nareen's class starts in five minutes."

They ducked into the nearest training preparation chamber, a room lined with individual partitions and spell-warmed screens. Liri continued talking as they changed, her voice carrying over the dividers.

"Do you think she'll make us spar right away? I heard she doesn't believe in warm-ups. Just throws you into it to see what you're made of. My cousin said she once made a first-year fight a practice dummy that hit back. Literally hit back, with actual force. Do you think that's true? It sounds true. She seems like the type who'd do that. Oh, do you think we'll use weapons today or just hand-to-hand? I'm better with a staff than bare-handed, but I don't know if—"

Cassara pulled on her training tunic, the high collar stiff against her throat. Liri's voice was a steady stream of nervous energy, questions tumbling out one after another without pause for answers.

It should have been annoying.

It wasn't. Not entirely.

"—and Barrett said his brother trained under her two years ago and she made him run the obstacle course in full gear in the rain, which seems excessive but I guess that's the point, right? To push you past what you think you can—oh, are you ready?"

Cassara stepped out from behind the partition, adjusting the fitted combat slacks reinforced at the knees. The fitted tunic was a deep crimson and bore Vallemont's silver thread insignia over her chest. No crest yet. That would have to be earned.

"Ready," she said.

Liri beamed, still chattering as they headed for the exit. "Good, because I really don't want to be late. Did I mention the thing about third-years? Because apparently—"

Cassara stopped listening once they reached the upper field and stepped into the packed stone yard, a wide training ring etched with chalk lines and faded sigils from long-forgotten bouts. Her boots scuffed against the ground, already powdered with dust.

Julian was already there, stretching casually near the center line, a rolled towel slung around his neck and his sleeves pushed back to expose his forearms. He looked unfairly composed in the uniform, his blond hair windswept like it had been styled that way on purpose. He caught her eye and offered a knowing smirk.

She didn't return it, but her gaze lingered a second longer than necessary.

He did look good, even if she didn't want to admit it.

At the far end of the field, Gideon turned from where he'd been adjusting the straps of his sparring gloves, his own uniform less crisp but somehow sharper for it. He rolled his shoulders, taut and loose at the same time, like a coiled spring walking. He didn't smirk, just met her stare with a flick of interest that sent heat up her neck.

Which, naturally, was when *she* arrived.

A flash of auburn hair and carefully choreographed malice. Verena swept past, shoulder angled hard. The collision wasn't accidental.

Cassara staggered half a step, teeth clenching as she whipped around.

"What the hell—"

"Ladies," came a voice like a blade drawn slow from its sheath.

Instructor Nareen strode onto the field, a long halberd slung easily across her shoulders, dark braids twisted back from her sharp-angled face. Her eyes cut between the two of them with dispassionate ease.

"There will be plenty of time to bloody each other," she said. "You want to throw a punch, you do it in the ring."

Verena's smile curled, clearly pleased by the implication. Cassara ignored her.

Nareen dropped the halberd with a metallic thud, letting its base settle in the center of the yard. Around them, the rest of the class filtered in, some still laughing, others already sizing up their competition.

"Welcome to Basic Combat," Nareen said, her voice carrying without needing to be raised. "The rules here are simple. You hit fast. You hit clean. You listen. The moment you forget, someone else gets to teach you why you're wrong."

She began pacing slowly, the halberd dragging a line in the dirt.

"We train as if your lives depend on it, because one day, they will. You'll learn strikes, holds, grapples. You'll learn how to fight without your beast and how to survive long enough to summon it. You'll learn what it means to face someone stronger and still win."

She stopped, glancing between them.

"And if you don't like getting hit, you better learn how to hit back harder or move faster."

Cassara's blood hummed.

Finally.

Nareen gave the group a long, measuring glance. "I can see you're eager," she said. "Good. Let's see if you're worth the bruises."

She moved to the edge of the ring, halberd in hand, and stabbed the butt of it into the dirt. "This is not a spar for prestige, though I am obligated to provide the points. It's an assessment. I want to see how you move. Your form. Your speed. How you handle a live opponent."

The class shifted, murmurs rising as students straightened, eyes sharpening.

Nareen barked a few names, pairing off students. The first matches were quick and unremarkable. A girl with blonde hair managed to land a solid hit before getting swept off her feet by her opponent's counter. Another pair circled each other cautiously, trading half-hearted jabs that Nareen criticized for lacking commitment. A third match ended when one student overextended and took an elbow to the ribs that left him wheezing on the ground.

Cassara watched with detached interest. Adequate technique, but nothing impressive. No one moved with real confidence, and most were too focused on not getting hit to actually land anything meaningful.

When Nareen reached the middle of the list, her eyes flicked between two standing apart from the others.

"Tremaine. Delvanir. You're up."

Julian raised an eyebrow and gave a long-suffering sigh that couldn't quite hide his excitement. "Going straight for the crowd-pleasers, are we?"

Across from him, Gideon said nothing. He just stepped forward, eyes narrowed, not at Julian, but at the space between them.

Cassara folded her arms as the two entered the ring, watching closely. Julian loosened his stance like a duelist preparing to perform, smiling faintly as he rolled his shoulders. Gideon didn't smile. His expression never changed.

Nareen raised a hand. "Begin."

Julian struck first, fast and clean, a classic forward lunge aimed low. Gideon dodged, twisting just out of reach, and countered with a sweeping leg aimed at Julian's feet intending to knock him off balance. Julian hopped it easily, pivoted into a backhanded feint, and their rhythm snapped into motion.

Cassara leaned forward slightly, analyzing their forms. She'd seen Julian spar countless times at embassy functions and private lessons. His movements were predictable to her, the slight twist of his wrist before a feint, the way his left foot pivoted when he was setting up a combination. It was strange seeing those familiar patterns deployed against someone who wasn't playing by the same rulebook.

It was clear they'd both been trained, their movements were fast, two distinct styles clashing in the dust. Julian moved like someone who'd learned from books and personal tutors, refined, flashy, confident. Gideon was all instinct and tension, controlled but reactive, like he was waiting for a real fight to start.

The first strike landed with a sharp crack of contact: Julian's elbow against Gideon's ribs.

"Point Tremaine," Nareen called, her voice cutting through the tense silence.

Cassara caught the flicker of satisfaction in Julian's eyes. That familiar spark of pride when he executed something perfectly. She'd seen it a hundred times, usually followed by that same glance toward the audience, seeking admiration.

But Gideon didn't falter. He twisted, ducked, and returned a jab to Julian's shoulder that would've knocked someone less prepared to the ground.

"Point Delvanir," Nareen acknowledged, circling the edge of the ring.

Julian's jaw clenched, a small tell that only someone who knew him well would notice. Cassara felt an unexpected twist in her stomach. She should be rooting for Julian without question. He was her... what? Friend? Ally? Almost-fiancé? Yet part of her couldn't help admiring the raw efficiency of Gideon's movements, how little he seemed to care about looking good while fighting.

A breath passed. Another flurry of movement, bodies blurring in controlled aggression. Julian landed a precise strike to Gideon's upper arm.

"Point Tremaine," Nareen announced. "Two-one."

Julian's smile returned, sharper now. Cassara recognized the dangerous edge to it, the same look he got when someone challenged him at embassy galas. That practiced charm hardening into something more territorial. His next combination was flashier than necessary, designed to impress rather than simply win.

The tension in the ring shifted. Julian's confidence swelled visibly, his movements becoming more theatrical. Gideon's expression hardened, his focus sharpening. In a sudden burst of speed, he feinted left, spun right, and caught Julian with a sweep that nearly took his feet from under him.

"Point Delvanir," Nareen called. "Two-two."

Cassara's breath caught. She hadn't expected that. Neither had Julian, judging by the flush creeping up his neck. That wasn't embarrassment, it was anger. *Real* anger, the kind he usually kept carefully hidden behind protocol and pedigree.

She found herself unexpectedly torn, uncomfortable with her own uncertainty. Julian was supposed to win. That was the natural order of things in their world. Yet watching Gideon match him point for point stirred something rebellious in her chest. If Julian could be challenged here, what else wasn't as certain as she'd been taught?

The final exchange was lightning-fast. Both fighters abandoned caution, each seeking the winning point. Their strikes connected simultaneously, Julian's palm to Gideon's chest, Gideon's forearm across Julian's collar.

"Draw," Nareen declared, stepping between them. "Final score: two-two."

Julian straightened first, flicking a bit of dust off his sleeve. "Not bad," he said, glancing toward the watching students like he'd meant it for them. But Cassara didn't miss the tension in his shoulders, the way his fingers flexed and curled at his sides. He was furious beneath that smile.

Gideon didn't respond. He simply left the ring, but not before his gaze slid briefly toward Cassara. There was no triumph there, no seeking of approval. Just a quiet, measuring look that made her skin prickle with awareness.

She glanced away first, unsettled by her own reaction. By all rights, she should be disappointed for Julian. Instead, she felt oddly relieved at the tie, as if some decision had been postponed, some choice she wasn't ready to make.

Nareen's eyes lingered on them both, undecipherable. Then she gestured for the next pair.

"Halvorsen. Ashton. You're up."

Liri stepped into the ring with a hesitant bounce in her step, her hands flexing at her sides. Across from her, Evie looked a bit uncomfortable, offering a small smile as she adjusted the grip on her training staff.

Nareen didn't waste time. "Begin."

Evie moved first, tentative, controlled. Her stance was steady, grounded, but her hesitation was obvious. She'd been trained to defend, not push. Liri, in contrast, danced around the edge of the ring with more speed than power, staying light on her feet, eyes darting, calculating.

Cassara watched from the sidelines, arms crossed. This match didn't have the tension of the last. There was no fire, no quiet seething beneath the surface, just two girls who didn't want to hit each other.

Still, Liri surprised her.

The moment Evie went for a clumsy forward swing, Liri dropped low, slipped under it, and tapped her on the ribs with a swift, controlled blow.

"Point Halvorsen," Nareen called. "Again."

Cassara blinked, reassessing everything she'd assumed about Liri. The awkward, scattered girl who could barely keep her books together had just moved with unexpected precision. There was muscle memory there, the kind that came from training, not random luck.

They reset.

This time, Evie tried to strike first again, but Liri was faster. She ducked, twisted, and landed another clean touch to Olivette's thigh. Gentle, but undeniable.

"Point Halvorsen. Two-zero"

Cassara found herself leaning forward, studying Liri's footwork. It wasn't the polished technique of formal training like Julian's. This was something else, practical, efficient, almost instinctive. Where had a scholarship student learned to move like that? Not at any academy Cassara knew of.

Liri landed a third point and Nareen called the match.

Evie stepped back, cheeks flushed, but not angry. "You're quicker than you look," she said, brushing off her sleeves.

Liri smiled sheepishly. "Sorry."

"Don't be. That was impressive."

Still, as Liri returned to the sidelines, Cassara caught the way her shoulders were hunched, like she was disappointed in herself for winning. The posture reminded her uncomfortably of herself in those moments when she'd outperformed the expectations her father had set, how she'd learned to temper her own successes to avoid drawing attention. She nudged Liri lightly with her elbow when she reached her side.

"You're allowed to be good, you know," Cassara muttered.

Liri's cheeks went pink. "Right. Sorry. I mean, thanks."

Cassara's gaze lingered on Liri a moment longer. Perhaps there was more to her roommate than met the eye, and perhaps she wasn't the only one at Vallemont with secrets worth keeping.

"Next match, Allencourt and Norran."

Movement at the edge of the field caught her attention before she could step forward. Auren had appeared near the observation platform, hands in his pockets, posture casual. He didn't announce himself, just settled against one of the stone pillars like he'd been passing by and decided to linger.

Cassara's stomach tightened. Of course. The one instructor who already thought she was reckless had decided to show up and watch.

Nareen's gaze flicked toward him, one eyebrow rising. "Didn't realize first-year sparring was worth your time these days, Veth."

"Had a gap between classes," he said easily. "Thought I'd see what this year's cohort has to offer."

Cassara stepped forward trying to ignore the weight of Auren's presence at the edge of her vision. Across the training ring, Talia took a single step toward the center.

Then Verena cut in front of her, striding into the ring with a smile that was all confidence and calculated provocation.

"You're not Norran," Nareen said, already moving to intercept.

"I know," Verena said, her tone light but pointed. "But I thought we'd give you something more interesting to watch. Let Allencourt show us all what a legacy really looks like."

Her eyes flicked briefly toward Auren as she said it, making sure he was paying attention.

Cassara's jaw tightened, but she kept her expression neutral as she entered the ring without a word. She wouldn't give Verena the satisfaction of a reaction.

Nareen frowned but didn't stop them. "Fine. Same as before. First to three wins. You break the rules, I bench you both."

Cassara took her place, settling into a ready stance. Across from her, Verena rolled her shoulders once, her copper hair pulled back tight, her eyes sharp and calculating.

And somewhere behind her, just out of sight, Auren was watching. Probably waiting to see if she'd do something reckless again.

She wouldn't.

"Begin," Nareen called.

CHAPTER EIGHT

Verena moved first, aiming high with a clean strike meant to intimidate. Cassara blocked with her forearm, the impact jarring, but she didn't give ground. She twisted, pivoted low, and came up with a counter-strike.

Their arms clashed with a dull thud of flesh against flesh.

Verena grinned. "Come on, Allencourt. I thought you were supposed to be a prodigy."

Cassara didn't answer, instead she let her feet do the talking.

Verena overcommitted on a sweep. Cassara slipped inside her guard, shoulder slamming into Verena's ribs with controlled force. As she staggered back, Cassara struck across her side with a clean, resounding blow.

"Point Allencourt," Nareen called.

Verena's smile vanished.

They reset. Verena's eyes had gone cold now, dangerous in a way that should have concerned Cassara more than it did. Her gaze flicked briefly to Cassara's right arm, the same arm that had been scraped raw during the airship attack. The bandage was visible just below her sleeve, a hint of white against her skin.

"Still sore from your little adventure?" Verena asked, voice low enough that only Cassara could hear. "Must be hard fighting when you're already damaged."

Cassara kept her expression neutral, but inwardly she tensed.

Verena circled this time, slower. Then she struck, hard and low. Cassara deflected, but not fast enough. Verena's kick clipped her thigh with bruising precision.

"Point Montero."

One to one.

They squared off again. This time, Verena shifted her stance, angling herself to force Cassara to defend with her injured arm. It was subtle, calculated, the kind of tactic that wasn't explicitly against the rules but walked the line of fair play.

Cassara felt a flare of pain as she raised her arm to block Verena's next strike, the impact sending a shock through her shoulder. She didn't flinch, didn't falter, but Verena's smile told her the discomfort had shown in her eyes.

"What's wrong?" Verena murmured. "Need Instructor Veth to catch you again?"

The words hit harder than the strike. Cassara tried not to think of Auren watching from the edge of the field. Watching her struggle. Watching Verena land hits on her injured arm. The instructor who already thought she was reckless, now watching her prove she couldn't even handle a first-year sparring match without showing weakness.

They clashed again, and this time it was more than sparring. The tempo changed. Neither of them held back. There was pride in every strike, defiance in every dodge. Each movement was sharper, faster. Students on the sidelines murmured, drawn to the tension that crackled in the air.

Verena drove another strike toward Cassara's injured side. This time, Cassara was ready. She twisted away from the blow, letting it pass harmlessly by her ribs, and in the same fluid motion, brought her elbow around in a controlled arc that caught Verena's shoulder, clean and square.

"Point Allencourt," Nareen announced, her sharp eyes missing nothing.

Two to one.

Verena's next attack was faster and sloppier, fueled by spite. Her composure cracking under the pressure of potential defeat.

She faked high, then aimed for Cassara's ribs, but Cassara was already moving. Despite the throbbing in her injured arm, she spun, planted her heel, and drove her fist into Verena's stomach hard enough to knock the wind out of her.

Verena staggered. The match was over.

"Point Allencourt. Match concluded," Nareen called, stepping between them.

Cassara lowered her guard, breathing hard but controlled. Her injured arm burned with exertion, but the pain felt almost satisfying now. She'd won not despite her injury, but with a sharper focus because of it.

Verena straightened, her expression a careful mask once more. "Lucky strikes," she said, but the words lacked conviction.

Cassara met her gaze evenly. "Wasn't luck," she replied, voice low. "And it wasn't a show, either."

As she turned to leave the ring, her eyes swept toward the observation platform. Auren was halfway down the steps, his back to the field as he walked away. He didn't look back. Didn't acknowledge the match he'd just watched. Just left, as casually as he'd arrived.

She caught Gideon watching from the sidelines. His expression was neutral, as usual, but there was reassessment in his eyes. She looked away first, not wanting to acknowledge the small flicker of satisfaction that came from his attention.

Nareen stepped forward before either of them could say another word.

"You disobeyed a direct order," she said flatly. "Impressive footwork, both of you, but this isn't your personal grudge ring. Pull that again and you'll be eating lunch with the medics."

Cassara held back a smirk.

Verena didn't.

They turned without a word, walking opposite directions.

Liri met Cassara with wide eyes and a grin that she was clearly trying to suppress.

"Did you see Instructor Veth?" Liri whispered, leaning close. "He watched your entire match. Didn't look away once."

Cassara's pulse kicked up, but she kept her expression carefully neutral. "He was evaluating the match."

"Maybe," Liri said, her tone suggesting she didn't believe that for a second. "But Instructor Nareen seemed surprised he showed up at all. And he didn't leave until after you won."

Cassara didn't reply. Instead she forced herself to focus on steadying her breathing, on ignoring the lingering burn in her injured arm.

"Remind me not to spar with you," Liri added after a moment, her voice returning to its usual lightness.

Nareen paced the center of the field with her staff resting across her shoulders, watching the last few students catch their breath and rejoin the gathered ranks. Her gaze lingered on Cassara and Verena as they returned to their places, muscles still tight with adrenaline.

“Let me be clear,” Nareen said, voice crisp. “This is not a dueling pit.”

Silence fell. Even the wind pulling through the arena stilled like it was listening.

"This was an evaluation. A chance to assess what you bring to the table. Skill, instinct, control. What I saw today? Plenty of the first two." Her eyes flicked toward Cassara, then Verena. "Not so much of the third."

A few students shuffled uncomfortably.

Nareen stepped closer. "You may think it doesn't matter. That raw talent will carry you through. It won't. Out there—" she jabbed her staff toward the jagged cliffs beyond the field "—talent means nothing if you can't follow orders. If you can't control your emotions when it counts."

Cassara held her ground, jaw tight. She could feel eyes on her, but she didn't flinch.

Nareen tilted her head slightly. "That said… I've seen worse first days. First-year assessments are complete. Preliminary prestige standings have been logged."

The buzz on the training field dimmed.

"Top marks, Cassara Allencourt. Form, control, response time. You earned it. Keep earning it."

Cassara didn't move, didn't smile, but the heat rising beneath her skin had nothing to do with the exertion. She felt dozens of eyes flicking toward her.

"Delvanir," Nareen continued, tone neutral, "Second. Clean execution. No wasted motion. Keep your temper out of your shoulders."

Gideon gave no visible reaction.

"Tremaine," she went on. "You favor power over adaptability. Don't confuse flash for strategy. Third."

Julian tilted his head, seemingly unbothered, but Cassara caught the faint tightening at the corner of his mouth.

"And Halvorsen. Fourth. Good instincts. Stop apologizing for them."

Liri let out the tiniest gasp beside her, then clamped both hands over her mouth like the sound had betrayed her.

Nareen turned. "As for the rest of you, your performance is your problem. Learn from it."

She didn't call Verena's name. Not once. But the silence after Halvorsen's rank was louder than any reprimand. Verena's shoulders were stiff, her expression dark. Someone whispered behind their hand and someone else laughed too quickly.

Cassara felt the shift happen, like a door quietly closing behind her. She hadn't just won a match.

She'd made her mark and now, they'd all be watching.

"Adequate for a first session," Nareen announced, addressing the entire class. "But adequate doesn't keep you alive in the field. Each of you is required to log at least twelve additional training hours per week in the combat halls outside of class. Your Codex will track your progress, and yes, I will know if you're training or just standing around gossiping."

She paced the edge of the ring, gaze sweeping over the students.

"Those who demonstrate exceptional progress will earn privileges. The top ten performers by week's end will be granted access to run the training Rift."

A murmur rippled through the group. The Rift was notorious, a grueling obstacle course that simulated real combat conditions against illusion beasts. It was usually reserved for second-years and above.

"This isn't about legacy names or raw talent," Nareen continued, her eyes lingering briefly on Cassara, then Gideon. "It's about who wants it most. Who puts in the work when no one's watching."

Cassara felt her pulse quicken. The Rift would be an opportunity to prove herself beyond sparring matches, a chance to show real combat readiness just weeks before the Wildes expedition.

"You'll train in groups starting next week," Nareen continued. "Teamwork drills. Tactical matches. Until then, expect bruises. Earn your place. And if you've got something to prove, prove it with discipline or don't prove anything at all."

With that, she stepped back, staff spinning once in her grip before coming to rest by her side.

"Dismissed."

Cassara let out a slow breath as students began to scatter, many already discussing training schedules and the Rift opportunity. Liri bumped her shoulder lightly.

"The Rift?" she whispered, eyes wide with a mixture of excitement and terror. "I heard a second-year broke her arm in there last term. The illusion beasts might not be real, but the walls definitely are."

"Good," Cassara replied, her mind already calculating how to fit those twelve hours into her schedule, and how to ensure she'd be among the top ten. "Real walls make for real training."

Liri gave her a look that suggested Cassara might be slightly unhinged. "You're really excited about this, aren't you?"

Cassara didn't answer, but the corner of her mouth lifted in a small, determined smile.

"Let's get changed," she said at last, not waiting to see if Liri followed.

The training field had cleared by the time Cassara returned, boots clean of dust, hair damp from a quick rinse, and the sharp lines of her uniform restored. Her muscles still thrummed with exertion, the pulse of the match with Verena echoing in her limbs.

She was nearly to the stone archway when Nareen's voice stopped her.

"Allencourt."

She turned to see Instructor Nareen standing at the edge of the corridor, still dressed in her instructor gear, her braids wind-tossed but tight.

"Walk with me."

Cassara obeyed without argument. They moved in silence down a side corridor, the stone beneath their boots smooth from years of wear. Overhead, the sigils flickered faintly, pulsing with the soft breath of active magic. A sharp gust of wind hissed through the slats as they climbed a set of narrow stairs and stepped onto one of the upper balconies, the air high and thin but the space secluded.

Nareen didn't speak until they reached the far end, where the balcony overlooked the training fields below. The sprawl of stone and sand and glyph covered dummies shimmered in the afternoon light.

Unlike the upper field they'd just left, the main training grounds weren't empty. A group of second-years had assembled in tight formation, weapons drawn, their movements synchronized with practiced precision. At their center, unmistakable even from this distance, stood Auren.

His coat was gone, replaced by a close-fitting training uniform that revealed the lean muscle beneath. He moved between the students with predatory grace, occasionally correcting a stance or demonstrating a technique with such speed that Cassara could barely follow the motion.

She tried not to let her gaze linger too long, but found herself studying his form despite herself. This wasn't the frantic combat from the airship attack, this was controlled, deliberate, each movement a lesson in efficiency. Even from here, she could see why the students watched him with such intensity. There was nothing wasted in how he moved. Nothing for show.

One of the second-years attempted a complex maneuver and faltered. Auren stepped in, repositioned the student's arm with a quick, precise adjustment, and stepped back. When the student tried again, the movement flowed perfectly.

Cassara pulled her attention away, conscious that she'd been watching longer than necessary. She noticed Nareen observing her wordlessly.

"Did you need something, instructor?" Cassara asked at last, shoulders squared, hands clasped behind her back.

Nareen glanced down at the fields, then sideways at Cassara. "Your mother used to stand here after drills. Same fire in her posture. Same refusal to rest after a win."

Cassara fought a frown. "You knew her?"

"She came through Vallemont the same year I did. Always two strides ahead of the rest of us. Gods, she was driven. Would've crossed her own shadow if it meant outpacing it." Nareen leaned her hands on the railing. "But it wasn't the strength that made her exceptional. Everyone here's strong. It was the way she carried people with her. The way she made them want to keep up."

Cassara stayed quiet, watching the wind stir dust across the abandoned rings below.

Nareen didn't look at her. "You've got her fire. I saw it today."

"I'm not trying to be her."

"No. You're trying to be better," Nareen replied, finally looking at her again, one brow raised. The instructor's gaze held hers for a moment, thoughtful but not unkind. "Just remember, even the best can fall behind if they're running a race no one else is in."

Cassara didn't answer.

Nareen gave her a nod, not quite approval, not dismissal either. "You've got the edge, Cassara. Learn when to cut with it. And when to sheathe it."

With that, she gave Cassara a light pat on the shoulder and walked way.

For a long while Cassara just stood there, the wind catching loose strands of hair around her face. The echo of her mother's words pressing in on her.

You win everything. And still, you are alone.

She shook it off.

She didn't come here to be warned. She came to win.

And she wasn't about to apologize for the fire in her blood.

By the time Cassara stepped into the Great Hall, the scent of roasted meat, garlic potatoes, savory gravy, and warm bread already filled the air. The long tables stretching the length of the room were already filled with first-years. At the far end, platters refilled themselves in slow, graceful loops of magic, roasted fowl carving clean off the bone, berries tumbling into bowls, steam curling from silver pitchers of honeyed tea.

Evie spotted her and lifted a hand, waving Cassara toward a half-filled bench near the center of one of the lower tables. Sonia sat beside her, already halfway through a plate of grilled squash and smoked fish, chewing delicately while pretending not to watch Cassara approach.

"I saved you a spot," Evie said with a small smile, scooting over to make room. "Before the upper-tier vultures swoop in and claim it for clout."

Cassara sat, grateful for the buffer. "How thoughtful," she murmured, reaching for a plate as a platter drifted into range, offering carved lamb with a drizzle of golden glaze.

"Just doing our part for the underdog legacy," Sonia said lightly, not looking up. Her tone was sweet, her expression practiced. "Though I suppose you're more of a dark horse at this point."

Cassara's fork paused mid-stab and Evie shot Sonia a look over her mug of tea, but said nothing.

Before Cassara could craft a reply, Liri arrived, tray wobbling precariously in her hands. She slid into the open seat beside Sonia, who greeted her with a too-sweet smile.

"Did you have to bring half the buffet?"

Liri flushed. "I-I wasn't sure what I'd want."

Cassara's eyes narrowed but before she could snap back, a loud, trilling laugh rang out from a table near the center aisle.

Verena.

She sat surrounded by a small cluster of first-years, mostly boys, hanging on her every word. She tossed her hair over one shoulder, leaned in, and pointed directly toward their table.

Another laugh accompanied by a ripple of snickers. Someone looked over and then quickly away when Cassara met their gaze.

"What do you think she said?" Evie muttered, her fork stabbing a slice of apple.

"Something petty and insecure, probably," Liri offered. "That's usually the flavor."

Cassara didn't answer. Her eyes stayed locked on Verena for one second too long. She hadn't said a word, but the laughter echoed all the same.

She turned back to her food and forced herself to remain calm as she cut the lamb into clean bites and let the warmth of the tea soothe the tightness in her chest.

"Don't," Evie said softly, nudging her elbow. "She wants the reaction. Don't give it to her."

Cassara gave the faintest nod. But the air still felt charged.

"Do you mind if I join you ladies?" Julian's voice drifted over them laced with the smooth confidence of someone already knowing the answer.

"Plenty of room," Sonia said, already shifting her tray to make space.

Julian circled the table and dropped into the open seat beside Cassara, his coat slung loose over one shoulder, hair still tousled from combat drills. He looked maddeningly relaxed, the faint gleam of exertion still clinging to his skin like a crown.

"Miss me?" he asked, voice pitched low for her alone.

"Not even a little," Cassara replied without looking at him. Of course that did little to hide the warmth coloring her cheeks when he spoke like that.

He poured himself a drink, casually letting his leg brush against hers beneath the table. "Liar."

Evie cleared her throat, cheeks a little pink as she focused very intently on her soup.

"You should eat more," Julian added, tone breezy but pointed. "You'll need the energy. I heard Nareen's taking first-years into the agility courses tomorrow."

Liri perked up. "Wait, I thought we weren't starting those until next week?"

"You're not," Julian said without turning. "But Cassara's not exactly on the standard track, is she?"

Cassara, still not looking at him, reached for the bread instead of giving into the temptation to twist her fork into someone's thigh. "Don't you have anyone else to bother?"

"Wouldn't be nearly as fun," he said, and leaned back just enough for her to feel the weight of his gaze.

Liri looked like she wanted to say more, but settled on stabbing a strawberry instead.

Across the hall, another ripple of laughter broke out from Verena's table. She was still surrounded by half a dozen first-years, basking in attention like it was light and she was the only one who deserved to glow in it.

Julian's voice dropped again, almost conspiratorial. "Ignore her."

Cassara glanced at him and immediately wished she hadn't. His smile was warm and disarming, the kind that made forgetting why she was annoyed with him dangerously easy. He leaned in closer. "She's all theater. You're the one people actually watch."

Sonia leaned her elbow against the table, chin in hand. "You were impressive out there, yourself, Julian. Sharp. Focused. Very... compelling."

Cassara's knife paused halfway through her fruit. The blade hovered just above the rind. Julian's smile curved, faint, indulgent, but his eyes didn't leave Cassara. "I try to deliver a show."

"Gideon didn't make it easy," Sonia added, her voice a touch too bright. "But you handled him. Maybe you can show me a few blocks when you have some time?"

Cassara didn't look up. She resumed slicing, the next piece of fruit sliding clean off the blade and onto Julian's plate. "Your favorite."

Julian's brow arched. Then he grinned, the kind of grin that carried weight, history, and a thousand memories. He picked up the fruit without looking away from her, his fingers brushing hers for the briefest moment, intentional, lazy, and unmistakably possessive.

It wasn't about the fruit, it was never about the fruit.

Cassara was making a declaration, reminding Sonia of her place in the grand scheme of things. A warning.

Sonia's smile faltered and Cassara set another piece on his plate. "Thought you might be low on sugar. Wouldn't want your focus to slip next time."

"Worried about me, Cass?" Julian held the fruit between his fingers.

She tilted her head, a faint smirk playing at her lips. "Only that you'll embarrass yourself."

He bit into the fruit before chewing thoughtfully. "I'm flattered."

"Are you planning to walk me to afternoon classes?" she asked, already knowing the answer.

"Only if you ask nicely," he murmured, causing Evie's already pink cheeks to darken further.

Sonia blinked, her smile faltering just slightly as she glanced between them. Cassara finally met her gaze, satisfied the point had been made.

The bell chimed low and final above the Great Hall, signaling the end of the midday reprieve. Around her, benches scraped, laughter waned, and students began gathering their things, some with sluggish reluctance, others with sharp-eyed urgency.

Cassara rose last.

Afternoon lessons waited, and Fenric's name alone had turned half the first-years pale. She gathered her Aether Codex and didn't pull away when Julian's hand came to rest against her hip.

Sonia was still watching after all.

CHAPTER NINE

Unlike the structured halls and vaulted ceilings of Vallemont's main building, the courtyard where they gathered for their first class in ACS handling felt raw, less curated. Cracked training dummies leaned along one wall, and a few second-years were dragging in crates of equipment.

Overseeing it all, giving orders and pointing, was Fenric Caldane. Even if he hadn't made such an impressive introduction on the first day, he would be impossible to miss. He was thick-armed and weather-worn, his half-buttoned shirt revealing runic burns old enough to have stories, and the twin prosthetic fingers on his right hand clinked softly as he adjusted the strap of his reinforced apron. A tiny metal beetle perched on his shoulder, wings twitching in a rhythmic stutter.

"Eyes up, first-years," he barked without turning. "If you were expecting a lecture, you thought wrong," a few whooping cheers followed before, "this is where you learn how not to die."

The students formed a loose half-circle around the crates. Cassara kept her arms crossed, gaze steady. Gideon stood across the group from her, alone. Verena wasn't in this time slot. Julian wasn't either. For once, the silence wasn't heavy. It was just hers.

Fenric kicked open a crate with a hiss of steam. From within, a second-year pulled out a crystal on a thick black cord, pale, milky, and faintly pulsing.

"This," Fenric said, holding it up, "is an Arclight Shard. It is the only reason you won't get your face bitten off in six weeks' time. You will wear it. You will sleep with it. You will not 'accidentally' leave it in your dorm. Because if it hasn't attuned to your signature by the time you go hunting for a bond, you'll be lucky if the beast walks away uninterested. Unlucky?" He smiled. "Well. That's why we keep the south wall reinforced."

Cassara accepted the shard when it was passed her way, inspecting the smooth, faceted crystal, the way the energy it emitted tingled across her fingertips.

Fenric's voice cut back in. "Demonstration."

Two second-years stepped forward. One knelt, placing a circular magitek anchor on the ground while the other activated an embedded ACS panel strapped to his shoulder. The humming noise rose, arcane threads lashing between beast and tamer as a sleek, feral creature shimmered into view, a projection of a previous bond.

Cassara leaned forward despite herself.

Fenric circled them like a vulture. "The ACS, Arcane Conduit System, connects you and your beast in a feedback loop. It regulates commands, synchronizes positioning, and prevents accidental soul hemorrhage. Unless, of course, you overload the core or forget your bindings. Then it gets, well, messy."

As if on cue, the projection stuttered. Sparks flared. The second-year swore and yanked his hand back as the projection distorted with a shriek.

Fenric grinned. "Anyone still think this is just gear maintenance?"

Cassara narrowed her eyes. This was new, more complicated than she'd expected, but still intriguing.

Fenric's grin didn't fade as he lifted a hand and gestured sharply. A small group of older students peeled away from the perimeter of the field, second-years in personalized ACS rigs that gleamed in the afternoon sunlight. The segmented armor fit close to the body, light and maneuverable, and each set shimmered with the faint, liquid pulse of active soul-thread circuits.

"Pair up," Fenric barked. "Your handlers'll walk you through the basics, get your preliminary measurements, and start calibration. You won't get your personal rigs until we have sufficient enough data."

Cassara's second-year, a girl with long dark hair and sun-gold skin, offered her a smile. "You're Cassara, right? I was hoping I'd get you."

Cassara tilted her head. "Have we met?"

"Not officially," the girl admitted, holding out a hand. "Reya Lorenta. My cousin was a crestbearer under your mother back in the day."

Cassara blinked, unsure how to respond to that. Reya didn't wait.

"Come on," she said, waving her toward a polished table stacked with fresh ACS components. "Let's talk armor."

Reya moved in a whirlwind of technical terms and calibrator wands. "This is the base skeleton of the ACS. Like Instructor Caldane said, you'll get your full rig before beast pairing, but we fit the framework now so it can begin attuning to your energy signature."

Cassara studied the curved plating, the sleek copper alloy etched with faint silver tracery. Soul-thread channels ran like veins through the frame, pulsing dimly.

"It syncs with the beast?" she asked.

"More like it syncs with you, and then mirrors that through your beast. The color feedback here," Reya tapped the glowing bar running down the forearm brace, "tells us how stable your sync is."

The light was a soft, steady teal. Cassara watched it shift slightly as Reya adjusted the alignment at her wrist.

"Blue to green is what you want. Resting state. Harmony between tamer and beast, if the beast is bonded," Reya said. "Yellow is still clear, but it means there is strain or tension, you'll see it spike in combat. Red?" She winced. "Red means instability. That's dangerous territory. You either calm the bond, or you're going to be in big trouble."

"And purple?" Cassara asked, because it had been whispered more than once already this week.

Reya hesitated. "We don't talk about purple."

Cassara arched a brow.

Reya lowered her voice. "It's misrepresented as a perfect sync. Fifty-fifty. Tamer and beast share full command. In theory? Ultimate trust. But it's dangerous and the few who have tried it... well... it has always ended poorly. The tamer should always retain higher control. Sixty-forty at least."

Cassara thought of her Echo trial. Of standing in that hall, alone.

"It's risky," Reya continued. "Too easy for a beast to override a human if the bond slips. When it happens... well, that's how you get names etched into the memorial wall. They say your mother went purple before..." She stopped, eyes widening. "Sorry. I didn't mean—"

Cassara shook her head. "It's fine."

Reya offered a quiet smile, finishing the last adjustments on the brace. "There, all set," she said. "Remember, don't try to cheat the link. Genuine connection is an important part of the bond."

Cassara flexed her fingers.

She had no intention of cheating anything, but if she could master this, master it all? Let the others worry about colors. She was here to win.

Fenric's voice rose above the din.

"This isn't a toy. It's not armor. It's a living conduit. Built to amplify your sync rate, channel beast feedback, regulate burst flow, and keep your overconfident ass from detonating mid-charge. If you forget any one of those functions, congrats. You've just turned yourself into a walking mana grenade."

He tapped the schematic again, enlarging a glowing blue core. "These are tuned to your resonance signature. Tamper with that? You fry your own nervous system."

Liri winced audibly.

Fenric turned, unbothered. "That's the happy ending. If it syncs wrong and tries to bond with your beast instead... well, best case, the beast rejects it and you black out. Worst case... it doesn't reject it, and you wake up with half your brain hijacked."

The class had gone quiet.

"Glad we understand each other." Fenric's tone lightened a degree, not much, but enough to be dangerous. "You'll be partnered today. Each pair gets a broken ACS rig and partial schematic. Your homework is to troubleshoot. Diagnose the issue. Begin repairs."

He started calling names, pointing with a metal stylus that sparked faintly with residual energy.

"Gideon and Morris. Lirien and Talia. Cassara and Oliver."

Cassara blinked.

"Oliver?" she asked under her breath, glancing around.

"Here," came a quiet reply. The boy she had been seeing all day, the one with the short cropped hair and wiry frame. He wore a pair of round, rune-rimmed glasses and a slightly rumpled shirt which she took notice of when he slipped into the seat beside her. His sleeves were already rolled up and tools poked from his belt like makeshift armor.

Fenric finished listing off names and set his codex to the side.

"Now," he said, slapping a sparking conduit into a containment crate, "before I let you all scamper off with your homework, a little light horror story for the road."

He leaned forward on the bench, oil-streaked hands steepled. "About six years ago, a pair of students thought they could shortcut the bond. One was a prodigy, top of his year. The other? A tinkerer, not unlike some of you. Thought he could 'correct' the link imbalance. Make the ACS respond faster. Stronger. More instinctively."

His smile didn't reach his eyes. "They forced the sync. Tamer and beast, equal mental load. Full parity. You know what we call that?"

He tapped a rune on the wall. The projection flared, a shimmering ACS schematic, its link core glowing purple.

"Going violet," he said quietly. "It looks beautiful and feels euphoric. But it's a lie. It's not trust. It's surrender. The beast takes what you give it, and if you're not stronger than your instincts, than the beast is, then what you are fades. Fast."

Cassara thought about what the girl had said, about her mother. Was it true? Was that why she had never come home?

"The prodigy's name isn't on the memorial wall," Fenric added. "Because we never recovered his body. Anyone caught slipping to violet gets flagged for override review." He let his eyes sweep the room. "You think you're the exception? I'll tell you right now, you're not. You let that pulse hit fifty-fifty, and we pull your rig before your beast pulls your lungs out."

Fenric began handing out broken components to each person. "Troubleshoot it. Fix it. Return it in working condition next class. No blood, no complaints."

Clink, his mechanical beetle, chirped ominously.

"Class dismissed," Fenric announced.

Cassara looked for Oliver and spotted him ahead, already striding toward the far exit of the practice field, his coat half-buttoned, boots scuffing faintly against the packed dirt. The jagged chunk of their assigned ACS component was still tucked under her arm, heavier now that the class had ended and expectations had been set.

She quickened her pace, closing the distance before he could disappear entirely.

"Oliver, right?" she said, falling into step beside him.

He didn't slow.

"I'm Cassara. Allencourt," she added, with the kind of ease that usually sparked recognition. A flicker of surprise. Something.

Nothing.

He barely glanced over, just enough to confirm she was still talking.

"I was going to ask when you wanted to meet for the repair," she continued, holding out the component. "We're partners, after all."

Oliver looked up, a smudge of dirt on his cheek catching the light. He blinked once. Then again.

Cassara offered a smile, polished and well practiced. "I figured we could find time after dinner. Unless mornings work better for you?"

He didn't answer. Just held out a hand.

She hesitated, then passed over the broken piece of gear.

He turned it in his hands, brow furrowing. "This one's practically a joke," he muttered. "Poor soldering. Misaligned conductors. I can do it faster myself."

And before she could respond, before she could even decide whether to be offended, he turned and walked away.

Cassara stood there, eyebrows lifted, hands empty, lips parting around a soundless scoff.

"Charming," she muttered.

He didn't look back.

The light in the Great Hall had softened by the time the last course was cleared. Faint arcs of magelight flickered above, tracing lazy spirals across the ceiling as the energy in the room ebbed. The buzz of first-day nerves had dulled to low chatter, laughter, and clinking cutlery. Cassara sat back in her chair, a half-finished tart pushed to the side, and allowed herself a rare moment of stillness.

One day down.

It hadn't gone perfectly. Verena still grated. Gideon had managed to crawl under her skin with fewer words than seemed fair. And Oliver, gods help her, might be the only partner at this entire academy who looked through her like glass instead of being remotely impressed. Still, she'd won her match. She'd kept her footing. She'd survived Thendrick, Marlowe, and Fenric without losing her mind.

That counted for something, right?

At the head table, the headmistress rose. The Hall hushed instantly.

"You've taken your first steps," she said, her voice like a low, striking bell. "Tomorrow, you'll take more. Some forward. Some back. Make them count."

And with that, she inclined her head, and the instructors stood, followed shortly by the students as benches scraped against polished stone and the crowd began to spill out into the halls.

Cassara was halfway to the dormitory corridor when a hand closed gently, but insistently, around her wrist.

She turned, startled, just as Julian leaned in close.

"Come with me," he said, his voice pitched low, conspiratorial.

She blinked. "Julian, what—"

"No arguments." His grin widened. "It's a surprise."

Before she could protest, he was already guiding her away from the crowd, his grip light but unwavering as they slipped down one of the narrower halls branching off the main stairwell.

Cassara knew she should have insisted on going back, but she was curious and couldn't help but wonder what exactly Julian thought counted as a surprise.

The corridor narrowed into a dim side passage that was barely lit. Despite having just arrived, Julian moved like he knew every twist of it, his pace casual, hand still loosely wrapped around her wrist. Cassara kept up without question, at first. His coat caught the occasional flare of magelight as they passed, throwing fractured glints across the stone.

"Where are we going?" she asked, not quite whispering.

"You'll see."

He sounded smug. Pleased with himself in a way that both irritated and intrigued her.

They slipped through an iron-bound door that creaked against old hinges, the warmth of the academy giving way to the sharper, wilder air outside. Night had settled properly now, skies clear and velvet-dark above the silhouette of the cliffs. Stars pulsed bright above, and beneath their boots, a narrow trail twisted down from the main path, away from the spire, away from the sanctioned dormitories and halls.

Cassara's steps faltered. Professor Marlowe's warning about beast activity and warded areas echoing in her mind.

"Julian," she said, pulling slightly against his grip. "This is off-campus."

"We're not going far."

"There's a curfew," she reminded him. "And the whole rules-and-boundaries speech? Pretty sure this breaks all of them."

Julian glanced over his shoulder, not slowing. "Since when do you follow rules?"

"Since getting expelled would mean marrying you?"

Cassara wasn't sure why she said it, they hadn't talked about it at all and Cassara knew deep down that was part of the reason she had been keeping her distance.

She waited for him to get annoyed. Instead, he huffed a laugh, tightening his grip only slightly as he led her past a low outcropping of rock. The path narrowed more here, the foliage brushing her coat, mist curling low through the grass

"Relax," he said, glancing back again. "We'll be back before anyone notices. Trust me."

Cassara did, or at least she wanted to, and that was the problem.

She didn't stop him. She furrowed her brow and kept pace, heart ticking faster in the dark. Something about the way he said it, that easy, assured drawl, like they'd done this a hundred times. Like nothing could touch them.

It made her nervous, but it also made her want to see what came next.

She was still sorting through her conflicting impulses when Julian finally slowed his pace and she realized they'd reached a thin, rusted gate marked by a weathered sign bearing a faded warning: *Closed by Academy Order, Unstable Terrain.*

He caught her hesitation and chuckled softly. "It's fine. They've been saying that for years."

She lifted an eyebrow. "And you know this because?"

"Because the third year who told me about this spot got caught out here once and told me exactly where *not* to go. So naturally," he pushed open the gate with a loud creak. "that's exactly where we're going."

Cassara rolled her eyes, but she stepped through after him anyway, curiosity winning out. Beyond the gate, the path dipped sharply, twisting through a tangle of low-hanging branches and ivy-coated stones. The air thickened, damp with mist, scented faintly of minerals and damp earth. It felt secret, untouched.

As they emerged from the trees, Cassara stopped short, eyes widening. Hidden between two jutting cliffs lay a series of pools shimmering faintly under the moonlight. Steam curled lazily above the water, casting the secluded grove in a hazy, dreamlike glow. The hot springs were eerily beautiful, wrapped in silence broken only by the quiet lapping of water against stone.

Julian watched her expression closely, lips quirking up. "Told you it'd be worth it."

Cassara hesitated, drawn forward despite herself. "It's...beautiful."

His smile widened, genuinely pleased. “It suits you.”

She cut him a sharp glance, warmth creeping up her neck despite the cool air. “Does that line usually work on the other girls?”

“I wouldn’t know,” he said, smoothly moving closer, his voice low enough that she instinctively leaned in to catch it. “I haven’t tried it on anyone else.”

Cassara bit back a smile, pulse skipping in her throat. She didn’t move away when Julian reached up, lightly brushing a loose curl back behind her ear. His fingertips lingered against her cheek, a careful touch, almost a question. The air between them felt charged with possibility, drawing taut as he leaned closer, close enough that she could count every freckle across his nose, the faint reflection of moonlight in his eyes,

Her breath caught. He paused, waiting, expectant. Tempting.

Cassara exhaled softly, purposefully stepping back. “Careful, Julian. You’re starting to believe in your own charm.”

Surprise flashed briefly in his eyes before giving way to amused resignation. He dropped his hand, unruffled by her rebuttal. “Maybe. But you came along, didn’t you?”

She snorted softly, shaking her head even as she admitted quietly to herself that part of her *had* enjoyed the risk, the reckless rush of slipping away under cover of darkness. But another part, deeper and quieter, knew it wasn’t enough.

The thought lingered as she dipped her fingers into the spring, watching ripples blur her reflection. “We shouldn’t stay long.”

“Just a little longer,” he murmured, voice quiet and coaxing. “When’s the next time you’ll get to just breathe?”

He had a point, and she hated that he did. Closing her eyes for just a moment, she felt the steam brush softly across her skin, inhaling deeply the wild, forbidden stillness. The weight of expectations felt distant here, easier to bear. Just for a moment, she let herself lean into that feeling, even knowing it couldn’t last.

When she finally opened her eyes again, Julian was watching her closely, head tilted, his expression unguarded. “You’re impossible, you know.”

She smirked softly, straightening, forcing her usual confidence back into place like armor. “Is that a compliment or a complaint?”

“Both,” he answered without hesitation, eyes dancing. “Always both.”

Cassara eased away, suddenly restless under the weight of Julian’s gaze. She trailed her fingers along the smooth stones bordering the spring, stepping slowly along its edge as she tried to recapture her composure.

"How did this place even get here?" she wondered aloud, grasping at conversation. The words felt weak in her mouth, an awkward attempt at distance. She tilted her head, eyes tracing the ribbons of steam curling lazily upward.

Behind her, Julian's footsteps thudded lightly against damp stone. "Natural formation, I think. Magical runoff did the rest," he explained, voice carrying a smug undertone of amusement, his pace carefully matching hers.

Cassara knew he was closing in, and found she didn't entirely mind. The nervous flutter in her chest gave way to a quiet thrill. She would allow him to play his little game, to let him think he had her cornered.

He stepped closer, voice low. "Are you running away, Cass?" he teased.

She tossed a playful glance over her shoulder, arching an eyebrow. "Are you chasing?"

"Always." His grin flashed brightly in the moonlight, all lazy charm and easy confidence.

He had her backed nearly to the end of the path, the steaming water close at her heels. Her breath caught in her chest when he closed the remaining distance between them, his arm slipping around her waist and pulling her flush against him.

He leaned closer, voice gentle but edged with quiet certainty.

"You know," he murmured softly, tracing his thumb lightly along her cheek, "you don't have to fight so hard. Prestige, ranks, proving yourself, it won't matter once we're married. Our families have already seen to that."

Cassara stiffened immediately, the tender haze evaporating into cold clarity. Her palm pressed against his chest, pushing him back, not harshly, but with enough force to catch him off guard.

Julian stumbled, arms pinwheeling in surprise, before losing his balance completely. He hit the hot spring with a startled splash, surfacing a moment later, coughing and sputtering indignantly.

She stood over him, arms crossed, irritation masking her amusement. "Careful, Julian. That sounded dangerously close to ownership."

He blinked water from his lashes, scowling petulantly as he slicked his hair back. "Was that really necessary?"

"Absolutely."

Despite his obvious irritation, a reluctant smile tugged at the corners of his mouth, dripping and defeated. "You're a menace, Cass."

"Always," she echoed back sweetly, stepping neatly away from the edge. "Now come on, we really should get back before someone notices."

He sighed dramatically, hauling himself from the water. "I suppose it's too much to hope this stays between us?"

She tilted her head, eyes glittering with mischief. "We'll see how well you behave."

Julian sighed dramatically, dripping as he began to climb out. When he reached the edge, his expression shifted, a flash of playful rebellion sparking behind his eyes. Before Cassara could fully register it, he lunged upward, caught her hand, and fell backwards into the spring again.

Cassara toppled forward with a startled yelp, landing in the water beside him in an entirely undignified splash. She broke the surface sputtering, water streaming from her hair and down her face as she glared incredulously at Julian.

"Julian Tremaine, have you lost your mind?"

Julian smirked triumphantly, thoroughly pleased with himself. "Now, who's behaving?"

Cassara shook her head, laughter breaking free despite herself. "You're incorrigible."

"But you wouldn't have me any other way," he shot back smoothly, pushing soaked hair out of his eyes with a grin.

Cassara rolled her eyes, splashing water at him half-heartedly as she fought, and failed, to suppress her smile. Shaking her head, she turned and began climbing out of the hot spring, soaked clothing clinging heavily to her skin.

"That's your first mistake," she said lightly, glancing over her shoulder with wicked amusement. "Thinking I want you."

Julian pressed a dramatic hand to his chest, feigning injury. "Ouch, Cass. Brutal."

She tossed him one last playful smile, already turning away toward the trail back to campus. "You'll live."

His laughter followed her into the darkness, but she didn't slow, and she didn't look back.

CHAPTER TEN

Hurrying through the empty corridors, Cassara tried to ignore the water dripping from her clothes, leaving an incriminating trail in her wake. The chill air sent goosebumps dancing across her skin, but her heartbeat was still light, buoyed by the lingering thrill of mischief. She was nearly back to the dormitory hall when voices echoed from behind her, breaking the quiet.

"—telling you, Evie, someone must've left a window open. The floor's all wet." Liri's voice floated forward, curious and slightly puzzled.

Cassara froze, glancing down at her dripping coat and damp boots, wincing. Gods.

"I don't think windows leave footprints," Evie's voice came next, dryly amused. "Maybe it rained?"

"Rain doesn't leave footprints either..."

Cassara turned sharply toward the dormitory, attempting to quicken her pace without outright running. But Liri's steps sped up behind her, shoes tapping rapidly against the stones.

"Wait—Cass? Is that you?"

She exhaled slowly, accepting her fate, and turned around with a sheepish smile just as Liri caught up, Evie just a few paces behind.

Liri's eyes widened. "Cassara, you're—you're soaked! What happened?"

Cassara offered a casual shrug, forcing nonchalance despite the flush warming her cheeks. "Little misadventure. Nothing serious."

Evie raised an eyebrow, folding her arms skeptically. "That adventure wouldn't have involved a certain tall, irritatingly confident blond legacy student, would it?"

Cassara struggled to keep from grinning, turning away with exaggerated dignity. "I plead ignorance."

Liri burst into laughter, linking arms with her, ignoring the way water soaked into her sleeve. "Come on, let's get you back to the room before anyone else decides to investigate the trail."

Cassara groaned softly, resigned, but allowed herself to be tugged gently forward toward their dorm, warmth blossoming in her chest at the effortless camaraderie. "Fine. But not a word to anyone."

"Wouldn't dream of it," Evie replied smoothly, eyes sparkling with amusement as she followed behind them, voice dropping to a conspiratorial whisper. "Not yet, anyway."

They reached the door to the dorm room just as Cassara managed to wring a final stream of water from the hem of her coat. Liri gave her a theatrical once-over and muttered something about finding towels and possibly a mop. Evie reached forward to push the door open.

Cassara had hoped the dorm would be empty. Unfortunately, it was not. Sonia lounged on her bed, brushing out her hair with long, practiced strokes, while Talia sat cross-legged at her desk, reading in silence, barely glancing up.

Sonia didn't bother hiding her smirk as Cassara stepped inside, trailing water and damp confidence in equal measure.

"Well, someone had an eventful evening," she said, eyes gleaming as they flicked pointedly to the puddle forming beneath Cassara's boots. "Let me guess, you decided to wrestle a leviathan in the showers?"

Cassara smiled sweetly, peeling off her coat and draping it over the chair by her desk. "Not quite. Though I wasn't the only one who ended up drenched."

Sonia's brush paused mid-stroke.

Cassara continued, hanging her coat over the back of her chair and turning with a faintly wicked tilt to her mouth. "I imagine he's still trying to dry off somewhere. Possibly reevaluating his choices and tending to his bruised ego."

Evie coughed behind her hand, trying to smother a laugh. Liri looked between them, eyes wide with the dawning realization that this was definitely about Julian.

Talia, still flipping a page, muttered, "Poor bastard."

Cassara offered no names, no clarifications, just a languid stretch and a casual stroll toward her trunk, the picture of amused satisfaction.

Sonia's jaw tightened ever so slightly before she turned back to her mirror with a too-casual toss of her hair. "How charming."

Cassara didn't answer. She didn't need to.

"I'm going to take a shower," she said casually after gathering her things from her trunk and making her way towards their shared bathroom.

By the time Cassara emerged, skin flushed from the hot water and her hair damp but free of steam, the dorm had quieted into the hush that always came just before lights dimmed. She padded in on bare feet, now dressed in soft nightclothes, black with subtle embroidery at the cuffs, regal even in rest. The flicker of magelight had dimmed to a low golden glow, casting gentle shadows across the room.

The other girls were already in bed. Sonia's curtains were pulled tight, a faint rustle suggesting she still fidgeted under her covers. Liri's were half-drawn, a soft snore already rising from within. Evie's, of course, were neatly closed, with the glow of a reading crystal still faintly visible beneath.

Only Talia remained awake, still seated at her desk, spine straight, head slightly bowed. Cassara passed behind her on the way to her own bunk and glanced down, then slowed.

Talia wasn't reading, and she wasn't taking notes either.

She was drawing.

Ink flowed clean and confident from her pen, sweeping into curved horns and thick, armor-plated limbs. The creature had a lean body like a hound, but its head was crowned with a jagged crest of bone, and its eyes, four of them, were wide and feral, ringed with flame or maybe smoke. A long tail curled along the bottom edge of the page, and beneath it, in small, spidery script, was a label:

"Wyrd-beast. Name unknown. Possibly extinct."

Cassara hovered, just a second longer than she meant to. "What is that?"

Talia looked up, startled, though not flustered. "Just a thing I saw once, in a dream."

Cassara raised a brow, considering, but didn't press. "Looks dangerous."

Talia offered a quiet shrug. "The interesting ones usually are."

She smirked faintly at that, then turned toward her own bed without another word.

Once nestled behind her curtains, she reached beneath her pillow and withdrew the small, worn journal she kept tucked there, the once-gilded lettering on the cover now dulled to bronze—K. L. Her mother's initials: Katrinel Lorellan.

She ran her fingers over them before letting the weight of the journal settle into her lap, the cracked leather soft beneath her fingers. For a heartbeat she hesitated, then flipped past the first few pages, dates and entries she remembered from years ago when she'd snuck it from her father's study, too young to understand half the words and too stubborn to stop reading anyway.

She found the place she was looking for, near the beginning, where the ink was still strong and the handwriting neat with effort. Her mother's voice rose from the page like a whisper reaching across time:

First Day, Vallemont.

I still can't believe I'm here.

The spires are taller than I imagined, and the glass dome in the Orientation Hall actually sparkled when the Trial of Echoes started. Everyone said it was only refracted light, but it felt like something more.

My Echo was...strange. I saw a version of myself standing at the head of a Crestboard, beast at my side, flames all around. Not burning. Not harming. Just...warm. Like belonging. Like home. That's what I want, I think. Not the fire, but the place it lights up.

I met my roommates tonight. Isadore, the pretty legacy, is exactly what you'd expect. Graceful, perfectly postured, already ranking herself against the rest of us. But she smiled when I complimented her braid, so maybe she's not all frost.

Then there's Nareen. She's rough around the edges, all elbows and laughter. I like her. She elbowed a second-year who tried to steal her dessert and didn't even flinch when they threatened her. I think she's fearless.

I want to be like that.

ACS class was a disaster. I could barely get the conduit straps fastened without slicing open my thumb. Why does magitek have so many wires?

No. I didn't cry. I didn't quit. And I already have two friends who I think will last a lifetime.

That has to count for something, right?

Cassara's eyes lingered on the page, her thumb tracing the edge of her mother's looping "K" at the bottom of the entry. There was a strange tightness in her chest, not sadness, not exactly. Just... a sense of closeness. A reminder that Katrinel had once sat in a bed like this, worried about beast rankings and ACS class, hoping for friendship and dreaming of fire.

A girl trying to belong.

Cassara exhaled quietly, then closed the journal and pressed it gently back beneath her pillow, the warmth of the words still flickering behind her eyes.

The last class of the day had let out into the late afternoon sun, the buzz of voices spilling into the courtyard outside the eastern hall. Students clustered along the stone paths and low walls, some reviewing notes, others already forgetting them. Cassara was halfway to the dorms, still mentally untangling the mess that was the morning's resonance drill, when a familiar tone caught her attention—sharp, clipped, and unmistakably Verena.

"I'm just saying," Verena was telling someone, loud enough to draw a small cluster of onlookers, "if you can't handle basic extraction drills, maybe you're better suited to maintenance work."

Curious, Cassara veered slightly, enough to catch a glimpse of Oliver standing stiffly a few paces from Verena, his shoulders hunched and his gaze pointed somewhere just beyond her. A few students nearby were pretending not to listen. No one moved to intervene.

Oliver kept his voice low. "I didn't ask you to step in for me."

"No," Verena said coolly, "but you are slowing people down, me included. I'm just being honest."

Cassara stepped forward, her stride smooth, voice sliding in like a blade. "Funny. You're not usually this talkative when Gideon's around."

Verena's head whipped toward her. The shift in expression, surprise first, then irritation, was brief but telling.

Cassara didn't stop and turned her attention instead to Oliver. "There you are, Straton," she said with exaggerated relief, weaving through the small crowd. "I've been looking everywhere for you. We've got ACS repairs, remember? Hope you haven't wasted too much time."

Oliver blinked at her like she'd started speaking another language.

Verena folded her arms. "Interesting choice of allies, Allencourt. Since when do you waste time on dead weight? Thought you were more practical than that."

Cassara's smile turned cold. "I am practical. Which is why I know talent when I see it. You clearly don't."

A few scattered chuckles from the surrounding students punctuated the silence that followed. Verena's glare darkened.

Cassara turned to Oliver and gave him a meaningful look. "Coming?"

He hesitated for a breath, then nodded stiffly. Cassara took his arm and walked him away without another word. He didn't resist, not until they rounded the next corner and the sound of voices faded behind them.

He jerked his arm back immediately, expression drawn tight with irritation. "You didn't need to do that."

Cassara blinked, confused by his sudden hostility. "You're welcome?"

He glared. "Don't act like that was about me. You just saw a chance to put Verena in her place and used me to do it. If it had been anyone else but her, you'd have kept walking."

The words hit sharper than she expected, and worse, he wasn't entirely wrong. She probably wouldn't have gotten involved if she hadn't heard Verena's voice. But still...

"That's not true," she said, following as he turned and stalked off toward the west wing archway. "I mean—maybe I noticed because it was her, but I wasn't just—"

He didn't slow.

Cassara scowled and picked up her pace. "Look, I actually do want to work on the ACS repairs. I wouldn't have said anything if I didn't mean it."

He shot her a skeptical glance over his shoulder. "Really? Because you didn't look all that interested in class yesterday."

Cassara crossed her arms, trying to look more indignant than flustered. "Well, I am now."

"Why?"

"Because—" Her voice caught. "Because my pride won't let me turn in shoddy work or let someone else do it for me. And because I'm your partner, and I don't like looking like I coasted."

Oliver slowed, frowning, then finally stopped. "You're serious."

"I just said I was."

He studied her a moment longer, then gave a small, begrudging sigh. "Fine. Meet me in the library in an hour. Bring the component Fenric gave you."

Cassara lifted her chin, victorious. "I will."

He turned without another word and walked off.

Cassara watched him go, then muttered under her breath, "You're welcome, again," before heading off in the opposite direction.

The library's quiet wrapped around her as she stepped through the arched entrance, swallowing the sound of her boots the moment she crossed the rune-etched threshold. She paused when she reached the central reading circle, gaze drifting upward to the great dome overhead. Starlight filtered through the glass and shimmered through the slow-turning lens above, scattering refracted constellations across the high ceiling like a celestial map in motion. A magelight drifted by like a curious firefly, its glow soft and golden.

Cassara found a bench near the edge of the circle, setting her satchel beside her. The broken ACS component clinked faintly as she pulled it out. She stared at it for a moment, brow furrowing, then pulled the repair schematic she'd copied onto her 'Dex. She didn't understand half of it, and she hated that.

A book passed by on its own, hovering lazily before one of the higher shelves, pages fluttering, before it slid itself into a slot Cassara could've sworn hadn't been there a moment before.

This place was alive, intuitive and watching.

She smiled faintly and leaned back against the cushions. "Don't suppose you have a tutorial for being less humiliated in front of a boy who thinks you're ornamental," she murmured under her breath.

The library, wisely, offered no comment.

She heard him before she saw him, his steps quiet and unhurried, prompting her to look up as Oliver approached, his uniform jacket hanging open, his ever-present case tucked under one arm.

"You're early," he noted, as if mildly surprised.

"Believe it or not," Cassara said, lifting the ACS rig slightly, "I do actually want to learn how this thing works."

Oliver didn't answer right away. His gaze flicked from her to the broken component in her hand, then to the schematic she'd laid out.

Finally, he sat beside her with a soft sigh and began pulling tools from his kit.

"Fine," he said. "But if you blow something up, I'm blaming you twice, once for the fire, and again for pretending you knew what you were doing."

Cassara couldn't help but grin. "Fair enough."

She didn't thank him, not aloud, but she leaned in when he started explaining, elbows braced on the wooden desk, her brows already drawn in tight concentration. Oliver began with the basics—terms she half-recognized from class, though they slid through her memory like water through cupped hands.

"The conduit array regulates mana output through sync channels. These," he gestured to the coiled wires and slotted plates in the open ACS rig between them, "are your resonance filters. If the signal bleeds, the rig doesn't know what to reinforce."

Cassara stared at the tangle of etched metal and glowing crystal like it had personally insulted her. "...That's not English."

Oliver sighed. Not loudly, but enough.

She straightened, crossing her arms. "I'm trying."

"I know." He rubbed his temples, then adjusted the angle of the schematic. "Okay. Think of it like this, you're dancing with your beast. If you're off-beat, the music's distorted. The filters are the sheet music. They help the system know what steps to amplify and what to ignore."

Cassara blinked. "So these," she pointed to the smaller etched nodes, "are like... tuning forks?"

His eyes flicked to her, surprised. "Exactly."

"Huh." She tilted her head, the concept starting to click. "And if one's off, the whole thing wobbles."

"Worse," he muttered, pulling a cracked filter from the unit. "It shatters. And takes you with it."

Cassara winced as he set the tiny shard on the desk, the edges faintly scorched. "This happened to someone?"

Oliver didn't answer right away. "...Once."

Something in his tone made her pause, but she didn't press. Instead, she shifted closer, watching as he carefully replaced the broken piece with a new one. His hands were steady, movements precise. When he spoke again, his voice had softened.

"Here. You try." He passed her the replacement and the alignment tool.

Cassara hesitated. "If I break it..."

"You won't," he said, not unkindly. "I'm watching."

Her fingers weren't as sure as his, but they didn't tremble. She followed his instructions slowly, carefully seating the crystal with the prongs of the tool until it clicked into place.

It glowed faintly: blue, steady.

Oliver began packing his tools away with methodical precision, each piece slotted into its designated place in his kit. Cassara watched him work, the question forming before she could stop it.

"Why are you here?"

Oliver's hands stilled for just a moment, then continued their careful arrangement. "Vallemont?"

"You're good with this," she gestured to the repaired ACS rig between them. "Really good. You could be at the Arcanum studying magitek engineering, or any of the universities. So why beast taming?"

He was quiet for a moment, closing the tool case with a soft click, then opened it again to adjust tools that didn't need adjusting.

"Does it matter?" he said finally.

"I'm curious."

"Why?"

Cassara shrugged. "Because you don't seem like someone who'd choose this path. You seem like someone who got stuck with it."

For a moment she thought he wouldn't answer at all, that he'd just stand up and leave. But instead he set the tool case down and stared at it.

"I didn't choose it," he said quietly. "My older brother was supposed to be here. Ansel. He was good at this, the combat, all of it. He was born for it."

Past tense.

"There was an accident two years ago," Oliver continued, his voice flat and careful. "He survived, but his leg... it didn't heal right. It can't handle the physical demands anymore." He exhaled slowly. "So my parents decided I'd take his place. Carry on the family legacy."

"And you just... agreed?"

Oliver's smile was bitter. "What was I supposed to do? Tell them no? That I'd rather build things than fight with them?" He shook his head. "The Straton family has sent tamers to Vallemont for five generations. Someone had to continue that."

Cassara studied him, seeing the weight he carried more clearly now. "That's not fair to you."

"Fair doesn't matter." Oliver picked up his case and stood. "It's done. I'm here."

She wanted to say more, to tell him it wasn't too late to choose differently, but the closed expression on his face stopped her. She could tell that he had shared more than he'd intended to already.

"For what it's worth," she said instead, "you're better at this than you think."

Oliver paused at the edge of the desk, glancing back at her. Surprise, or perhaps gratitude flickered across his face.

"Thanks," he said. Then he turned and left, his footsteps quiet against the library's enchanted floors.

Cassara sat alone for a moment longer, the repaired ACS rig still glowing faintly beside her.

She tried to imagine it. Being here, in this place she'd fought so hard to reach, and not wanting it at all. Waking up every day to pursue someone else's dream while your own gathered dust in some corner of your mind you weren't allowed to touch.

It was the future she faced if she failed.

Cassara gathered her things slowly, tucking the ACS rig carefully into her satchel. The library hummed quietly around her, whisperlamps drifting overhead in their lazy patterns.

At least now she understood the difference between them. She was here because she'd clawed her way toward something she wanted. He was here because he'd given up something he'd wanted more.

The lecture had finally ended, and Cassara had a narrow window before combat drills with Nareen. Enough time to change into training gear and maybe grab a bit to eat if she didn't waste it. She gathered her notes and was slinging her satchel over her shoulder when movement blocked her path.

Verena stood there, arms crossed, eyes glittering.

"You think you're clever."

Cassara arched a brow. "Depends on the day."

Verena's smile was cold. "Humiliating me in front of everyone like that? Using him to do it?"

"Oh. That's what this is about. It's been a week and you're still hung up on that?"

"Don't play dumb," Verena snapped. "You made me look like a bully."

Cassara's laugh was short and sharp. "You are a bully."

Verena stepped in closer. "You think throwing a few snide lines makes you special? You're just another legacy bitch who walked through those gates because of her name. You don't belong at the top, Cassara. You haven't earned it."

Cassara grit her teeth. She was tired of this. Tired of being dismissed, underestimated, reduced to nothing but her family crest.

"And yet," she said quietly, "I'm still here. Still ranked higher than you. That must really bother you."

"Keep mouthing off and you'll find out what happens when someone finally puts you in your place."

Cassara didn't flinch. "Is that a threat or just your usual attempt at personality?"

That was it, that was all it took to push Verena over the edge. Her hand shot out, aimed to shove her back, but she'd never get the chance.

Cassara moved on instinct. She caught Verena's wrist, twisted, and swept her legs in one clean, efficient motion.

Verena hit the floor hard with a breathless yelp.

Cassara looked down at her, still holding her wrist. "Looks like we figured out who belongs where."

"What the hell."

Cassara immediately released Verena's arm and took a step back, breath still tight in her chest

"It's not—"

"What the hell is wrong with you?" he barked, crossing the space between them.

"She shoved me," Cassara snapped back. "I defended myself."

But Gideon wasn't listening. He was already kneeling beside Verena, steadying her with one hand as she pushed herself up with exaggerated effort, letting out a soft groan like she'd been flung across the battlefield.

"She attacked me," Verena said, barely hiding the shake in her voice. "I-I just asked her a question, and she lost it."

Cassara's hands clenched at her sides. "That is not what happened."

Gideon helped Verena to her feet, his arm braced under hers. "You're bleeding," he muttered, eyeing a scraped elbow that was barely more than a scratch.

Verena leaned into the attention like it was a performance. "I didn't even raise my voice."

Cassara scoffed. "You never have to. You just pick your moments."

Gideon turned on her, his expression unreadable but cold. "Do you think this helps you? Picking fights in a classroom? Proving what exactly?"

"I didn't start it."

"But you finished it," he said, sharply. "And that's what people will remember. But maybe that's exactly what you want."

Cassara stared at Gideon, fury churning in her chest. He hadn't been there for the shove. He hadn't heard her threats, or the venom in her voice. But none of it mattered.

He was looking at her like she was the problem.

Before she could speak again, another voice cut through the tension. "What happened?"

They all turned as Julian strode in from the corridor like a storm, his eyes immediately locking on Cassara, then shifting to Verena who was leaning into Gideon's grip like she'd just survived a duel.

Cassara opened her mouth, but Julian was already speaking.

"Just who do you think you are, Delvanir?" he demanded, stepping between them.

"Let's just go," Cassara said, not wanting the altercation to escalate further.

"She was on the ground," Gideon said flatly, still holding Verena's arm. "And Cassara put her there."

Julian scoffed. "So? Maybe she deserved it."

"She just threw me down," Verena added softly, her voice trembling with the perfect edge of victimhood. "I didn't touch her."

Cassara took a step forward, fists clenched at her sides. "That's a lie and you know it."

Julian turned toward her, eyes narrowing, not with suspicion, but with that sharp, possessive fury she knew too well. "You don't have to explain yourself. Not to them."

She stood stiff between them, the heat of Julian's protectiveness burning at her back, the chill of Gideon's judgment pressing from the front. She could feel the tension coiling tighter by the second, anyone with eyes could see it was about to snap.

"Come on," she tried again, catching his arm.

Julian shrugged her off.

"We both know what this is really about," he said. "If you've got a problem with me, Delvanir, have the backbone to say it to my face. Leave Cassara out of your mess."

Gideon's eyes narrowed. "She's not out of it if she's throwing people to the ground."

Julian stepped forward. "Please. You just don't like that she makes you feel small. But that's not new, is it? I imagine most things have felt out of reach since your family torched their name."

Cassara saw the shift in Gideon's expression as his hands curled into fists at his sides. This was about to get ugly.

"Julian, please—" She grabbed his arm, trying to pull him back before this escalated further.

"I can handle it," he snapped, shaking her off with a hard shove.

Cassara staggered back at the same instant that Gideon lunged towards Julian. For a brief moment their eyes met and she saw his grow wide as he registered what was about to happen. He tried to pull back, but momentum carried him forward. She twisted away, trying to avoid impact, but his elbow clipped her shoulder hard enough to send her crashing sideways into a desk. Pain exploded through her side as the edge drove into her ribs leaving her gasping for air.

Everything stopped.

Gideon froze, breath heaving, his face going white when he saw her clutching her ribs, face flushed, teeth gritted against the pain.

"Cass!" Julian was at her side instantly. "You're hurt."

"I'm fine," she said breathlessly, doing her best to curb the anger. She pushed his hands away and glared up at Gideon, fury sparking through her pain.

Gideon didn't move. His hands were half-raised like he meant to reach for her, but didn't dare.

Verena, conveniently silent until now, made a soft, horrified sound, like the whole thing had shocked her the most.

Cassara pushed herself upright, every breath tight.

"Next time you two want to prove who has the bigger *legacy* complex," she said coldly, "try not to use me as the battlefield."

And then she walked out leaving both of them standing in the silence she left behind.

CHAPTER ELEVEN

Returning to her dorm, Cassara found the room empty, giving her much needed privacy. She sat on the edge of her bunk, wincing as she drew the curtain partway closed.

She pulled her shirt carefully over her head, teeth clenched as fabric brushed across the side of her ribs. The bruise was blooming violet-blue across her skin, darkest where the edge of the desk had caught her ribs. It was ugly. What was worse? It ached when she breathed too deep.

Tears stung in the corners of her eyes but she blinked them away. This was no time for self pity. In just two days the top ten first year students would be announced and they'd run the Rift for the first, and only, time until they started their second year. She wasn't about to miss out on a chance to prove herself, to beat Verena, because of a little bruising.

Cassara was prodding lightly at the edges, wondering if she could sneak into the infirmary for some ointment, when she heard the door open. She flinched, yanking the edge of her shirt down and twisting toward the wall.

But it wasn't fast enough.`

Talia's voice came quiet and flat from across the room. "That looks bad."

"It's nothing."

"You bounced off a desk," Talia said simply. "Pretty sure it's not nothing."

Cassara narrowed her eyes. "Who told you that?"

If word started spreading that she was injured, if it somehow got back to the instructors...

Talia shrugged. "I happened to be in the hall when it happened."

Cassara remained silent, watching as Talia crossed the room and knelt beside her trunk. There was a soft click of the latch giving way followed by shuffling and the faint clink of glass. Cassara turned away, pretending not to be curious, when she felt a thud beside her on the bed.

When she looked she saw a small jar made of pale blue glass. It was wax-sealed and had a thin ribbon of string tied around its rim.

Cassara glanced towards Talia. "What's this?"

Talia crossed her arms loosely around her waist. "A salve. My grandmother makes it. Helps with bruises. Soothes the inflammation. It won't fix you overnight, but it'll get you closer to healed than nothing."

Cassara stared at the jar. "What's in it?"

"Wyrdroot, flame-leaf, a bit of duskspore." Talia shrugged. "Old recipe. Been passed down through five generations of bone-setting midwives."

Cassara eyed her now, not just the jar. "Where are you from?"

Talia's gaze flicked away. "Outer isles. Charthorne."

Charthorne. She knew the name, but barely. A speck on the edge of the Empire's trade routes, known more for its storms and dangerous passage than prestige.

"I'm the first in my family to get in here," Talia added, voice quiet but steady. "They didn't expect me to last a week."

Cassara didn't answer right away, instead she picked up the jar and turned it slowly in her hand. "So is this how you plan to last longer? By drugging your competition?"

Talia gave a dry smile. "If I wanted you gone, I'd have let you limp into the Rift without it."

Cassara snorted, despite herself.

She uncorked the jar. The scent that rose was sharp and herbal, earthy with something cool beneath it. "I won't thank you," she muttered.

Talia was already walking back toward her desk. "Didn't ask you to."

Dipping two fingers into the salve, Cassara found the texture thick, slightly gritty, but not unpleasant. She hesitated, eyeing the purpling bruise along her ribs, then braced herself and dabbed the ointment on.

It stung, not the screaming sort of sting, but a sharp, prickling heat that spread instantly through the skin. Her breath caught which caused another stab of pain from somewhere deeper. Then, just as suddenly, the pain began to dull, easing into a warm throb instead of the fire it had been before.

Her shoulders dropped a fraction. It wasn't a miracle cure, but it was better. Much better.

She glanced toward Talia, who was already bent over her desk, scribbling with quick, easy strokes. Cassara considered saying something but instead she recorked the jar, shoved it beneath her pillow. Finally, after much contemplation, "This doesn't make us friends," she said.

Talia didn't look up. "Tragic."

Cassara rolled her eyes, stripped down the rest of the way, and tugged her nightshirt over her head. The ambient glow of the dorm's magelight had dimmed to a soft pulse, casting the alcoves in half-shadow.

She climbed into her bunk, tugged the curtains the rest of the way closed, and stretched out as slowly and carefully as she could. Her ribs ached, but not enough to keep her from sleep.

For the first time since classes began, she didn't lie awake counting every mistake.

Just one.

But it hurt less now.

Two days later the bruises still bloomed dark across her ribs. Despite using the ointment regularly, they were still tender to the touch and wrapped in a tight, pulsing ache that throbbed with every breath. Talia's salve had helped more than she wanted to admit, but not enough to erase the pain entirely.

But Cassara hadn't expected it to, and she hadn't wanted it to. It served as a lingering reminder of that moment between Gideon and Julian, when everything insufferable and stupid in her life collided.

She moved a little slower when no one was looking, shifted carefully when dressing, but when asked how she was, she smiled and said fine. If anyone suspected the truth, they'd pull her from the Rift before she ever set foot on the first platform.

So she told no one.

And when the summons came, she reported without complaint.

By the time the top ten first-years gathered at the mouth of the Rift chamber, the atmosphere had turned electric. Magitek sigils pulsed along the curved walls, their glow sharpening with each footstep, and the course below waited in preparation, stone shifting, the air laced with mana.

Cassara stood near the edge, ACS rig clipped in place, tension coiled beneath her skin.

Across the platform, Verena was preening. Julian leaned casually against the rail like he owned the Rift itself. Gideon stood still and quiet, gaze fixed on the shifting terrain as if memorizing every obstacle. Several other students that Cassara couldn't name were scattered throughout the waiting area, all of them trying their best to look casual and disinterested.

Instructor Nareen stepped into the center of the platform, her halberd resting across her shoulders.

"You're here because someone saw potential," she said, tone clipped. "Probably not me. But we'll see if they were right."

A few scattered laughs. None from Cassara.

"You're about to run the training version of the Rift. No beasts. Just your ACS rig, your reflexes, and the charming instinct to survive. You'll be split into pairs."

A girl near the front brightened slightly. "We'll have a partner?"

Nareen's smile was sharp. "No. An opponent."

The girl's expression fell.

Nareen paced the platform's edge, halberd balanced across her shoulders. "Running against another student isn't about ranking, though that's a nice bonus for those of you obsessed with the prestige board. It's about learning to think when someone else is taking your options away. When the route you planned gets blocked. When the timing you counted on shifts because another living, breathing variable is moving through the same space."

Cassara glanced towards Verena who offered a smirk in return.

"Out in the field, corrupted beasts don't follow patterns. They adapt. They react. They force you to make split-second decisions with incomplete information." Nareen's tone hardened. "The Rift does the same thing. Your opponent isn't your enemy—they're chaos given form. And if you can't handle another student making your life harder, you have no business facing something with claws and teeth that actually wants you dead."

A few students shifted uncomfortably.

"So you'll compete," Nareen continued. "When one of you seals a route, the other scrambles. When platforms collapse, you adjust. When everything goes wrong at once—" She smiled coldly. "—you figure it out or you fail. Simple as that."

She raised a pale crystal etched with runes. "Pairings will be determined by resonance sort. The system's not random, it's responsive. It analyzes tension, rivalry, and the kind of unresolved friction that makes teams combust."

"Sometimes it'll pit you against someone you hate. Sometimes," Nareen added, her tone sharp, "it'll pair you with someone you don't trust to catch you when you fall. Its purpose is to make you see each other."

She flicked the crystal.

The runes launched into the air, names unraveling like constellations in motion. Arcs of light shimmered and shifted as they aligned above the platform. Every student tilted their head back to watch, breath held, posture tight. The Rift was choosing.

Cassara Allencourt.

Her name lit first in silver-white, bright and steady, hanging at the center of the spellwork.

She braced herself, refusing to look at Verena even as her name started to form, red-gold threads curling into place, the pairing nearly complete.

Then something changed.

The glow around Verena's name flickered, warped like heat haze. It destabilized, unraveling in a spiral of dimming light before vanishing entirely.

A quiet gasp slipped through the group.

Verena's eyes widened, then narrowed.

Another name flared beside Cassara's, this one cooler in tone than Verena's had been.

Gideon Delvanir.

Cassara went still.

Julian's face darkened and for half a heartbeat Cassara thought he might protest. Across the platform, Verena's expression sharpened, though she said nothing.

Nareen glanced up at the shifting display, one brow lifting with mild interest.

"Oh," she said, a touch too pleased. "Well that's interesting."

The rest of the pairings came faster now. Julian Tremaine sparked next, paired with a girl named Mara Cavalle.

Julian did nothing to hide his scowl. Verena got stuck with Egan Odanis, a silver-ranked boy from the east islands.

Nareen flicked her wrist again and let the constellation dissolve.

"Looks like the Rift has taste," she announced. "All pairings, report to your lanes. First up, Allencourt and Delvanir."

The platform erupted into movement. Students scattered toward the preparation chambers, voices rising in a mix of anticipation and dread. Some were already strategizing aloud, others walking in tense silence.

Cassara didn't move immediately. She stood there, staring at the space where her name had hung beside his, trying to process what the Rift had just decided for her.

Behind her, she heard Julian's voice, low and irritated, talking to someone about his pairing. Verena swept past without a glance, her expression carefully neutral but her posture rigid.

Taking a deep breath, Cassara finally turned and headed for the prep chamber.

The narrow room was all stone and steel, lined with benches and equipment racks. A few other students were already gearing up, checking straps, testing their ACS synchronization.

Cassara sat on the edge of a bench, gauntlet straps half-tightened, the air around her charged with nerves and frustration. The Rift shimmered beyond the prep chamber walls, glowing like it could sense her heartbeat.

Across from her, Gideon was checking his codex in silence—calm, methodical and detached.

The Rift had sorted them out of a storm of rivalries and still decided he was the one she needed to face. Not Verena. Not Julian.

Him.

Cassara couldn't decide if it was a curse or a challenge, but either way, it was too late to figure it out.

The warning bell sounded.

Cassara's boots snapped against the pressure seal as the Rift's entry gate opened. A rush of cool air hit her, scented with charged stone, forged metal, and the coppery tingle of old magic.

Across the mirrored divide, she saw Gideon stepping into motion, every inch of him fluid, composed, sharp as a drawn blade.

Let him be. Let him look perfect.

She was going to beat him anyway.

The first phase surged to life—a wide chamber littered with platforms, hanging chains, pivoting stone ledges, and elevated rune-points etched into the walls.

Cassara's gaze snapped toward the nearest trigger rune, one of six, glowing faint gold. She needed three to open the gate. The moment she activated a rune, its twin would seal on Gideon's side, locking him out of the easier options.

She ran.

The first jump was clean, off a rotating ledge and onto a suspended beam. She didn't hesitate, springing to the right where the lowest rune hummed just within reach. She pressed her hand to the carved surface, mana surging from her rig's core into the stone.

The rune flared.

A corresponding rune on Gideon's side went dark.

Good.

Cassara pushed off before the beam twisted. Took a higher route, narrow stones rotating on invisible axles. She had to keep momentum. The second rune was wedged in a steep corner, above a narrow climb.

She scaled it with grit rather than grace, breath hissing between her teeth as the strain hit her ribs. One slip, one flare of pain, and she still made it. Palm to stone.

Two.

Below her, the stone shuddered. On the far side, she caught a glimpse of Gideon rerouting. He'd gone for the central pillar, only to find its rune dead.

He looked up at her, just for a second.

Their eyes met.

No words. No pause.

But something passed between them. A pulse of rivalry that seemed to say: *you're faster than I thought.*

She dropped down to her third point and took the longer path to avoid the one she'd seen him eyeing at the start. If she got there first, she'd block it entirely.

Stone rumbled again.

A sharp white flash to her left.

Gideon had just triggered his second, cutting off the last remaining easy rune.

Cassara grinned. Perfect.

She swung from a chain, caught the edge of a high turning platform, dragged herself over the lip just as the last viable rune came into view.

It was high and almost out of reach.

No time to question it.

She leapt and hit the wall, kicking off before catching a hanging rung. From it she swung and slammed her palm against the rune just as it pulsed gold.

Three.

A deep grinding sound filled the chamber.

Her gate began to open: carved metal sliding into stone. She dropped to the platform and ran toward it, sparing a glance over her shoulder.

Gideon was still moving, still calculating. He'd have to find one of the advanced runes hidden in the upper chamber, ones that required higher mana output or riskier acrobatics.

He'd be out soon, but she'd made damn sure he'd earn his place in the next round.

Taking advantage of the head start, Cassara burst through the gate into a new chamber—and nearly slipped right off the edge.

The floor beneath her shimmered with a thin sheet of ice.

Wider platforms rose ahead like broken glacier shelves, layered with frost and pulsing with subtle arcane glow. Streams of freezing water rushed between them, fast-moving, narrow channels churning with mana currents.

High above, wind glyphs spun lazily, decorative at first glance, until a gust hit her from the left, trying to unbalance her mid-step.

This wasn't just a path, it was a storm.

Another gust struck, stronger this time, causing her to stagger, the soles of her boots fighting for purchase. She went down on one knee, palm slapping against the frozen surface to keep from toppling over entirely.

Her ribs screamed in protest but she ignored them, pushing herself back to her feet and leaping to the next platform. She slid half a step, then used a low crouch and momentum to ride the slick surface to the edge before springing onto a jagged ledge. The ice snapped underfoot but didn't give entirely.

Another gust struck. She ducked, braced—

Splash.

From somewhere behind her, water surged and a body hit the course hard.

Gideon had crossed the threshold.

She didn't look back. Instead, she scaled a narrow ledge slick with frost, each grip burning with cold. The rune markings in the ice gave her just enough foothold to keep climbing. At the top: a fire glyph flaring intermittently. If she passed beneath it during a flare, it would strike the platform with a burst of heat that would melt the path and her rig.

Cassara paused, watching the rhythm.

One... two... flare.

One... two...

She moved. Slid under the arch as it dimmed, boots skating over melting frost just before the glyph erupted again in a hiss of steam behind her.

A shadow passed overhead prompting her to look up.

Gideon had taken the high path, leaping a wind-carved ledge above her. His coat flared behind him like a banner, his landing almost silent as he moved from icy outcrop to icy outcrop, choosing elevation over balance.

Smart, but risky.

The higher platforms twisted in a slow spiral, forcing him to take more steps and follow a less direct route.

Cassara kept to the low road, watched the patterns, and calculated the pulses of the glyphs.

Fire. Wind. Water. Ice.

It was like dancing across an elemental heartbeat. She slipped twice. Swore once. But she moved, and the path unfolded beneath her in a rhythm of risk and momentum.

She was nearing the final jump, the exit ledge carved into a frozen slope with barely an edge to land on.

One shot.

Cassara built speed across the slick, uneven frost, her breath ragged, legs aching with every push, ribs howling. Her boots struck the final ridge, a jagged, rune-scored ledge barely wide enough to count as footing, and she launched. It was a perfect leap, timed between the shifting gusts of wind glyphs spinning overhead.

Almost.

A sudden gust struck mid-air, stronger than any before it, slamming into her like a wall. Her trajectory veered. Her balance shifted mid-flight, and her hip slammed hard against the lip of the next platform. The pain was instant and blinding, a white-hot flare beneath already-bruised ribs.

She hit the ice and skidded, breath wrenched from her lungs in a sharp gasp.

For a moment, she hovered at the edge, boots scrambling, fingers clawing across frost-slick stone as the platform shuddered beneath her weight. One slip and she'd be down in the chasm.

But she didn't fall.

With a growl of effort, Cassara hauled herself up, chest heaving. A rough cough tore from her throat as the cold hit her again, hard and sharp and merciless.

Behind her, the soft crunch of boots on ice.

Gideon landed cleanly on a higher ledge, his descent fluid and controlled. He dropped into a slide that arced down the slope, his timing perfect.

Cassara was already standing by the time he reached the same platform.

They were neck and neck now, just a few paces apart.

Their eyes locked across the frost-scarred stone. No words. No false politeness. Just breath, visible in the cold between them, and the weight of everything that hadn't been said.

Both of them were marked, frostbite edging their gloves and sleeves, grit clinging to their boots, bruises blooming under armor. She was scraped and battered. He was flushed and wind-creased. They'd bled for this.

But they were both still standing.

The Rift shuddered around them as the next gate activated. Runes crawled across the archway behind them, burning gold.

Shared Arena Initiating.

Cassara tasted copper and lifted a trembling hand to her mouth. Blood came away on her glove. She must have bitten through her lip at some point and hadn't even noticed.

The gate hissed open to reveal a narrow ledge curling around the edge of a vast, open chamber.

She stepped toward it and froze.

Before her stretched a chasm lit by molten light. Floating stone discs hovered over a pit like scattered coins tossed by the gods. They glowed faintly, pulsing in strange, shifting rhythms.

There was no rhyme or reason, no pattern that Cassara could discern, and none of them were marked.

Gideon joined her without a word, the archway sealing shut behind them.

Objective: Cross the Rift.

Reach the final seal.

First to touch it wins.

Cassara sucked in a breath, ignoring the sting of her busted lip and trying to drown the fire roaring through her ribs. Every breath scraped raw against bone. Her legs trembled, burning from exertion. Her skin slick with sweat beneath her uniform.

But she wasn't done.

Not yet.

The first disc pulsed beneath her boot, a burst of pale blue light, and she launched forward.

Gideon moved a heartbeat later.

Cassara hit the second disc clean, the third with a jolt that rattled her spine. The fourth wobbled under her pivot and she shoved off hard, teeth gritted as she aimed for the fifth.

It blinked out of existence mid-air.

"Shit—!"

She twisted mid-leap, back arching, boots scrambling for purchase. Her foot clipped the nearest disc at a brutal angle and she slammed down sideways. Her knee struck first. Pain lanced up her thigh as she skidded across the stone's surface. The disc tilted under the impact, groaning ominously, but held.

Behind her, Gideon adjusted. He arced wide, choosing a longer but steadier route. The disc he landed on shimmered beneath him, but he shifted his weight low and centered, and it held.

Cassara didn't wait. She surged to her feet and drove forward again.

The path ahead still offered no pattern. No logic. Some platforms vanished the moment she touched them. Others waited, teasing stability, only to disappear without provocation. One disc shivered violently and dropped with a sickening hiss the second her foot left it.

There was no way to predict which disc was safe. They could only rely on speed and reflex.

And then the field changed.

At the midpoint, their routes locked, two glowing platforms aligning side by side. One forward path remained.

Cassara hit it first, boots slamming down with a jarring thud that vibrated through her. Her breath tore in and out, raw in her throat, every inhale agony. A half-beat later,

Gideon landed beside her, the platform dipping with a groan beneath their combined weight.

The disc vibrated beneath them, a low, uneasy hum thrumming through the soles of her boots.

Too much pressure. It wouldn't hold long.

She didn't look at him. "You first."

He didn't move. "Afraid?"

Her jaw clenched, pain flickering across her side. "Only that you'll fall and I'll get blamed for it again."

He exhaled sharply. "You threw Verena."

"She deserved it."

Their eyes met, heat colliding in the narrow space between them. The disc trembled beneath their feet, magic twitching like a nervous pulse.

"Is that how you decide what's fair?" Gideon stepped forward slowly, testing the edge of the next platform with a quiet confidence. "By what people deserve?"

"Better than standing around like a coward letting them walk all over everyone." Her voice lowered. "Unless that's all the great Delvanir name is good for these days."

His expression darkened, just enough to show it hit, but he didn't bite. Not the way she wanted him to.

Instead, he moved.

Without warning, he darted for the next stone. Cassara surged forward after him, teeth clenched against the pain flaring through her side, using his momentum to judge her own next move. Her eyes flicked across the field, analyzing the shifting platforms, the flickering glyphs beneath each surface.

They landed. The stone held. Barely.

Another leap. Another test. The next platform cracked under Gideon's boots and dropped, but he caught a chain mid-swing and used the momentum to throw himself to the next. Smooth. Controlled. Frustratingly graceful.

Cassara aimed higher, taking the elevated path. She pushed too far, misjudged the landing, her foot skidded, and she crashed sideways, ribs shrieking as her ACS flared to soften the blow. Even then, it wasn't enough. She slammed into the edge of the next disc with a breathless grunt.

Don't stop. Don't slow.

She forced herself to roll clear of the collapsing platform and launched again, catching the lip of the next stone with a hard, bone-jarring impact. A burst of pain shot through her chest, but she made it.

She looked up.

Gideon was a full stone ahead.

No.

Cassara narrowed her eyes as she studied the field, watched the rhythm-less chaos of the platforms, the twitch of unstable glyphs beneath their surfaces.

Waited. Waited—

Two discs pulsed side by side.

The left looked steadier.

So she took the right.

It dropped, slow, late.

She launched higher, catching a rotating chain overhead and letting it whip her across the field. The wind snapped past her face and she landed hard, shoulder-first, just as Gideon reached the final segment.

The last bridge.

Only three stones remained, spaced across a chasm of air and shadow. Each one trembled with barely contained energy. No guarantees. No mercy.

The seal was embedded in the far wall, glowing gold. Waiting.

Gideon glanced over, panting slightly. "Last chance. Give up now. Save the fall."

Cassara grinned, teeth bared. "You first."

He moved.

One, two—

She followed, matching his pace, teeth grit through the pain and fire burning in her chest.

The first disc held.

The second trembled beneath her boots, a spiderweb of cracks blooming from the center.

Gideon prepared to jump, arms stretching for the seal.

Cassara leapt first.

Her hand caught the corner of the final platform. It dipped under her weight as she scrambled, slipping, one boot caught the edge, the other left dangling.

She managed to pull herself up as Gideon's fingers stretched towards the seal, slamming her palm down a half-second before his touch could claim it.

The platform lit beneath her, golden light flaring outward like a miniature sun exploding under her hand.

Match complete.

The platforms groaned, the air bleeding static as the magic began to drain. Slowly, the discs began to retract, fading back into their hidden anchors with a resonant hum.

Cassara didn't move.

The light dimmed, fading from her vision. She was still kneeling, body trembling with aftershock. One hand braced on the cool stone. The other curled protectively around her side, where the pain now spiked with every breath. Her pulse thundered in her ears.

Everything hurt.

The bruises had deepened, layers of impact pulsing outward like rings on a target. Her vision shimmered, edges curling in, black fog licking at her focus. She swayed.

"Cassara."

She couldn't answer.

Slowly she staggered to her feet and instantly regretted it as the world began to tilt, her breath escaping in shallow gasps.

A hand caught her arm, pulling her steady.

She looked up in surprise. It was Gideon. She blinked hard, trying to surface through the fog. "I'm fine," she rasped. The lie cracked in her throat.

"You're stubborn as hell, you know that?" he snapped, sounding angry. No, not angry... worried maybe?

"Are you concerned about me, Delvanir?"

Before he could answer, her knees gave out. He cursed, his arm catching her and pulling her into him. "You never make anything easy, do you?"

"I thought I told you I didn't need saving?" There was no heat to her words, she was too tired.

"You say a lot of things." His voice dropped lower, gentler. "Doesn't mean I believe them."

That was the problem wasn't it? What Cassara didn't understand was why.

For once, she didn't have the energy to argue. Her body made the choice her pride wouldn't, relaxing against him as the world swayed and her thoughts began to scatter like smoke.

The edges blurred. Sound became distant—voices, footsteps, the hum of magic draining from the arena. She felt herself being lifted, arms shifting beneath her knees and back, and then there was only warmth and the steady rhythm of movement.

CHAPTER TWELVE

The roar of the Rift faded away as Cassara drifted in and out of awareness. All that remained now was the gentle, rhythmic sensation of being carried.

Her head lolled slightly and she turned into the warmth surrounding her despite the alarm bells going off in the back of her mind. Her cheek pressed into the rough fabric of a training tunic and she felt the subtle press of muscles shifting with each step.

She was drifting towards darkness again when a quiet voice jerked her back to awareness.

"One of these days you're going to get killed because you're too stubborn to ask for help."

It was Gideon.

Her heart skipped and she struggled to focus her gaze, not that she needed to see his face to know what it probably looked like. She'd seen his disapproving frowns often enough that she could see them in her sleep.

Not that she dreamed about him.

She tried to speak, her lips parting, but her tongue felt too thick and refused to form sounds let alone cohesive words. This was *not* good. Shifting, she tried to say with her body what she couldn't articulate with words.

"Stop moving or you'll end up hurting yourself more," Gideon admonished without looking down at her. She felt more than heard him sigh. "Just... let me help you."

Help. It seemed so simple, so easy, but reliance on anyone was a weakness she couldn't afford. It might not cost her now, but the price would be paid eventually. The question now was simple. Would it be worth it? Cassara grit her teeth and finally gave up, allowing the tension to drain from her limbs.

Darkness pressed in again and this time, she let it swallow her.

When she surfaced once again, Cassara found herself staring up at the vaulted ceiling of the infirmary. Runed arches pulsed faintly with soft, calming light. Her ACS rig had been removed and her limbs felt weightless without it.

She tried to sit up and instantly regretted it, groaning as fire lanced through her side.

A chair scraped nearby.

"You're awake!"

Cassara looked to see Liri leaning over the edge of the bed, face practically glowing with excitement.

"Barely," Cassara grunted. "What are you doing here?"

"You passed out," Liri said. sitting back. She was practically vibrating with anticipation. "After you won, after that jump. Gods, Cass, you were amazing and then you went down like," she mimed a collapsing tower with her hands, "whoosh."

"I remember, I was there." Cassara dropped her head back to the pillow. It was worse than she'd originally thought. Everyone had seen her pass out. She groaned inwardly. She could hear it now, the rumors that Cassara Allencourt had fainted.

Verena was going to be insufferable.

Liri beamed. "Oh no, wait. It gets better."

Cassara didn't move, she simply stared at the ceiling and braced herself. Better? Somehow she doubted it.

"Do you remember who caught you?"

Her heart began to race. *Stop, let me help you.*

No, that had been a hallucination, a dream, a figment of her imagination.

"It was Gideon." Liri said, whispering like it was both a secret and a gift. "He carried you out, in front of everyone. Like some exiled prince out of a trashy romance."

Cassara closed her eyes. "No."

"Yup."

"No."

"*Yes.*"

Cassara threw her arm over her face, groaning from a place deeper than pain. Maybe she should have just died in the Rift, it would be better than facing Gideon later.

Liri laughed, far more amused by the turn of events than Cassara was. "You should've seen Julian's face! And Instructor Nareen? She just raised an eyebrow and let him pass like she was impressed." Liri paused for dramatic effect. "Oh, and you're currently number three on the Crestboard. You're officially a threat."

Cassara said nothing. She simply lay there, arm still draped across her eyes, wrapped in pain and mortification and wondering if throwing herself from the overlook would be too dramatic. She remembered, just faintly, the way Gideen's voice had sounded, how he hadn't hesitated. Not once.

She should've been furious.

Instead, her pulse still hadn't slowed.

"You want to know the best part?"

"There's more?"

Liri kept going as though she hadn't heard a thing. "Verena. I swear to the skies, Cass, the look on Verena's face when Gideon carried you out," Liri flung a hand in the air, practically vibrating with delight. "She looked like she'd just bitten into a lemon—"

The infirmary door burst open and Julian came striding into the room. His blond hair was damp with sweat, his cheeks still flushed from exertion, and his ACS rig showed fresh scuffing across one shoulder.

"Are you insane, Cassara? What the hell were you thinking running the Rift with an injury? This is the exact reason your father didn't want you here. You're irresponsible, reckless—"

Liri let out a small squeak of distress causing Julian to cut his tirade short. He took a deep, steadying breath.

"I didn't know you had company. Do you think you could give us some privacy?" he said, his voice low.

She hesitated, glancing towards Cassara.

"I'll see you back at the dorm,"

Liri frowned. "Okay," she started for the door, pausing by Julian. "She's hurt. Maybe don't make it worse?" She slipped out, and the door clicked softly behind her.

Hesitating a moment, Julian moved to the edge of the cot. He didn't sit, he just stood there, his eyes moving over her like he was scanning for damage the healers might've missed.

"I'm sorry, I shouldn't have yelled. I just... when I saw you—you scared me."

Cassara looked up at him. She always seemed to scare him these days.

"I'm fine," she said, too tired to offer more than that.

"Fine? You passed out cold, Cass."

"Does it matter? I won."

Julian huffed, shaking his head. "Yeah. You did." He glanced away for a second before meeting her eyes again. She saw the fear there, but she saw something else too, something that went deeper. "And then he picked you up like it was his place."

Cassara's brows drew together. Was that what had brought him running? It certainly hadn't been her well being, he hadn't even asked her if she was okay, or how she felt. No, it was all about him, how he felt, it was *always* about him.

"Would you rather he just left me on the ground?"

Julian's mouth curved slightly, but there was no humor in it. "He could've flagged a medic, or an instructor, but no, he carried you. Right through the middle of the field. Slow enough to make sure everyone saw."

"Why does that matter?"

"Don't you get it yet, Cassara? Gideon Delvanir is spitting in the face of what it means to be a tamer. Ever since his family fell he's blamed mine."

Cassara shifted against the pillow. "You think he did it for you?"

Julian shrugged. "I think he doesn't do anything unless there's a motive. So yeah, I think he saw an opportunity to make me look bad and took it."

She studied him, trying to find the boy she knew lost within the tangle of the man he was becoming. "Maybe he just wanted to help."

When Julian smiled it was soft, almost sympathetic, and it made her want to slap him. "Cass. You don't honestly believe he did it out of the goodness of his heart."

She didn't answer, so he took that as permission to keep going.

"I get it. He caught you, said the right thing, looked the part, but don't forget what he's actually done. He took Verena's side when she humiliated you in front of the first year cohort. He's the reason you got hurt to begin with, or did you forget?"

Her throat felt tight, but she maintained her silence. He wasn't wrong, but that didn't mean everything else he said was right.

Julian leaned in just slightly. "Don't let one act of charity blind you to the truth. Gideon comes from bad blood. I don't want to see you fooled into believing otherwise."

Cassara's eyes stayed locked on the ceiling as she took a deep, steading breath.

"I know this is going to be hard to believe, but not everything is about you," she said at last.

Julian stilled and the air in the infirmary seemed to press in around them.

"You're defending him now?" he asked, anger creeping into his voice. "After everything?"

"All I am saying is that maybe it wasn't as calculated as you're making it out to be," She turned to meet his gaze. "Maybe he just did what anyone decent would've done."

Julian let out a short breath, almost a laugh, but not a kind one.

"Right," he said, stepping back. "Because Gideon is just full of noble instincts."

Cassara didn't rise to the bait. She didn't need to. The sting of her ribs and the heat in Julian's voice said more than either of them had time to unpack.

Fortunately, the infirmary door swung open again and Nareen strode in like a storm bottled in black leather and restrained judgment. She took one look at Julian and didn't bother with pleasantries.

"Tremaine, out."

Julian hesitated. "We weren't finished,"

"You are now." Her eyes didn't even flick toward him. "You can argue about... whatever, later, but if you delay my evaluation, I *will* write you up and dock points."

Julian glanced at Cassara and for a moment she thought he might argue. He seemed to think better of it and finally left without another word.

Nareen crossed to the side of the bed and folded her arms. "How long."

Cassara blinked. "What?"

"How long," Nareen repeated, "have your ribs been compromised."

"Since... before the Rift," Cassara admitted, shifting uncomfortably in the bed.

"That much was obvious. Care to be more specific?"

No, but she didn't have much of a choice. "Four days."

Nareen exhaled through her nose. "Gods above," she muttered, mostly to herself. "Do you have any idea how much worse you could've made your injuries running a full trial course like that?"

Cassara opened her mouth but Nareen cut her off.

"Don't. Don't answer. I know the answer. You do, you just didn't care."

Nareen paced away and then back again, "I'm not going to dress you down in front of your classmates. You earned your position out there, and frankly, you performed better injured than half the class on a good day." She looked down and frowned. "But don't mistake my respect for your determination as a license to be reckless."

Cassara swallowed the sting in her throat.

Nareen sighed. "You're restricted from combat trials and obstacle courses for the next five days. Minimum. Until the ribs are re-stabilized and cleared."

"What! I can't miss that much training! I'll fall behind, I'll—"

Nareen raised a brow. "Five. Days."

Cassara fell quiet.

"You can watch drills, you can observe matches, but if you so much as think about engaging in any physical activity before clearance, you will be pulled from rotation and won't be allowed to join your cohort when they go to the Wilds. Have I made myself clear?"

Cassara wanted to argue but knew that it would only make things worse. "Understood."

Nareen gave a short nod. "Good. Heal fast. You're starting to make them nervous." And with that, she turned on her heel and walked out.

She sank deeper into the bed.

Five days.

It shouldn't have mattered as much as it did, it was just time after all, just drills she already knew by heart. She supposed it was the reason, not the punishment. She should've said spoken up, should've let someone help, but help always came with strings.

So instead, she'd lied and now she was here, too sore to sit up straight and too proud to regret it.

Cassara exhaled slowly, eyes drifting shut for a moment.

It would be fine.

She would heal, she always did, and the next time she'd win without collapsing to prove it.

It had only been two days since the Rift and Cassara felt like she was going to crawl out of her skin. The wind off the cliffs carried the scent of chalk dust and scorched mana, the kind that clung to your skin no matter how long you stayed on the sidelines. She stood just beyond the boundary flags of the training field, arms crossed, ribs bandaged beneath her coat, watching the students run drills she should've been participating in.

Pairs moved in tandem through the obstacle sequences and from here, it was easy to see which ones flinched before impact, easier still to spot the ones who wouldn't last.

Cassara found her gaze drawn to the far side of the field, where the familiar cadence of steel on steel rang through the air.

A cluster of second-years had formed a loose circle around two figures moving with lethal grace, but it wasn't the students that made her breath catch—it was their instructor.

Auren Veth had discarded his usual training jacket, leaving him in boots, dark trousers and nothing else. The afternoon light played across the lean muscle of his shoulders and back as he moved, and Cassara found herself transfixed by the casual display of strength she'd only guessed at beneath his typically austere attire.

He wasn't just observing today, he was actively sparring with one of the older students—a broad-shouldered boy she didn't recognize. The student was good, his movements confident and precise, but watching Auren move was like watching lightning choose its path.

Don't stare, she told herself, but her eyes refused to cooperate.

Every shift of his body was economical, purposeful and when the student lunged forward with an overhead strike, Auren didn't block so much as redirect, his bare torso twisting with fluid grace as he caught the boy's wrist and used his own momentum against him. The move sent the student stumbling, and Auren followed through with a strike that stopped just short of connection.

"Again," his voice carried across the training ground, calm and unbothered despite the exertion.

Cassara's mouth had gone dry.

She'd seen him fight on the airship, had felt the controlled power in his arms when he'd caught her, but this? This was different. This was Auren unguarded, focused entirely on the art of combat, and the sight of him like this? It left her feeling ways she wasn't entirely ready to confront.

The student reset his stance and attacked again, this time with a series of quick strikes that should have been impossible to counter, but Auren moved like he could see the blows coming before they were thrown, his body responding with an elegance that made her think of deadly things like serpents striking or hawks diving for their prey.

When he caught the student's blade on his forearm guard and twisted, the muscles of his back shifted and bunched beneath sun-bronzed skin, and Cassara felt something squeeze in her chest that had nothing to do with her injuries and everything to do with the way the late light carved shadows along the plane of his shoulders.

The spar ended with Auren's practice blade at the student's throat, both of them breathing hard but neither winded. When Auren stepped back and nodded his approval, the gesture was small but somehow devastating in its restraint.

"Better," he said simply, and the student's face lit up like he'd been given the highest praise imaginable.

That was when Auren's gaze swept the training ground and found her. Their eyes met across the distance, and Cassara suddenly felt exposed, pinned like a butterfly under glass. His expression was unreadable for the most part, but for the briefest of moments something flickered there. Awareness, perhaps, or annoyance at her presence where she didn't belong.

Cassara looked away before he could see the flush she could feel burning across her cheeks and read whatever foolish thoughts were surely written across her face.

She took a deep breath, preparing to leave, when a voice rose from behind her.

"You're not supposed to be training."

Auren's voice was dry, neutral. Cutting in its quiet way. Just like when he'd told her that heroics made poor habits.

Cassara spun around, startled. She hadn't even noticed he had left the training field let alone come to join her. "I'm not."

He came to stand beside her, close enough that she could feel the difference in stillness between them. He didn't lean or pace, he just stood, watching. It was the same controlled presence she'd felt when his arms had locked around her mid-air, steady and sure despite the chaos of the fall.

She kept her gaze fixed determinedly on the training field, refusing to acknowledge the expanse of sweat-streaked skin in her peripheral vision.

"Sulking isn't any better."

Cassara scoffed. "And you're here to lecture me again?"

"Lectures require an audience capable of learning from them," he said with a shrug.

She frowned, glancing towards him.

"I heard about the Rift," he continued.

Cassara looked back toward the arena. "So? Who hasn't." A student overreached and caught a blow to the ribs, just off balance enough to hurt. She didn't wince, but the ache in her own side flared anyway.

"You shouldn't have run it."

"Everyone keeps saying that."

"Because you nearly made it worse."

"Does it matter? I still won. Everyone seems to forget that part."

"I know why you did it," he said. "The same reason you climbed that stabilizer. To prove something, but next time, don't expect it to end in applause."

Her fingers curled around her arms. "You're wrong," she said quietly. "I didn't do it for anyone else. I did it for me."

He didn't answer, but the look he gave her said he wasn't convinced.

Silence settled between them and Cassara found herself growing anxious. Had he come over just to repeat what half a dozen people had already said? He hadn't struck her as someone with that kind of time to waste. "Was there something else you needed, Instructor Veth?"

Auren was quiet for a moment, as though trying to decide the best way to proceed. "Your instructor gave me clearance to work with you. During your downtime."

She frowned, not quite sure she understood. Nareen had been adamant about no training until she had been cleared. "What? Why?"

"To keep you from acting reckless out of boredom." He offered a shrug. "Nareen seems to think you're high risk. Judging by your track record, she's not wrong to be concerned."

The way he said it, quiet, flat, certain, hit harder than it should've. It was like he'd cataloged her entirely based on assumptions.

She narrowed her eyes. "And if I refuse?"

"You won't." His gaze lingered on her injured side for just a heartbeat too long.

He turned before she could respond, stepping back into the archway without so much as a glance over his shoulder.

"Training room two. Six a.m."

Then he was gone.

Cassara stood there, ribs aching, heart pounding harder than it should've. She told herself it was frustration at being reduced to a problem that needed solving, but the heat curling beneath her skin said otherwise.

And beneath that, a stubborn determination. She'd show him she was more than just reckless impulse. She'd prove she belonged here, not just at Vallemont, but under his attention.

Even if she wasn't entirely sure why that mattered so much.

She'd barely made it three steps from the field when footsteps closed the distance behind her.

"Cassara."

She stopped, turning to find Gideon there. He stopped a few steps away, his hand flexing at his side. His gaze dropped briefly to her ribs, then lifted again.

"You alright?"

"Fine." She kept her tone even, though her ribs were screaming.

"You don't look fine."

She gave a short, breathless laugh despite herself. "Well, I'm standing. That's something."

They stood there in awkward silence for a moment, the noise of the training ground swelling and falling behind them.

"Impressive work yesterday."

Cassara raised a brow. "Wasn't aware you gave out compliments."

"I don't," he said and Cassara couldn't help but notice the way his eyes shifted from hers when he said it. "But it would've been worse to pretend you didn't earn it."

His words caught her by surprise. There was a rawness to them that was unexpected after weeks of animosity.

She shifted where she stood, suddenly feeling watched though Gideon had yet to return his gaze. "Thanks."

Gideon was quiet after that and she thought perhaps that might be the end of it. Before she could excuse herself, however, he spoke again. This time he seemed reluctant. "Julian came to find me. After the match."

"What? Why?" Even as she uttered the question she knew the answer.

"He came to tell me off." Gideon's tone was flat and Cassara could tell he was unimpressed by Julian's behavior. "He warned me to stay away from you. As if that was ever going to be a problem. Said he wouldn't tolerate me trying to steal what's his. "

What's his.

“He said that?” Cassara's hands had curled into fists.

“Among other things.” He paused, head tilting, strands of dark brown hair falling across his forehead.

“He had no right—”

“Doesn’t he?” Gideon smirked. “Rumor has it you're practically engaged to him.”

She crossed her arms tighter, ignoring the protest from her ribs. "That's not—it's not like that."

"Are you sure? Because from where I'm standing, it looks exactly like that. He draws a line, and you just... accept it."

"I don't accept anything from him," she snapped.

"Then why are you defending him right now?"

Cassara bristled. Her ribs throbbed with every breath, and after the conversation with Auren, she had no patience left for this. "I'm not defending him. But maybe if you hadn't—" She stopped herself, but it was too late.

"Hadn't what?" Gideon's voice went cold. "Carried you? Should I have just left you there? Let you crawl across the finish line to prove some point?"

"You could've just called for help."

"Maybe." He glanced down, then back at her. "But then you wouldn't have had your moment."

Her eyes narrowed. "What is that supposed to mean?"

"You ran that course injured," he continued. "You thought you'd be paired with Verena—everyone did. Don't act like you weren't planning to either gloat if you won or play the sympathy card if you didn't."

"Are you serious?"

"You're not exactly shy about making a scene."

The words cut deeper than they should have. He'd reduced everything—her training, her pain, her refusal to quit—into theatrics. He saw her as nothing more than a girl succumbing to pride. Just like her father did. Just like Julian did.

Cassara straightened, every muscle in her back going tight. "I ran it because I earned my spot and I wasn't going to let anyone take it from me. I don't need sympathy and I sure as hell wasn't looking for a stage."

She saw a shift in his eyes, saw him realize he'd crossed a line, but it didn't matter anymore. He'd already shown her exactly who he was.

"You know what? Maybe Julian is right," she said, stepping back. "I thought you might be different, but in the end you're all the same. Nobody does anything without a reason."

She turned and walked away without waiting for a response.

Cassara was headed towards the dorms. Not hers—his. Julian's.

Her fingers were clenched so tightly they ached, nails biting into her palms. Her ribs were throbbing, but she hardly felt it. What burned deeper was the audacity of Julian going to Gideon, telling him to stay away from her like she was some possession that needed guarding.

She turned sharply down the next hall, her boots striking hard against the stone, cutting through the low murmur of students enjoying a well deserved afternoon break.

Cassara spotted two upperclassmen exiting one of the stairwells and intercepted them.

"Julian Tremaine?"

The shorter one straightened. "Common room, I think. West alcove. Playing charstones with the—"

"Thanks."

She didn't wait for them to finish.

The common room was all carved alcoves and floating game boards, lit with enchanted skylights that filtered the sun into golden shards. A few students lounged on the curved benches, laughter spilling from one corner as a cluster of first-years bantered over an illusion-casting game.

Julian sat in the center, a charstone grid in front of him, coat slung with effortless care across the back of his chair. His sleeves were rolled, and his smile was lazy as he moved a glowing token across the board. Vash and Jonas sat on either side of him, Jonas leaning in to track the game, Vash half-reclined with a smirk like he was already bored of winning.

He looked up when she stepped into the space.

The shift in his expression was immediate—surprise first, then pleasure. She so rarely sought him out on her own it was no surprise he was pleased.. because the warmth gave way to concern.

He started to rise. "Cass—"

She didn't stop her approach. "We need to talk."

Julian stepped around the bench, intercepting her. "Sure, but let's take it somewhere else."

"No," she said, loud enough for Vash to straighten and Jonas to glance up.

"You went to Gideon?"

The room stilled.

Julian's eyes narrowed slightly. "Not here."

"You told him to stay away from me?" Her voice shook with fury. "Like I'm some possession you get to fence off?"

He exhaled slowly, already trying to reach for calm. For control.

"I was looking out for you."

Cassara stared at him, stunned for half a heartbeat.

Looking out for her.

"No. You weren't doing it for me. You made it about you. You always do."

"Cass, this isn't the place—"

"It became the place when you went behind my back."

Vash shifted on the bench. Jonas had frozen mid-move, the charstone still glowing beneath his fingers.

Julian's voice dropped. "This is exactly what I was worried about, what I tried to warn you about. You don't know what he's like. He's manipulative and—"

"It doesn't matter. You don't get to decide my life for me."

The tension in the air was thick now. Too many eyes. Too much space that suddenly felt too small.

Cassara's pulse thundered. She felt the flush creep into her cheeks. The weight of every stare. A part of her hated it, the spectacle, the weakness of letting it boil over here.

But the rest of her was too angry to care.

"You think I'm yours to manage or control." She didn't shout, but her voice cut clean. "But you're wrong."

"Everyone is watching, you're making—"

"Let them."

Julian took a step closer.

"You really want to pick this fight here?" he asked, voice low and fraying. "Make a big scene? In front of them?"

You're not exactly shy about making a scene.

"I didn't come here for a fight."

"Then what did you come for?"

She stared at him. The answer wasn't as clear as it should've been.

"I came to remind you that I don't belong to you," she said. "No matter how many times you try to act like I do."

"Cassara," Julian called as she turned away.

She didn't stop. Didn't look back. Whatever he wanted to say—apology, excuse, another attempt to spin this into something reasonable—she didn't want to hear it. She was done listening to men tell her who she was allowed to be.

By the time she reached the girls' dorms, Cassara's breath was shallow and her ribs were screaming. The stairs were brutal, but she took them anyway.

She didn't stop when she passed Liri napping on the common room cushions, or when Sonia glanced up from her perch on the windowsill with a smirk she didn't bother to hide. Cassara didn't speak. She didn't even blink.

She shut herself in her alcove, tugged the curtain closed, and sat on the edge of her bed.

The ache behind her eyes wasn't physical. Not exactly.

After a moment, she reached beneath her pillow and pulled out the worn journal.

Cassara flipped it open without thinking, letting the pages fan until one caught on her thumb. Midway through. Mid-year.

She recognized the curve of the script instantly, quick, confident strokes, the ink faded in places where fingers had lingered too long.

We ran drills today. Nareen nearly sent her partner to the infirmary, and Isadore keeps tripping over her own shadow but won't admit it. I'm not sure what the instructors saw in me, but I'm starting to think I belong here.

We're behind, but not broken. That counts, right?

I still don't know what I'm going to bond with. Something magnificent, I hope. A beast with wings.

Every time I pass the overlook, I pretend I can feel the wind lifting me. Hopefully, someday I won't have to pretend. I think I'm falling in love with the air up here.

Cassara stared at the page. Her thumb brushed the edge of the ink, careful not to smudge what time hadn't already claimed.

She didn't know what she'd expected. Something stronger, wise maybe. But the words were real. Unpolished. Hopeful in a way Cassara hadn't let herself be since she was a child.

She didn't close the journal, she just sat with it open in her lap, eyes drifting to the corner of the page where the ink had bled faintly from being read too often.

The dorm was quiet. Just the low hum of magelight, the muffled sound of water pipes shifting behind the walls, the occasional creak of someone turning in their bunk.

Leaning back against the wall of her alcove, the journal still open across her knees, her eyes drifted over the page again, slower this time. Not really reading, just remembering.

Her mother had been young here. Full of dreams and scraped knuckles and the same gnawing need to matter. It felt distant and close all at once.

Cassara closed the book gently but she didn't put it away. She caught the edge of the blanket by her feet and dragged it over herself. Beyond the drawn curtain, the dorm light dimmed to its softest flicker, and she lay still beneath it all, eyes open, thoughts sharp, heart restless.

CHAPTER THIRTEEN

The training room was cold at six a.m.

Not frostbitten like the higher terraces, but sharp with still air and shadow. The enchantments that warmed the space during peak hours hadn't kicked in yet, and the only light came from a few slits of early dawn filtering through the high windows.

Auren was already there in the far ring, moving through a series of warm-up drills. He pivoted low, swept high, his arms cutting through the air in controlled arcs that barely made a sound. He was dressed in black sparring gear, and she couldn't help but notice how the fabric moved with him, tracing the lines of muscle across his shoulders as he shifted his weight.

She watched longer than she should have, captivated by the way he moved—certain, deliberate, like someone who'd spent years learning exactly what his body could do and never had to prove it.

Heat crept up the back of her neck and she forced her gaze away, focusing instead on the weighted rods and reinforced balance markers laid out near the edge of the ring.

"Planning to watch all day, or are you actually going to train?"

Of course he'd caught her staring. He hadn't even turned around. How did he always know? She stepped into the room and crossed to the mat, boots scuffing against the chalk-dusted edge. "I'm here, aren't I?"

"On time, even." He adjusted one of the weighted rods without looking up.

"Gee, try not to sound so pleased."

"I'm not."

She rolled her shoulders, testing the stretch across her ribs. Still sore, but better. "So what's the plan? Boredom by repetition? Or do we skip straight to condescension and balance drills?"

That earned his gaze.

He turned just enough to meet her eyes—steady, unreadable, like she'd walked into a blade he hadn't drawn yet. The intensity of his focus made her skin prickle with awareness.

"If you're done performing," he said, "we can start."

She shrugged. "Ready when you—"

Without warning, he tossed her a baton. It was weighted and heavier than she expected. She caught it one-handed, the impact jarring through her wrist, but she didn't flinch.

"Precision drills," he said. "Control over power. No flares. No bursts. No shortcuts."

"Because of my ribs," she muttered, adjusting her grip.

"Because you're sloppy when you're angry."

Cassara grit her teeth. "Maybe I perform better when I'm angry."

"No," he said, stepping into her space without hesitation. "You perform louder. There's a difference. Get in position."

Cassara took her stance, feet spaced apart, shoulders squared, the baton held level with the precise angle taught in standard combat training. Professional. Controlled. Exactly how she'd been drilled.

He moved behind her, and suddenly she was aware of every inch of space he occupied. The air felt warmer at her back.

His fingers brushed her elbow, adjusting the angle with brief, deliberate pressure. The touch was clinical, impersonal even, but her pulse kicked up anyway. She hated that her body reacted before her mind could stop it.

"Strike."

She struck.

"Slower."

Another strike.

"You're compensating."

"I'm injured," she bit out.

"Then stop pretending you aren't."

Heat flared in her chest. "You're enjoying this."

"I'm surviving it," he said.

Fine. If he thought she was favoring her ribs, she'd prove she wasn't.

She reset her stance and moved into the next sequence, deliberately distributing her weight evenly, forcing her injured side to bear the load it had been avoiding. The baton cut through the air—

The pivot came with full commitment, no compensation, exactly as it should be. But her ribs weren't ready for it. Pain lanced through her side, sharp enough to steal her breath. Her weight pitched forward and her vision blurred at the edges.

He caught her around the waist to stop her from falling, and she suddenly found herself pressed against his chest, fingers twisting without conscious thought into the fabric of his shirt. She could feel his heart beating against her palm, the rhythm faster than it had any right to be.

"Damn it." The word came out rough. "This was a mistake. You're too reckless. You're—"

"I'm fine." She wasn't fine. Her ribs were screaming and she was shaking and his hand was splayed across her lower back, fingers pressed firm enough that she could feel the heat of them through her training gear.

"You're not." She lifted her gaze to meet his eyes and noticed a flush had crept up his neck, faint but unmistakable against his skin. "That's enough for today."

"No." She forced herself to straighten, but his arm stayed locked around her waist. "I can keep going."

"I told you—"

"I said I'm fine." Her voice shook and she hated it. Hated that his hand was still on her, that she could feel every point of contact between. His eyes dropped to where her hand still gripped his shirt, then back to her face. She watched his throat work as he swallowed.

"Let go," he said quietly.

For a heartbeat she didn't know if he meant her hand or the argument.

Then his arm loosened at her waist and his hand slid from her back with deliberate slowness, fingertips dragging across fabric in a way that felt anything but professional.

She released his shirt and stepped back. The air between them felt colder without his body heat.

"Slower, then," he said, and his voice had gone carefully neutral again. Professional. Like the last thirty seconds hadn't happened. "And if you so much as wince like that again, we're done. Understand?"

She nodded, not trusting her voice, and reset her stance with movements that were deliberately controlled this time.

Auren circled slowly, his presence deliberate without ever becoming invasive. He didn't correct her again, not with touch, but she could feel his gaze mapping her movements, cataloging every shift of muscle and balance. He didn't look away, either.

They moved through the set twice more, the rhythm sharpening. The only sound between them was the muted thud of her boots against the training mat and the quiet drag of breath.

By the time he called it, her hands ached and her body trembled from the stillness, not exertion, but control.

Auren stepped back. "That's enough for today."

Without another word, he turned and began gathering the rods. She once again found herself watching the flex of his forearms, the controlled precision of his hands, and quickly turned away, heading towards the door.

She was nearly there when he spoke.

"Same time tomorrow."

It wasn't a question.

Cassara paused, hand on the frame, but she didn't look back.

"Yeah," she said. "I figured."

Then she stepped out into the hall, breath still tight in her chest and for the first time in days, not entirely from pain.

The dining hall buzzed with midday noise—cutlery clinking, steam rising off charmed dishes, and the low churn of mana from the overhead runes adjusting the light. Cassara sat in their usual alcove near the east windows, half-listening as Liri interrogated her about training in between mouthfuls of food.

"Okay. So," she said, leaning in, "you're just casually training alone with Auren Veth now? Like, normal thing, no big deal?"

Cassara didn't look up. "It's not like that."

"It's exactly like that," Liri hissed gleefully. "He's terrifying, but in a pretty way. I've never seen anyone dodge like that and still look like he was judging your life choices."

"He judges everyone's life choices," Cassara muttered. She stabbed a piece of potato on her plate with more force than necessary, trying to ignore the unbidden image of Auren's focused gaze that flashed through her mind. "It's not personal."

Liri beamed. "That's what draws the eye, isn't it? The danger beneath the control."

Cassara looked up, deadpan, hoping her face didn't betray the treacherous part of her that, for just a heartbeat, couldn't entirely disagree. "You need better taste."

Liri rested her chin on her fist. "Did he have to correct your stance? With his hands?"

Cassara made a face, her skin warming at the memory of his fingers against her elbow, brief but deliberate. "You're depraved."

"Mmm. Maybe. Was it cold and emotionally confusing?"

Cassara gave her a long, hard look. "He's just a combat instructor."

"No. He's Auren Veth," Liri whispered dramatically. "I heard he graduated a year early and became a breach commander right after. Youngest in history."

Cassara rolled her eyes and stabbed at the last bite of roast on her plate. "Am I supposed to be impressed?"

Before either Liri could reply, Talia slid onto the bench beside her. She didn't make eye contact. Just set her food down, calm as ever, like sitting with them was as natural as breathing.

Cassara blinked. "You're sitting with us now?"

Talia shrugged once, her tone casual. "It was loud over there."

They waited for her to elaborate. She didn't. Of course she didn't.

Liri suddenly perked up. "Talia! You've heard things. About Auren. Haven't you? Wasn't he born in the Outer Isles?"

Cassara's shoulders stiffened. "Don't start—"

But Talia didn't look up from her food and Cassara hoped she would simply ignore the question. "Only things my cousins have said, nothing verified, it's all rumors."

So much for silence.

Liri straightened, visibly leaning in. "Go on."

"He used to lead advanced breach units. Off-record missions. Leviathan zones. Wilds reclamation." She paused. "Had a perfect record for over a year before it happened."

Cassara found herself listening even though she'd told herself she didn't care. When Talia didn't continue, she found herself growing impatient. "What happened?"

Talia glanced at her briefly before responding. "He lost a squad."

Cassara's breath caught, just for a second.

The buzz of the dining hall seemed to fade around them, the low voices and clinking dishes softening under the sudden quiet at their table.

Liri blinked. "What, like... they just went missing?"

"No. Dead. All of them. Three years ago I think." Talia dipped her bread into her stew. "They said it was a miscalculation. His call. No one talks about it."

Cassara went still. He'd lost a whole squad?

She wasn't sure what to make of that revelation. Auren had always seemed distant and controlled to the point of coldness. She had assumed it was discipline, but was it truly? Or was he simply a man holding himself together through sheer force of will? The realization made him suddenly, disconcertingly human in a way that left her feeling off-balance.

Liri glanced at Cassara, then back at Talia. "How do you even know this stuff?"

"I listen," Talia said.

That was all the explanation she offered.

Cassara didn't speak again for the rest of lunch. She couldn't seem to settle back into her skin. Her thoughts kept looping, catching on Auren's silences, his sharp corrections, his refusal to praise.

She'd called it arrogance, but now it sat differently in her chest.

For some reason, it felt less like pride and more like grief.

It was a brokenness trying hard not to be noticed. She recognized it because she'd learned young how to wear the same mask—how to bury pain so deep that no one could see it bleeding through. Grief, after all, was weakness and tears were failure.

It had been one of the many lessons her father had taught her after her mother had died.

Maybe Auren had learned the same lesson.

The training room was empty when Cassara arrived.

She stood in the doorway for a moment, taking in the silence, the neat arrangement of equipment already set out for the session. The stone walls still held their faint chill, though the air felt less sharp than it had yesterday.

It was empty.

She told herself the flicker of disappointment was about the wasted effort, nothing more.

Cassara stepped inside and began her warm-ups without waiting. Her ribs protested less today—Talia's salve had worked its magic, the deep bruising faded to mottled yellow-green. Still tender, but healing.

She moved through the sequences with more ease than she had in days. Rotations, stretches, flowing from one position to the next with a fluidity she hadn't allowed herself when Auren was watching. No need to prove anything to an empty room.

Her body found its rhythm. She rolled her shoulders, testing the give, then sank into a deeper stretch, one arm extended overhead, her spine arching as she breathed through the pull on her injured side.

The prickling awareness hit her between one breath and the next.

The feeling of being watched.

Cassara straightened and turned.

Auren stood in the doorway.

Not just arrived—standing there, one shoulder against the frame, arms crossed. The way he held himself suggested he'd been there long enough to settle into the position. Long enough to watch.

His eyes were on her. Not her form, not her technique. *Her.*

For one unguarded moment, he looked at her like a man instead of an instructor. Then the realization seemed to hit him and his expression closed off, neutral and controlled once more. But her heart was already hammering against her ribs.

The silence stretched.

Neither of them spoke.

Heat crept up her neck. She forced herself to hold his gaze even as her heartbeat thundered in her ears.

"Do you always lurk in the shadows watching students?" The words came out more defensive than she had meant them too, perhaps trying to break whatever had just passed between them.

Auren didn't respond immediately.

He just pushed off the doorframe and stepped into the room. Measured. Deliberate. Each footstep steady on the stone floor as he crossed the threshold into her space.

He stopped a few feet away. Close enough that she had to tilt her chin up slightly to maintain eye contact.

"You're still compensating," he said finally, his voice level. Professional.

But he moved closer.

Cassara's breath caught as he circled behind her, and suddenly she was acutely aware of every inch of space he occupied. The heat radiating from him. The steady rhythm of his breathing.

"Here." His hand settled on her left shoulder, fingers pressing just firmly enough to adjust her posture. "You're dropping this side."

The touch was clinical. Professional. Exactly the kind of correction an instructor would make.

Except his hand didn't move.

His palm was warm through the thin fabric of her training shirt, and she could feel each individual finger where they rested against her shoulder. His other hand came to her waist—steadying, correcting the angle of her stance.

"Distribute the weight evenly," he said, close enough that she felt the words against her ear more than heard them.

She tried to focus on the correction, on adjusting her position, but all she could think about was the heat of his hands on her body. The way his thumb pressed against her lower back, firm and sure. The fact that he was still touching her.

Her pulse jumped visibly at her throat.

"Like this," Auren continued, his hands guiding her into proper alignment.

But they lingered.

Not long. Not inappropriately. Just a half-second longer than necessary before he released her and stepped back, putting professional distance between them once more.

Cassara's skin burned where his hands had been.

She exhaled slowly, forcing her breathing to steady, and adjusted her stance as he'd directed. The correction was sound—she could feel the difference immediately, the way her weight distributed more evenly, taking pressure off her injured side.

"Better," Auren said, his voice carefully neutral again.

He moved to the equipment without looking at her, checking the resistance bands with methodical precision.

But something had shifted in the air between them. A charge that hummed beneath the surface, unacknowledged but undeniable.

Cassara flexed her fingers once, trying to shake off the sensation of his touch still ghosting across her skin.

"Ready?" he asked, holding out one of the bands.

She nodded, not trusting her voice, and crossed to take it from him.

Their fingers brushed in the exchange—brief, accidental—but she felt it like a spark up her arm.

His hand stilled for just a heartbeat before he released the band and stepped back.

Neither of them mentioned it.

They moved into the drills with that same careful distance, that same studied professionalism. But Cassara couldn't shake the awareness thrumming through her veins.

The way he'd looked at her in the doorway.

The way his hands had felt on her body.

The way neither of them had acknowledged any of it.

When they finished the final set, Auren gave a single nod toward the door. "Same time tomorrow."

Cassara hesitated, fingers flexing once at her side. "That's it?"

"For now."

She nodded, slowly.

As she turned to leave, she felt his eyes follow her—a heat against her back that lingered all the way to the door.

The corridor leading back to the dorms was blissfully quiet. Most students were still at brunch or finishing drills, and Cassara moved with purpose—sweat still clinging to her neck, muscles sore from Auren's circuit, ribs burning in a steady pulse beneath her shirt.

She needed a shower and space.

She spotted Julian before he saw her—leaning against the wall near the dormitory entrance, clearly waiting. Her steps slowed, but it was too late. He'd already looked up.

"Cass."

She didn't stop. "Don't."

“I’m not here to fight.”

“You’re always here to fight.”

He fell in step beside her, posture loose and apologetic. “Just give me a minute.”

“I really don’t have the energy for this.”

He angled ahead of her, not blocking her exactly, just enough to make her pause before the dormitory stairs. "One minute."

Cassara crossed her arms and leaned into the stone. Her ribs flared in protest. "You're wasting your sixty seconds."

Julian gave a crooked smile, though it didn't reach his eyes. "You remember when we were thirteen, and you got caught sneaking into the old conservatory behind the estate?"

She frowned.

"I told your father it was my idea," he said. "Said you were just following me."

Cassara remembered. "And he believed you."

"Of course he did. I'm very convincing."

"You also got grounded for a week."

"Worth it."

Julian reached into his coat and pulled out a small velvet pouch. It was deep blue and worn at the corners. Cassara recognized it immediately.

"You gave me this," he said. "Said it would protect me during my training."

"I said it might," she corrected. "If you didn't lose it in your laundry bin."

He smiled faintly. "I was thinking maybe you could use it more than me now."

Cassara stared at it. There was something practiced in his charm, polished in his concern—so different from Auren's raw honesty. Julian wielded his emotions like perfectly balanced weapons, each smile calculated for maximum effect. Auren's silence carried more weight than Julian's carefully chosen words.

The comparison came unbidden, unwelcome. She shoved it down before it could take root.

Julian's voice dropped, softer now. "I don't like when things are so cold between us."

Cassara didn't answer, she just stared at the pouch. Part of her wanted to refuse, to shove it back and walk away from whatever peace offering this was meant to be. But she couldn't quite make herself do it. Because Julian hadn't always been like this—treating her like a thing to be owned. There had been a time when his gestures felt genuine, when she'd actually wanted his attention. She hated that she still remembered that version of him. Hated more that some small part of her still hoped he might come back.

Finally she took it, but she didn't open it, just held it, the weight of it small and familiar against her palm.

Julian stepped aside, giving her the space she'd been silently demanding since he'd appeared. "I'll let you go," he said, quieter this time. "Just don't forget I'm still here."

Cassara waited until Julian's footsteps faded completely, until she was certain he'd turned the corner and wasn't lingering to see what she'd do next.

Then she ducked into the nearest alcove, back pressed against cool stone, her breath still not quite steady. Her ribs ached. Her muscles burned. But neither of those things were why her hands trembled slightly as she looked down at the pouch.

The drawstring was half-frayed, one corner darker where the dye had worn from years of being tucked into pockets and forgotten satchels. It smelled faintly of cedar and dust. Old things. Familiar things. Things that belonged to a version of herself she was trying very hard to leave behind.

She opened it.

Inside sat a tiny carved feather, no longer than her pinky joint. Pale wood, delicately etched with glyphs, clumsy ones, unaligned and slightly uneven. She remembered the day she'd made it, cutting the shape from driftwood. They'd been twelve.

A folded scrap of parchment sat beneath it.

She pulled it free and unfolded the note.

Don't burn out before the good part. I still owe you that rematch. —J

Cassara slid the charm into her palm and closed her fingers around it.

Her ribs ached. Her throat ached worse.

But she didn't cry.

She stood there for a long time, eyes fixed on the tiny curl of burnt wood, trying to remember when Julian's promises had stopped feeling safe.

And why part of her still wanted to believe them anyway.

CHAPTER FOURTEEN

The third morning arrived cloaked in haze.

Fog clung to the windows of the training room and what little light filtered through was thin and cold, casting the mats in soft gray shadow. Cassara entered with as much indifference as she could muster. Today her hair was pulled back in a ponytail that sat low at the nape of her neck and the sleeves of her training uniform were pushed to her elbows in display of casual defiance.

Her ribs still twinged if she twisted too fast, but she could breathe again without it catching, which was a relief. Especially since after yesterday's session, breathing around Auren had become its own challenge.

Today he waited by a resistance post, arms crossed, expression severe. The fog-filtered light outlined his silhouette, casting his features in shadow and relief. It shouldn't have made him more striking, but it did.

"You're late."

"By one minute."

"Which is still late."

She moved to the mat without comment, aware of how his eyes tracked her movement. He tossed her a baton, slightly heavier than before.

Cassara caught it clean, the weight settling into her palm like an extension of herself.

"Three strikes. Forward, sweep, pivot."

She launched into the first drill. Crisp. Controlled. Her steps were sharper today, less fluid. More force than finesse. Auren didn't stop her.

"Again."

She reset.

Strike. Sweep. Pivot.

"Your weight's off-center."

"I know. I'm compensating."

"Then fix it."

Cassara wanted to snap back, but instead she struck again. The exertion brought heat to her face, a flush she was grateful he couldn't see in the dim light.

He moved around her without comment, silent corrections in every step he didn't take. She could feel the scrutiny, his gaze a tangible weight that traced her form with maddening precision. It made her chest tight, her movements sharper, more deliberate.

"Back foot's dragging."

"I noticed."

"Then correct it."

Her baton slammed against the strike post with a sharp crack. "Gods, do you ever say anything nice?"

"When it's earned."

She turned on him. "Earned? You won't even say good when it is."

His expression didn't change, but his eyes grew darker, more intense. "You don't need praise."

"Why not?" she snapped. "Because I'm a legacy and I'm supposed to already be perfect?"

"No," Auren said quietly. "Because you'll cling to it instead of fixing the next mistake."

Her breath caught. Fury bubbled fast behind it, complicated by the fact that she was suddenly acutely aware of the space between them—how little there was and how easily it could disappear.

She stepped closer despite knowing full well that she should just walk away before her frustration got the better of her.

But the heat in her chest was raw and she was tired of being made to feel small.

"That's what you're trying to do, right? Knock me down before someone else does it better?"

He didn't move. Just stood there, watching her with that infuriating stillness that made her want to reach out and shake him, to provoke some reaction, any reaction, that proved he wasn't entirely unmoved by her.

It wasn't fair that he was so unaffected while she felt like she was drowning.

"I didn't ask for this," she went on. "I didn't ask for your drills, your orders, your disdain. I don't even want to train with someone who gets people killed."

The words tumbled out before she realized what she was saying and Cassara felt her heart stop. What the hell was she thinking?

Auren's posture shifted, almost imperceptibly. His gaze grew colder.

For what felt like an eternity, he looked at her. Not through her, not over her, but at her. The intensity of it made her want to step back, or move closer, she couldn't say for sure.

"Do you think I wanted this?" he asked, his voice carrying an unexpected edge. "To be stuck training a spoiled, pampered princess who throws herself into danger just to prove... what exactly are you trying to prove?" He turned his back and crossed the mat to the rack without looking at her again.

"You don't get to call me pampered." Her voice cracked on the word. "You don't know what I'm fighting against. What happens to me if I fail here, if I'm not strong enough to—" She cut herself off, fists clenched at her sides. He didn't get to know. Didn't deserve to know.

"Everyone here is fighting something," he said without turning around. "Reset your stance."

Cassara didn't move.

The heat in her throat pulsed sharp. Her pride twisted beneath it, bruised and howling. She grabbed her towel off the bench and turned.

She made it halfway to the door.

"I didn't take you for a quitter."

Her grip on the towel tightened. She didn't stop walking.

"Arrogant... impulsive, reckless," Auren continued behind her. "But not a coward."

Cassara stopped cold.

"Coward," she echoed, turning slowly to face him.

Auren didn't look smug. He wasn't smirking. Just watching her in his usual measured and intolerably calm way.

"You want everyone to think you're above being shaken," he said. "Fine. You're good at that. But don't walk out now and expect me to believe you're walking out on me. You're walking out on yourself."

She stared at him. A storm building in her chest and nowhere to send it.

"You think you know me," she said.

"I know what you show."

"You don't see a damn thing."

He stepped toward her then.

"You want me to tell you you're special?" he asked quietly. His voice had dropped, the controlled baritone sending a shiver down her spine. "You are. You're the best I've seen in years. Maybe ever. But you're also brittle. You break harder than you bend, and the moment someone sees the cracks, you lash out."

Cassara's hands curled into fists. "And what do you do, Instructor? Hide behind drills and dead-eyed silence until no one can remember you used to matter?"

She knew she was going too far, overstepping boundaries that she shouldn't. But she didn't care. If he was going to cut her open, examine her like a specimen in Professor Marlowe's anatomy class, she'd return the favor.

He didn't flinch, but for the first time, she saw a crack in his composure, a flash of genuine emotion that made her breath catch.

She kept going, ignoring every bit of instinct that screamed at her to stop before she dug herself any deeper.

"I know why you're here and not in the field," she said, breath shallow now. "I know about your squad."

The silence that followed wasn't just heavy, it was suffocating.

Cassara's heart beat hard in her ears and she became very aware of how alone they were in the training room, how the rest of the world seemed to have fallen away.

Auren didn't speak right away. He held her gaze for a breath. Two. His eyes had narrowed, the usual mask slipping to reveal raw emotion.

"And what is it you think you know?" His voice was unexpectedly quiet.

Cassara had expected fury, shouting, and would have preferred it over the quiet accusation threaded through a seemingly simple question.

"That I got them killed leading them into a fight they weren't prepared for? That I was chasing glory? That I sacrificed them for personal gain?" He offered a grim smile. "The truth is, I did nothing, and oftentimes inaction is the worst offense of all."

She didn't know what to say to that. The vulnerability in his admission stripped away her anger, leaving complicated feelings in its place.

He stepped back, turned his attention to the mat.

"This is the part where you leave, if you're going to."

She didn't look at him, she looked past him, at the sparring marks on the floor, the faint scuff from her last strike, the imprint of her boot still visible in the chalk-dust line.

Auren hadn't moved.

Cassara hated him for that, for standing there like she hadn't just torn into a festering wound. She hated herself more for being exactly what he had accused her of being.

She turned halfway and stopped, letting the silence settle.

Then, she made a choice. "Reset the markers," she said as she stepped back onto the mat. She didn't look to see if he would acknowledge her, she didn't need to, she felt him move.

He was quiet for a long moment. "Good." The word was soft, almost to himself, before he moved to reset the markers. "Let's go again."

At some point the tension between them had shifted. It felt like more than just pride or determination, but a dangerous recognition.

By the time Cassara reached the dorms, the hallway noise had thinned to a low murmur. The aches from training hadn't fully set in yet. Those always came later, once the adrenaline left her body, but the bruises were blooming warm beneath her ribs.

What lingered more persistently was the memory of Auren's voice, low and raw with admission. The rare vulnerability in his eyes when he'd spoken of his squad. The charged space between them that neither had been willing to cross.

Her skin still hummed with awareness, as if some part of her remained in that fog-wrapped training room, suspended in that moment of recognition.

She pushed open the door to the common room and stepped inside.

Liri was curled in the corner armchair, blanket wrapped around her shoulders like a throne, holding a cup of tea that was probably too sweet, knowing her, and talking in low, animated bursts to Sonia.

They both glanced up at her entrance.

"Look who's returned from the underworld," Liri said, raising her cup in mock salute.

Cassara lifted a brow, forcing her thoughts back to the present. "What?"

"Your training sessions with Veth," Liri explained, leaning forward. "Half the first-years think you're being punished. The other half think you're being groomed for something classified."

"I'm just training," Cassara said flatly.

Just training. As though lying to herself would make it any more true.

Sonia traced the rim of her mug with one finger. "Not according to Jace Kingston. He says Nareen's never assigned private sessions this early in the term."

"Even Instructor Eravian mentioned it in tactics," Liri added. "Asked if anyone had seen 'the Allencourt girl who challenged the Rift.'"

"People need to find better things to talk about," she muttered, crossing to her bunk alcove.

Liri shrugged. "When Darius Eravian himself tells a story about how you staggered out of the Rift, refused help, and then collapsed dramatically into Nareen's arms—"

"That's not what happened," Cassara cut in.

"—people tend to remember," Liri finished. "Besides, you have to admit, doing things the unnecessary hard way is your specialty."

Talia looked up from her desk, her pen pausing mid-stroke.

"If they're guessing, let them guess," she said, voice low and measured. "Gossip is only dangerous when it holds truth."

Cassara paused, caught by the unexpected insight.

Talia held her gaze for a beat longer than usual. "Some secrets should stay buried."

The cryptic nature of her words made Cassara wonder which secrets Talia meant, her injury, her recklessness in running the Rift, or something else entirely.

She ducked into her alcove without answering, drawing the curtain closed, and sat on the edge of her bed. Cassara waited until the voices fell back into whatever quiet conversation they'd been having before she arrived and then reached beneath her pillow for the journal and left.

The sky had dimmed to that particular shade of violet that came just before true night, when the last of the light clung to the clouds and the stars hadn't yet made their entrance. Cassara sat with her back to the stone wall of the Overlook, legs curled beneath her, journal in her lap.

She hadn't meant to end up here. Her feet had simply wandered after the common room, carrying her toward quiet, toward open air. The aches from her session with Auren still lingered in her limbs, but the deeper bruises were finally fading. Tomorrow she had her post-recovery assessment. If all went well, she'd be cleared to return to team drills with the other first-years.

It should've been relieving, knowing that tomorrow would be her last session with Auren. No more early mornings in the cold, no more silent drills or sharp corrections, and, most importantly, no more of him, standing too close and saying too little, his presence as steadying as it was infuriating.

So why did it feel... hollow?

She shook the thoughts from her head. It wasn't worth dwelling on. He was just an instructor. A frustrating, maddeningly unreadable one. That was all.

Even as she thought it, her fingers gripped the edge of the journal a little tighter.

She flipped through the time worn pages, scanning the contents, not sure what she was hoping to find. Most entries were technical, battle tactics, beast behavior, shorthand notes about mission reports she couldn't decipher. Her mother's script was sharp and elegant.

Near the middle, she found something different.

The ink was messier here. Smudged in places, as if written in haste, or with trembling hands.

Some days I wake up and the weight of what I'm supposed to be settles in before my feet even touch the floor. Everyone says I'm meant for greatness. I don't know what that means, not really. Maybe they think I'll become some kind of symbol, like that's enough to make a person unbreakable.

But I'm tired. And I hate admitting that.

There are mornings where I don't feel brave. I just feel... small. Not because I can't do it, but because I'm afraid I won't do it well enough.

Still. One step. One hour. One breath at a time. That's all I can promise.

And like my mother used to say: "Even the fire rests between sparks."

Cassara's eyes lingered on the words, her thumb brushing the margin where ink had bled slightly, either from a spill or a tear long dried, but the words held firm.

Even the fire rests between sparks.

She'd heard that before. Not often, but enough. Whispered on mornings when her mother had returned home from the front, bone-weary and silent. Tucked between lessons about posture and poise, like an afterthought too gentle to be remembered on command.

It had sounded strange to her then, she hadn't understood it.

But now?

Now it settled differently in her chest, like a weight she'd been carrying without knowing it. A kind of permission she never realized she'd been granted.

Cassara swallowed hard, her fingers curling at the edge of the page.

Her mother had once woken unsure, uncertain, scared she wouldn't live up to what was expected of her, and still, she'd persevered. One step, one hour, one breath at a time.

Closing the journal carefully, she stared at the worn cover for a long moment before setting it aside, her heart beating a little slower than before.

She wasn't sure she could afford doubt. But just for tonight, she let the quiet truth of it sit beside her.

Even the fire rests between sparks.

And maybe... maybe that was okay.

Dawn hadn't yet broken when Cassara woke, the dormitory still silent around her. She dressed in the dark, movements careful and practiced, aware of every breath, every stretch. Her ribs no longer protested when she twisted or bent, the bruising had faded to a watercolor smudge of yellows and faint greens against her skin.

Today was the day.

The thought shouldn't have left such a hollow space beneath her ribs. This was what she'd wanted from the beginning, to be cleared, to rejoin her cohort, to stop being singled out for remedial work. To stop being his project.

And yet.

She slipped from the dormitory without waking anyone, Julian's charm tucked into her pocket where she'd kept it since yesterday. She told herself it was sentiment, not attachment, that made her carry it, but her fingers closed around it as she approached the training room door.

The room beyond was darker than usual, the pre-dawn gloom deepened by storm clouds that seemed to press against the high windows. The air felt charged, electric with the promise of rain.

She pushed the door open without knocking.

Auren stood in the center of the mat, back to her, moving through a sequence she'd never seen before, his body a controlled arc of power as he shifted from stance to stance.

He wore only a sleeveless training shirt and loose pants, feet bare against the mat. No pretense of formality today.

He finished the sequence without acknowledging her, though she knew he'd heard her enter. Only when the final form was complete did he turn, eyes finding hers across the dim space.

"You're early," he said.

His voice seemed different. Quieter. The edge of authority softened in a way that felt considerably more vulnerable.

"Couldn't sleep," she admitted, setting her things down at the edge of the mat. She hadn't meant to confess even that much, but the words slipped out before she could catch them.

Auren watched her for a beat too long, then nodded toward the center of the room.

"No drills today," he said.

Cassara paused in the middle of rolling up her sleeves. "Then what?"

"Combat. Real movement." He stepped onto the mat, stance relaxed but alert. "Your ribs are nearly healed. Time to test them."

She stared at him, trying to read past the carefully neutral expression. After yesterday's raw confession, she'd expected...what? Distance? Coldness? Not this strange, quiet focus.

"You'll go to your evaluation after we're through," he continued.

Cassara stepped forward, taking her place opposite him on the mat. "Anxious to be rid of me?"

The question came out sharper than she'd intended.

Auren's expression didn't change, but his eyes tracked her movement with that same intensity that made her skin warm despite the room's chill.

"I'm not the one who tried to walk out yesterday," he reminded her.

She felt heat rise to her face. "That was different."

"Was it?"

Cassara didn't answer.

Instead, she settled into a ready stance, chin lifted in silent challenge.

Auren mirrored her, his posture deceptively casual. "Three touches," he said. "First to land them wins."

"What do I win?" The question slipped out unbidden, carrying a hint of the dangerous tension between them yesterday.

His mouth curved slightly, not quite a smile, but less guarded than his usual expression.

"Bragging rights," he said. "And maybe a straight answer to one question."

Cassara's pulse quickened. One question. One honest answer from the man who revealed nothing unless cornered.

"And if you win?" she asked.

"Then I get the same."

They circled each other slowly, neither making the first move. The storm clouds outside deepened, casting the room in shadow broken only by the faint glow of mage-lights along the wall. Their reflections ghosted across the window glass, two figures in a dance too tense to be called practice, too controlled to be called combat.

Cassara struck first.

She feinted right and then came in low from the left. He blocked with infuriating ease, deflecting her arm with a precise motion that used her own momentum against her.

"Telegraphing," he said. Not criticism but an observation.

She didn't reply, just reset and circled again. This time when she moved, it was with a swift combination that forced him to actually defend rather than simply evade.

From there they fell into rhythm, a language of movement neither had to translate. Strike. Parry. Advance. Retreat. The space between them electric with unspoken awareness.

His hand caught her wrist once, not to restrain, but to redirect. The contact lasted only a heartbeat, but it sent a spark through her that had nothing to do with combat.

"One," he said, tapping her shoulder with his free hand before she could counter.

She broke away, breathing harder than she should have been. "Lucky shot."

"No such thing."

They reset. Circled again. This time, she was more careful, more patient. She'd watched him long enough to know his patterns, the way he favored his right side, the slight tell before he shifted his weight.

When she moved, it was with a feint meant to draw him forward before a quick sidestep and pivot let her slip past his guard and tap his ribs with an open palm.

"One," she echoed, unable to keep the satisfaction from her voice.

His eyes narrowed slightly, reassessing. She'd surprised him.

The next exchange was faster, more intense. Neither willing to give ground, both reading each other's moves with uncanny accuracy. At one point, they ended up locked in a momentary stalemate, faces inches apart, breath mingling in the cool air.

"Not bad for someone who couldn't breathe a week ago," he murmured.

"Impressive, for someone stuck teaching first-years," she countered.

A ghost of a smile touched his lips, there and gone before she could be sure she'd seen it.

He broke the lock with a swift movement, almost too fast to track. But Cassara was ready, turning with the momentum, using his own technique against him to slide inside his guard.

Her palm connected with his chest, directly over his heart.

"Two," she said, voice steady despite her racing pulse.

She could feel his heartbeat beneath her hand, strong and surprisingly fast. Neither of them moved for a moment that stretched far longer than it should have.

Then Auren stepped back, his posture shifting with new found intensity and a focus that hadn't been there before. When he moved again, it was with a fluidity that made their previous exchanges look like practice.

He caught her next strike effortlessly, redirected her second, and with a motion almost too swift to follow, swept her legs from under her.

Cassara landed on her back, the impact controlled enough not to hurt but decisive enough to knock the breath from her lungs. Before she could recover, Auren was above her, one hand braced beside her head, the other tapping her collarbone lightly.

"Two," he said, voice low.

She stared up at him, suddenly aware of their position, his body poised above hers, his face close enough that she could see a faint scar above his left eyebrow she had never noticed before and found herself wondering how he had gotten it.

Neither moved.

Outside, the storm that had been threatening all morning finally let loose. Rain began to fall, fat drops striking the windows in a rhythm that matched her heartbeat.

Cassara should have pushed him away. Should have reset. Instead, she found herself studying the line of his jaw, the controlled intensity in his eyes, the slight parting of his lips as he drew breath.

"Last point," she said, voice barely above a whisper.

Auren's gaze flickered to her mouth, just for a moment, before he pushed himself up and extended a hand to help her rise.

She took it, the contact sending another jolt through her system. His palm was warm, his grip firm as he pulled her to her feet, perhaps a bit closer than necessary before releasing her.

They reset one final time.

This time, their movements were almost choreographed, each anticipating the other's strategy, each countering with increasing precision. It wasn't combat anymore. It was conversation, challenge, an exchange where neither was willing to concede.

When the final point came, it was simultaneous.

His hand found the hollow of her throat at the exact moment hers pressed against his sternum. They froze, connected by two points of contact that seemed to burn through cloth to skin.

"Three," they said in unison.

A draw.

They stayed like that for a heartbeat too long, neither willing to be the first to break contact. The storm outside intensified, rain lashing the windows, thunder rolling in the distance.

Finally, Auren stepped back, his hand falling away from her throat with what felt like reluctance.

"You've improved," he said, voice rougher than usual.

"Good teacher," she replied, surprising herself with the admission.

A moment of silence stretched between them, filled only by the sound of rain and their gradually slowing breaths.

"Your ribs?" he asked.

"Fine." And they were. Even the fall hadn't triggered pain.

Something flickered in his expression, there and gone too quickly to interpret.

"Good," he said. But there was a finality to the word that left a hollow feeling in her chest. "We're finished."

Cassara gathered her things slowly, neither of them acknowledging the draw or the promised question. Perhaps because a draw meant neither won, or because they both knew there were too many questions that needed answers.

At the door, she paused, hand on the frame. The impulse to look back, to speak, was nearly overwhelming.

"Auren," she said, not turning.

"Cassara."

Her name in his voice sent an unexpected shiver down her spine. It was the first time he'd used it, not "Allencourt," not a clipped command. Her actual name.

"Same time tomorrow?" The question slipped out before she could stop it, vulnerable in its hope.

A pause, filled with the sound of rain.

"You'll be cleared after today," he said, voice carefully neutral. "You'll rejoin your cohort."

"Right. Of course," she said, nodding once before she stepped through the doorway.

It wasn't until she was halfway down the corridor that she realized she was still holding her breath, as if some part of her was still caught in that charged moment on the training mat, his hand at her throat, her palm against his heart.

She exhaled slowly, the emptiness beneath her ribs spreading wider with each step that took her away from the training room.

This was what she'd asked for. Group training. Distance. An end to his relentless observations and impossible standards.

So why did getting it feel wrong?

CHAPTER FIFTEEN

The infirmary was colder than Auren's training room had been. Cassara sat on the edge of the long examination bench, the chill from the polished stone bleeding through her training pants. She kept her hands folded in her lap as the senior healer flipped through her chart.

"Mobility?" he asked without looking up.

Cassara lifted her arms, twisted her torso, inhaled sharply—no twinge, no pull. "Unrestricted."

"Pain?"

"Only when people talk too much."

The healer huffed a laugh. He scribbled a final note on a device similar to her Codex, then tapped twice to seal the assessment.

"You're cleared," he said simply. "Effective immediately. Welcome back to the meat grinder."

Cassara slipped from her perch. "Thanks."

He gave a grunt of acknowledgment and turned to organize a shelf of vials, already halfway to forgetting her.

She exited the infirmary into late morning air, the wind off the higher terraces carrying the promise of cooler weather. Vallemont's upper halls were already buzzing, students weaving between classes, instructors barking reminders, the forge tower chiming out a mid-morning strike.

The combat grounds had already been chalked and restructured for group drills by the time Cassara arrived. Half the cohort was already warming up in groups of five or six going through a series of warm ups and stretches.

Her name was listed at the bottom of the assignment board.

Allencourt, assigned to Group 4, drill partner: Delvanir.

Her stomach sank.

Gideon stood off to the side watching a low-spar session unfold on the mats. His stance was relaxed but alert, like someone who'd rather be doing anything else, but would still win if pushed. His gaze flicked to her the moment she stepped into range and didn't look away.

She squared her shoulders.

Nareen's voice rang out over the grounds. "Allencourt, good to have you back. You're with Delvanir. Pair up. Group Four will be running tactical reentry drills. Five rotations, with weapon restrictions. And don't make me regret rebalancing the teams."

Cassara took her mark beside him without comment.

"You're behind," Gideon said without looking at her.

"Don't worry, I'll go easy on you."

He didn't smile, but he didn't scowl either.

Their first sequence was clean. Dispassionate. Until she pushed harder. Faster. When he feinted, she didn't dodge, she countered. When he circled, she pressed. He grunted at one particularly aggressive sweep he barely avoided.

"You still trying to prove something?" he muttered.

"I don't need to prove anything to you."

They rotated through three more sets in silence, and by the end of the fourth, sweat slicked her spine and her arms burned, but she held her own.

When Nareen called time, Cassara left the sparring circle. She moved to retrieve her outer jacket and was pulling it on when Gideon's voice rose from behind her.

"You could've asked for a different partner."

She paused, halfway through adjusting her collar. "Didn't seem necessary."

He nodded once, brushing a hand through his hair. "I think you're pushing too hard."

"I'm fine."

"I didn't say you weren't. Just said you're pushing."

"Gods, you're frustrating," she muttered before she turned toward him fully, expression unreadable. "Why do you care?"

There was a beat of silence between them.

"Because no one else here will tell you when to slow down."

It wasn't a challenge, it was almost gentle, and Cassara didn't know what to do with that. He looked like he wanted to say something else, then thought better of it.

"Just say it," she said, crossing her arms.

She expected him to tell her she was overdoing it, that catching up wasn't worth exhausting herself. What she got was different.

"I'm running drills this evening. If you want the extra time, I'll be on the upper deck."

Cassara froze, not visibly, not enough to give it away, but just enough that her fingers curled tighter around her towel.

Before she could reply, another voice sliced between them.

"She won't need extra time. She's fine."

Julian stepped into the circle like he owned it, every inch of him composed and deliberate. His jacket hung unfastened, a thin sheen of sweat glistening against his throat. His expression was unreadable as his eyes cut to Gideon before shifting back to her.

"You're back. That's what matters. Don't waste time taking scraps from someone who can barely keep up with you on a bad day."

Her jaw locked. She could feel Gideon watching her now, waiting to see what she'd do.

She looked at Julian, then back to Gideon.

"I'll be there," she said, voice calm.

Julian's posture tensed, just slightly. Gideon only gave a curt nod.

Cassara didn't wait for another argument to break out. Instead, she turned and strode toward the outer ring, heart pounding.

Whether out of spite, or pride, or something more dangerous, she would train tonight.

She didn't stop until she found a quiet corner near the weapons rack, bracing one hand against the cool metal frame as she forced her breathing to slow. The combat circle still buzzed behind her with movement and the low hum of instructors shouting corrections, but she couldn't hear any of it clearly, her pulse was too loud.

"Your footwork's tighter. That drop-pivot on the second set would've earned a point in open spar."

Cassara looked up to see Nareen striding towards her. "Thanks."

Nareen gave a small nod, then leaned in just enough to speak over the noise. "Looks like Auren working with you paid off. I wasn't sure it was a great idea at first, with the injury, but he seemed confident."

Cassara stilled.

"What?"

"Your counters. Smoother than last week," Nareen said, glancing back toward the sparring circles. "He's brutal, but effective."

She swallowed. "No, the other part... didn't you ask him to work with me?"

Nareen gave a soft snort. "No one asks Auren Veth to do anything. Keep it up, Allencourt."

Cassara barely registered that Nareen was walking away, calling out instructions to an incoming group. The world felt strange in her ears, too quiet in some places and too loud in others. Her mind cycled through every moment in that training room, every clipped command, every correction he delivered without warmth.

I didn't ask to train you either.

Her blood heated.

Not just from the betrayal, but from something deeper. A gnawing tangle of confusion and disbelief.

Cassara didn't change out of her training gear, didn't stop to collect her thoughts or cool down or pull herself back into balance. She left the training grounds with her fists clenched and her eyes locked on one destination.

The training hall.

Where she knew exactly where to find him.

The training room was almost empty when Cassara arrived, its high windows streaked with the dim gray of a sky nearing dusk. Mage-lights flickered low along the walls, casting long shadows across the padded floor.

Auren stood at the far side of the room, rolling up the reinforced mats into neat coils and returning sparring gear to its proper place.

Cassara stepped inside without a word.

He didn't look up at first. "If you're here to use the space, give me two minutes."

"I'm not."

That made him pause.

He straightened slowly, turning toward her. His expression was unreadable. The edge of a bruise still colored his jaw from a second-year sparring session earlier that week, and the sight of it, fresh, imperfect, twisted something sharp in her chest.

Cassara didn't approach him, she stayed near the door, arms folded, heart pounding hard enough to hear.

"You said Nareen asked you to train me."

Auren's face didn't change. "She did."

"No," Cassara said, her voice flat. "She didn't."

Auren exhaled, just once, as if the fight had landed exactly where he expected it to but hoped it wouldn't.

"She said *you* offered," Cassara continued when he gave no explanation. "That no one asks the infamous Auren Veth to do anything."

His gaze shifted away for the first time.

"Why did you lie?"

The question landed softer than she meant it to, less accusation and more hurt. She hated how vulnerable it made her sound.

Auren looked back at her and finally spoke. "Because it was easier."

"For who?" she asked, heat blooming beneath her skin. "For you? For me?"

"For both of us."

"That's not your call to make."

His eyes flickered. "You were injured. You were restless. I didn't want you to do something reckless."

"Oh, so you volunteered to babysit," she snapped.

"No," he said sharply. "I watched you run yourself into the ground in the Rift just to prove you could. I thought that maybe if I kept you moving, you wouldn't try to set yourself on fire again."

She stared at him. "You had no right to decide what I could handle."

"I never said you couldn't handle it."

"Then why lie?"

Auren took a step forward.

"I lied because I didn't want you to look at me like this," he said, voice low, each word clipped and controlled. "Because if you knew I wanted to be there, you'd start asking why. And I didn't have an answer I could give."

Cassara's breath caught. The words reframed everything. Every session. Every touch when he adjusted her form. Every time she'd caught him watching her like he was memorizing something he couldn't keep. She'd convinced herself it was nothing, that she was reading into professional distance. But he'd asked for this. Chosen it. Chosen her, and then pretended he hadn't.

The betrayal of it burned hotter than the revelation itself.

"You don't get to act like it didn't mean anything," she said, quieter now, but no less fierce. "You don't get to stand there and pretend you didn't choose this. You did. And now I don't know what was real."

His gaze snapped to hers.

"It was all real."

The silence between them pulsed.

Cassara took a step forward. "Then say it."

Auren didn't move and for a moment, Cassara was afraid he might refuse.

"I wanted to train you," he said at last. "I asked Nareen because I saw what you were capable of and I couldn't watch from the sidelines while you burned yourself out for people who only wanted to see you fail."

The words settled over her, heavy with meaning that went beyond instruction manuals and proper form. He'd watched her. Cared whether she succeeded or destroyed herself trying. That wasn't simple duty. That wasn't professional distance.

That was something else entirely.

"Is that all it was?" Her voice came out quieter than she intended. "Training?"

Auren went very still. She watched the muscles in his jaw work, watched his hand curl into a fist at his side—tight enough that his knuckles went white. Like he was physically restraining himself from reaching for her.

"No," he said finally, unable to meet her eyes. "It wasn't."

Something broke inside of her. All the careful distance she'd maintained, all the reasons she'd told herself this was nothing—they shattered in the face of what he'd just admitted. He'd chosen her. Not because he had to. Because he couldn't stand not to.

She knew she should walk away. This was her instructor, this was impossible, this would only end badly, but in that moment common sense didn't matter.

She didn't know who closed the distance first, if her hands were pulling or if his were already there. One moment there was air between them, the next he was everywhere.

His fingers tangled in the fabric at her waist. His breath ghosted across her cheek. The moment before contact stretched impossibly long, like even gravity had gone still.

And then—

Their mouths collided.

It wasn't tentative. There was no slow discovery, no testing the edge. It was a crash. All fire and fury and pent-up denial. Her back hit the wall with a thud that echoed across the quiet room, and he followed, crowding her in with the weight of something that felt inevitable. His hand braced beside her head. The other found her hip, anchoring her like he thought she might vanish.

Cassara's hands twisted in the front of his shirt, dragging him closer. She didn't care how rough it felt. Didn't care how breathless she already was. All that mattered was that he was finally kissing her like all the times he hadn't had cost him.

His lips moved against hers with quiet desperation, not sloppy but sure, like he'd imagined this too many times to get it wrong. She opened to him without thinking, without planning, a sound catching in her throat as his mouth deepened against hers and her knees nearly gave out.

He caught her.

Not with tenderness. With strength. A hand under her thigh, hitching her leg up around his hip so he could press even closer, her body fitting to his like muscle memory. She could feel the hard line of his control breaking under the way she kissed him back, mouth greedy, reckless, hungry.

Auren pulled away just enough to look at her, their breath mingling in the narrow space between.

"I didn't—" he said roughly, voice frayed. "Not like this."

"Then stop," she breathed.

But he didn't.

He kissed her again, harder.

And she let him.

Her fingers slid up the back of his neck tangling in his hair. He made a low sound at the contact, like even that small softness undid him. His hand gripped her tighter, fingers spreading across her ribs. She felt his thumb move, achingly slow, sweeping just under the curve of her breast but not quite touching. Like even now, he was holding himself back. And gods, she hated how badly she wanted more.

She tilted her hips forward and felt him tense.

He broke the kiss, just barely, lips brushing hers as he spoke.

"We shouldn't."

"I know."

"But I want to."

"So do I."

He groaned softly against her mouth, half curse, half prayer, and captured her lips again, gentler this time, but no less intense. Like he needed her, like she was the only thing keeping him grounded.

Until the sound of footsteps echoed faintly in the corridor outside.

They both froze.

The noise was distant, unhurried, someone passing by, or maybe approaching, the rhythm just steady enough to send a jolt of reality back into the air between them.

Cassara shifted.

Not much. Just enough to turn her face slightly, the edge of her jaw brushing his. Her leg slid back down from his hip and the sharp press of her body against his began to ease. Her hand slipped from his hair, fingers skimming his shoulder on the way down, but she didn't move far. She couldn't. His arm was still braced beside her head, the wall firm at her back.

Auren didn't move immediately. His forehead still rested against hers. His breath was ragged. His hand lingered too long at her waist before finally falling away.

Cassara's pulse thundered in her ears. Not from fear, or shame, but from the jagged awareness of what they'd just done. What they might have done if the hallway had stayed silent a moment longer.

Her skin still burned where he touched her. Her lips were swollen, her body ached, not with pain but with the slow, unbearable retreat of something she hadn't been ready to let go of.

And beneath it all, beneath the heat, the hunger, the thunder in her blood, was a sharp, startling spike of self-consciousness.

What had she just done?

What had *they* just done?

"I should go."

Auren finally lifted his head. His face was unreadable again, but his eyes still held that same wild, fractured heat. He nodded once, like that was the only answer he trusted himself to give.

Cassara waited until he stepped back, until the pressure of his body and the press of his arm were no longer keeping her there, before she slid past him toward the door. She didn't run. Didn't rush. But the moment her hand found the handle, she realized she'd left her training gear rumpled, her braid half-loosened, her shirt tugged unevenly along her ribs.

She didn't fix it.

She walked out anyway.

And Auren didn't follow.

Cassara didn't remember the walk back.

Not the turns she took, not the stairs, not the students she passed, if there were any. Her limbs moved on instinct, muscle memory guiding her.

She only knew that she couldn't stop, because if she stopped, she might turn around.

The moment she reached her dormitory floor, she slipped into the nearest empty alcove beside the common room and leaned back hard against the wall, hand pressed over her mouth like it might trap the breath still shivering out of her lungs.

Gods.

Her pulse hadn't calmed. Her body still buzzed. Every inch of her skin felt hypersensitive, like it remembered his touch too well. She could still taste him. Still feel the drag of his mouth, the heat of his hand on her waist, the way his voice had sounded when he said he wanted her.

She squeezed her eyes shut, head thudding gently against the stone.

What did you just do?

It hadn't meant anything.

It was adrenaline.

Residual heat.

The tail end of an argument that had no place in her life right now.

She kissed him because she was angry and tired. Because she wanted to prove something, to him, to herself, to every part of her that had started to crave the weight of his presence each morning and hadn't known how to name it.

That was all.

It had nothing to do with the way he said her name with meaning.

Nothing to do with how steady he always felt, even when everything else was chaos or how he looked at her like she was fire worth getting burned for.

Cassara pushed off the wall, fingers tightening into fists.

Impulse. That's all it was.

He kissed her back, sure, but he hadn't asked for any of it. And neither had she. It just... happened. The way lightning struck when the air got too heavy.

A one-time thing.

A mistake.

So why did her legs keep wanting to turn back?

She paced halfway down the hall before catching herself, teeth clenched, eyes wild, and pivoted, slamming herself through the door to her dorm without stopping to consider who might be there.

Everyone, naturally.

Talia glanced up from her desk. Liri looked up from her essay, parchment and reference books scattered around her in careful disorder.

"Everything okay?" Liri asked.

"Fine," Cassara muttered, brushing past them and vanishing into her sleeping alcove. The curtain snapped shut behind her.

She sat on the edge of her bed, staring at the wall, and pulled the tie from her braid with fingers that trembled just slightly.

It didn't mean anything.

She was just tired. She was just...

Her lips parted on a shallow breath.

It meant *everything*.

She pressed the heels of her hands to her eyes, willing the feeling away.

This wasn't just about them. Auren was an instructor, even if he wasn't much older than some of the upper years. If anyone saw them... if anyone even suspected...

Nareen would remove him from teaching. The academy would question every assessment he'd given her, every skill she'd earned. They'd call it favoritism, manipulation, a breach of trust. Everything she'd worked for would be tainted. And Auren? He'd lose what little he had left.

All because she couldn't control herself.

And still, traitor that she was, every part of her wanted to go back.

As she lowered her hands, her gaze caught on the edge of her mother's journal peeking out from beneath her pillow. The worn leather corner seemed to watch her, a silent witness to her turmoil. She brushed her fingers over it, remembering the words she'd read just days ago.

Some days I wake up and the weight of what I'm supposed to be settles in before my feet even touch the floor.

Her mother had written that, the Iron Songbird, the untouchable legend, confessing doubts no one else had been allowed to see. Had she ever felt like this? Caught between what she should want and what she did want?

One step. One hour. One breath at a time. That's all I can promise.

Cassara withdrew her hand. One breath at a time. Right now, she couldn't even manage that without feeling Auren's lips on hers again.

She stood abruptly, tucking the journal deeper under her pillow. She couldn't afford to be this distracted. Not with the Wildes expedition approaching. Not with her father's ultimatum hanging over her.

Not with the taste of Auren still on her tongue.

She needed air.

She needed distance.

She needed to move.

The upper training deck was quieter than the main grounds, the sound of combat and chatter fading into wind and distance as Cassara stepped into the open space. The sun had dipped low, casting long shadows across the wide floor. Lanterns hadn't been lit yet, but mage-lights flickered faintly at the four corners, catching the thin sheen of moisture on the stone.

She spotted Gideon near the far edge, stretching out one shoulder, coat shrugged off and folded beside his gear. He looked up at her approach.

"You're late."

"By two minutes."

He gave her a look. "That's late."

She rolled her shoulders. "Then let's not waste more time."

They squared off in silence.

There was no warmup, no banter, just Cassara sinking into stance, her movements sharp and controlled. Every strike came faster than it should've, each dodge more forceful than needed.

Gideon blocked her next blow, and this time he didn't let her reset. He held the contact longer, forcing her to meet his gaze.

"You're not here," he said.

She yanked back. "I'm right in front of you."

"You're somewhere, but it's not here."

"I'm just focused."

"No. You're distracted and angry."

Cassara stepped back, raising her fists again. "Maybe I have a lot to be angry about."

He didn't take the bait. "Did I do something? Or did someone else?"

She hated how steady he sounded. How much more it made her want to hit something.

Gideon shifted forward, pressing the rhythm harder this time. Not cruelly, but with purpose. He struck low, swept wide, forcing her to think.

"Again," he said, and it wasn't a suggestion.

Cassara came at him fast. He blocked. She pivoted. He caught her wrist.

"Your form's slipping."

"I don't need commentary."

"You do when your balance is off."

Their eyes locked.

"I meant it," he said, voice low. "When I offered to help. You don't have to punish yourself just because you missed a few drills."

She wrenched her arm free, taking two quick steps back.

"I'm not punishing myself."

Gideon tilted his head slightly. "Then what are you doing?"

She opened her mouth and promptly closed it again. She didn't have an answer. Not one she could say out loud.

Not *I kissed someone I shouldn't have.*

Not *I can still feel his hands.*

Not *I came here because if I didn't move, I'd go back to him.*

"I don't need this right now," she said, too quickly.

"Cassara."

"I said I'm fine."

Gideon took a step back, frustration flickering across his features. "Fine? The Wildes expedition is in less than two weeks, and you think you're fine?" His voice lowered, almost concerned beneath the irritation. "You're not the only one with something to prove out there. We all need to be ready."

The mention of the Wildes sent a jolt through her system, another obligation, another expectation, another test she couldn't afford to fail. It momentarily cut through the fog of Auren still clouding her thoughts.

She turned away like she could outrun the heat still rising in her chest.

But she knew Gideon was still watching her, and gods help her, a part of her was glad.

CHAPTER SIXTEEN

The training field smelled of chalk dust and steel. Morning light cut across the arena in sharp angles, catching on the mist that still clung to the edges of the practice grounds. Students moved in synchronized patterns, the rhythm of combat drills echoing across stone.

Cassara executed each form with mechanical precision. Strike. Block. Pivot. Advance. Her muscles remembered what her mind wanted to forget.

But forgetting proved impossible.

Three days had passed since the training room and her world had tilted on its axis and refused to right itself. She'd avoided the training hall, taken different routes to class, buried herself in drills and texts, anything to escape the ghost of his hands on her skin.

It hadn't worked.

She could still feel the pressure of his mouth, the heat of his breath, the low sound he'd made when she'd touched him. It lingered like a bruise beneath her skin, invisible but throbbing whenever her guard dropped.

"You're leaving yourself exposed," Gideon said. Before she could react, his hand tapped her ribs—light, controlled, but enough to prove his point.

Cassara jerked back, heat flooding her face. She would have blocked that. Should have seen it coming. The fact that she hadn't—that she had been lost in the memory of Auren's fingers tangled in her hair—made fury coil hot in her chest. She was mad at herself for being so pathetically distracted. At Auren for crawling under her skin and refusing to leave. At Gideon for noticing, for always noticing.

"Sorry," she muttered, resetting her stance.

"Sorry doesn't mean much when you're dead." His tone was flat, matter-of-fact. "Out there, that mistake costs you. Take five to get your head in the right space."

She watched him walk away, the sarcasm from moments ago tasting bitter on her tongue. He wasn't needling her. He was genuinely concerned. And here she was, taking out her frustration on someone who didn't deserve it.

Across the field, Julian stood with his training group, his gaze occasionally drifting toward her. She could feel his attention like a weight, the careful calculation behind his eyes whenever Gideon stepped too close.

She wondered, with a sharp twist of irony, what Julian would think if he knew where her thoughts actually lingered. Not on Gideon. Not on him. But on an instructor who'd lied about why he wanted to train her and then kissed her like he'd been drowning for years and she was the first breath of air.

“Again,” Nareen called from the front of the field. “From the beginning. Accuracy over speed.”

Cassara took a deep breath and forced her focus back to the present.

She couldn’t afford distraction. Not with the Wildes expedition only two weeks away. Not with her father’s ultimatum hanging over her like a blade.

Gideon rejoined her without saying a word and they moved through the forms again, each strike more controlled than the last. *Push it down. Lock it away. Focus.*

By the end of the session, sweat clung to her skin despite the chill in the air. Her muscles burned pleasantly, the physical exertion finally quieting the chaos in her mind. For a moment, she almost felt like herself again.

Until she looked up and saw him.

Auren was at the far side of the training grounds, speaking with one of the third-year instructors. His posture was rigid, controlled, nothing in his stance betraying what had happened between them. Nothing in his expression revealing the man who had pressed her against a wall and kissed her until she couldn’t remember her own name.

Their eyes met across the field.

Just for a moment. A heartbeat, maybe less.

Then he turned away, continuing his conversation as if he hadn’t seen her at all.

This, she realized, was how it would be. Distance. Silence. Pretending.

As if the kiss had never happened at all.

The beast identification hall was unnaturally quiet, save for the soft scratch of fountain pens against parchment and the occasional rustle of turning pages. Sunlight filtered through tall, narrow windows, catching dust motes that danced in lazy spirals above the long wooden tables.

Cassara stared at the classification chart before her, trying to focus on the distinctions between alpha and beta ridge patterns on leviathan subspecies. The differences were subtle, a matter of millimeters in scale spacing, variations in color that might mean the difference between a beast that could be redirected and one that would strike without hesitation.

She'd been at it for hours. The day had blurred into a haze of taxonomic hierarchies and anatomical sketches, threat assessments and behavioral notes. Her eyes burned from strain, and her hand was cramped from transcribing key identifiers.

Five days since the kiss, and still her concentration fractured at the smallest provocation.

Professor Marlowe paced between the tables, occasionally pausing to examine a student's work before moving on. "Remember," she said to the room at large, "in the Wildes, you won't have time for second guesses. You'll have seconds, maybe less, to determine whether the creature before you is a potential bond or a potential death sentence."

Cassara rubbed her eyes, trying to banish the fog of fatigue. She needed to master this, to know these distinctions well enough to recognize them in a heartbeat, even under pressure. Even when afraid.

Even when distracted by thoughts of an instructor who hadn't spoken to her since she'd left him standing in the training room, lips still wet from her kiss.

"Allencourt."

She looked up. Professor Marlowe stood beside her table, one eyebrow raised expectantly.

"The distinguishing marker between venomous and non-venomous ridge serpents?"

Cassara straightened. "Secondary scale coloration along the throat. Venomous variants display a deeper ochre undertone, while non-venomous specimens maintain a consistent jade coloration throughout."

"And the exception?"

"Highland variants during mating season," Cassara replied without hesitation. "The males develop temporary ochre coloration regardless of venom status. In those cases, you look to the eye ridges for confirmation."

The professor nodded once, satisfied, and moved on.

Cassara sighed. At least her academic retention hadn't completely abandoned her.

She gathered her notes, preparing to move to the reference section for a text on aquatic variants, when voices from the corridor outside caught her attention.

"—student evaluations before the expedition. Standard procedure. I can bring yours when I bring mine."

Nareen.

"That won't be necessary. I can deliver the assessments myself."

The voice was low and unmistakably his. Auren.

Their footsteps grew closer, echoing against stone. Without thinking, Cassara abandoned her notes and slipped between the tall shelves of the adjacent archive room. Her pulse thundered in her ears as she pressed herself against the cool stone wall, hidden from the main corridor but close enough to hear their conversation continue as they passed.

"Your evaluation of the first-years is particularly interesting," Nareen was saying. "Especially Allencourt."

Cassara went still. She shouldn't be listening. She knew she shouldn't. But her feet refused to move, and she found herself leaning, ears straining for his answer.

"She's capable," Auren replied, his tone revealing nothing. "More so than most."

"High praise, coming from you."

A pause, long enough to make Cassara wonder if they'd moved beyond hearing range.

Then, quieter: "She works hard. That's all."

Their voices faded as they continued down the corridor, leaving Cassara alone in the shadows, her heart still racing, her skin flushed with heat that had nothing to do with exertion.

She's capable. More so than most.

She closed her eyes, pressing her palms flat against the cool stone at her back.

This was ridiculous. Hiding in archives to avoid him. Analyzing his words like they might contain some hidden message. Feeling her pulse quicken at the mere sound of his voice.

She was acting like a lovesick child, not a Vallemont initiate with less than two weeks until the Wildes expedition. Not an Allencourt with everything to prove.

Pushing away from the wall, she felt a renewed sense of determination. She would master these classifications. She would prepare for the Wildes. She would stop thinking about him, stop letting three minutes define every waking moment. The kiss, the intensity, all of it would fade into something manageable.

It had to.

The gardens were quieter than the common areas, especially in the early evening when most students retreated to the dining hall. Lanterns hung from curved iron posts, not yet lit despite the deepening shadows. The air smelled of fresh rain and damp earth.

Cassara hadn't meant to accept Julian's invitation for a walk. She'd been heading to the library when he'd appeared beside her, his smile casual but his eyes intent.

"Just half an hour," he'd said. "Fresh air. No pressure."

Six days since the kiss with Auren, and she was desperate for any distraction.

So here they were, walking the stone paths between carefully tended beds of herbs and flowers, their conversation meandering through safe topics, training progress, upcoming assignments, memories of simpler days at the estate. Julian was careful not to mention their arrangement, the looming threat of return if she failed to excel. For once, he seemed content just to be near her.

"Remember when we snuck into your father's study to look at the old battle maps?" Julian asked, his shoulder occasionally brushing hers as they walked. "You were so determined to memorize every leviathan sighting from the last decade."

Cassara smiled faintly. "I thought if I knew where they'd been, I could predict where they'd go next."

"You plotted an entire migration pattern. At thirteen."

"And I was wrong," she reminded him. "The southern ridge breach happened exactly where I said it wouldn't."

Julian shook his head. "You were thirteen," he repeated, his voice softer now. "And you still knew more than half the so-called experts."

She glanced at him, surprised by the warmth in his tone. For a moment, she glimpsed the boy she'd grown up with, the one who'd climbed trees with her, who'd stood up to her father when no one else would, who'd looked at her like she hung the moon even when she was covered in mud and full of wild ideas.

Before expectations had twisted everything between them.

They paused near a small fountain, its water catching the last rays of sunlight. Julian turned to face her, his expression suddenly serious.

"I miss you," he said quietly. "The real you. Not this... armor you've been wearing ever since we arrived."

Cassara stiffened. "I'm still me."

"Are you?" His eyes searched hers. "Because the Cass I knew wasn't afraid to let people see her. Wasn't afraid to feel things."

"I'm not afraid," she said, but the words rang hollow even to her own ears.

Julian stepped closer, his hand coming up to brush a strand of hair from her face. The gesture was achingly familiar, he'd done it a hundred times over the years, when they were children, when they were almost more.

"Then why are you running?" he asked. "From me. From everyone."

From Auren, she thought, and immediately hated herself for it.

Julian's fingers lingered against her cheek, and she didn't pull away. She was so tired of fighting against her father's expectations, against Julian's persistence, against her own traitorous heart that still raced whenever she thought of Auren.

"I'm not running," she said, the lie bitter on her tongue.

Julian's gaze dropped to her mouth. "Prove it."

Cassara knew what would happen next. Could see it unfolding like a page already written. He would lean in. She would let him. And maybe, just maybe, the taste of him would overwrite the memory of Auren. Maybe it would give her something simple and uncomplicated to hold onto.

When Julian's lips touched hers, she didn't pull away.

The kiss was gentle, almost hesitant, so different from the desperate collision with Auren. Julian's hand cradled her face, his mouth moving against hers with practiced care.

Cassara closed her eyes, trying to lose herself in the moment. but instead of clarity, all she felt was emptiness.

Julian deepened the kiss, his other hand finding her waist, drawing her closer. She let him, her own hands coming up to rest against his chest. She could feel his heartbeat racing beneath her palm, his breath catching with want.

She felt nothing but absence.

No fire. No thunder. Just a void in her chest where desire should have been.

Julian pulled back slightly, his forehead resting against hers, his breathing uneven. "I've missed that," he whispered.

Cassara opened her eyes, reality crashing back with brutal clarity.

What was she doing?

This wasn't fair, not to Julian, not to herself. Not when every cell in her body was still humming with the memory of another man's touch. Not when she'd closed her eyes and wished, just for a moment, that it had been Auren's voice murmuring against her skin.

She stepped back, breaking contact. "Julian, I—"

"Don't," he said, his smile small but genuine. "Don't apologize. Don't overthink it." His fingers traced her cheek one last time before falling away. "Just remember that not everything has to be complicated. That some things can be simple if you let them."

But nothing about this felt simple. Not the guilt twisting in her stomach, the emptiness where desire should have been, or the realization that no matter how hard she tried, she couldn't kiss away the memory of Auren's heated touch.

Movement at the edge of the garden caught her eye. A tall figure passing between lanterns, pausing just long enough for her to recognize the familiar silhouette.

Auren.

Their eyes met across the distance, his expression unreadable in the gathering shadows.

Had he seen? Did it matter if he had?

He continued walking without acknowledgment, disappearing around the curve of the path as if he'd never been there at all.

Cassara turned back to Julian, who was watching her with a mixture of renewed hope and uncertainty.

"It's getting late," she said, her voice steadier than she felt. "We should head back."

Julian nodded, offering his arm. She took it, allowing him this small victory, even as her mind raced with the implications of what she'd just done, and what she hadn't felt.

One thing was devastatingly clear, she couldn't kiss away Auren's memory.

And she wasn't sure she wanted to try anymore.

Rain lashed the upper training field, turning packed earth to mud, and stone to slick, treacherous ground. Students ran the perimeter in staggered formation, boots splashing through puddles, uniforms soaked through despite weather-resistant enchantments.

Cassara pushed herself harder with each lap, lungs burning, muscles screaming. The cold rain stung her face, plastered her hair to her neck, seeped through every layer until she could no longer tell where the water ended and her own sweat began.

She welcomed the discomfort. Craved it.

Seven days since Auren. One day since Julian.

One day since she'd made everything infinitely more complicated.

"Faster!" Nareen barked from beneath the shelter of the observation pavilion. "The Wildes won't slow down because you're tired!"

Cassara dug deeper, forcing her legs to push harder against the muddy terrain. She overtook two students, then three, her breath coming in ragged gasps that fogged in the cold air. Each step was a punishment, each stride a desperate attempt to outrun her own thoughts.

Had Auren seen her with Julian? Did it matter if he had?

She wasn't accountable to him. Owed him nothing. He'd lied about why he wanted to train her, then kissed her like she was oxygen, then walked away like she was nothing.

And Julian... gods, Julian. The look in his eyes after she'd let him kiss her. Hope. Triumph. As if one moment of weakness meant she'd finally surrendered.

She pushed harder, muscles screaming, lungs burning.

Around her, other students began to falter as the rain intensified, the wind cutting across the field like a blade. A few dropped to a walk, hands braced on knees, chests heaving.

Cassara didn't slow.

"Allencourt!" Nareen called, her voice sharp through the downpour. "That's enough!"

She pretended not to hear and kept running, kept punishing her body for the chaos in her mind.

Until a figure stepped into her path, forcing her to skid to a halt, mud spraying from beneath her boots.

Auren.

He stood before her, mouth set in a grim line, eyes cold, rain streaming down his face and dripping from the edge of his jaw. His training gear was soaked through, clinging to the lean muscle beneath. He must have been running drills with the upper years on the adjacent field.

"Instructor Nareen gave you an order," he said, voice flat.

Cassara's chest heaved, her breath coming in painful gasps. "I'm fine."

"You're not." His gaze was clinical, detached. "You're pushing too hard. Risking injury before the expedition."

"Since when do you care about my limits?" she shot back, too breathless to care who might overhear.

"Since it became my job to keep first-years from killing themselves out of stubbornness." His voice was cold, as if the training room had never happened at all. As if he hadn't seen her in Julian's arms just yesterday.

It was infuriating.

Cassara straightened, pushing wet hair from her face. "Is that concern, Instructor? Or jealousy?"

The words were out before she could stop them, low enough that only he could hear but sharp enough to draw blood.

Auren's expression didn't change, but she saw the muscle in his jaw flex. "Pack it up, Allencourt," he said. "Unless you want to face disciplinary action."

He walked away without waiting for her response.

Cassara stood frozen, rain streaming down her face, heart pounding with exertion and something dangerously close to regret. Around her, the remaining students continued their laps, giving her a wide berth, curious glances sliding over her and then away.

She'd wanted a reaction. Any reaction.

And she'd gotten exactly what she deserved—nothing. Just empty air where something real had been.

Later, in the armory mirror, she caught sight of herself as she changed out of her sodden gear. Pale face, dark circles beneath her eyes, hair tangled and dripping. She looked haunted. Hollowed out.

Like someone she barely recognized.

Was this what she'd become? Someone who kissed one man to forget another, then lashed out when neither gave her what she wanted?

She turned away from her reflection, disgusted.

Ten days until the Wildes expedition. Ten days to get her head straight, to focus on what mattered. To remember who she was supposed to be.

Not a girl tangled between two men.

But an Allencourt with everything to prove.

CHAPTER SEVENTEEN

The tactical theory exam was the final hurdle before weapon specialization assignments. Fifty questions on deployment strategies, beast classification response protocols, and emergency field procedures. Students hunched over their exams throughout the hall, pens scratching, pages turning, tension thick in the concentrated silence.

Cassara finished early, her answers precise and thorough. Eleven days since Auren's kiss. Five since Julian's. Four since the confrontation in the rain.

Four days of Auren treating her like a stranger, which somehow cut deeper than any anger could have.

She gathered her materials and slipped from the hall, handing her exam packet to the proctor with a nod. The corridor outside was empty, most students still wrestling with scenarios involving compromised field positions and corrupted beast encounters.

She needed air, a place to think beyond the confines of tactical hypotheticals and the approaching Wildes expedition.

The east wing corridor was rarely used this time of day, its large windows overlooking the mist-shrouded cliffs beyond Vallemont's floating perimeter. Cassara made her way along the passage, fingers trailing against cool stone, mind still half-caught in exam questions and half-lost in memories she couldn't seem to banish.

She was so distracted she almost didn't notice the figure emerging from the side passage until they were nearly upon each other.

Auren stopped short, regarding her with that maddening neutrality he'd worn like armor since the training room. Since the garden. Since the rain.

"Allencourt," he said, the formal address like a wall between them.

Cassara straightened, chin lifting slightly. "Instructor."

They stood in tense silence, neither moving aside, the corridor suddenly too narrow despite its generous proportions. Beyond the windows, rain threatened again, clouds gathering in dark masses that mirrored the tension coiling between them.

"Exam finished?" he asked, voice flat, professional.

"Yes."

"Confident?"

"Always."

He nodded stiffly. "Weapon assignments are tomorrow. Make sure you're prepared for whatever Fenric assigns you."

"I'm always prepared," she replied, the words coming out sharper than intended.

Auren's eyes narrowed slightly. "Are you? Because lately you've seemed... distracted."

"Have you been watching, instructor?" Cassara said, feeling heat rise to her cheeks. "I'm focused on what matters."

"And what would that be?" he asked, voice dropping lower. "Your training? The expedition?" A pause, barely perceptible. "Or Tremaine?"

Cassara frowned. "That's not your concern."

"No," he agreed, his voice too controlled. "It's not."

He moved to step past her, the conversation clearly over in his mind.

Something in Cassara snapped.

"That's it?" she demanded, turning to face him as he passed. "Eleven days of silence, and all I get is a cold warning about weapon assignments?"

Auren stopped, his back to her, shoulders tense beneath his instructor's coat. "What did you expect?"

"I expected you to at least acknowledge what happened."

"Nothing happened that should be acknowledged."

"We both know that's a lie," she said, voice low but intense. "Another one to add to your collection."

He turned then, eyes growing dark. "Careful, Allencourt."

"Or what?" she challenged, stepping closer. "You'll report me? Ignore me? Pretend I don't exist? Oh wait, you already did that."

"Because what happened was inappropriate—"

"Because you're a coward," she said, the words a quiet blow.

Auren moved so swiftly she barely had time to register it. One moment they were facing off in the corridor, the next he had pulled her into an empty classroom, the door clicking shut behind them.

"A coward," he repeated, voice dangerously soft. He stood close, too close, and she could feel the heat radiating from him, could see the tension coiled in every line of his body. "Is that what you think?"

"I think you're running," she said, refusing to back down despite every fiber of her being that told her to. "I think you're hiding behind rules and protocols because you're afraid of what happened between us."

"You know nothing about what I'm afraid of," he said, each word sharp, but beneath it, she heard the strain, the crack in his composure.

"Then tell me," she challenged. "Tell me why you kissed me. Tell me why you can barely look at me now. Why do you walk around like it doesn't affect you when I can barely—nevermind."

She moved to push past him, but he caught her arm and swung her around to face him. His eyes locked with hers, searching, assessing.

"You want honesty, Cassara? Fine. I kissed you because I've wanted to since I watched you climb that stabilizer like you had something to prove. I ignored you because I crossed a line, one that I know I'll cross again given the chance and I can barely look at you now because every time I do, all I see is you in Tremaine's arms."

"That wasn't—" she began.

"What?" he cut in. "What wasn't it? Because from where I stood, it looked exactly like what it was."

"It wasn't what I wanted," she said, voice barely above a whisper.

Auren regarded her carefully. "Then what *do* you want?"

Cassara didn't answer with words.

She closed the distance between them in one step, hands curling into the front of his coat, and pulled him down to her.

Their mouths collided with the same desperate heat as before, but this time there was no hesitation, no surprise. Only hunger. Auren's arms wrapped around her waist, lifting her slightly as he backed her against the classroom wall, his body pressing against hers with delicious weight.

Her back hit the stone wall hard enough to rattle the chalkboard beside it, the edge of a desk biting into her hip. She barely noticed.

She gasped against his mouth, fingers sliding into his hair, gripping tight enough to earn a low groan that vibrated through her entire body. His lips were demanding, almost punishing, teeth grazing her lower lip in a way that made her arch against him.

"This is a mistake," he murmured against her mouth, even as his hands traced the curve of her waist, slipped beneath the edge of her uniform top to find bare skin.

"I know," she breathed, tilting her head back as his mouth trailed down her throat, leaving a path of fire in its wake.

"We can't—" His words broke off as she tugged his hair again, bringing his mouth back to hers.

"You keep saying that," she gasped, before kissing him again, deeper, slower, her tongue sliding against his in a way that made him shudder against her.

His hand found her thigh, hitching it up around his hip just like before, pressing closer until she could feel every part of him, the evidence of his desire impossible to miss. The room was silent save for their ragged breathing and the soft, desperate sounds that escaped when his teeth found the sensitive spot where her neck met her shoulder.

"Cassara," he groaned. "If we don't stop—"

"Don't," she whispered, hands sliding beneath his coat, feeling the heat of him through his shirt, the rapid thunder of his heart that matched her own.

For one breathless moment, she thought he might listen.

Then, with visible effort, he pulled back just enough to look at her, his eyes dark with desire and something far more complicated.

"Not like this," he said, voice rough. "Not rushed. Not angry."

She started to protest, but he silenced her with another kiss, gentler this time, devastating in its restraint.

"Not when there's so much at stake," he murmured against her lips. "The Wildes expedition. Your standing. My position."

He was right, of course, but that didn't make it any easier.

Cassara let her forehead rest against his chest for just a moment, allowing herself this small comfort before the inevitable separation.

"So what now?" she asked, voice steadier than she felt. "More silence?"

She wasn't sure she could stand it.

Auren's hand came up to brush a strand of hair from her face, the tenderness of the gesture at odds with the heat still simmering between them.

"Now we focus on what matters," he said quietly. "Your training. The expedition. Becoming the tamer I know you can be."

"And after?" The question slipped out before she could stop it, vulnerable in its hope.

His expression softened, just slightly. "After... we'll see."

It wasn't a promise, but it wasn't a rejection either.

Auren finally stepped back, creating distance between them, though his eyes never left hers. She could see the effort it took for him to rebuild his composure, to straighten his coat, to become the instructor again when moments before he'd been simply a man wanting a woman.

"One week until the Wildes," he said. "Be ready."

Cassara nodded. "I will be."

He moved to the door, pausing with his hand on the latch. "And Cassara?"

She looked up, heart still racing.

"Whatever you felt with Tremaine... was it anything like this?"

Cassara met his gaze and smiled. "Not even close."

Something flickered in his eyes, satisfaction, perhaps, or relief. He nodded once and slipped out, leaving her alone with tingling lips and the lingering heat of his touch on her skin.

The forge classroom smelled of scorched metal and hot iron woven with the sharp ozone tang of stored spellwork. Cassara stepped inside with the others, her boots clicking on the soot-streaked stone as the heavy door sealed behind them.

Racks of weapons lined the walls in neat formation. They shimmered faintly with arc-thread stabilizers, each marked by glyph-locked containment fields. No two were alike. Blades, gauntlets, staves, whips, guns, all gleaming with restrained potential.

Fenric stood at the center of the room, oil-streaked, bronze-skinned, goggles perched atop his forehead. He looked half-bored and fully unimpressed.

"Congratulations, first-years," he said, arms crossed. "You've managed to survive long enough to be trusted with something sharp."

A ripple of nervous laughter passed through the group.

"Your assignments," he continued, gesturing to the projection crystal beside him, "are based on aptitude evaluations, projected compatibility, and combat behavior.

These are not mere gifts. These are extensions of who you are. Fail to earn them, and they'll turn on you just as easily as any beast."

The projection spun to life: names and glyph signatures cycling in slow rotation. Students leaned closer.

"Try not to drool," Fenric muttered. "Tremaine. You're first."

Julian stepped forward without hesitation, all perfect poise and aristocratic swagger. Fenric didn't speak. He simply gestured toward a sealed rack, which hissed open with a click.

The weapon in question gleamed gold and crimson in the low light.

A high-alloy arc-saber with a collapsible lance extension, its hilt threaded with command runes. A plaque bore its name—Ceravolt.

Julian took it in both hands, and the blade hummed in response. Arrogant as he was, the resonance was undeniable.

He met her eyes and smiled. Cassara looked away.

"Delvanir."

Gideon moved next. Quiet, unhurried. Fenric didn't even glance up, just keyed a different rack. What emerged was a dense, layered gauntlet with expanding plates and a flicker of shieldlight already activating.

It's name, Lockstep. A defender's weapon.

Gideon slid it onto his arm like he'd done it a hundred times before. His eyes didn't leave the glyphs as they stabilized.

"Halvorsen."

Liri bounced forward, nervously wringing her hands.

Fenric arched a brow at her, muttered something under his breath about "overclocked optimism," and motioned to two compact fans folded like flower petals.

She blinked. "Fans?"

He smirked. "Unfold them."

She did and the fans snapped outward into graceful, razor-edged rings. Arc-thread lit along the rims, and for a moment, the blades shimmered like water kissed with moonlight.

Liri gasped softly. "They're beautiful."

"Nimbrush," Fenric said. "Try not to stab yourself with them. Allencourt."

Cassara stepped forward, pulse steady even as her hands felt too warm.

Fenric eyed her for a moment then he reached behind the console and drew out a long, slender case. It hissed open at a touch.

Inside lay a simple rod no longer than her forearm. It was sleek, rune-inlaid, polished to a mirrored gleam. She looked at him questioningly.

What exactly was she supposed to do with a stick?

“This is Spireglass,” he said, unbothered by her lack of enthusiasm.

She lifted it gently and found it was cool to the touch, cooler than expected, but not dead. Something stirred beneath the surface.

“It might not look like much,” he explained, “but don’t treat it like a toy. It’s a glaive-blade when extended. Syncs with movement. Partial resonance calibration built in, pending full beast bond.”

Cassara pressed the release.

The rod expanded with a low *shhkt*, unfolding into a full-length polearm of mirrored steel. Light caught along its surface making it gleam and the weight felt perfectly balanced in her hands.

A shimmer rippled across its surface, a faint pulse of energy, like it recognized her.

Fenric watched with a glint of something unreadable in his eyes. “It responded. You’re not bonded yet. But it’s listening.”

Cassara said nothing. She didn’t trust her voice.

“Control that,” he said. “It’ll cut through armor, beasts, and pride if you let it.”

She nodded.

As she stepped back into the ranks, weapon in hand, the others murmured around her, but she didn’t hear them. Her focus narrowed to the hum still alive in her grip. The reflection of her own eyes in the mirrored blade.

Spireglass. Hers.

Seven days to the Wildes.

Seven days to become what she was meant to be.

The ACS calibration wing was colder than the forge.

High ceilings. Silver-glass panels embedded in the floor. Rows of glowing nodes suspended above the platforms, each tethered to a magewired console manned by technicians in dark robes etched with diagnostic glyphs. The air buzzed with power, not magic, exactly, but the hum of something waiting.

"Welcome to your final preparation before the Wildes," the lead technician announced, his voice carrying easily through the chamber despite its hushed tone. "The Arcane Combat System calibration will determine how efficiently you can channel mana through your personal conduits. Over the past few weeks you've used training gear. Today, you receive programmed units based on data collected from your instructors. This affects not only your combat effectiveness but your ability to establish and maintain a beast bond."

"Allencourt," he called, consulting his list.

Cassara stepped onto the platform.

"Your ACS unit will be calibrated to enhance this natural tendency," the technician explained, selecting one of the harness systems from a specialized rack.

"Shoulder harness first," he instructed, helping her slip her arms through the leather straps. The harness settled across her shoulder and chest, its organic curves following the natural lines of her body. Multiple blue crystals were embedded throughout the metalwork, each one pulsing gently with contained energy.

Next came the bracer component, which locked into place along her left forearm with a series of precise clicks. The moment the connection was complete, all the crystals flared to life, creating a network of magical conduits that ran from her shoulder down to her wrist.

Cassara gasped as power flowed through the system. It felt like her essence had suddenly been amplified and refined, every pathway enhanced and stabilized.

"The crystals will respond to your mana signature," he continued, making final adjustments to several of the nodes. "Each one serves as both a conduit and a regulator, helping you maintain optimal flow even under stress."

A middle-aged technician, lean, sharp-eyed, precise, gestured her forward.

"Reset your stance. Relax the wrist. Good." He tapped his screen. "Running preliminary resonance scan."

Light spilled from the arc anchors at her feet, crawling up her legs and spine in a quiet, shimmering wave. The ACS bracer lit with responsive pulse, steady at first, then flickering.

"Hm," the technician murmured. "Interesting. High base capacity, but some... irregularities in flow pattern."

Cassara kept her expression neutral. "What does that mean?"

"It means your baseline mana readings are all over the place. High peaks, sudden drops. Inconsistent." He frowned at the display. "Have you experienced any emotional stress recently?"

She nearly laughed.

Emotional stress had become her operating state. Kissing Auren. Kissing Julian. Running herself raw in the rain, trying to outrun the weight of things she couldn't name.

"Some," she said.

"Mm. Emotional turbulence can affect mana stability." His tone was matter-of-fact. "Try to center yourself. Think of something that brings you peace."

Peace. Right.

She closed her eyes.

Instead of calm, she felt heat, mouths crashing, hands gripping, breathless want against stone and silence. Auren's voice, rough with restraint. The tension that hadn't left her body since that locked-door moment when it had almost been more.

The light flared.

Crystals around the platform brightened, casting silver patterns across her skin. The technician leaned in, eyes narrowing.

"Fascinating," he murmured, making notes. "Your resonance is stabilizing under emotional intensity rather than calming meditation. Most unusual."

Cassara opened her eyes. "What does that mean?"

"It means you may be what we call a stress channeler," he said. "Someone whose magic tightens under pressure. A rare alignment. High potential. Higher risk."

He tapped the bracer. "Push too hard without regulation, you'll burn yourself from the inside out. But if you channel correctly?" He gave her a slight smile. "You could break records."

Cassara stepped off the platform, the flickering glow of her ACS rig still dancing faintly across her wrist.

"Noted."

She didn't tell him that pressure was the only thing that ever made her feel clear anymore. That standing still felt more dangerous than anything she could face in the Wildes.

As she left the calibration wing, her reflection shimmered for a heartbeat in the polished wall panel, ghosted and bright, the bracer glowing softly at her side.

A girl built for the storm.

Evening had settled across Vallemont, the sky outside stained gold and rose through the tall arching windows of the second floor common room. The flicker of mage-light danced across worn rugs and deep cushions, casting soft shadows that made the wide stone space feel warmer than it was.

Liri and Evie were sprawled on the low rug near the central hearth, a game of charstone spread out between them, the rune-etched tokens flickering with elemental glow as they clacked across the board.

"I'm telling you, I don't want anything with wings," Evie declared, sweeping up a wind-glyph tile and smacking it onto the corner of the board. "Flight training is for sadists."

"You say that now," Liri countered, twirling a glimmering ember tile between her fingers, "but imagine bonding a phoenix serpent. You'd never have to wait in a line again."

Evie snorted. "I'd trade that for something small and sneaky. Like a burrowling or a duskcrawler. Compact. Non-murdery."

"You're not allowed to bond anything 'non-murdery.' You're already too nice."

Cassara sat curled in one of the deep chairs beside them, legs tucked up beneath her. She wasn't playing or participating at all, really. She hadn't spoken in ten minutes, simply letting the gentle banter of her dormmates wash over her in a way that was oddly soothing.

She wasn't thinking about beasts.

At least not the kind they would face in the Wildes.

She was thinking about Auren's voice against her neck, the feel of his breath when he said her name, and what it meant that he'd stopped and she hadn't wanted him to.

"Cass," Liri called gently, not looking up. "If you had to pick, fangs or feathers?"

Cassara blinked. "What?"

"Beast traits," Evie supplied. "Fangs or feathers. Which would yours have?"

Cassara glanced down at her bracer, the soft thrum of its recent calibration still pulsing in her fingertips.

"Fangs," she said, quiet but certain.

Liri and Evie exchanged a look, both nodding solemnly like they approved of this savage leaning.

Before the conversation could shift again, the scry crystal mounted above the hearth flared to life, projecting light into the center of the room.

A few students stood while others whispered amongst themselves.

"What is it?" Liri asked, her voice low.

"That's a Council-grade relay. They only light it that color if it's bad."

The crystal's hum deepened. Then a voice, calm but far from comforting, broke through.

"This is an emergency transmission from Watchtower Fourteen. As of this hour, the southern floating isle of Kareth's Edge has fallen. Full breach confirmed. Leviathan presence, Class B, has overrun containment. All tamer communications from the island ceased at 17:03 standard. Last known beacon registered inside the perimeter. Status of defense team: unknown."

The projection shifted to an overhead map showing Kareth's Edge had gone dark.

The room fell silent.

"Kareth's Edge?"

Evie's brow creased. "That was a stronghold, one of the largest. It wasn't..."

"It wasn't supposed to fall," Cassara finished, voice low.

The map faded, replaced with a static glyph—*Council Lockdown Directive: Wildes Quadrant Three. Expedition Protocol Reassessment Pending.*

And then the crystal went dark.

Liri set her game piece down slowly, her fingers trembling. "They had fourth years stationed there, didn't they?"

"Graduates," Evie said quietly. "Fully ranked. That was an elite deployment."

Cassara didn't speak.

Her gaze stayed locked on the now-dark crystal, her fingers curling tight into the fabric of the chair. Somewhere a girl was crying while another tried to console her.

"Her brother was stationed there," Evie continued, voice cracking.

Goosebumps prickled across her arms..

Not quite fear, but the distinct understanding that what they were training for wasn't just a theory anymore. The Wildes weren't a proving ground, they were a warzone, and one day soon, it wouldn't be someone else's island.

It would be hers.

CHAPTER EIGHTEEN

The days that followed blurred together in a haze of preparation and intensity.

Training sessions stretched longer, pushing past the usual boundaries as instructors drilled expedition protocols with grim efficiency. The news from Kareth's Edge had changed everything, what was once theoretical preparation became urgent reality. Students practiced emergency beacon procedures, reviewed corrupted beast identification charts until they could recite them in their sleep, and ran endless combat scenarios in the training yards.

Cassara threw herself into mastering Spireglass with single-minded focus. The weapon was unlike anything she'd trained with before, longer reach than a sword, more versatile than a staff, requiring perfect balance and timing to wield effectively. In the early hours before breakfast, she could be found in the practice yards, working through forms until sweat dripped from her brow and her muscles screamed in protest.

The glaive responded to her moods in ways that both thrilled and unsettled her. During moments of frustration, when a sequence wouldn't flow correctly, the mirrored blade would grow heavier, more resistant. But when she found her rhythm, when anger or determination surged through her, Spireglass sang, light as air, cutting through practice dummies like they were made of mist rather than reinforced leather.

"You're fighting it," Instructor Nareen observed on the third day, watching her struggle through a defensive rotation. "Stop trying to control the weapon. Let it be part of the movement."

Easier said than done. But gradually, she began to understand. Spireglass wasn't meant to be dominated, it was meant to be partnered with, a dance between wielder and blade that required trust rather than force.

By the fourth day, something clicked. As she moved through a complex sequence—thrust, pivot, sweeping arc, reverse grip—the weapon flowed with her like liquid silver. For a brief, perfect moment, she felt what it might be like to fight with a bonded beast, that seamless unity of purpose and power.

The moment shattered when she noticed Auren watching from the doorway.

Their eyes met across the training yard, and she felt that familiar heat rise in her chest, part attraction, equal parts frustration. He nodded once then turned and walked away.

The message passed through the first-year dormitories like wildfire, whispered from room to room with the kind of excited secrecy that only unsanctioned activities could inspire.

Tonight. The ruins. Midnight after the banquet. Fourth-year tradition.

Cassara found the note slipped under her door when she returned from training, written in an unfamiliar hand on expensive parchment that suggested one of the legacy students had connections among the upper years.

She looked up to find Liri practically vibrating with excitement, clutching a similar note.

"Are we going? Tell me we're going," Liri whispered. "I mean, if we get caught..."

"We won't get caught," Talia said quietly from her bed, not looking up from the book she was reading. "The instructors know about the tradition. They just pretend they don't."

Cassara raised an eyebrow. "How do you know that?"

"I asked around," Talia replied simply.

They had one more day until the expedition. The formal banquet was in a few hours—academy tradition before every Wildes departure.

Common sense said they needed to rest, to make sure they were in top form when they descended to the ground. Staring down at the note in her hands, Cassara couldn't help but wonder if maybe one night of forgetting wasn't mere indulgence—it was armor.

"Wait," Liri said, panic creeping into her voice as she stared at her open trunk. "What am I supposed to wear? I only brought one nice dress but it's so... plain. It's not meant for something formal—"

"Breathe," Evie said, already moving to her own trunk. "I have options. We'll figure it out."

Cassara left them to their own devices and crossed to her trunk. She lifted the upper panel, revealing the second layer beneath the standard-issue gear. Gowns in dusky jewel tones lay folded in precise rows, silk and satin catching the light like spilled moonlight.

She chose a deep garnet gown, sleeveless, open-backed, with a high neckline that dipped slightly at the collarbone. It hugged her waist, held in place by laces, then flared in layers to the knee. The fabric shimmered faintly with arcane threadwork, catching light with every movement.

It was perfect for the formal banquet, and for slipping into the ruins after midnight.

"Cass," Evie breathed, pausing mid-search through her own gowns. "You're going to kill someone tonight."

Liri nearly dropped the dress she was holding. "That's... that's illegal. That's war crime level. That's—"

"Tailored," Cassara said simply, turning back to the mirror.

She unpinned her braid, shaking her hair free until it fell in soft chestnut waves down her back. She left it loose. Untamed. *Hers*. She lined her eyes with a practiced hand, added a touch of shimmer to her cheekbones, and fastened a set of black gem cuffs around her wrists—tokens that looked far more like heirloom blades than jewelry.

"You've worn that before," Talia observed quietly. "That gown. It's important to you."

Cassara's reflection stilled for a beat. Then she nodded. "It belonged to my mother, it was the last dress she wore before she died."

"Here," Evie said, breaking the silence. She pulled out a midnight blue gown and held it up to Liri. "Try this one. It'll look beautiful on you."

Turning from the mirror, she moved to Liri's side, helping pin her unruly hair back with steady hands. She added a streak of metallic liner just above her lashes, soft enough to feel magical, strong enough to feel brave.

Across the room, Sonia fastened the clasp on her own dress—elegant, understated silver that caught the light without demanding it. She met Cassara's eyes in the mirror.

"I'll sit through the speeches and formality. But sneaking off to the ruins afterward? You lot are on your own for that part."

Cassara shrugged. “It’s not like anyone will notice.”

Talia finally set her book aside and rose. Cassara watched her, curious to see what sort of attire the girl from the Outer Isles would have brought. Talia produced a dress of deep forest green, simple but striking against her umber skin.

Turning, Cassara glanced at her own reflection one last time.

For the first time in weeks, she didn't feel like a soldier.

Just Cassara Allencourt, heir to a legacy of light and fire, and tonight, walking into ceremony and midnight like she belonged to both.

The Grand Hall had been transformed.

Mage-lights floated in clusters overhead, casting warm golden light across long tables draped in deep blue cloth embroidered with silver thread. Candles flickered in crystal holders, their flames steady despite the gentle current of air from the high arched windows.

First-years filed in through the main doors, their voices hushed despite the grandeur. Cassara entered with Liri and Evie, aware of the way heads turned, the way conversations paused just long enough to notice who wore what, who stood with whom.

She didn't let it touch her.

The upper years were already seated at tables near the back, their relaxed postures a stark contrast to the nervous energy radiating from the first-years. Instructors lined the dais at the front of the hall, standing behind a raised table set with fine china and silver goblets. Cassara's gaze swept across them—Nareen, stern and watchful; Thorne, arms crossed; Roderick, expression unreadable.

And Auren.

He stood near the end, hands clasped behind his back, his dark instructor's uniform immaculate. His eyes found hers for the briefest moment, then moved away as if she were just another student in the crowd.

"This is incredible," Liri whispered, eyes wide as she took in the decorations, the sheer scale of the event.

"It's tradition," Evie said, though her voice carried a note of awe too. "My sister told me about it. They do this every year before the Wildes expedition."

Cassara's attention shifted as more students entered, the hall filling with the low hum of conversation and the rustle of formal attire. She caught sight of Gideon near one of the side tables, the dark gray of his formalwear a stark contrast to the colorful gowns and ornate coats around him. He was listening to Oliver—no doubt prattling on about glyph patterns or crystal resonance—when his gaze shifted and stopped on her.

His expression changed from abject boredom to... surprise?

She told herself she'd imagined it.

Turning back to Liri and Evie, she let herself be pulled into their conversation about table assignments and whether the food would actually be good.

"Allencourt."

The voice came from directly behind her. She turned to find Gideon standing closer than she'd expected, hands sliding into his pockets, his posture casual but his eyes sharp.

"Delvanir," she said evenly.

His gaze flicked down, then back up, so quick she almost missed it. "You clean up well."

The words were simple. Matter-of-fact. But the way he said them—like he hadn't meant to, like they'd slipped out before he could stop them—made her pulse kick up.

"Thanks," she said, keeping her tone light. "You too."

Before either of them could speak again, Verena appeared at Gideon's side, her gown a shimmering gold that hugged every curve. She smiled, but it didn't reach her eyes.

"Cassara," she said, her voice smooth. "I almost didn't recognize you without all the mud and bruises."

"I could say the same, but I think you wear yours on the inside," Cassara said, keeping her expression neutral.

Verena's smile tightened. "Charming. I suppose desperation looks different on everyone."

"Verena." Gideon's voice cut through, quiet but firm. He didn't raise it, didn't shift his stance, but the weight of his tone was enough to make her pause. "She looks fine. Leave it."

Verena blinked, clearly taken aback. For a moment, she looked like she might argue, but then she just laughed—brittle and forced—and turned away without another word.

Gideon didn't watch her go. He met Cassara's eyes for a second longer, then stepped back. "See you after," he said, and walked off before she could respond.

Cassara stood there, still processing what had just happened.

"What did he say?"

She turned to find Julian at her elbow, his expression pleasant but his eyes watchful. He was dressed impeccably, as always—dark blue coat with silver buttons, his blond hair perfectly styled.

"Nothing important," she said.

Julian's gaze followed Gideon's retreating form, then returned to her. "Didn't look like nothing."

Before she could answer, a chime rang through the hall—clear and resonant. Conversations died instantly as students moved toward their assigned tables. Julian offered his arm, and Cassara took it, letting him guide her to a seat near the front.

The headmistress rose from her place at the dais.

Her silver-streaked hair was pulled back in an elegant knot and her robes were Vallemont colors—deep crimson edged with gold. When she spoke, her voice carried effortlessly through the hall.

"First-years of Vallemont Academy," she began, her tone formal but warm. "Tonight, we gather as we have for generations—to honor those who will soon embark on the Wildes expedition. This is not merely tradition. It is a rite of passage that has shaped tamers for centuries."

She paused, her expression growing somber.

"Before we continue, I ask that we observe a moment of silence for those we lost at Kareth's Edge. Tamers and civilians alike who gave their lives defending against the breach. Their sacrifice reminds us of the stakes we face, and the responsibility we carry."

The hall fell silent. Cassara bowed her head, the weight of the words settling over her.

After a long moment, the headmistress spoke again.

"The bond between tamer and beast is sacred. It is forged in trust, in strength, and in the willingness to face the unknown together. Once made, it cannot be undone. It is forever."

Her gaze swept across the room, landing on each first-year in turn.

"You stand on the edge of that bond. Soon you will enter the Wildes. You will face creatures of immense power, and if you prove worthy, one of them will choose you. Not because you are strong, though strength matters. Not because you are skilled, though skill is essential. But because you are compatible. Because something in you calls to something in them."

She raised her goblet.

"To the first-years. To the bonds you will forge. To the legacy you will carry forward. May you return with honor, with strength, and with a companion who will stand beside you for the rest of your days."

The hall echoed with the sound of goblets raised, voices joining in the toast.

"To the first-years."

Cassara lifted her own glass, the weight of the moment pressing down on her. Around her, students drank, the formal ceremony giving way to the meal that followed.

But she couldn't shake the feeling that everything was about to change.

The ruins rose like broken teeth beneath the moon, half-swallowed by vines and moss, their crumbling arches glowing with intermittent pulses of magic from centuries past. Lanterns floated in lazy arcs overhead, bobbing through the air like captured stars. Somewhere within the ancient stone, the sound of conversation and laughter, mingling with the sound of the fire crackling at the heart of the clearing.

It was beautiful. Reckless. Wild.

Cassara stepped into the glow and felt every eye that turned.

Her gown caught the firelight, garnet rippling like flame with every step. Her hair cascaded in soft waves, her posture highborn and untouchable. She moved with the kind of presence only someone raised in court could wield, not because she wanted attention, but because she knew she'd draw it regardless.

Even Julian looked momentarily stunned, as though he hadn't expected to see her there.

He stood near the fire, his coat now open at the throat, silver clasps undone to show just a hint of collarbone. He was devastating like this, hair touselled, a glass of wine already in hand, and a smile that barely masked intent.

He recovered quickly, crossing to her with a grin that tried to be casual.

“Didn't think you'd actually come.”

Cassara's mouth quirked. “I'm full of surprises.”

“Mm, and still, seeing you now?” His eyes trailed her like a brand. “Wasn’t prepared.”

He offered her his glass. She took it, sipping without comment. The wine was rich and heady, plums and spice and unspoken intentions that hummed just beneath the surface. Julian poured himself another from the nearby table, already surrounded by empty cups.

Beyond the fire, she caught sight of Gideon where he stood beneath an ivy-draped archway, Verena standing close, smiling, laughing too brightly, a possessive hand looped through his arm.

Julian leaned closer. "Come on. Just for a minute."

Before she could refuse, he took her hand and tugged her past the fire and down a half-collapsed corridor glowing with moonlight and old sigils that pulsed gently beneath their feet. The ruins were vast, layered in forgotten halls and hidden alcoves, each one whispering of secrets and stolen moments.

He stopped abruptly and she felt his hands on her waist.

"Julian—"

He kissed her without warning, his mouth hot from wine, his grip confident, hands slipping lower than they should have.

Her heart stuttered and for a moment she couldn't think, couldn't react. Her hands went flat against his chest.

"Julian," she gasped, pulling back. "Stop."

He didn't. Not right away. His fingers tightened.

"Don't worry, no one will see us," he murmured, mouth dipping to catch hers again. This time she was able to turn and his mouth met her cheek instead.

"I mean it."

"You're always doing this," he said, voice edged with anger. "Drawing me in, then pulling away. You think I don't see what you're doing? Wearing that dress, letting me walk you here, kissing me when it suits you and then acting like I'm the problem when I want more."

She shoved him, hard.

He stumbled back a step, face flushed from wine and frustration fueled anger.

"You've been dangling yourself in front of me for weeks," he continued, his voice rising. "Playing the victim, making me chase you, and now you're going to pretend you didn't know exactly what you were doing? That you didn't want this?"

"I never wanted this," she said, her voice shaking with fury. "You're delusional."

"Am I?" He stepped forward again, backing her toward the stone wall. "Because last time you kissed me back. You didn't pull away then. So what's different now, Cassara? What changed?"

"Everything," she spat. "Get away from me."

But he didn't. His hand caught her wrist, pulling her closer.

"You don't get to do this," he said, quieter now but no less intense. "You don't get to make me feel like I'm losing my mind and then act like you're innocent. I know what I saw. I know what you—"

He moved to kiss her again, his grip tightening on her wrist.

Before he could close the distance, he was yanked off his feet and dragged backward into the shadows, cursing as he landed hard on stone. His voice rose in confusion, but he couldn't see who had grabbed him, just empty air and torchlit fragments of ruin.

CHAPTER NINETEEN

Julian was still shouting and her mind was still reeling when a hand wrapped around her wrist. She found herself being pulled in the opposite direction, away from Julian and deeper into the ruins. Her first instinct was to pull away, but when a familiar voice met her ears, she could have wept with relief.

"I've got you."

"Auren," she gasped.

"Quiet."

The single word came out clipped and Cassara didn't need to see his face to know that he was furious. She could feel it in the grip of his hand and in the barely controlled violence radiating from him with every step.

She stumbled once, her slipper catching on the edge of uneven stone, but he caught her, steadying her by the waist for one burning second before releasing her again. Like he didn't trust himself to hold on longer.

By the time he stopped, the sounds of the gathering had faded behind them, the crackling of fire reduced to a distant echo among crumbling stone.

He released her hand and paced away, movements sharp and restless. She watched him stop, watched his shoulders rise and fall as he took a deep breath that did nothing to calm the storm she could see building in him.

Cassara glanced back the way they came, breath still uneven. "Julian didn't see you, did he?"

Auren shook his head, voice low and dangerous. "No."

She nodded once and folded her arms, mostly to hide the way her fingers trembled. Was he angry at her? For being reckless, for letting Julian pull her away—

"You didn't have to do that."

"I did."

Simple and honest, but edged with something sharp.

He stepped forward, his hand rising as though to touch her, only to curl into a fist and fall back to his side. His eyes searched hers.

"He touched you. Put his hands on you—"

The words came out rough, and the anger in them made her stomach twist. She needed him to know she hadn't wanted it, that she hadn't asked for any of this.

Cassara's voice came soft. "I didn't want him to."

"I know, Cassara, I know." The response was immediate, the fury in his voice shifting. "I heard you and I tried to get to you faster—gods, I should have killed him. I should go back and tear him limb from limb."

His anger wasn't directed at her, she realized, but at Julian and at himself.

"No, Auren," Cassara said, catching his hand. "It's fine. *I'm* fine."

"It's not," Auren countered, his free hand rising to cup her face. She felt the tremor in his fingers. Fear? No, not fear. It was barely controlled rage mixed with concern.

"What if he did see you? What if—"

"He didn't," Auren assured her, thumb brushing her cheek. "And if he did? So be it."

"You say things like that," she said, barely above a whisper, "and I forget what's at stake."

"Good," he said quietly. "Because watching him touch you nearly broke something in me I'm not sure I can fix."

She reached for him, her hands caught the front of his jacket and she pulled, closing the space between them in one sharp movement. His mouth met hers halfway.

It was heat and hunger and a week's worth of restraint torn apart in a single breath. His hands found her waist, her back, the curve of her ribs, everywhere at once, like he couldn't decide what to hold and so tried to hold all of her. She felt the press of him through every inch of her dress, the shudder in his breath when she arched into him without meaning to.

He kissed her like he'd been waiting for this moment through fire and silence and sleepless nights. Like he'd memorized her mouth in memory and was only now being allowed to taste it again.

Her back hit stone, cold and solid, an ancient column or maybe a fractured wall. She didn't care. The edge of it bit into the small of her back, grounding her even as the rest of her went molten. Somewhere behind them, laughter drifted across the ruins, but it felt far away, dreamlike. Nothing mattered outside the heat of his mouth, the way his tongue flicked against hers, coaxing, claiming. The way he made a low sound in his throat when she kissed him harder in return.

She wanted more, more of his hands, his breath, his weight. More of the way he needed her like this, wild and wordless.

The kiss deepened, slower now. Hungrier. He took his time tracing the shape of her mouth with his own, until she was breathless, dizzy, her lips swollen and her thoughts reduced to nothing but the feel of him.

His hand slid from her cheek down the curve of her neck, hesitating at her collarbone. She felt the tension in his fingers, the slight tremor that betrayed his struggle for control.

"Auren," she whispered against his lips, her voice raw with need. His name was both plea and permission.

His eyes met hers, the moonlight filtering through the crumbling ruins caught the sharp angles of his face, illuminating the conflict there. Instructor and student. Forbidden and necessary. The rules that had always stood between them seemed paper-thin now, dissolving with each ragged breath.

Cassara reached for his hand and guided it lower, over the delicate fabric of her dress. Her heart hammered against her ribs as his palm curved around her waist, fingers splaying across her bare back. The sensation of his hand against her skin sent electricity coursing through her veins.

"We shouldn't," he murmured, but his body betrayed him. His lips found the sensitive spot below her ear, trailing fire down her neck.

"We already are," she answered, arching into him.

His grip tightened, pulling her closer as his restraint crumbled.

A gasp escaped her as his hand slid lower, tracing the curve where her dress met skin. The world narrowed to the feel of his mouth on her throat, his chest against hers, and the wall at her back. She couldn't think, didn't want to. Her fingers fumbled with the buttons of his shirt, each one a small victory as more of his skin was exposed to her touch.

Auren's breath hitched when her hand slipped beneath the fabric and her palm flattened against his chest, feeling the rapid thunder of his heart. It matched her own, wild, desperate, afraid to stop. His muscles tensed beneath her exploring fingers, and something primal surged through her at knowing she affected him this way.

"Tell me to stop," he whispered against her collarbone, his voice rough with restraint even as his hands continued their maddening journey across her back. "Tell me now, Cassara."

But she couldn't. Wouldn't. The rules that had seemed so important hours ago were distant shadows compared to the reality of him. She answered by pulling his mouth back to hers, tasting the groan that vibrated through him.

His hands found the ties at the side of her dress, hesitating there. Cassara arched into him, silent permission granted in the press of her body against his. Her skin tingled, every nerve alive with sensation as his fingers worked the knots free. When the laces fell open, she felt the cool night air kiss the newly exposed skin of her hip, sending a shiver through her that had nothing to do with cold.

Auren's eyes sought hers again, dark with want, but still questioning. Still giving her one last chance to retreat.

Cassara answered by guiding his hand to the remaining ties. Her heart hammered against her ribs, excitement and nervousness braiding together in her chest. The dress loosened further, fabric whispering against her skin as his hands explored the curve of her waist, the touch igniting something primal within her.

"You're trembling," he murmured against her ear, his breath hot against her skin.

"So are you," she countered, feeling the slight quiver in his fingers as they traced patterns on her bare skin.

A half-smile curved his lips. "Terrified," he admitted. "Not of this. Of how much I want it."

Her mind clouded with sensation as Auren's fingers moved with gentle insistence, slipping beneath the loosened bodice of her gown. The fabric gave way beneath his touch, sliding down to reveal the curve of her shoulder. Cassara was taken aback by the intensity of his gaze as it followed the path of his hands.

"You're beautiful," he whispered, voice rough with desire as he traced the exposed line of her collarbone, then lower.

Heat bloomed across her skin, a flush that spread from her cheeks down her neck to where his fingers now played at the edge of her bodice. She felt vulnerable and powerful all at once, watching his expression darken as more of her was revealed to him. The garnet fabric pooled at her elbows, caught on the last remaining ties.

With deliberate slowness, Auren's fingers worked at the remaining fastenings, each one giving way in silent surrender. Cassara held her breath as the dress slipped lower, baring her breasts to his heated gaze. She fought the instinct to cover herself, to shield her body from the moonlight that silvered her skin.

"Don't," he murmured, catching her wrist gently when she moved. "Let me see you."

Her pulse quickened as his eyes took in every inch of exposed skin. No one had ever looked at her with such reverence, such hunger.

Cassara's breath came in shallow bursts as Auren's hands hovered just above her skin, the heat of him radiating between them without touching. When his fingertips finally made contact, tracing the delicate curve where her neck met her shoulder, she couldn't contain the soft sound that escaped her lips.

"I've imagined this," he confessed, as his palm skimmed downward, following the slope of her collarbone, then lower still. "But imagination pales against reality."

When his hand finally cupped her breast, Cassara's head fell back, eyes fluttering closed as his thumb brushed across her nipple. The jolt of pleasure that followed made her gasp, her body responding instinctively, arching into his touch as heat pooled low in her belly.

"Look at me," Auren whispered, and she forced her eyes open to find his gaze locked on hers, pupils blown wide. He held her there, trapped in that stare as his other hand joined the first, learning the weight and shape of her breasts with exquisite attention.

He lowered his head, his tongue moving slowly, deliberately, tracing a path along the delicate curve of her skin with teasing persistence. Light as breath, it traveled a merciless line, following the contours of her bare shoulder, across her collarbone, and down to the swell of her breast.

Another soft noise escaped her, barely audible but loaded with need, as he took his time. Each moment seemed impossibly long before his mouth finally found her nipple. She gasped at the sensation, the contact sending shockwaves of pleasure cascading through her body in wild, unpredictable waves. Her spine arched, pressing into him with a desperate urgency that matched the whimpers escaping her throat.

His hand, not satisfied with its distance, moved with a mind of its own, raising up to mirror the actions of his mouth on her other breast, fingers curving as his thumb circled tight and tantalizing in patterns that made her breath hitch.

"You're exquisite," he murmured against her skin, his breath hot and damp. "Perfect."

The reverence in his voice made her heart stutter. This was madness, the combat instructor and his student, half-dressed in abandoned ruins where anyone might find them, but Cassara couldn't bring herself to care. His hands slipped lower to explore the curve of her waist, the small of her back. Each touch left trails of fire in its wake.

His mouth found hers again, hungrier this time, and she met his intensity with her own. Their tongues danced as his hand slid down, slipping beneath the bunched fabric of her skirt.

She gasped against his lips as his fingers traced delicate patterns along her inner thigh, each circle drawing closer to where heat pooled between her legs. Her head fell back against the stone, a soft moan escaping her as Auren's mouth traveled to the sensitive skin of her neck. The contrast between his battle-hardened hands and the gentleness of his touch made her tremble.

His fingers found the edge of her undergarments, and she arched against him in anticipation. The cool air against her exposed skin only heightened her awareness of every point where their bodies connected.

"Tell me if you want me to stop," he murmured against her throat, even as his fingers traced the edge of silk, teasing.

"Don't stop," she breathed. "Please don't stop."

His fingers slipped beneath the fabric, and Cassara's breath caught at the first deliberate touch. It was nothing like her own fumbling explorations in the privacy of her room—this was different, overwhelming in its intensity. He moved slowly, exploring, learning what made her gasp, what made her grip his shoulders harder. When he found the spot that made her whimper, he focused there with maddening patience, circling with gentle pressure that built heat low in her belly.

"You're so wet," he whispered, wonder and hunger mixing in his voice. The crude honesty of it sent a fresh wave of arousal through her.

She couldn't form words, could only nod as her hips moved against his hand, seeking more. His free hand braced against the stone beside her head, holding himself steady as he watched her face, tracking every reaction. The intensity of his gaze should have made her self-conscious, but instead it heightened everything—knowing he was watching her unravel, that he wanted to see it.

His fingers moved with more purpose now, sliding through her slickness before one pressed inside. Cassara gasped, her body tensing at the unfamiliar intrusion. She'd touched herself before, but never like this, never with someone else's hands, never with this kind of certainty.

"Relax," he murmured against her temple, his voice soothing even as his thumb found her clit and began to circle. "I've got you."

She tried to breathe through it, tried to let her body adjust to the sensation. The slow rhythm he set, it was too much, building toward something she'd never quite let herself reach. Every time she'd gotten close before, alone in her bed with her own trembling fingers, the intensity had frightened her. The loss of control. The way her body seemed to spiral toward something unknown and overwhelming.

She'd always stopped.

But Auren didn't stop. His finger curled inside her, finding a spot that made her cry out softly, and his thumb maintained that relentless pressure.

"Shh," he murmured, though his own breathing had gone ragged. "We have to be quiet."

The tension was building faster now, coiling tighter in her belly, and panic flickered at the edges of her consciousness. It felt like standing at the edge of a cliff, and every instinct screamed to pull back, to retreat to safety.

"Auren," she gasped, her fingers digging into his shoulders. "I don't—I can't—"

He must have heard the uncertainty in her voice because he paused, his movements gentling. "Have you done this before?" he asked quietly.

She shook her head, heat flooding her cheeks. "I've tried. By myself. But I always... it gets too intense and I stop."

Understanding softened his expression. He pressed a kiss to her forehead, tender and reassuring. "Do you trust me?"

"Yes," she whispered without hesitation.

"Then let go," he murmured. "I won't let anything happen to you. Just feel it. Don't fight it."

He resumed the rhythm, slower this time, more deliberate. Increasing the pressure of his thumb while his finger moved inside her with practiced care. The pressure built again, and this time when the panic rose, she focused on his voice, his presence, the solid warmth of him surrounding her.

"That's it," he whispered as her body began to tremble. "Don't run from it. I want to feel you come apart."

The sensation climbed higher, her breath coming in short gasps. Every nerve ending felt alive, sparking with electricity. The coil of tension wound tighter and tighter until it felt like something inside her might break.

He added a second finger, and the stretch combined with the pressure on her clit pushed her dangerously close to that edge she'd always retreated from.

"Auren," she gasped, a warning and a plea. "I'm scared—"

"I know," he murmured, his lips brushing her ear. "But you're safe. I promise. Just let it happen."

His fingers curled inside her again, hitting that devastating spot while his thumb pressed harder, and suddenly she was falling over the edge she'd never dared cross.

The pleasure hit her like a wave, crashing through her body with an intensity that stole her breath. Her mouth opened in a cry, and Auren's hand immediately covered her lips, muffling the sound as her body convulsed around his fingers. It was overwhelming, terrifying, perfect—every muscle tensing and releasing in waves she couldn't control. Her hips jerked against his hand as he worked her through it with gentle persistence, prolonging the sensation until she thought she might shatter completely.

She was still trembling when the sound of voices drifted through the ruins—closer this time, multiple people laughing and talking as they explored.

Auren's fingers stilled inside her, though he didn't withdraw. His other hand remained over her mouth, and she felt his breath hot against her ear as they both froze. Her body was still pulsing with aftershocks, oversensitive and raw.

"—think they went this way?" a female voice called.

"Maybe. Or they found somewhere more private," another voice answered, followed by laughter.

Cassara's heart hammered against her ribs, the lingering pleasure mixing with sudden panic. Auren's hand slowly left her mouth, his fingers carefully withdrawing from between her legs. The loss made her whimper softly, her body still hypersensitive from what had just happened.

His eyes found hers in the darkness—heated, satisfied, protective.

The voices grew closer. He helped her straighten her undergarments with gentle hands, smoothing down her skirt before adjusting the bodice of her dress. His fingers worked the ties with practiced efficiency, though she noticed the slight tremor in them.

"Behind here," he whispered, guiding her deeper into the alcove, behind a crumbling column. He positioned himself in front of her, his body blocking her from view, one hand braced against the stone above her head.

She could still feel the ghost of his touch between her legs, her body still trembling with the aftermath of her first real orgasm. Her mind felt hazy, dreamlike, as if she'd crossed into some new territory she couldn't return from.

Two silhouettes passed by the archway—third years, from the sound of their conversation. Cassara pressed herself against the stone, grateful for Auren's solid presence shielding her. Her legs felt weak, unsteady.

The footsteps faded. The voices grew distant.

Slowly, the tension in Auren's shoulders eased. He looked down at her, and in the moonlight filtering through the ruins, the satisfaction in his eyes gentled into something tender, almost awed.

"Are you alright?" he asked quietly, his hand coming up to cup her face.

Cassara nodded, still not entirely trusting her voice. She felt raw, exposed in a way that had nothing to do with her partially unlaced dress.

"That was..." she trailed off, unable to find words for what she'd just experienced.

"Your first," he said softly. Not a question.

"Yes," she whispered.

Something fierce and possessive flashed in his eyes. "Good," he murmured, his thumb brushing across her still-swollen lips. "You're beautiful when you come undone. I wanted to watch you without having to muffle your sounds. Wanted to hear my name on your lips when you fell apart."

Heat flooded her cheeks. The vulnerability of it—that he'd seen her like that, felt her lose control completely—should have embarrassed her. Instead, she felt trust. Intimacy deeper than the physical act itself.

"Next time," she whispered, surprised by her own boldness, by the certainty that there would be a next time.

His eyes darkened with promise. "Next time," he agreed. Then, more seriously, "They'll notice you're gone."

She nodded but made no move to leave. Her body still felt languid, heavy with satisfaction.

Auren rested his forehead against hers, his breathing finally steadying. One hand still rested at her waist, as if he couldn't quite bring himself to let go completely.

"One more day until the Wildes," she said quietly.

"This complicates everything."

Cassara met his gaze steadily, seeing her own desire reflected there, along with something deeper. What they'd just shared had changed things, crossed a line that couldn't be uncrossed. "I don't care."

His smile was slow, dangerous, full of promise. "Good."

He kissed her once more, soft and lingering, before helping her fully adjust her dress and smooth her hair. His hands were gentle, almost reverent, as he made sure no evidence of what had transpired remained visible.

"You should go back first," he said.

Cassara nodded, though leaving him felt wrong somehow, like walking away from something essential. She took a step toward the archway, then turned back.

"Auren?"

"Hmm?"

"Thank you. For earlier. With Julian." She paused. "And for... this. For not letting me be afraid."

His jaw tightened at the mention of Julian's name, but his expression softened at her second admission. "Always," he said simply.

She believed him.

CHAPTER TWENTY

The sky skiffs descended in a slow spiral, glyph woven sails catching the morning sun like fractured glass. The Wildes spread beneath them—dense and unruly, a vast sprawl of shadowed trees, tangled undergrowth, and mist-choked glens that pulsed with ancient magic. Cassara stood near the rail, hands braced, watching as the land rose to meet them.

She didn't flinch when the skiff jolted upon landing, didn't spare a glance at the other first-years clustered behind her, some wide-eyed, others trying too hard to look unimpressed. Her focus was on the forest, on the place where legacy and instinct would either converge or implode.

At the far end of the hold, Auren stood watch, gaze sweeping over the first-years with quiet scrutiny. He wasn't in training gear today but his more formal, instructor attire. His coat was unbuttoned at the collar, gloves tucked at his belt, and his posture held the same coiled composure as always.

Cassara felt her heart skip at the sight of the wind dragging through his hair, already recalling how it had felt tangled between her fingers.

They'd barely spoken since the ruins, both agreeing to maintain a careful, professional distance until after the expedition. It was easier than before. There was none of the fear or uncertainty, none of the wondering, just confidence that soon, somehow, they'd find a way to be together.

"First Year Cohort. You will have three days to track and procure a beast bond." Auren's voice seemed to find her even across the crowded deck, as if he were speaking directly to her despite addressing the group. "Should you find yourself in trouble and require extraction, you will use the emergency flare included in the survival packs you were given when you boarded. You will find enough rations to sustain you, and I would advise against eating anything you might find, no matter how appealing."

"He's talking about you, Evie," Sonia whispered, eliciting a chuckle from some nearby students. Evie's face turned bright red.

"Keep talking, Sonia," Cassara said coldly. "See how funny it is when you're bonded to a moss slug."

Sonia's smirk faltered. For a moment, genuine anger flashed across her face before she masked it with indifference. "Whatever," she muttered, but her voice lacked its usual bite.

Auren's voice drew their attention back. "....a bond is not a trophy. It's a partnership forged in mutual respect. Force will get you killed. Arrogance will get you abandoned. If you approach a beast with anything less than absolute certainty that you're willing to give as much as you take, don't approach at all."

The same warning and expectations that had been repeated a hundred times since they'd first arrived.

For Cassara, everything felt different now.

Not just because of Kareth's Edge, though the memory of the ruined island hung heavy in all their minds. It was the air here—charged, feral, thick with the possibility of fate snapping its teeth shut.

A few students shifted. Others straightened.

"If you're lucky," he continued, "you'll return with more than scars."

But when his eyes swept the group, found hers, the air in her lungs stalled. Just for a moment. Gone was the careful neutrality he'd worn for days. What remained was concern, stark and unguarded, edged with hunger he couldn't quite mask.

Be careful, his eyes seemed to say. *Come back to me.*

They held each other's gaze.

No smile. No expression. Just a single nod, barely perceptible, but she felt it like a touch, like the ghost of his hands at her waist in moonlit ruins.

She nodded back, her pulse thundering beneath her skin.

The moment shattered when someone coughed nearby, and Auren's attention moved on, becoming the instructor once more. But Cassara's cheeks burned with the memory of what had passed between them.

Julian stood off to the side, glancing her way and shifting his weight like he was waiting for something—approval, attention, or maybe just the right moment to insert himself.

Cassara's stomach turned but she managed to keep her expression neutral while angling her body slightly away from him. The memory of his hands on her, his mouth, his anger, the way he'd backed her against that wall—she wanted to hit him, to expose him to the world. But if she reacted, if she flinched or accused or even acknowledged what had happened, he might mention the invisible force that had dragged him away and start asking questions that led back to Auren.

It was a risk Cassara was unwilling to take.

So she said nothing.

"You're really going alone?"

Cassara looked up to see Gideon standing nearby, arms crossed, watching her. She turned away, tightening the strap on her survival pack, grateful for something to distract her. "Why? Would you like to come hold my hand?"

He didn't take the bait, just looked at her for a beat too long, then said, "Don't forget your signal flare. Just in case."

She didn't answer. Her mind was still half-caught on the weight of Auren's gaze, the unspoken promise hidden there, and on Julian, hovering too close, acting like nothing had happened.

As if summoned by the tension, or perhaps unable to help himself, Julian moved to join them. "You don't have to prove anything, you know. No one would think less of you for going with a team."

Every instinct screamed at her to step back, to put distance between them. Instead, she held her ground, kept her voice even. "I would."

Julian offered a slow smile that didn't reach his eyes. "Then I'll save your place beside me on the ride back."

The casual presumption of it made her skin crawl, but she couldn't let it show. Couldn't give him any reason to think she was upset with him and risk him mentioning last night to anyone who might listen too closely.

"Don't bother," she said simply, and turned away before he could respond.

Ahead of her, the ramp hissed as it lowered and the Wildes spread out before them.

At that moment, everything else fell away. Julian. Auren. The tension coiled in her chest. None of it mattered.

This was it.

This was what she had been waiting for.

Cassara stepped off the ramp with her head high and her grip steady on Spireglass, the metallic haft of her glaive cool and certain against her palm.

Before her the forest rose like a living thing. Moss carpeted the ground in thick, uneven swaths, broken by jagged roots that twisted like serpents frozen mid-strike. Pale light filtered through the canopy in shifting columns, catching on mist that crept across the ground. The trees were massive, ancient, their bark scored with patterns made by creatures larger than her imagination could fathom.

Cassara didn't wait for instructions, the second her boots met earth beyond the landing point, she moved.

Every step forward steadied something inside her that had been fracturing for weeks. This wasn't about proving herself to her father, or Julian, or the academy. This wasn't about rankings or reputations or living up to a name she'd been born into.

This was about becoming the tamer she'd always known she could be.

The forest swallowed her within minutes. Behind her, voices faded to nothing. The landing zone disappeared behind walls of green. She moved slowly, scanning the undergrowth, reading the signs the instructors had drilled into them—broken branches, disturbed earth, claw marks on bark. Her ACS adjusted constantly to the shifting arcane pressure, crystals pulsing warm against her skin. Spireglass hummed in her grip.

The terrain shifted as she walked. The ground grew softer, more treacherous. Moss gave way to damp earth that squelched beneath her boots.

She stepped through a narrow thicket, pausing to adjust her grip on Spireglass. Ferns the size of blankets draped over stone outcroppings. Strange vines dangled like necklaces from the branches overhead, slick with dew and speckled with bloom-like pods.

Too late, she noticed one of them shifting.

It dropped fast, a thick, sinuous coil of green and gold wrapping around her wrist with a snap of instinct.

Cassara twisted, yanking her arm back on reflex, but it held tight. Another vine uncoiled from above, angling toward her face like a striking serpent.

Spireglass surged to life in her other hand.

She sliced upward, the blade catching the vine mid-lunge with a crackle of arcane backlash. The vine coiled around her wrist spasmed, then went limp, slithering back up into the canopy. The pulsing flowers along the vineline closed in slow, eerie unison, no longer curious, but sated.

Cassara stood still, chest rising hard with each breath.

A scratch marked her forearm. Not deep, but already tinged with a strange purple-red where the vine's sap lingered. Her ACS flickered a warning: foreign compound detected. She activated the filtration glyph stitched into her glove, hissing as it glowed hot against her skin, burning the toxin clear.

She swallowed hard, and did her best to dismiss the fear that had curled cold in her gut for just a moment.

Then she started walking again.

Slower, this time, more aware of how the forest breathed around her.

The Wildes were beautiful, yes, but beauty here was just another way to lie.

By mid-afternoon, the trees began to whisper—a low murmur that sounded almost like her name.

Cassara's steps slowed. She told herself it was nothing, just wind through leaves, but the air hung too still for that. The sound came again, closer this time.

Her grip tightened on Spireglass.

She squared her shoulders and kept moving. The Wildes wanted to unsettle her, that was all. It was part of the challenge and she wouldn't let it get under her skin.

Ahead of her a glade appeared like a mirage—one moment she was surrounded by trees, the next, she was in open space. Mist clung to the clearing like a veil, low and ghost-pale, rising from the ground as if the earth itself was exhaling. It was beautiful in a way that made her feel anxious. Something about it was too quiet.

Cassara stepped into the mist, Spireglass held low, and then she saw it.

A flicker just beyond the shimmer of fog. It was small and quick, affording the barest glimpse of mirror-sheen fur which caught the light like polished silver. It was gone before she could blink or question if it had even been real.

She moved toward where it had disappeared when her eyes caught claw marks on the nearby trunk, deep and fresh. Below them more impressions in the moss, large, spread wide, the spacing of a predator with serious weight behind it.

Cassara knelt, brushing away debris.

Beast prints. The wrong shape for a drake, too small for a leviacat. But the rear pressure, she leaned closer, gauging the depth, suggested a leaper. Possibly a glider.

High rank, she thought. Maybe S-class.

Yes.

This was what she had trained for.

She barely glanced back toward the glade. The silver-furred creature, whatever it had been, was forgotten.

The tracks led her up into rockier terrain, the lush forest thinning into clusters of jagged stone and narrow ledges. The moss here was slippery, the incline steep. Mud clung to her boots, sucking at every step. She slipped once, catching herself with a hiss as her knee slammed against stone.

Thunder rumbled overhead, the only warning she received before the rain began.

Not a soft drizzle, but a sudden, lashing curtain that blurred the world to shadow and water. Within minutes, her hair was soaked, loose curls flattened against her neck, rivulets trailing down her spine. Her ACS flickered erratically, trying to recalibrate. Her pack grew heavier with each step, her coat saturated and clinging.

Still, she climbed.

She couldn't stop now. The tracks curved toward a narrow ledge that hugged the side of a cliff before it opened into a hollow with enough dry space to pitch a temporary camp.

By the time she reached it, her fingers were numb, her clothes were plastered to her skin, and her legs sore from navigating the mud-slick incline. An overhang kept the worst of the rain at bay, and for the first time in hours, she could breathe.

Cassara stripped off her outer layer and wrung it out, teeth chattering, before unpacking a single firestarter crystal from her kit. She cracked it against the stone, and a low, steady flame sprang to life in the center of the little alcove. The light was warm, golden, and she crouched beside it, rubbing her hands together. Steam rose from her skin as the heat slowly soaked in.

Her body ached and her pride simmered. She needed this, to prove that she didn't need a team, and didn't need anyone's help. She would come back with something exceptional, something worthy, no matter what it took.

Hunching closer to the fire, she drew her knees up and lay Spireglass across her lap. The heat licked her skin as she stared into the flame and whispered to herself that tomorrow, tomorrow, would be the day she proved them all wrong.

Cassara woke to silence.

Not the eerie kind, or the kind laced with whispers or distant cries, but the heavy, waiting kind.

The fire had burned down to faint embers. The overhang had kept her dry, but the air was different now, hot, wet, and clinging. Her clothes, still damp from the day before, clung to her skin as she sat up and stretched aching limbs.

Outside the alcove, the forest stirred. Birds she couldn't name trilled high in the canopy, their songs sharp and strange. A glimmer of light filtered through the leaves, dull, colorless. The sun hadn't broken the horizon yet, but it was coming.

So was something else.

Cassara stilled when she saw tracks just beyond the edge of her camp.

Large pawprints, deep-set in the softened earth, leading away from the alcove and into the dense underbrush.

They were fresh.

And Cassara?

She was already moving.

No time for food. No time to second-guess. This could be the same beast she had been tracking the day before, or something new. Either way, she wouldn't let it get away.

Every step through the underbrush soaked her boots anew. Insects whined in her ears. The ACS rig on her bracer buzzed occasionally, reacting to flickers of ambient magic or fauna movement she couldn't see.

Once, a nest of vine-limbed creepers stirred beneath her feet, sharp-limbed and snatching, but she spun Spireglass into a wide arc, severing the writhing roots before they could wrap around her leg.

She didn't stop.

Hours passed and the sun climbed above the trees and the tracks seemed to keep shifting directions. Once, they disappeared entirely, until she spotted a broken fern and a splash of mud against a stone.

Cassara pressed on even as the forest seemed to close in around her, every shadow a threat, every flicker of movement a possibility. The humidity had turned suffocating, curling her damp hair tighter around her temples. Her shirt clung to her back, slick with sweat, and her legs ached from hours of trudging through uneven terrain. Her stomach gave a low, bitter twist of protest, but she ignored it. She had half a ration bar in her pack and no intention of stopping.

Not until she found it.

A rustle up ahead indicated something large cutting through the underbrush. She held her breath and crouched low, easing past a gnarled root to peer through the curtain of leaves.

There, just beyond a break in the trees, a massive form moved like shadow and smoke. Four-legged, broad-shouldered, with muscles that rippled beneath thick, dark fur. The beast didn't lumber, it flowed.

That's it.

Her fingers tightened on the haft of Spireglass and she surged forward without a second thought, pushing branches aside, boots slamming into moss and stone. The world narrowed to the shimmer of that fur, to the pounding of her heart in her throat.

The ledge came out of nowhere—a jagged, half-concealed break in the forest floor, shrouded in vines and shaded by overgrown brush. One moment her foot hit packed earth, the next, there was none.

The world tilted and Cassara fell.

Air rushed past her ears and the breath whooshed from her lungs, stolen by gravity and shock.

She had just enough time to twist, arms flailing. Her hand caught the thick, gnarled curve of a root jutting from the cliff wall. The impact wrenched her shoulder with a violent jolt, a cry of pain ripping from her throat. Her grip nearly failed.

She dangled, her boot tips scraping open air, her breath ragged.

For a second, she thought she might lose it. That her fingers would slip and she'd plummet into whatever waited below.

But she didn't.

Her other hand scrabbled wildly, catching a tangle of moss-slick stone. Dirt crumbled beneath her nails. Her muscles screamed as she fought gravity, arms trembling with effort, shoulder burning with every inch of movement.

Come on. Don't let go.

With a growl that came from somewhere low and guttural inside her, Cassara hauled herself up. Every inch felt like war. Her arms shook. Her core ached. But she didn't stop.

She would not stop.

The edge of the cliff rose beneath her and she scrambled over it, elbows and knees hitting the ground in a graceless heap, breath punching from her lungs as she collapsed in a sprawl.

For a long moment, all she could do was lie there, her cheek pressed to the wet earth, chest heaving, her heartbeat roaring in her ears.

Spireglass glinted just a foot away, half-buried in the moss. She reached for it, fingers curling around the haft like it might anchor her to the world again.

Around her, the forest was still. The beast, whatever it had been, was gone. No sound, no shimmer of movement, just the whisper of wind through the high canopy and the thrum of blood still pounding in her veins.

Cassara shut her eyes.

You're not beaten, she told herself, breath shallow. Not yet.

She forced herself to sit up, every muscle protesting. Her hands were scraped raw, dirt caked beneath her fingernails. A bruise was already blooming across her ribs where she'd slammed into the cliff face. She tested her ankle, rolling it slowly—tender, but functional.

Good enough.

She pushed to her feet, swaying slightly before her balance returned. Spireglass felt heavier than it should in her grip, or maybe she was just that tired. Either way, it didn't matter. She'd come too far to turn back now.

The tracks she'd been following weren't hard to find again—disturbed earth, broken ferns, claw marks gouged deep into bark. Whatever she'd been chasing hadn't gone far.

Cassara wiped her palm along her thigh, trying to ignore the ache in her calves and the pulse that throbbed in her temple like a warning.

She had just picked up the trail again when she realized she wasn't alone.

"You're relentless," came Julian's voice from above, sounding amused. "I'll give you that."

Cassara turned her head slowly, already bristling. He stood on the slope ahead, framed by a tangle of leaves and slanting light. He looked infuriatingly untouched by the Wildes, no mud, no torn fabric, no sign of effort made to survive. Just cool elegance and that faintly mocking curve to his mouth.

At his throat, his Aether Shard pulsed with life which meant he'd already caught his beast.

Damn it.

Cassara gritted her teeth and kept on moving. "Go away."

He fell in beside her anyway, his steps silent. "I thought you'd be happy to see me. I'm certainly happy to see you."

She didn't answer. Her eyes stayed on the trail ahead. The earth was disturbed. The tracks were real.

"I saw the look on your face," Julian continued, quieter now. "At the ruins. Right before you disappeared."

Her pace faltered, just for a second.

"I thought maybe it was the wine," he said, and his smile was softer now, charming in a dangerous way. "But I've had time to think."

Was he seriously doing this now?

Cassara forced a scoff. "You should be careful, Julian, that sort of thing gets you into trouble."

He hummed, not buying it for a second. "Me? Trouble seems to be your specialty these days."

Her stomach turned. There was a quiet fury beneath his words, sharp and cold. The kind of anger that didn't shout, it smiled.

"I don't know what story you've written in your head, Julian," she said. "But I don't have time for it."

He stopped walking. She didn't, not at first, but his next words made her freeze.

"I know you're hiding something, or perhaps someone."

She spun to face him, startled by how close he stood. "This isn't the time or place—"

He took a step closer, casually moving into her space and once again she found herself fighting the urge to step back. As much as he repulsed her, she refused to give him the satisfaction.

"Tell me no one else touched you that night." His hand moved toward her face but stopped short of touching. The impulse to knock it aside was immediate, but she held still.

For the first time in her life, she was afraid of Julian Tremaine and the terrifying, gnawing possibility that he might guess who.

Her thoughts whirled even as she struggled to maintain her composure. She shifted her tone, let her posture soften. "I don't know what you're talking about."

He scoffed and shook his head. "Don't you?"

"Julian—"

"I'm not stupid," he continued. "You think I haven't noticed that something's changed?"

"I told you I don't have time for this," she said, her patience finally reaching its limit. Before she could make her retreat, his hand shot out and curled around the back of her neck, restraining her.

"You can lie if you want," he said, voice low, his thumb stroking the curve of her throat like a lover's touch. "But don't forget, I *know* you. I know what your body says even when your mouth is too proud to speak."

His fingers slid down her arm, slow and deliberate. Cassara stiffened, but didn't move.

"I know what makes you shiver," he murmured, leaning in, breath grazing the curve of her jaw. "What makes you gasp."

His lips brushed just below her ear and she swallowed hard to keep from screaming. "You've been mine for years, Cass. Whether you want to admit it or not."

His fingers tightened and he pulled her closer. "When I find out who it is," he whispered. "I'll make him regret the day he thought he could take what belongs to me."

Finally his hand dropped away and he stepped back, all smiles again, like he hadn't just threatened her.

"See you at pick up," he said quietly, his voice carrying just enough edge to make it sound like a warning. "Good luck, Cassara."

He disappeared into the trees without another word, as silent as he'd arrived.

CHAPTER TWENTY ONE

Focus she told herself, gripping Spireglass tighter. *The tracks. The beast. That's all that matters now.* The undergrowth gave slightly beneath her boots as she moved. She tried to focus on the trail and the clawed impressions in the softened earth, but her thoughts were not where they should've been.

Julian's voice still clung to the edges of her mind, coiled and insidious.

You'll always come back to me.

Like it was an inescapable fate.

He didn't know the truth about Auren, not yet, but he was circling it. If he did find out who had pulled him into the dark that night, Auren would lose everything and so would she.

A marriage to someone like Julian, no matter how unbearable, was still a possibility regardless of her transgressions. But Auren? Instructor. Superior. *Forbidden.* If Julian exposed that secret—

Her heart skipped, not from guilt but fear. Raw, gut-deep fear.

Cassara forced herself to breathe slower, quieter. This wasn't the place for panic. If she failed now, she'd be sent home and nothing else would matter.

The tracks led uphill, where the trees thinned and the underbrush began to give way to far more treacherous terrain—slick, mossy, stone. As she crested the incline, a wide cavern yawned open before her. It was massive. The kind of place that could shelter a dozen creatures, maybe more. The tracks continued straight in, the soil at the mouth disturbed, the stones scattered.

Crouching, she brushed her fingertips against the marks. There were no exit prints. Whatever had gone in, hadn't come back out.

She rose slowly, gaze sweeping the treeline. The sun was already sinking, throwing amber fire across the horizon. She didn't have time to hesitate. The beast was likely nocturnal; if it emerged, it would do so soon.

Cassara unshouldered her pack and set to work.

The binding circle was elegantly simple. A series of pressure glyphs etched into an expandable ring, designed to project a larger boundary when activated. At its center, she placed her aether shard—the one she'd been attuning to since her first day at Vallemont, weeks of her mana soaking into the crystalline structure.

She checked each sigil twice, then pressed her hand to the center ring.

It flared to life with a glow that matched the color of her Codex-bound aura: ember-pale gold. The ring expanded outward, projecting a wider circle of light across the forest floor before fading to near-invisibility. The aether shard began to pulse, sending out waves of mana in steady rhythms—a beacon. A call.

I am open to a bond. Do you accept?

Now all she could do was wait.

She turned to the trees, scanning for height and branch structure. There, a towering spindlevine maple, its limbs wide and easy to navigate. There was no obvious vine infestation but she still tapped its bark with Spireglass once and waited.

When there was no sign of movement, Cassara started to climb.

The bark scraped her palms, her shoulder burned in protest, but she reached a wide crook overlooking the cave entrance and nestled in. From here, she could see everything while she waited.

If this was the beast, then by dawn, it would be hers.

But even as she stilled her breath and settled in for the long watch, her thoughts drifted again. To the press of Auren's body against hers, to Julian's grip on her wrist and his thinly veiled threats, and to the terrible truth that she was already caught in a snare of her own making.

And no trap she laid tonight would be half as dangerous as the one she was already in.

Minutes passed into hours and as the sun set below the horizon, the shadows around her deepened. Her limbs ached from holding so still, and her stomach had been growling since sunset, but her eyes never left the cave's mouth.

Just as she was beginning to wonder if she had miscalculated, there was movement.

Cassara held her breath as a massive shadow stepped from the cave. She recognized the creature instantly—a Cinderback Auroch. S-Rank. Attack class. It was enormous. Easily triple her size. Four-legged, low to the ground, with massive shoulders and gleaming horns that arced back over its skull. The fur along its spine shimmered dark gold and red in the moonlight, almost metallic, and the air around it warped faintly, whether with heat or magic she couldn't tell.

This was it.

This was everything.

The beast stalked toward the ring.

Her pulse pounded and she shifted her weight, preparing to drop from the branch and claim her moment.

Before she could make her move, a silver blur bounced out of the underbrush beneath the tree.

Cassara blinked, confused.

The auroch paused, snorting once, eyes narrowing.

The blur leapt again, small and ridiculous. It paused long enough for Cassara to catch a glimpse of a round little fox-cat-rabbit hybrid with a gleaming mirror-sheen coat and ears too large for its head. Its tail swished like a silk streamer as it bumbled forward with disarming confidence—straight into the binding circle.

Cassara's heart stopped.

"No," she breathed. "No, no, no—"

The moment the creature crossed the threshold, mana threads rose from the pressure glyphs like living things, weaving around the small body in intricate patterns. A sphere of containment formed, shimmering gold and translucent, holding the creature suspended in gentle stasis.

The little beast blinked once, luminous opal-flecked eyes meeting hers through the barrier.

"No!"

The aether shard flared brilliant gold as the bond snapped into place like a lock turning, immediate and irreversible.

The auroch let out a low sound of distress, startled by the sudden surge of magic, and bolted into the trees.

The mana sphere dissolved. The threads retreated. The creature landed on all four paws with a soft thump and a cheerful *mrrp.*

Cassara could only watch in horror.

Her beast. Her moment. Her everything.

Gone.

All that remained was a ridiculously shiny puffball sitting in the center of her binding circle, tail swishing contentedly, like he'd just accomplished something marvelous.

Cassara remained in the tree, stunned silent, rage and disbelief twisting in her chest like a blade.

She had spent days surviving storms, tracking elusive signs, pushing herself to the brink...

And this. This is what she'd bonded with.

The creature canted his head, whiskers twitching, watching her.

Cassara pressed a hand over her mouth, not to stifle a cry, but to keep from screaming.

After several steadying breaths, she climbed down from the tree like a ghost moving through fog. Her muscles ached from stillness, her boots scraped bark and moss, but none of it registered. Not over the roaring silence in her ears.

It wasn't supposed to happen like this.

The beacon should have called something worthy, a beast that was fierce and rare and grand enough to shut every mouth that had ever doubted her. Not... not this.

She approached slowly, not wanting to look at the curled, silver-furred shape sitting just beyond the binding circle's edge. The mana threads had dissolved. The containment sphere was gone. It was free to leave.

But it hadn't.

It just sat there, calm and patient, like it was waiting for her to catch up to something it already understood.

No. No, she could fix this.

She had time.

One day. Twenty hours, give or take. Maybe the bond hadn't fully taken. Maybe the shard's flare had been a warning, not a confirmation. If she could just... reset somehow. Try again. The Cinderback Auroch could still be close by, she still had a chance.

Her chest tightened as she stepped forward. The early morning mist clung to the undergrowth, casting everything in a pale blue haze. The creature's fur shimmered faintly in the gloom, all mirror-sheen and shadow, eyes glowing softly like distant stars. It tilted his head, watching her approach with eerie calm.

As if it had chosen her rather than the other way around.

"This was a mistake," she whispered, stopping a few feet away. "You weren't meant to be here."

The creature blinked slowly. Not scared. Not even wary. Just... present.

Cassara's hands trembled at her sides. Maybe if she didn't get closer. Maybe if she just walked away, the bond wouldn't complete. Maybe—

Her ACS bracer flared to life.

A sharp, crystalline tone rang out as the conduit lines etched across her wrist lit up silver-white, threading up her arm in intricate patterns. Her aether shard flared from the center of the binding circle, pulsing in sync with her ACS.

"No— no, stop," she gasped.

But it was already happening.

The creature's body tensed slightly, then relaxed, curling his tail around himself like he'd been waiting for exactly this.

The sync had locked into place and her ACS now hummed with new resonance, the vibration settling into her bones. A report flickered across the bracer's crystal face:

BEAST LINKED. MALE. CLASS UNKNOWN. COMPATIBILITY... 97.4%.

Her vision blurred and she blinked hard to clear the tears.

She'd felt the shard flare, but she'd hoped—gods, she'd hoped it wasn't permanent yet. That there was still time. That she could undo it somehow.

But the system didn't lie.

The bond had taken root the moment he'd accepted. And now, standing this close, her ACS had registered him, synced with him, locked him into her magical signature permanently.

This wasn't the beast she'd dreamed of. He was small and strange. He looked like a fox and a rabbit and a star had been melted into something too elegant to be threatening. He didn't growl, or snap, or posture.

And worst of all?

He looked at her like he already belonged to her, like he had always known this moment would come.

Cassara backed away, every thought collapsing under the weight of singular horror—she couldn't undo it.

This was what they'd announce at the gala and what she'd be judged for. She'd show up not with a Cinderback Auroch but... whatever this was.

The silence pressed in, not peaceful, but suffocating. The kind of silence that followed ruin.

Was it even worth going back?

Cassara buried her face in her arms.

It hurt. Not even in her pride anymore. It hurt somewhere deeper, in a place she didn't have words for. A hollowed-out ache that echoed *you're not enough* with every breath.

She wanted to scream. She wanted to tear off the ACS, to crush the aether shard into the dirt and forget this ever happened.

But instead, she just sat there feeling small and tired in a way that had nothing to do with travel or pain.

Then... she felt it.

Not a noise or movement.

A presence.

Inside her mind.

It was subtle, gentle. Not invading, just there. Brushing up against the raw edges of her thoughts with quiet curiosity. A flicker of warmth, soft as candlelight against cold stone. She felt it like a breath. No pity, no questions, just comfort.

She leaned into it without thinking and for one suspended heartbeat, it soothed something jagged inside her.

And then she realized what it was.

Her body jerked like she'd been burned.

No.

The bond. It wasn't just locked in. It was active.

The creature had reached for her.

Cassara recoiled from the sensation, shoving it out, if she could even do that. She didn't want its comfort, didn't want its presence in her mind.

Her rejection must have registered because she felt the faintest shift. A quiet withdrawal. Not in pain or anger, just confusion, as if the creature didn't understand why she'd turned away.

The weight of that made her stomach twist. But she refused to feel guilty.

She hadn't asked for this. She hadn't chosen this. And she sure as hell hadn't come into the Wildes to bond with some wide little thing that had ruined everything.

Cassara curled tighter into herself, the bond's fading warmth leaving her even colder than before.

The area was quiet now save for the slow drip of water from the overhang and the faint rustle of leaves stirred by wind.

Cassara remained sitting, staring at nothing.

The creature remained curled a few feet away, still watching her with those wide, uncanny eyes, head tilted like he was waiting for something. She couldn't bear to look at him directly.

Her nails dug into the packed earth beneath her as images began to surface, unbidden and sharp.

Julian's knowing smile when she returned defeated. The way he'd tower over her, satisfied that she'd finally been brought low.

Verena's barely concealed delight, whispering to anyone who'd listen about how the great Cassara Allencourt couldn't even manage what every other first-year had accomplished.

Her father's letter, arriving within days. Cold and self-righteous. *I told you this was folly, Cassara. Pack your things.*

The wedding invitations would go out before summer's end.

The anguish that had been building to suffocating proportions in her chest solidified into something bitter and resigned.

She looked at the creature. He wasn't what she'd wanted. He would never be what she'd wanted. But he was what she had.

"I am Cassara Allencourt," she said quietly. "And apparently, you're all I'm getting."

She pushed herself to her feet, legs unsteady.

The creature yawned, revealing needle-sharp teeth that should have been impressive but just felt like mockery.

Cassara's mouth set in a grim line.

"Come on then," she muttered, moving toward him with all the enthusiasm of someone walking to their own execution.

The binding circle still lay on the ground, inactive now, the aether shard resting at its center. She bent down and retrieved it, the crystal warm against her palm. Her shard. Bonded now.

She turned to the creature, mind scrambling. What had the instructors said about recall? Something about intent, about the bond acting as a conduit. Or was it a command? She tried to remember Thorne's demonstration—had he spoken aloud or just willed it? Her thoughts felt sluggish, tangled.

The creature sat there, staring up at her with those too-intelligent eyes. Waiting. Watching.

Like he knew she had no idea what she was doing.

Heat crawled up her neck. "If you're so smart," she snapped, "then you figure it out."

For a heartbeat, nothing happened.

Then his form began to shimmer, dissolving into particles of light that streamed toward the shard like water flowing downhill. Silver and gold motes swirled in the air before being pulled into the crystal with a soft pulse of warmth.

The shard flared once, then settled, glowing faintly.

Cassara stared at it. She could feel him there—a presence, a weight that hadn't existed before. Not heavy, just... there. Tucked inside the crystal like he'd always belonged.

She hated it.

With a sigh, she looped the leather cord holding the shard around her neck, gathered the binding circle, and started walking.

The ACS bracer pinged after the first hour.

Cassara glanced down at the display. A beacon marker had appeared, pulsing green at the edge of her range. An extraction point. Not the one she'd started from—closer. Maybe two hours away if she kept moving.

The forest passed in a blur of green and shadow. This time there was no tracking to slow her down. Just the singular goal of getting out.

The aether shard rested against her chest, warm and silent. The creature hadn't stirred or attempted to reach out through the bond again. Maybe it had learned his lesson.

Or maybe it was just waiting.

She didn't want to know which.

The terrain shifted as she walked, the dense undergrowth giving way to rockier ground, then to sparse trees and patches of open sky. Her legs ached and her injured arm throbbed with every movement, but she didn't slow.

Two days to get in. Three hours to get out.

Funny how that worked.

The extraction point appeared ahead—a small clearing marked by a ring of glyphs carved into the stone, pulsing with faint blue light. Standard Academy work. She'd passed a dozen of these on the way in, too focused on her hunt to consider using them.

Cassara stopped at the edge of the circle and pulled the emergency flare from her pack.

It was a simple cylinder, etched with runes. Twist the base, and it would send up a colored signal visible for miles. Green for successful bond and ready for pickup. Red for emergency extraction. Yellow for complications.

Her hand hesitated over the base.

Green meant she'd completed the expedition and was coming back with a beast.

With this beast.

She twisted it anyway.

The flare shot into the sky with a sharp hiss, exploding into a burst of brilliant green light that hung in the air like a star. The glyphs in the clearing flared in response, acknowledging the signal.

Now all she had to do was wait.

Cassara sank onto a flat rock at the clearing's edge, letting her pack slide from her shoulders. Her whole body felt heavy, exhausted in a way that went beyond physical strain.

She stared at the aether shard. Still glowing faintly. Still warm.

Still holding the creature that had destroyed everything.

The pickup skiff arrived within the hour.

It was smaller than the main vessel—a retrieval craft meant for ferrying students from extraction points back to the primary skiff. The pilot didn't speak as Cassara climbed aboard, just gestured to the bench seating along the hull.

Two other students were already there. A girl with a bandaged arm and a tired smile and a boy who looked like he hadn't slept in days.

Neither of them looked at her long enough to ask questions.

Cassara was grateful for that.

The skiff lifted with a lurch, propulsion glyphs flaring beneath the hull as it rose above the canopy and banked toward the distant shape of the main vessel. Through the open sides, she could see the Wildes spreading out below—endless green, mist-shrouded and wild.

She'd survived it.

She'd bonded.

And now she had to go back and face what came next.

The main skiff grew larger as they approached, its dark wood hull inlaid with glowing runes that pulsed in rhythmic patterns. She could see figures moving on the deck. Other students. Instructors.

They were waiting.

Her stomach twisted.

The retrieval skiff landed close by with a gentle thud, arcane anchors engaging with a hum of energy. The pilot secured the vessel and lowered the ramp.

Cassara stood, took a deep breath, and forced herself to walk forward.

She saw Gideon first, arms folded, his coat still streaked with dried mud and scuffed in places that hadn't been there before. He looked up the moment her footstep hit the ground. Their eyes met and he offered a short nod of acknowledgement.

Talia was seated on a supply crate, bandaged at the wrist and muttering something to Liri, who looked rumpled and radiant all at once. Evie sat beside her, coat askew, grinning tiredly at something none of them had said aloud.

Julian was there, leaning casually against a railing. When he saw her, that familiar smirk curved his lips upwards.

Liri bounced up from where she'd been sitting beside Evie, both girls looking tired but triumphant. "You made it back! Was it terrible all alone? Did you get something magnificent?"

Cassara managed a smile. "Did you doubt I would?"

"Never," Liri said warmly, though her eyes swept over Cassara's disheveled appearance with obvious concern. "You look..."

"Victorious," Cassara finished smoothly, before Liri could say whatever she'd actually been thinking.

She let her gaze wander until she found him standing with the other instructors, codex in hand, his expression carefully neutral. When their eyes met across the space, she caught the flash of relief that crossed his features, so brief she might have imagined it, but real enough to make her heart squeeze in her chest.

He'd been worried about her.

The thought sent warmth spiraling through her, followed immediately by cold dread. Julian's words echoed in her mind. *I know you're hiding something*. She quickly averted her gaze. She couldn't afford to give either of them away, not with Julian so determined to discover her secret.

"So," Julian called, as he sauntered over to her, "successful hunt?"

The question seemed casual on the surface, but there was something sharp beneath it.

Cassara's hand drifted to the Aether Shard at her throat, feeling its subtle warmth against her skin. Inside, she could sense the creature's presence, like a distant hum she couldn't quite tune out. He had been mercifully quiet during the trek back, curled up in whatever space the shard provided, but she still felt... wrong. Off-balance. Like wearing clothes that didn't quite fit.

"Everything went exactly as planned," she said, injecting just the right amount of smugness into her voice. "But you'll have to wait for the gala like everyone else."

The lie tasted bitter on her tongue, but she delivered it flawlessly. Years of court training, of smiling through galas while her father criticized every breath she took, had taught her how to perform confidence even when her world was crumbling.

Julian's smile widened. "I'm sure it did. You always were good at getting exactly what you wanted."

There it was again, that edge. That knowing tone that made her skin crawl.

"Usually," she agreed, meeting his gaze steadily.

Auren cleared his throat, drawing their attention. "All right, everyone aboard. We're heading back to Vallemont."

As the students began filing up the ramp, Cassara hung back, pretending to adjust her pack straps. In reality, she needed a moment to breathe. To remind herself that she could do this. She'd survived the Wildes. She'd bonded with... something. She would get through the gala, figure out what came next, and—

"Cassara."

Auren's voice was quiet, meant only for her. She turned to find him approaching, his expression carefully neutral but his eyes intense.

"You're all right?" he asked, low enough that the others couldn't hear.

The question caught her by surprise. Well, not the question itself, but rather the tone. Nothing about it felt perfunctory or like he was just checking a box. He actually wanted to know. She couldn't remember the last time someone had asked after her wellbeing like that—like the answer actually mattered to them, not just what it meant for their plans or reputation.

For one dangerous moment, she wanted to tell him everything. About the creature she'd never wanted, Julian's threats, and how scared she was that everything was about to fall apart.

Instead, she pushed it down and smiled. "Never better."

He studied her face and she was afraid he could see through the lie, that he could read the tension in her shoulders, and the careful way she held herself. But he simply nodded.

"Good," he said quietly. "I'm glad you're safe."

The warmth in his voice nearly undid her. There was no judgment, no expectation, just genuine relief that she'd made it back. She started to step closer, drawn to that rare feeling of being seen as more than a name or a ranking or a problem to be managed.

But she caught herself. Julian was watching her from the deck above, and she couldn't risk it.

“See you at the gala, Instructor,” she said instead, injecting just the right amount of formal distance into her voice.

Uncertainty flickered in Auren’s eyes and he stepped aside to let her pass.

As Cassara climbed the ramp, she could feel the weight of multiple gazes on her back. Julian’s calculating stare. Gideon’s quiet assessment. Auren’s concerned attention.

She acknowledged none of them, but rather kept her shoulders squared and her smile in place.

The skiff crested the final ridge, Vallemont rising into view like a mirage of steel and stone. Banners fluttered from the observation decks. Students and faculty lined the platforms, anxiously awaiting the return of the first year cohort.

Cassara stood near the bow, chin high, hands folded loosely behind her back. Her body ached and her feet throbbed. Her beast, if you could even call it that, remained curled and silent within the shard at her neck.

She felt like a cracked mirror, but she kept smiling anyway.

Applause erupted as the skiff hissed and settled into place, ramps lowering with a practiced clatter allowing the students on board to disembark.

As they descended, the crowd parted. The headmistress stood at the base of the platform, flanked by the faculty.

"Welcome home, first-years," Headmistress Kalisandra said, her voice carrying effortlessly through the courtyard. "You've crossed one of the most sacred thresholds in the taming arts and survived. For that alone, you've earned the respect of this academy and all those who came before you."

Murmurs of pride rippled through the gathered students. Liri beamed beside Talia. Gideon, as ever, stood straight-backed and unreadable. Julian rested one hand lazily on his belt, gaze flicking sideways toward Cassara.

She did not meet it.

The Headmistress continued. "Though you have been victorious, remember this. You have returned with bonds still fresh and untested."

The elation in the crowd dimmed.

"Over the next week, you must solidify the bond you have begun. You must learn to communicate with your beast, to understand its nature, to work as a unified pair. Those who cannot achieve this level of partnership will undergo a final assessment."

The words hung heavy in the air. Everyone knew what that meant—potential dismissal. Being sent home in disgrace. For Cassara it meant a life shackled to Julian.

"I must impress upon you the gravity of this task," Kalisandra continued. "It is exceedingly rare for a tamer to receive a second opportunity to bond with a beast. This is your moment. Do not waste it."

Cassara's smile never wavered, but inside, panic clawed at her chest. A week to bond with a creature she couldn't even stand to acknowledge. A week to somehow make partnership work with something that felt more like a cosmic joke than a worthy companion.

She could do this. She had to.

A hush fell across the courtyard. Even the wind seemed to hold its breath.

"That being said, tonight I implore you to rest, savor this moment, celebrate this milestone. Tomorrow the real test begins."

With that, the headmistress took her leave and the students began to disperse, some elated, most pale with renewed anxiety.

Cassara paid them no mind and kept walking, each step echoing with more dread than triumph. Her creature stirred faintly in the shard, a flicker of awareness she shoved back down like a secret too dangerous to voice.

As they entered the academy proper, the weight of the next week settled on Cassara's shoulders. Seven days to forge a partnership she didn't want with a creature she couldn't respect.

Seven days to save her future.

CHAPTER TWENTY TWO

The bonding chambers were tucked into Vallemont's lower levels, each one a small sanctuary of stone and soft light designed to foster the delicate connection between tamer and beast. Cassara sat cross-legged on the moss-cushioned floor, watching her creature with mounting frustration.

It had been an hour. One hour of trying to establish the most basic communication, and what did she have to show for it?

A small, silver-furred menace that was currently batting at dust motes like they were the most fascinating things in existence.

"Focus," she said quietly, trying to project calm authority. "We need to work on synchronization."

The creature paused mid-swipe, tilted his head at her with those impossibly large eyes, then promptly scampered up to the nearest wall to investigate a crack in the stonework.

Cassara pressed her palms against her temples. Through the walls, she could hear muffled sounds from the neighboring chambers. Soft laughter from one direction. The rhythmic thud of coordinated movement from another. Success. Progress. Everything she wasn't achieving.

A gentle knock on her door made her straighten. She quickly pressed her palm to the Aether Shard at her throat, recalling the creature in a flash of silver light just as it was mid-pounce toward a spider.

"Come in."

Liri peeked inside, her face glowing with exhaustion and joy. "How's it going?"

Cassara glanced around the now-empty chamber. "Wonderfully. How about you?"

"Oh, Cass, it's incredible!" Liri's eyes sparkled as she stepped into the chamber. "I can't show you yet, obviously, but when I laugh? She sings. Sings! This beautiful, haunting melody that makes my heart feel like it might burst."

Cassara's smile felt brittle. "That sounds amazing."

Liri bounced slightly on her toes. "What about yours? Any breakthroughs?"

"We're taking things slowly," Cassara said, her hand unconsciously drifting to the shard where she could feel the creature's presence, mercifully quiet for once. "Building trust."

"That's wise. Gideon mentioned his took a while to warm up too, but now they've found their rhythm." Liri's expression softened. "You look tired. Are you getting enough sleep?"

"I'm fine."

Liri didn't look convinced, but she didn't push. "Well, I should get back. We're working on something called harmonic resonance. I have no idea what that means, but it sounds important."

After Liri left, Cassara waited a full minute before pressing her palm to the Aether Shard again. Silver light spilled from the crystal, coalescing into the familiar small form of her creature.

He materialized in the exact same position he had been in when she'd recalled it mid-pounce, tiny paws stretched toward where the spider had been. Finding nothing there, he landed with a confused chirp and looked around the chamber as if wondering where his prey had gone.

"The spider left," Cassara said flatly.

Why?

The question caught her by surprise. It was the first time the creature had spoken to her since they'd returned from the Wildes.

He tilted his head at her, ears twitching, then padded over to investigate the spot where Liri had been standing. He sniffed delicately at the air, nose wrinkling.

She smells happy, came the soft whisper in her mind. *Why don't you smell happy?*

Cassara stared at him. "Did you just... analyze her emotional state through scent?"

The creature blinked at her with those impossibly large eyes, tail swishing uncertainly. *Was I not supposed to?*

For a moment, Cassara felt a flicker of intrigue. An empathic creature that could read emotional states could actually be useful in certain situations. Strategic, even.

Then the creature spotted another dust mote floating in a shaft of sunlight and immediately forgot she existed, leaping after it with renewed enthusiasm.

The flicker of hope died as quickly as it had come.

"Focus," she said, more to herself than to the creature. "We need to work on basic commands."

But even as she opened the bonding manual again, she couldn't quite forget that moment of unexpected insight. Or the fact that it had been right, Liri had smelled happy. She had been happy. Radiantly, obviously happy.

Unlike herself.

The next morning brought no improvement.

If anything, her creature seemed more distracted than ever, and somehow, impossibly, kept escaping the Aether Shard without her permission.

The first time it happened, Cassara had been reviewing tactical formations in the library when she felt the telltale warmth of materialization. She looked down to find him curled up in her lap, tiny paws tucked beneath its chin, fast asleep.

"How did you get out?" she hissed, quickly scooping him up and glancing around the library. Thankfully, the section she'd chosen was deserted.

He blinked at her sleepily and gave a soft chirp, as if this were perfectly normal behavior.

The second time she'd been walking to her afternoon lecture when she felt that familiar flutter of presence. She spun around to find him batting at flower petals that were drifting down from the academy's garden terraces, completely oblivious to the fact that half a dozen students could see it if they just looked down.

She'd barely managed to recall it before a second year named Randall rounded the corner.

Cassara was hurrying away from the gardens when she nearly collided with someone rounding the corner.

"Careful there."

Auren's hands came up to steady her, and for a moment she was close enough to catch the familiar scent of leather and chalk dust. Her pulse jumped at the contact—or maybe it was still racing from nearly being discovered.

"Instructor Veth," she said, stepping back quickly. "My apologies."

Something flickered in his eyes, confusion, perhaps, at the formal address. "Cassara, are you-"

"I'm fine. Just late for my next class." She clutched her books tighter, using them as a shield. "If you'll excuse me."

She moved to step around him, but he shifted slightly, not blocking her path but clearly wanting to continue the conversation.

"You've seemed distracted lately," he said. "If there's anything—"

"Everything is perfectly fine, Instructor." The title felt like glass on her tongue. "I should go."

This time she didn't wait for a response, walking briskly down the corridor without looking back. She could feel his gaze following her, and could practically sense his confusion at her sudden coldness.

It wasn't until she was safely around the next corner that she realized her hands were trembling.

She hated it. The confusion in his eyes, the careful distance she'd forced between them, it felt wrong. Everything about this situation felt wrong. But it also felt necessary.

She was still replaying the conversation in her mind when she felt it again, the subtle shift in the air that meant her creature had somehow freed itself from the Aether Shard.

Again.

"Damn it," she grumbled, spinning around in the corridor. Where was he this time?

She hurried toward her dormitory, checking every alcove and shadow along the way. Other students passed her with curious glances as she peered under benches and behind tapestries, but she was beyond caring about appearances.

She finally found him in the dormitory common area, somehow wedged upside down in one of the shoe cubbies near the entrance, looking perfectly content.

"You can't keep doing this," she said, scooping him up and retreating quickly to her room before anyone could see. Her hands were still shaking, from the Auren encounter, from the constant fear of discovery, from everything.

She held it at eye level once her door was safely closed. "Someone is going to see you."

He tilted his head, ears drooping slightly. *But I get lonely.*

The simple admission hit her harder than she'd expected. She set him down on her desk with perhaps more gentleness than strictly necessary.

"We have scheduled bonding time," she said firmly. "You need to stay in the shard until then."

Why do you hate me?

There it was again. That soft, uncertain question that made her chest tighten with guilt she had no business feeling.

She didn't answer. How could she explain that she didn't hate him, exactly? That her frustration had nothing to do with what he was and everything to do with what it represented? Every mocking smile Verena might wear. Every expectation her father would wield like a blade. Every whispered conversation about how the great Cassara Allencourt had managed to bond with something so... ordinary.

Why are you so sad?

The second question was worse than the first. Not accusatory or confused, but genuinely concerned. As if this tiny, escape-artist of a creature actually cared about her emotional state.

Cassara shoved the thought away with such force that her shard pulsed hot at her throat, the connection fraying for a breath before settling again.

The creature flinched, ears flattening against his head. *I'm sorry. I didn't mean to make you angry.*

"I'm not angry," she said quietly, though they both knew it was a lie. "I'm just... we need to work on staying put."

She reached for the shard to recall him, but the creature had already padded over to her pen case, investigating it with the same curiosity he showed everything else. When he looked back at her, there was something almost hopeful in those too-large eyes.

Can we practice now? I want to learn.

Despite everything, Cassara felt her expression soften slightly. He wasn't malicious. He just didn't understand. And the worst part was... he wanted to.

"Fine," she said. "But this time, you have to actually listen."

The creature's entire body seemed to perk up, tail swishing with what could only be described as excitement.

Ten minutes later, she found him hanging upside down from her curtain rod, having apparently decided that was the most comfortable position from which to watch her demonstrate basic commands.

She buried her face in her hands and wondered if it was too late to become a hex mage instead.

Cassara was halfway across the training field when she saw him.

Auren stood at the center of the upper-year practice circle, barking corrections at a group of third-years running formation drills. Sunlight caught the edges of his black hair, and even from this distance, she could see the power in the way he moved, the quiet authority that made students snap to attention.

She should have looked away and kept walking toward Nareen's combat class like nothing had happened. Instead, she found herself slowing, her grip tightening on Spireglass's haft.

As if sensing her gaze, Auren turned.

Their eyes met across the field, and for one suspended moment, the rest of the world seemed to fade. His expression shifted to surprise, then something deeper, warmer in a way that made her pulse quicken despite every rational thought telling her to keep moving.

She was about to offer a brief smile in return when he abruptly turned back to his students, but not before she caught the frustration that flickered across his features.

That's when she felt an arm slip around her shoulders from behind.

Julian's voice was warm honey in her ear, his hand settling just over her pounding heart. "Interesting view?"

Cassara stiffened but didn't pull away. She couldn't, not without making a scene in front of half the academy. "I was just heading to class."

"Mmm." His breath stirred the hair at her temple. "You seemed rather... focused. Tell me, is it one of the third-years?"

The question sent ice through her veins. "What?"

"Your mysterious admirer." Julian's fingers traced along her collarbone, casual and possessive. "I've been watching. The way you look at things. People in particular." His voice dropped lower. "Is it Garrett? He's been staring at you during meals. Or perhaps Davies—he did ask you to spar with him during open training."

Relief and terror warred in her chest. He suspected a student. Not an instructor. Not Auren.

"You're imagining things," she said, proud of how steady her voice sounded.

"Am I?" Julian's arm tightened slightly. "Will you tell me which one? I promise I won't be too harsh with him."

Her pulse thudded against his arm, traitorous and loud.

"There is nothing to tell."

"I could guess," he offered, still close enough that his lips almost brushed her skin.

The casual threat in his tone made her skin crawl. "There's no one, Julian."

"We both know that's not true." He pressed a kiss to her temple, soft and chilling. "But don't worry. I'll figure it out eventually."

He released her as suddenly as he'd grabbed her, stepping back with that familiar, charming smile.

"Don't be late for class," he said lightly, as if they'd just been discussing the weather.

Cassara forced herself to walk away at a normal pace, every instinct screaming at her to run. Behind her, she could feel Julian's gaze following her across the field.

And somewhere to her left, though she didn't dare look, she knew Auren was watching too.

Cassara pushed her food around her plate, her appetite long since vanished. She couldn't stop thinking about that moment on the training field, the way Auren had looked at her, then deliberately turned away. Had he seen Julian? Was that why he'd averted his gaze so quickly, so pointedly?

The memory of Julian's arm around her, his breath against her ear, made her skin crawl all over again. The casual possessiveness, the veiled threats. And underneath it all, the terrifying knowledge that he was getting closer to the truth.

"Mind if I join you?"

Cassara looked up to find Sonia approaching with her lunch tray, blonde hair perfectly styled despite the afternoon heat. Without waiting for an answer, she slid into the seat across from Cassara with practiced grace.

"You look tired," Sonia observed, her tone carrying just enough concern to sound genuine. "The bonding process taking its toll?"

"I'm fine," Cassara replied automatically.

"Of course you are." Sonia's smile was bright, but there was something calculating in her pale blue eyes. "I'm just so excited to see what you managed to bond with. Four days until the gala, can you believe it? It feels like we just got back from the Wildes."

Four days. The reminder hit Cassara like a physical blow. Four days to figure out how to present her creature, her butterfly-chasing, curtain-hanging, impossible little creature, to the entire academy without becoming a laughingstock.

"Time does fly," she managed.

“Is it just me,” Liri said, settling beside Cassara with her own tray, “or have Vash and Jonas been around a lot lately?”

Sonia’s eyebrows rose with interest. “Oh? What do you mean?”

Cassara looked up from her barely touched meal, a new thread of unease weaving through her already frayed nerves. “Have they?”

“I mean everywhere we go, there they are.” Liri lowered her voice, glancing around the dining hall. “Yesterday I saw Jonas in the library when you were there, Cass. And this morning, Vash was lurking near the bonding chambers when I came out of my session.”

A chill ran down Cassara’s spine. “They’re first-years too. They have every right to be in those places.”

“I guess,” Liri said, but she didn’t sound convinced. “It just feels off. Like they’re watching for something.”

Or someone, Cassara thought, but kept the observation to herself. Julian’s words echoed in her mind: *I’ll figure it out eventually.*

“How paranoid,” Sonia said with a light laugh, though her eyes had sharpened with interest. “Though I suppose the pressure is getting to all of us. Some more than others.” Her gaze flicked meaningfully to Cassara’s untouched plate. “You really should eat something. You’ll need your strength for the final preparations.”

“Since when were you so concerned about my health, Sonia?”

"I care about all my friends." Sonia leaned forward slightly, voice dropping to a conspiratorial whisper. "Between you and me, I think everyone's a bit anxious about the reveals. Though I suppose those of us who bonded with something... impressive... have less to worry about."

The comment hit its mark perfectly. Cassara's fingers tightened around her fork, but she kept her expression neutral. "I'm sure everyone will do fine."

"Oh, I'm certain you will," Sonia said sweetly. "After all, you're so good at making the best of... challenging situations."

Liri frowned, clearly picking up on the undercurrent of hostility. "What's that supposed to mean?"

"Nothing at all," Sonia replied, her smile never wavering. "Just that Cassara has always been remarkably adaptable. Haven't you, Cass?"

Before Cassara could respond, Sonia was already standing, gathering her things. "Well, I should get back to my bonding session. Not much time left, can't waste a moment."

She paused, looking down at Cassara with that same false concern. "Do try to eat something. And maybe get some rest. You look like you haven't been sleeping well."

After she left, Liri stared after her with obvious confusion. "What was that about?"

Cassara watched Sonia's retreating figure, noting how she stopped to speak briefly with a group of students at another table. Even from here, she could see them glancing in her direction.

A cold thread of unease worked its way down her spine. The way Sonia had said *impressive*. The pointed comment about *challenging situations*. Did she know? Had she somehow seen the creature when he'd popped out of the shard uninvited?

No. That was impossible. Cassara had been careful, always alone when it happened.

But still. The doubt lingered, small and insidious.

"Nothing," she said quietly, forcing the worry down. "Just Sonia being Sonia."

The bonding chamber was eerily quiet at this hour, the soft glow of the practice runes casting long shadows across the stone walls. Cassara sat cross-legged on the stone floor, her creature perched on a low stone ledge nearby, watching her.

It was well past midnight and she should have been in bed hours ago, but sleep seemed impossible when every passing day brought her closer to the gala and no closer to a functional bond.

"Let's try again," she said, holding out her hand. "Come here."

The creature tilted its head, ears twitching. He padded over obediently enough, but when she tried to guide him through a simple synchronization exercise, he immediately became distracted by a moth that had found its way into the chamber.

"Focus," Cassara said, more sharply than intended.

I am focusing, came the soft response in her mind. *The moth is very interesting.*

"The moth is not part of our training."

Why can't training be interesting too?

Cassara pressed her palms against her temples. Three days until the gala, and she couldn't even get her creature to pay attention for more than thirty seconds.

Around them, the other bonding chambers were dark and silent. Everyone else had made progress. Everyone else had figured this out and yet here she was watching her creature chase insects.

You're sad again, the creature observed, abandoning the moth to study her face. *Why are you always sad?*

"I'm not sad," she lied. "I'm frustrated."

Is there a difference?

The innocent question hit harder than it should have. Cassara looked at her creature—really looked at him. The silver fur that caught the light like star-shine. The intelligent eyes that seemed to see too much. The way he tried so hard to understand her, even when she pushed him away.

"I wanted something different," she admitted quietly. "Something that would make people respect me."

Don't they respect you now?

"Not enough." The words tasted bitter. "Never enough."

The creature's ears drooped slightly. *I'm sorry I'm not what you wanted.*

Guilt twisted in her chest. This wasn't the creature's fault. It was hers. Her pride, her expectations, her inability to see past what she thought she needed to what she actually had.

"It's not your fault," she said softly. "It's mine. I just don't know how to—"

A sound from the corridor made her freeze. Footsteps, slow and deliberate, coming closer.

No one should be down here at this hour. The bonding chambers were locked after evening sessions ended. She'd had to get special permission to practice late.

Cassara quickly pressed her palm to the Aether Shard, recalling her creature in a flash of silver light just as the chamber door opened.

The man who entered was no one she recognized. Middle-aged, unremarkable in appearance, wearing clothes that suggested money but not nobility. He moved with the quiet confidence of someone who belonged wherever he happened to be.

"Miss Allencourt," he said, his voice smooth and cultured. "Forgive the intrusion."

"How did you get in here?" Cassara's hand drifted instinctively toward where Spireglass would have been if she'd brought it.

"I have my ways." He smiled, and it wasn't entirely pleasant. "This isn't my first visit to Vallemont, I assure you. Though the security has improved since my student days."

"You're not supposed to be here."

"Many of the best solutions involve things we're not supposed to do." He stepped further into the chamber, hands clasped behind his back. "Word is you're having some difficulty with your bonding process."

Cassara's blood turned to ice. "I don't know what you're talking about."

"Of course you don't." His smile widened. "But perhaps you'd be interested in a solution to a problem you definitely don't have."

He reached into his coat and withdrew a small leather pouch. From it, he produced six Aether Shards, each one pulsing with a different colored light.

"A-rank and S-rank beasts," he said casually, setting them on the stone ledge where her creature had been sitting moments before. "A simple swap, and your troubles are over. No one would ever know."

Cassara stared at the shards, her heart pounding. Each one represented everything she'd dreamed of. Power. Prestige. The kind of beast that would make her father proud, that would silence every doubt and whisper.

"You're talking about cheating," she said, though the words felt hollow.

"I'm talking about practical solutions to unfortunate circumstances." He gestured toward the shards. "Take your pick. The fire drake is particularly impressive, bred from champion stock. Or perhaps the storm hawk? Magnificent in aerial combat."

Her fingers twitched toward the shards almost involuntarily. A fire drake. She could picture it now, sleek and deadly, breathing flames that would make the entire academy gasp in awe. Her father's face when he received word that his daughter had bonded with an S-Rank drake. The look of shocked respect in Julian's eyes. The way Verena's smug confidence would crumble.

"The storm hawk," she whispered, almost to herself. "What can it do?"

"Lightning strikes. Flight speeds that put pegasi to shame." The stranger's voice was hypnotic, painting pictures of glory she could almost taste. "Imagine walking into that gala with such a creature at your side."

She *could* imagine it. Could see herself standing tall as the crowd fell silent, watching her storm hawk spread its magnificent wings. No whispers about disappointing bonds. No pity or laughter.

No more marriage contract hanging over her head like an executioner's blade.

"My father," she said quietly, her voice barely audible. "He expects me to fail. He's already planning my wedding."

"Ah." The stranger nodded with understanding. "Family expectations. Always so... limiting. But this could change everything, couldn't it? Success has a way of rewriting the rules."

Did it? He wasn't wrong, it would change everything, but at what cost?

Her hand moved closer to the shards, hovering just inches above the storm hawk's crystal. The light within pulsed like a heartbeat.

But then another memory surfaced. Small paws tucked beneath a tiny chin as her creature slept in her lap. The innocent questions. The way it had apologized for not being what she wanted, as if its existence was somehow a burden she had to bear.

"What happens to my current bond?" she asked.

The stranger shrugged. "Released back to the wild, most likely. Or used for training purposes. Does it matter? It's clearly unsuitable for your needs."

I get lonely. Can we practice now? I want to learn.

Cassara frowned, suddenly feeling defensive of the creature she didn't even want. "It's not unsuitable. It's just... different."

"Different doesn't win competitions, or impress fathers, or silence critics." His voice grew softer, more persuasive. "You know what they'll say when you reveal your current bond. You know how they'll look at you."

She did know. She could already hear the whispers, see the barely concealed smirks. Poor Cassara Allencourt, reduced to bonding with something so disappointing. Her father would read the reports with that familiar expression of resigned disappointment. Julian would comfort her with false sympathy while secretly reveling in her failure.

The marriage contract would be signed within the month.

"I could be powerful," she said, more to herself than to him. "I could be everything they expect me to be."

"You could be more than they expect," he corrected. "You could be legendary."

Her fingers trembled as they moved closer to the storm hawk's shard. Just one touch. One moment of decision, and everything would change. She would walk into that gala as the tamer she'd always dreamed of being.

But even as she reached for it, she heard her creature's voice again. *I'm sorry I'm not what you wanted.*

The memory stopped her cold. When had anyone ever apologized to her for simply existing? When had anyone ever tried so hard to please her, despite getting nothing but coldness in return?

"He chose me," she whispered.

"I beg your pardon?"

"My creature. He chose me." She pulled her hand back slightly, staring at the shards with growing uncertainty.

"Sentimental attachment," the stranger said dismissively. "Hardly a basis for strategic decision-making."

But it wasn't sentiment, was it? It went deeper and felt suspiciously like integrity.

She wanted to win on her own terms, she'd always wanted that. The storm hawk might bring her victory, but it would be a hollow one.

A lie she'd have to carry for the rest of her life.

CHAPTER TWENTY THREE

"I ..." she began, then stopped, still staring at the shards.

The internal war raged on. Fear of failure warring with the need to do what was right. The desperate desire for her father's approval fighting against the small voice that whispered she might be making the biggest mistake of her life.

"I can't," she said finally, the words barely above a whisper. "I can't do this."

The poacher's expression remained passive. "Are you certain?" he asked smoothly. "Once I leave, this opportunity won't—"

Footsteps echoed in the corridor outside. Distant, but approaching.

The poacher's head snapped toward the door. For a heartbeat, he went perfectly still, listening.

"Unfortunate," he said quietly, scooping up the shards in one sweep of his hand and tucking them away. "Most unfortunate."

He gave a short bow and slipped through the door, gone as quickly and silently as he'd arrived. The latch clicked shut behind him.

Cassara stood frozen, staring at the empty space where the shards had been. Her heart hammered against her ribs. The room felt too small suddenly, the air too thin.

She'd been tempted. Gods, she'd been so tempted.

Her hands trembled as she pressed them against her thighs, trying to steady her breathing. The weight of what she'd just refused settled over her—not relief, not pride, just exhaustion.

The footsteps grew louder, closer, and her pulse spiked. Whoever was coming would find her here, alone, looking guilty. Would they know? Could they tell just by looking at her that she'd been offered a deal?

The door opened.

Auren stepped inside.

He moved with his usual quiet grace, but there was something different in the set of his shoulders, the careful way he closed the door behind him. His gaze swept the room once before finding hers, and she saw relief flicker across his features.

"There you are," he said, his gaze sweeping the room before settling on her again. "I've been looking for you."

Cassara's heart hammered against her ribs. Did he know? Had he heard something? Seen someone leaving? Her mind raced through possibilities, each one more terrifying than the last.

"I was just finishing up," she said, taking a step toward her things. "I should head back to the dormitory."

But Auren was already moving closer, concern creasing his brow.

"Hey." He reached out to touch her arm. "Are you all right? You look—"

She jerked back from his touch like it burned, wrapping her arms around herself. "I'm fine. I just need to go."

The words came out harsher than she meant for them to, and she saw him freeze, his hand still extended outward. His expression shifted, concern giving way to hurt, then something harder.

"Cassara." His voice was quiet, but there was steel beneath it. "What's going on?"

"Nothing." She moved toward the door, but he stepped sideways making it clear he wasn't going to let her escape without an explanation. "Auren, please. Someone could see—"

"There's no one here but us." His eyes searched her face, and she could see him cataloging every detail, the way her hands shook, how she wouldn't meet his gaze, the careful distance she kept between them. "The other training rooms are empty."

"That doesn't matter." She hugged herself tighter, wishing she could disappear. "We can't keep doing this."

"Doing what?" The question was soft, but she heard the edge creeping in. "Having conversations? Because that's all this is, Cassara. Two people talking."

But they both knew it wasn't that simple. Even now, with several feet separating them, she could feel the pull of him. The way her body wanted to lean toward his warmth, the way her pulse quickened just from being in the same room.

"You know it's more than that," she whispered.

"No, I don't." He took another step closer, and this time she had nowhere to retreat. "Because you won't tell me what's wrong. For days now, you've been treating me like a stranger. In public, I can understand. But here? Now? When it's just us?"

His voice cracked slightly on the last words, and the vulnerability in it nearly undid her.

"I'm trying to protect us both," she said desperately.

"From what?" He stepped closer. "Cassara, talk to me. Please."

She wanted to. Gods, how she wanted to tell him everything. But the image of Julian's satisfied smile, the way he'd touched her with such possessive confidence, it all crashed over her at once.

"I can't," she breathed.

Something snapped and Auren's hands came up to frame her face, gentle but insistent, forcing her to look at him.

"Yes, you can," he insisted. "Whatever it is, whatever's frightening you this badly, you can tell me."

The tenderness in his touch, the way he looked at her like she was something precious, broke through her defenses like a dam bursting.

"Julian knows," she whispered.

Auren went very still, his thumbs tracing along her cheekbones. "Knows what?"

"Not about you. Not specifically. But he knows someone was with me that night. He's been asking questions, making... implications." The words tumbled out in a rush, relief and terror warring in her chest. "He said he'd figure it out eventually. That it doesn't matter who I... that in the end I'll still belong to him."

The change in Auren was immediate and frightening. The gentleness in his touch remained, but his eyes went cold, dangerous in a way she'd never seen before.

"The hell you will," he said, voice low and deadly.

The possessive fury in his voice terrified her almost as much as it thrilled her. She could see the storm building behind his eyes, could practically feel the violence he was holding back.

"He can ruin everything, Auren. His family—he could destroy you." She pressed her palms against his chest, feeling the rapid thunder of his heartbeat beneath her hands. "Promise me you won't do anything reckless."

"Reckless?" His laugh was sharp, bitter. "You think confronting him would be reckless?"

"I think it would be stupid," she said desperately. "And dangerous. If he even suspects you're the one, he won't need proof."

"Then what?" His hands tightened slightly on her face, not painful but insistent. "You'll just keep letting him terrorize you? Let him stake his claim while you suffer in silence?"

"I can handle Julian."

"How?" The question cut through her protests like a blade. "By avoiding me? By pretending nothing happened between us? Because that strategy isn't working, Cassara. He's only getting bolder and I… I am tired of pretending."

She opened her mouth to argue, to insist she had everything under control, but the words died in her throat. Because he was right. Julian was getting bolder. More possessive. More certain of his eventual victory.

"I'll figure something out," she said weakly.

"Will you?" Auren's voice dropped to a whisper, his breath warm against her cheek. "Because from where I'm standing, it looks like you're drowning. Avoiding me, avoiding this, isn't going to save either of us."

"Auren, please—"

His mouth crashed against hers with desperate hunger, swallowing her protests in a kiss that was raw and claiming. There was nothing gentle about it this time, it was need and frustration and days of forced restraint finally snapping.

Cassara melted into him despite herself, her hands curling in his shirt as she kissed him back with equal desperation. This was what she'd been denying herself, what she'd been pushing away out of fear. The heat, the connection, the way he made her feel like she was coming alive.

When he finally pulled back, they were both breathing hard.

"This," he said roughly, his forehead pressed against hers, "is not something you can just handle or figure out and I'm not going to stand by and watch Julian destroy it."

She stared up at him, seeing the fierce determination in his eyes, the way he looked at her like she was worth fighting for. When had anyone ever looked at her like that?

"I'm scared," she whispered, the admission torn from somewhere deep inside her. "Of losing you."

"Hey." His thumbs brushed away tears she didn't even realize had fallen. "You're not going to lose me. Not to him. Not to anyone."

The tenderness in his voice, the absolute certainty, was too much. All the fear and frustration and desperate longing she'd been holding back came rushing to the surface.

"I've missed you," she breathed. "These past few days, pretending you meant nothing to me, it's been killing me."

His expression shifted, the anger giving way to something deeper, hungrier. "Show me," he said quietly. "Show me how much you've missed me."

This time, she was the one who closed the distance between them, pouring weeks of suppressed longing into the kiss. His response was immediate and overwhelming, his hands sliding into her hair, angling her head to deepen the contact until she was drowning in the taste and heat of him.

"Cassara," he groaned against her lips.

Her hands found the buttons of his shirt, fingers fumbling with urgent need. She needed to feel him, needed the reassurance of skin against skin and to prove to herself that this was real.

He helped her, shrugging out of the fabric before his hands found the hem of her training shirt. The question in his eyes was clear, and she answered by raising her arms, letting him lift the garment away.

The cool air of the chamber kissed her heated skin, but it was nothing compared to the fire in his gaze as he looked at her.

"Beautiful," he whispered, his hands skimming along her sides with reverent care. "So damn beautiful."

His hands mapped the curve of her waist, fingers tracing patterns along her ribs that made her shiver. When his thumbs brushed just beneath the curve of her breasts, she gasped, arching into his touch.

"I've thought about this," he murmured, pressing kisses along her jaw, down the column of her throat. "About touching you like this. Every night since the ruins."

His mouth found the sensitive spot where her neck met her shoulder, and she made a sound that was half sigh, half moan. Her hands explored the broad expanse of his chest, marveling at the play of muscle beneath skin.

"Auren," she breathed.

He backed her against the stone wall with deliberate purpose, his body caging her in. The cool stone against her bare back was a stark contrast to the heat radiating from him, and the sensation made her dizzy with want.

His mouth traveled lower, pressing open-mouthed kisses along her collarbone before finding the swell of her breast. When his tongue flicked against her nipple, she cried out, fingers threading through his dark hair.

"I love the sounds you make," he murmured against her skin, lavishing attention on first one breast, then the other.

Cassara's skin tingled at his praise, a flush spreading across her chest and up her neck. Her body was a live wire, every nerve ending electrified by his touch. When he drew her nipple into his mouth again, she felt the sensation echo between her legs, an answering pulse of desire.

"I can't help it," she admitted breathlessly. "You make me feel things I never—"

Her words dissolved into a gasp as his teeth grazed the sensitive peak, sending sparks of pleasure racing through her. His hand traced the curve of her waist, fingers splaying across her ribs before drifting lower. The anticipation was almost unbearable as his touch skimmed her abdomen, pausing at the laces of her pants.

With deft movements that spoke of his combat training, Auren loosened the ties while his mouth continued its sweet torture on her breasts. Cassara's head fell back, her eyes fluttering closed as sensation overwhelmed her.

"Is this still alright?" he asked as he began to ease her pants lower.

"Please," was all she could manage, her hips shifting restlessly against him.

His fingers slipped beneath the waistband, stroking the sensitive skin just below her navel. Cassara's breathing stuttered as he ventured lower, through the soft curls until he found the slick heat of her. When his finger slid against her she bit her lip to stifle a moan.

"Don't hold back," he commanded softly. "I want to hear every sound." His eyes were dark with desire as he watched her reactions. His finger circled her entrance, gathering moisture before sliding up to brush against her clit.

Cassara gasped, clutching at his shoulders, her nails leaving half-moon impressions in his skin.

When the finger finally slipped inside her, she let out a whimper, her inner walls clenching, her body instinctively seeking more.

He added a second finger alongside the first, stretching her gently. His thumb found her clit, circling it until she was quivering with need.

"That's it," Auren whispered against her neck, his breath hot on her skin. "Let me hear you."

Another whimper escaped her lips, soft and vulnerable. Her hips bucked against his hand, seeking more pressure, more friction, more of everything he offered.

"Auren," she moaned again, her voice cracking as his fingers curled inside her. "Please," she begged, though she wasn't entirely sure what she was begging for. Her body knew, even if her mind couldn't articulate it.

His free hand tangled in her hair, tugging gently to expose her throat. His mouth descended, teeth grazing the tender skin where her pulse hammered wildly. The feel of his fingers between her thighs and his mouth on her neck drew a low cry from deep within her.

Her breasts heaved against his bare chest, sensitive nipples brushing against heated skin. Each point of contact sent new sparks of pleasure coursing through her veins.

As his thumb increased its pressure, circling faster, Cassara felt herself climbing higher. Her thighs began to tremble, muscles tensing as her body chased the release it craved.

"I can't—" she gasped, eyes flying open to meet his gaze. The intensity there nearly undid her, hunger and tenderness mingled in equal measure.

"You can," he assured her, his voice a rumble she felt more than heard. "Let go for me, Cassara."

As if on command, the wave crested and broke. She cried out his name, a sound that started deep in her chest and emerged as something between a sob and a scream. Her body clenched rhythmically around his fingers as pleasure radiated outward from her core, washing through her limbs in tingling ripples.

Auren worked her through it, slowing his movements as the aftershocks rippled through her. When she finally sagged against him, boneless and panting, he withdrew his hand and wrapped his arm around her waist to steady her.

"You're exquisite," he whispered against her hair.

Cassara looked up at him through half-lidded eyes, taking in his flushed face and the barely contained hunger in his gaze. A newfound boldness surged through her, washing away the last of her nervousness.

"I want more," she said, her voice hoarse but determined. "I want all of you."

Auren's gaze intensified at her words, the last thread of his restraint snapping visibly. He claimed her mouth with savage intensity, his lips crushing against hers with a groan that reverberated through her body. Cassara gasped into his kiss, her back pressing harder against the wall behind her as his hands found her hips.

"Are you sure?" he breathed against her lips.

"Yes," she whispered.

His fingers dragged her pants down her thighs with agonizing slowness.

Heat bloomed across Cassara's face, but she refused to look away. The vulnerability of standing half-naked before him was overwhelming, yet strangely empowering. Her damp undergarments followed her pants, sliding down her legs until she could kick them aside.

His hand slid between her thighs again and he brought his lips close to her ear.

"I want to taste you," he whispered, his lips trailing down her neck as his fingers continued to tease her.

Cassara wasn't sure what he meant, at least not until he sank to his knees before her, looking up at her with reverence. In this moment, she wasn't just a beast taming student, and he wasn't her combat instructor. They were equals in desire, partners in this ancient dance.

His palms skimmed up her outer thighs, his warm hands creating delicious friction against her smooth skin. Cassara's breath caught as he gazed up at her, his eyes dark pools of hunger. The stone wall behind her was the only thing keeping her upright as her knees threatened to buckle.

"Steady," Auren murmured, his breath warm against her inner thigh. His hands gripped her hips firmly, anchoring her. "Let me help you."

With gentle pressure, he guided her right leg up and over his broad shoulder. The position opened her completely, leaving nothing hidden from his view. She felt exposed in a way she'd never been before. A tremor ran through her body, not from cold or fear, but from the intensity of his gaze as he studied her most intimate place.

"You're beautiful here, too," he said, his voice rough with desire.

Cassara's fingers found purchase in his hair, partly for balance and partly from an instinctive need to hold onto something solid as sensation threatened to overwhelm her. "I haven't—" she began, her voice faltering as his thumbs parted her gently.

"I know," he whispered, pressing a kiss to the tender curve of her thigh. "Trust me."

The first touch of his mouth against her core tore a startled cry from her throat. His tongue traced her entrance with agonizing slowness before sliding upward to circle her clit and had her clutching his hair tighter. The wet heat of his mouth was unlike anything she'd ever experienced, more intense, more intimate than his fingers had been.

"Auren!" His name escaped her lips as a desperate plea.

He hummed against her in response, the vibration sending new waves of pleasure coursing through her body. Her head pressed harder against the wall, her back arching as he explored her with abandon. Each stroke, each gentle suck drew sounds from her she'd never made before.

The leg supporting her weight trembled dangerously. Sensing her instability, Auren's arm wrapped around her thigh on his shoulder, his hand splaying across her lower back to support her. His other hand gripped her hip, thumb making soothing circles against her hipbone.

Cassara looked down, and the sight of him kneeling before her, his face buried between her thighs, nearly undid her. Their eyes met, and the raw hunger in his gaze sent a fresh wave of heat pooling low in her belly. She was at his mercy, yet somehow in this moment of complete vulnerability, she felt powerful beyond measure.

"I can feel you trembling," he murmured before his tongue delved deeper, exploring her with thoroughness that had her gasping for breath. When he returned his attention to her clit, alternating between gentle flicks and firm pressure, she gasped, one hand tangling in his hair, not knowing whether to pull him closer or push him away as the pleasure built to an almost unbearable intensity.

His hands moved lower to grip her thighs more firmly, holding her in place as he redoubled his efforts. When he slipped one finger inside her, curling it upward while his tongue continued its relentless assault, the last of her resistance crumbled. The tension that had been building snapped, and she cried out as waves of pleasure crashed through her body, more powerful than the first time.

Auren didn't relent, drawing out her climax until she was whimpering, her body hypersensitive and trembling. Only then did he slowly rise to his feet, his eyes never leaving hers as he wiped his mouth with the back of his hand. The primal gesture sent another pulse of desire through her despite her recent release.

"Beautiful," he murmured again, pressing his body against hers, the hard planes of his chest against her soft curves. She could feel his arousal pressing insistently against her stomach through the fabric of his remaining clothes.

"I want to touch you," Cassara whispered, surprised by her own boldness as she reached for the fastenings of his trousers. Her fingers fumbled slightly, betraying her inexperience, but the hunger driving her was unmistakable.

Auren caught her hands, bringing them to his lips. "Are you sure? We don't have to—"

"I've never been more sure of anything," she interrupted, her voice steady despite the nervous flutter in her stomach. This wasn't just desire, it was claiming.

With a groan that seemed torn from deep within him, Auren shed the last of his clothing. Cassara's eyes widened as she took in the sight of him fully naked, powerful and unashamedly aroused. He was magnificent, his body honed by years of combat training, marked with scars that told stories she longed to learn.

He lifted her effortlessly, and she wrapped her legs around his waist, gasping as the movement brought them into intimate contact. The stone wall supported her back as Auren positioned himself at her entrance, pausing there as their eyes locked.

"This might hurt," he warned. "Tell me if you need me to stop."

Cassara cupped his face between her trembling hands, nodding as heat bloomed through her body like wildfire.

"I trust you," she whispered, her voice catching as he pressed forward, slowly breaching her for the first time.

The initial discomfort made her breath hitch, a small whimper escaping her lips. Auren froze immediately, his forehead pressed against hers, muscles quivering with the effort to remain still.

"Breathe," he murmured, pressing gentle kisses to her temple, her cheek, the corner of her mouth. "Just breathe with me."

Cassara inhaled deeply, giving her body time to adjust to the unfamiliar intrusion. The pain ebbed away, replaced by a curious fullness that sent sparks of pleasure radiating through her.

"More," she commanded, surprising herself with her boldness as she tightened her legs around his waist.

Auren obliged, pushing deeper with exquisite slowness until he was fully seated within her. The sensation was overwhelming, completion, connection, as if some missing piece of herself had finally clicked into place. Her fingernails dug into his shoulders as she arched against him.

He groaned against her neck, words failing him.

When he began to move, drawing back before easing forward again in a gentle rhythm, Cassara could focus on nothing else save the points where their bodies touched. Each thrust sent surges of sensation cascading through her, building upon themselves one after the other.

Her inhibitions melted away with each rock of his hips. The careful, considerate pace he'd set was no longer enough. Cassara rolled her hips to meet his thrusts, drawing him deeper. The beast tamer in her recognized something primal awakening, a hunger that wouldn't be satisfied with gentleness.

"Faster," she gasped.

Auren's control visibly frayed. His eyes, locked on hers, darkened as he gave in to her demands. One hand braced against the wall while the other gripped her hip, fingers pressing into her flesh as he drove into her with newfound intensity.

The change in pace stole her breath. Each powerful thrust pushed her higher, the coil of tension within her winding tighter until she felt she might shatter. Sweat slicked their bodies as they moved together, the combat instructor's disciplined strength now focused entirely on her pleasure.

His hand slipped between them, finding the sensitive bundle of nerves at her core once more. Cassara gasped as Auren's deft fingers worked in tight circles, perfectly matched to the rhythm of his thrusts, sending jolts of lightning through her.

The pressure of him buried deep inside her, combined with the relentless motion of his fingers, drove Cassara closer to the edge. Her thighs began to tremble, muscles clenching involuntarily around him.

Auren groaned, his rhythm faltering for a heartbeat before becoming more determined. His eyes, unguarded in a way they never were during training sessions, now burned into hers with an intensity that stole what little breath remained in her lungs.

"I can't—I don't know how to—" she stammered, overwhelmed by sensations she'd never experienced before.

"You do," he assured her, adjusting his angle slightly until she cried out, her eyes widening. "There. Just feel."

Cassara surrendered to him, her body arching as waves of ecstasy crashed through her. She cried out his name, uncaring who might hear, clutching him desperately as her world narrowed to nothing but this moment, this man, this overwhelming pleasure that shattered her completely.

Auren groaned against her skin, his rhythm faltering as her body gripped him. She felt him swell within her, his powerful body tensing as he followed her over the edge, spilling himself deep inside with a hoarse cry that echoed her own.

For several moments, they remained locked together against the wall, trembling and gasping for air. Cassara's mind swam in a haze of pleasure and wonder, her body still pulsing with aftershocks. As the waves began to recede, Cassara became aware of her surroundings again, of the distant sound of water dripping somewhere in the training facility, the scent of their mingled sweat, the weight of Auren's forehead resting against hers as they both struggled to catch their breath.

He kissed her then, softer than before, a tender press of lips that spoke of something beyond physical desire. Cassara's heart fluttered with a different kind of vulnerability as she returned the kiss, her hands sliding up to cup his face.

"That was..." she whispered when they finally parted, unable to find words adequate enough to describe what had happened between them. Auren's thumb traced her lower lip, his eyes searching hers. The disciplined combat instructor had somehow transformed before her eyes. Gone was his usual stern demeanor, replaced by something raw and vulnerable that made Cassara's heart flutter against her ribs like a caged bird.

Eventually, reality began to seep back in. Auren set her gently on her feet, his hands steadying her when her legs proved unwilling. The tenderness in the gesture made her heart flutter anew.

"No regrets?" he asked quietly, echoing his words from their first kiss.

"Never," she replied, meaning it completely.

He helped her dress with the same reverence he'd shown when removing her clothes, his fingers gentle as he smoothed her shirt back into place, as he carefully tied the laces of her training pants. Each touch was a small worship, a promise of care that made her throat tight with emotion.

When they were both clothed again, he cupped her face in his hands, thumbs tracing her cheekbones.

"Whatever happens with Julian, with the academy- this was real. We're real."

She nodded, storing his words like armor against whatever storms awaited them. "I know."

"And Cassara?" His voice was soft. "You're not alone in this anymore."

The promise settled in her chest, warm and reassuring. For the first time in weeks, she felt like she could breathe freely.

CHAPTER TWENTY FOUR

Cassara felt like she was floating as she made her way back across the school grounds. Her body hummed with a contentment she'd never experienced before, every step a reminder of Auren's touch. The soreness between her thighs was a delicious ache that made her cheeks warm with remembered pleasure.

For the first time in weeks, the knot of anxiety in her chest had loosened. *You're not alone in this anymore.* The promise echoed in her mind, wrapping around her like armor.

She was so lost in the memory of his hands on her skin, that she almost didn't notice the familiar warmth of materialization until a small weight settled across her shoulders.

She looked over to find her creature draped there like a shoal, his eyes studying her face with curious intensity.

You seem happy now. Much happier than before. You smell different too.

Heat flooded her cheeks as it dawned on her what he might be picking up on. "You're supposed to stay in the shard," she whispered, but there was no real irritation in her voice. How could she be anything but content right now?

But you're not sad anymore, the creature observed, tilting his head with that innocent curiosity. *I wanted to see what changed. Your heart beats differently now. Calmer.*

Despite everything, Cassara found herself smiling, a real, genuine smile that felt foreign after a lifetime of hiding behind pretense. "I suppose I am happier."

Good, he said simply, as if her happiness was the most important thing in the world. *I don't like when you're sad.*

The genuine care in that small voice made her heart ache. "Go back to the shard now. Someone might see."

Will you still be happy tomorrow?

"I hope so," she said softly, meaning it.

The creature nuzzled against her cheek once before allowing himself to be recalled in a flash of silver light. Cassara pressed her palm to the shard, feeling the warmth of his presence settle there, comforting in a way she wasn't ready to admit.

She turned down a side path that wound its way through the gardens, already picturing the warm comfort of her bed, the slow crawl of memory that would keep her flushed and giddy for hours yet—

Her breath caught as a figure stepped from the shadows, blocking her.

Julian.

He didn't speak at first, just looked at her.

And then, he smiled.

It wasn't the polished one he wore for galas or his condescending smirk from class. This smile was sharp and held the promise of cruelty. It told her everything she needed to know before he even opened his mouth.

"I've been waiting a while," he said casually, as if this were a friendly chat and not a noose tightening. "Hope I'm not interrupting anything."

Cassara didn't answer, instead she tried to step sideways, but his hand shot out, bracing against the wall beside her head. Trapping her.

"Move," she snapped.

"I don't think I will." His eyes swept over her, taking in details she hadn't even realized were visible—her slightly mussed hair, the way her clothes sat differently on her body, the lingering flush in her cheeks. "You have that look, Cassara. That glow that comes after... well. *After*."

She tried once again to move around him, but he mirrored her movement, keeping her cornered as he leaned in close and inhaled deeply.

"You smell like sex."

Her stomach twisted.

"I said move," she said, hating how small her voice sounded. "Get out of my way."

Instead, he stepped in, tightening the cage of his arms until her back hit stone.

"No." His eyes swept over her, invasive and cold. "I want to know who it was. Which one of them touched you."

"You've lost your mind," Cassara insisted before she tried to duck under his arm. He caught her arm in one hand and her chin with the other, his fingers digging in like iron as he yanked her back. "Look at me."

She did because she had no choice.

His face was beautiful, his features carved with aristocratic perfection, but up close like this, she could finally see the cracks in the facade. The cold fury. The hunger.

"Who?" he repeated, his voice dropping to a dangerous whisper. "Was it Gideon? Is that why you've been sniffing around him lately? Or was it someone else?" His lips curled. "One of the third years, maybe? You always did like a challenge."

"Let go of me," Cassara snapped, trying to twist away.

"Not until you answer me." His fingers dug deeper into her jaw, forcing her head back against the wall. "I have every right to know who touched what's mine."

"I'm not yours." The words came out as a growl, but her voice shook.

"Aren't you?" His thumb traced her lower lip with mock tenderness, the gesture made obscene by the violence in his grip. "Your father seems to think otherwise. The marriage contract is already drafted, you know. Just waiting for the right moment."

"You're lying."

"Am I?" His smile was razor-sharp. "Ask him yourself. Better yet, don't. I'd hate to spoil the surprise."

Before she could react, his mouth crashed against hers in a bruising kiss that tasted of possession and cruelty. There was nothing of Auren's reverence in it, nothing tender or caring. Just dominance and the bitter tang of her own fear.

She couldn't move, couldn't think, just tasted him, sharp and sour, felt the crushing press of his body pinning her to the stone.

Her mind screamed.

Cassara wrenched her face away, tearing her mouth free with a gasp.

And then she hit him.

Her open palm cracked across his face causing Julian's head to snap sideways from the force. His hand fell from her, and for the briefest second he looked more shocked than hurt.

"You little—"

She drew back her hand to strike him again, but he was faster. His fingers caught around her wrist, not crushing but firm enough to stop her momentum.

"Enough," he said through gritted teeth. "I think you've made your point."

His grip was iron, holding her arm suspended between them as he leaned in once again.

"But don't think for a moment that this changes anything. You can fight me all you want, Cassara, but we both know how this ends."

Then—

A scream.

Not hers.

Julian bellowed in pain, his entire body jerking as he stumbled back.

Cassara blinked through the blur, and there, just below the hem of his pants, was a streak of silver fury.

The creature.

He clamped onto Julian's ankle with a snarl that seemed far too large for something so small. His teeth sank in deep, his tail whipping furiously as he latched on with feral vengeance. Cassara heard the crunch of expensive leather giving way under fangs like needles.

Julian tried to shake him off, but the creature held fast, claws scrabbling at his shin, ripping at fabric and skin with wild determination. He shouted, cursing, stumbling back against the wall as it tore into him again.

"What the hell?!" he yelled, trying to kick, but the creature vanished with a shimmer, only to reappear a second later clamped onto his other leg.

This was her creature. Her moth chasing, spider eating, infuriating little creature had turned out to be her brave, fierce, protective little creature. He held on with grim determination, growling like a miniature dragon as he gnawed Julian's flesh through his boot.

Go! came the urgent voice in her mind. *Run! Now!*

Cassara didn't hesitate. She pushed off the wall and ran, her feet flying as Julian's curses echoed behind her. She could hear him still trying to dislodge her protector, his voice rising in pain and confusion.

She burst through the entrance to the girls' wing, not stopping until she was well past the barrier that would keep Julian out. Only then did she allow herself to slow, pressing her back against the cool stone wall as she struggled to catch her breath.

The corridor was blessedly empty, lit only by the soft glow of mage-light. She could hear the distant murmur of voices from behind dormitory doors, late-night conversations and muffled laughter that spoke of a normalcy she couldn't even fathom right now.

Her hands were shaking. Her lip throbbed where Julian's brutal kiss had split it, and she could still taste copper on her tongue. But worse than the physical discomfort was what he had claimed.

The marriage contract is already drafted.

A flash of silver light announced her creature's return. He materialized in her arms, looking remarkably pleased with himself despite a small smear of blood on his muzzle.

Are you hurt? he asked immediately, silver eyes wide with concern as they searched her face.

Cassara touched her swollen lip gingerly. "I'll live. But you—" Her voice caught. "You saved me."

Of course I did, he said simply, as if there had never been any question. *You're mine to protect.*

The words cut deep. All this time, she'd been resenting him for not being what she wanted, when it turned out he'd been exactly what she needed. Brave. Loyal. Fierce when it mattered.

"Thank you," she whispered, meaning it more than she'd ever meant anything.

He nuzzled against her cheek, warm and comforting. *Always.*

Cassara took a few more minutes to compose herself, using the small mirror mounted near the washrooms to check that her hair was properly arranged and her clothes were in order.

When she finally slipped into her dormitory room, moving as quietly as possible, she was relieved to find it dark and peaceful. Soft breathing came from the other beds indicating her roommates were asleep.

Cassara changed into her nightgown in the darkness, every movement careful and silent. Her creature remained recalled in his shard, but she could feel his presence there, warm, protective, devoted.

As she finally settled into her bed, pulling the covers up to her chin, she tried to reconcile the events of the evening. The incredible joy and connection with Auren felt like a lifetime ago, overshadowed now by Julian's threats and the terrifying certainty that things were escalating beyond her control.

But beneath the fear, something else flickered. For the first time, her creature had shown her exactly what he was capable of.

Not disappointment or failure, but pure, unwavering loyalty.

The morning sun filtered through the haze like a held breath, casting pale ribbons of gold across the gravel-strewn training circle. Cassara stood at the edge, the aether shard warm in her palm. Her body still carried echoes of the night before, a sore ache between her thighs, a lingering heat beneath her skin, but it was the weight of this moment that coiled tight around her spine.

She wasn't here for battle practice.

She was here for him.

With a thought, she released the creature.

He materialized in a shimmer of silver light, his fur caught the light like moonlit fog, and for once, he didn't skitter away or vanish into the rafters. He just sat there, tail curled around his feet, staring up at her like he was waiting.

Cassara crossed her arms. "Well? Are you going to sit there like a stuffed toy or do something useful?"

He tilted his head.

She sighed and crouched to his level. "They expect something presentable tonight. Not just tricks or talking. They want proof of a bond."

His ears twitched. *We have a bond. I chewed that boy's ankles for you.*

"You know what I mean," she muttered. "They want sync. Unity. Power."

A pause. *But that's not what you want.*

Cassara's mouth tightened. "No. I want to win."

The creature didn't flinch or disappear this time. He simply padded forward on silent paws, stopping just shy of her knees. He sat again, lifting one paw to bat gently at her shin. *Do you still hate me?*

She exhaled. "I never hated you."

Then why do you always sound like you do?

Because I hate what you mean, she thought. Because you're a mirror of everything I can't control. Of the path I didn't choose. Of a future that isn't mine.

She didn't say any of that aloud.

Instead, she reached out, slowly, and ran her fingers between his ears. "You're not what I wanted," she said, the words soft but unflinching. "But you're what I've got. And... you protected me. You comforted me."

He leaned into her touch. *You were scared. I didn't want you to be alone..*

She pulled her hand back, suddenly too full of feeling. Her voice shook when she said, "You need a name."

The creature blinked up at her.

She hesitated, looking at the way his fur shimmered like living starlight, the way his body moved like candlelight caught in a draft. Always flickering. Never still.

"Flicker," she said quietly. "That's what you are. And what you do. You flicker."

His entire body stilled.

Then a warmth bloomed in the aether shard so sudden and fierce it nearly knocked her back. The link surged between them like a current snapping into place. Flicker's eyes widened, and she felt it—not words this time, not fragmented emotion, but a burst of recognition, of something settling.

Cassara, he whispered in her mind.

It wasn't a question.

It was trust.

A single thread, fine and fragile, but real.

Cassara swallowed hard, standing slowly. Her heart felt too big for her chest. "We're not perfect," she said aloud. "But we might be enough."

Flicker tilted his head again, then bounced to his feet and trotted in a slow circle around her. When she pivoted instinctively to track him, he mirrored her steps exactly, tail swaying in time with her balance, paws matching her footfalls. It wasn't graceful yet. Not show-worthy.

But it was sync.

It was something.

And for once, Cassara didn't feel like she was faking it.

She just... was.

And Flicker was with her.

The midday bells had barely faded by the time Cassara reached the dormitory steps. Her hair clung damp to her temples, her hands still faintly trembling from the charge that had surged through her when Flicker accepted his name. The bond was still new, tenuous, but it was there.

The dormitory door creaked open to warm light and quiet voices. Liri was cross-legged on her bunk, humming softly as she polished a shell-shaped comb. Talia was by the mirror, fixing a pin into her braid. Evie leaned against the windowsill, a half-eaten roll in hand.

Sonia sat on her own bed, perfectly poised, eyes cutting to Cassara the moment she stepped inside.

"Something came for you," she said, gesturing to the end of Cassara's bunk. "Just after you left this morning."

Cassara followed her gaze.

There, resting on the folded blanket at the foot of her bed, was a long, elegant box sealed with red wax.

She didn't have to check the crest to know. The weight of it was enough.

Allencourt.

Her stomach clenched as she crossed the room, every step slow, cautious. The box was made of fine lacquered wood, the seal unbroken. Beside it sat a folded parchment, ivory vellum, her name written in her father's sharp, cold script.

The air felt heavier just touching it.

She broke the seal with a snap and unfolded the letter.

Cassara,

I will be attending the gala this evening, as will Lord Marcel Tremaine and his family. You would do well to ensure your appearance reflects the dignity of your bloodline.

Julian has been most accommodating in keeping me informed of your progress, and I am pleased to hear you've been spending time together as intended.

I expect you to comport yourself with grace and propriety—and to give no cause for embarrassment.

You know how this evening will be perceived.

Do not disappoint me.

—Father

No greeting. No warmth. Just directives dressed in courtesy.

Cassara's fingers trembled as she set the letter aside.

"What's it say?" Liri asked, already inching closer, wide-eyed with curiosity.

Evie had abandoned her roll and Talia had stopped braiding. Even Sonia was leaning forward now, interest barely veiled.

Cassara didn't answer. She turned to the box, lifted the lid.

Inside, nestled in tissue-soft folds of crimson silk, was the most stunning gown she'd ever seen.

The fabric shimmered with a liquid sheen, red as molten rubies, tailored to skim every curve without clinging. Delicate gold chains draped across the shoulders and down the exposed back like a constellation. At the collarbone, rubies glittered in an arcane filigree—half necklace, half ward. The back dipped scandalously low, held together only by the weight of the gold chains crossing her spine like gossamer armor.

For a moment, no one spoke.

Then Liri exhaled like she'd been holding her breath. "Stars."

Evie let out a low, appreciative whistle. "That's not a dress. That's a weapon."

Talia touched the edge of the fabric, reverent. "Is it from your family?"

Cassara nodded, resisting the urge to toss the entire box, dress included, into the fireplace.

Sonia's eyes flicked toward the letter. "Your father has taste, at least," she said, and though her voice remained cool, there was a note of surprise Cassara hadn't heard before. Admiration, even.

Expensive taste, Cassara thought grimly. It was beautiful, yes, but it was also a statement. A reminder of exactly what she stood to lose if she disappointed him.

Cassara didn't answer.

She was too busy trying to remember how to breathe.

The warmth she'd carried from the morning, Flicker's trust, that first step toward real partnership, was already cooling beneath the weight of expectation. Her father would be there. Julian's family too. This dress wasn't a gift. It was a command in silk and chainmail.

She'd have to wear it.

She'd have to smile and act like the creature she summoned tonight was exactly the one she wanted.

"We should all start getting ready," Liri said anxiously. "The gala starts in a few hours. I still don't know what to do with my hair."

"I can't wait to see how it looks on you," Evie added, her eyes bright with genuine excitement.

Cassara wanted to refuse, wanted to shove the dress back in the box and pretend this night wasn't happening. But her roommates were already bustling around, clearing space and chattering about hair arrangements and jewelry.

She stood and lifted the gown from its tissue paper, carrying it behind the changing screen in the corner of their room. The dress fit like it had been made for her, which, of course, it had. Her father's seamstresses knew her measurements by heart.

Cassara took a deep breath and turned to face the mirror. She hardly recognized the young woman staring back at her. The crimson gown transformed her into something ethereal and dangerous—silk flowing like liquid fire, gold chains catching the lamplight as they traced delicate patterns across her bare shoulders and down her spine.

She looked every inch the perfect noble daughter. Beautiful. Untouchable. Exactly what was expected of Cassara Allencourt.

The thought made her stomach clench.

"You look like a queen," Liri breathed from behind her.

"Or a sacrifice," Cassara murmured, then immediately regretted the words when she saw her roommates' expressions in the mirror.

"Don't say that," Evie said firmly.

Even Sonia nodded approval. "Julian won't be able to take his eyes off you."

The comment struck a nerve and she fought the urge to scream. Julian. Her father. Marcel Tremaine. All of them watching, judging, maneuvering her into whatever position served their interests best.

Tonight she would be performing a careful dance of submission, to her father's expectations, to Julian's advances, to the academy's judgment. All while presenting Flicker to a crowd that would see him as proof of her failure.

She pressed her palm to the aether shard at her throat, feeling the warm pulse of Flicker's presence. At least she wouldn't be entirely alone.

You're worried, came his soft voice in her mind.

Terrified, she corrected silently.

I'm with you, he promised, and somehow that made the tight knot in her chest loosen just slightly.

Through the window, Cassara could see the academy's grand hall glowing with warm light, already filling with elegantly dressed figures.

It was time.

She took one last look in the mirror, at the girl in crimson silk who looked like she could conquer the world, even as she felt like she was walking to her execution.

Then she squared her shoulders, lifted her chin, and prepared to meet whatever waited for her beyond that door.

When she reached the barrier at the entrance to the girls' wing, she paused, taking one last steadying breath. The moment she stepped through, there would be no retreating, no sanctuary until the evening was over.

Julian was waiting just beyond the threshold.

He looked magnificent and she hated that she noticed. His formal coat was deep crimson to match her gown, a coordination that hadn't been accidental, with gold embroidery at the cuffs and collar that caught the light as he moved. His blond hair was perfectly styled, his posture radiating the easy confidence of someone who had never doubted his place in the world.

When he saw her, his expression shifted from casual waiting to something more intense. His eyes swept over her, taking in every detail of the gown, the way the gold chains draped across her skin, the elegant line of her throat where the rubies glittered.

"Breathtaking," he said, offering her a perfect bow that managed to be both respectful and possessive.

The compliment sent a chill down her spine, but she forced her expression to remain neutral. "Julian. You look very handsome."

"Do I?" His smile was charming, but there was something sharper beneath it. Something that reminded her of the way he'd cornered her in the garden and the bruising grip of his fingers. "I was hoping you'd approve."

He offered her his arm with practiced gallantry. "Shall we? I believe our fathers are eager to see us together."

Cassara stared at his offered arm, knowing that the moment she took it, she was accepting more than just an escort to the gala. She was stepping into whatever web he and her father had woven around her.

But what choice did she have? To refuse would cause a scene, would give him ammunition to use against her later. And her father was watching, always watching.

She placed her hand lightly on his sleeve, hating how right they looked together. How perfectly matched in their crimson and gold, like figures from a fairy tale.

"Wonderful," Julian murmured, covering her hand with his own. His touch was warm, possessive, a silent reminder of ownership. "You know, Cassara, you've never looked more radiant than you do tonight."

"Thank you," she managed, though the words felt like ash in her mouth.

As they began walking toward the grand hall, Julian leaned closer, his voice dropping to an intimate whisper that sent unwelcome chills across her skin.

"I do hope you'll save me more than one dance tonight. After all," his fingers tightened slightly on hers, "we are going to have so much to celebrate."

CHAPTER TWENTY FIVE

The grand hall had been transformed into something from a dream, or perhaps a nightmare given Cassara's current state of mind. Crimson and gold banners hung from the vaulted ceiling, interwoven with strands of enchanted light that pulsed gently. The academy's colors blazed from every surface, turning the vast space into a glittering jewel box.

Students and faculty mingled in elegant clusters, their formal attire a sea of rich fabrics and gleaming jewelry. But tonight, the usual academy hierarchy felt different. Parents moved through the crowd with the easy authority of wealth and power, their presence transforming what should have been a student celebration into something far more political.

Cassara's eyes swept the room automatically, cataloging faces, alliances, potential threats. Near the far wall, she spotted her father deep in conversation with a man she recognized all too well—Marcel Tremaine. Julian's father shared his son's aristocratic features, though his were harder and far more calculating. Both men exuded the quiet authority of those accustomed to having their will obeyed without question.

"There she is—Allencourt's daughter."

"Tremaine and Allencourt. Makes sense, doesn't it?"

She felt Julian's fingers tighten slightly when they were noticed, knew he was basking in the moment, believing he'd won. In spite of the growing desire to sink into the floor and disappear, Cassara kept her chin high and smiled just enough to convince the people around her that she wanted to be there.

"Magnificent, isn't it?" Julian murmured beside her, following her gaze. "Though I confess, I'm far more interested in the company than the decorations."

Before she could respond, the soft strains of music began to drift from the orchestra positioned on a raised dais. Couples began to form on the polished marble floor that served as a dance area, their movements graceful and practiced.

"I believe this is our cue," Julian said, offering her his hand with that same perfect smile. "Shall we show them how it's done?"

Cassara glanced toward where their fathers stood watching, noting the way her father's eyes had already found them across the crowded room. There was expectation in his gaze, approval in the slight nod he gave when he saw her hand resting on Julian's arm.

She was trapped, and they all knew it.

"Of course," she said, accepting his hand and allowing him to lead her onto the dance floor.

Julian was an excellent dancer, she'd known that from years of social gatherings, but tonight there was something different in the way he held her. His hand at her waist pressed more firmly than necessary, drawing her closer than propriety strictly allowed. His fingers intertwined with hers in a grip that felt more like ownership than partnership.

"You're tense," he observed as they moved through the opening steps of the waltz. "Surely you're not nervous? You've been dancing since you could walk."

"Just thinking about the evening ahead," she replied carefully.

"Ah yes, the grand revelation." His smile turned predatory. "I'm quite looking forward to seeing what you've managed to bond with."

Cassara's heart skipped. Did he know something? Or was this just Julian's usual cruelty, assuming the worst because he wanted to see her fail?

"Though between you and me," Julian's voice dropped to barely above a whisper, meant only for her ears, "I suspect the real entertainment will come afterward."

"I don't know what you mean."

"Don't you?" He spun her expertly, bringing her back against his chest with perhaps more force than the dance required. "You've been so... tense lately. So secretive about your progress. When someone's confident about their achievements, they tend to boast, don't they? But you..." His smile widened. "You've been remarkably quiet."

He's fishing, Cassara realized with a mixture of relief and dread. He didn't know for certain, but he suspected.

"When your father sees whatever disappointing creature you've managed to bind yourself to," Julian continued, "when he realizes that all his investment in your education has been wasted... well, I imagine he'll be quite eager to discuss alternative arrangements."

The threat was delivered with such casual charm that anyone watching would think they were sharing sweet whispers. But Cassara felt each word like a blade between her ribs.

"You seem very confident about my failure," she managed.

"I seem realistic about your limitations." His hand slid lower on her back, fingers tracing the edge of where her gown dipped low. "But don't worry, darling. I'll be there to comfort you when it all falls apart."

She tried to put distance between them, but his grip tightened, keeping her locked against him as they continued their elegant circuit of the dance floor.

"Speaking of comfort," Julian continued, his breath warm against her ear, "I do hope you've been careful regarding your evening activities. It would be such a shame if rumors were to reach the wrong ears."

Ice flooded Cassara's veins.

"I have no idea what you're talking about," she said, proud that her voice remained steady.

"Of course you don't." His smile was razor-sharp. "But just remember, Cassara—I see everything. And I protect what's mine. Especially after seeing how lovely you look tonight."

Did he?

As if summoned by her distress, her eyes found Auren across the room.

He stood near the faculty section, dressed in formal evening wear that transformed him from combat instructor to something altogether more dangerous. The dark fabric of his coat emphasized the breadth of his shoulders, and his hair was styled back from his face, revealing the sharp angles of his cheekbones. He looked magnificent.

And absolutely furious.

Their eyes met across the crowded dance floor, and she saw the barely concealed rage simmering behind his careful mask. His hands were clasped behind his back, knuckles white with the effort of restraint as he watched Julian's possessive display.

For one wild moment, she imagined him cutting across the dance floor, tearing her away from Julian's grip, claiming her in front of everyone. The fantasy was so vivid she almost stumbled.

But reality crashed back as Julian's grip tightened, reminding her exactly how trapped she was.

"Careful," Julian murmured, following her gaze across the dance floor to where other couples swayed in elegant formations. "Admiring the competition? Though I can't imagine any of these boys could offer you what I can."

His voice dropped lower, possessive. "I do hope you're not getting any foolish ideas about your options, Cassara. We both know how limited they really are."

The casual cruelty in his voice made her want to slap him again. But here, surrounded by hundreds of witnesses including both their fathers, she could do nothing but smile and continue the dance.

The music swelled toward its conclusion, and Julian spun her one final time before drawing her close for the ending pose. To everyone watching, they looked like the perfect couple—beautiful, wealthy, well-matched in every way that society valued.

"Beautiful as always, my dear," Julian said loudly enough for nearby couples to hear. Then, quieter, for her alone: "Make sure you remember tonight and how good we look together. How right this all is."

As the music ended and polite applause rippled through the crowd, Cassara forced herself to curtsy gracefully. But inside, she was screaming.

"Come," Julian said, offering his arm again. "I believe our parents are eager to greet us."

Julian led her with the confidence of someone born to wield people like weapons. His stride was sure and Cassara matched him, step for step, mask for mask, all the way to the dais.

Her father stood like a statue carved from frost. His silvered hair was immaculate, his emerald coat tailored to an unforgiving line. The Allencourt crest shimmered faintly at his shoulder, a flare of gold thread catching the ballroom light.

To his left stood Lord Marcel Tremaine—taller, broader, his presence no less commanding. Julian's eyes, cold and proud, were a mirror of the man beside him. Lady Tremaine was there as well, all velvet and poise, her smile a study in pleasant cruelty.

"Father," Cassara said with a slight curtsy, every motion precise.

"Cassara." His gaze swept over her, lingering not on her face, but the gown. "You wear it well."

She couldn't tell if that was approval or a warning.

Julian leaned closer to his mother and kissed her cheek. "Lady Tremaine."

"Darling." Her voice was honeyed. Then she turned to Cassara, her expression softening. "My, my. You've grown into such a striking young woman. Almost makes me forget how wretchedly behaved you were as a child."

Cassara offered a cool smile. "A compliment, then. Thank you."

The older woman laughed, clearly delighted. "Oh, I do like her."

Lord Tremaine's eyes narrowed. "Charm isn't a substitute for strength."

Julian's hand curled possessively at her waist. "She has both."

Cassara's stomach turned.

Her father cut in, voice low and clipped. "Julian, I've received your latest correspondence regarding her progress. There are a few points I'd like clarified. Shall we?"

"Of course, Lord Allencourt." Julian gave Cassara a brief look, something smug flashing in his eyes. "Will you be alright, dearest?"

She smiled too sweetly. "I'll try to survive without you."

Julian chuckled, brushing his lips to the back of her knuckles in a performance that made her skin crawl. Then he turned to follow her father, already discussing Crestboard rankings and projected career paths like she was a pedigree asset to be traded.

Lady Tremaine turned to Cassara. "Why don't you sit with us, darling? I'm sure we'll be hearing your name called soon enough."

"Of course," Cassara said. "But if you'll excuse me, I need a moment of air."

She didn't wait for permission.

Cassara turned from the dais and walked with calm, measured steps through the gathering crowd until she was able to slip through one of the side doors and toward a stone archway that opened onto the darkened upper terrace.

She exhaled slowly, palms braced on the cold marble of the terrace rail, her gaze tracing the constellations suspended above Vallemont's gleaming towers. Behind her, nobles danced, toasts were raised, alliances were brokered. The pageantry of power played on inevitably.

But here, in this quiet pocket of darkness just beyond the ballroom's reach, she could finally breathe.

"You shouldn't be out here alone."

Cassara spun, her heart leaping into her throat.

Auren emerged from the shadows. His eyes, when they found hers, burned with something too fierce to be mistaken for indifference.

"Careful," she said, her voice quiet. "Someone might see."

"They already saw," he murmured, stopping just before her. "You, on his arm."

"I didn't have a choice," she said, turning her face back to the wind. "My father's here. So are the Tremaines. It's a performance."

"I know." His voice dropped. "That's what makes it worse."

Cassara's hands clenched against the stone. "You think I wanted to dance with him? Smile for him? Pretend I'm proud to be paraded around like a well-trained pet?"

"I think," Auren said, stepping closer, "you shouldn't have to play this game at all."

She felt his hand curl around her waist as the other ghosted up her spine, fingers brushing the delicate gold chains that hung there. Cassara turned to face him only to discover there was no space left between them, only the press of heat and the sharp awareness of every inch of bare skin his palm touched.

"You look," he said, voice low and dark with want, "like sin wrapped in starlight."

Her breath caught.

"This dress," he murmured. "Do you have any idea what it's doing to me? Watching you move in it, knowing that beneath all this silk and gold, you're the same woman who came apart in my arms?"

"And you're making it very, very difficult," he continued, lips brushing her cheek, "not to kiss you until your legs forget how to work."

Heat flooded her cheeks, but she didn't look away. "We can't do this here."

"Can't we?" His hand slid lower, fingers burning through the thin silk as they traced the curve of her hip. "Right now I'm finding it hard to care about anything except you."

"Liar." The word slipped out sharper than intended. "You care more than anyone."

He stilled against her.

"You're thinking about my reputation," she continued, voice softening. "About what happens to me if we're discovered. You always are."

A rueful smile played across his lips. "You know me too well."

"So when you say you don't care about propriety," she traced a finger along his collar, "what you really mean is you're trying very hard not to care. There's a difference."

"Perhaps," he admitted, though his grip on her didn't loosen. "But do you know what I was thinking about during that dance? When I watched him hold you too close, touch you like he owned you?"

She shook her head, not trusting her voice.

"I was thinking about all the ways I could make Julian Tremaine disappear," he said, and there was something in his voice that suggested he wasn't entirely joking. "Make it look like an accident, of course. A training mishap. Very tragic."

"Auren—"

"Hypothetically speaking," he added. "I'm far too responsible an instructor to actually follow through. Wouldn't want to set a bad example."

Despite everything, she found herself fighting a smile. "How considerate of you."

"I am the picture of restraint," he murmured, pressing a kiss to the corner of her mouth that proved exactly the opposite. "Most of the time."

"They'll miss me," she said weakly, even as her hands came up to rest on his chest. "Julian will come looking."

"Will he?" Auren's lips found the sensitive spot below her ear. "Because from what I saw, he was plenty absorbed with your fathers' scheming."

Auren's lips traced along her throat. "One more minute," he murmured against her skin. "Give me one more minute to memorize every inch of you I can."

He didn't wait for an answer.

His mouth found hers, hot and hungry, as his hand slid to the small of her back, drawing her impossibly closer, until there was nothing between them but heat and silk and the sound of her gasp as he kissed her like he'd been starving for it.

Her hands slid up into his hair, fingers twisting in soft strands as her back hit the stone railing. The gold chains pressed cool against her skin, a sharp contrast to the fever building between them. When his teeth scraped her lower lip, she whimpered, soft, involuntary, and Auren groaned like he'd been holding back too long.

He pulled back just enough to speak, forehead resting against hers.

"Say the word," he said, voice ragged. "Tell me to stop, and I will."

Cassara's chest heaved, but she couldn't say it.

Instead, she ran her hands down his chest, over the firm lines of muscle hidden beneath the fine fabric. "They're going to come looking if—"

"I'll cause a distraction."

"You *are* the distraction."

"You came out here for air," he said, his lips brushing her jaw. "You can have mine."

He kissed her again, slower this time. His lips lingering as if gentleness might save them both from everything they couldn't say. As if despite everything, the danger, the eyes, the future, this moment still mattered. Still belonged to them.

And it did.

But eventually, she pulled back, trembling and flushed, her lip still tingling where he'd kissed her raw. "Later," she whispered, palm flat on his chest. "I'll come to you later."

His eyes closed for half a second, like he was trying to memorize her just as she was. "Promise?"

"I promise."

He kissed her forehead, then her temple, then stepped back into shadow.

Cassara waited a moment longer, allowing her racing heart to settle before making her own retreat.

She hadn't moved three steps before Julian found her, eyes narrowed. But Cassara only offered him her sweetest smile.

"I've been looking for you. Mother said you ran off."

"I needed some air," Cassara replied. "It's almost time for the Revealing Ceremony. Shall we?"

And just like that, the performance resumed. But behind the mask, her lips still tingled and her heart no longer felt like it was in someone else's hands.

They were halfway across the ballroom when Auren intercepted.

For a moment, Cassara's heart stopped. Was he going to challenge him? Right there in front of everyone? Fear gripped her, but she couldn't deny the thrill that sparked deep in her chest.

She couldn't meet his gaze, afraid that if she did she would betray herself. When he finally spoke, his voice was calm and unbothered.

"Miss Allencourt, Mr. Tremaine, first years are to report to the holding chamber in preparation for the Revealing Ceremony," he said, motioning towards a door several other students were already gravitating towards.

The breath she had been holding escaped in a low rush and she nodded. He offered a short bow and then moved on without another word.

"Charming," Julian murmured, adjusting his cuffs. "Nothing quite like watching grown men reduced to herding first-years like livestock."

"How fitting," Cassara replied with a sweet smile. "I suppose that makes us livestock. Though I'm curious which category you'd place yourself in. Pig perhaps?"

Julian scoffed. "I prefer to think of myself as the one who owns the farm."

Cassara let the comment hang between them as they joined the stream of first-years moving toward the eastern corridor. Around them, nervous chatter filled the air, but she barely heard it over the memory of Auren's voice, the way he'd looked at her without looking at her at all.

The flow of students carried them forward through wide double doors that had been draped in academy banners and past upperclassmen checking names against scrolls.

Julian's presence beside her felt like a weight she couldn't shake, his earlier words echoing with the kind of casual ownership that made her want to vomit. But as they were directed toward the staging area, she forced herself to focus on what lay ahead rather than the arrogance radiating from the boy at her side.

They were being gathered into a holding chamber behind the arched eastern corridor. Beyond the curtain, the space had been transformed from a ballroom into a theater.

Ringed arrangements of circular seating were spaced at even intervals, each table bearing the emblem of a noble house, of an instructor's domain, or a visiting dignitary's crest.

Mage-lights floated in staggered tiers overhead, their golden glow caught in the shimmering glyphs etched into the polished obsidian floor, forming a spiraled path that curved gently around a central stage.

At the far end, atop a tiered dais, stood Headmistress Kalisandra, draped in Vallemont crimson, her silver hair swept into a crown of living flame. No ornament, only spellwork. She held no script, needed no fanfare. Her presence alone commanded the silence.

"Welcome, honored guests, council members, and sponsors of Vallemont Beast Tamer Academy," she began, her voice carrying across the room without enchantment. "Tonight, you witness more than pageantry. You witness promise. Bond. Legacy."

A hush settled across the hall.

"Each of our first-year tamers has, by now, forged a link with a creature that reflects their spirit. Their strength. Their weaknesses. Their future." Her gaze cut sharply toward the hidden corridor where the students waited. "You will see not only beasts tonight, but the shape of the years to come. The future of your alliances. The next generation of Vallemont's elite."

A flick of her hand, and an illuminated display materialized above the central spiral, Vallemont's Crestboard, shimmering in real time, alive with color and motion.

"Though Crestboard rankings are traditionally updated at week's end," Kalisandra continued, "tonight we mark a singular occasion. For the first time since the academy's founding, I present to you the mid-term standings."

A collective breath rippled through the assembled first-years. These rankings, normally visible only in the great hall, carried a new gravity when spoken aloud before an audience of nobles.

"In tenth place, demonstrating admirable dedication to her studies, Miss Olivette Ashton."

"Ninth, Mr. Marcus Whitmore. Eighth, Miss Vera Castell."

The headmistress moved through the names with precise cadence, each met with polite acknowledgment. But when she reached the upper ranks, the air sharpened with focus.

"In fourth place, showing exceptional promise in defensive tactics, Miss Verena Montero."

"In third place, demonstrating remarkable combat innovation, Mr. Julian Tremaine."

Julian's smile was visible even behind the screen, measured, assured. Third was exactly where someone of his stature belonged: high enough to command respect, not so high as to invite suspicion.

"In second place, maintaining excellence across all disciplines despite considerable challenges, Miss Cassara Allencourt."

Cassara felt her breath catch. There was a beat of stunned silence before the polite applause began, hesitant at first, then building.

"And in first place," Kalisandra continued, her voice cutting clean through the hall, "for achieving the highest marks in both combat assessment and tactical application, Mr. Gideon Delvinar."

The response was louder this time, more confident. Gideon's family name had once carried gravity. Pride, legacy, and power all rolled into one. It was evident it could do so again. Behind the screen, Cassara didn't have to look to know Julian's jaw had likely tightened.

Gideon, as always, said nothing.

The screen shimmered again before fading and resetting.

Now came the part that mattered most.

The headmistress spoke again. "Let the reveal begin."

With that, the hall shifted. Music hummed to life from unseen instruments, low strings and delicate woodwinds, and the curtain separating the first-years from the guests dissolved into light.

"Row one, enter."

Cassara watched as the first group moved forward, led by Julian.

He stopped just before the threshold, his hand moving to the aether shard at his chest. The crystal flared with pale blue light, and his beast materialized in a cascade of shimmering particles. The Moonlit Wyvern prowled forward, sleek and obsidian-scaled, wings that shimmered faintly even at rest. A floating screen appeared beside them, displaying the beast's name, class, and rank in elegant script. Attack Class. Rank A.

Julian didn't just walk—he glided, his posture perfect, the tether between him and his beast taut with control. Every movement was calculated, meant to show off. And it worked. Guests leaned forward. One woman fanned herself. His mother beamed.

Behind him, Gideon summoned his own beast with quiet efficiency. His aether shard pulsed gold, and the Skyreaper Griffin emerged in a blur of light and feathers, fierce and gleaming. It didn't snarl or preen—it watched, golden eyes slicing the room like blades. The synergy between them was almost painful in its precision. No wasted motion. No falter in step. Attack Class. Rank A.

Whispers swept the room. Nobles shifted in their seats. House heads exchanged glances that promised negotiations in the weeks to come.

The line continued. Verena summoned her Ironclad Manticore, Evie and her stoic Pangolar, Talia her ethereal Aether Sprite, and then—

"Cassara Allencourt."

The crowd had fallen into a hush of anticipation.

She stepped forward, slowly moving towards the center of the stage. She took a deep breath and raised her hand to the aether shard.

"Wait."

The words rang out, clear and venom-laced, slicing through the room like a thrown blade.

Cassara froze.

The headmistress turned, brow lifting with elegant precision. "Miss de Kere?"

Sonia stepped forward from the cluster of first-years, her expression composed save for the glint of calculation in her eyes.

"I believe there's been a breach of academy protocol," she said, loud enough for her voice to carry. "A violation of the taming oath."

Whispers flared instantly. Across the ballroom, Cassara saw her father straighten in his seat, his eyes meeting hers for the briefest of moments before returning to Sonia.

Headmistress Kalisandra's voice remained calm. "You are aware of the weight of your accusation, Miss de Kere?"

"I am." Sonia's hands folded demurely before her. "I saw Cassara Allencourt making contact with a poacher. She accepted a private offer, an exchange. She replaced her original bonded beast with something else."

A collective gasp. Somewhere, a glass was set down too hard.

"What? She's lying," Cassara said, before she could stop herself.

Kalisandra raised one hand, silencing both girls with the gesture. "Do you have evidence?"

Sonia didn't falter. "I have my word, and if that's not enough, I suggest you examine the beast she presents. If she swapped creatures, there will be a mismatch in her aura signature. Traces of the original bond will still linger."

The headmistress turned her gaze to Cassara. "Miss Allencourt. Do you refute this claim?"

Cassara's fists clenched at her sides. "I've never broken the taming oath. My beast is ... mine."

"Then," Kalisandra said evenly, "we will allow the beast to answer."

Silence fell over the hall as Cassara took one step forward.

Are you ready?

Are you? came Flicker's gentle response.

No, she admitted. *But let's do it anyway.*

She pressed her hand to the aether shard.

Light bloomed from her palm, silver, soft, almost gentle, and then a shape materialized at her side.

Tiny. Shimmering. Wholly unimpressive.

Flicker blinked up at the crowd with ever curious eyes. His ears twitched. His tail curled delicately around his feet. He looked more like an overgrown kitten than a combat partner. His stats flared to life above them.

Unknown Class. Rank C.

Silence.

Then—laughter. Muted at first but spreading quickly.

A few guests tried to mask it behind handkerchiefs. One man coughed conspicuously into his wine. Someone in the upper tier let out a faint scoff.

Cassara didn't move.

She stood perfectly still, spine straight, lips pressed into a line, as Flicker padded over to her feet and sat like a statue, unbothered by what was happening around him.

Julian's eyes were bright with satisfaction. He thought he'd won, and he very well might have.

Gideon's eyes had narrowed, not mocking, just watchful.

And Sonia?

Sonia looked confused. Visibly and thoroughly confused.

She opened her mouth only to close it again. She hadn't expected this. She'd expected something dark, something monstrous, something visibly powerful. Not Flicker.

Headmistress Kalisandra descended the dais slowly, stopping only a few feet from Cassara. She studied the creature at her side.

Flicker tilted his head up, expression unreadable.

"Miss de Kere," the headmistress said without turning, "thank you for your... concern. But it seems Miss Allencourt's bond is very much intact and very much hers."

Sonia's mouth opened again, but the headmistress was already turning away.

"Next."

The ceremony resumed. More beasts entered, announced and admired. But Cassara heard none of it. Her blood was roaring too loud in her ears.

She didn't look at the crowd.

Her attention was on her father and the satisfaction curling behind his cool, flat gaze.

No words had been exchanged. He didn't need them.

The message was clear.

I warned you.

He rose, said something to Lord Tremaine, and then disappeared.

The applause had barely faded. The last of the first-years were still returning to their seats, some flushed with pride, others trailing their beasts with quiet resignation, when Lord Allencourt appeared at her side.

"Walk with me," he said without greeting.

Cassara followed. There was no choice in it, there never had been, only the foolish illusion of choice she had allowed herself to believe. They moved through the low murmur of the crowd, past nobles sipping wine and instructors offering polite congratulations. None stopped them. No one dared.

When they reached the edge of the floor, near a curtained alcove shadowed from the candlelight, he turned.

His eyes swept over her gown, her face, and finally, the small creature seated at her heel.

"So," he said softly. "That's what you chose to present."

It wasn't a question.

Cassara straightened. "His name is Flicker. And he—"

He held up a hand. "Spare me the sentimental narrative."

The pause that followed was more brutal than any raised voice could've been.

"You've wasted enough time," he said at last. "We'll be leaving in the morning. Your things will be packed."

Her stomach dropped. "What?"

"You've made your decision. Now I'm making mine." His gaze flicked again to the creature by her feet. "You had the chance to distinguish yourself. To secure a future, and instead, you've chosen mediocrity."

"I didn't cheat," she began, anger flaring in her chest. "If that's what this is about—"

"It's about optics, Cassara." Her name came out cold. "It's about strength. Status. The legacy you were so determined to represent. And you've shown none of it tonight."

She felt her pulse spike. "The school year isn't over—"

"Stop with this foolishness," he snapped. "There are better uses for your time. Like writing up the guest list for your wedding."

The air seemed to collapse inward.

"No," she said, too quickly.

But before he could respond, before she could unravel, another voice slid into the silence.

"Forgive the interruption, Lord Allencourt," Headmistress Kalisandra said, her tone cool and calm as ever. "I couldn't help but overhear."

Cassara hadn't even heard her approach. Auren stood just behind her, tense and unreadable.

The headmistress's gaze swept from father to daughter to the tiny beast beside them. "While I understand your concerns, I must remind you that Miss Allencourt signed a binding contract upon enrollment. She is required to complete the academic year in full, unless formally expelled or otherwise incapacitated."

Lord Allencourt's eyes narrowed. "Are you threatening to interfere with my daughter's future, Headmistress?"

"Not at all," she said, with a smile that didn't reach her eyes. "Merely reminding you of the Academy's legal protections. You're a businessman. Surely you understand the importance of keeping one's word."

Silence stretched between them. Then he inclined his head, curt and cold.

His jaw tightened almost imperceptibly. "Of course. How foolish of me to forget such... important details."

"Not foolish at all," Kalisandra replied with gracious magnanimity. "These are complex matters. I'm sure you'll find the remaining months will pass quite quickly."

Lord Allencourt's gaze swept over Cassara one final time, and in it she saw a promise that this reprieve was temporary at best.

"Indeed," he said coldly. "I'm sure they will."

Without another word, he turned and strode away, leaving Cassara standing alone with the headmistress and Auren. She watched her father's retreating figure until he disappeared into the crowd, no doubt to find Julian's family and discuss accelerated wedding plans.

"Curious," Kalisandra murmured, her gaze dropping to Flicker, who had remained perfectly still throughout the entire exchange. The small creature looked up at her with those impossibly large eyes, as if he were studying her in return.

"You've acquired an interesting companion," Kalisandra said, though interesting was not the word that Cassara would have chosen to describe Flicker. "I look forward to seeing how the two of you grow. Good evening, Miss Allencourt." Then she was gliding away, leaving Cassara alone with Auren and the wreckage of her public humiliation.

Auren took a step closer, his eyes searching her face with barely concealed concern. "Cassara—"

But she was already moving, scooping Flicker into her arms and turning away from the lingering crowd, from the whispers, from everything that reminded her of how spectacularly she'd just failed.

She needed to disappear. Now.

Before anyone else could see her break.

CHAPTER TWENTY SIX

The stars stretched wide above the academy, endless and suffocating all at the same time. Cassara stepped onto the overlook, the wind biting through silk and chain, her breath shallow in her throat.

It was moments like this she loathed the silence. It left too much room for other things to fill it, like her spiraling thoughts and the crushing weight of failure and what it meant for her future.

The scuff of a boot against stone caused her entire body to stiffen. She didn't need to look to know who it was. The overlook was off the beaten path and in the months since she'd arrived there was only one other person she'd ever seen there.

Glancing over her shoulder she saw Auren hovering in the archway, not hesitant to approach, but simply watching her with those too-knowing eyes.

He looked at her, gaze steady, and she hated how that almost broke her.

"I don't need comfort," she said before he could speak.

"I didn't offer any."

That should have helped, but it didn't.

She moved closer to the railing, crimson skirts swirling, arms tight across her ribs. The chain at her throat felt like it was choking her.

"They all saw it," she said. "Julian. The creature. Me. I played the part, smiled at the right people. Let Julian hold me like I was his."

Her voice shook, anger, not tears. Not yet.

"I was supposed to prove something tonight. That I belonged. That I earned this. Instead, I revealed a beast that looks like a pet. I guess Flicker and I have that in common, don't we?"

Auren stepped closer, silent. Watching.

"And Julian? He thinks he won. The marriage contract is already drafted, Auren. My father has it all planned out. He used Vallemont as a distraction, he was never going to let me choose my own path."

"Cassara."

"No." The word came out fierce, desperate. "Don't try to make it better. Because it won't be, will it? This thing between us, it's dangerous. For both of us. And Julian knows it, and my father would destroy you if he found out, and I—"

Her breath hitched.

She blinked hard, jaw tightening like she could force the next words back down. But they slipped out anyway.

"I couldn't survive that."

The silence that followed wasn't empty. It pressed against her ribs, thick and unbearable.

Something inside her gave way.

Not loudly, not visibly.

She took one step toward him, then another, and it was too much. The careful walls she'd built, the control she'd clung to, it all crumbled at once.

She reached for him like someone grabbing the edge of a cliff.

Her body hit his with more force than either expected. Her fingers curled in his coat, her head found his shoulder, and her knees gave out like her strength had been a borrowed thing all along.

He staggered slightly, caught her on reflex, arms wrapping around her. With surprising gentleness he shifted them both down, knees to stone, back against the railing. He pulled her into his lap, one arm braced behind her, the other at her waist.

"I tried so hard," she whispered, voice so small it didn't sound like hers. "I've been trying for so long, and I'm still not enough. I'll never be enough."

That's when the tears came.

Not the kind you could swallow, or the kind you could hide.

The kind that tore through you like something ripping free. Her lungs seized, stealing breath in jagged gasps. The sobs came in waves that shook her entire frame, each one wrenching sounds from her that she couldn't control.

She was breaking apart in Auren's arms where anyone could find them.

The thought should have stopped her. Should have made her pull back, compose herself, rebuild the armor.

But she couldn't. She was so tired of holding it together.

Her fingers twisted tighter in Auren's coat, desperate for something solid when everything else felt like it was crumbling. All the fear and rage and suffocating pressure poured out of her in waves—for the mother she'd never known, for the father who saw her as currency, for Julian's threats and her own failures, for every year she'd spent trying to be enough and never quite reaching it.

Auren didn't speak. He didn't try to shush her or offer words that would change nothing. He only held her closer, one hand curling at the nape of her neck, his chin resting lightly atop her head as if afraid too much pressure would break her further.

His steadiness was almost unbearable. Like he could weather this, like her falling apart wouldn't make him pull away.

Minutes passed. The sobs dulled into tremors and her breathing became less ragged. Cassara stirred against him, but she didn't lift her head, only shifted enough for her cheek to find the crook of his neck.

She felt empty in the way that came after purging, like a fever finally broken. Hollowed out but somehow lighter, like she'd been carrying too much for too long and her body had finally forced her to set it down.

"Tell me something real," she said at last, her voice quiet but stronger than it had been a moment before.

She felt him go still, every muscle tensing beneath her. For a moment she thought he wouldn't answer, that even now there were still walls he wouldn't let her breach.

Then he sighed, long and slow.

"Her name was Lya."

Cassara's fingers stilled. She didn't move, didn't speak.

"We were sent into Vire Hollow to extract an A Rank corrupted beast. Lya was brilliant, reckless, too smart for her own good and bonded to a plasma wyvern she could barely contain. She thought she could end the threat alone."

His voice had gone flat.

"I saw the danger. I could've ordered her back. I should have. But I hesitated, told myself to trust her, let her prove it. She lit the Hollow instead."

Cassara's breath caught.

"The explosion triggered a cascade. Her wyvern lost control and by the time I reached her..." He swallowed. "There was nothing left to save."

He looked down at her.

"I dragged the rest of the squad out and resigned the next day. My mentor always told us that a true leader never hesitates and he was right. I hesitated and it cost me everything."

She touched his chest and lifted her head to meet his eyes.

"I must be exhausting to watch," she said, voice quiet. Almost a joke. Almost not.

A breath of silence.

Then, he huffed a quiet laugh. It wasn't sharp. It was worn at the edges, like something that had lived in his chest for weeks.

"You have no idea," he said, gaze warm despite everything. "But I'd watch you a thousand times over before I let anyone else try."

He didn't give her time to deflect or let the moment turn. His voice softened again.

"I see the same fire, the same defiance. The way you throw yourself into the storm just to prove you can come out breathing." His voice cracked slightly. "And it terrifies me. Because I know now what it costs to love someone like that."

She didn't look away, didn't speak, just leaned in and kissed him.

It wasn't birthed of heat or desire, but need, as though in that moment it was the only solid thing she could reach.

He didn't hesitate. The moment her mouth touched his, Auren was moving, his hand sliding into her hair, the other tightening at her waist like he'd been holding back too long. He kissed her like he knew her. Like he remembered every place they'd touched and couldn't bear the space between them a second longer.

It wasn't rough or rushed, but it wasn't careful, either.

Their mouths moved with unspoken urgency, her breath hitched when his fingers brushed the bare skin at her neck, and her grip in his coat clenched tighter as if letting go would mean unraveling all over again.

His lips parted against hers, deeper now, and she leaned into him fully, body pressed to his as if she could disappear there. She didn't need words. Didn't want them. She just needed this. Needed him. The warmth of his hands. The press of his chest. The way he held her like nothing about her fear or fury scared him off.

When they broke apart, it wasn't because either of them wanted to.

It was because they needed air.

But even then, she didn't pull away. Her forehead pressed to his, their breath shared in the small, quiet space between them.

She didn't say anything and he didn't try to fill the silence.

He only whispered her name, low and rough like it hurt him to say.

And in the hush that followed, she finally breathed.

Cassara pushed open the dormitory door, wanting nothing more than to collapse onto her bed and let the night settle around her in blessed silence.

Instead, she found Sonia methodically packing a trunk.

The other girl didn't look up immediately, just continued folding clothes with precise movements, stacking them neatly beside an open chest. Her belongings were already half-sorted—books in one pile, toiletries in another, the systematic dismantling of her corner of the room.

Cassara stopped in the doorway.

"Leaving?" she asked, her voice flat.

Sonia glanced up, and something cold flickered across her features. Not guilt. Not embarrassment. Satisfaction.

"I requested a room transfer," Sonia said simply, returning to her packing. "Thought it best, given the circumstances."

"The circumstances," Cassara repeated slowly, stepping fully into the room and letting the door close behind her. "You mean the ones where you accused me of cheating in front of the entire academy?"

"I simply reported what I was told." Sonia's tone was practiced, smooth. "What happened after that wasn't my fault."

Cassara's hands curled into fists at her sides. "What you were told? Who exactly informed you about a private conversation with a poacher?"

Sonia's hands paused, just for a fraction of a second, before resuming their methodical folding. "I can't say."

"That's convenient."

"Is it?" Sonia picked up a stack of books. "Or maybe you were just careless."

"I wasn't careless." Cassara took a step closer. "I was alone. In a private training room. So unless you were following me—"

"Is it that important?" Sonia cut in, her composure cracking slightly. "You were approached. That's the truth, isn't it?"

"But I didn't take the deal," Cassara said slowly, watching Sonia's face. "So why accuse me?"

"Because I saw your beast." Sonia's voice hardened. "That ridiculous little creature. I saw what you bonded with and I knew—"

She stopped abruptly, realizing she'd said too much.

Cassara went very still. "You saw Flicker. Before the reveal. When?"

"Does it matter when? I saw him and—"

"What? Thought that I'd be desperate enough to cheat?"

"You should have been desperate!" Sonia said, her careful mask finally cracking. "Anyone with half a brain would have taken that deal. You could have had something actually useful, something that wouldn't make you a laughingstock. You turned down a fire drake—"

"How do you know what he offered?" Cassara interrupted quietly.

"Because I gave him the perfect opportunity!" Sonia exploded, throwing the books down into the chest. "I saw your pathetic excuse for a beast and I thought, 'here's a chance.' I arranged it. I made sure he'd approach you with something good enough that you couldn't possibly refuse—"

"You hired him," Cassara breathed.

"So what if I did?" Sonia's face flushed with anger. "You were supposed to take it! But no, precious Cassara Allencourt is too noble, too principled—"

"You tried to frame me."

"I tried to expose you for what you are!" Sonia stepped forward, all pretense gone now. "You get everything! The rankings, the attention, *Julian*—and you act like you don't even want it! Like it's all such a burden!"

There it was.

Cassara stared at her, disbelief cutting through the anger. "This is about Julian?"

"He's obsessed with you," Sonia spat, stepping closer, her voice rising. "Follows you around like a lovesick fool and you can't even be bothered to appreciate it! You have everything I've ever wanted handed to you on a silver platter and you just—"

She jabbed a finger toward Cassara's chest.

"You don't deserve any of it," Sonia hissed. "Not him. Not your ranking. Not the attention. Nothing."

Cassara's hand shot out and knocked the items from Sonia's other hand. Personal effects scattered across the floor—a jewelry box, a framed portrait, bottles of perfume that rolled under beds.

The sharp crack of breaking glass punctuated the silence.

"You want Julian?" Cassara's voice was ice. "Take him. He's yours."

Sonia's expression twisted. "You don't mean that."

"I mean every word." Cassara held her gaze. "You think he's some prize? You're welcome to him."

"Liar," Sonia hissed. "You're just saying that because you know he'd never choose me over you—"

"I'm saying it because I don't want him." Cassara stepped closer. "I never did. Whatever fantasy you've built in your head about him, about me—it's just that. A fantasy."

"You're so smug," Sonia said, her voice shaking with fury. "So convinced you're better than everyone else. Well look at you now. Obsidian. Bottom of the rankings. And it's exactly where you deserve to be."

Cassara's hands curled into fists at her sides. It would be so easy to hit her.

One punch. Just one.

"You hired someone to destroy my future because you're jealous of something I don't even want," she said quietly. "That's pathetic, Sonia."

"At least I'm honest about what I want!" Sonia shot back. "At least I don't pretend to be above it all while manipulating everyone around me—"

The door opened behind them. Liri stood there, eyes wide, Evie just behind her. They took in the scene—the scattered belongings, the two girls standing too close, the tension in the air.

"What's going on?" Liri asked carefully.

Sonia stepped back, her chest heaving. For a moment, Cassara thought she might say something else.

Instead, she crouched and began gathering her scattered things with jerky, angry movements.

"Nothing," Sonia said coldly. "I was just leaving."

She shoved the last of her belongings into the trunk with more force than necessary, then hauled it toward the door. Liri and Evie pressed against the wall to let her pass.

Sonia paused in the doorway, glancing back.

"For what it's worth," she said, voice flat, "I don't regret it. You deserved everything you got."

Then she was gone.

The silence that followed felt suffocating.

"Cass?" Liri's voice was gentle. She stepped forward, hand reaching out. "What happened? What was she talking about?"

Cassara stared at the space where Sonia had been, at the empty corner that would soon belong to someone else.

"She hired the poacher," Cassara said, her voice hollow. "The whole thing. She set me up."

"What?" Evie's voice cracked. "But—why?"

"Because she's jealous." The words tasted bitter. "Because she wants things I don't even want and can't stand that I have them."

Liri moved closer, clearly wanting to comfort her. "Cass, I'm so sorry. We should tell someone, the headmistress—"

"No." Cassara cut her off. "It doesn't matter. She admitted it to me, not anyone who matters. It's my word against hers and we both know how that goes."

"But—"

"Liri." Cassara turned to face her friend, exhaustion settling into every bone. "I can't. Not right now."

"Okay," she said softly. "But we're here. When you're ready."

Cassara nodded once, unable to find words.

She sank onto her bed, still in her gala gown, the gold chains cold against her skin. Liri and Evie retreated to their own beds, giving her space.

Alone with her thoughts, Cassara stared at the ceiling.

She should feel something. Rage, maybe. The desire for revenge.

Instead, she just felt tired.

So impossibly tired.

Cassara walked onto the main training with her back straight and her chin lifted, every step confident. She could feel the eyes on her, curious, pitying, amused. Let them look. She'd given them plenty of reasons to.

Every first-year had been summoned. Dozens lined up in ranked order, backs stiff, uniforms neat, beasts pacing or perched nearby. And above them all, the Crestboard loomed, alive with shifting glyphs and cold, unfeeling truth. Names flickered like stars in a dying sky, each one stamped with a color-coded sigil. Platinum at the top and at the bottom...

Cassara's breath caught.

Obsidian.

The sigil flared beside her name like a brand. She'd known her fall had cost her and that her performance in the Reveal had been a mess of pain and panic and shame. But Obsidian?

From top to bottom overnight.

The sight made her stomach twist. It didn't matter that she'd survived a corrupted beast, or that she'd stood tall in front of the entire school after false accusations of cheating, it hadn't been enough. Not for the board. Not for the academy. Not for the vultures waiting in the sidelines.

She heard the murmurs, knew they were watching. Wondering. Remembering the girl who had once walked with her chin high and now stood a failure.

Flicker nudged her leg.

He mimicked her stance like he didn't quite understand why they were standing still. His eyes flicked up at her, trusting. As if the world hadn't shifted under her feet.

Sonia caught her eye and smiled with false sympathy. The kind of smile that said how the mighty have fallen.

Cassara smiled back.

Sharp as glass.

"First-years." Headmistress Kalisandra's voice cut through the morning air, drawing every eye to the center of the field. She stood before the Crestboard, hands clasped behind her back.

"The Reveal has concluded. Your individual trials are over. From this point forward, your success, and your survival, depends not on personal achievement, but on your ability to function as a unit."

Nervous whispers swept through the crowd. Cassara listened with the stillness of someone who'd already lost everything and had nothing left to fear.

"The top six ranked students will serve as unit captains," Kalisandra continued. "Each captain may select up to five additional members for their team. These units will train together, fight together, and be evaluated together. Your Prestige rankings will rise or fall based on individual and collective performance."

Collective. The word tasted bitter in Cassara's mouth. She'd spent her entire life being judged by her individual merit, or lack thereof. Now even that small comfort was being stripped away.

"Captains," the headmistress said, "you have one hour to make your selections. Choose wisely. The students you recruit today will determine your fate for the remainder of your time at Vallemont."

One by one, she called the names. Gideon Delvanir stepped forward first. Even from across the field, Cassara could see the tension in his shoulders, the way he held himself apart from the others. First place, but still an outsider.

Julian's name came second. He moved with easy confidence, that familiar smile playing at his lips as he took his position. Several students immediately gravitated toward him, drawn by his ranking and his family's influence.

The other four captains barely registered. Cassara watched the proceedings with detached interest, noting who approached whom, who was ignored, who tried too hard to seem valuable. It was fascinating, in a distant sort of way. Like watching ants reorganize after someone kicked their hill.

"The selection process begins now," Kalisandra announced. "Captains, make your choices."

And then the real show began.

Teams began forming with the efficiency of a market exchange. Julian's squad filled quickly, ambitious students who saw his political connections as a path to advancement. Gideon moved more slowly, more deliberately, speaking quietly with potential recruits who approached him with careful respect.

Cassara remained where she was, arms crossed, watching.

Waiting.

The fury that had been building since she'd seen her ranking burned steady and cold in her chest. Not at Flicker, never at Flicker again. But at all of them.

The ones who whispered and laughed, who looked at her with pity or dismissal or vengeful satisfaction.

The ones who reminded her, with uncomfortable clarity, of herself just days ago.

She remembered the way she'd dismissed Oliver, the quiet boy who preferred working alone. The way she'd categorized people by their usefulness, their potential, their worth to her goals. Standing here now, watching others do the same to her, left a foul taste in her mouth.

"Cassara."

Julian stepped forward like a god in a story he'd written for himself. His smile held no kindness. "Want to redeem that golden debut? I've got one spot left." he said, voice rich with false generosity. "I'll even carry your weight, if you're sweet enough about it."

His eyes flicked to her feet, where Flicker sat grooming his silver fur with meticulous care, apparently unbothered by the conversation.

"All you have to do," Julian continued, stepping closer, "is ask nicely."

The words hung in the air between them. Around them, other students had stopped their conversations to listen. This was entertainment now. The fallen prodigy, brought low, begging for scraps from her almost-fiance.

Cassara held his gaze a beat longer, then turned her face away.

He didn't take it well.

"Suit yourself," Julian muttered, doing little to mask the bitterness in his tone. "We'll see how long it takes before you come crawling back."

She didn't dignify his assumptions with a response.

The field buzzed around her, a tide she couldn't quite reach.

And then—

Boots crunched beside her. She looked up sharply expecting to see Julian returned for another round.

Instead Gideon stood there, arms folded, watching her like he was trying to solve a puzzle that wouldn't sit still.

"I'm surprised you didn't take him up on it," he said. "Tremaine always did have a soft spot for pretty things that break easy."

The disgust that flashed across Cassara's face was swift and visceral, gone almost before it appeared.

Her spine straightened instinctively. "Come to add your insult to the pile?"

Flicker turned toward Gideon with curiosity, then, without hesitation, started nibbling at his boot laces. Little, hopeful tugs.

To his credit, Gideon didn't move. He just reached into his coat pocket and pulled something out.

A unit pin, plain black.

He held it out to her.

Cassara stared. “What is that?”

“A place. On my unit.”

She blinked. “Why?”

His eyes didn’t waver. “Because you’re not afraid to burn.”

She let out a laugh. “You don’t even like me. And he’s useless.”

Flicker paused in his play to chirp softly, as if agreeing with the assessment. The sound was so matter-of-fact that it almost made her smile.

“No,” he said, and stepped in closer. “But I respect you.”

He caught her wrist gently, pressed the crest into her palm, closed her fingers around it like a promise.

“Training starts tomorrow at nine. Don’t be late.”

And then he turned, leaving no room for argument, no time to second guess.

“Well,” she murmured, fingers brushing over the velvet rise of Flicker’s ears, “looks like we’ve got ourselves a team.”

He chirred at her touch, leaning into it with a contented flutter.

Cassara’s gaze swept the training field once more.

“Come on,” she said quietly. “Let’s get out of here.”

She hadn’t gotten far when Julian’s voice cut through the air behind her.

“Cassara. Wait.”

She didn’t stop, didn’t even turn around. But she heard his footsteps following, quick and determined.

“I said wait.” His hand closed around her wrist, spinning her back to face him. The crest in her palm pressed sharp against her fingers where his grip tightened.

“Let go of me,” she said quietly.

Julian’s eyes were bright with something ugly. Jealousy, maybe. Or wounded pride.

“So that’s how it is,” he said, voice pitched low enough that only she could hear. “All this time, acting like you were above such things. But you’re not, are you? You’re just like every other ambitious little—”

“Careful,” Cassara warned.

“It was him, wasn’t it?” Julian’s grip tightened, his thumb pressing into her wrist. “That night you came back late? I could smell him on you. Delvanir. Did you think I wouldn’t figure it out?”

Heat flooded Cassara’s cheeks, but she kept her voice level. “I don’t know what you’re talking about.”

"Don't lie to me." His smile was sharp, predatory. "It doesn't matter, you know. Whatever arrangement you have with him. I can offer you something better. More secure. You wouldn't have to debase yourself, slumming it with damaged goods from a disgraced family."

Cassara tried to pull away, but Julian's grip held firm.

"Think about it," he continued, leaning closer. "My team. My protection. My bed, if you're willing to be reasonable about it. Much more civilized than whatever desperation led you to—"

"Get your hands off her."

The voice came from behind Julian, cold and steady. Gideon stood there, his eyes fixed on the hand wrapped around Cassara's wrist.

Julian turned, his grip loosening slightly but not releasing. "This is a private conversation, Delvanir."

"No," Gideon said, taking a step forward. "It's not."

"Gideon," Cassara started, but he wasn't looking at her. His attention was focused entirely on Julian, on the space between them that was shrinking with each deliberate step.

"Was I not clear enough, Tremaine? Let. Her. Go."

"Or what?" Julian's voice carried that familiar edge of entitled amusement, his grip tightening causing Cassara to wince. "You'll make me? We both know your family doesn't have the influence to—"

Gideon's fist connected with Julian's jaw with a sound like breaking wood.

Julian staggered backward, releasing Cassara's wrist as his hand flew to his face. Around them, the field erupted in gasps and excited whispers. Students pressed closer, sensing blood in the water.

"What the hell," Julian started, but Gideon was already moving again.

"Maybe if you spent less time talking, you'd be able to hear better," Gideon's voice was low, lethal.

The second punch caught Julian in the stomach, doubling him over. He wheezed, spittle flying from his lips as he struggled to breathe.

"That's enough."

Auren's voice cut through the chaos as he strode across the field, students parting before him like water. His expression was carefully neutral, but Cassara caught the flash of something fierce in his eyes as he took in the scene, Julian on the ground, Gideon standing over him with bloody knuckles, herself with finger-shaped bruises already blooming on her wrist.

"Tremaine, get up," Auren ordered. Julian struggled to his feet, one hand pressed to his ribs, the other dabbing at his split lip.

"He attacked me!" Julian protested, voice higher than usual. "Unprovoked assault! I demand—"

"Detention," Auren said calmly. "One week. Evening sessions with Instructor Nareen."

"What?" Julian's voice cracked. "But he hit me! I'm the victim here!"

"You're also the one who grabbed a fellow student after she told you to let go," Auren replied, eyes flicking meaningfully to Cassara's wrist. "That's grounds for disciplinary action."

"This is ridiculous! My father will hear about this! You can't—"

"Your father," Auren cut in, "can take it up with the headmistress. If he has concerns about our discipline policy."

Julian's mouth opened and closed like a fish gasping for air. Around them, the other students watched with rapt attention, clearly enjoying the spectacle of Julian Tremaine being dressed down in front of everyone.

Auren turned to Gideon. "Delvanir. Same punishment. One week detention."

Gideon shrugged, wiping blood from his knuckles with clinical detachment. "Worth it."

The simple acceptance in his voice, the complete lack of regret, sent something warm and complicated spiraling through Cassara's chest. She pressed her lips together to keep from smiling.

Auren's gaze lingered on Gideon for a moment before he turned to address the crowd.

"Show's over," he announced. "Return to your team selections."

The students began to disperse, reluctantly, still buzzing with excitement over what they'd witnessed. Julian stood there for another moment, dabbing at his lip and shooting venomous looks at both Gideon and Cassara before stalking away to rejoin his team.

Gideon turned to go as well, but Cassara caught his sleeve.

"Why?" she asked quietly.

He looked down at her hand on his arm, then back to her face. For a moment, she thought he might answer and explain why he'd chosen her, why he'd defended her, why he'd been willing to take detention for the privilege of bloodying Julian's nose.

Instead, he just pulled free of her grip and walked away.

But not before she caught the ghost of a smile at the corner of his mouth.

Cassara stood there, holding his crest in her palm, watching him go.

Tomorrow at nine, he'd said.

She wouldn't be late.

CHAPTER TWENTY SEVEN

The dormitory was silent when Cassara finally returned, the corridors empty save for the faint glow of enchanted sconces that never quite went dark. Her muscles ached from hours spent alone in the training yard, pushing herself through drills until exhaustion finally outweighed the churning in her chest.

She'd stayed away as long as she could. Long enough for Sonia's satisfied whispers to fade, for Liri's well-meaning concern to settle into sleep, for Evie's gentle questions to remain unasked. She wasn't ready for any of it, the betrayal, the pity, the careful navigation of friendships that might not survive what she'd become.

Her boots thudded against stone as she made her way to her room, careful not to wake anyone. The door opened with barely a sound, and she slipped inside to find her roommates' beds curtained and still. Safe, for now.

Cassara sank onto her own bed without bothering to change, every movement deliberate and quiet. Her training clothes stuck to her skin with dried sweat, and her hair had long since escaped its pins to hang loose around her shoulders. She should wash. Should sleep. Should do any number of practical things.

Instead, she reached under her pillow and pulled out her mother's journal.

The leather was soft beneath her fingers, worn smooth by years of handling. She'd read these pages so many times she could recite them from memory, her mother's hopes, fears, the careful documentation of a young woman trying to find her place in a world that demanded more than she thought she could give.

But tonight, instead of reading, Cassara flipped toward the back where blank pages waited like held breath.

She stared at the empty parchment for a long moment, pen hovering uncertainly in her hand. The silence stretched, broken only by the soft breathing from behind the other curtains and the distant sound of wind against the windows.

I've never done this before, she finally wrote, the words small and uncertain on the page.

Her hand stilled. What was there to say? That she'd fallen further than she'd ever imagined possible? That the girl who'd arrived at Vallemont with fire in her chest and her mother's legacy as armor had been stripped bare in front of everyone who mattered?

Today I became everything I once looked down on, she wrote. Obsidian. Bottom tier. The charity case that someone took pity on.

The words felt clumsy, inadequate. How did you capture the weight of humiliation in ink? How did you explain the particular ache of watching Julian's satisfied smile, of seeing Sonia's false sympathy, of knowing that everything she'd worked for had crumbled in a single evening?

But Gideon chose me anyway. I don't understand why. I don't understand him.

Her pen paused again. The memory of his fist connecting with Julian's jaw sent something warm and complicated through her chest. The way he'd said "worth it" about the detention, like bloodying Julian's nose had been a privilege rather than a punishment.

Julian thinks I slept my way onto Gideon's team. Maybe others think it, too. Maybe it doesn't matter what they think anymore.

The admission felt dangerous, even written in her own hand. But there was something liberating about it too, the possibility that their opinions might not have the power to destroy her after all.

She tried to write more, about Auren and the way he'd looked at Julian's hand on her wrist, about the strange comfort of Gideon's matter-of-fact acceptance of her, about the slow burning realization that she might not be as alone as she'd thought. But the words wouldn't come. They tangled in her throat, too complicated and raw to pin down with something as simple as language.

Finally, she closed the journal and shoved it back under her pillow with more force than necessary.

The movement stirred something warm against her side. Flicker materialized from her shard without being summoned, his small form silver-bright in the darkness. He looked at her for a moment then padded across the blanket to curl up beside her hip.

Cassara stared down at him, this creature that everyone called useless, this bond that had somehow become the catalyst for her downfall. He was grooming his fur again, completely unaffected by her mood or the day's events. Content, somehow, just to be near her.

Flicker's purr was so quiet she almost missed it. He'd settled into the curve of her body as if he belonged there, as if he'd always belonged there, and the simple acceptance of it made her throat tight.

You're not what I wanted, she thought. *But maybe... maybe that's not your fault.*

The little creature's ear twitched, and his purr deepened in response, not hurt by the admission, but somehow pleased by her honesty. He knew what she was thinking, felt her resentment, and yet he'd chosen to stay anyway.

Cassara stood outside the training annex, arms crossed, weight tilted into one hip, clearly not staring at the door. Her reflection ghosted faintly in the glass: braid sharp over one shoulder, boots polished, posture defiant. Nothing to be nervous about. Nothing at all.

Flicker circled lazily beside her, nosing at the edge of a nearby bench, then hopping up onto it to sprawl in a ridiculous puff of ears and tail. The little creature stretched, yawned, and rolled over onto its back, legs twitching in the air as if asking her for belly rubs.

Cassara resisted the urge to groan.

"Planning to stand out here all day?" came a voice from behind her.

She twisted, startled, and found Gideon standing at her shoulder, hands in his pockets, watching her expectantly. "You're blocking the door," he added, coolly, stepping around her before she could respond.

Cassara scowled at his back and moved, catching the faintest twitch at the corner of his mouth as he brushed past. He paused at the entrance, glanced over his shoulder with a subtle lift of his brow. "Well? Are you coming or not?"

She exhaled sharply, lifted her chin, and followed him in. Flicker hopped down with a delighted chirp and trotted after, tail swishing like a banner.

The training room was one of the smaller annex fields, hex-glass ceiling panels, ambient magelight pulsing through the floor in thin, circuit-like lines.

Three other teammates were already there.

Cassara's eyes caught on the first, red curls tied in a lopsided knot, bag slung half open, and a grin mid-formation even before she turned fully around.

"Liri?" Cassara said before she could stop herself.

Liri's eyes widened. "Cassara!" she yelped, bounding forward like a wind-up spring. "Oh my stars, are you on our- I mean- wait, is this your team too?!"

Cassara blinked, half-expecting a catch, but the sheer relief that bloomed in her chest was so sharp it caught her completely off guard. "Apparently," she muttered.

Behind Liri, another figure stood near the wall, arms folded, expression neutral behind rectangular lenses. Oliver. Cassara barely tilted her head in acknowledgment, unsurprised. "Figures," she said under her breath.

His brow twitched. "Pleasure to see you again, too."

And next to him was a boy, taller, broad-shouldered, nervously adjusting the strap of his bracer like it was strangling him.

She'd seen him around. His name started with a B.

"Brian?" she guessed.

"No," said Gideon, without missing a beat. "That's Barrett. Barrett. Everyone calls him Rett."

"Right. Barrett," she repeated. "I knew that."

Gideon glanced at the clock on the wall. "One more. Then we'll begin."

As if on cue, the door swung open.

Verena sauntered in, hair perfect, uniform crisp, boots echoing on the reinforced floor. She smiled at Gideon, until her gaze slid past him and caught sight of the wrong person standing too close.

Her whole body froze.

"Is this a joke?" she snapped. "Are you kidding me, Gideon?"

The silence snapped taut like a wire pulled to its limit. Even Flicker stopped mid-stretch, one paw still in the air.

The temperature in the room seemed to drop several degrees. Liri's Sparkfly Moth, Nym, paused mid-flutter. Oliver looked up from his equipment and Barrett had gone still, his gaze sliding from one person to the next as though cataloging each reaction to examine later.

Cassara felt Flicker press against her ankle, a warm, steadying weight that somehow made it easier to keep her chin up and her expression calm.

"Problem, Verena?" Gideon's voice carried no particular inflection, but his posture had changed. His weight shifted forward slightly, shoulders squaring, every line of his body suddenly alert and focused.

"The problem," Verena said, taking a step forward, "is that I gave up a captain position to be on this team. *Your* team. And you've filled it with charity cases and academy jokes."

Her gaze flicked to Cassara with undisguised contempt.

"Did you really think no one would notice? The girl who collapsed in the Rift, ranked dead last after her precious gala disaster? What possible use could she be to anyone?"

Each word cut deep, perfectly aimed to find the softest spots in Cassara's armor. But she'd been expecting this. Had been preparing for it since the moment she'd seen her name at the bottom of that damned board.

"I'm standing right here," Cassara said.

"Unfortunately," Verena replied without missing a beat.

Cassara's fingers clenched at her sides, but before she could speak, Flicker trotted over to Verena's manticore, tilted its head, and booped its armored leg.

It blinked once. Twice.

Then hissed like a furnace cracking open.

"Get your house pet away from Kaddock," Verena snapped. "I don't need you crying because it gets stomped on or eaten."

Flicker was entirely unphased by the display from the much larger beast. He simply stared up at the snarling fortress of a creature and let out a chirp that sounded suspiciously like a giggle.

Liri stifled a laugh. "I love him."

"That's enough."

Gideon's voice cut easily through the tension, silencing all of them. When Verena turned to him, her expression was a mixture of disbelief and wounded betrayal.

"You're defending her? After what happened with Julian? After being accused of cheating?"

"Accused and cleared."

Silence stretched between them and Cassara could feel the weight of everyone's attention, the careful way they were all watching this power struggle unfold.

Verena's jaw worked for a moment before she found her voice again. "This is a mistake, Gideon. And when it costs us, when *she* costs us, don't say I didn't warn you."

"Noted," he replied evenly.

Verena stared at him for another long moment then turned on her heel and stalked to the far side of the room, her manticore following with heavy, deliberate steps that made the floor vibrate.

"Well," Oliver said, his voice startlingly loud in the quiet. "This should be fun."

Gideon clapped his hands once. "We've wasted enough time. Spread out. We're running core coordination drills. You don't have to like each other, but you do have to work together."

Verena rolled her eyes. "Says the one who forgot to mention he was bringing in a charity case."

Cassara stepped forward, eyes flashing. "Say that again."

"Stop." Gideon's voice cracked like thunder, short, sharp, and silencing. "Cassara. Position three. Verena, flank right. Oliver, pair with Barrett. Liri, center with me."

As they moved into place, Verena muttered, "I'm not taking orders from her."

The moment they moved into formation, the tension doubled.

Barrett stood still as stone, his eyes kept flicking toward Liri. Oliver adjusted his bracer twice, muttering something about field calibration. Verena didn't even try to hide her sneer when Cassara passed her.

Cassara took her position, arms crossed. Flicker circled her ankles once and then sat back with the serenity of a creature that hadn't just insulted a manticore.

Gideon took a slow breath, then stepped forward, voice steady and even.

"This isn't a sparring match," he said, gaze sweeping over all of them. "And it's not about raw power."

Liri stopped fidgeting. Oliver straightened. Even Rett looked up from adjusting his gauntlet.

Gideon nodded toward the hex-lined floor beneath them, the faint magelight already starting to pulse in patterns. "These drills are about cohesion. Timing. Reading your teammates without needing a shout or a signal. When we're in the field, you won't have time to argue or second-guess. This drill forces your ACS to adapt to team-based feedback and spatial mapping. It records how well you move as a unit and uses that to help find weak spots."

"And what exactly are we moving for?" Verena asked, voice too sweet.

"You're tracking formation rotations based on real combat layouts," Gideon replied without looking at her. "Rotations simulate shield coverage, line-of-sight for beasts, and pressure-point shifts during battlefield engagement. If one of you lags, the whole formation collapses."

Barrett shifted slightly. Liri bit her lip, glancing down at the pulsing lines.

"This is about awareness, movement, and trust. On my mark, you'll rotate positions in sequence. Cassara, you start the rotation."

"Why her?" Verena cut in immediately.

"Because I said so," Gideon answered. "Mark."

Cassara moved, fluid, focused, silent. It wasn't flawless, but it was sharp. She side-stepped, ducked under Barrett's shoulder as he pivoted left, spun around Liri, and rotated into Gideon's blind spot like she belonged there.

"Next!" he barked.

When Verena moved it was intentionally too slow.

Cassara narrowly avoided a collision and bit her tongue as she snapped into her next position. "You're dragging," she said without looking.

"Some of us don't have to cheat to keep up," Verena hissed.

Liri stumbled trying to shift wide, clipped by Oliver's elbow as he pivoted. Barrett caught her with one arm before she hit the ground, but the timing shattered. Gideon stepped in with a frustrated sigh, voice taut. "Reset. Again."

They realigned. Again.

Flicker, unimpressed, began circling the group, small paws padding through glowing glyph trails left by the floor's mana. He occasionally stopped to tap a rune with his nose, blinking each time the glyph sparked in response.

Oliver glanced down, distracted. "Is he... learning the circuit patterns?"

"Flicker," Cassara hissed. "Stop being odd."

Flicker promptly rolled over onto a mana node and hummed.

Liri beamed. "Did I mention I love him?"

Verena scoffed. "No wonder your training's a disaster."

Cassara's teeth ground together. "I swear, if you say one more—"

"Enough!" Gideon cut in again. "Verena, reset your stance. Cassara, you're in lead rotation this time. Let's try not to mess this one up."

Cassara positioned herself at the edge of the formation circle, watching the flow of movement like she was reading a complex equation. The mana-lit nodes beneath their feet pulsed in rhythm, waiting for synchronization that kept slipping just out of reach.

Oliver moved first, his Stoneshade Mantis Ilza, mirroring his careful, calculated steps. But his feint angled too wide, throwing off the balance they needed. Barrett shifted instinctively to cover Liri's position, his protective instincts overriding formation discipline. Liri herself wavered, uncertain whether to hold center or adjust to compensate for the others.

And Verena—Verena was already preparing to cut her arc short, impatience radiating from every line of her body as Kaddock rumbled its disapproval.

Cassara saw it all unfolding like a slow-motion disaster.

"Hold center, Liri," she called out, her voice cutting through the confusion. "Barrett, take her flank but maintain distance. Oliver, stagger left instead—smaller increments."

It wasn't loud, but it carried absolute clarity. Authority born not from rank but from understanding of patterns.

They listened.

Barrett adjusted his position smoothly, giving Liri the space she needed while still maintaining protective proximity. Oliver corrected his angle, his movements becoming more precise, more controlled. Even Liri seemed to find her confidence, the glow from Nym brightening as she settled into the center point.

The pattern clicked into place like puzzle pieces finding their home.

The mana nodes responded, their pulsing synchronizing into a steady, harmonious rhythm that seemed to hum with satisfied energy. Even Gideon paused at the edge of the circle, his dark eyes narrowing, not in disapproval, but satisfaction.

He was impressed.

Verena stopped dead in her tracks.

"What was that?" she demanded, rounding on Cassara with fire in her green eyes.

"A fix," Cassara answered, meeting her gaze without flinching. "You were about to throw the timing off again."

"You think you get to command this team?" Verena took a step forward, heat radiating from her like a forge. Behind her, Kaddock shifted restlessly, responding to its tamer's rising temper.

"No," Cassara said, her voice calm and level. "But I think I just saved it."

A soft, musical warble drew everyone's attention downward. Flicker sat perfectly positioned on the very center node of the formation ring, his silver fur glowing with the same gentle radiance as the arcane channels beneath his paws. The light pulsed in perfect synchronization with his purring, as if he'd become part of the magical circuit itself.

Even Oliver looked startled, his usual analytical composure cracking. "How did it—? The resonance frequency alone should have—"

He trailed off, staring at the little creature with the kind of fascination usually reserved for impossible equations that somehow solved themselves.

I made it hum.

Cassara stared at Flicker, who stared back at her with those wide, innocent eyes that held depths she was only beginning to understand. There was something almost smug in his expression, like he'd been waiting for them to figure out what he figured was already obvious.

"Again," Gideon said, his voice carrying quiet command. "Cassara—call it."

Cassara blinked, certain she'd misheard. "What?"

"You saw the pattern. You understood the flow." His dark gaze fixed on her with an intensity that made her pulse quicken. "Fix it. Again."

She hesitated, acutely aware of every eye on her, but only for a second.

"Liri, tighten your arc by half a step," she called out, her voice growing more confident with each instruction. "Barrett, stay opposite me but watch your spacing—you're crowding the energy flow. Verena—" She paused, meeting the other girl's venomous glare directly. "Try not to get in the way this time."

Verena looked like she might explode, her face flushing red as her manticore let out a low, threatening rumble. For a moment, Cassara thought she might refuse outright or storm out of the formation, damn the consequences.

Whether it was pride, pragmatism, or some combination of both, Verena took her position with sharp, angry precision that somehow worked within the larger pattern and for the first time since they'd started training together, the sequence ran smooth.

Not perfect—Oliver still moved with mechanical motions that lacked intuitive flow, and Barrett's protective instincts occasionally overrode formation discipline. But it was functional. Aligned. The mana nodes sang with harmonious energy, and their beasts moved in complementary patterns that spoke of genuine synchronization.

Cassara didn't say anything when they finished, she didn't need to.

Her pulse still thrummed in her ears as she stepped out of formation, Flicker trotting faithfully at her heels. Across the room, Liri was beaming like she'd just won a tournament, while Barrett offered her a small, quiet thumbs-up.

Flicker bumped against her calf, soft and solid, and flopped down dramatically across a glowing node with a pleased little grunt.

"Better, not great, but better," Gideon said.

Verena stared hard at him looking like she might combust. Without a word she turned, grabbed her bag, and stalked toward the exit without waiting for dismissal.

"Verena," Gideon said, calm but commanding.

She stopped just shy of the door but didn't look back, not right away.

"You're expected at afternoon drills. If you skip them, I'll report it."

Verena looked over her shoulder. Her smile was cold as ice. "Then I suppose I'll see you there."

She left without another word.

Cassara exhaled, long and quiet. "Do we get a medal for surviving that?"

Gideon didn't flinch. "No. But I'd call this progress."

The words startled her, not because of what he said, but how he said them. Not as a backhanded note or passive formality. It almost sounded like praise.

She blinked. "Did you just say something nice?"

"You saw what needed fixing," he said. "And you acted, they listened. That's the whole point of the exercise."

Cassara hesitated. "Thanks," she said, quietly.

"I didn't say it was perfect," he added.

She arched her brow. "You really don't know how to make a compliment, do you?"

Again, a corner of his mouth twitched. Not quite a smile, but close. "Take a break. Get some water. Reset your ACS. We've got two hours until combat drills."

And with that, he turned and left. Was he going to look for Verena? To apologize for being so harsh to her in front of the team?

Cassara didn't have time to dwell on it. Her attention shifted to Oliver, who was watching Flicker with more interest than she'd ever seen him direct at something living.

Flicker was sitting in front of him like a very fluffy statue, lazily scratching his ear with a back paw and sending faint ripples through the mana lines beneath him.

"You're triggering the circuit," Oliver murmured, fascinated. "But not through pressure... you're syncing with the ley pattern. How—?"

Flicker yawned wide enough to show all four little fangs.

Oliver blinked. "Right. I'll try again after you nap."

"I'm starving," Liri announced, bouncing to her feet. "And if we stay in here any longer, I'm going to eat part of the ACS paneling. Cassara, come on."

Cassara blinked. "What?"

"We're going to lunch." Liri grabbed her arm like this had always been the plan. "You've earned real food and gossip."

"I don't—"

"Too late, I'm already dragging you."

Barrett fell into step behind them with quiet inevitability. Oliver followed a beat later, still scribbling a note into his Codex while occasionally glancing back at Flicker, who now trailed behind them like a smug cloud with ears.

And just like that, they left the training annex.

Together.

For the first time—not as strangers. Not as rejects.

But as a team.

The drills blurred together.

Day after day, the team returned to the same hex-lit training annex, rotating through cohesion exercises, formation tests, and mana sync calibrations. The circuits changed, but the outcome rarely did.

Cassara called formations. Sometimes they worked. Usually, they didn't, but not because they couldn't. Rather, because the unity between them was fleeting.

Liri stayed upbeat until the bruises on her shins outnumbered her jokes. Oliver scribbled theories between sets and tried to fine-tune his ACS interface mid-run. Barrett was steady but slow to adjust when the formation shifted under pressure. Verena never passed up a chance to throw blame, usually at Cassara, occasionally at everyone else.

Flicker stopped glowing during drills. He curled by the back wall or wandered the edge of the mana field, occasionally flicking a glyph with his tail, but he no longer brightened when Cassara made a correct call. He seemed bored. Disappointed, even. And Cassara hated how that bothered her.

Every success felt like a fluke while every failure felt earned.

"Hold left!" Cassara barked, skidding into position as the light-trail pattern changed mid-rotation. "Rett, you're late—Liri, cover the gap—Verena, shift back, you're out of—"

"I know where I'm supposed to be," Verena snapped, voice hot with venom. "Maybe if the rest of you kept up—"

The formation broke.

A flare of red light pulsed beneath their feet: failure signal.

Again.

Cassara's shoulders tightened as she froze in the center of the circle. Heat prickled behind her eyes, not from effort but frustration. Around her, the others pulled to a stop, staggered and breathless, no one looking at each other.

Flicker let out a soft, unimpressed chirp from where he lounged atop the bench, one paw dangling dramatically over the edge like this was a poorly rehearsed stage play.

"That's the third failure today," Verena said. "Maybe we should stop pretending this team ever had a chance."

"Oh, please," Cassara bit back. "You're the only one who's off every time we sync. You can't hold a simple defensive pattern for more than thirty seconds!"

Cassara's voice echoed off the training hall walls, sharp with a week's worth of accumulated frustration. Sweat beaded on her forehead despite the cool fall air, and her ACS readings flickered—stress channeling at its finest.

"Maybe the pattern would hold if certain people stopped barking orders like they owned the place," Verena shot back, Kaddock pawing the ground with barely restrained aggression. "News flash, Allencourt, being at the bottom of the rankings doesn't make you team leader."

"No, but understanding basic tactical formations apparently does," Cassara retorted. "Which seems to be beyond your—"

"My what?" Verena stepped forward, green eyes blazing. "My abilities? My intelligence? Please, enlighten us all about what the great fallen prodigy thinks I lack."

"Common sense, for starters—"

"Both of you, stop." Liri's voice cut through their argument, but it lacked its usual gentle authority. She looked exhausted, Nym's glow dim and erratic. "This isn't helping anyone."

"Tell that to the princess here," Verena snarled. "She's the one who thinks she can fix everything with her brilliant insights."

"At least I'm trying to fix something instead of actively sabotaging—"

"Enough."

They fell silent as Gideon stepped forward, arms crossed, his face unreadable. Not angry. Just... done.

"Three days," Gideon said, his voice deadly quiet. "In three days, we face another squad in exhibition combat for the first time. Full tactical engagement, ranked evaluation, academy-wide observation." His dark gaze swept over each of them in turn. "The results will determine our standing for the next quarter's prestige rankings."

He let that sink in for a moment. Around the circle, faces went pale as the implications hit home.

"Every team has been training together for the same week we have," Gideon continued. "The difference is they've been working as a unit while we've been playing out petty grievances and ego games." His eyes found Verena, then Cassara. "If you want to hand them an easy victory, keep doing exactly what you're doing."

Rett shifted uncomfortably, his massive frame somehow managing to look smaller. "What happens if we lose?"

"Bottom tier placement," Gideon said bluntly. "Reduced training resources. Limited advancement opportunities. And for those of you already struggling with rankings," his gaze lingered meaningfully on Cassara, "potential review for continued enrollment."

Cassara felt the blood drain from her face as the full weight of their situation settled over her. She'd fought so hard to stay at Vallemont, only to face the possibility of losing it all because they couldn't function as a team.

Gideon's gaze moved across them, pausing longer than necessary on Cassara and Verena.

"I said this at the start. You don't have to like each other," he said. "But you do have to work together. Because this team is all you've got. No reassignment. No second chances. And no one, no one, is going to carry anyone else through it."

He looked at each of them again.

"So," Gideon said, crossing his arms over his chest. "Are we going to waste the next three days repeating this performance? Or are we going to figure out how to fight together instead of against each other?"

"I..." Cassara started, then stopped. The angry words that had been building died in her throat as she looked around the circle at her teammates.

Oliver, clutching his modified equipment like a shield against his own inadequacy. Liri, exhausted from trying to keep them all from destroying each other. Barrett, protective instincts at war with team dynamics he didn't understand. And Verena whose face now showed a flicker of fear beneath all that rage.

Gideon took their silence for acceptance. "Follow me," he said before turning and walking out of the annex.

CHAPTER TWENTY EIGHT

Gideon led them into another room that looked empty at first glance. A simple square, floors and walls paneled and lined with rune circuitry glowing a faint blue. He turned to a panel on the wall beside the door and engaged a series of glyphs. The lines on the floor flared brighter and panels in the floor and walls, and even the ceiling, slid aside to reveal an obstacle course—platforms of varying heights, narrow beams, swinging pendulums, and what looked like a maze of hanging ropes.

"Trust exercises," he said, his tone implying this wasn't a suggestion. "You'll work in pairs, one person navigating blindfolded while their partner guides them through verbal commands only."

Cassara felt her stomach clench. After everything that had just happened, the last thing she wanted was to depend on someone else's guidance while she stumbled around blind.

"This is ridiculous," Verena grumbled, but there was less venom in it than usual.

"Verena, you're with Barrett," Gideon continued, pulling black cloth strips from a storage compartment. "Oliver, Liri. Cassara, you're with me."

He handed out the blindfolds, ignoring the various expressions of reluctance around the circle.

"Barrett, Verena—you're first."

Verena approached the starting line with her usual aggressive confidence, but Cassara caught the slight tension in her shoulders as Barrett moved to tie the blindfold around her eyes. His hands were gentle—the same way he might handle an injured creature.

"Can you see anything?" Barrett asked.

"Nothing."

"Okay. Take three steps forward, then there's a platform about knee-high."

Verena moved without hesitation, but the moment her foot found the platform, uncertainty crept into her posture. The Verena who commanded every room she entered was suddenly just a girl trying not to fall.

Barrett's directions were methodical, patient. "Left two steps. There's a beam—narrow, but stable. I've got eyes on you."

For a few minutes, it seemed to work. Verena navigated the first few obstacles with growing confidence, Barrett's steady voice guiding her through each challenge.

Then she reached a gap between platforms that required a careful jump.

"About two feet," Barrett said. "You can make it easily. Just go slow and be careful."

Verena gathered herself and leapt—but misjudged the distance, landing hard and stumbling as her ankle twisted.

"Damn it!" She ripped off the blindfold, whirling on Barrett with familiar fire in her eyes. "You said two feet!"

"I said about two feet," Barrett replied, maddeningly calm. "You jumped too far."

"I jumped where you told me to jump!"

"I also told you to be careful. You weren't listening to the whole instruction."

Verena's face flushed, and for a moment Cassara thought she might hit him. Instead, she just stood there, breathing hard, before finally stalking away.

"Oliver, Liri," Gideon said into the tense silence. "Your turn."

Liri accepted the blindfold from Oliver with a small, encouraging smile. "I trust you," she said simply.

Oliver's cheeks reddened. "I'll... try to be more precise than Barrett."

And he was. Painfully, overwhelmingly precise.

"Left four and three-quarter inches," he called out as Liri felt her way forward. "Duck seventeen degrees from vertical—no, wait, horizontal reference point—"

"Oliver," Liri said, halfway through an awkward crouch. "What does seventeen degrees mean in actual movement?"

"It means... um..." Oliver's voice cracked slightly. "Duck? A lot?"

Liri tried to adjust, but the pendulum caught her shoulder anyway, sending her spinning sideways into a foam barrier. She went down hard, Nym immediately materializing to flutter anxiously around her head.

"I'm sorry," Oliver said, staring at her with something approaching horror. "The angular calculation was imprecise, and I didn't account for reaction time variables, and—"

"Oliver." Liri pushed herself up, brushing foam particles from her hair. "It's fine. Really."

But it wasn't fine, and they all knew it.

"Cassara." Gideon stepped forward with the blindfold.

She stared at the black cloth like it might bite her. Around the room, four pairs of eyes watched her with varying degrees of expectation and skepticism.

"I don't need to prove anything to them," she said quietly.

"No," Gideon agreed. "You need to prove it to yourself."

Cassara took the blindfold and tied it around her eyes, the world disappearing into soft darkness. Immediately, her other senses sharpened—the sound of breathing, the scent of charred ozone that meant Gideon's griffin Vangal was near.

"Three steps forward," Gideon's voice came from beside her, low and steady. "Platform, knee-high."

She moved carefully, finding solid wood exactly where he'd said it would be.

"Good. Left about four feet. There's a beam. It's narrow, but you can handle it."

His confidence in her was unexpected and steadying. Cassara stepped onto the beam, arms out for balance, and found her footing.

For several obstacles, it worked. Gideon's directions were clear without being overwhelming, and his voice held an assuredness that made it easier to trust. She navigated platforms, ducked under pendulums, even managed the gap that had tripped up Verena.

Then she reached the final challenge—a narrow ledge that required edging along a wall while avoiding hanging ropes.

"Careful," Gideon said. "Rope about six inches from your face."

Cassara felt forward, found nothing, and took another step.

"Stop." His voice was sharper now. "The rope—"

"I don't feel any rope," she said, irritation creeping in.

"Trust me. It's there."

But doubt crept in with his words. Trust me. She'd learned young that trust was a weapon people used when they wanted something. Her father wielded it to secure alliances. Julian had tried to trap her with it. Even here, at Vallemont, everyone angled for advantage, assessed value, measured what you could offer against what they might gain.

She took another step.

The rope caught her across the throat, and she stumbled backward, foot slipping off the ledge. Strong hands caught her before she could fall.

Cassara ripped off the blindfold to find herself staring up into Gideon's dark eyes, his arms steady around her waist.

"You didn't trust me," he said quietly.

"No," she admitted. "I didn't."

The silence that followed was heavy with disappointment—not just from Gideon, but from herself.

"Right," Gideon said, helping her straighten. "Again. All of you."

"Again?" Verena's voice cracked slightly.

"You think real combat gives you one chance to get it right?" Gideon's expression was unforgiving. "Again. Barrett, Verena—different approach this time."

The second attempt went better. Not perfect, but better.

Barrett learned to give Verena time to process his instructions, to read the tension in her shoulders that meant she was overthinking. Verena learned to listen to the whole instruction instead of just the first part, to trust that Barrett wouldn't let her fall.

Oliver discovered that Liri responded better to simple, clear directions than technical precision. "Big duck" worked better than angular measurements. "Careful jump" was more useful than distance calculations.

And Cassara...

Cassara learned that Gideon's voice stayed steady even when hers wavered, that his hands were there to catch her even when she didn't trust his words.

By the third run, something had shifted.

"Left," Barrett said as Verena felt her way along a beam. "Trust me."

And she did.

"Duck now," Oliver called to Liri, and she dropped without hesitation, the pendulum swinging harmlessly overhead.

"The rope is there," Gideon told Cassara at the final obstacle. "Six inches out. Duck under it."

This time, she believed him.

When they finished the fourth run—clean, synchronized, successful—the silence in the training hall was different. Not heavy with frustration, but light with possibility.

"Better," Gideon said, approval in his voice.

Verena was breathing hard, but her shoulders had lost some of their rigid tension. Oliver was actually smiling, a small, proud expression that transformed his usually serious face. Liri beamed at everyone, her Sparkfly Moth's glow steady and warm.

And Cassara...

Cassara felt something she hadn't experienced in weeks. Not confidence, exactly, but its foundation. The sense that maybe, just maybe, they could figure this out.

"Same time tomorrow," Gideon said, already moving toward the exit. "And remember—two days until the arena."

As the others began to gather their things, Cassara found herself standing next to Verena. Neither of them spoke, but the earlier hostility had dimmed to something more manageable.

Cassara found refuge in the east wing library—a narrow, tall-ceilinged hall stacked with ancient tomes and still-ticking rune compasses. The scent of parchment and crystal dust calmed her nerves more than it should've. It was one of the few places Julian never came. Too quiet, too studious, too beneath him.

The silence settled around her as she spread her notes across a corner table, magelight casting a soft glow over pages of careful observations.

Tomorrow's arena exhibition loomed like a storm on the horizon. Cassara had spent the evening cataloging everything she could remember about their potential opponents—team compositions, individual strengths, the little behavioral tells that might reveal tactical preferences.

Her own team's pages lay open beside the others, filled with brutally honest assessments she never intended anyone else to see. Oliver's technical brilliance balanced against his tendency to overthink. Liri's unexpected combat instincts undermined by her reluctance to take aggressive action. Barrett's protective nature that could be both asset and liability depending on positioning.

And Gideon...

She'd filled nearly a full page with observations about their captain, ranging from tactical assessments to things she definitely shouldn't have noticed. Like the way he always checked on Barrett first after difficult exercises, knowing the gentle giant took failures personally. Or how his jaw tightened when instructors questioned his training methods, pride and defensiveness warring beneath that calm exterior.

Footsteps echoed through the library stacks, too measured to belong to a wandering student. Cassara quickly flipped her notes over, but not quite fast enough.

"Planning our victory strategy?" Gideon's voice carried a hint of amusement as he approached her table.

She kept her tone light, casual. "Something like that." Her hand moved, resting protectively over the papers. "Shouldn't you be getting rest before tomorrow?"

"Couldn't sleep." He settled into the chair across from her. "Thought I might find you here. You've been avoiding the common areas."

"I don't avoid anything."

"No?" His eyes held a knowing glint. "Then you won't mind if I see what's got you so absorbed."

Before she could stop him, he'd flipped over the nearest page. His eyebrows rose as he took in her meticulous handwriting, the detailed behavioral observations, the tactical assessments arranged in neat columns.

"This is... thorough," he said, clearly impressed. Then his gaze caught on something that made his mouth curve into a genuine smile. "What's this about my 'insufferable need to have the last word in every conversation'?"

Heat flooded Cassara's cheeks. "Those are private notes."

"'Tactical assessment: excellent situational awareness, possibly the result of mild paranoia,'" he read aloud, his smile widening. It was a rare sight and Cassara found her breath catching despite herself. "'Physical capabilities: unfairly competent at everything he attempts. Probable theory: made some sort of deal with dark forces.'"

"Give that back." She reached for the paper, but he held it just out of reach.

"'Leadership style: thinks brooding in corners makes him mysterious. Don't tell him, but it works.'" Gideon's laugh was low and warm, entirely too pleased with himself. "Should I be flattered or concerned that you've analyzed my brooding technique?"

"You're insufferable," Cassara muttered, but there was no real heat in it.

"Wait, there's more." His expression shifted to something softer as he continued reading. "'Puts team before personal recognition. Chose Oliver knowing others would question it. Defended my placement despite obvious political cost. Either secretly noble or terrible at self-preservation.'"

The last comment settled between them, more honest than she'd intended. Gideon's eyes found hers across the table, something unreadable flickering in their depths.

"Terrible at self-preservation," he said at last. "Definitely that one."

Before the moment could stretch too far into dangerous territory, he flipped to the next page. His expression sharpened as he took in her notes on the other teams.

"These observations—how did you gather this much detail?"

"I pay attention." Cassara leaned forward, grateful for the safer topic. "Julian's team has obvious power, but they've barely trained together. Vash and Jonas follow his lead without question, which could be useful if we can force Julian into making impulsive decisions."

Gideon nodded slowly, his tactical mind clearly engaged. "And Morrison's squad?"

"More cohesive, but predictable. Their captain favors direct confrontation, probably because his beast is built for it. If we can force them into terrain that doesn't favor their approach..."

"You've been watching their training sessions."

"From a distance," Cassara admitted. "The library has an excellent sight line to the practice yards."

"Clever." Gideon pulled the papers toward himself, studying her assessments with growing interest. "But you're missing some context. Morrison's second—the girl with the ice drake—she's got a temper problem. Push her too hard and she'll break formation to chase personal vendettas."

"Really?" Cassara grabbed a fresh sheet, making quick notes. "What about Julian's team composition? I know Vash and Jonas, but the other two..."

"Magda is bonded with a wind serpent, fast but fragile. She'll hang back unless she's certain of victory. And Marcus..." Gideon's expression darkened slightly. "His family specializes in enhancement potions. Not illegal, but his beast performs significantly better than its natural capabilities should allow."

They worked together after that, building strategies around observed weaknesses and unexpected strengths. Cassara found herself appreciating Gideon's analytical mind—the way he considered multiple angles before committing to a plan, how he factored in not just tactical considerations but psychological ones.

"This formation here," she said, sketching out a rough diagram. "If we can get them to commit to direct assault, Barrett and Verena could hold the center while the rest of us—"

"Won't work," Gideon interrupted gently. "Barrett won't hold center if it means Liri's exposed on the flanks. His protective instincts override tactical positioning."

"So we use that." Cassara's mind raced. "Position Liri where we want him to go, let his instincts guide the formation shift..."

"That's..." Gideon stared at her diagram, then looked up with something approaching admiration. "That's actually brilliant. Turn his weakness into a strategic advantage."

"We all have our patterns," Cassara said. "The trick is making them work for us instead of against us."

They continued planning until the candles burned low, filling pages with contingency strategies and backup plans. By the time they finally gathered the papers together, they had something resembling a comprehensive battle plan.

"The others should see this," Gideon said, carefully stacking their work. "Before tomorrow."

"Will they listen?" The question slipped out before Cassara could stop it. "I'm not exactly the most popular strategist on the team."

Gideon was quiet for a moment, considering. "They'll listen. And this—" He gestured to their accumulated plans. "This gives us a real chance."

As they prepared to leave, he paused at the edge of the table. "For the record, I don't brood."

"You definitely brood," Cassara replied without hesitation. "Right now, for instance. That's a classic brooding stance."

Gideon glanced down at himself—one hand braced against the table, shoulders angled just so, that familiar intensity in his dark eyes. "This is strategic contemplation."

"Strategic contemplation," she repeated, barely suppressing a smile. "Is that what we're calling it?"

"I prefer it to 'brooding.' Brooding implies unnecessary drama."

"And standing dramatically in corners while staring pensively into the distance is what—tactical positioning?"

"Exactly." His mouth twitched. "I'm maintaining visual superiority over the training yard."

"Of course you are." Cassara gathered her notes, shaking her head. "And here I thought you were just trying to look mysterious and tortured."

Gideon's mouth curved. "Does it work?"

She looked up at him then, taking in the way magelight caught the angles of his face, the strength in his posture, the intelligence that flickered behind his carefully neutral expression.

"I'm sure someone finds it charming," she managed at last.

Silence hung between them for a moment before Gideon cleared his throat, some of his composure slipping back into place.

"We should get some rest," he said. "Tomorrow's going to be interesting."

"I never took you for an optimist," Cassara replied.

Walking back through the darkened corridors, their makeshift battle plans tucked safely between them, Cassara found herself stealing glances at her enigmatic captain. Maybe her assessment had been more accurate than she'd realized.

The brooding definitely worked.

The arena stretched before them like a colosseum built for gods, its massive walls rising toward a dome of crystalline panels that would shift to mimic whatever environment the magical systems conjured. Students filled the tiered seating that surrounded the combat floor, their excited chatter creating a buzz of anticipation that made Cassara's nerves thrum with electric tension.

On the arena floor, eight teams stood in neat formations while Instructor Nareen's voice carried across the space with crisp authority.

"First-years," she began, her halberd planted firmly at her side like a ceremonial staff. "Today's exhibition match will test more than raw strength. You'll be judged on coordination, strategy, and field awareness. The objective is territorial control."

Auren, who had been standing beside her, stepped forward. "There are nine beacon points throughout the arena. Eight are scattered across varied terrain. The ninth—" He flicked his fingers, and an illusion formed behind him, revealing a high-floating platform gleaming with runes, utterly exposed. "—is central. Worth three points, but harder to hold."

A murmur ran through the assembled teams.

Nareen continued. "The match duration is forty-five minutes. Victory goes to the team controlling the most beacons when time expires."

Cassara felt her stomach clench as the rules sank in. Forty-five minutes of sustained tactical combat, with terrain that could shift beneath their feet at any moment.

"The arena environment will be randomly selected and unknown until combat begins," Auren added, his gaze sweeping over the assembled teams. "Adaptation will be as crucial as preparation."

"You'll have one hour of prep before deployment," Nareen finished before turning her attention to a rune-crystal display that flickered to life between them, shifting to show the match pairings. Murmurs broke out again—some surprised, some smug.

Delvanir appeared across from Morrison and a ripple of tension surged through Cassara's squad. Verena muttered something like a curse. Oliver looked pale. Rett's fingers flexed nervously at his side. Liri gave a tiny, audible gulp.

Cassara's heart hammered against her ribs. Morrison's team—one of the many scenarios she and Gideon had planned for, but somehow hearing it made official sent fresh waves of anxiety through her chest.

"Teams will have one hour to prepare before combat initiation," Auren announced. "You're dismissed."

As the groups began to disperse, Cassara caught sight of Julian standing at the opposite end of the platform, his expression dark as he watched her team file toward their assigned preparation chamber. The weight of his attention felt like a target painted between her shoulder blades.

The preparation room was smaller than Cassara had expected, fitted with basic equipment racks and a tactical planning table that projected a three-dimensional map of potential arena configurations. Her teammates clustered around it with varying degrees of confidence.

Liri looked pale, her usual brightness dimmed by anxiety. "Morrison's team is more cohesive."

"And stronger," Oliver added glumly, adjusting his ACS bracer with nervous precision. "Their average beast ranking is nearly a full tier above ours."

Barrett said nothing, but his body was tense in a way that suggested he was preparing for the worst.

Verena crossed her arms, her expression skeptical. "So what's the plan? Hope they underestimate us and get lucky?"

"Actually," Gideon said, moving to the tactical table, "we have something better than luck."

He and Cassara exchanged a look, and she felt heat creep up her neck as she remembered their late-night strategy session. The way he'd looked at her across that library table, the easy banter about brooding and tactical positioning...

"We spent some time analyzing the other teams," Cassara stepped forward, calm and collected as she unrolled a scroll and dropped it onto the table in front of them. "Morrison's squad has predictable patterns we can exploit."

Gideon followed, unfurling a second sheet—a detailed arena mockup with notes already inscribed across each quadrant. "We've noted their tendencies, triggers, and best of all, their weak points."

Oliver blinked. "When—?"

"Library sightlines," Cassara said simply. "Gideon and I compared notes."

Verena's eyes narrowed. "You and Gideon? When exactly was this happening?"

"Does it matter?" Gideon's tone carried a warning edge.

"It matters if our captain is making tactical decisions without consulting the team." Verena's voice was dangerously quiet. "Especially if those decisions involve... private strategy sessions."

Cassara frowned and forced her voice to remain steady. "The analysis is sound regardless of when it was conducted."

"I'm sure it is," Verena replied, but her smile was sharp as broken glass.

"We don't have time for this." Gideon interjected. "We have forty minutes to prepare for combat. Personal grievances can wait."

He activated the tactical display, projecting their carefully planned formations. Cassara stepped beside him, tapping a marked point on the southern ridge. "Morrison's unit is predictable. Direct. He'll push straight for central control and try to brute-force their way into dominance."

Oliver leaned forward across the tactical table, squinting at the projected formation. "They have a Stone Titan, right? Massive tank-class?"

"Exactly," Cassara said, pointing to the central position on their display. "He'll park it at a central chokehold and dare anyone to move him."

Liri shifted nervously in her chair, one hand fidgeting with her gear strap. "But what about that ice girl? She seems... stabby."

"Kira," Gideon confirmed, moving around the table to adjust the projection angle. "She's fast and aggressive, but she's got a temper problem. She breaks formation if she feels insulted."

Cassara's smile turned sharp as she leaned back against the equipment rack. "Which is why we're going to insult her."

Verena straightened abruptly in her seat. "We're going to what now?"

"We'll fake a collapse on our left flank," Cassara said, pushing off from the wall to trace the movement on the display with her finger. "Draw her in. She'll think we're scrambling and break ranks to finish the job. That'll leave Morrison's core vulnerable."

Gideon nodded, circling to the opposite side of the table. "Dalyn will turtle up. That's what he does—he'll over-defend if he thinks Morrison's being flanked."

Barrett, who had been standing quietly near the door, stepped closer to get a better view of the tactical breakdown.

"And when that happens," Oliver said, rising from his chair as understanding dawned, "he'll lock himself in a position that cuts off his team's mobility."

"Exactly." Gideon tapped the projection, highlighting the predicted defensive positions. "Derek's mole won't be able to flank fast enough if we keep shifting beacon control. And their Wind Hawk? Harassment only goes so far when they don't have clean line-of-sight."

Cassara moved to stand beside Gideon, close enough that their shoulders almost touched as she gestured toward the center beacon. "We play them like a storm. We keep moving, never meet them full-force. Make them chase us. Make them react."

Verena frowned. "That's a lot of moving pieces. And what if they don't take the bait?"

"They will," Gideon said. "Because they always do."

"Our job isn't to outpower them," Cassara added. "It's to outthink them."

Gideon smiled—a rare expression that transformed his usually serious features. "There's one more thing." He reached into his equipment bag and withdrew a collection of blackened steel pins, each bearing an intricate design of crystalline spears arranged in a wing-like sunburst pattern around the lower half of a woven steel ring.

"Our official unit designation," he announced. "Auric Vow."

Cassara stared at the crest, recognizing the elegant artistry that had gone into its creation. The golden crystals seemed to catch and hold light, while the black center gave the impression of depth, of potential waiting to be filled.

"It's beautiful," Liri breathed, accepting her pin with reverence.

"Where did you—" Oliver started, then stopped. "Never mind. It's perfect."

Even Verena handled her crest with something approaching respect, though her eyes still held traces of earlier irritation.

As they pinned the crests to their combat uniforms, Cassara felt something shift in the room's atmosphere. They weren't just a collection of individuals anymore—they were Auric Vow.

Whatever they would become, they would do it together.

"Fifteen minutes until arena activation," came an announcement from outside their chamber.

Gideon looked around the circle of his team—his squad, his unit—and nodded once.

"Time to show them what we're made of."

CHAPTER TWENTY NINE

The crowd surged when they emerged from the preparation room. Students were packed into the overlook stands, their cheers echoing through the crystalline arches of the exhibition chamber. Upper years jostled for better views while the professors and instructors stood as quiet sentinels behind the enchanted barriers, ready to assess.

Cassara stood with her unit at the ready platform as Nareen's voice rang out across the arena.

"The battlefield is set."

A low hum trembled through the stone beneath her boots. The floor of the chamber cracked, not broken, but shifting. Entire slabs folded away like panels of an enormous puzzle, revealing the true arena below: a jagged spread of rocky cliffs, ridgelines, and narrow bridges, suspended in midair by humming arc pillars.

Crumbling spires jutted from the terrain as mist rolled along the deeper drops, obscuring the chasms between platforms. At the center, glowing faintly, floated the triple-value beacon, exposed and untethered on its elevated perch.

"No two exhibitions are ever the same," Auren called from the instructor's observation platform. "This arena was designed for environmental control, mana-anchored terrain morphing, and strategic adaptation. Remember that."

Cassara barely heard him. The cliffs gleamed with veins of silver. Chokepoints. Fall hazards. Excellent cover for ranged interference, but brutal if you got cornered.

Good, she thought, squinting toward the distant shapes of the opposing team. Let them come at us head-on. Let them think they've already won.

Beside her, Gideon watched the terrain with steady calculation. The wind caught the ends of his dark scarf, his combat bracer already aglow with a soft shimmer of mana.

Above, the scoreboard rune flared to life. Auric Vow on the left. Ironhold on the right. Nine beacon runes shimmered across the display, eight faintly pulsing, one in the center glowing brightest of all.

Across the battlefield, Morrison's satisfied grin was visible even at a distance. His stone golem rumbled into existence beside him, a massive, granite-plated behemoth that looked like it had been carved from the mountains themselves. The beast's eyes glowed with the same confidence as its tamer as it surveyed terrain that might as well have been designed for its specifications.

"Well," Oliver muttered, adjusting his crossbow's scope. "They look pleased."

"Lots of elevation," Gideon muttered. "Favors their assault team, but the flanking routes are tight."

"We can work with tight," Cassara said, scanning the terrain again. "If we keep them funneled, Oliver can mark their rotations. We'll control their field of vision."

Gideon glanced sideways. "Think you can hold up under pressure?"

"Don't I always?" Her tone stayed light, but one hand drifted toward the hilt of Spireglass, the sleek glaive-rod strapped across her back. Her fingers grazed the mirrored surface, already warm with latent sync.

Through her ACS, she could sense Flicker's presence, calm, curious, ready.

"Teams, take positions!" Nareen's voice echoed across the arena. "Combat begins in sixty seconds!"

"Remember," Cassara said quietly, "we're not here to match their strength."

"Combat begins... NOW!"

The arena erupted into motion.

Morrison's team surged toward the central plateau exactly as predicted, the stone golem's massive footsteps shaking the arena floor as it claimed the high ground. Kira's ice drake prowled ahead, frost already beginning to coat the rocks beneath its claws in anticipation of easy prey.

But Auric Vow scattered like quicksilver, boots pounding over stone and moss-slicked ridges.

Verena's voice crackled through the comm runes. "We don't have the range to control the south flank. They'll box us in if we overcommit."

"You're not wrong," Gideon replied evenly. "That's why we're not overcommitting. Maintain your post. Wait for Oliver's mark."

"Copy," she muttered, but her tone was laced with irritation.

From a ledge above the field, Cassara crouched low beside Liri, watching flickers of movement on the far plateau. Morrison's stone golem lumbered forward in massive strides, flanked by the ice drake sweeping low like a living glacier. "There," Cassara said, pointing to a curve in the path. "He's baiting us. He wants us to intercept early."

Liri squinted. "Shouldn't we?"

"No," Cassara said quickly. "Let them pass. Oliver, tag the rear."

A whisper of arcane glow rippled through the comm-link. "Marked," Oliver's calm voice confirmed. "Two seconds later and I wouldn't have had line of sight. Thanks, Cassara."

Verena's response came a beat late. "You're giving her calls now?"

Rett grunted through the channel. "Pretty sure she's the one watching the enemy's backline. So unless you've got second sight, Verena..."

Silence.

Cassara ignored the jab and pressed her palm to her comms glyph. "We hold the northern ridge. Gideon and I will fake toward the center beacon when the clock hits thirty. Liri, you're with us for visual disruption. The rest of you stay tight on the perimeter until directed otherwise."

"Understood," said Gideon.

"Got it!" Liri replied.

Verena didn't answer.

Cassara exhaled slowly. Her fingers hovered near Spireglass, the weapon now shimmering faintly against her spine. She could feel Flicker stir in the shard. Not afraid, curious.

Below, the central beacon thrummed once, like a heartbeat building in the earth.

Thirty-five minutes left.

Cassara crouched behind a jagged outcrop, her breath steady despite the storm thudding in her chest. Just ahead, Oliver's voice crackled through the comms.

"Target Derek. South flank. Trap cluster Alpha deployed. Bait movement... now."

Beneath her, the ground pulsed, faint tremors echoing from Ilza crouched low in shadow, antennae twitching as it mirrored Oliver's calculation. A hum of glyphs lit under the ridge. Smoke glyphs, delay snares and flashbursts, all interlocked with eerie precision. Oliver's signature.

Derek's mole burst from the stone, claws flaring, only to trigger a pulse mine. The blast staggered him mid-surge. He barely recovered before a terrain fracture opened beneath him, collapsing his footing. He tumbled with a strangled curse and disappeared from sight.

"Trap confirmed," Oliver called. Ilza shifted forward like living granite, her crystalline wings refracting light into fractured, flickering decoys. "Disrupting terrain flow."

"Now," Cassara ordered.

She and Liri burst forward from opposite ledges, one a glinting ripple of motion, the other a blur of golden shimmer. Above, Nym unfurled, growing in size as its bioluminescent wings pulsing in time with her breath. Nimbrush spun in Liri's hands, casting illusion-ring distractions that bloomed like fireworks in fog. The moth spiraled overhead, scattering light distortions that danced across the field, false shadows of a tamer who couldn't be pinned.

Kira took the bait.

Cassara caught the shift, Kira's sudden burst of speed, the way her ice drake veered off course with her, spitting frost and fury in twin arcs. The drake's wings snapped tight as it dove after the mirage.

Too predictable.

Cassara cut hard left, boots skidding. Spireglass deployed with a crisp, mirrored snap. The blade gleamed, catching Kira's lunge with the illusion of a strike. Not a hit, just a suggestion. A shimmer of movement, an echo of intent.

The blade didn't need to land. Kira's reflexes did the rest. She pulled back, twisted to avoid a phantom blow, and lost tempo.

Behind them, the east beacon flared crimson.

Auric Vow claimed it.

More pulses followed, Beacon Five. Beacon Seven. Each one a beat of progress, a breath drawn deeper.

"They're overcorrecting," Gideon called out. "Focus. We hold the net, not the center."

Cassara scanned the field's heart.

Morrison's stone golem was charging.

The ground shuddered beneath its weight, each step another threat of collapse. But it hadn't reached the central platform. Not yet.

Because Gideon was already there.

Lockstep flared open at his side, tower plates snapping outward into a fortress-shield. Vangal screamed overhead, circling in a tightening spiral. With each cry, its wings cut through the wind, sending slicing gusts down at the advancing golem.

Cassara watched as Morrison's charge faltered. Lockstep glowed, locking into Overwatch Mode. Gideon stood unmoved, braced behind the kinetic shield, his beast funneling power through the barrier. A hurricane of force crackled between them.

"Center is stalled," he reported. "Push edge control."

To the west, Rett and his razorspine raptor, Skelli, swept in like a blade. His battle hammer, Gravemaul, slammed into stone with a seismic crunch, anchoring them at Beacon Three. Skelli coiled beside him, its plated tail twitching, yellow eyes fixed forward, waiting for the next opening to lunge.

Liri landed nearby, panting, Nym hovering protectively above. The moth's wings pulsed, sending faint golden waves toward her teammates, small, almost imperceptible, but enough to smooth their breathing, sharpen their clarity.

Even Verena, tight-lipped and poised, held position without protest. Whispercoil rested at her side, the obsidian blade humming softly. Kaddock growled low, crouched behind her like a living fortress, its molten seams beginning to glow in anticipation.

Cassara took it all in.

Every line held, every step taken.

Across the field, Ironhold was struggling to recalibrate and for the first time, this didn't feel like a scramble or a survival, it felt like momentum, like victory wasn't just possible, it was inevitable.

The plan was working.

Until the first drops of rain struck Cassara's face like ice, and she looked up to see storm clouds gathering across the dome with supernatural speed. Within moments, what had been clear skies became a torrential downpour that turned the rocky terrain treacherous.

Morrison's stone golem, so perfectly positioned on the central plateau, suddenly found its footing uncertain as water cascaded down the rock faces. The beast that had seemed immovable was now struggling just to maintain its position.

The downpour should have been their advantage, Morrison's team suddenly struggling with footing, their careful positioning disrupted by the shifting battlefield. Cassara spun Spireglass in a defensive arc, rain streaming off the mirrored blade as she moved toward their next objective.

"Liri, northeast beacon!" she called, trusting the others to maintain formation as they pressed their advantage.

Nym pulsed with acknowledgment, its stained-glass wings carrying her toward the exposed beacon point. But when Cassara glanced back to confirm their positioning, her blood turned to ice.

Verena wasn't there.

The space where their heavy hitter should have been covering Liri's advance was empty except for rain-slicked stone. Cassara's eyes swept the battlefield frantically, finally spotting the distinctive gleam of Whispercoil's extended chain, far from where it should have been, chasing what looked like Kira.

Liri was completely exposed.

"There!" Morrison's voice boomed across the arena, and Cassara watched in horror as every member of his team pivoted toward the unprotected beacon point. "The support! Cut her down!"

Kira's ice drake was already mid-dive, its wings beating hard against the downpour, carving gusts through the storm-thick air. Rain sluiced over its sleek, horned head, claws outstretched, frost curling in coils behind it like the tail of a comet. Liri stood exposed, fans only half-raised, Nym flaring bright with a defensive pulse, but they weren't ready.

Cassara ran.

Her boots skidded across the soaked shale, catching, sliding, catching again. Every stride threatened to bring her down, the slope nothing but jagged stone and mud now, the earth liquefied beneath the storm.

"Liri!" she shouted, but the wind ripped the name away.

Cassara didn't think, she didn't plan, she threw herself into the path of the strike.

Kira's beast opened its jaws and frost surged from within, white-blue and blinding, a direct blast meant for Liri.

Cassara gritted her teeth and braced herself for impact.

Light tore through the storm with a violent crack, sharp as metal breaking. A silver-blue arc erupted beside her, Flicker slamming into existence.

The frostblast struck, full force, roaring down in a spiral of jagged magic, and hit the mirror of his body with a sound like glass bending, not breaking, but redirecting. The attack folded in on itself, split and scattered in a ring of distorted light, harmlessly cast aside as if it had been misfiled by the laws of physics.

Cassara staggered backward, thrown by the shockwave, but not cut. Not frozen. Her boots caught again, slid, and she dropped to one knee as mist rose around her in spirals.

The ground hissed.

Flicker hovered in place, unbothered as always.

His body shimmered with residual glow, rain sliding off his gleaming surface like he barely registered the storm at all. No heaving breaths. No trembling limbs. He blinked slowly, tilting his head toward Cassara, the way a child might after squashing a bug they didn't quite understand.

She stared.

He'd shielded her, without hesitation, without effort and there wasn't a scratch on him.

And he was already drifting sideways again, gaze snagging on something behind her, perhaps a shift in wind, perhaps a beetle in the mud, acting as if he hadn't just stood between her and potential death.

The rain roared down harder, pounding on stone and skin alike. The terrain was slipping apart beneath their feet every step now a risk.

Liri, soaked and scraped but alive, was already rising behind her. Nimbrush whirled beside her in a bright, defensive spiral of light. The sparkfly's wings flared, catching the rain like broken prisms. Liri's fans glowed, ready to move.

Her eyes met Cassara's across the storm.

"What just happened?" Liri breathed.

"Flicker happened," Cassara said, spinning Spireglass as her weapon's enhanced afterimages scattered their remaining attackers. "Now let's finish this."

Ahead, Kira reared her drake back with a sharp whistle, eyes narrowing. But the opening was there. She'd overreached, leaving the beacon exposed. Cassara could take it.

A flash of victory, right there—hers, if she moved now.

She turned, not toward the beacon, but to protect Liri's flank.

Spireglass arced through the rain, a mirrored warning as she intercepted Kira before the other girl could recover. Kira's drake hissed, claws tearing deep gouges through the rock as it skidded, trying to reorient.

But Cassara stayed between them, feet planted, blade raised. She didn't attack. She didn't need to.

Her presence, sharp and unyielding, was enough to hold the line.

Behind her, Liri shouted something indistinct through the storm, and Nimbrush let out a flare of radiant color, wings blooming outward like a living lantern. The Sparkfly lifted her into the air in a single graceful pulse of magic, fans flashing like twin stars at her sides.

"Go, Liri! Go now!" Cassara shouted without looking back.

She felt the rush of light as Liri soared over the ridge on Nym's back, water trailing from her boots, the center platform just ahead, unguarded, untouched.

Flicker shimmered beside Cassara, no longer defensive, but calmly watching Kira's drake as though it were a mere curiosity. His form pulsed once with residual magic, silver fractals echoing across his translucent fur, then he promptly sat in the mud again, seemingly more interested in the falling rain than the standoff before him.

The beacon behind them erupted in a shock of gold.

Auric Vow: Central Point Captured

The arena shuddered, not from magic, but from the roar of the crowd.

It echoed through the glass-lined observation walls, over the storm, louder than thunder. Above them, the scoreboard flared to life. All nine beacons flashed in real-time, a flickering dance of dominance.

Cassara's Codex buzzed.

The timer stopped.

Match Complete.

Auric Vow – 7 | Ironhold – 4

Cassara lowered her weapon.

Across the platform, Kira stood frozen, rain sliding down her face as her beast paced behind her in slow, frustrated circles. She didn't speak, didn't curse, but her glare was molten.

Cassara let it fall away.

Instead she turned toward the center, where Liri touched down in a spin of light and mud, laughing with exhilaration as the sparkfly dimmed to a gentle glow and began to shrink. Gideon stood at the base of the ridge, watching her, not like a captain, but like someone who saw her.

He nodded once and Cassara felt an unfamiliar ache in her chest.

From the side, Morrison's furious bellow broke through, some harsh reprimand to his team, one of whom had dropped their weapon entirely. His stone golem let out a mournful, ground-cracking stomp.

Oliver joined her at the slope, wiping rain from his lenses, the Stoneshade Mantis perched ghostlike in the rocks behind him.

"That shouldn't have worked," he muttered. "Flicker shouldn't be able to do what he just—"

He stopped.

Flicker was now lying on his back in a puddle. He flopped lazily, tail swiping the mud like he was painting with it. His body shimmered every few seconds, still refracting bits of Kira's ice attack, as if unconcerned by physics or reality.

Oliver stared. "He's... rolling in the mud."

Cassara smirked, a small breath of laughter escaping her throat.

"Let him," she murmured. "He earned it."

Oliver wandered off shaking his head and muttering, fingers flying across his Codex. Cassara sank to one knee, Spireglass retracting to its compact form as adrenaline finally gave way to exhaustion. Around her, her teammates were similarly spent, but there was something different in their postures now. They weren't just a collection of individuals anymore.

They were a real team.

"Not bad," Gideon said, offering her a hand up. His rare smile made the victory feel even sweeter.

"Not bad at all," she agreed, accepting his help.

On the observation platform, she caught sight of Julian, his expression a mixture of shock, anger, and ...fear? He was finally beginning to understand that she was no longer the girl he believed he could control.

The thought made her smile.

Good, she thought as she turned away. Let him be afraid.

Auric Vow was just getting started.

And so was she.

The preparation room buzzed with the kind of euphoric energy that only came after surviving the impossible. Barrett had claimed a corner bench and was methodically cleaning mud from Gravemaul's grip, but his shoulders had lost their perpetual tension. Oliver sat cross-legged on the floor, dismantling and reassembling his crossbow's scope with the satisfied focus of someone whose calculations had finally paid off.

And Liri—Liri was practically bouncing off the walls.

"I'm having chocolate cake for dinner," she announced, still flushed with victory. "And those little cream pastries from the dining hall. And maybe that berry tart. Actually, you know what? I'm having nothing but dessert for the entire week."

"Your stomach will hate you," Oliver pointed out without looking up from his work.

"My stomach can complain after I've properly celebrated not dying horribly in front of the entire academy," Liri shot back, spinning in a circle.

"No one would have let you die..." Oliver said, before adding, "Probably."

Gideon leaned against the equipment rack, arms crossed, watching the chaos with something Cassara had never seen on his face before, genuine amusement. Not his usual half-smile, but actual warmth that softened the sharp angles of his features and made him look younger somehow.

The sight made something flutter in her chest that she definitely wasn't ready to examine.

Cassara lingered near the door for a breath too long, unsure why her boots suddenly felt too loud and her Codex too bright in her hand.

It worked.

The plan had worked.

She crossed the room slowly before stopping beside him, not looking directly at his face. "You were right," she said, quietly. "About the edges, about the net. About the team."

Gideon turned his head slightly, eyes finding hers.

"You were the reason it held," he said. "You could've taken the center. You didn't."

The compliment hit differently than she'd expected. Not the grudging acknowledgment she was used to, but genuine recognition from someone whose opinion had somehow started to matter more than she wanted to admit.

"I couldn't have done it without—"

The door burst open with enough force to rattle the frame.

Verena stalked in, soaked to the skin and splattered with mud, her red hair plastered to her skull and her expression thunderous. She looked like she'd been dragged backward through the arena, which, Cassara reflected, wasn't entirely inaccurate.

"Well," Verena announced, shaking water from her sleeves with sharp, angry movements. "That was a complete disaster. Morrison's team fights like barbarians, no finesse, no tactical awareness. And the arena conditions were absolutely unacceptable. Rain in the middle of combat? What kind of—"

"Stop."

The single word cut through Verena's tirade like a knife. The room went dead silent, even Liri's celebration freezing mid-bounce.

Gideon straightened from the equipment rack, eyes narrowing in on Verena.

"What did you just say?" His voice was quiet and bore the kind of control that suggested violence barely held in check.

Verena blinked, apparently oblivious to the danger radiating from him. "I said Morrison's team—"

"No." Gideon took a step forward, and Cassara saw Barrett tense in her peripheral vision. "You said 'that was a complete disaster' about the match we just won. The match where your team—" Another step, predatory and precise. "—pulled off a tactical victory against superior odds."

"Well, yeah, but the conditions—"

"The conditions? What about how you abandoned your assigned position?" His voice never rose, but somehow it seemed to fill the entire room. "Where you left Liri exposed to pursue your own personal vendetta. Where you nearly cost us everything because you couldn't follow a simple formation plan."

Verena's mouth opened and closed like a fish gasping for air. Around the room, the others watched with the fascination of people witnessing a controlled detonation.

"You want to know what disaster looks like?" Gideon continued, closing the distance between them until Verena had to crane her neck to meet his eyes. "Disaster is watching Morrison's entire team converge on an unprotected teammate because someone decided personal glory was more important than unit cohesion. Disaster is realizing that everything we'd worked for, every strategy we'd built, meant nothing because one person couldn't be trusted to do their job."

"I—" Verena started, but he cut her off with a look that could have frozen flames.

"You nearly got Liri hurt and nearly lost us the match. Then you walk in here complaining about the rain?" He glared down at her. "If you ever, *ever*, put this team at risk like that again, you'll find out exactly how much personal history matters against a formal disciplinary review."

Verena's face had gone pale beneath the mud, and for the first time since Cassara had known her, she looked genuinely rattled.

"Now," Gideon said, his voice returning to its normal tone, though the edge remained. "I suggest you clean up, reflect on what happened out there, and decide whether you want to be part of this team or continue playing solo games that endanger everyone around you."

Verena stood frozen for another heartbeat, then spun on her heel and stalked toward the washroom without another word. The door slammed behind her with enough force to make the walls shake.

In the silence that followed, Liri let out a low whistle. "Well," she said finally. "That was terrifying and impressive."

Barrett nodded slowly. "Remind me never to piss off the captain."

Oliver looked up from his crossbow with something approaching awe. "I don't think I've ever seen anyone shut Verena up that effectively."

But Cassara just stared at Gideon, seeing him in an entirely new light. She'd known he was protective of the team, had seen hints of it in training, in the way he'd recruited each of them despite their obvious flaws. But this was something else entirely.

This was a man who would go to war for the people under his command.

And somehow, inexplicably, that included her.

CHAPTER THIRTY

The common room buzzed with celebration, voices layered over the clink of mugs and the occasional burst of laughter that came with victory wine. Liri had claimed the largest armchair and was holding court about her aerial maneuvers, gesturing wildly with a chocolate tart in one hand. Barrett sat quietly beside her, his usual reserved smile softened by genuine contentment. Even Oliver had emerged from his corner to demonstrate crossbow trajectory angles using dinner rolls and increasingly elaborate hand gestures.

Cassara lifted her mug to her lips again, savoring the warm burn of the spiced wine as it settled pleasantly in her chest. Not drunk, she wasn't stupid, but she had drunk enough that the edges of everything felt softer and she felt bold enough that the voice in her head telling her to be careful had finally shut up.

They'd won. She'd led them to victory and she was tired of pretending she didn't want things she couldn't have.

"I need some air," she announced, setting down her half-empty mug and slipping toward the door before anyone could protest.

The corridors beyond the common room were cooler and certainly quieter, but instead of sobering her up, the contrast only heightened the pleasant warmth spreading through her veins. She'd earned this. Earned the victory, earned the celebration, earned the right to want things without apology.

Her feet found their way to the overlook without conscious direction, muscle memory guiding her up the familiar stone steps.

She leaned against the stone railing, tilting her face up to the stars and finally allowing herself to feel it, the intoxicating rush of having proved everyone wrong. Including herself.

"Trouble sleeping?"

The voice came from behind her, low and familiar, and instead of the usual flutter of nerves, warmth bloomed in her chest.

"No trouble at all," she said, not turning around. She was feeling brave, or perhaps reckless. Let him come to her. "Just enjoying the view."

She held her breath and waited, resisting the urge to turn around. Within moments she felt his presence at her back like warmth from a fire. Close enough to touch, if she wanted to.

And oh, she wanted to.

"Celebrating?" he asked, and she caught the note of amusement in his voice that meant he'd most likely noticed her slightly flushed cheeks and the way she swayed.

"Thoroughly." She turned then, offering him a smile that was pure challenge. "Care to join me?"

Auren's gaze swept over her face, taking in the brightness in her eyes, the way she held herself with liquid confidence. "How much have you had to drink?"

"Enough to stop caring about being careful," she said, taking a deliberate step closer. "Not enough to do anything I'll regret."

"Cassara—"

"Do you know what I was thinking about out there today?" she interrupted, moving closer. "When Flicker saved my life, when we won, when everything finally came together?"

"What?" His voice was carefully controlled, but she caught the way his breathing had changed.

"I was thinking about you." Another step. "About how you believed in me when I didn't believe in myself. About how you see me, not just the name or the legacy or the expectations, but the real me. The messy me."

"You should go back to your celebration," he said, but he didn't move away.

"Should I?" She reached up, fingers trailing along the edge of his collar. "Or should I stay here and tell you all the other things I've been thinking about?"

"This isn't a good idea."

"Probably not." Her smile turned wicked. "But I've had several very good ideas today, and where did that get me? Victory. Recognition. Everything I wanted." Her hand flattened against his chest, feeling his heartbeat racing beneath her palm. "Maybe it's time I tried a bad idea, just to see what happens."

"Cassara." Her name came out rough, warned.

"Say it again," she whispered, pressing closer until she could feel his breath against her lips. "I like the way you say my name when you're trying not to want me."

"I'm not trying not to want you," he said, his hands finally moving to her waist. "You've been drinking. I'm trying to protect you."

"From what? From whom?" She laughed, the sound bright and dangerous. "I just led my team to victory against impossible odds. I think I can handle one overly serious instructor."

"You're playing with fire."

"Good thing I'm not afraid of getting burned."

That broke something in his control. His grip on her waist tightened, pulling her flush against him as his mouth crashed down to hers.

She kissed him back with wine-bright boldness, her hands tangling in his hair, her body arching against his like she was trying to erase every inch of space between them. When they broke apart, they were both breathing hard.

"This is dangerous," he said against her lips. "Someone could—"

"Everything worth having is dangerous," she replied, nipping at his lower lip just to watch his eyes darken. "The question is—are you brave enough to want it anyway?"

His answer was another kiss, deeper this time, as his hands slid lower, fingers digging into the curve of her hips with a possessiveness that sent lightning through her veins. Cassara gasped against his mouth, feeling her control, the control she'd been wielding like a weapon, start to slip away. The wine-warm confidence in her blood transformed into something hotter, more urgent.

"You want to play games?" Auren growled, breaking the kiss to trail his lips down the column of her throat. His stubble scraped deliciously against her sensitive skin, making her shiver.

"I don't hate them," she replied, tilting her head to give him better access. Her fingers found the buttons of his shirt, fumbling in her eagerness. "Especially when I'm winning."

He pressed her back against the railing, his hands sliding beneath her shirt, palms mapping the soft skin of her waist, her ribs, higher still.

"Is this what you wanted?" he asked, his voice rough with desire as he stopped just shy of her breasts. "To break my control?"

"Yes," she admitted, arching into his touch. "And it worked."

"Are you sure?"

Before she could respond, he captured her mouth again, this time with a deliberate slowness that made her whimper. Gone was the desperate clash of their first kiss—this was calculated, methodical, designed to drive her mad. His tongue teased hers, retreating when she tried to deepen the kiss, setting a rhythm that had her clutching at his shoulders.

"You think you've won," he murmured against her lips, one hand sliding up to cup her breast. His thumb circled her nipple, never quite giving her the pressure she craved. "But I'm just getting started."

Cassara shuddered at his words, the promise in them making her knees weak. His thumb finally pressed against her stiffening peak, drawing a gasp from her lips that turned into a moan when he rolled it between his fingers.

Without warning he spun her around in one fluid motion, his chest pressing against her back as his hands slid down her sides to her hips. The railing bit into her palms as she caught herself, the stone cool and rough beneath her fingers. He nudged her legs apart with his knee, the fabric of his trousers brushing against her inner thighs causing her to tremble.

"Is this what you imagined?" he whispered in her ear, as he leaned over her. His body caged hers, warm and solid, one hand sliding down her side to grip her hip the other moving up her spine, applying gentle but insistent pressure between her shoulder blades until she bent forward over the railing. "What about when you were out there being reckless and brilliant today, is this what you thought about?"

"Yes," she admitted, voice husky with desire as his hand tangled in her hair, not pulling but holding, a gentle restraint that made her pulse quicken.

His lips found the curve of her throat, teeth grazing the skin before soothing it with his tongue. The sensation made her moan, louder than she'd intended, the sound carrying out into the night.

"Careful," he warned, his voice amused even as his hand tightened in her hair. "Unless you want the entire academy to hear what a beast tamer sounds like when she's being tamed."

His hand at her hip slid lower, fingers bunching the fabric of her skirt, dragging it upward until cool air kissed the backs of her thighs.

"Auren," she gasped, pressing back against him instinctively.

"Patience..." he murmured, but his own control was slipping, she could hear it in the roughness of his breathing, feel it in the hardness pressing against her. His hand skimmed up her inner thigh, fingertips tracing patterns that made her quiver.

When his fingers finally brushed against her through her undergarments, Cassara bit her lower lip to stifle the moan that threatened to escape. The thin fabric was already damp, and his touch sent fire through her core.

"Remember," Auren whispered against her ear, his voice a dangerous rumble that sent shivers cascading down her spine, "not a sound. Even out here, the night carries voices." His teeth grazed her earlobe as his fingers pushed the fabric aside and pressed inside of her.

Her hands gripped the railing tighter, knuckles whitening as she fought to maintain her composure. The stars blurred above her as her eyes lost focus, pleasure spiraling outward from his skilled touch. How had simple teasing led to this? She'd challenged him, but never expected him to call her bluff so thoroughly.

Each thrust of his fingers drew her closer to the edge, her breath coming in short, desperate pants that she struggled to keep silent.

"Please," she breathed, barely audible, her hips moving unconsciously against his hand.

The pressure of his touch increased, finding a rhythm that made her tremble. The thought of being so exposed, bent over the railing with him behind her where anyone might see only heightened her arousal.

He withdrew his fingers momentarily, and she nearly whimpered at the loss before she felt him shift behind her. The rustle of clothing, the sound of a belt being unfastened—each noise heightened her anticipation until she thought she might combust from wanting alone.

"Is this what you want?" he asked, his voice strained with his own need.

"Yes," Cassara breathed, her voice barely audible above the night breeze that caressed her exposed skin. "Gods, yes, Auren. Please."

She felt his chest press against her back, his hand sliding possessively around her hip. The head of his cock teased against her entrance, and she pushed back instinctively, desperate for more.

When he finally pushed inside, it was with exquisite restraint, a slow, careful claiming that made her gasp. Her body yielded to him, accepting each measured inch.

"Look at the stars," he murmured, his chest pressed to her back as he slowly, achingly pushed deeper. "I want you to remember this moment every time you look up at them."

Cassara's gaze lifted to the vast expanse above, the glittering star scape swimming in her vision. Waves of pleasure cascaded through her body, her inner walls stretching to accommodate him.

"Oh gods," she gasped when he was fully seated within her. The feeling of completeness overwhelmed her senses.

Then he began to move. His thrusts were agonizingly slow, gentle, a stark contrast to the fierce intensity of his earlier touches. His hands found her hips, holding her steady as he withdrew almost completely before sliding back in.

"You feel incredible," he groaned, his breath hot against her neck. One hand slid up her side. Pushing fabric aside to cup her breast, thumb circling her bared nipple in time with his languid strokes. She arched her back, changing the angle slightly, and a soft moan escaped her lips as he struck something deep within.

"There," she managed, her voice breaking. "Right there."

Auren complied, his rhythm steady but gradually increasing in intensity. His hand slid up her spine to tangle in her hair, tugging just enough to arch her neck back. The subtle display of dominance from her usually composed combat instructor made something primal awaken inside of her.

"You're perfect," he growled, his controlled pace finally beginning to falter. His thrusts grew deeper, more insistent, the gentleness giving way to something more urgent.

She pushed back against him, meeting his increasingly powerful thrusts with equal fervor. Her body was no longer her own but an instrument being played, every nerve ending alive with sensation.

When his hand slid around to find her clit, Cassara nearly sobbed with need. Her release built rapidly under his skilled touch, the dual stimulation threatening to unravel her completely.

Cassara gripped the railing tighter, her knuckles turning white, each thrust driving her closer to the edge, her legs trembling with the effort to remain standing.

"Auren," she gasped, the syllables of his name breaking apart as he increased his tempo. "I can't— I'm going to—"

His hand left her hair and clamped firmly over her mouth. The gesture was both commanding and intimate, sending another wave of heat through her core.

"Shhh," he whispered against her ear, his breath hot and ragged. "What I'm about to make you feel isn't for anyone else to hear." She moaned against his palm, her body tightening around him, each circle of his fingers sending her higher.

When the orgasm hit, Auren held her firmly against him, his fingers still working relentlessly against her sensitive flesh as he chased his own release. The strokes prolonged her climax, drawing it out until she thought she might shatter completely. Through the haze of her pleasure, she felt his rhythm falter, his breathing harsh against her neck as his body tensed.

With a final, powerful thrust, he buried himself completely inside her. She felt him pulse within her as he reached his own climax, his hand pressing harder against her mouth, silencing the whimpers that continued to escape her. His groan was barely contained against her shoulder as he bit down gently on the sensitive skin there. The sharp sting only heightened her pleasure, drawing out the aftershocks that still rippled through her body.

Slowly, he removed his hand from her mouth, replacing it with his lips in a kiss that was surprisingly tender after such intensity.

"Are you alright?" he murmured, his hands now gentle as they smoothed over her hips, her waist.

Cassara nodded. Her legs felt like water, her mind deliciously empty of everything but sensation. Auren turned her in his arms, his expression a mixture of concern and lingering desire as he studied her face. His thumb brushed across her lower lip, red and swollen from their kisses and her own attempts to stay quiet.

"I didn't hurt you?" he asked as he carefully helped her stand upright, steadying her when she swayed slightly.

"No," she finally managed, her voice hoarse. "That was..." Words failed her, and she laughed softly, resting her forehead against his chest. "I don't think I can walk back to my room yet."

His chuckle rumbled against her cheek as he held her close, one hand stroking soothingly down her spine. "Give it a moment."

She nodded, her eyes drifting closed as she savored the feeling of his heartbeat, the rapid thudding gradually slowing, matching the calming rhythm of her own. Auren's warmth enveloped her, his arms a sanctuary she hadn't known she needed.

"I never realized it but... I've wanted this for so long," she admitted, the words escaping before her usual defenses could silence them. The victory wine still hummed in her veins, making honesty easier than it had been before. "Not... *this*. But someone. Like this. Like you. Seeing me. Just me."

His fingers tangled in her hair, tilting her face up. The tenderness in his eyes made her breath catch.

"I've always seen you, Cassara." His thumb traced the curve of her cheek. "That's been the problem."

He kissed her then, so unlike the hungry desperation from before. This kiss was soft, the gentle press of his lips against hers making her heart flutter in ways that both terrified and thrilled her.

When they parted, she felt strangely shy, despite the intimacy they'd just shared. "What happens now?" she asked, her voice small.

Auren's smile held a touch of wryness. "Now I make sure you get back to your room without being seen looking thoroughly debauched by your instructor."

"Debauched?" She laughed, the sound breaking some of the tension. "Is that what they're calling it these days?"

"What would you call it?" His eyes held that dangerous glint again, the one that made heat pool low in her belly even as her body still trembled from release.

"A victory celebration," she replied, finding her confidence again as she pressed a kiss to the underside of his jaw.

He groaned softly. "You're dangerous, beast tamer."

Cassara smiled, still catching her breath. "I know."

She stepped back slightly, testing her legs. They still felt shaky, but no longer like they would collapse beneath her. Carefully, she adjusted her clothing, smoothing down her skirt and redoing the buttons of her shirt with fingers that only trembled slightly.

Auren watched her with heavy-lidded eyes, making no move to hide his appreciation. When she finished, he reached out to tuck a strand of hair behind her ear.

"You're beautiful," he said.

The compliment, delivered without artifice or agenda, made her cheeks flush anew. She'd been called beautiful before, usually by people who wanted something from her or her family. But the way Auren said it, like he was simply stating a fact about the world, made it feel true for perhaps the first time in her life.

The dormitory was blissfully quiet when Cassara slipped back inside, her roommates either still celebrating or long since asleep. She moved carefully through the darkened space, hyperaware of every creak of floorboard, every rustle of fabric. The last thing she needed was questions about where she'd been or why her hair looked like she'd been caught in a windstorm.

Once safely behind her bed curtains, she sank onto the mattress with a soft exhale. Her body still hummed with contentment, muscles loose and pliant in ways that made her want to stretch like a cat in sunlight. She could still feel the memory of Auren's hands gripping her hips, still taste him on her lips.

Flicker materialized without being summoned, his small form padding across the blanket to curl against her hip with a satisfied chirp. He looked up at her and she could swear there was approval there, or maybe amusement at her thoroughly disheveled state.

"Don't look at me like that," she whispered, but there was no real reproach in it. "You're the one who decided to be heroic today."

Happy.

The singular word echoed in her mind.

He purred softly, settling into his chosen spot like he belonged there. Which, she supposed, he did.

Cassara reached under her pillow and pulled out her mother's journal, the leather warm and familiar in her hands. She flipped past pages of her mother's careful script to find the next blank sheet, pen poised over parchment for a long moment before she began to write.

Today we won. Not just the match, but something more. I led them and they followed. Even when Verena broke formation and nearly cost us everything, we adapted. We survived. We triumphed.

I understand now what you meant when you wrote about finding your place. It's not about being the strongest or the smartest or living up to everyone else's expectations. It's about becoming who you're meant to be, even if that person surprises you.

Especially then.

She paused, pen hovering over the page as warmth spread through her, not from wine this time, but from memory. From the way he'd looked at her afterward, like she was precious. Like she mattered.

And after... there was someone waiting.

Her lips curved without her permission, slow and certain.

I can't write his name, can't risk it.

But it's someone who saw all of it and didn't flinch. Who let me be fierce and messy and victorious, and wanted me anyway.

For the first time, that feels like enough, maybe more than enough.

I think I'm falling in love with him. The terrifying, reckless, completely impractical kind that changes everything. I should be scared. Part of me is. But mostly I'm just... grateful. That someone like him exists. That somehow, impossibly, he chose me too.

I wish you were here to tell me what to do. But maybe that's the point, I have to figure this out myself. Make my own choices. Live with my own consequences.

I think you'd like him. I think you'd understand.

Cassara set down her pen and closed the journal, tucking it back under her pillow beside Flicker's warm bulk. Outside her curtains, the dormitory remained peaceful, her roommates safely asleep and unaware of how thoroughly she had been undone by starlight and gentle hands.

She settled back against her pillows, one hand resting lightly on Flicker's fur. Tomorrow would bring complications, it always did. Julian's suspicions, her father's expectations, the careful dance of pretending that nothing had changed between her and her instructor.

But tonight, she was exactly where she belonged. In her own bed, in her own skin, with her own choices written in her own hand.

For the first time in her life, that felt like victory enough.

She fell asleep smiling and didn't dream of expectations, or failure, or legacy.

Only of stars.

And fire.

And a voice in the dark saying her name like it meant something.

CHAPTER THIRTY ONE

Cassara moved quickly through the halls of the training wing, boots ringing against stone as she hurried toward practice. Spireglass rested easy across her shoulders now—less weapon, more extension of self. She was late, and Gideon would have something to say about it, but she hadn't rushed breakfast. Not when students were still stopping her in the dining hall to congratulate her.

She was rounding the corner when a hand shot out from the shadows, catching her wrist in an iron hold.

She spun, breath catching.

Julian.

Before she could pull away, he dragged her into the alcove, twisting her around so that her back hit the wall while his body moved to pin hers in place.

She tried to jerk her wrist free, but he didn't loosen his hold. "Julian. This is really getting old. I'm already late."

"For practice?" His voice was low, his thumb brushing idly over her pulse like he was counting the beats for himself. "Or for another private celebration with your dear captain?"

Cassara went still.

"Tell me," he murmured, "did Gideon earn your loyalty in the training yard—or somewhere... quieter?"

"What the hell is that supposed to mean?"

But even as she snapped at him, she saw the suspicion in his eyes. It wasn't just jealousy anymore.

"You've changed since the gala," he said, his free hand planting against the wall beside her head. "The way you walk. The way you carry yourself. That look in your eyes. Confidence, yes… but more than that. There's a softness in you now and I'd bet good money it has something to do with Delvanir."

"You're imagining things."

"Am I? You look like a girl who's been thoroughly ruined."

Heat surged to her cheeks, not embarrassment, but fury. She shoved at his chest. He didn't budge.

"You're being ridiculous."

"I'm being realistic." His grip tightened. "I saw the way he touched you. The way you looked at him after the match. You think I don't know what happened after you slipped away from the party?"

"No one—"

"No one's claimed you?" His smile turned cruel. "We played this game last time, Cassara. From where I'm standing, it looks like Gideon has already had his way with you on several occasions. I wonder what your father would think. An Allencourt heir, tangled up with a Delvanir. All it would take is a single letter."

"You wouldn't."

"You think so?" His thumb stroked her wrist again. "Your father already doubts your priorities. Imagine what he'd say if he knew you were whoring yourself out to a disgraced bloodline. That glow of yours? It'll fade fast once the wrong person sees the wrong kind of closeness. The kind that violates conduct codes. The kind fathers and headmistresses don't take kindly to."

She shoved at him again. "You manipulative bastard—"

"Come now, Cassara," he cut her off. "We both know this was never about affection. This was about control. Yours slipping, mine tightening. And from where I'm standing, you've been very… uncontrolled lately."

"Tell me," he breathed, leaning closer, "was he good to you? Did he make you feel special? Safe? Was it worth it?"

She bared her teeth. "I told you there is nothing to tell."

"Then prove it." His hand left the wall to cup her face, fingers digging in with just enough pressure to border on painful. "Kiss me. Right here, right now. Remind me who you belong to."

Revulsion twisted through her gut. The thought of Julian's mouth on hers after what he'd done, what he'd tried to do.

"No."

A dangerous gleam flared in Julian's eyes. "No?" His voice sharpened. "You still think you get to say no to me? I am inevitable. The contract is signed. The decision has been made. You can keep playing pretend, but in the end, you'll belong to me."

"Go fuck yourself, Julian," she said.

His smile vanished. The hand at her jaw squeezed, and his other rose—fist or palm, she couldn't tell. His voice dropped to something lethal. "You're going to regret—"

"Cassara."

Gideon stood at the end of the hall, framed by shadows, posture rigid. No instructors. No students. Just intent.

"You're going to be late," he said, but his attention was fixed on Julian with predatory focus.

Julian didn't release her, didn't step back. "We were just having a conversation about old times. Weren't we, dearheart?"

The endearment made Cassara's skin crawl, but it was the possessive way Julian said it, like a claim, or a warning, that made Gideon grit his teeth. "Nevertheless, let her go."

Julian's grip stayed fixed, but something in his shoulders twitched. His smile returned, ugly at the edges. "Why? Afraid she might remember where she comes from?"

"Julian," she warned. Still, he ignored her.

"What exactly do you think you can offer her, Delvanir?" Julian's voice dripped venom. "A tarnished name? A ruined house? Nothing but scraps from your father's failures? Cassara is promised to me. That's not something you can charm your way around with gallant little stares and battlefield speeches."

Gideon didn't rise to it. He only extended his hand toward her. "The rest of the team is waiting."

Cassara hesitated only a moment, but it was long enough for Julian's fingers to clamp down harder than before, fingers digging into flesh and bone with unbridled malice.

"We're not finished," Julian hissed. "She stays with me."

"Is that so?" Gideon said with a low laugh. He slowly began rolling up his sleeves. "You know, Tremaine. The last time you ran your mouth, there were instructors watching. You really want to try again without an audience?"

Julian's jaw flexed but his grip didn't ease.

Gideon moved closer until he stood inches away. "No one's watching now."

Julian faltered, only slightly. "Touch me, and I'll file a report so fast—"

"You already did, didn't you?" Gideon's voice didn't rise, didn't crack. "Implied she violated code. Suggested something improper. All very careful, very clean. But I wonder, did you think that would protect you from me?"

Cassara could feel the shift. The cold burn of Gideon's fury, it wasn't explosive—which made it that much more frightening.

Julian sneered. "I'm a Tremaine. You so much as bruise me, and your family sinks permanently. You don't have the weight to make threats."

"I'm not making a threat." Gideon's eyes never left Julian's face. "I'm making a promise. Let her go—or I will make sure the next time you touch her, it's with a broken hand."

Julian held his stare for a moment before his grip slowly loosened, his fingers sliding away from her wrist with deliberate reluctance, like he was savoring every last moment of contact. Cassara jerked away from him, her wrist throbbing, angry red marks already beginning to surface.

Gideon's hand was there before she even looked up, steady and waiting.

She hesitated, pride warring with the sick twist in her stomach, but her fingers found his, and the moment they touched, the tremble in her spine steadied. He didn't squeeze, didn't speak, just held her hand like it was the most natural thing in the world.

But Gideon's expression darkened as his eyes focused on her wrist and the marks Julian had left behind. "You bastard," Gideon breathed, his voice deadly quiet.

Julian straightened his jacket with casual arrogance, smoothing down the fabric like nothing had happened. "Careful, Delvanir. Your feelings are showing."

He moved to brush past them, but paused just close enough that his words would carry. "Don't worry, Cassara," he said. "Once we're properly married, I'll make sure to leave marks where no one else can see—"

Gideon moved before the words finished leaving Julian's mouth.

His fist collided with Julian's jaw in a sharp, brutal arc, the crack of bone on bone echoing off the corridor walls. Julian staggered, teeth bared in shock, and immediately retaliated with a hook to Gideon's ribs, fast and practiced. He didn't waste time with insults, Julian wasn't the type to scream, just the type to aim for damage.

They crashed together in a tangle of fists and fury. Julian might have preferred psychological warfare, but his body moved with the fluid precision of someone who'd been trained to fight from childhood. His fist found Gideon's mouth; Gideon's knee drove toward Julian's stomach in return.

"Stop!" Cassara shouted, but they were beyond hearing her.

"You think this changes anything?" Julian hissed between clenched teeth as they locked arms. "She'll wear my name. She'll bear my mark. And every time she tries to run, I'll be there to remind her of who she belongs to."

"You won't get the chance," Gideon growled, and this time, when his fist connected, it split Julian's lip.

"Stop!" Rett's voice boomed, his arms hauling both men apart with a force that rocked all three of them. Gideon's chest heaved, blood on his knuckles, jaw tight. Julian shook off Rett's grip, spitting red onto the floor as he adjusted his collar.

Liri skidded in next, eyes wide. "What's going on? Cass, are you—are you okay?"

She nodded, swallowing thickly. "I'm fine."

"You sure?" Liri's eyes flicked to her wrist and the bruises blooming there. Her whole expression hardened. "You don't look fine."

Oliver emerged from behind them, crossbow in hand though he lowered it when he realized the threat was internal. "Are you insane? Fighting in the corridors where anyone could see?"

More footsteps, and then Verena rounded the corner, her expression shifting from confusion to fury as she took in the scene. "What the hell is wrong with you people?"

"You might want to ask your captain why he's so eager to throw punches over someone else's fiancée," Julian spat.

"Get out," Gideon said, his voice deadly quiet despite Barrett's restraining hand.

Julian's smile was all teeth and poison. "Gladly. But Cassara?" His gaze found hers across the group. "This conversation isn't over. Neither is our engagement. Some things are bigger than schoolyard infatuations and noble gestures."

With that Julian walked away, his footsteps echoing with casual arrogance.

"Is everyone okay?" Liri asked anxiously, pulling a handkerchief from her pocket. "Gideon, your face—"

"I'm fine," he said curtly, but accepted the cloth to dab at the cut on his cheekbone.

"Fine?" Verena snapped. "Are you completely out of your mind?"

All eyes turned to where she stood rigid with suppressed fury. "This is exactly what I was talking about," Verena continued, her voice rising. "This is what happens when you drag the team into your personal drama!" Her accusing stare fixed on Cassara. "He just risked everything—his position, his reputation, the team's standing—because you can't handle your own problems!"

"Verena—" Cassara started, but the other girl wasn't finished.

"Don't! Just don't! You think because you had one good match, because you got lucky with a few tactical calls, that makes you worth destroying everything we've worked for?" Her voice turned shrill. "He's going to get disciplinary action! Julian will report this! All because you couldn't keep your mess away from the team!"

"Verena, that's enough," Gideon said.

"Is it? Because from where I'm standing, it looks like you've completely lost perspective! You're supposed to be our captain, not her personal knight in shining armor!" Verena's composure cracked completely.

"I said that's enough," Gideon snapped, louder this time. "Training is canceled."

The silence that followed was immediate and jagged.

Verena's mouth parted in disbelief. "You're punishing the whole team?"

"No. I'm making sure no one trains when they're distracted or bleeding. If you've got a problem with that, take it to the headmistress, or find a new team."

Liri opened her mouth to protest, but Barrett caught her arm, shaking his head slightly. Oliver was already backing away, clearly wanting no part of whatever was happening here.

Verena stood frozen, her face pale except for two bright spots of color high on her cheekbones. "Gideon, I didn't mean—"

"Yes, you did." His dark eyes were unforgiving.

He turned without another word, brushing past Verena without even glancing back. His hand found Cassara's again, gentler now.

"We're leaving," he said simply.

For once, Cassara felt no desire to argue and followed.

The room Gideon guided her inside was small, the sterile glow of the arcane lamps flickered faintly overhead as he nudged the door shut behind them. Cassara stood awkwardly for a beat, her adrenaline fraying into soreness now that the incident in the hallway was behind them. Her wrist ached but it was nothing compared to the way her heart still raced.

Gideon crossed to one of the supply cabinets. "Sit," he said gently, motioning to the padded bench against the wall.

She didn't protest.

He retrieved a small pack of ice, a jar of salve, and a roll of gauze before kneeling in front of her. No words, just care. His fingers were deft but cautious as he inspected the damage.

When she flinched, he froze.

"Sorry," she murmured quickly.

Gideon's gaze flicked up to meet hers. "You don't need to apologize. Not for that. Not for him."

"I mean it," she said softly. "For getting you involved. For... dragging the team into my mess."

He sighed, but his voice was calm. "You didn't drag anyone. Julian's the one who crossed a line. Again."

She swallowed. "He wasn't always like this."

"You sure about that?"

Cassara's mouth parted, then closed. Was she sure? Her voice went quieter. "Maybe I didn't want to see it. When I stayed in line, followed the rules, did what I was supposed to... he never pushed."

"And now?"

"Now I can't unsee it." She flexed her fingers as he secured the bandage. "The way he talks about me like I'm property. The threats."

"It's not your fault he can't stand losing you."

"Verena," she said, watching his expression shift. "You care about her."

"I do," he admitted. "My parents took her in when she was twelve. She watched hers die during a leviathan breach. She was the only one who made it out. After that, she barely spoke. Wouldn't eat. Had constant night terrors. My mother sat by her bed every night for a year just in case. When she finally started to live again, she clung to the one constant she had left."

"You."

He nodded, quiet. "She sees me as something I've never been to her and no matter how many lines I draw, she doesn't want to believe they exist."

Cassara's chest ached with the weight of it all. Gideon began packing the supplies back into the kit, his movements automatic.

"Wait." She rose, stepped toward him, and pressed her hand to his arm.

He turned to look at her, his expression guarded.

Cassara reached past him, picked up a clean cloth, and wet it with a flick of the tap. Then, without waiting for permission, she stepped into his space, reached up, and gently dabbed at the blood smeared high on his cheekbone.

"Thank you," she murmured.

Gideon tilted his head slightly, a lopsided smile playing at his lips. "No need. I never pass up the chance to punch that pompous idiot in the face."

She huffed a laugh.

"No," she said, her hand still cupping the side of his face. "Well, I mean yes. But also thank you for giving me a chance. From the start."

Gideon's smile softened.

"You earned it," he said. "I just happened to notice."

And in the space between their breaths, something settled. Not finished. Not resolved. But steady. And very, very real.

His hand rose to catch hers as she dabbed at the cut. She didn't pull away.

Instead her pulse fluttered, a quiet, unsteady thing, and when she looked up, Gideon was watching her. The light above cast soft shadows down the strong line of his jaw, catching on a faint smear of blood she'd missed.

Gideon's eyes were darker than usual. Not stern or commanding, just quiet.

She knew that look. She had seen it once before. On the overlook. Right before Auren had kissed her like the world might end.

But this felt different.

Not desperate or heated.

Just... honest.

Gideon reached up, hand brushing gently against her jaw, hesitating only when he felt her breath hitch.

"I shouldn't," he murmured. "But I want to."

His thumb traced lightly along her cheekbone. She didn't move. Couldn't.

And then he leaned in.

For a second, her eyes fluttered shut. Just for a heartbeat.

But the unexpected warmth came tangled with something colder. A flicker of guilt. A hand tangled in her hair. Auren's voice in the dark.

Cassara turned her face gently, Gideon's kiss landing on the curve of her cheek instead.

"I'm sorry," she said quietly, not looking at him. "I just... I don't know what this is."

He froze, but didn't pull away completely. His hand dropped from her face, curling into a loose fist at his side.

"You don't have to explain," he said, after a moment. "I should be apologizing."

"It's okay," she said quickly, but her voice came out breathless, shaky. She stepped back, putting distance between them, one hand pressed to her cheek where his lips had touched. "It's fine. It's just—"

"You're with someone." It wasn't a question. The realization was written clearly across his face and the way he suddenly wouldn't meet her eyes.

"Yes," she whispered, then stronger: "I am."

But even as she said it, her heart was racing for reasons that had nothing to do with the almost-kiss and everything to do with the way her body had leaned toward him before her mind caught up. The way part of her, a part she didn't want to examine too closely, had wanted to let it happen.

"Julian was right about one thing. You have been different. Happier. More confident." His smile was rueful, self-deprecating. "I should have realized there was someone else."

Cassara's chest ached with guilt and confusion. "Gideon—"

"Don't." He said, running a hand through his hair. "Don't apologize. I overstepped. I just..." He trailed off, shaking his head. "Forget it happened."

But she couldn't forget it. Not the way her pulse had spiked when he'd started to lean in, or the moment of want that had flashed through her before loyalty kicked in.

"We should get back," she said, her voice carefully controlled.

"Right." He moved toward the door, then paused. "Cassara? This doesn't change anything. Between the team, I mean. Whatever's happening with your personal life, we'll figure it out."

"I know." But even as she said it, she wondered if that was true. Because something had changed, something she didn't know how to define or deal with.

They walked back toward the training area in silence, the weight of the almost-kiss hanging between them like a storm cloud. And Cassara tried very hard not to think about why her lips tingled with the phantom sensation of what might have been.

CHAPTER THIRTY TWO

The training glyph flared too early and Cassara jerked sideways as the barrier wall snapped into place half a second ahead of schedule, forcing her into an awkward dodge that nearly sent her sprawling. The arc-light shimmered too fast, too sharp, and her ACS unit buzzed hot against her forearm like it had skipped a beat.

She caught herself with a grunt and rolled back onto her feet, breath sharp in her chest.

"Having trouble?" Liri asked, jogging over with her battle fans still spinning lazily around her wrists. Nym fluttered overhead, wings pulsing with a steady glow that made Cassara's erratic readings look even more pronounced.

Cassara winced and tapped the control dial on her bracer. "That one wasn't me. The glyph pulsed early."

Rett, manning the illusion reset panel, looked up. "Didn't touch anything."

Before she could reply, Oliver was already making his way toward her, the loose strap of his Codex bag slung across one shoulder, brows drawn together. "That's the third misfire this week."

Cassara frowned. "It's not my timing. It jumped ahead again. I barely made the dodge."

"Could be harmonic interference," he replied. "Beast signatures can destabilize if there's a mismatch between the ACS calibration and actual output."

Cassara looked at him hopefully. "Can you fix it?"

"Let me see." He stopped in front of her and held out a hand, hesitant but focused. "If it's misfiring this close to the match, we should check the diagnostics."

She offered her wrist without argument, and Oliver crouched slightly to better inspect the runework etched into the ACS shell.

"Huh. That's... unusual."

"Bad unusual or interesting unusual?"

"Both." Oliver's frown deepened as he cycled through different diagnostic modes. "The latency buffer's off again, and the projection flare is looping too early. That shouldn't be happening unless your core sync is destabilizing."

Cassara glanced toward the still-active glyph wall. "Is it something I did?"

"I don't think so," he said. "You haven't changed your configuration in the last few days, right?"

"No."

Oliver nodded slowly, thoughtful. "It's not corrupted, but... it's not stable either. Your beast data's acting strange. Energy patterns keep shifting. Too many peaks and dips, like the signature can't settle."

Cassara tensed. "Is it dangerous?"

"Not yet," he said. "But I have a theory. It might be Flicker."

Her brow furrowed. "What about him?"

"Well... his sync pattern isn't consistent. It keeps adjusting—sometimes in tiny increments, sometimes in bursts. That could throw off your ACS readings if the system can't keep up."

"You think he's doing it on purpose?"

"No. But it might be part of how he's wired. Or how he's... evolving." Oliver looked up at her, hesitant. "The data spikes remind me of something I saw in some data records. There was a shapeshifter beast bonded to a third-year who had similar signature variance. Constant growth threw the system out of calibration unless they resynced almost daily."

Cassara blinked. "So I'm going to need daily syncs?"

"Maybe not forever. But until I know more, it's a possibility. I'll take your ACS and run a few tests. I'm going to need to recalibrate your entire harmonic matrix. Maybe install some adaptive filters to smooth out the fluctuations."

She hesitated, then nodded. "Okay. Thanks, Oliver."

His ears flushed faintly, but he gave her a brisk nod and started unfastening the bracer with quick, careful fingers. "Try not to push too hard until I get this sorted. No more weird lunges into ghost walls, okay?"

She managed a wry smile. "You're no fun."

"I'm all numbers and logic. Fun terrifies me."

But there was worry in his voice. And beneath it, an unease neither of them could name. Not yet.

Four days of training without her ACS had been torture. Cassara felt disconnected from Flicker, clumsy with Spireglass, out of sync with everything that had finally started to feel natural. Oliver had kept her updated with progress reports, adaptive algorithms, harmonic recalibration, predictive matrices, but the technical jargon only made her more anxious.

Now, on the morning of their match, the preparation room buzzed with pre-match energy, but Cassara's attention was fixed on Oliver, who sat hunched over her ACS unit with the intensity of someone defusing a bomb.

Her ACS bracer sat in pieces across his lap, a fine scatter of copper-touched plating and rune-threaded wires gleaming in the overhead light.

"You're sure it's not going to short out mid-match?" Cassara asked.

"I'm sure if it does it won't kill you," he muttered.

"That's hardly reassuring."

Oliver didn't look up. "If you'd rather fight with manual glyphs and no beast sync, I can reattach the casing right now and we can both panic quietly."

"Fine," she said, flopping onto the bench again, but her knee kept bouncing.

Around them, the rest of the team was going through their final preparations. Gideon checked Lockstep's defensive matrices while his griffin preened its storm-colored feathers. Liri practiced quick-draw maneuvers with Nimbrush, her moth providing gentle pulses of calming light. Barrett methodically inspected Gravemaul's weight distribution, Skelli coiled nearby in patient readiness.

Even Verena seemed focused, running Whispercoil through its extension sequences while Kaddock rumbled with barely contained energy.

"Oliver," Gideon's voice carried a note of warning. "Five minutes to deployment."

"I know, I know!" Oliver's hands moved with practiced precision, making final calibrations. "The resonance patterns were more complex than I anticipated. Her beast's signature keeps shifting, so I had to build in predictive algorithms to—"

"English, please," Liri called out, though her voice held more amusement than impatience.

"Done," Oliver said suddenly.

Cassara blinked. "Really?"

He held out the newly restored ACS. "Mostly. I've rerouted the sync to a modulated channel. It won't fix Flicker's fluctuations, but it'll give the system a moment to breathe between surges. Might delay his response time by half a second. You'll feel it."

"Will I?"

He gave her a flat look. "You'll either notice it, or the match will go great and I'll pretend I was a genius."

Cassara smirked and strapped it on. "Genius it is."

What followed was perhaps their smoothest arena performance yet. The terrain, a series of floating platforms connected by narrow bridges, should have favored their opponents' ranged specialists, but Auric Vow moved like a single organism across the battlefield.

Each member slid into position without the need for orders. Gideon launched first, his griffin streaking overhead, wind trailing in slicing arcs that disrupted their opponents' positioning.

Rett's raptor flanked hard left and drove two enemy tamers into a trap line Oliver had already seeded. Liri darted through the chaos, Nym's light blinding and disorienting, disrupting shield glyphs and leaving the enemy wide open.

And Cassara... Cassara felt like she was flying. Spireglass responded to her every thought, creating afterimages that confused and misdirected their opponents and teleporting her seamlessly, putting her exactly where she needed to be to tip the balance in their favor.

Flicker, meanwhile, seemed content to observe from various perches around the arena, occasionally absorbing stray attacks with his usual casual indifference. To outside observers, he appeared to be doing very little. But Cassara could feel his presence through their bond, steady, supportive, ready to act if truly needed.

And just like that, it was over.

The final beacon flared gold in their favor. The opposing team fell back, panting, bruised, but not broken. They knew it. Everyone watching knew it.

Auric Vow had dominated.

"Drinks tonight?" Liri suggested as they gathered in the center of the arena, still breathless from exertion but glowing with triumph.

"Absolutely," Gideon agreed, his rare smile making an appearance. "We've earned it."

Even Verena seemed genuinely pleased, her usual edge softened by the satisfaction of a perfect performance.

"Not bad," she said, which, from her, was high praise.

As they filed off the arena floor to the cheers of the watching students, Cassara caught Auren's eye in the instructor's section. His nod was subtle, professional, but she caught the pride flickering behind his carefully controlled expression.

The next morning frost coated the training yard, the air carrying a chill that promised of encroaching winter. The team moved through drills in near-perfect sync, Gideon calling out rotations, Rett locking formation, Liri darting between simulated cover as her moth cast sweeping light to mimic evasive flares. Cassara's glaive spun in a blur, her ACS humming steady against her wrist.

"Let's reset for the beacon run," Gideon said. "Cassara, flank on—"

The sound of approaching bootsteps broke the rhythm.

Auren and Nareen strode across the yard, flanked by a third figure in uniform-gray robes. The academy tech, instantly recognizable by the silver insignia gleaming at his collar, carried a reinforced case and a neutral expression that screamed problem.

Her first instinct was to smile, to catch Auren's eye the way she had yesterday after their victory. But when his gaze swept across the assembled team, it passed over her without the slightest flicker of acknowledgment. No subtle nod. No hint of warmth. Nothing.

Not a single glance.

Cassara's heartbeat kicked up.

Gideon stepped forward, tension rolling off his shoulders. "Instructors. We weren't scheduled for oversight today."

"We need to speak with Cassara Allencourt," Nareen said, and there was something in her tone that made every member of the team go still.

Cassara's mouth went dry. "I'm here."

She glanced towards Auren who still didn't look at her. His gaze remained fixed on some point over her shoulder, professional distance radiating from every line of his body.

"We're going to need you to surrender your ACS unit for inspection," Nareen said, her voice matter-of-fact but not unkind.

"What? Why?"

Nareen's gaze stayed steady. "A formal complaint's been filed."

Cassara blinked. "By who?"

"I can't disclose that."

"Then what's the complaint?"

Nareen sighed. "Tampering. Data manipulation. The report alleges that you've altered your ACS sync settings to falsify and enhance your beast's combat performance in a way that is both a danger to your beast and yourself."

It didn't register at first. The words bounced in her skull like hail, hitting too fast to absorb. "What?" Cassara's world tilted sideways. "You're saying... I cheated? That's—that's impossible. I would never—"

"Nevertheless, we need to examine your equipment." The tech held out his hand, expectant. "Please remove your ACS unit."

For a moment, Cassara couldn't move, couldn't breathe. The accusation was so absurd, so completely contrary to everything she'd worked for, that her mind simply couldn't process it.

"Cassara," Nareen's voice was gentler now, but implacable. "Your ACS unit."

Cassara's throat closed. With trembling fingers, she undid the latch, detached the bracer, and handed it over. Her wrist felt cold without it.

Liri stepped closer, alarm creasing her face. "That's insane. Flicker's been acting weird, sure, but she's not cheating. Why would she?"

Rett stayed silent, eyes fixed on the ground.

"Any tampering will be verified by academy tech," Nareen added. "If the claim is baseless, it'll be dismissed."

"And if it's not?" Cassara asked, voice barely above a whisper.

Nareen didn't answer.

Auren turned away.

The tech bent over the case, his fingers working fast and unflinching as he connected her ACS to the scanner. Runes lit across the interface in waves: white, then blue, then a flicker of pulsing amber.

Cassara tried to speak, to explain. "If there's something wrong with it, it wasn't me. You can ask—"

"Please, Cassara," the tech interrupted, polite but firm. "Let the scan finish."

Each second dragged.

And then the color shifted, amber deepening into red. The scanner chimed. The tech straightened, eyes flicking to Nareen.

"Preliminary scan shows evidence of system modification," the tech announced after what felt like an eternity. "The harmonic signatures have been altered, and there are traces of unauthorized code in the resonance matrix."

Cassara felt the ground drop out from under her. "No. No, that's not—Oliver worked on it! He was fixing sync issues, that's all!"

"I'm sorry," Nareen said, and this time there was something like regret in her voice. "You are suspended from all academy training, including team sessions, Rift access, and arena participation until further notice."

"But—" Her voice cracked. "I didn't do anything."

"The evidence says otherwise," the tech said quietly. "You'll have a chance to speak at the hearing."

"What hearing?"

"There will be a formal hearing to determine if disciplinary action is warranted," Nareen explained.

"Disciplinary action?" Cassara already knew the answer.

"Suspension though expulsion is a possibility," Nareen said quietly. "Data fraud violates the academy's core principles of integrity and fair competition."

Cassara's knees nearly gave out. Everything she'd fought for, everything she'd earned, was crumbling in her hands.

"Additionally," Nareen added, and her voice carried genuine regret now, "academy policy requires that we notify your family of any formal investigation. Your father will be informed of the charges."

That was the final blow.

Her father. Who already doubted her worth, who saw her as a disappointment, who would view this as confirmation of every suspicion he'd ever harbored about her judgment.

"This is insane!" Liri burst out, her usual gentle demeanor replaced by fierce loyalty. "Cassara would never cheat!"

But Cassara barely heard her. She was drowning in the weight of stares, in the terrible silence from Auren, in the growing doubt she could see taking root in Gideon's eyes.

After everything. After proving herself, after finding her place, after finally believing she belonged, it was all being ripped away by an accusation she couldn't even comprehend.

And the worst part was the tiny voice in the back of her mind whispering the question she was afraid to examine too closely:

Why did everyone suddenly look like they weren't sure they believed her?

The overlook was empty in the deep hours of night, just as Cassara had hoped. She stood at the railing, gazing out across the training fields that lay dark and silent below. Somewhere out there, in those very yards where she'd finally learned what it meant to belong, her reputation was being torn to shreds by whispers and speculation.

Cheater. Fraud. Liar.

The words had followed her through the corridors like poison, spoken just loudly enough to ensure she heard every syllable. Students who'd congratulated her on yesterday's victory now looked at her with suspicion.

Tomorrow afternoon would bring with it the hearing that would determine her fate along with her father who would be there to witness the end result.

"You aren't thinking of jumping, are you?" The voice came from behind her, familiar and warm despite its teasing tone. "I didn't bring my glider with me. Be a shame if I had to jump after you without it."

Cassara didn't turn around, couldn't bear to see whatever expression Auren might be wearing. "Depends. Would you really jump?"

"For you? Probably." His footsteps approached slowly, giving her time to object if she wanted solitude. "Though I'd prefer we find a less dramatic solution to your problems."

The casual certainty in his voice, that he would jump, that her problems could be solved, made the tears she had been fighting all evening burn in the corners of her eyes.

"Do you believe it?" she asked softly, the words trembling more than she wanted. "Do you think I cheated?"

Silence.

It dragged long enough for her stomach to twist.

And then she felt him step in. His arms wrapped around her waist from behind, firm and steady, and pulled her against his chest. His breath stirred her hair, his voice a murmur.

"No. I don't."

She let herself lean into him, just a little. "Why?"

"Because you're too damn proud. Too stubborn. And if you were going to rig your stats, it wouldn't be for a win you earned." He paused. "You would've done it the night the poacher came."

She stiffened and turned to look at him. "You knew?"

Auren's expression didn't shift. "I saw him sneak in. Knew you were still down in the bonding rooms, pushing yourself too hard like usual. I followed. Watched. Overheard enough to understand what he was offering

She stared. "You didn't stop him."

"It wasn't my place." His tone was calm, edged with something quieter, something close to pride. "It was a choice you had to make on your own."

Cassara looked away, the ache in her chest dulling for the first time in hours. "I don't know what to do."

"You wait," Auren said simply. "You let them scramble and you trust your team."

She gave a soft, humorless laugh. "My team's falling apart. Gideon won't even look at me. They all think I'm guilty."

"Gideon is being careful. There's a difference between doubt and caution." He pulled back just enough to meet her eyes. "Give them time to process. Give them a chance to prove their loyalty."

Before she could respond, he kissed her—soft and sure and full of the kind of faith she'd forgotten how to have in herself.

When they broke apart, his forehead rested against hers. "You're not alone in this, Cassara. And you're not done. Not yet."

The afternoon sun did nothing to warm the courtyard.

Cassara paced beneath the marble arches, boots scuffing the same worn path she'd walked a dozen times already. Her Aether Codex weighed heavy at her hip, but it was the silence that pressed heavier.

Her fingers fidgeted with the hem of her sleeve, tugging it down to hide the fading bruises that ringed her wrist. Her pulse skittered with every shadow.

"You always did look lovely in distress."

Cassara froze.

Julian stepped into view, posture relaxed, hands folded behind his back like a nobleman out for a stroll. His smile was all teeth. "Though I think I preferred you flushed with victory rather than panic."

She took a step back.

Julian's gaze dropped to her wrists, where the finger-shaped bruises from their last encounter had faded to a sickly yellow-green. His smile sharpened.

"Easy," he said, holding up his hands in defense. "I'm not here to touch. I'm here to talk."

"I'm not interested."

"That's unfortunate," Julian mused. "You used to hang on my every word. How quickly things change."

Her fingers curled into tight fists.

"Where's your knight in shining armor now?" he asked, glancing around the empty courtyard with mock concern. "Or has Gideon finally realized his damsel's not worth the trouble? Funny how quickly people abandon you when your reputation becomes... questionable."

"He's not abandoning me." But even as she said it, doubt crept into her voice. She hadn't seen Gideon since yesterday's devastating revelation, hadn't spoken to any of her teammates except for Liri's brief, fierce hug in the corridor.

"Could have fooled me," Julian took another step forward, close enough she caught a hint of the clove-oil cologne he favored. "I was thinking," he said airily, "once all this blows over and your name's tarnished beyond repair, we should consider a summer wedding. I've always liked the gardens at your family's estate."

"I'd rather jump off the edge of this island than marry you," she hissed.

His smile didn't falter. "Noted. Though I'm confident it won't come to that. You know, I'll miss our little chats once you're no longer attending Vallemont. But don't worry..." He leaned in slightly, voice dipping to a whisper. "I'll visit often. Wouldn't want you forgetting your place."

Her nails bit into her palms, fury crackling at the edges of her vision.

"Miss Allencourt."

They both turned to see Auren standing at the entrance to the covered walkway, perfectly composed except for the rigid set of his shoulders and the careful way he wasn't quite looking at Julian.

"You're needed for the hearing," he continued, his tone professionally neutral. But Cassara could see the tension radiating from every line of his body, could practically feel the violence he was holding in check.

Julian straightened, brushing invisible lint from his jacket. "Ah, Instructor Veth. How thoughtful of you to escort our dear Cassara to her... appointment."

The pause before 'appointment' was deliberate, weighted with implication.

"Miss Allencourt," he repeated, not acknowledging Julian's presence.

Cassara moved toward him quickly, grateful for the excuse to put distance between herself and Julian's predatory smile. But as she passed, Julian's voice followed her.

"Good luck, dearheart. I'm sure everything will work out exactly as it should."

Auren fell into step half a pace behind her as they left the courtyard, his presence a solid, reassuring weight at her back. But she could feel the coiled tension in him, could sense how close he'd come to abandoning professional restraint entirely.

"Thank you," she said quietly once they were out of Julian's earshot.

"For what?"

"For not killing him. Though part of me wishes you had."

Auren's laugh was short and humorless. "The day is young."

CHAPTER THIRTY THREE

Cassara stepped into the hearing chamber with Auren beside her. He didn't speak again, didn't glance her way, but his presence steadied her just enough to keep walking. Her boots echoed off the polished marble tiles, each step a measured act of defiance against the sinking weight in her chest.

High-backed chairs were arranged in a semicircle facing a central table where her ACS unit sat like evidence in a murder trial, its familiar weight now transformed into something alien and damning under the harsh magelight. Two ACS technicians stood nearby, whispering quietly, their attention centered on the object between them.

Auren's hand barely brushed her elbow as he guided her to the defendant's chair, but she caught the subtle pressure. Then he was gone, taking his place among the faculty with the same professional distance he'd maintained since yesterday's disaster.

"The disciplinary panel will now come to order," Headmistress Kalisandra announced, her voice carrying the weight of institutional authority.

Cassara's gaze swept the room, taking in the faces that would determine her fate. The headmistress sat at the center of the panel, flanked by four figures in formal academy robes, alumni who'd returned to sit in judgment of current students. Three were strangers, their expressions carefully neutral.

The fourth made her blood turn to ice.

Lord Marcel Tremaine. Julian's father. His blue eyes, so like his son's, regarded her with smug satisfaction. The slight curve of his mouth suggested he was exactly where he wanted to be.

Across the chamber, her father sat in a visitor's gallery. Straight-backed and unmoving, his gaze never shifted to meet hers.

Cassara's team sat to the left, huddled together, Liri's arms crossed tight over her chest, Oliver hunched, fidgeting. Rett stared straight ahead, unreadable. And Gideon... Gideon tracked her entrance like a hawk.

Verena was not with them.

She sat alone to the far right, near the board. Not a teammate now.

Her red hair was pulled back severely, and she sat with the rigid posture of someone preparing for battle. When their eyes met for a brief moment, Cassara saw something she couldn't quite identify flicker across Verena's face.

Guilt? Fear? Or just the satisfaction?

"Before we begin," the headmistress continued, "let me remind everyone present that these proceedings are confidential and protected under academy privacy statutes. The charges brought today are serious and will be treated with the gravity they deserve."

A chime resonated through the room indicating that the hearing had officially begun.

The headmistress rose from her seat, gaze sweeping the room before settling on Cassara. No smile, no malice, only the weight of centuries-old tradition behind her voice.

"This hearing is now in session," she said. "We are gathered to assess the validity of a formal complaint submitted to the Academy Review Board concerning possible academic misconduct and breach of code by first-year student Cassara Allencourt."

The headmistress continued, folding her hands atop the marble in front of her. "The complaint alleges that Miss Allencourt's ACS unit was tampered with to enhance the perceived performance of her bonded beast during ranked evaluations, both in training and official combat. The implication is clear: manipulation of performance data to gain an unfair advantage. If proven true, this would constitute grounds for immediate expulsion and formal blacklisting from all bonded academies within the jurisdiction of the Skybound Concord."

A low murmur rose from the upper tiers. It was quickly silenced by another chime.

Cassara's palms were slick against her thighs. Her breath came slow, too slow, held tight in her chest until the headmistress turned fully to her.

"Miss Allencourt," she said. "How do you respond to the charges brought against you?"

The chamber fell silent. Cassara could hear her own heartbeat, could feel the expectant tension radiating from every corner of the room.

Cassara stood slowly, her legs shakier than she'd expected.

When she spoke, her voice carried clearly through the chamber despite the tremor she felt inside.

"I plead innocent to all charges," she said. "I have never tampered with my ACS equipment. I have never falsified performance data. And I have never attempted to gain unfair advantage through deception or fraud."

Another beat of silence.

The headmistress nodded once, as if checking a box.

"So noted," she said. "We will now proceed to the presentation of evidence. I believe we will first hear from the Technical Assessment team." She gestured toward the two uniformed figures in the faculty section.

The senior technician, the same man who'd delivered yesterday's devastating verdict, rose and approached the central table where Cassara's ACS unit sat. His movements were precise, clinical, as he activated a projection array that filled the air above the table with swirling data streams.

"Honored alumni," he began, his voice carrying the neutral authority of someone accustomed to delivering expert testimony. "Our examination of the defendant's ACS unit reveals extensive evidence of unauthorized modification."

The projections shifted, displaying what looked like cascading waterfalls of numbers and symbols that meant nothing to Cassara but seemed to carry damning weight for those who understood them.

"First, the calibration logs." He gestured, and a section of the display highlighted in red. "Standard ACS units maintain detailed records of all adjustments and modifications. Miss Allencourt's unit shows multiple instances where these logs have been corrupted or deliberately overwritten."

Cassara's stomach dropped. She wanted to protest, to explain that Oliver had been working on the unit for days, but something told her that speaking out of turn would only make things worse.

"Furthermore," the technician continued, "we discovered unusual signature alignments that don't match the baseline readings for her registered beast." Another gesture brought up side-by-side comparisons: jagged, erratic patterns next to suspiciously smooth, optimized curves. "The modified signatures consistently show enhanced performance metrics across all categories."

Lord Tremaine leaned forward with interest. "How significant are these enhancements?"

"Substantial," the technician replied without hesitation. "Combat effectiveness increased by approximately thirty percent, synchronization stability improved by forty-five percent, and magical resonance amplified by nearly sixty percent. These are not natural fluctuations- they represent systematic optimization."

Cassara felt the walls of the chamber pressing closer, the weight of suspicious stares growing heavier.

"Most concerning," the second technician added, rising to join his colleague, "is the altered sync data itself. The modifications were sophisticated—someone with considerable technical knowledge went to great lengths to make the falsified readings appear legitimate."

He activated another display showing timestamp data and access logs. "The tampering occurred over multiple sessions, suggesting premeditation rather than a single impulsive act."

Cassara's hands clenched in her lap. Every piece of evidence painted her as a calculating cheater who'd spent weeks systematically undermining the academy's most fundamental principles. The technical language made it sound impossible to refute.

"In conclusion," the senior technician said, "the evidence clearly demonstrates deliberate and extensive tampering designed to provide unfair competitive advantage. The modifications required both technical sophistication and prolonged access to the equipment."

Cassara stared at the projection, her pulse thudding in her ears. Her lips parted, but nothing came.

She had no logs.

No alibi.

No defense except the sick, hollow truth in her chest.

"I didn't do that," she said softly. "I don't even know how to do that."

As the projections faded and the technicians returned to their seats, silence settled over the chamber like a funeral shroud. Cassara stared at her ACS unit, the piece of equipment that had finally made her feel connected, competent, worthy, now transformed into the instrument of her destruction.

"We will now hear character testimony regarding the defendant," the headmistress announced. "Captain Delvanir, as Miss Allencourt's team leader, you may speak first."

Gideon rose from the student section with measured composure, but Cassara caught the tension in his shoulders as he approached the center of the chamber. When he turned to face the panel, his expression was carefully neutral, the same mask of professional control she'd seen him wear during difficult tactical briefings.

"Honored panel," he began, his voice steady but formal. "I have served as Cassara Allencourt's team captain for the past several weeks. In that capacity, I have observed her conduct both in training and in combat situations."

He paused, choosing his words with deliberate care. "Cass- Miss Allencourt has consistently demonstrated dedication to improvement through legitimate means. She trains longer hours than required, seeks additional instruction when struggling, and has never requested modifications to equipment or evaluation standards."

Cassara felt a flicker of hope, but something in Gideon's careful tone suggested he was walking a diplomatic tightrope.

"Her tactical contributions to our team's success have been substantial," he continued. "She has shown willingness to sacrifice personal advancement for team objectives and has never exhibited behavior consistent with someone seeking unfair advantage."

Lord Tremaine leaned back in his chair. "And yet, Captain Delvanir, the evidence suggests otherwise. Would you not agree that sophisticated cheating might be difficult to detect through casual observation?"

"I can only speak to what I have observed directly, my lord. Miss Allencourt's actions in my presence have been honorable."

The careful phrasing sent ice through Cassara's veins.

In my presence.

Not a ringing endorsement, but a cautious statement that left room for doubt about what might have happened when he wasn't watching.

Gideon returned to his seat without meeting her eyes.

"Instructor Nareen," the headmistress called next.

Nareen rose with the rigid bearing of a career military officer. "Miss Allencourt has been in my combat instruction courses for the past term. Her improvement has been notable, though achieved through conventional training methods."

"You observed no unusual advancement that might suggest artificial enhancement?" one of the alumni asked.

"Her progress was rapid but not unprecedented," Nareen replied diplomatically. "Some students experience breakthrough periods where multiple skills converge. However, I cannot speak to the technical aspects of her equipment modifications."

Another careful non-endorsement that felt more damaging than helpful.

Professor Thendrick was called next, his barefoot approach to the panel lending an air of otherworldly detachment to the proceedings.

"The young woman shows genuine empathic connection with her beast," he said simply. "Such bonds cannot be artificially manufactured through equipment tampering. However, enhanced readings might mask the true depth, or limitations, of such connections."

Even Thendrick's mystical support came with qualifications that suggested reasonable doubt.

As the character witnesses returned to their seats, Cassara felt the weight of their carefully neutral testimonies. No one had called her a liar outright, but no one had offered the kind of unequivocal support that might counterbalance the technical evidence either.

The message was clear—she was a decent person and a dedicated student, but decent people could still make desperate choices when cornered.

The headmistress consulted her notes. "Unless there are additional witnesses or evidence to present, we will proceed to—"

"I'd like a chance to speak on behalf of my teammate."

Cassara turned, startled. So did half the room.

Oliver stood slowly, hands clasped in front of him, expression unreadable behind his lenses. His voice, though quiet, carried easily.

The headmistress raised an eyebrow. "Mr. Straton, you are not listed as a character witness."

"No, ma'am. I'm here as a technical expert." Oliver set his toolkit on the table beside Cassara's ACS unit. "I've been analyzing the data independently, and I believe there are... discrepancies in the evidence."

"How can a student be a technical expert?" Lord Tremain protested.

Kalisandra studied Oliver a moment. "I think it's prudent we hear all the information before making a decision. A student's reputation and scholastic life is at stake. Please proceed, Mr. Straton."

Oliver activated his own projection array, filling the air with data streams that looked far more complex than the technicians' earlier display.

"The tampering is real," he began, and Cassara's brief hope plummeted. "Someone definitely modified the ACS unit. But the question isn't whether it happened, it's who had access to do it."

He gestured, and the projection shifted to show a timeline marked with colored indicators. "For the past week, Cassara's ACS has been in my possession for diagnostic work. She's had no physical access to it during that period."

Lord Tremaine frowned. "Are you suggesting the tampering occurred while the device was in your care?"

"Exactly." Oliver's voice carried the confidence of someone on familiar technical ground. "But here's where it gets interesting. ACS units automatically log proximity to other active devices—it's part of their synchronization protocols for team combat."

The projection changed again, displaying a complex web of connection logs and timestamps. "According to these logs, another ACS unit was detected in close proximity to Cassara's device while it was secured in the tech lab overnight."

Cassara leaned forward, hope beginning to stir again.

Around the chamber, she could sense the shift in attention as people tried to follow Oliver's technical explanation.

"The proximity signature matches..." Oliver paused, consulting his notes with theatrical precision. "ACS unit registration number 4-7-Alpha-9. Registered to..." Another pause as he double-checked his data. "Verena Montero."

The silence that followed was deafening. Cassara's gaze snapped to Verena, who had gone rigid in her seat.

"This is circumstantial evidence at best," the senior technician interjected. "Proximity logs can be triggered by routine maintenance or equipment checks."

"Agreed," Oliver nodded. "Which is why I dug deeper." His hands moved over the glyphs on his Codex, bringing up another display. "The proximity was detected at 6:47 AM, during a period when the tech lab was secured and no maintenance was scheduled."

One of the alumni leaned forward. "Are you accusing Miss Montero of the tampering?"

"I'm presenting data," Oliver replied carefully. "The interpretation is up to you. But the timing is... troubling. Especially since Cassara can be definitively placed elsewhere during that window."

Verena finally found her voice, though it came out higher than usual. "This is ridiculous. Oliver could have fabricated those logs easily. He had access to both devices!"

Oliver turned to stare at her, and for a moment his usual mild expression gave way to something much sharper. The insult seemed to hit him on a level that surprised everyone in the room.

"Excuse me?" His voice was dangerously quiet. "Are you seriously suggesting that if I wanted to frame someone, I'd be sloppy enough to leave proximity logs lying around?"

The chamber went silent. Even the headmistress looked taken aback by the sudden shift in Oliver's demeanor.

"I mean," Oliver continued, his tone growing more offended by the second, "if I were going to orchestrate something like this, which I absolutely would not, do you really think I'd be amateur enough to leave such obvious digital fingerprints? Please. Give me some credit for basic competence."

He gestured at his projection with something approaching indignation. "If I'd done this, there wouldn't be any evidence to find. The logs would be clean, the timestamps would be perfect, and we'd never be having this conversation because no one would ever know anything had happened."

Cassara found herself staring at Oliver with a mixture of gratitude and mild alarm. She'd never seen him so personally affronted.

"Not that I would do such a thing," he added quickly, seeming to realize how his defense might sound. "I'm simply saying that your accusation is insulting to my technical abilities. If you're going to accuse me of something, at least accuse me of being competent at it."

Verena's face had gone pale, her earlier confidence shaken by Oliver's vehement response to the suggestion that he might be a sloppy criminal.

The headmistress cleared her throat. "Mr. Straton, while we appreciate your... professional pride, perhaps we could return to the evidence at hand?"

"Of course," Oliver said, his composure returning as quickly as it had cracked. "My point is simply that proximity logs don't lie. And whoever did this clearly didn't understand how team synchronization protocols work."

His gaze flicked back to Verena with barely concealed disdain. "Amateur hour, seriously."

"This is absurd!" Verena's voice cracked through the chamber like a whip, her careful composure finally beginning to fracture. She half-rose from her seat, green eyes blazing with desperation. "He's lying! Oliver's making this up to protect his precious teammate!"

The outburst drew sharp looks from the panel. Lord Tremaine raised an eyebrow at the breach of protocol, while Kalisandra frowned at the interruption.

"Miss Montero," the headmistress said coolly, "you will have an opportunity to respond when called upon. Please remain seated."

Verena sank back down, but her hands were clenched white-knuckled in her lap. "He could have fabricated all of this. Proximity logs, timestamps, he's had days to manufacture whatever evidence he needed."

One of the alumni nodded thoughtfully. "The board acknowledges that Mr. Straton's findings are... interesting. However, as has been noted, proximity data alone is circumstantial. Without more concrete evidence—"

"Oh, I have more," Oliver interrupted mildly, his fingers dancing over his controls. "Much more."

The projection shifted, displaying what looked like official academy security logs. "These are the access records for Tech Lab Seven, where Cassara's ACS was secured for overnight diagnostics. As you can see, there was only one unauthorized access during the critical timeframe."

The data highlighted a single entry: V. MONTERO - 06:47 AM - AUTHORIZED PERSONNEL OVERRIDE

"Miss Montero used her academy credentials to access not just the lab, but specifically to unlock the diagnostic containment unit where the ACS was housed." Oliver's voice carried the satisfaction of someone presenting an airtight case. "The timestamp correlates exactly with the proximity detection from her personal ACS unit."

Cassara felt her breath catch. Around the chamber, she could see the mood shifting as the weight of real evidence settled over the proceedings.

"Furthermore," Oliver continued, bringing up side-by-side technical readouts, "here are the before and after calibration patterns. On the left, you can see Flicker's actual signature-erratic, unstable, constantly fluctuating. This is what I was trying to compensate for with my diagnostic work."

The display showed the chaotic, spiking patterns Cassara remembered from her malfunctioning equipment.

"And on the right," Oliver's voice hardened, "the falsified signature that was uploaded after Miss Montero's access. Perfectly optimized, artificially stable, and completely inconsistent with any natural beast synchronization I've ever documented."

The contrast was stark even to Cassara's untrained eye. The real readings looked like a seismograph during an earthquake; the fake ones resembled a textbook diagram of ideal performance.

"I have to admit," Oliver continued, a note of professional embarrassment creeping into his voice, "I missed this initially. We were so rushed to get the unit functional before the arena match that I focused on the immediate sync issues rather than running a full forensic analysis. The tampering was... sophisticated enough to blend with my own modifications at first glance."

He turned to face the panel directly. "But once I knew to look for it, the evidence was unmistakable. Someone with limited technical knowledge attempted to overwrite Flicker's natural signature with idealized data. They did a decent job of hiding their tracks, but they didn't understand the deep-layer logging protocols that record every change to core calibration matrices."

In her seat, Verena had gone white, her earlier defiance crumbling as Oliver methodically dismantled any possible innocent explanation for her presence in the lab.

"The question," Oliver said with quiet finality, "is why Miss Montero felt the need to access secured academy equipment at 6:47 in the morning, and why that access resulted in systematic falsification of combat data."

"This is fabricated!" Verena's voice cracked with desperation as she shot to her feet. "Oliver altered those logs! He's had access to all the academy systems for days! He could have changed anything he wanted!"

The accusation hung in the air for a moment before Oliver turned to look at her with the kind of cold disdain usually reserved for malfunctioning equipment.

"Really?" His voice was dangerously quiet. "You think I'd alter official academy security logs and then present them as evidence in a formal hearing? What exactly do you take me for?"

He gestured dismissively at his projection. "If I were going to falsify access records, do you honestly believe I'd be stupid enough to leave my digital fingerprints all over the academy's security infrastructure? Please. I may be many things, but incompetent isn't one of them."

Oliver's professional pride was clearly wounded. "For your information, I was in my dormitory room at 6:47 AM, as confirmed by the automated door logs that track every student's movements. Unlike some people, I don't feel the need to sneak around academy facilities in the early morning hours."

"But you can't prove-" Verena started.

"Actually," Cassara interrupted, her voice cutting through Verena's protests, "I can verify the timeline. I was conducting extra training drills with Instructor Nareen that morning. We started at 6:30 AM."

All eyes turned to Nareen, who rose with military precision. "Confirmed. Miss Allencourt was under my direct supervision from 6:30 AM until approximately 8:15 AM. We were working on advanced defensive formations in training yard C."

The simple statement landed like a hammer blow. Cassara had an ironclad alibi, witnessed by an instructor, during the exact time window when her ACS had been tampered with.

Verena's face went ashen. Her gaze darted frantically around the chamber, looking for any escape from the closing trap, before finally settling on the student section.

"Gideon," she said, her voice breaking with desperation. "Tell them. Tell them I was with you that morning. We were studying together in the library, remember? We talked about tactical formations and—"

But Gideon didn't respond. He sat perfectly still, staring straight ahead with the kind of stone-faced silence that spoke louder than any words. His jaw was set, his dark eyes fixed on some point beyond Verena's pleading face.

He didn't even look at her.

"Gideon, please," Verena's voice cracked completely now, all pretense of composure shattered. "You know I would never—I was with you, I swear I was with you—"

Still nothing. Not even a flicker of acknowledgment.

The silence stretched until it became unbearable, Verena's desperate pleas echoing in a chamber where no one came to her defense. Her teammates sat in horrified silence and the faculty watched with professional detachment.

Finally, Verena seemed to understand that she was utterly alone.

She sank back into her chair, her face crumpling as the full weight of her choices crashed down on her. She was cornered and abandoned by the very person she'd betrayed everyone to protect.

Headmistress Kalisandra cleared her throat, her voice carrying new authority. "I believe we have heard sufficient evidence to reach a conclusion in this matter. The panel will now deliberate."

The five-member board huddled briefly, their voices too low to carry across the chamber. Cassara sat frozen in her chair, hardly daring to breathe as her fate hung in the balance.

After what felt like an eternity but was only minutes, the headmistress straightened.

"In the matter of allegations against Miss Cassara Allencourt," she began, her voice carrying formal weight, "the panel has reached its decision."

Cassara's heart hammered against her ribs.

"The vote is four to one in favor of dismissing all charges. Miss Allencourt, you are hereby cleared of all accusations of academic fraud and equipment tampering."

Relief crashed over Cassara like a wave, so sudden and overwhelming that she nearly sobbed aloud. Around the student section, she heard Liri's quiet cheer and saw Barrett's shoulders drop with released tension.

But Kalisandra wasn't finished.

"However," she continued, her gaze shifting to Lord Tremaine, who sat with obvious displeasure at being outvoted, "I must note that one panel member maintains concerns about the circumstantial nature of the evidence."

Julian's father stood and adjusted the cuffs of his coat, his gaze not fixed on her but... her eyes flicked toward the gallery.

A glance passed between the two men.

A decision regarding her fate had been made before this room had ever filled and the evidence had been presented.

One that had failed to go according to plan.

Cassara couldn't believe it.

Like father, like son.

"The minority opinion notwithstanding," the headmistress continued, "the panel finds the evidence presented by Mr. Straton compelling and definitive. Miss Allencourt's ACS unit will be returned to her immediately, and all academic restrictions are hereby lifted."

One of the technicians approached with her familiar bracer, and Cassara's hands shook slightly as she strapped it back onto her forearm.

"As for Miss Montero," the headmistress's voice turned cool, "separate disciplinary proceedings will be initiated immediately. The charges include academic fraud, equipment tampering, filing false accusations, and violation of academy trust protocols."

Verena sat hunched in her chair, no longer the proud, defiant girl who'd entered the chamber. She looked smaller somehow, diminished by the weight of her exposed betrayal.

"Pending the outcome of those proceedings," the headmistress continued, "Miss Montero is immediately suspended from all team activities and academy privileges. Should the charges be substantiated, expulsion will be recommended to the Board of Regents."

The words fell like a gavel. Verena's academic career, possibly her entire future, lay in ruins because of her jealousy and desperation.

As the chamber began to empty, Cassara caught sight of her father rising from his seat. For a moment, she thought he might approach, might offer some acknowledgment of her vindication.

Instead, he walked toward the exit without so much as a glance in her direction.

Cassara didn't think, she moved.

CHAPTER THIRTY FOUR

Her boots echoed sharply against the polished floor as she cut across the aisle, ignoring the eyes that still lingered on her. "Father."

He didn't stop.

"Father." Sharper this time, angling into his path.

He paused, finally, near the arched double doors. The set of his jaw was unreadable. "You should be grateful this embarrassment didn't cost you everything."

"You tried to make sure it did." Her voice came out steadier than she expected. "You and Lord Tremaine. Don't bother denying it."

"Denying what? That I took steps to protect my investment? Unfortunately, Miss Montero proved less reliable than Julian assured me she would be. Jealous girls are so easily directed, but apparently not easily managed."

Not his daughter, but his investment. That was all she really was to him, all she had ever been. Julian's involvement came as no surprise, but Verena? She had been nothing more than a convenient tool, easily discarded when she failed to deliver the desired result. Cassara would never have believed Verena would risk own career just to get rid of her. In the end, they'd all conspired to destroy her—not because she'd done anything wrong, but because she'd dared to want something for herself.

"You wanted me to fail from the start," she said, her voice rising. "You were hoping they'd send me home in shame. Straight into Julian's arms, exactly where you always planned to put me."

His expression didn't change. No guilt. No remorse. Just cold calculation. "What I wanted was for you to understand the consequences of defiance. Clearly, that lesson didn't take."

"It's not defiance to want a life of my own."

His face hardened. "Watch your tone, Cassara."

"Or what? You'll orchestrate another tribunal?" Her voice cracked. "Mother knew what you were. That's why she kept going back to the border. It was the only place you couldn't control her."

The strike came fast.

A sharp crack of skin on skin that snapped her head to the side. Pain bloomed across her cheek, red-hot, and the breath rushed from her lungs.

Her father stepped closer, and suddenly she was small again. A child who'd learned that defiance had consequences. His voice dropped to something deadly quiet. "You think you've won? You think—"

Gideon was suddenly there, stepping between them with deliberate calm.

Rather than face her father, he turned his back to him and faced her. One hand lifted to gently cradle her face.

“Let me see,” he murmured. His fingers traced the edge of the bruise, feather-light but sure.

“It’s okay,” Cassara murmured. She wanted to tell him to leave, not to get involved, but the words lodged themselves in her throat.

“No, it’s not. If you ever touch her again—” He turned his head, just enough to meet Lord Allencourt’s eyes over his shoulder. “—you’ll regret it.”

Her father’s laugh was sharp and bitter. “So this is the one? The Delvanir boy? I suppose I shouldn’t be surprised.” His voice turned venomous. “Julian mentioned some interesting observations about my daughter’s... nocturnal activities. Late-night absences. Changes in behavior.”

Gideon went very still, but his hand didn’t move from Cassara’s face.

“Tell me, boy,” Lord Allencourt continued, “has my daughter been warming your bed? Is that why you’re so eager to defend her? Or has she been trading other favors for advancement?”

Cassara felt her cheeks burn with humiliation, but it was the dangerous stillness that had settled over Gideon that truly frightened her.

“Lord Allencourt,” Gideon said quietly, finally turning to face him fully, “I suggest you choose your next words very carefully.”

“Is that a threat? From a disgraced family’s son to a peer of the realm?” Lord Allencourt stepped closer, his voice dropping to a whisper. “Your family has already lost everything once. How much more are you willing to sacrifice for a girl who was never meant for the likes of you?"

For a moment, Cassara thought Gideon might hit him. The tension coiled between them like a spring wound too tight, violence waiting just beneath the surface.

Instead, Gideon smiled, cold and sharp and lacking even a hint of humor.

"You're right about one thing," he said. "My family does know about sacrifice. We know what it costs to stand by our principles instead of our profit margins. And we know the difference between honor and expedience."

His voice carried the quiet authority of someone who'd never needed to raise it. "Cowards hit their daughters and call it discipline. Cowards orchestrate tribunals and call it justice."

Her father's jaw twitched.

Gideon turned slightly, offering Cassara his arm without taking his eyes off her father. "Cassara, you don't have to listen to this."

She looked between them, her father's face twisted with rage and disgust, Gideon's steady presence offering protection and respect in equal measure. The choice should have been harder than it was.

It wasn't.

She took Gideon's arm and walked away from her father without looking back, leaving Lord Allencourt standing alone in the corridor with his fury and his political machinations.

"This isn't over," her father called after them.

Gideon paused at the corridor's end. "No," he agreed quietly. "It isn't."

As they passed the chamber doors, Cassara caught a glimpse of movement in her peripheral vision. Auren stood in the shadowed alcove near the faculty entrance, perfectly still, watching. Not with anger or jealousy, but regret.

His hands were clenched at his sides and the rigid set of his shoulders spoke of barely leashed restraint. Like a man forced to watch something he couldn't bear to see but couldn't look away from and could do nothing to stop.

Their eyes met for just a moment, long enough for her to see the protective rage burning there before his mask slipped back into place. Then Gideon was guiding her around the corner, and Auren was lost to shadow.

They walked in silence down the corridor until Gideon finally steered them into an empty alcove. Afternoon light filtered through the glass, catching dust motes in the air.

Only then did he release her arm, focusing his attention on something beyond the window.

Cassara's cheek still throbbed where her father had struck her, but that pain was nothing compared to the knot tightening in her chest.

"You shouldn't have done that," she said quietly.

Gideon turned to face her fully. "Which part?"

"Any of it. All of it." Her voice wavered. "My father will—"

"I don't care what your father does."

"You should." She insisted. "He has influence, connections. He could make things difficult for you, for your family—"

"Cassara." Gideon's voice cut through her spiraling thoughts. "Stop."

She closed her mouth, throat tight.

He sighed and Cassara had worked with him long enough now to know what it looked like when he was growing frustrated. "Your father hit you. Did you think I was going to stand there and let that happen?"

"But it's not your fight—"

"Yes, it is." His voice was quiet but absolute. "The moment he put his hands on you, it became my fight."

Cassara's breath caught. She wanted to argue, to push back, to tell him he didn't understand the cost of crossing her father. But the steadiness in his gaze stopped her.

"You could lose everything," she whispered.

"I've already lost everything once." His expression shifted revealing a shadow of old pain. "When my family became outcasts, I learned what actually matters. And it isn't influence or connections or political favor."

"Then what is it?"

"Standing up when it counts." He held her gaze. "I won't apologize for that. Not to your father, not to anyone. And I'd do it again."

The certainty in his voice nearly undid her. No hesitation. No regret.

"Why?" The question slipped out before she could stop it.

Gideon was quiet for a moment, his eyes searching hers. When he finally spoke, his voice was softer. "Because you deserve better than being treated like property. You don't deserve someone who hits you and calls it love."

Her vision blurred. She blinked hard, willing the tears back.

"And because," he continued, even quieter now, "someone needed to show you that not everyone will stand by and let it happen."

Cassara couldn't speak. Couldn't find words for the tangle of emotions knotting in her chest—gratitude and fear and something dangerously close to hope.

"Thank you," she finally managed, voice rough.

Gideon's expression gentled. "You don't need to thank me for basic decency, Cassara."

"Yes, I do." She met his eyes. "Because apparently it's not as common as it should be."

A beat of silence passed between them, heavy with unspoken understanding.

"Your cheek," Gideon said, his hand rising as though to touch her face before he caught himself. "You should have the medics look at it."

"It's fine."

"It's not fine." His voice carried an edge again. "None of this is fine."

"No," she agreed quietly. "It isn't."

The days following the hearing had settled into an uneasy routine. The training annex echoed with the familiar rhythm of combat drills, boots against stone, the whistle of practice weapons through air, the occasional grunt of exertion. Without Verena's barked criticisms and aggressive charges, the space felt oddly hollow, like a song missing its bass line.

Cassara moved through the defensive sequence, her body finding the gaps where Verena should have been. They'd been compensating for three days now, pretending the empty space didn't throw off their entire formation. Pretending they didn't all know what was coming.

"Hold," Nareen's voice cut through their movements.

They turned to find her standing at the entrance, her expression more severe than usual. The afternoon light streaming through the high windows caught the edge of her halberd.

"I have news regarding your teammate."

No one asked which teammate. They all knew.

"The disciplinary board has reached their decision," Nareen continued, her tone carefully neutral. "Miss Montero has been formally expelled from Vallemont Academy. She was escorted from the premises this morning."

The silence that followed wasn't shocked, it was exhausted. They'd all been waiting for this particular blade to fall.

Liri's shoulders sagged slightly, her usual brightness dimming. Barrett said nothing. Oliver simply nodded, as if confirming a mathematical equation he'd already solved.

And Gideon... Gideon's expression didn't change at all. His dark eyes held that particular stillness that meant he'd known this was coming long before Nareen walked through the door.

"The board's decision is final," Nareen added unnecessarily. "You'll need to adjust your tactical formations accordingly."

"We're down to five," Oliver said, because someone had to state the obvious, and he'd always been good at that. His fingers moved unconsciously, already calculating. "More importantly, we've lost our primary defensive tank. Verena's manticore could hold a line against three opponents simultaneously. Without that anchor point, our entire defensive strategy needs restructuring."

Cassara found herself nodding along with his assessment, even as guilt twisted in her chest. She'd wanted Verena gone, had dreamed of it after every cutting remark, every deliberate sabotage. But standing here in the aftermath, all she could think about was the fierce pride in Verena's eyes when Kaddock had been revealed. The potential that had burned so bright before jealousy poisoned it.

"We've handled worse," Gideon said, his voice cutting through her thoughts. There was something almost gentle in his tone, a captain reassuring his team even when the odds had shifted against them. "We'll adapt. We always do."

"The defensive gap," Oliver started.

"Will be addressed," Gideon interrupted smoothly. "I'll use the upcoming break to restructure our formations. Work out new patterns that play to our remaining strengths."

Cassara's head snapped toward him. "You're staying here for break?"

"My presence at home would be... complicated, given recent events. I thought I'd make better use of the time here."

Complicated. Cassara could only imagine what House Delvanir would be like right now, with Verena's fresh expulsion hanging over family dinners like a storm cloud.

"Well," Barrett said quietly, the first words he'd spoken since Nareen's announcement. "At least we'll have time to figure it out without the pressure of matches breathing down our necks."

"Indeed," Nareen agreed. "Those of you departing for break should make your preparations. The academy transport leaves at dawn the day after tomorrow." Her gaze swept over them one more time before she left as abruptly as she'd arrived, leaving the five of them standing in an uncertain circle.

"I should start packing," Liri said into the silence, her voice smaller than usual. "My family's expecting me."

"Mine as well," Oliver added, though he looked like he'd rather calculate defensive formations than face whatever waited at home. "The statistical probability of my mother not interrogating me about team rankings for the entire break is approximately zero."

Barrett just nodded, already moving to collect his gear. His family's expectations were quieter than most, but no less weighty for their silence.

"Go," Gideon said. "Get some rest, you've all earned it. When we get back, we'll be stronger for it."

They dispersed slowly, reluctantly, as if leaving might make Verena's absence more real.

Cassara lingered, watching Gideon reset the training markers with mechanical motions. He moved like someone who'd learned to find comfort in routine, in the things he could control when everything else spiraled beyond reach.

"She was talented," Cassara said quietly.

Gideon's hands stilled on the markers. "She was."

"It's a waste."

"Yeah." He straightened, meeting her gaze directly. "But talent without wisdom is just destruction waiting to happen. She made her choices."

The words were matter-of-fact, but Cassara caught the tightness around his eyes. He'd known Verena longer than any of them, her loss had to sting.

"I'm staying too," Cassara found herself saying. "For break."

His eyebrows rose slightly. "What about your father?"

"Would prefer I come home and submit to his plans," she finished, not admitting the truth. She was scared of what might happen if she went back now. "Which is exactly why I won't."

He nodded in understanding. They stood there for a moment, two people choosing empty halls over complicated homes, finding solidarity in their mutual exile.

"Well then," Gideon said finally, the ghost of a smile touching his lips. "I suppose we'll have to suffer through the peace and quiet together."

The late morning sun was just climbing into view as Cassara made her way across the frost-covered grounds toward the training halls. Most students were packing for tomorrow's departure, the dormitories alive with the chaos of trunks and farewells. But she had other plans, starting with finding Auren before the morning's second-year session ended.

As the second-year students filed out of the training hall in chattering clusters, Cassara waited in the shadow of the doorway, letting them pass before stepping inside. She knew his schedule as well as her own—second-years until eleven, then weapon maintenance, then advanced combat theory. She'd timed this perfectly.

Except the figure cleaning up scattered training equipment wasn't Auren.

A third-year she vaguely recognized was collecting practice blades, his movements efficient but lacking Auren's particular grace. Her stomach dropped.

"Where's Instructor Veth?"

The third-year glanced up, seemingly unsurprised by the question. "Left last night. Emergency leave, apparently." He shrugged, continuing his work.

The floor seemed to tilt slightly. "Left?"

"That's what I said." The student's tone suggested he'd already answered this question multiple times today. "Tav's covering his classes until further notice."

"When will he be back?"

"Didn't say."

Cassara stood frozen as he finished gathering equipment and left, the hall suddenly too quiet, too empty. No note. No word. No goodbye. After everything, after the ruins, after promises whispered against stone, after stolen moments between careful distances, he'd just... left.

The walk back to the dorms blurred together, her thoughts churning. Maybe there'd been a family emergency. Maybe the headmistress had sent him on urgent academy business. Maybe, maybe, maybe. Each possibility felt hollower than the last.

She'd been so careful, planning how to tell him she was staying. How they'd finally have time without Julian's suspicious gaze, without the constant fear of discovery.

She'd imagined quiet evenings, actual conversations that didn't have to be cut short by approaching footsteps.

Stupid. She'd been so stupid to hope for some normalcy.

The common room door was ajar, soft humming drifting through the gap. Cassara pushed it open to find Liri surrounded by what looked like a craft store explosion. Ribbons trailed across the floor, paper scraps dotted every surface, and several small wrapped packages sat in a careful pile beside her.

"Oh!" Liri looked up, a smudge of paint on her cheek. "I thought everyone had gone to lunch. Sorry about the mess, I got a bit carried away." She gestured helplessly at the chaos. "I'll clean it up, I promise. I just wanted to finish these before the transport tomorrow."

Cassara blinked, trying to shift her focus from Auren's absence to the immediate present. "You made all of those?"

Pink colored Liri's cheeks. "It's a tradition in my family. Handmade gifts for the winter celebration. Nothing expensive or fancy, just..." She shrugged, suddenly self-conscious. "Something to show you're thinking of someone."

Before Cassara could respond, Liri was digging through her pile, producing a small package wrapped in silver paper that had clearly been recycled from something else.

"This is for you," she said, holding it out with both hands. "I know it's not much, and the wrapping's a bit wrinkled, and honestly I'm not very good at this kind of thing, but..."

"Liri." Cassara accepted the gift, its weight surprising her. "You didn't have to do this."

"I wanted to." Liri's smile was soft, genuine. "You're my friend. That's what friends do."

The paper crinkled as Cassara carefully unwrapped it, revealing a small leather journal. The cover had been hand-tooled with delicate patterns, swirling designs with tiny stars scattered throughout. It wasn't perfect; she could see where the tool had slipped in places, where the pattern didn't quite match up at the edges. But it was beautiful in its imperfection, clearly made with hours of patient work.

"It's for your observations," Liri explained, fidgeting with a ribbon. "I noticed you're always making notes on scraps of paper, and I thought... well, maybe you'd like something proper to keep them in."

Cassara traced the patterns with one finger, her throat suddenly tight. She'd received gifts before, expensive ones, usually. But they'd all been transactions, investments in her future potential.

This was different. This was just... because.

"I didn't get you anything," she admitted.

Liri's laugh was bright. "I didn't give it to you expecting something back. That's not how gifts work." She tilted her head, studying Cassara. "Haven't you ever gotten a gift just because?"

"Not like this." The admission slipped out before Cassara could stop it. "Not without... conditions."

Something shifted in Liri's expression, understanding mixed with a sadness that made Cassara want to look away.

"Well," Liri said gently, "now you have. No conditions. No expectations. Just a gift between friends." She paused, then added with deliberate lightness, "Though if you wanted to help me clean up this disaster zone, I wouldn't object."

Cassara found herself almost smiling as she surveyed the craft explosion. "What were you even trying to make?"

"Bookmarks, mostly. Some hair ribbons. A terrible attempt at a carved whistle for my younger brother." Liri held up what might generously be called a piece of wood with holes in it. "I don't think it's supposed to look like it's screaming."

This time Cassara did smile, settling down among the chaos. "Show me how."

"Really?"

"I've never made anything before. Not like this." She picked up a piece of unmarked leather, testing its weight. "Might as well learn."

Liri beamed, immediately launching into an explanation of basic tooling techniques. As she demonstrated, chattering about leather grain and proper pressure, Cassara felt some of the hollow ache in her chest ease.

Auren had left without a word. That hurt would still be there tomorrow. But right now, in this moment, she had a friend who gave gifts without expectation, who had paint on her cheek and absolutely no idea her "screaming whistle" looked like a tortured carrot.

"Alright," Cassara said, adjusting her grip on the tool. "Show me again. Slower this time."

Liri grinned and launched back into her explanation, and for a little while, the world narrowed to just the two of them and the simple act of making something with their hands.

CHAPTER THIRTY FIVE

The silence woke her.

Not the usual pre-dawn quiet of students trying to sleep past the first bell, but something deeper, the peculiar hush that came with an empty dormitory. Cassara lay still for a moment, disoriented by the absence of Liri's gentle breathing, the missing sounds of footsteps in the corridor, the lack of muffled conversations through thin walls.

Winter break had officially begun.

The transport had left the day before, carrying away most of Vallemont's students toward warm homes and warmer welcomes, leaving behind the few who had nowhere else to go, or nowhere else they wanted to be.

Still no word.

The thought slipped in before she could stop it. It had been three days now since Auren had vanished without explanation.

Cassara reluctantly slid from beneath the blankets, the chill seeping up through the floor making her toes curl. She padded barefoot to the arched window alcove, tucking her arms around herself as she leaned closer.

The world beyond had transformed overnight. Where yesterday there'd been dead grass and gray stone, now everything was draped in white. Snow blanketed the grounds in thick, pristine layers, turning the familiar landscape into something from a fairy tale. Ice crystals clung to the window glass, fracturing the morning light into tiny rainbows.

Cassara pressed her palm against the cold pane, mesmerized.

She had never seen snow before, not real snow, not like this.

At the estate, winter came with dry winds and frostbitten windowsills. The fireplaces roared hotter, the servants rotated in thicker layers, and everything outside was kept at bay. The cold was something endured, not embraced.

Here, it felt like something sacred.

Cassara stared for a long moment, forehead pressed against the glass. She hadn't cried when Auren left, or when the dorms emptied, not even when Liri vanished down the corridor with a cheerful wave.

She was used to being left behind, what she wasn't used to was feeling the loss that came with it.

Back in the bed, Flicker stirred. He blinked sleep from his eyes, then padded over and pressed his little face to the glass too. His breath left a delicate bloom beside hers.

She wasn't alone. Not entirely.

What are we looking at?

"Snow. Shall we go outside?"

Can we eat it?

Cassara laughed and moved to her trunk. Beneath the gowns and gear were winter clothing she hadn't anticipated needing.

She dressed quickly, layering wool and leather against cold she'd never experienced. The clothes felt foreign, thick boots that changed her gait, gloves that muffled sensation, a hat that threatened to slide over her eyes. But the scarf, at least, was perfect. Deep crimson wool, soft and long enough to wrap twice around her neck. If she was going to stumble through her first snowfall, she'd at least look elegant doing it.

The dormitory echoed with her footsteps, abandoned common rooms yawning empty on either side. Even the ever-present hum of daily academy life had faded to nothing. Just her and the silence and the weight of questions without answers.

Outside, her first breath crystallized in the air, and she watched it dissipate with childlike wonder. The snow crunched beneath her boots, a sound she'd never heard before, couldn't have imagined. Each step required more effort than expected, the powder deeper than it looked.

"Flicker," she called softly, knowing he'd materialize when ready. A faint shimmer in her peripheral vision caught her attention, but she wasn't sure if it was him or the light catching on fresh snow. With his silver-white coloring, he'd practically vanished into the landscape.

She wandered without purpose, following paths made foreign by their white blanket. The training grounds looked softer, less militant. The gardens had become abstract sculptures. Even the austere academy buildings seemed gentled by their coating of ice and snow.

A soft poof sound made her turn. Flicker had materialized in the snow nearby, only his eyes and pink nose visible against the all white backdrop. He blinked at her once, then promptly shoved his entire face into a snowdrift.

"What are you—" Cassara started, then stopped as he emerged with snow clinging to his whiskers, looking incredibly pleased with himself. He sneezed, sending tiny ice crystals flying, then dove in again.

This time he disappeared entirely, only a Flicker-shaped hole marking where he'd gone. A moment later, the snow erupted three feet away as he tunneled up like some sort of arctic mole, chirping excitedly.

I like snow.

"You ridiculous creature," she murmured, but found herself smiling as he began what could only be described as a frenzied snow dance, pouncing on invisible prey, rolling until his fur was more snow than silver, then shaking it all off only to start again.

When he discovered that snow retained paw prints, he spent several minutes walking in careful circles, admiring his own track patterns. Then he tried to catch a falling snowflake, leaping straight up with surprising height, jaws snapping at nothing.

When he finally tired of his snow games, he bounded over to her, leaving a chaotic trail of prints and body-shaped indentations. His fur stood up in frozen spikes, making him look like a tiny, disheveled storm cloud.

"You're a mess," Cassara informed him, reaching down to brush some of the accumulated snow from his back. He purred, then immediately ruined her efforts by performing what appeared to be a celebratory backflip directly into another drift.

A figure in the distance caught her attention, a dark shape moving across the white expanse. The stride was familiar, the set of those shoulders unmistakable even at a distance.

Gideon.

He headed toward the eastern grounds, where the academic buildings gave way to rougher terrain. It was less maintained than the school grounds, a stretch of rocky outcroppings and hardy trees that the academy used for advanced survival courses.

What was he doing out here, alone in the snow? She'd assumed he'd spend the break in the library, restructuring their formations, planning for a five-person future.

Without quite deciding to, she found herself following his tracks. The deep impressions made it easy, even for someone who'd never tracked anything through snow before. He moved with surprising confidence across the unfamiliar terrain, as if he knew exactly where he was going.

You're being ridiculous, following him like some kind of—

Her foot found a hidden dip in the ground, snow giving way to nothing. She windmilled, fighting for balance, and managed to catch herself on a nearby tree. Snow cascaded from the disturbed branches, coating her in a fine layer of white.

When she looked up again, Gideon had stopped walking. He stood perhaps fifty yards ahead, his back still to her, but something in his posture suggested awareness.

Caught.

A shimmer of movement near her feet revealed Flicker, his tiny form barely visible.

You're bad at this.

"Traitor," she muttered, brushing snow from her scarf.

Ahead, Gideon still hadn't turned. But she could almost swear she saw his shoulders shake slightly.

Was he... laughing at her?

The indignity of it burned through her embarrassment. She'd faced legendary beasts, survived academy politics, endured public humiliation. She would not be defeated by frozen water and uneven ground.

Lifting her chin, Cassara stepped out from behind the tree and continued forward, following his tracks with as much dignity as she could muster while wearing a hat that kept sliding sideways.

If he wanted to pretend he hadn't noticed her ungainly pursuit, she could pretend she'd meant to be there all along.

Gideon waited until she'd closed half the distance between them before finally turning. His expression was perfectly neutral, but she caught the telltale twitch at the corner of his mouth.

"Fancy meeting you here," he said, voice dry.

Cassara lifted her chin, brushing a rebellious strand of hair back under her slipping hat. "Yes, well. I was taking a walk."

"A walk." His dark eyes flicked to the obvious trail she'd left following his footsteps. "What a coincidence."

"Complete coincidence," she agreed, tugging her scarf higher to hide the heat creeping up her neck. "The grounds are quite lovely in the snow."

"Mm-hmm." He studied her for a moment longer, taking in the snow still clinging to her coat from her earlier tree collision. "And you always take your morning walks creeping behind other people?"

"I strive to maintain a respectful distance from all fellow pedestrians."

"How considerate of you."

They stood there in the crystalline morning, the absurdity of the exchange not lost to either of them. Finally, Gideon's mouth curled into a smile.

"Well," he said, "since we're coincidentally walking in the same direction..." He tilted his head toward the eastern path. "Shall we?"

He offered an arm but Cassara ignored it.

"I can walk."

He chuckled and shook his head. "Suit yourself."

She fell into step beside him, pretending her curiosity wasn't eating her alive. "Where exactly are we coincidentally going?"

"You'll see."

The terrain grew rougher the further they moved away from the manicured grounds. Walking beside him proved no easier than following, the snow seemed determined to hide every root, rock, and dip in the earth. She managed perhaps a dozen steps before her boot caught on something invisible.

She pitched forward with a startled yelp, but Gideon's hand shot out, catching her elbow and hauling her upright before she could face-plant in the snow. The momentum brought her stumbling against his chest, her gloved hands splaying against his coat for balance.

"Careful," he murmured, steadying her with both hands now. "The snow is beautiful but can be treacherous when you don't know what's hiding underneath."

She looked up to find his face much closer than expected, close enough to see amusement lighting up his eyes.

"I'm starting to think," he continued, voice dropping lower, "that you might need assistance after all. Unless you're planning to throw yourself at every tree between here and our destination?"

The words sent heat flooding through her despite the cold. "I wasn't—I didn't throw myself at anything!"

"No?" His hands were still on her arms, steadying. "My mistake. Must have been gravity."

"Gravity," she repeated flatly, trying to ignore how warm his hands felt even through layers of wool.

"Terrible thing, gravity. Always pulling people in unexpected directions." His thumb brushed against her sleeve, possibly by accident. "We should probably keep moving before it strikes again."

He released her then, stepping back with that same almost-smile, leaving Cassara to follow on legs that felt decidedly less steady than before.

They walked in silence after that, Gideon occasionally offering a hand when the path grew particularly treacherous. Cassara reluctantly accepting the help with as much dignity as she could muster, which wasn't much when she kept needing it every few yards.

Finally, the trees opened up to reveal their destination—a small pond, its surface frozen into a perfect mirror of ice. Morning sun scattered diamonds across its surface, and near the shore sat a modest wooden shack, weathered but well-maintained.

Cassara stopped short, staring at the scene. "This is where you were going?"

"Problem?"

She gestured at the frozen pond, then at him, trying to reconcile this pastoral setting with Gideon's usual intensity. "I just... what exactly are we doing here? Secret training? Hidden beast observation? Some sort of tactical—"

"Sometimes," Gideon interrupted, already heading for the shack, "things are exactly what they appear to be."

"Which would be what?"

But he'd already disappeared inside. She heard rummaging, the scrape of wood against wood, and then he emerged carrying two pairs of what looked like boots with blades attached to the bottoms.

"These should fit," he said, offering her a pair with the same casual air he might use to hand her a practice blade.

Cassara stared at them like he'd just presented her with a live explosive. "You want me to strap knives to my feet."

"That's... one way to look at it."

"And then do what? Walk on ice? On knife-shoes?"

The corner of his mouth twitched again. "The general idea is to glide, not walk."

"Glide," she repeated, voice climbing slightly. "On a frozen pond. On blades. Attached to my feet."

"Have you never—" He stopped, reading something in her expression before understanding finally dawned. "You've never skated before."

It wasn't quite a question, but Cassara felt compelled to defend herself anyway. "There aren't many frozen ponds in the southern provinces. It's all temperate coastline and managed forests. Snow is... theoretical."

"Theoretical," Gideon echoed, and now he was definitely smiling. "Well then. Consider this your practical examination."

He sat on a cleared log near the pond's edge, already working on his own skates with ease. After a moment, Cassara joined him, handling the skates like they might bite.

"For someone who scaled a failing stabilizer mid-flight," he observed, "you look remarkably concerned about recreational footwear."

"That was different. Physics on an airship makes sense. These are just—" She gestured helplessly at the skates. "Chaos with laces."

"I promise," Gideon said solemnly, though his eyes danced with suppressed laughter, "the skates have no documented casualties. Well. Minimal documented casualties."

"That's not reassuring."

"I'll catch you if you fall."

And somehow, that was even less reassuring. Because the memory of his hands on her arms, his chest solid against her palms, was still far too fresh. And the prospect of repeating that experience, possibly multiple times, on ice...

Theoretical snow had been so much simpler.

Cassara stared at the skates in her lap like they were a particularly complex glyph structure. The laces seemed to go everywhere and nowhere, through holes that made no logical sense.

"Here," Gideon said, and before she could protest, he was kneeling in the snow in front of her. "May I?"

She knew she should say no, insist she could manage herself and maintain the careful distance that kept things... uncomplicated. Instead, she found herself nodding, extending one booted foot.

His hands were sure as he unlaced her winter boot, fingers working with the same confidence he brought to combat drills. When he slipped the boot off and cradled her foot to slide on the skate, Cassara had to focus very hard on the tree line to avoid thinking about how gentle his touch was. How his thumb brushed her ankle as he adjusted the fit.

"Too tight?" His voice was perfectly professional, but when she glanced down, there was something else in his expression. An awareness that matched her own.

"It's fine," she managed.

He bent his head to the laces, dark hair falling across his forehead. Each pull was careful, tightening the skate enough for support without cutting off circulation. His fingers skimmed along the leather, checking the fit, and Cassara found herself holding her breath.

Stop being ridiculous, she told herself firmly. He's helping with footwear. Knife footwear. Nothing more.

But when he switched to her other foot, his hand lingered just a moment at her calf and she remembered other hands. Other promises. The ghost of Auren's touch that still haunted her skin, the ache of his absence that sat heavy in her chest.

"There." Gideon rocked back on his heels, surveying his handiwork. "Think you can stand?"

"Of course I can stand." The indignation helped mask whatever else was threatening to show on her face. "I'm not completely helpless."

His mouth curved. "We'll see."

Standing proved to be optimistic. The moment she put weight on the blades, her ankles wobbled alarmingly. She grabbed for the nearest support, which happened to be Gideon's shoulder.

"Graceful," he observed.

"Shut up."

"Like a newborn fawn."

"I said shut up."

"If fawns were particularly angry and wore knife-shoes."

She tried to glare at him, but it was hard to look dignified when clinging to someone for dear life. "Are you always this irritating when you're not captaining?"

"I have hidden depths." He stood slowly, letting her use him as support. "Ready to try the actual ice?"

"No."

"Excellent. Let's go."

The journey from log to pond edge took approximately forever. Cassara shuffled forward in tiny, wobbling increments, Gideon's arm steady under her death grip. Every step felt like balancing on sword edges, which, technically, she supposed she was.

"This is impossible," she announced when they finally reached the ice. "People don't actually do this for fun. You're lying to me."

"Would I lie to you?"

"Yes."

He pressed a hand to his chest in mock offense. "Your faith in your captain is truly inspiring."

"My captain doesn't usually try to kill me with footwear."

"First time for everything." He stepped onto the ice with infuriating ease, turning to face her while skating backward. Backward! "Come on. One foot, then the other."

Cassara stared at the ice. It looked solid enough, but she'd thought that about snow-covered ground too, and that had betrayed her repeatedly.

"Cassara." Gideon's voice was gentle. "I meant what I said. I'll catch you if you fall."

The echo of his earlier promise sent warmth through her chest. Which was dangerous. Which was complicated. Which was—

She stepped onto the ice.

For exactly three seconds, she stayed upright. Then physics reasserted itself with violent enthusiasm. Her feet shot in opposite directions, her arms flapped frantically, and she would have crashed spectacularly if Gideon hadn't darted forward to catch her.

"I hate this," she informed his chest.

"You've been on the ice for less than five seconds."

"Five seconds too long."

His laugh rumbled through his chest, and she realized belatedly that she was essentially hugging him in the middle of a frozen pond. She started to pull back, but her skates had other ideas, sliding again.

"Okay," he said, steadying her with hands at her waist. "New plan. Hold onto me and let me pull you. Get used to the feeling first."

Pride warred with self-preservation.

Self-preservation won.

She gripped his hands as he skated backward, drawing her slowly across the ice. It was terrifying. Her legs kept trying to do different things, her balance non-existent. But after a few minutes, she started to understand the glide, the way momentum carried her forward.

"Better?" he asked.

"Marginally."

"Such high praise. I'm overwhelmed."

She squeezed his hands in retaliation, then immediately regretted it when her skates wobbled. "Why are you being like this?"

"Like what?"

"You know what. Teasing. Relaxed. You're practically... cheerful."

His eyebrows rose. "I'm not allowed to be cheerful?"

"You're Gideon Delvanir. You brood in corners and make tactical assessments and look disapproving. You don't make jokes about fawns."

"Maybe," he said, pulling her into a gentle turn, "I only brood when there are people around to see it."

"So the mysterious captain thing is an act?"

"Would you respect me less if it was?"

She considered this as they glided, well, as he glided and she clung. "Depends. How much is act versus actual brooding?"

"Seventy-thirty."

"Which way?"

His grin was answer enough.

"You're impossible," she muttered, but found herself fighting a smile. This version of Gideon, light, teasing, unguarded, was dangerously appealing. It made her wonder what else hid beneath his carefully curated mask. Made her want to find out.

Which she shouldn'tt want. Because she was with—

Her skate caught on something, sending her lurching forward. Gideon caught her again, but the momentum carried them into a graceless spin that ended with her back pressed against his chest, his arms wrapped around her middle to keep them both upright.

"Definitely a fawn," he murmured near her ear. "The angriest fawn in Vallemont."

She elbowed him, which only made her skates slide again, which made him tighten his hold, which made everything infinitely worse and better and—

"I'm going to master this," she declared, as much to herself as to him. "And then I'm going to skate circles around you."

"I don't doubt it." His voice was warm in a way that made her heart flutter. "You're Cassara Allencourt. You don't know how to fail."

The words should have been simple encouragement. Instead, they cut deeper than Gideon had meant. She had failed. Failed to see through Julian. Failed to see the real threat Verena posed. Failed to stop her heart from racing when Gideon held her steady on the ice.

"Teach me properly," she said, pushing the thoughts away. "I want to learn."

He turned her carefully to face him, keeping hold of her hands. "All right. First lesson—stop fighting the ice. You're trying to control it instead of moving with it."

"I always try to control things."

"I've noticed." His thumbs brushed her palms through the gloves. "But this isn't combat. It's more like... dancing."

"I'm terrible at dancing too."

"Now that," he said, beginning to draw her backward again, "I don't believe for a second."

Time blurred. What started as graceless flailing gradually evolved into something resembling actual skating. Cassara's death grip on Gideon's hands loosened to fingertips, then to occasional steadying touches, until finally, miraculously, she was gliding on her own.

"Look at that," Gideon called from several feet away, skating backward in lazy circles. "The fawn has found her legs."

"I am not," Cassara said with as much dignity as she could muster while wobbling, "a fawn."

"My mistake. Clearly you're a natural. Poetry in motion."

She narrowed her eyes at his teasing tone. He was just out of reach, maintaining the distance with infuriating ease every time she tried to close it.

"Come here and say that."

"And risk those knife-shoes?" He spun in a neat circle, showing off. "I've seen what you can do with actual blades. I'm not giving you an advantage."

"Coward."

"Strategic retreat." He glided further back, grinning. "Besides, you're doing so well on your own."

The praise might have warmed her if it wasn't delivered while he skated away from her. Cassara shuffled forward faster, determined to wipe that smirk off his face. Her newfound confidence lasted exactly four strides.

Her blade caught wrong, balance vanishing in an instant. She pitched backward with a yelp, arms seeking purchase and finding nothing but air. Gideon's eyes widened as he rushed toward her, but momentum was not their friend. He caught her around the waist just as her skates went out from under her entirely.

They hit the snowbank at the pond's edge in a tangle of limbs. Cassara's back hit the soft snow, air whooshing from her lungs, and then Gideon's weight followed, his hands bracing on either side of her head to keep from crushing her completely.

Snow settled around them in gentle silence.

Cassara blinked up at him, acutely aware of everywhere they touched, his hips bracketing hers, chest nearly pressed to chest, his face so close she could see gold flecks in his hazel eyes. Her hat had gone completely askew, dark hair fanning out across the pristine white snow like spilled ink.

Gideon seemed frozen above her, arms trembling slightly with the effort of holding himself up, or maybe from something else entirely. His gaze traveled over her face, her flushed cheeks, her parted lips, the way her chest rose and fell with quick breaths.

"Cassara." Her name came out rough, barely voiced.

The way he was looking at her, intense and hungry and tender all at once, made heat pool low in her stomach despite the snow seeping through her coat. His head lowered fractionally, and she could feel his breath against her lips, could see the question forming in his eyes.

For a moment, she almost let it happen. Almost lifted her head those scant inches to close the distance. Almost forgot about complicated truths and absent instructors and promises made in stone corridors.

Almost.

Instead, she planted both hands against his chest and shoved.

"Off," she managed, voice not quite as steady as she'd like. "You're heavy."

He rolled to the side immediately, landing on his back in the snow with a soft whump. For a moment they both lay there, staring at the winter sky, breathing too hard for such a simple fall.

"Well," Cassara said finally, proud when her voice came out almost normal, "I think we've established that ice is vindictive and not to be trusted."

Gideon remained on his back for a moment longer, staring at the sky like it might provide answers. Then he huffed a laugh that was equal parts amusement and something else.

"Vindictive ice," he repeated. "Of course."

She struggled to her feet, which was significantly harder with skates still attached. "Have you had your fill of trying to kill me with knife-shoes? Because I'm starting to think this was all an elaborate assassination attempt."

"Caught me." He sat up, snow cascading from his hair. "The captain of Auric Vow, laid low by recreational activities."

"I knew it." She offered him a hand up, which he accepted with a wry smile. "No one is naturally that good at skating backward. Dark forces were clearly involved."

"Just practice," he said, and somehow they were standing too close again, her hand still in his.

She pulled away, adjusting her wayward hat. "Yes, well. Some of us had better things to do than practice knife-shoes."

"Like following people through the snow?"

"That was reconnaissance."

"It was stalking."

"Tactical observation." She lifted her chin. "Completely different thing."

His laugh was warm, genuine, so different from his usual controlled responses.

She laughed too, but the tremor beneath it wasn't all from the cold. Her lips still tingled from his breath, from the kiss that hadn't happened but somehow felt more real than ones that had.

"Your hat gave up," Gideon said, reaching past her to pluck the wayward item from the ground where it had finally admitted defeat, half-buried in the snow. "I think it's plotting against you."

"Traitorous thing," Cassara muttered, glaring at it like it had personally offended her. "First the knife-shoes, now the hat. Everything's conspiring today."

"Maybe they know something you don't," he said lightly, then stepped closer. "Hold still."

Before she could protest, he was settling the hat gently over her disheveled hair, his fingers brushing her temples as he adjusted it. The gesture was careful, tender, and far too reminiscent of how he'd helped with her skates earlier.

"There," he murmured, hands lingering just a moment before dropping away. "Though I'm not sure it's learned its lesson."

Cassara had to clear her throat before she could speak. "Clearly needs more discipline. I'll have it running drills by tomorrow."

"Come on," Gideon said, already moving toward the pond's edge, though she caught the slight roughness in his voice. "Let's get these death traps off before you decide to attempt revenge."

CHAPTER THIRTY SIX

The box of craft supplies sat on her desk like a coiled viper waiting to strike.

Cassara glared at it from across the room, where she'd retreated after her third failed attempt at "simple leather wrapping." Liri had made it look so easy. A little folding here, some careful stitching there, and voilà: a perfectly wrapped gift.

Cassara's attempts looked like leather had gotten into a fight with itself and lost.

"One more try," she muttered, approaching the desk with the same level of caution she'd use for a hostile beast. Oliver's notes lay spread beside the disaster zone, his neat handwriting explaining mana-circuit integration with helpful diagrams. That part she'd managed. The tiny tracking crystal now sat properly embedded in its magitech housing, calibrated to emit a unique signature that could be traced by its paired receiver.

She was quite proud of that bit. Oliver would be impressed that she'd managed the frequency alignment without his help.

It was everything else that was going wrong.

"Right." She picked up the leather cord, eyeing it suspiciously. "You're going to cooperate this time."

The leather did not cooperate.

Ten minutes later, she'd somehow managed to wrap it sideways, creating lumpy bulges where the crystal housing showed through. The paint she'd tried to use for a decorative border had smeared, and—

"No, no, no- Flicker, don't—"

Too late. Her familiar materialized directly on the workspace, silver paws landing squarely in the open paint pot. Blue paint. *Expensive* blue paint that was supposed to add "elegant detail."

This is nice.

He chirped happily, then proceeded to walk across Oliver's notes.

"You absolute menace!" Cassara lunged for him, but Flicker interpreted this as a game, bouncing away and leaving a trail of blue paw prints across her remaining clean leather. "That was my last piece!"

Flicker paused in his destruction to bat at a ribbon, sending it rolling off the desk and under her bed. When she dove to retrieve it, she heard the distinctive sound of a paint pot tipping over.

She emerged to find blue paint spreading across her desk like a small lake, Oliver's notes now artistic interpretations of themselves, and Flicker sitting in the middle of it all, tail swishing with satisfaction.

"Don't follow me," she said flatly.

She gathered what supplies remained untainted, the wrapped (badly wrapped) tracking device, some backup leather scraps, fresh ribbon, and her last pot of paint, red, and fled her contaminated workspace.

The common room was empty and paint-free. She commandeered the large table, spreading everything out with military precision. This time would be different. This time she'd maintain control.

"Stay," she commanded Flicker, who'd naturally followed despite being explicitly not invited.

I want to help.

"I don't need help," she insisted as she rewrapped the device, managing something that looked almost presentable if you squinted. The leather only bulged in two places instead of five. Progress. Now for the decorative elements.

The paint immediately pooled in all the wrong places. Somehow, *somehow*, it seeped into the tiny gaps in the housing, definitely contaminating the carefully calibrated mana channels. The device sparked once, weakly, and the leather wrapping came undone again.

"How is this harder than syncing an entire ACS array?" she demanded of the universe.

Flicker offered a helpful chirp and knocked over the ribbon spool with his nose.

By the time she'd rewrapped it, attempt number seven, added what might generously be called "decorative painting"—it looked like someone had sneezed color onto leather—and tied it with a ribbon that was definitely crooked, Cassara was ready to burn the entire craft industry to the ground.

She held up her creation and examined it. It was... functional. Probably. The tracking spell still hummed beneath the paint-contaminated surface. The leather wrapping held if you didn't look too closely at where she'd given up and just tied extra knots. The painted design could be interpreted as abstract art if you were feeling generous.

Or drunk.

Possibly both.

"He'll hate it," she told Flicker, who was now decorated with several paint colors himself. "It looks like I let you make it."

What's wrong with that? Flicker preened, apparently taking this as a compliment.

She set the poorly wrapped gift aside and surveyed the carnage. Paint on the table. Leather scraps everywhere. Ribbon in places ribbon should not be able to reach.

This was supposed to be simple. A thoughtful, practical gift that showed she'd been paying attention, that she cared about his safety, that she—

Footsteps in the corridor made her freeze.

No. No, no, no. Everyone was supposed to be gone. The common room was supposed to be empty. She looked around wildly at the disaster zone she'd created, then at herself: paint under her nails, bits of leather in her hair, one sleeve rolled up and the other mysteriously stained red.

The door opened.

Gideon paused in the doorway, surveying the scene with raised eyebrows. His gaze traveled from the paint-splattered table to the leather scraps scattered like confetti, to Flicker, now rainbow-colored, and finally to Cassara herself, frozen mid-reach for a ribbon that had somehow ended up stuck to her elbow.

"Should I come back later?" he asked, fighting a smile. "After the explosion finishes?"

"It's a controlled crafting environment," Cassara said, immediately shifting to block his view of the table. Behind her back, she frantically swept the wrapped device under a pile of leather scraps. "And it's private. You should go."

"Private?" He stepped fully inside, closing the door behind him. "Is that why you murdered a craft store in the common room?"

"I didn't murder anything." She sidled along the table, keeping herself between him and her disaster. "Flicker knocked over some paint. In my room. So I had to relocate."

"Ah." Gideon's gaze tracked to where Flicker sat perched on the sofa arm, tail swishing proudly. "And he followed you here to continue his reign of terror?"

"He's helping," Cassara said, still maintaining her human shield position. "From over there. Away from the... project."

"Projects," Gideon corrected, circling toward the seating area. "Plural. Unless all of this destruction is for one project?"

"Maybe I'm making several." She moved with him, maintaining her human shield position. The common room suddenly felt much smaller with this ridiculous dance. "It's efficient. Mass production."

"Mass destruction, more like." He changed direction, heading for the other side of the table.

Cassara darted that way too, nearly tripping over a chair in her haste. "Don't you have formations to plan? Maps to brood over?"

"Finished this morning." He was definitely enjoying this now, the corner of his mouth curling into a smile. "I thought I'd take a walk. Imagine my surprise when I heard what sounded like someone fighting furniture."

"I wasn't fighting—" She cut off as he feinted left then went right, nearly getting past her guard. She grabbed a paint-stained cloth and threw it over the suspicious lump of leather scraps. "Would you stop moving?"

"Would you stop acting like you're hiding a body?"

"I'm not hiding anything!"

Flicker chose that moment to hop from the sofa to the table, landing directly on her cloth-covered secret. The impact sent a small spark of mana fizzling out from beneath.

They both stared at it.

"That's..." Cassara began.

"Sparking," Gideon finished. "Your nothing is sparking."

"It's supposed to do that." Another fizzle, this one larger. "Mostly."

He stepped closer, and she had nowhere left to retreat unless she wanted to climb onto the table itself. Which she considered.

"Cass," he said. "I'm not going to judge whatever craft massacre you're attempting. Though I am curious why it's trying to set itself on fire."

"It's not—" She pressed her hands flat on the cloth, trying to smother the sparking. "It's just... temperamental. Like everything else today."

"Including you?"

"Especially me." She glared up at him, very aware that he was now close enough to see the full scope of her disaster. "This was supposed to be simple."

His expression softened further. "What was?"

"I can't tell you that," she said, then immediately wanted to kick herself. Way to make it obvious she was making something secret.

"Ah." His eyes lit with understanding. "Gift making. That explains the devastation."

"I don't need help," she said quickly, even as another spark escaped her smothered project.

"Of course not." He moved to the chair across from her, settling in with the air of someone who had nowhere else to be. "I'll just sit here. In case your nothing achieves full combustion."

"It's not going to—" A particularly enthusiastic spark shot out. "Oh, for the love of—"

She yanked the cloth away, revealing her lumpy, paint-splattered disaster. The leather wrapping had come partially undone again, and somehow there was now blue paint on parts that had definitely been clean before.

"Don't look at it," she ordered, gathering it protectively against her chest.

"Bit late for that." But he obligingly focused on her face instead. "Though I'm more concerned about why you look like you've been in battle."

She glanced down at herself, properly taking in the damage. It was worse than she'd thought. "Leather is vindictive. Like ice."

"Starting to sense a pattern with you and inanimate objects." He leaned back in his chair, apparently settling in for the long haul. "Sure you don't need help?"

"No."

"Honest? Because from here it looks like the leather is winning."

"I said no." She turned her back to him, trying to rewrap the stupid thing one-handed while keeping it hidden. The leather immediately rebelled, unfurling with what felt like malicious glee.

Behind her, she heard him shift in his chair. "The trick with wrapping is consistent tension."

"I have been consistently tense this entire time," she shot back.

His laugh was warm. "Different kind of tension. Here—"

She heard him stand, move around the table. Panicked, she spun to block him, clutching her project against her chest like state secrets.

"No helping!"

"I'm not even looking at it," he said, hands raised in surrender. "Just... let me show you on a spare piece. Unless all your leather is currently winning individual battles?"

She grudgingly grabbed a clean scrap, shoving it at him while keeping her actual gift hidden behind her back. "Fine. Demonstrate your superior leather-taming skills."

He took the scrap, moving to the clear end of the table. Close enough to help, far enough that she didn't feel like he was about to unmask her terrible secret.

"See? Even pressure, overlapping edges." His fingers moved with surprising dexterity, turning the rebellious material into something cooperative. "You're probably gripping too hard. Leather responds better to coaxing than force."

"Everything in my life requires force," she muttered, but she watched his technique carefully.

"I've noticed." He finished the demonstration wrap, setting it aside. "Your turn. On whatever you're definitely not hiding behind your back."

She glared at him suspiciously. "You won't look?"

"I'll even close my eyes if it helps." He made a show of covering them with one hand. "Though that does increase the risk of Flicker ambush."

As if summoned, the paint-covered creature chose that moment to investigate, hopping from the table directly onto Gideon's shoulder.

"Why is he wet?" Gideon asked, still covering his eyes as Flicker's paint-covered paws left prints on his collar.

"That would be the paint incident I mentioned," Cassara admitted, using his distraction to attempt a proper wrapping. Even pressure. Overlapping edges. Don't strangle the leather into submission.

She managed three whole overlaps before it started to rebel. "Oh, come on!"

"Too tight," Gideon diagnosed, eyes still covered. "Ease up a bit."

She tried again, looser this time and it finally started to cooperate. "How do you know about leather working anyway?"

"Weapon maintenance. Sometimes you have to rewrap handles, repair straps." He pecked through his fingers. "Better?"

"Don't look!" She clutched it protectively again.

"I'm not looking at what it is," he protested. "Just the technique. Completely different thing."

"That's... actually true," she conceded, relaxing slightly. The wrapping was holding. Mostly. If you ignored the parts where paint had definitely seeped into places paint shouldn't be.

"See? I can be helpful without ruining surprises." Flicker chose that moment to walk down his arm, leaving a trail of blue pawprints. "Though Flicker seems determined to use me as a canvas."

"He's an artist," Cassara said defensively. "He doesn't understand conventional boundaries."

"Clearly." Gideon was now decorated with red and blue paint on his previously white shirt, blue pawprints down one arm, and what looked like a purple tail-swipe across his collar. "Am I his masterpiece?"

"You're certainly... colorful." She bit back a smile at how ridiculous he looked, the composed captain of Auric Vow covered in paint like a children's art project.

"Still not as colorful as you." He reached out, plucking something from her hair. "Is this an entire spool of ribbon?"

"That's... tactical ribbon storage."

"Of course it is." He set it on the table, then noticed her elbow. "And that one?"

"Emergency backup ribbon."

"Very strategic." His eyes dropped to her partially wrapped project. "It's holding better now."

She looked down, surprised to find he was right. It still looked like something a blindfolded child might have made, but at least the leather was staying in place.

"I suppose that's something," she admitted grudgingly.

"Progress." He stood, stretching. Paint crinkled on his shirt. "Though I should change before this dries permanently. Unless you need more help with your definitely-not-secret project?"

"I think I've got it from here," she said, then added more quietly, "Thank you."

"Anytime." He headed for the door, pausing to look back. "For what it's worth, whoever gets that gift? They'll love it."

"How could you possibly know that?"

"Because you made it," he said simply. "Even if it does occasionally spark."

The door closed behind him before she could formulate a response, leaving her standing there with her lumpy, paint-stained, occasionally sparking creation.

Maybe it wasn't so terrible after all.

Then it sparked again, singeing her thumb.

"Vindictive leather," she muttered, and got back to work.

The last traces of blue paint had finally surrendered to her aggressive scrubbing twenty minutes ago. Cassara examined her nails one more time in the mirror, grateful for the empty dormitory that meant no one had witnessed her day-long battle with craft-related evidence. Liri would have asked questions. Evie would have giggled. The solitude of break was proving useful already.

She adjusted the deep plum velvet bodice one final time. She'd chosen it deliberately, rich enough to honor the occasion, but not so elaborate as to seem like she was trying too hard. The silver embroidery traced delicate constellation patterns across the fabric, and the layered skirts of lighter lavender and cream moved like water when she walked. It was armor of a different sort, one she knew how to wear well.

For once, she'd left her hair mostly loose, only the front sections pinned back with silver clasps. The style felt strange after years of practical braids, but tonight called for something different.

The great hall had been transformed. Where normally hundreds of students filled long tables, tonight there was only one round table set near the massive hearth, intimate and glowing with candlelight. Evergreen garlands draped the walls, dotted with tiny magelight stars that pulsed gently. The vaulted ceiling reflected an enchanted winter sky, constellations spinning slowly through their ancient patterns.

To one side, a small space had been cleared for dancing, marked by more candles and what looked suspiciously like enchanted snow that fell but never accumulated.

"Cassara!" A third-year she vaguely recognized—Mira?—waved from the table. "We were starting to think you'd gotten lost."

Six students were already seated, cups of something steaming in front of them. Professor Thendrick sat cross-legged on his chair like it was a meditation cushion, while Nareen occupied her seat with military strictness despite the festive atmosphere.

"Not lost," Cassara said, taking one of the empty chairs. "Just... delayed."

"Craft incident?" Thendrick asked mildly, and she wondered if he could somehow see the paint she'd scrubbed away.

"Something like that."

A second-year named Fenn grinned. "We've all been there. Last year I tried to make enchanted candles and nearly burned down my room."

"The key," Thendrick said, accepting a cup from a floating tray, "is to embrace imperfection. The universe delights in flawed creation."

Nareen snorted. "The universe also delights in students who don't set things on fire."

"Where's the wonder in that?" Thendrick countered, eyes twinkling.

More students trickled in, another third-year, a quiet first-year who looked overwhelmed by everything. Cassara found herself checking the door each time it opened, definitely not waiting for anyone in particular.

The table was filled with easy chatter, stories of previous winter celebrations, complaints about the academic year so far. It felt strange, sitting here without the usual hierarchies and pressures. Just students and professors sharing a meal as snow fell silently outside.

She was reaching for her cup when the door opened again.

Gideon entered. He traded his usual training attire for formal evening wear—a deep forest green doublet with silver buttons over dark trousers, cut perfectly to his frame.

Their eyes met across the room.

"Gideon!" Fenn called out. "Perfect timing. We were about to start the first course."

He took the last empty seat, directly across from her, offering a general greeting to the table. But his gaze lingered on her for just a moment longer than necessary, taking in the velvet, the loose hair, the way candlelight caught on her skin.

"You look..." he started, then seemed to catch himself, clearing his throat. "Purple suits you."

Heat crept up her neck. "Thank you."

His fingers drummed once on the table, the only sign he wasn't as composed as he appeared. "Hair's different."

"Well, I thought I might try something new." She touched one of the silver clasps self-consciously. "Though I'm already regretting the impracticality."

"Don't." He cleared his throat again. "It's... nice."

The moment stretched between them, weighted with unspoken things, snow and skating and almost-kisses, until Mira's cheerful voice broke through.

"Oh good, everyone's here! They can bring out the food now!"

CHAPTER THIRTY SEVEN

As if summoned by Mira's enthusiasm, the doors to the hall swung open again, and the real celebration began.

The feast unfolded in waves of decadent abundance. Roasted winter birds glazed with starfruit honey, root vegetables that sparkled with edible gold dust, bread so warm it still steamed when broken. Each dish came with stories, Fenn explaining how his region saved the wishbones for midnight fortune-telling, Mira describing ice wine that could only be harvested under a full moon.

"In the eastern provinces," the quiet first-year, a girl named Dania, offered shyly, "we write our hopes for the new year on paper and burn them in the solstice fire."

"Beautiful," Thendrick murmured. "The smoke carries dreams to the stars."

"Or sets the curtains on fire," Nareen added dryly. "As we discovered three years ago."

Laughter rippled around the table. Cassara found herself relaxing into the warmth of it, the easy camaraderie so different from formal dinners at home where every word was measured, every gesture calculated.

"Cassara," Mira asked, passing a dish of honeyed carrots, "what are southern traditions like?"

"We..." She paused, realizing she had no idea. Her father had never celebrated anything that didn't involve contracts or political advantage. "We keep things simple."

"Simple can be profound," Thendrick said, saving her from elaboration. "Sometimes the absence of ritual is its own tradition."

Across the table, Gideon caught her eye. He'd been quieter than usual tonight, contributing to conversations but always seeming half-focused on something else. On her, she realized, with a flutter of heat. Every time she looked up, he was looking away just a moment too late.

"Oh!" a second-year named Edwin suddenly exclaimed. "They're bringing the fortune tarts!"

A collective murmur of appreciation rose as a floating tray descended, bearing the most beautiful desserts Cassara had ever seen. Each tart was a small work of art—delicate pastry cups cradling crystallized berries that caught the light like tiny gems. The sugar work on top formed unique patterns of frost, no two alike.

"Frost Blossom Fortune Tarts," Fenn explained to Dania. "You can only make them on the winter solstice when the berries are perfect. The frost pattern predicts your fortune for the coming year."

"Mine has three spirals!" Mira announced, examining hers with delight. "That means new friendships."

"Crossing lines for me," Edwin added. "Journey or adventure, supposedly."

One by one, the others selected their tarts, interpreting the sugar patterns with varying degrees of seriousness. Nareen's had what looked like a sword shape.

"How predictable," she muttered, while Thendrick's showed a perfect circle.

"Completion of cycles," he mused, looking pleased.

Cassara waited, always more comfortable observing than rushing forward. Gideon seemed to have the same instinct. By the time the tray floated between them, only one tart remained.

It was perfect—berries so deep purple they were nearly black, the frost pattern elaborate and mysterious, like a constellation she couldn't name.

They reached for it at the same time.

Their fingers collided over the delicate pastry, his warm against her cool skin. Both froze, hands touching, neither pulling back.

"Oh no!" Mira's gasp broke the moment. "You both touched the last fortune tart!"

Cassara started to withdraw her hand, but Edwin practically shouted, "Don't! That's worse!"

"What?" She looked around the table, confused by the sudden intensity on everyone's faces.

"If two people touch the last fortune tart, they have to share it," Fenn explained, grinning. "Otherwise, you're stealing each other's luck for the year."

"That's..." Cassara began.

"Ancient tradition," Thendrick confirmed solemnly, though she swore she saw his eyes twinkling. "To split a fortune without sharing its blessing invites calamity."

"Calamity," Cassara repeated flatly. "From a pastry."

"Not just any pastry," Edwin insisted. "The last fortune of the solstice! Do you want to risk it?"

She looked at Gideon, who had remained remarkably silent through this explanation. His expression was carefully neutral, but there was something dancing in his eyes—amusement? Anticipation?

"Fine," she said. "We'll share. Cut it in half and—"

"No!" This time it was a chorus. Even Nareen looked mildly alarmed.

"You can't cut a fortune," Mira explained patiently, like Cassara was missing something obvious. "That definitely splits the luck. You have to..." She paused, suddenly looking everywhere but at them.

"Have to what?" Cassara demanded, though she had a sinking feeling she knew where this was going.

"Share the blessing," Fenn supplied helpfully. "With a kiss. To seal the fortune between you."

The table went very quiet. Even the enchanted snow seemed to fall more softly.

Heat flooded Cassara's face. "That's the most ridiculous—"

"It's tradition," Mira said.

"A very serious tradition," Edwin added, fighting a smile. "Terrible things happen to those who split a solstice fortune. There was a couple in my village who refused—separate storms followed each of them for months."

"Storms," Cassara said. "Really."

"And the livestock incidents," Fenn added gravely.

"Don't forget the turnip blight," Mira chimed in.

Cassara looked at Nareen for help, but the instructor just sipped her wine, apparently finding the ceiling fascinating. Thendrick was definitely hiding a smile behind his cup.

"We're really doing this," she muttered.

"Unless you want to risk the turnip blight," Gideon said, speaking for the first time since they'd touched the tart. His voice was steady, but she caught the slight upturn of his mouth.

She glared at him.

He was enjoying this.

"Fine," she said, lifting her chin. "For the sake of the turnips."

"And the livestock," he added solemnly.

"Can't forget the chickens."

They were still holding the tart between them, fingers touching. The entire table watched with poorly concealed delight as Gideon leaned forward slightly.

"Where?" he asked quietly, and she realized he was giving her the choice—cheek, forehead, hand. Letting her set the boundary.

"Cheek," she managed, voice steadier than her pulse.

He leaned across the small space between them. She turned her face slightly, offering her left cheek, and tried not to think about how this was happening in front of everyone, how Thendrick was definitely going to say something cryptic about it later, how—

His lips brushed her cheek, soft and warm and lasting just a heartbeat longer than strictly necessary. His breath stirred the loose hair by her ear.

This doesn't count, she told herself firmly as her skin tingled from the contact. It's just tradition. Just superstition. Auren would understand.

Would he?

The thought crept in unbidden as Gideon pulled back. Auren, who'd kissed her with desperate hunger against ancient stone. Who'd whispered promises in the dark. Who'd left without a word of explanation.

If he'd been here, she wouldn't be sharing fortune tarts with Gideon. If he'd stayed, if he'd trusted her enough to explain, if he'd—

No. That wasn't fair. There had to be a reason. There was always a reason with Auren, layers of duty and honor and things he couldn't say.

But the small, traitorous voice in her mind whispered: *He still left.*

"There," Edwin announced cheerfully. "Fortune preserved! Now you can eat the tart."

"Right," Cassara said faintly, guilt twisting in her stomach. "The tart."

They divided it carefully, with their hands, not a knife, as apparently that was also bad luck, and ate in silence while conversation resumed around them. The berries burst on her tongue, sweet and tart and perfect, but all she could taste was the ghost of almost-kisses and the promise of what if.

What if Auren hadn't left? What if she wasn't sitting here, skin still warm from another man's kiss, however innocent? What if her heart didn't race quite so fast when Gideon looked at her?

She had no right to feel abandoned. She and Auren had made no promises beyond "after"—after the Wildes, after the danger passed, after they could stop pretending. But "after" had come and gone, and he'd vanished like morning mist.

And now here was Gideon, solid and present and looking at her with eyes that saw too much.

When she finally risked a glance at him, he was studying his half of the frost pattern intently.

"What fortune did we get?" she asked, needing to say something normal, needing to stop the spiral of her thoughts.

He tilted the remaining sugar work toward the light. "Looks like... intertwining spirals that meet in the center."

"What does that mean?"

"Convergence," Thendrick said, having apparently been eavesdropping. "Two paths becoming one. Very auspicious for a shared fortune."

Cassara nearly choked on her last berry. Two paths. Like hers and Auren's were supposed to? Or like—

No. She wouldn't think it. Couldn't.

"Or it's just melted sugar," Nareen said dryly. "Sometimes a pastry is just a pastry."

But when Cassara caught Gideon's eye again, she knew they were both thinking the same thing.

Sometimes it wasn't just a pastry at all.

Sometimes, the people who stayed mattered more than the ones who left.

I'm sorry, she thought, not sure if she was apologizing to Auren, to Gideon, or to herself. But the warmth on her cheek remained, a gentle accusation and a sweeter promise all at once.

The empty dessert plates floated away as conversation mellowed into the comfortable fullness that followed a good meal. Fenn stretched, patting his stomach with satisfaction.

"I won't need to eat for a week," he groaned.

"Good thing we still have a few days before everyone gets back," Edwin laughed. "I couldn't lift a sword right now if my life depended on it."

"Speaking of movement," Mira said, eyes bright with mischief, "who's brave enough to start the dancing?"

A collective groan rose from several students, but Thendrick was already standing, offering his hand to Nareen with exaggerated courtliness.

"Instructor Nareen, would you honor me?"

She eyed him suspiciously. "If you step on my feet, mystic or not, I'm throwing you across the room."

"Fear not," he said cheerfully, leading her to the cleared space where the enchanted snow still fell without landing.

Music swelled from nowhere, or everywhere, filling the hall with a melody that was both ancient and immediate. Thendrick and Nareen moved with surprising grace, his flowing style somehow complementing her precise steps.

"Come on," Mira grabbed Edwin's hand. "Before all the good space is taken!"

Soon half the table had emptied onto the makeshift dance floor. Dania was coaxed up by Fenn, who promised not to let her embarrass herself. Even some of the third-years paired off, laughing as they tried to remember the steps to dances they'd learned years ago.

Cassara remained seated, watching. Unlike her claims during the ice skating debacle, she *could* dance, had been taught all the formal court dances since childhood. It made her no more eager to participate.

"Not joining?" Gideon asked. He'd stayed in his seat too, though she'd noticed him refuse two invitations already.

"I told you," she said, taking a sip of wine. "I'm terrible at dancing."

His mouth curved. "Liar."

"Excuse me?"

"I've seen the way you move through combat forms. You scaled a failing airship. You learned to ice skate in a single afternoon." He tilted his head, studying her. "There's no way you can't dance."

"Those are different."

"How?"

"They have..." She searched for the words. "Purpose. Dancing is just—"

"Joy?" he suggested. "Fun? Expression without agenda?"

"Exactly. Pointless."

"Ah." He nodded sagely. "And Cassara Allencourt doesn't do pointless."

"Now you're learning."

They sat in comfortable silence, watching Thendrick spin Nareen in a move that should have looked ridiculous but somehow didn't. The music shifted, becoming something slower, sweeter.

"What if," Gideon said carefully, "it wasn't pointless?"

She glanced at him. "Meaning?"

"Well, we've already weathered ice skating. This can't be worse." He stood, offering his hand with a slight bow that was only half-mocking. "For the sake of comparison. Purely academic."

"Academic," she repeated.

"Think of it as research. Cultural anthropology."

"You're ridiculous."

"Probably." But his hand remained extended, and there was something in his eyes that made her pulse skip. "One dance. You can critique my form the entire time if it helps."

She looked at his hand, steady, patient, familiar now from all the times he'd caught her on the ice. The warmth from his kiss still lingered on her cheek, mixing with guilt and want and the echo of Auren's absence.

One dance. What harm could one dance do?

"Fine," she said, placing her hand in his. "But only because I'm curious if you're as insufferably competent at this as everything else."

His fingers closed around hers, warm and sure. "Only one way to find out."

He led her to the dance floor, finding space between the other couples. The enchanted snow swirled around them, never quite touching, and the music wrapped them in its ancient melody.

"So," he said, settling one hand at her waist while keeping the other in hers. "Going to admit you know exactly how to do this?"

"I have no idea what you mean." But her body betrayed her, falling into position with practiced ease.

"Of course not." He guided her into the first steps, and she moved with him instinctively. "This must be natural talent."

"Must be."

They moved together, finding their rhythm within heartbeats. He was good, of course he was, leading without forcing, matching her pace perfectly. But there was something else, something that had nothing to do with the steps.

The way his hand felt at her waist, warm through the velvet. The careful distance he maintained, proper and correct, that somehow made her more aware of every inch between them. The way he looked at her, not at her feet or over her shoulder, but directly at her, like she was the only person in the room.

"You're thinking too loud," he murmured.

"I'm not thinking anything."

"Your shoulders just tensed."

"Maybe you're holding them wrong."

"Maybe you're holding yourself wrong." His thumb moved slightly at her waist, just a breath of motion. "Stop fighting it."

"I don't know how to not fight."

"I know." The words were soft, understanding. "But it's just a dance, Cass. Let it be simple."

Simple. As if anything in her life had ever been simple. As if dancing with him while her skin still remembered another man's touch could ever be simple.

But for this moment, with snow falling around them and music filling the air, maybe she could pretend.

So she let her shoulders drop, let herself move closer, let the dance be what it was, just two people moving together in the candlelight, sharing space and breath and something that didn't need words.

At least, not yet.

They danced through two more songs, each one drawing them incrementally closer until the proper distance became something more theoretical than actual. Other couples swirled around them, but Cassara found her awareness narrowing to the warmth of Gideon's hand at her waist and the steady rhythm of their movement.

When the third song ended, transitioning into something livelier, she expected him to step back, to return to their seats. Instead—

"Come with me," he said quietly.

"Where?"

He didn't answer, just tugged her gently toward the edge of the dance floor. She followed, curiosity overcoming confusion as he led her past their abandoned table, past Thendrick's knowing smile, toward the great hall doors.

"Gideon, what—"

"Trust me."

And despite everything, despite the bruised parts of her heart that still ached for explanations that never came, despite the guilt that whispered she had no business following him anywhere, she did.

The corridors were quiet, their footsteps echoing off stone as he led her through familiar paths made strange by candlelight and shadow. She recognized the route to the common room just as he pushed open the door.

The space was empty but warm, fire crackling in the hearth. And there, arranged along the mantelpiece, sat a collection of wrapped packages and bags—gifts waiting to be claimed.

"Did you—?" she began, but he was already moving toward the hearth, reaching for something at the end of the row.

A small black velvet bag, tied with silver cord.

He turned back to her, and there was something almost uncertain in his expression. "This is for you."

Cassara stared at the offering. "You got me something?"

"Is that so surprising?"

"I..." Yes, it was. She'd made him something out of obligation, out of Liri's gentle reminder about friendship and traditions. But she hadn't expected, hadn't thought...

"Open it," he said softly, pressing the bag into her hands.

The velvet was soft beneath her fingers as she loosened the cord. Inside, her fingers found leather, supple and worn smooth. She drew it out slowly, breath catching as lamplight revealed what he'd made.

A bracelet. But not just any bracelet.

The leather was braided with care, reinforced with what looked like shimmer-cord—the same material used in ACS bonds. Three beads caught the light, each one hand-carved with delicate runes. She touched them gently, recognizing the symbols.

One for Auric Vow—their team, their unit, their shared purpose.

One that captured the essence of Flicker in abstract swirls, not mocking or dismissive, but acknowledging the bond she'd thought everyone scorned.

And the last one… blank. Waiting.

"The glyphs," Gideon said, stepping closer to point out the subtle markings worked into the leather itself. "This one's for balance. I thought you might appreciate that after your battle with the ice. This one helps with focus during stress. And this—" His finger traced the third symbol. "—will glow faintly when you're near other members of our unit. So you can always find us."

So you're never alone.

The words hung unspoken between them, but she heard them anyway.

"I don't—" Her voice came out rough. She cleared her throat, tried again. "Gideon, this is—"

"Practical," he said quickly, like he was afraid of what she might say. "That's all. You needed something that could survive combat training, and I noticed you don't wear much jewelry, so I thought—"

"It's perfect," she interrupted, and watched his words stumble to a halt. "Help me put it on?"

His fingers were warm as they took the bracelet, wrapping it carefully around her left wrist. The leather settled against her skin like it belonged there, and when he fastened the simple clasp, she felt the glyphs hum to life, subtle, barely there, but unmistakably real.

"There," he murmured, but his fingers lingered on her wrist, thumb brushing where leather met skin.

She looked up at him, finding his face closer than expected. The firelight threw shadows across his features, highlighting the intensity in his dark eyes, the slight part of his lips.

"Thank you," she whispered.

Something shifted in his expression, heat and hope and barely leashed want. His hand was still on her wrist, and she could feel her pulse racing beneath his touch.

"Cass—"

"I have something for you too," she said quickly, stepping back before the moment could become something they couldn't take back. Her cheek still burned from his earlier kiss, and the bracelet felt like a brand on her wrist, marking her as something she wasn't sure she could be.

Not yet. Not with Auren's ghost still haunting her hollow spaces.

She moved to the mantel, finding her lumpy, paint-stained package tucked between more elegant offerings. Next to the others, it looked even more pathetic than she remembered.

"It's not—" She turned back to him, package hidden behind her back. "It's nothing like what you made. It's actually kind of a disaster."

"I'm sure it's—"

"No, really. There might be paint in places paint shouldn't be and the leather refused to cooperate. And as you know...Flicker helped, which means there are probably paw prints somewhere unfortunate."

He smiled. "Sounds perfect."

"You haven't seen it yet."

"Doesn't matter." He stepped closer, holding out his hand. "I told you before. You made it. That already makes it perfect."

The certainty in his voice gave her the courage she needed. She thrust the package at him before she could lose her nerve.

"Just... remember that the technical part works. Probably. Oliver would be proud. Of that part. Not the rest."

Gideon accepted the package with the same care he might use for unstable alchemical compounds. The wrapping alone told a story, multiple layers where she'd clearly started over, and what looked suspiciously like a blue paw print on one corner.

He peeled back the paper slowly, revealing her creation in all its... glory.

His expression didn't change. Not exactly. But Cassara saw the minute widening of his eyes, the way his jaw tensed like he was physically holding back a reaction. His mouth twitched once. Twice.

"It's..." He turned the leather-wrapped disaster carefully in his hands, examining it from different angles like that might help identify it. "This is..."

"Functional," Cassara supplied helpfully, though she could feel heat creeping up her neck. "Mostly."

"Right. Functional." He held it up to the light, where a suspicious spark fizzled from between the leather wrapping. "And it's a..."

Oh gods. He didn't even know what it was.

"It's a protection charm," she said quickly. "For weapons. Or ACS units. You can attach it to—" She gestured vaguely. "Things."

"Of course." He nodded seriously, though she caught the way his shoulders shook slightly. "I can see that. The, uh, the leather wrapping is very..."

"Lumpy?"

"Artistic." His finger traced one of the paint smears that had definitely seeped where it shouldn't have. "And this blue accent really adds..."

"That's not supposed to be there."

"Character," he finished, mouth definitely twitching now. "It adds character."

"You're laughing at me."

"I'm not." But his voice came out strained, like he was fighting a losing battle.

"You are. Your eyes are laughing even if your mouth isn't."

"My eyes are expressing joy," he corrected, turning on the charm again. He turned it over and something rattled inside. His eyebrows rose. "Is it supposed to make that sound?"

"No," Cassara admitted miserably. "I think some of the paint got into the mana channels. It might have... crystallized."

This time he couldn't quite suppress the sound that escaped, not quite a laugh, more like air escaping a bellows. "You got paint. In the mana channels."

"Flicker was helping!"

"Of course he was." He examined the leather more closely, noting what were definitely tiny paw prints pressed into the surface. "I can see his artistic influence."

"Just say it's terrible."

"It's not terrible." He looked up at her, and despite the mirth in his eyes, there was something genuinely warm there too. "It's... unique."

"That's what people say about things that are terrible."

"No, terrible would be if it didn't work at all." He held it up again, and another small spark escaped. "This clearly... functions. In its own special way."

"You don't even know what it does."

"Well," he said reasonably, "that does add to the mystery. Is it supposed to protect against something specific, or...?"

She grabbed for it, but he held it out of reach. "Give it back. I'll make you something else. Something that doesn't look like Flicker and I got into a fight with craft supplies and lost."

"Absolutely not." He clutched it protectively to his chest. "This is mine now. You can't take back a gift just because it has personality."

"Personality," she repeated flatly.

"Besides," he continued, finally letting the grin he'd been fighting break free, "how many people can say they own an original Allencourt artistic disaster? This could be valuable someday."

"I hate you."

"No, you don't." He was fully smiling now, examining his paint-splattered, lumpy, occasionally sparking gift with what looked like genuine delight. "This is perfect. It's like you somehow captured our entire afternoon crafting explosion in one small, chaotic package."

"That wasn't the goal."

"Which makes it even better." He attached it to his belt, where it hung crooked and immediately released another small spark. "There. Now I'm protected by... whatever this protects against."

"General threats," Cassara muttered. "And getting lost. It's a tracking charm. In case you misplace your ACS. Or yourself."

His expression shifted, the laughter fading into something softer. "You made me a tracking charm?"

"It's practical!"

"So I don't get lost," he repeated quietly.

"Your ACS is expensive. It would be irresponsible to lose it."

"Right. My expensive equipment." But his hand went to the charm at his belt, fingers tracing the lumpy leather with surprising gentleness. "That's very... thoughtful."

"It's very dysfunctional, is what it is."

"It's perfect," he said again, and this time there was no laughter in it at all. Just that same intensity from the dance floor, from the snowbank, from every moment where the space between them felt too full of possibility.

"Even with the paint?"

"Especially with the paint." He chuckled. "Though I do have one question."

"What?"

"If this is for tracking..." He tilted his head, studying her. "Does that mean you'll always know where I am?"

Heat flooded her face as the implication hit. She hadn't thought it through, hadn't considered how it might sound.

"Yes but for emergencies," she said quickly. "Only for emergencies."

"Of course." But his smile suggested he heard what she hadn't said. That she'd made him something to keep him safe. That she'd wanted to be able to find him.

That maybe, despite everything, she couldn't bear the thought of him disappearing without a word.

CHAPTER THIRTY EIGHT

The afternoon sun cast long shadows across the snow-covered grounds, turning the academy gardens into a glittering wonderland. Cassara stood at the edge of it all, arms crossed, watching a group of third-years attempt to build what might generously be called a snowman.

"The proportions are all wrong," she muttered to herself. "The base needs to be wider if they want structural integrity."

Nearby, two second-years shrieked with laughter as they pelted each other with loosely-packed snow. Another group had started what looked like snow angels, though why anyone would voluntarily lie in frozen water was beyond her comprehension.

Three days without proper drills. Three days of "rest" that left her feeling like a bowstring pulled too tight with nowhere to release. Her muscles ached for movement, for purpose, for something more than watching other students engage in... whatever this was.

Fun, a small voice in her head suggested. They're having fun.

She pushed the thought away. Fun was for people who didn't have legacies to uphold, rankings to maintain, hearts to sort out from their tangled mess of—

THWAP.

Something cold and wet exploded against the back of her head, sending her hat sliding forward over her eyes. Snow trickled down her neck, shockingly cold against her skin.

She spun sharply, hand already reaching for a weapon that wasn't there, to find Gideon standing twenty feet away. He tossed another snowball lazily from hand to hand, grinning like he'd just executed the perfect tactical maneuver.

"Your situational awareness needs work," he called out, that insufferable smirk widening.

Cassara shoved her hat back into place, glaring. "Did you just—"

"Hit you with snow? Yes." He shifted the snowball to his right hand, arm cocking back slightly. "The question is—what are you going to do about it?"

"I don't engage in childish—"

The second snowball caught her square in the shoulder.

"Oh, you're dead," she growled, diving for the nearest snow bank.

Her first attempt at forming ammunition was pathetic. The snow crumbled in her hands, too powdery to pack properly. Meanwhile, Gideon had somehow produced three more perfect spheres and was advancing with military precision.

"Having trouble?" he called out, dodging behind a topiary. "Need me to teach you this too?"

"I know how to make a snowball!"

"Evidence suggests otherwise."

She flung her malformed attempt at him. It disintegrated mid-air, dusting his coat with harmless powder.

His laugh was warm and infuriating. "Was that supposed to be an attack?"

This is ridiculous. Flicker's voice chimed in her head as he materialized near her feet. *You're terrible at this.*

"Whose side are you on?" she hissed, finally managing to pack something resembling a proper snowball.

The winning side, he replied primly, and then, the traitor, bounded across the snow toward Gideon, chirping happily.

"Flicker!"

"Smart creature," Gideon said, reaching down to pat Flicker's head while maintaining his supply of ammunition. "He recognizes superior tactical positioning."

He gives better treats, Flicker informed her without shame. *And he's not losing.*

"We'll see about that," Cassara muttered, using a stone bench as cover. She peaked around the edge just in time to see Gideon's snowball coming straight for her face. She ducked, heard it splatter against the stone, and immediately returned fire.

This time, her snowball held together. It caught him in the chest with a satisfying thump.

"Better!" he called out, but he was already moving, circling to flank her position.

What followed could only be described as warfare.

The other students, drawn by the commotion, quickly chose sides. Fenn and Edwin joined Cassara, while Mira and Dania backed Gideon. Snow flew in deadly arcs across the garden. Defensive positions were established behind benches, statues, and the increasingly malformed snowman.

"Left flank!" Cassara barked at Fenn, fully embracing the tactical nature of the engagement. "Edwin, suppress their position by the fountain!"

"This is a snowball fight," Edwin laughed, even as he followed orders. "Not a military campaign!"

"Everything is a military campaign if you're doing it right," she shot back, nailing Mira with a perfectly aimed throw.

Gideon had turned a decorative wall into a fortress, launching devastating volleys while Flicker, the absolute traitor, used his small size to scout enemy positions.

Behind the rosebush, Flicker reported to Gideon, apparently delighted by his new role in espionage. *She's making a big one.*

"Saboteur!" Cassara accused when her extra-large snowball was intercepted before she could throw it.

Strategic intelligence gathering, Flicker corrected, preening.

The battle raged on. Alliances shifted. The quiet first-year turned out to have a wicked throwing arm. Fenn accidentally hit a passing professor, who simply shook his head and muttered about "youth."

And through it all, Cassara found herself... laughing? When had that started? Somewhere between diving behind a hedge and watching Edwin get pelted by Mira's rapid-fire assault, actual joy had crept in.

She was having fun.

The realization distracted her just long enough for Gideon to break from cover. He charged her position, and she scrambled backward, trying to reload. But movement in snow was still her weakness, and her boots found a hidden dip in the ground.

"Oh no," she cried out as she went down. "My ankle!"

Gideon skidded to a stop immediately, snowball forgotten. "Cass?" He dropped to his knees beside her, hands hovering uncertainly. "How bad—"

She smashed a handful of snow directly into his face.

"You little—" He spluttered, wiping snow from his eyes.

"Tactical deception," she said sweetly, scrambling to get up.

But he was faster, catching her around the waist before she could escape. "Oh no. You don't get to fake an injury and just walk away."

"It's a legitimate strategy!"

"It's cheating!" But he was laughing as he said it, spinning her around to face him. "I was actually worried!"

"Your mistake," she managed, breathless from laughter and something else as his arms tightened around her waist.

They were close, too close. Snow clung to his dark hair, and his cheeks were flushed from cold and exertion. His hands were warm through her coat, and she could feel his chest rise and fall against hers.

The laughter faded slowly, replaced by that dangerous awareness that seemed to follow them everywhere now. His eyes dropped to her mouth, and she found herself leaning in slightly, drawn by something stronger than strategy or competition.

You're both very silly, Flicker observed from somewhere nearby. *But at least you're not boring anymore.*

The spell broke. Cassara pulled back, clearing her throat. "I should—"

"Right." Gideon's hands loosened but didn't quite let go. "The battle."

"The battle," she agreed.

They stood there for another heartbeat, snow falling gently around them, before Dania chose that moment to lob a snowball that caught them both.

"No fraternizing with the enemy!" Fenn called out, grinning.

And just like that, the war resumed. But something had shifted in that moment of closeness, something that made every subsequent glance feel weighted, every accidental touch spark with possibility.

By the time they finally called a truce—cold, soaked, and exhausted—the sun was setting. The other students drifted back inside, chattering about hot cider and dry clothes.

Cassara shook out her scarf, surprised to find herself reluctant for the afternoon to end.

"Same time tomorrow?" Gideon asked, brushing snow from his hair.

"I don't know," she said, fighting a smile. "I might be busy with something actually productive."

"Like brooding in the library?"

"Strategic planning."

"For the next snowball fight?"

She threw her last handful of snow at him, loose and powdery. He didn't even try to dodge.

"I'll take that as a yes," he said, grinning.

He's not wrong, Flicker piped up, shaking snow from his fur. *You had fun. Admit it.*

She scooped up her traitorous beast, who purred despite his soggy state. "You're supposed to be on my side."

I am, he said, nuzzling against her chest. *That's why I helped him win. You needed to laugh.*

And as she headed inside, warm despite the cold, she couldn't quite argue with that logic.

The common room had emptied as evening deepened, leaving Cassara alone with the crackling hearth and her tangled thoughts. She'd claimed the best spot, an oversized armchair that let her stretch her wool-socked feet toward the flames without quite touching the grate. The fire's warmth seeped through the thick wool, chasing away the last of the afternoon's chill.

She held her left wrist up to the firelight, watching how the flames caught in the small beads of Gideon's gift. The Auric Vow symbol gleamed, then the delicate swirls representing Flicker, then the blank one. Waiting. For what, she wondered, rolling each bead slowly between her fingertips.

The leather was already softening against her skin, like it belonged there. Like it had always been there.

A cup appeared beneath her nose, steam curling up with the rich scent of chocolate and something else, cinnamon perhaps? She followed the hand holding it up to find Gideon watching her with that expression she couldn't quite name.

"Thought you might enjoy something warm," he said simply.

She accepted the cup, wrapping both hands around it, grateful for something to do with them. "Thank you."

He settled into the chair beside hers with his own cup, close enough that she could smell the winter air still clinging to his clothes beneath the warmth of chocolate. For a moment they sat in comfortable silence, watching the fire dance.

"There's another tradition," he said eventually, gesturing toward the hearth with his cup. "On the last night of the year, you write down your regrets on paper and burn them. Start fresh."

Cassara raised an eyebrow. "Burn them?"

"Symbolic cleansing. The smoke carries them away, or so they say." He studied her expression, mouth quirking. "Let me guess, another one you've never heard of?"

"I'm starting to wonder if you're making these up."

"Were you raised under a rock?" The teasing in his voice took any sting from the words. "Next you'll tell me you've never made shadow puppets in the firelight or roasted cake over the flames."

"You don't roast cake over flames," she protested. "That would ruin the frosting."

"Exactly what someone raised under a rock would say."

She kicked at his chair with her foot, making him laugh. The sound did something uncomfortable to her chest.

"We didn't... do holidays," she admitted quietly, staring into her cocoa. "Not like this. There was always a formal dinner for the winter solstice. Dignitaries, nobles, political alliances dressed up as celebration. But we never..." She gestured vaguely at the room, at him, at the simple comfort of hot drinks by a fire. "This."

"No gifts?"

"Oh, there were gifts. Carefully selected ones. A rare book from Lord Pemberton to curry favor. Jewels from the Montrose family to remind us of their wealth. Everything had a purpose, a meaning beyond the giving."

"No frost blossom fortune tarts?"

She shook her head.

"No hot cocoa by the fire?"

"My father would consider it inefficient. Why sit doing nothing when you could be reviewing trade agreements?"

Gideon was quiet for a long moment. When she glanced at him, his expression had gone thoughtful, almost sad.

"That sounds lonely," he said simply.

The words hit harder than they should have. She took a sip of cocoa to avoid responding, but he wasn't done.

"We did all of it," he continued, voice softer now. "Before. Every tradition, every silly ritual. My mother loved the winter celebrations. She'd start planning weeks in advance, who to invite, what to cook, which room needed fresh garlands." His smile was distant, aimed at the fire rather than her. "My father would pretend to be exasperated, but he always helped. Usually ended up tangled in ribbon or covered in flour."

"That sounds nice," Cassara said carefully. She knew where this was heading, everyone knew the Delvanir fall had been spectacular and swift.

"It was." He shifted in his chair, and she could see him weighing his words. "Right up until it wasn't."

She waited, letting the silence stretch. Sometimes the best way to learn was to leave space for the telling.

"You know the story, I'm sure. Everyone does." His voice carried a bitter edge. "The downfall of Delvanir, house of cowards and murders."

"That's what they say," she agreed carefully.

"They're wrong," he said, staring into the fire. "Oh, we lost everything. That part's true. But it wasn't poor judgment or greed. It was the Tremaines."

Cassara straightened slightly. This wasn't the story she'd heard, the one Julian had told with such satisfied detail.

"My family was pioneering new ACS technology, beast enhancement protocols that could've revolutionized bonding. The Tremaines were our primary backers. My grandfather, Corman, led the research team." Gideon's hands tightened on his cup. "The technology needed more time. More testing. But Lord Evard Tremaine, Julian's grandfather, wouldn't wait. He saw profit slipping away with each delay."

The fire popped, sending sparks up the chimney.

"They forced us into field trials. My grandfather warned them, begged them, told them it wasn't ready. The bonding matrices were unstable. But Evard threatened to pull funding, to bury us in legal proceedings if we didn't comply." His voice went flat, like he'd told this story to himself too many times. "So they ran the trial."

"The Southmark Incident," Cassara breathed, pieces clicking together.

"Two tamers dead within minutes. The third..." He paused, jaw working. "The enhancement backfired through the bond. Her own beast tore her in half. And Evard, he was injured in the chaos. Not badly, but enough."

"Julian said—"

"I know what Julian says." Bitterness crept into his tone. "That my grandfather was a coward who fled the scene, leaving Evard to die. That the Delvanirs pushed untested technology. Every word a lie."

"What really happened?"

"Corman tried to save them. All of them. He shut down the matrix manually, took massive feedback damage doing it. Evard left him there, bleeding out on the testing ground. Left him for dead." Gideon stared into the fire. "Then testified that Corman had fled like a coward. That the Delvanirs had hidden critical safety data. That we'd murdered those tamers through negligence and greed."

The silence stretched, heavy with the weight of old pain.

"The trials were swift, closed to the public. We were ordered to pay reparations to the victims' families, which we gladly did. They deserved that much. But it emptied our coffers. And with our reputation destroyed, every contract was cancelled. Every partnership dissolved. The Tremaines acquired our research for a fraction of its worth. Our patents. Our prototypes. Everything."

"My mother tried to hold it together. Sold everything she owned to keep us afloat. But when the entire nobility turns its back, when every door closes..." He shrugged.

Cassara felt sick. She'd sat through dinners where this story was told, always Julian's version, always painting the Delvanirs as greedy fools who'd killed good people through arrogance. She'd believed it. Judged Gideon through that lens when they'd first met.

"I'm sorry," she said quietly. "I believed, when Julian told me."

"Why wouldn't you? The Tremaines tell it well. They've had years to perfect the narrative." His smile was sharp. "And who's going to believe the disgraced grandson over the war hero's family?"

"I believe you," she said firmly. "Now. I believe you."

Something in his expression softened. "Thank you."

"Is that why you came? To Vallemont?"

"Partly. The academy has access to archives, old records. Somewhere in there is proof, grandfather's original warnings, safety concerns he documented, something. And partly..." He looked at her directly. "Because I won't let them erase us entirely. Every time I excel here, every achievement with my name on it, it's proof we were more than they said we were."

"And Julian knows this."

"Oh, he knows. He delights in reminding me how his family 'saved' beast taming technology from our reckless hands. How they made it safe, profitable, respectable." His laugh was hollow. "With our research. Our innovations. Built on the bones of what they stole."

"Gideon,"

"I'm not telling you this for pity." He turned to face her fully. "I'm telling you because you should know, those calculated gifts, those political dinners? That's all that's left when the rest gets stripped away. And it's nothing. It's empty rooms and cold hearths and silence where laughter used to be."

"So you hold onto the traditions," she said softly, understanding.

"Every ridiculous one." His smile returned, smaller but genuine. "Burnt cake and all."

"There's no such thing as burnt cake tradition."

Flicker chose that moment to materialize on the arm of her chair, chirping curiously at their cups. He leaned precariously toward Cassara's cocoa, whiskers twitching.

"Don't even think about it," she warned.

It smells good, he protested. *Just one taste?*

"You don't even like chocolate."

How do you know if I've never tried it?

"Because last time you tried coffee you sneezed for an hour."

Flicker's investigation grew more determined, forcing Cassara to hold her cup out of reach. The movement brought her closer to Gideon, who was watching the exchange with amusement.

"He's persistent," Gideon observed.

"He's a menace." But she was smiling as she said it, trying to keep her cocoa away from Flicker's grabby paws.

The little creature made a particularly ambitious leap, and Cassara jerked back to avoid the collision. Her shoulder bumped against Gideon's chest.

Your heart's going to get loud again, isn't it?

"I should..." she started.

But Gideon was already leaning in, one hand coming up to cup her cheek. "Cass."

Just her name, nothing more. But the way he said it, soft and certain...

The kiss was nothing like their almost-moment in the snow. That had been sudden, charged with adrenaline and surprise. This was deliberate. Intentional. His lips were soft against hers, patient, like he was asking a question and giving her all the time in the world to answer.

She answered by shifting closer, her hand coming up to rest against his chest. She could feel his heartbeat through the wool of his sweater. He made a soft sound, surprise or pleasure or both, and deepened the kiss, his fingers threading into her hair.

He tasted like chocolate and cinnamon and something sweeter. The fire crackled beside them, Flicker purred somewhere above, and for one perfect moment, everything else fell away. No Julian. No expectations. No complicated emotions about instructors who left without a word. Just this, just them, just the warm, sweet pressure of his mouth on hers.

Reality crashed back like cold water.

Heat.

Not fire, but hands in her hair.

Not Gideon. Auren.

She jerked away. "I- I can't."

Gideon's hand was still raised, hovering between them. His eyes were dark, pupils blown wide, and his lips—

She couldn't look at his lips.

"Cass—"

"I'm sorry." She stood abruptly, cocoa sloshing dangerously. She set the mug down on a nearby table. "I shouldn't have, I can't."

"Wait." He started to rise, but she was already backing away.

"I'm sorry," she said again, and fled.

She made it to her room before her hands started shaking. Her lips still tingled. She could still taste chocolate and him.

But she could also remember stone walls and desperate promises, another man's hands in her hair.

Her heart hammered against her ribs, pulled in two directions at once.

What had she done?

What was she doing?

And worse, why did she want to go back downstairs and do it again?

CHAPTER THIRTY NINE

The creak of hinges pulled Cassara from restless dreams. Her mind, still thick with sleep, tried to make sense of the sound. Had Liri come back early? Or perhaps it was one of the other girls, confused after too much celebration wine?

She pushed aside her bed curtain, ready to redirect whoever had stumbled into the wrong room, and froze.

Auren stood, no, sagged, against the doorframe, one arm wrapped tight around his ribs. Even in the darkness, she could see the wet gleam of blood seeping through his fingers.

"Auren?" His name came out as barely a whisper.

He lifted his head with visible effort, and the moonlight from her window caught his face, pale, drawn with pain, but unmistakably him. "I'm sorry. I didn't... there was nowhere else..."

She was out of bed before conscious thought kicked in, catching him as his knees started to buckle. He was heavier than she expected, solid muscle that now trembled with exhaustion.

"What happened?" She tried to keep her voice low, aware that the rooms around them were empty but not wanting to risk discovery. "Who did this?"

"Can't." He sucked in a sharp breath as she shifted to better support his weight. "Please. Just... trust me."

A thousand questions burned in her throat. Where had he been? Why had he left? What was worth this, blood and secrets and showing up in her room like a ghost made flesh?

But his weight against her was real, warm despite the blood loss, and she found she didn't care about answers. Not yet. He was here, he was alive, barely, and for now that was enough.

"Your room," she decided. "Can you walk?"

He nodded, though she felt more than saw the gesture. Together they made their way through the silent corridors, Cassara bearing more of his weight with each step. She'd never been to his quarters before, instructors' wings were off-limits to students. But he guided her with mumbled directions, until they reached a door that looked identical to all the others.

His room surprised her. She'd expected something austere, military. Instead, it was... warm. Rich colors, worn leather furniture, books stacked on every surface. A fire burned low in the grate, as if he'd left it lit with plans to return to it.

"Medkit," he managed, gesturing vaguely toward a cabinet. "Top shelf."

She eased him into a chair by the fire and retrieved the kit, military grade, comprehensive. Of course he'd have quality supplies.

"I need to see," she said softly.

His hands shook as he worked at his coat buttons. She brushed them aside, taking over with careful efficiency. The coat came away heavy with blood. His shirt was worse, torn along the left side, fabric stuck to what looked like claw marks.

"Auren, what—"

"Please." His hand caught hers, grip surprisingly strong. "No questions. Not tonight."

She nodded, swallowing her demands. The shirt had to be cut away, too much blood, too much damage to pull it off normally. And then she forgot about questions entirely.

The wounds were deep but clean, three parallel gashes along his ribs. Claw marks, definitely, but from what? She worked in silence, cleaning and disinfecting, applying the healing salve that made him hiss through his teeth.

"Sorry," she murmured.

"'S fine." His head tipped back against the chair, eyes closed. "Had worse."

She believed him. Some of those scars were old, faded to silver. Others looked more recent. A whole history written on his skin that he'd likely never share.

The bandaging required her to wrap around his torso, bringing her close enough to feel his breath against her temple. His eyes opened then, dark and unreadable in the firelight.

"Thank you," he said quietly.

"Don't." She tied off the bandage with hands that wanted to tremble. "Don't thank me for this."

"For not asking, then."

"I want to." The admission slipped out before she could stop it. "I want to demand answers. Where you went. Why you left without a word. What did this to you. Why you came to me instead of the healers."

"But you won't."

"No." She sat back on her heels, studying his face. "Not tonight."

Relief softened the hard lines of his face before guilt chased it away, leaving behind only exhaustion. He reached out, fingertips brushing her cheek with phantom lightness.

"I thought about you," he said, so quiet she almost missed it. "Every day. Every night. You were..." He stopped, jaw working. "It wasn't supposed to be like this."

"Like what?"

But he was already standing, wavering slightly. "Stay here tonight."

"Auren."

"Please." He caught her hand, tugged gently. "Just... stay."

She let him lead her to the bed, wider and more comfortable than what they had in the first year dorms. He eased down carefully, favoring his injured side, then drew her down beside him. He simply held her close, pulled her into him, her back pressed to his chest, his arm careful around her waist, his breath warm against her neck.

"What happened?" she asked, despite saying she wouldn't.

"I can't tell you," he murmured into her hair. "I want to. But I can't."

"I know."

"I'm sorry."

"I know that too."

His arm tightened fractionally and she could feel his heartbeat against her back, could still smell the sharp tang of blood beneath the antiseptic.

All the anger she'd carried, at his silence, his absence, his secrets, melted away. Tomorrow she could be furious, she could demand explanations.

Tonight, she just wanted this. The solid warmth of him. The rise and fall of his chest. The way he pressed his face into her hair like she was air and he'd been drowning.

"Sleep," she whispered.

"You'll stay?"

"I'll stay."

His breathing slowly evened out, exhaustion finally claiming him. But even in sleep, his arm remained around her, holding on like she was the only real thing in a world of shadows.

It was enough to make her heart ache, hating that the warmth of Gideon's mouth still lingered while she was holding someone else together with shaking hands and silence.

Cassara stared at the dying fire, questions churning behind her ribs. Where had he been? What had those claws belonged to? Why her, why had she been the only one he could trust?

And underneath it all, guilty and persistent—the memory of another kiss, another taste, another pair of hands gentle on her skin.

She closed her eyes, trying to quiet her racing thoughts. Auren shifted behind her, murmuring something unintelligible into her hair. His warmth seeped into her bones, familiar and necessary and impossibly complicated.

Morning light filtered through unfamiliar curtains, and for a moment Cassara couldn't place where she was. The bed was too wide, too warm, and there was a weight around her waist that—

Memory crashed back. Auren. Blood. Bandages.

She shifted carefully, mindful of his injuries, and found him already awake. His dark eyes studied her with an intensity that made her breath catch.

"Hi," he said softly, and the smile that curved his lips was so unexpectedly tender it made her chest ache.

Before she could respond, he leaned in and kissed her, gentle, careful, like he was afraid she might vanish. His hand came up to cradle her face, thumb brushing her cheekbone with reverent lightness.

"I'm sorry if I scared you," he murmured against her lips.

She pulled back enough to stare at him. "If? You showed up bleeding at my door in the middle of the night. There's no 'if' about it."

His smile turned rueful. "Fair point."

All the questions from last night rose like a tide. Where had he been? What had attacked him? Why the secrecy? Why her? She could see him reading them in her expression, see the moment his walls started to rebuild.

"Don't," she said quickly. "I'm not asking. Not yet. I just..." She traced a finger along the edge of the bandage, careful not to press. "Are you all right?"

"I'll live." He caught her hand, pressed a kiss to her palm. "Thanks to you."

"Auren—"

"You should go." The words came out pained, like they cost him. "Everyone returns today. If someone sees you leaving the instructor wing..."

He was right. She knew he was right. But leaving felt like abandoning him, like if she walked out that door he might vanish again.

"The others can't know I'm back," he said quietly. "Not yet. Please."

"Why?"

His body tensed. "Because whoever did this might try again if they know I survived."

The words sent ice through her veins. "Someone tried to kill you?"

"Cassara." Just her name, but weighted with plea. "Please. Trust me. Just for a little longer."

She wanted to refuse, wanted to demand answers, truth, something more than shadows and secrets. But his hand was still wrapped around hers, and she could feel the tremor in it, pain or exhaustion or fear, she couldn't tell.

"Fine," she said finally. "But this conversation isn't over."

"I know."

She rose quickly, aware of his eyes tracking her movements. At the door, she paused, looking back. He'd pushed himself up despite the obvious pain it caused, sheets pooled around his waist, morning light catching on the silver scars across his chest.

"Be careful," he said.

"That's my line."

His smile was sad. "Not anymore."

The corridors were blessedly empty as she made her way back through the academy. Most students wouldn't arrive until the afternoon, and the early morning staff were busy preparing for the influx. She'd almost made it to the common room when footsteps made her freeze.

Gideon rounded the corner, clearly heading for the dining hall, and stopped short when he saw her.

For a moment, they just stared at each other. The memory of last night, firelight and chocolate and the soft press of his mouth, was suspended between them like a physical thing.

"Cassara." His voice was carefully neutral.

"Gideon."

Silence stretched, painful and awkward. She could see him struggling for words, trying to address what had happened without making it worse. She needed to say something, anything, to break this terrible tension.

"Is that blood?"

She followed his gaze to her sleeve, where a smear of red stood out against the pale fabric. Auren's blood. She'd been so careful.

"Paint," she said quickly, tugging her sleeve down. "Flicker got into my supplies again. You know how he is."

His brow furrowed slightly. "I thought you cleaned all that up days ago."

"He found more. Hidden stash. Very clever." She was babbling. She needed to stop. "I should go change."

"Cass—"

"The others will be back soon," she said, already backing away. "I need to... prepare."

She fled before he could finish, acutely aware of his eyes on her back.

By afternoon, the dormitory was chaos. Trunks everywhere, voices overlapping as everyone shared their break adventures at once. Cassara sat on her bed, letting the noise wash over her, only half-listening to Liri's tale about her younger brother's attempt to tame a particularly aggressive chicken.

"—and then Cassara, you won't believe what happened at the embassy dinner!"

She looked up to where Evie was perched on her bed, eyes bright.

"Julian was there, of course. Looking absolutely devastating in formal wear. That dark green really brings out his eyes, don't you think?"

Cassara made a noncommittal sound.

"Him and Sonia danced three times. He only danced with me once. He's an excellent dancer, but I'm sure you already know that. He seemed distracted. Kept looking toward the doors like he was waiting for someone."

"Fascinating," Cassara said flatly.

"He asked about you. Several times, actually. Wanted to know if you'd mentioned coming to the capital."

Cassara thought of controlling hands and possessive words and the way Julian's charm could turn to cruelty in a heartbeat.

"I decided to stay here."

"You're so dedicated," Evie groaned, flopping back.

But even as the conversation moved on, Talia quietly sharing something about her village's winter traditions, Liri bouncing between beds to distribute small gifts, Cassara's mind remained split.

Auren was back, wounded and secretive, trusting her with his presence but nothing else.

Gideon had kissed her, and she'd kissed him back, and now they couldn't even look at each other without the weight of it pressing down.

And somewhere out there, Julian was watching doors and asking questions, his attention a noose waiting to tighten.

The break was over.

Whatever simple peace she'd found in snow and firelight was already fading, replaced by the familiar tangle of secrets and wanting and impossible choices.

She pressed her fingers to the bracelet at her wrist, leather and promise and a blank bead waiting to be filled, and wondered if Gideon had spent his morning thinking about kisses too.

Wondered if Auren was safe in his room or already gone again.

Wondered how long she could balance on this knife's edge before everything came crashing down.

The practice arena echoed with the sound of failure.

"Again," Gideon called, but even he sounded tired.

They reset formation for the dozenth time that morning. Oliver took point with Thornweaver, his crossbow, Barrett anchored the left flank, Liri floated between positions, and Cassara held right. The space where Verena should have been gaped like a missing tooth.

"Defensive pattern C," Gideon commanded. "Rett, you need to—"

The formation crumbled before he could finish. Without Verena's manticore to hold the center line, Barrett had to overextend, which pulled Oliver out of position, which in turn left Cassara exposed, which—

"Stop." Nareen's voice cut across the arena. "This isn't working."

Really? Cassara thought, like they hadn't all noticed.

A week back, and they moved like strangers. Every drill highlighted what they'd lost, not just Verena's skill, but the brutal efficiency her presence had provided. Love her or hate her, she'd been a wall nothing could break through.

Now they had gaps everywhere.

"Take five," Nareen ordered. "Hydrate. We'll try pattern D next."

Pattern D. As if cycling through the alphabet would magically conjure a sixth team member.

Cassara grabbed her water, trying not to notice how Gideon stood apart from the group, shoulders rigid with tension. He'd been like this all week, distant during drills, barely speaking outside them. She knew why, of course.

"This is a disaster," Oliver muttered, adjusting his ACS bracer for the hundredth time. "We're down twenty percent on defensive coverage. The mathematical probability of success with our current formation is—"

"We know," Barrett said quietly. "We all know."

Liri fidgeted with her canteen. "Maybe if I pushed Nym to be more aggressive? I could try to fill some of the gap."

"Your moth isn't meant for defensive holds," Cassara said, then immediately regretted how sharp it came out. "Sorry. I just mean... we can't force beasts into roles they're not suited for."

"Unlike tamers," Gideon said, just loud enough to carry.

She looked up to find him watching her, something unreadable in his expression. The intensity of his gaze made her stomach flip, and she hated how her body responded, heat creeping up her neck, pulse quickening, the memory of his mouth on hers suddenly, vividly present.

She looked away first.

"Pattern D," Nareen called. "Positions."

They tried. Gods, they tried. But Pattern D failed just as spectacularly as A through C. Cassara found herself constantly out of position, either overcompensating for gaps or pulling back too far. It didn't help that every time Gideon corrected her stance, professional, distant, barely touching, her skin lit up like she'd been branded.

"Your left shoulder," he said during one reset, reaching out to adjust her form. His fingers barely grazed her, but she felt it everywhere. "You're telegraphing."

"I'm not telegraphing." She jerked away from his touch. "Maybe if the formation actually made sense—"

"The formation is fine. Your execution—"

"My execution is perfect when I'm not having to cover two positions at once!"

They glared at each other, weeks of careful teamwork evaporating. Around them, the others shifted uncomfortably.

"Perhaps," Nareen interrupted, "you could save your personal disputes for after practice. Run it again."

Heat flooded Cassara's face. Personal disputes. As if everyone couldn't see the crackling tension, couldn't guess at its source.

They ran it again. Failed again. By the end of the session, they'd cycled through every defensive pattern in the manual and invented three new ones. None worked.

"Dismissed," Nareen finally said. "Individual training tomorrow morning. Team drills in the afternoon. Find a solution or fail out. Your call."

The threat hung heavy as they dispersed. Two weeks until their next arena match. Two weeks to fix the unfixable.

Cassara lingered, watching the others file out. Gideon remained too, rolling his shoulders like he could shake off the morning's failures.

"We need to talk," he said quietly.

"About the formations? Because I think—"

"About why you can't look at me." He stepped closer, and her traitorous body swayed toward him before she caught herself. "About why you flinch every time I correct your form. About—"

"Don't." The word came out desperate. "Please. Not here."

"Then where?" Frustration crept into his voice. "You've been avoiding me all week. We can't lead a team like this."

He was right. She knew he was right. But how could she explain? That every time he got close, she remembered firelight and chocolate and the way he'd said her name? That she'd spent the week split between worrying for Auren, who remained frustratingly absent from public view, and this unwanted, persistent awareness of Gideon?

That kissing him had been a mistake, but she couldn't stop thinking about doing it again?

"I know," she said finally. "Just... give me time."

"Time." He laughed, short and humorless. "We have two weeks, Cass. Less than that."

The nickname made her shiver. He noticed, of course he noticed, and his expression shifted to something softer, more dangerous.

"Is it because of—" He stopped. "No. Forget it. Individual training tomorrow. We'll figure out the rest later."

He left without waiting for a response. Cassara stood alone in the empty arena, Flicker materializing at her feet with a concerned chirp.

You're being weird, he informed her.

"I know."

Both of you are being weird. It's affecting the team.

"I know that too."

So stop being weird.

If only it were that simple. If only she could compartmentalize, lock away midnight kisses and morning guilt, secret wounds and persistent want. Be the leader her team needed instead of a girl caught between two impossible choices.

But every time she closed her eyes, she saw Auren's blood on her hands.

And every time Gideon got close, she remembered exactly how he tasted.

Two weeks to fix their formation.

She wasn't sure that would be nearly enough time to fix herself.

Two weeks crawled by in a blur of failed formations and growing frustration. They were better, marginally. Oliver had developed a rotating coverage system that almost compensated for their missing defender. Barrett had learned to split his attention without leaving Liri exposed. But "almost" and "learning" weren't enough. Not with tomorrow's match looming.

Cassara moved through the afternoon's drills on autopilot, muscle memory carrying her through patterns they'd run hundreds of times. Her mind was elsewhere, on formations, on rankings, on the persistent ache between her ribs that had nothing to do with physical exertion.

Then she saw him.

Across the training grounds, leading his second-years through sword work like nothing had happened. Like he hadn't bled all over her hands. Like he hadn't vanished into his quarters for two weeks of silence.

Auren moved with his usual lethal grace, demonstrating a parry-riposte combination. No sign of injury. No indication that anything had changed.

Business as usual.

Something hot and sharp flared in her chest. She missed her next block entirely, earning a bruise from Barrett's practice sword and a concerned look from Gideon.

"Focus," he said quietly.

She wanted to laugh. Or scream. Focus? When Auren was right there, close enough to see but impossibly distant, acting like the last two weeks, the last everything, hadn't happened?

The rest of practice passed in a haze of barely controlled fury. The moment Nareen dismissed them, Cassara was moving. Not toward Auren, that would be too obvious, too public. But to her room, where she scrawled a single word on paper with hands that shook.

Overlook.

She slipped it under his door that evening, then made her way to their spot.

Night fell.

The air grew cold.

She waited.

He came so quietly she almost missed it. For a moment they just looked at each other, taking inventory, measuring changes. He seemed thinner, sharper somehow. The moonlight caught angles in his face that hadn't been there before.

"You look well," he said finally.

The banality of it snapped something inside her.

"That's what you lead with? 'You look well'?" She stepped forward, fists clenched. "Two weeks, Auren. Two weeks of nothing. Not a word about where you went, what happened, why you showed up bleeding."

"You know I can't—"

"Don't." The word cracked like a whip. "Don't tell me you can't. You came to me. You trusted me enough to help you, but not enough to tell me why?"

His expression hardened. "It's not about trust."

"Then what is it about?"

"Protection." He moved closer, and she could see it now, the careful way he held himself, the lingering stiffness that spoke of wounds not fully healed. "The less you know, the safer you are."

"From what?" She was nearly shouting now, weeks of fear and fury pouring out. "What could be worse than wondering if you're dead? Then seeing you across the field and not knowing if tomorrow you'll vanish again?"

"Cassara—"

"I kissed him."

She hadn't meant to say it, not like that, not as a weapon. But they were out now and there was no taking it back.

Auren went very still.

"Gideon," she clarified unnecessarily. "During break. I kissed him."

Pain flickered across his face, though it was gone too quickly to be sure. When he spoke, his voice was terribly gentle.

"Maybe that's for the best."

The quiet acceptance of it hit harder than anger would have. "What?"

"You should be with someone who can give you what you deserve." He looked away, toward the forest. "Someone who doesn't have to hide. Who can stand beside you in daylight instead of meeting in shadows."

"I don't want—"

"Yes, you do." He turned back, and his eyes were infinite and sad. "You want the truth, and I can't give it. You want certainty, and I offer only secrets. You want a future, and I..." He stopped, swallowed. "I can only promise you locked doors and lies."

"That's not—"

"It is." He stepped closer. "Maybe not today. Maybe not tomorrow. But eventually, you'll resent it. Resent me. The weight of what we can't have will poison what we do, until there's nothing left but bitterness."

"You don't know that."

"I do." His hand came up like he might touch her cheek, then fell away. "I've seen it happen. I've watched love turn to ash under the pressure of too many secrets. I won't—" His voice roughened. "I won't do that to you."

"So you're giving up?" Anger flared again, hot and desperate. "That's it? You're just... done?"

"I'm trying to save you."

"I don't need saving!" She shoved him, hard enough to make him step back. "I need honesty. I need to know you won't disappear every time things get difficult. I need—"

"Someone else." The words were quiet but final. "You need someone else, Cassara."

The certainty in his voice broke something inside her. She stared at him, this man who'd held her like she was precious, who'd kissed her like worship, who now stood there calmly dismantling everything between them for her own good.

"You promised we were in this together."

"I know, I'm sorry—"

"You're a coward," she whispered.

He flinched but didn't deny it.

"Fine." She stepped back, wrapping her arms around herself. "If that's what you want—"

"It's not about what I want."

"Right. It's about protecting me." The words tasted bitter. "How noble. How perfectly self-sacrificing. I'm sure you'll comfort yourself with that when you're alone."

She turned to leave, then stopped.

One last shot, one last truth to fling at him.

"I kissed him," she said without looking back. "But I thought of you."

She left before he could respond, fleeing down stone steps and through empty corridors. Only when she reached her room did she let herself fall apart. She sat on the edge of the bed shaking with fury, with loss, with the terrible finality of it all.

He was right about one thing—she did want more than shadows and secrets.

But gods help her, she'd have accepted all of it, if it had meant staying together.

Now she had nothing.

Tomorrow they'd face the arena. She'd have to stand strong, lead her fractured team, pretend everything was fine.

She pressed her face into her pillow and tried not to think about how "for the best" felt exactly like heartbreak.

CHAPTER FORTY

The arena materialized around them in a rush of green and shadow.

Ancient trees towered overhead, their canopy so thick it turned midday to twilight. The air hung heavy with moisture and the scent of moss, while somewhere in the distance, water roared. As Cassara's eyes adjusted, she caught glimpses of the terrain: twisted roots creating natural barriers, ravines cutting dark scars through the forest floor, and through it all, the glint of a river bisecting the arena like a liquid wall.

"Beacons are lighting," Oliver reported, his Ilza already blending into the bark beside him. "Three on each side of the river, two along the ravines, and-" He paused, calculating. "The center point is directly over the water. Suspended platform."

"Formation C," Gideon ordered, but his voice carried an edge that made Cassara grit her teeth. "Liri, high patrol. Oliver, eastern ravine. Barrett—"

"We practiced Formation D for this terrain," Cassara interrupted.

His eyes cut to her, dark and unreadable. "D leaves our right flank exposed without a proper tank."

"C puts too much pressure on Barrett. He can't hold two positions—"

"He can if you maintain your sector instead of overextending."

The criticism stung, mostly because it was true. She'd been overcompensating all week, trying to fill gaps that shouldn't exist.

"Positions," Gideon said with finality. "Match starts in thirty seconds."

They scattered into the forest, but the damage was done. That spark of conflict, small as it was, rippled through their coordination.

Cassara took her position among the twisted roots, Flicker materializing beside her in a shimmer of silver fur. His large eyes reflected her frustration back at her.

You're upset, he observed.

Not now.

Being upset makes you sloppy.

She wanted to argue, but the starting horn echoed through the trees, and suddenly there was no time for anything but survival.

Their opponents, Morrison's team again, because fate had a sense of humor, moved like they'd been born in forests. Their stone golem crashed through undergrowth like a living avalanche, while their scout's wind hawk provided aerial intelligence Liri's sparkfly couldn't match in the dense canopy.

"Eastern beacon under attack," Oliver's voice crackled through their comm crystals. "Two incoming—no, three. They're using the ravine for cover."

"Barrett, shift east," Gideon commanded. "Cassara, cover his—"

But she was already moving, Spireglass unfurling from her back in one fluid motion. The mirrored glaive caught what little light filtered through the canopy as she intercepted Morrison's flanker before they could exploit Barrett's movement. The clash of her blade against stone rang through the forest, the weapon's reach keeping the attacker at perfect distance.

"I said cover, not engage," Gideon's voice was hard.

"They were going to—"

"Cassara, center!" Liri's panicked call cut through their argument.

The warning came too late. By rushing to intercept, she'd left their middle beacon exposed. Morrison himself was already there, his ironhide boar smashing through their hasty defenses.

"Rotating," she called, but the formation was already fractured. Barrett was pinned at the eastern ravine. Oliver couldn't leave his position without sacrificing another beacon. Nym provided what cover it could, but against Morrison's raw power—

"Western beacon lost," Oliver reported, stress creeping into his usually calm voice.

They were being picked apart. Every move they made to cover one weakness opened two more. Without Verena's manticore to anchor their center, they were playing a defensive game with half the pieces.

"Regroup at the river," Gideon ordered, but Cassara could hear what he didn't say—retreat. They were giving up half the arena to consolidate what little they could hold.

She fell back, Flicker darting between her feet, reflecting her growing frustration in the agitated swish of his tail. Across the rushing water, Morrison's team had already claimed the suspended platform. Their tank stood like a monument to everything Auric Vow had lost, while their ranged fighters picked off any attempt to challenge the position.

"We need to take the platform," Cassara said, breathing hard as they huddled behind a massive root system.

"With what approach?" Gideon's control was fraying. "They have height advantage and defensive positioning."

"If we circle through the northern ravine—"

"That leaves our remaining beacons exposed."

"Then what do you suggest?" She asked, unable to temper her mounting frustration. "Sit here and slowly lose?"

"I suggest we follow the formation instead of improvising every—"

A blast of compressed air from the wind hawk sent them scattering, Morrison's team pressing their advantage. Cassara rolled aside, came up spinning, Spireglass cutting a silver arc through the air as she caught their scout across the shoulder. The blade's mirrored surface left confusing afterimages in the forest gloom, but it was desperate, reactive, everything they'd trained not to be.

"Southern beacon under attack," Barrett's strained voice reported.

"Eastern beacon lost," Oliver added.

The scoreboard floating above the arena told the story in stark numbers. Morrison's team controlled six of the nine points. The match was barely half over, and it was already finished.

They fought on, for pride, if nothing else. Cassara pushed herself harder, trying to be everywhere at once. But every spectacular individual effort only highlighted how badly they were failing as a unit. She saved the southern beacon only to lose the western one. Barrett held the bridge approach until sheer numbers overwhelmed him. Liri's moth grew to massive size in a desperate play for the platform, only to be swatted down by coordinated fire.

When the final horn sounded, they held exactly one beacon.

One, out of nine.

The arena dissolved around them, replaced by the academy's neutral grey. Morrison's team celebrated on their side, while Auric Vow stood in scattered positions, not even looking at each other.

"Well," Morrison called across the space, his grin sharp. "Guess the mighty do fall. What happened to your perfect record?"

Cassara's hands clenched around Spireglass, the weapon humming with her suppressed fury. But before she could respond, Gideon's hand fell on her shoulder.

"Don't," he said quietly. Then, louder: "Good match."

Morrison's laugh followed them off the field.

The walk to their preparation room felt endless. Students lined the corridors, whispers trailing in their wake. She caught fragments—

"completely destroyed"

"without Verena"

"Gideon and Cassara couldn't even..."

Inside their room, silence reigned.

"That was—" Oliver began.

"A disaster," Barrett finished, unusual bitterness in his tone. "We looked like first-weeks out there."

"We did our best with what we had," Liri offered weakly.

"Our best?" Cassara whirled on her, weeks of frustration boiling over. "That wasn't our best. That—"

"What?" Gideon snapped. "What was it, Cassara? Since you seem to have all the answers."

They faced each other across the room, the air crackling with more than exhaustion.

"We needed better coordination," Cassara said, voice tight. "The formations weren't working—"

"Because you broke off without signaling." Gideon's control finally cracked, heat flooding his voice. "Barrett had no idea where you'd gone. Neither did I."

"I made a judgment call—"

"You made a solo decision that left the rest of us exposed!" He stepped forward, frustration breaking through his usual composure. "We can't hold a formation when you're improvising!"

"At least I was trying something!" Her voice rose to match his. "Instead of clinging to strategies that clearly aren't working anymore!"

"Stop," Barrett said quietly, but neither of them heard him.

"The strategies aren't the problem," Gideon shot back. "The problem is we can't function as a team when you're—"

"When I'm what?" Cassara demanded, heart pounding. She knew what he wasn't saying. Knew he could see she was a mess, distracted, falling apart. That everything with Auren had gutted her and she was bleeding all over their team dynamics.

"When you're not communicating," Gideon finished, jaw tight. "When you're making calls without the rest of us."

But that wasn't what he'd been about to say. She could see it in the way his hands flexed, the careful control in his voice. They were fighting about tactics when the real problem was standing right between them—the kiss they weren't acknowledging, the tension that made every interaction feel like walking on broken glass.

"We're falling apart because we lost our defensive anchor," she said instead, redirecting to safer ground. "The formations don't work without—"

"Verena was expelled," Gideon cut in, voice going hard and flat. "We all knew what we were losing when that happened."

"I know that," she said, quieter but no less tense.

His expression shifted—frustration giving way to something that looked almost like regret. Like he hadn't meant for it to sound like that, but couldn't take it back now.

The silence stretched between them, heavy with everything they weren't saying.

"Rankings post tomorrow," Gideon said at last. "We should... prepare for the drop."

One by one, they filed out. Barrett squeezed her shoulder as he passed. Liri murmured something no doubt meant to be comforting. Even Oliver paused, adjusting his glasses like he wanted to say something before thinking better of it.

Finally, only she and Gideon remained.

“I'm sorry,” she said to the floor.

“So am I.” He sounded exhausted. “This isn't working.”

Her heart clenched. “The team?”

“Us.” He gestured between them. “Whatever this is. The kiss, the anger, the... everything. It's affecting everyone.”

She wanted to deny it. Wanted to say they could separate personal from professional. But the evidence was splattered across the arena floor in the form of their worst defeat ever.

"I know," she whispered.

"We need to fix this. Find neutral ground. Or- "

"Or?"

He met her eyes, and she saw her own fear reflected there. "Or we'll lose more than matches."

The door closed behind him with quiet finality. Cassara sank onto a bench, Flicker immediately crawling into her lap, purring anxiously.

We lost, he said unnecessarily.

"I know."

It hurt to watch.

"I know."

You still care about him.

She buried her face in his soft fur, not bothering to ask which 'him' Flicker meant. The answer was the same either way.

"I know."

The silver pin felt heavier than gold ever had.

Cassara turned it over in her fingers, watching morning light catch on the lesser metal. One catastrophic match, and they'd dropped an entire tier. The Crestboard rankings had been posted at dawn and Auric Vow now sat at a comfortable mediocrity that made her stomach turn.

"Stop brooding," Oliver said from across their usual table. "It's affecting your tactical assessments."

She looked up to find him surrounded by notebooks, each filled with his meticulous observations. When had he started documenting everything?

"I'm not brooding."

"You've been staring at that pin for six minutes and forty-seven seconds." He pushed his glasses up, fixing her with that unnervingly direct gaze. "Time better spent reviewing these."

He slid a notebook across the table. Her name was written on the cover, followed by '& Flicker - Behavioral Analysis.'

"What is this?"

"Everything I've observed since day one." He opened it to a page covered in diagrams. "Your beast is operating at approximately twelve percent capacity."

Flicker, curled in her lap, chirped indignantly.

"Twelve percent?" She couldn't hide her skepticism. "He's barely combat-functional as is."

"Exactly my point." Oliver flipped pages, showing chart after chart. "Look at his resonance patterns during high-stress situations. Here, during the Verena match. Here, when Julian cornered you. And here—" He tapped a spike on the graph. "When Gideon was injured in training last week."

Each spike was dramatic, the readings far exceeding what a C-rank beast should produce.

"These are instrument errors," she said, but even she could hear the doubt.

"Seven different instruments? Across four months?" Oliver shook his head. "Cassara, your beast reacts to emotional stimuli in ways that defy classification. He's holding back."

Am not, Flicker protested in her mind.

Are too, she shot back.

"We have one match left," Oliver continued. "One chance to avoid complete mediocrity. I think it's time you stopped treating him like a pet and started treating him like the weapon he could be."

The words stung more than they should have. Maybe because she'd been avoiding hard truths all week.

Like how she'd crossed halls to avoid Auren, that careful dance of schedules and routes that kept them from occupying the same space. She'd caught glimpses, his rigid posture during instructor meetings, the way he never quite looked in her direction during assemblies. They were strangers again, polite and distant, as if midnight bandages and whispered rejections had been a dream.

And Gideon...

She glanced across the dining hall to where he sat with Barrett and Liri, reviewing formation diagrams. He'd been nothing but professional since their fight. Perfectly correct and captain-like. It was worse than anger would have been.

"Cassara." Oliver's voice pulled her back. "Are you listening?"

"Yes. Emotional stimuli. Hidden potential." She closed the notebook. "What do you suggest?"

"Intensive bond training. Push boundaries. Stop protecting him, and yourself, from discomfort."

I don't like him, Flicker announced.

He's trying to help.

He smells like chalk and judgment.

Cassara stood, Flicker flowing up to perch on her shoulder. "When do we start?"

"Now, ideally. The—"

"Cassara!"

Liri appeared at her elbow, slightly breathless, Barrett a steady presence behind her. "Team meeting in ten minutes. You too, Oliver."

"About?"

"New formations," Barrett said quietly. "Gideon thinks he's found something."

Of course he had. Something brilliant and logical that would require perfect coordination between two people who could barely look at each other.

"We'll continue this later," she told Oliver, who was already packing his notebooks.

"Don't put it off," he said. "That twelve percent won't improve itself."

The meeting was held in their usual practice room, formation diagrams already projected on the walls. Gideon stood at the center, and for a moment, just a moment, their eyes met. Something flickered there, gone too fast to name.

"Right," he began, voice carefully neutral. "We've been approaching this wrong. Trying to replace what we lost instead of building on what we have."

He gestured to a new formation, unlike anything in the standard manual. "Oliver's beast excels at area control. Nym has been growing stronger, more responsive. Barrett can anchor a line if we stop asking him to cover two. And Cassara—"

He paused, and she held her breath.

"Your agility is our greatest asset. We've been trying to make you a defender when you're built for surgical strikes."

"And Flicker?" The question slipped out before she could stop it.

Another pause. "Oliver's research suggests untapped potential. We should explore it."

Cassara nodded.

"One week," he continued, addressing the group. "We'll train twice daily. Morning conditioning, afternoon tactics. Questions?"

"What about our opponents?" Liri asked. "Do we know—"

Gideon glanced towards Cassara.

"Julian's team."

Of course. Of course it would be Julian.

"They're ranked gold, riding a five-match winning streak," Gideon said evenly. "Their formation is aggressive, beast-heavy. They'll expect us to be defensive after last week."

"So we won't be," Cassara said, understanding. "We'll attack."

"Precisely." For just a second, his professional mask slipped, and she saw a fleeting glimpse of approval. "They won't expect precision from a wounded team."

We're not wounded, Flicker protested.

But they were. Fractured by loss, complicated by feelings nobody would acknowledge, held together by pride and necessity. One week to forge themselves into something functional.

"Dismissed," Gideon said. "Individual training starts in an hour."

As she turned to go, Gideon called out. "Cassara. A moment."

Her heart jumped, but she kept her expression neutral as the others left. When they were alone, he moved to the window, not quite looking at her.

"Oliver's right about Flicker," he said quietly. "I've seen the readings."

"Everyone has opinions about my beast lately."

"That's not—" He stopped and took a breath. "I'm trying to help."

"I know. I'm sorry. I'm just—"

"Frustrated. Angry. Confused." He turned to face her, and the careful distance he'd maintained cracked slightly. "I know the feeling."

They stood there, the space between them filled with everything they couldn't say. She wanted to apologize again, wanted to explain about Auren.

Instead, she said, "One week."

"One week," he agreed.

"We'll win."

"We have to."

Neither of them moved to leave. Finally, Gideon cleared his throat.

"Cassara..."

"I should go," she said quickly. "Oliver's waiting. Bond training."

"Of course. Train hard."

She left before either of them could make things worse, Flicker a warm weight on her shoulder.

That was painful to watch, he observed.

Not now.

You still want to kiss him.

I said not now.

And you're still angry at the other one.

She didn't dignify that with a response. Because Flicker was right, as usual. She was angry at Auren for his noble stupidity, for pushing her away, and for being right about how the secrets would poison everything. And she *did* want to kiss Gideon again, wanted to know if that fire was real or just reaction to the feeling of abandonment.

Most of all, she was angry at herself for the mess she'd made, for the hearts she'd tangled and for the team she was failing.

She headed to the bonding chambers, Oliver's notebook under her arm. If Flicker had hidden potential, she'd find it. If the team needed her to be a weapon, she'd sharpen herself to a killing edge.

And if her heart needed clarity?

Well. That would have to wait until after they proved they weren't broken.

Silver might be heavier than gold, but she'd be damned if she'd let it drag them down.

The bonding chamber hummed with residual energy, mana particles still dancing in the air from another failed synchronization attempt. Cassara sat cross-legged on the floor, breathing hard, while Flicker paced in agitated circles around her.

"Again," she said.

No, he protested, sitting down firmly. *It hurts when the connection snaps.*

"It hurts me too." She held up her ACS bracer, where warning lights flickered amber instead of steady blue. "But Oliver says we're at fifteen percent now. That's progress."

Three percent in four days. At this rate, we'll be ready when we're dead.

She couldn't argue with his math. Every push forward came with backlash. The ACS was struggling to regulate the surges of power that shouldn't exist from a C-rank beast. Oliver's modifications helped, but they were bandages on a breaking dam.

"Cassara?"

She looked up to find Oliver in the doorway, carrying what looked like a portable workshop in his arms. Tools, crystals, and a set of schematics covered in multiple handwriting styles.

"New modification," he said without preamble, already setting up on the chamber floor. "The current framework is restricting flow. We need a different approach."

"Different how?"

He produced two mana crystals, each about the size of her thumb, gleaming with internal light. "Direct regulation through synchronized crystals. One embedded in your ACS, one in a collar for Flicker. They'll create a stabilized channel between you."

Flicker padded over to investigate, sniffing at the crystals suspiciously. *They smell like lightning.*

"That's... is that legal?" Cassara asked, remembering all too well the cold scrutiny of a disciplinary tribunal. "Modified equipment in official matches-"

Oliver shrugged.

The casual gesture was so unexpected from him that all she could do was stare. "Did you just... shrug? At regulations?"

"Perhaps," he said, but she caught the tiniest twitch at the corner of his mouth.

"Oliver Straton. Did you just make a joke?"

"I never joke about modifications." But the twitch was definitely there now. "The regulations specify that ACS systems must maintain the original manufacturer framework. These crystals don't alter the framework, they create a parallel processing path. Completely legal."

"You absolutely made a joke."

"I made a regulatory clarification that happened to cause amusement." He was already disassembling her bracer with practiced efficiency. "Hold still. This requires precision."

She watched him work, noting how his usual rigid focus had softened slightly. Four days of intensive training together had worn down some of his sharp edges, revealing glimpses of dry humor beneath the analytical exterior.

"There." He sat back, the first crystal now seamlessly integrated into her bracer. "Flicker?"

Do I have to wear a collar? Flicker's ears flattened. *I'm not a pet.*

"He doesn't want to wear a collar," Cassara explained.

"It's a tactical enhancement device," Oliver said seriously. "Shaped like a collar for practical reasons."

Still feels demeaning.

"I'll make it silver," Cassara offered. "To match your fur."

...acceptable.

The collar was elegant, more like jewelry than equipment. The crystal sat at the front, pulsing gently with Flicker's heartbeat. The moment it clicked into place, Cassara gasped.

The bond exploded open.

Where before there had been a narrow channel, constrained and difficult, now there was a river. She could feel Flicker's emotions with crystalline clarity—his curiosity, his frustration with their limitations, his deep, unwavering loyalty. And underneath it all, power. Waves of it, simply waiting.

Oh, Flicker said, his mental voice clearer than ever. *This is better.*

"This is incredible," she breathed, watching her ACS readings steady into perfect blue. "Oliver, you're brilliant."

He ducked his head, adjusting his glasses unnecessarily. "It wasn't entirely my design."

Something in his tone made her stomach tighten. "What do you mean?"

"Gideon came to me three days ago. He had notes, partial schematics. Said he'd been working on it but couldn't finish the calculations." Oliver gestured to the scattered papers. "I just filled in the blanks."

Cassara looked down at the bracer. Gideon had done this. Had seen her struggling and, instead of approaching her directly, had found another way to help.

"I see," she managed.

"He specifically asked me not to mention his involvement," Oliver added, then paused. "Which I've now done. Hmm."

"Why tell me?"

"Because secrets are tactically unsound." He began packing up his tools. "And because credit should go where it's due. Even if it makes things... complicated."

Complicated. That was one word for it.

After Oliver left, Cassara sat in the empty chamber, Flicker curled in her lap. Through their newly opened bond, she could feel his concern, warm and steady.

You should thank him, Flicker said.

I know.

But you won't.

No.

Because you're scared.

She stroked his fur, not bothering to deny it. She *was* scared. Scared that thanking him would mean acknowledging what he'd done. Scared that acknowledging it would mean admitting she'd noticed, that she cared, that despite everything, she still felt that pull toward him.

"Stand," she said instead. "Let's test these new crystals properly."

They moved through forms together, and it was like dancing with a part of herself she'd never known existed. Flicker anticipated her movements, power flowing between them in perfect synchronization. Twenty percent. Thirty. The readings climbed steadily, no backlash, no strain.

By the time they finished, she was grinning despite herself.

Tomorrow they would face Julian and his team in the arena and she'd have to navigate team dynamics and unspoken gratitude and the weight of what they'd lost.

But she wasn't worried. Now she had this, a bond finally opening like a flower in sunlight, and the knowledge that somewhere in the academy, Gideon Delvanir was still trying to save her, even if it was from a careful distance.

CHAPTER FORTY ONE

The preparation room felt like a tomb.

Cassara adjusted Spireglass for the third time, the weapon's weight both familiar and foreign against her back. Around her, the team moved through final checks in unusual silence. No banter. No last-minute strategy debates. Just the quiet intensity of people who knew what waited beyond those doors.

"Two minutes," Gideon said, voice steady despite the tension radiating from his shoulders.

Through the window, she could see Julian's team in their own preparation space. He caught her looking and smiled, that particular curve of lips that promised pain. Beside him, Jonas cracked his knuckles, his battle axe propped against one massive shoulder. Vash's fingers danced along his staff's threads. They were a picture of confidence.

"Remember the plan," Gideon continued. "They'll expect us to be defensive. We use that. Oliver, your traps—"

"Already memorized the likely positions," Oliver said, adjusting his Shadepiercer with mechanical precision.

"Liri, aerial reconnaissance but don't overextend."

"Got it." Her usual brightness was muted, Nym's wings flickering nervously.

"Barrett—"

"Hold the line. I know."

"And Cassara..." Gideon's eyes found hers, holding something unreadable. "Trust the bond. Trust Flicker."

The mana crystal at her wrist pulsed in response, Flicker's presence a warm constant in her mind.

We can do this, he said, though she felt his nervousness bleeding through their connection.

Together, she agreed.

The stone beneath her boots vibrated with distant thunder, deep, molten, and alive. Cassara adjusted her grip on Spireglass, exhaling slowly as the gates ahead began to part. Heat licked through the seams of her gear, dry and biting, but it wasn't the temperature that made her tense.

It was the match.

The stakes.

The weight of everything riding on it.

She could feel the others behind her, Gideon silent at her right, Barrett murmuring something to Liri too low to catch. Oliver tapped twice on the side of his Codex like it could steady his nerves. Flicker pressed lightly against her neck, warm and alert, mirroring her every breath.

Then the gates opened.

A volcanic arena sprawled before them, black glass and blistered rock, split by glowing fissures that pulsed like veins beneath a dying world. Sulfur scorched the air. Brimstone shimmered in the sky above, caught in a swirling updraft of ash and smoke. Every breath stung, dry and metallic on the tongue.

Flicker shrank closer, ears flattened, his fur prickling with static. His body hummed with nervous energy, matching hers beat for beat.

Cassara swallowed hard.

Across the basin, the opposing gate yawned open.

Dawnpierce stepped out in perfect formation, their silhouettes sharp against the searing light. Their beasts moved like extensions of will, practiced, polished, and lethal. Julian stood at the center, Ceravolt resting against one shoulder, his moonlit wyvern coiled behind him in languid menace.

He looked straight at her.

Cassara held his gaze, spine stiffening as if defiance alone could be armor.

Julian tilted his head in a slight nod. A silent dare.

This arena was built for fire. Let's see if you burn.

Her stomach coiled. Not from fear, but from knowing he wanted her to crack first.

Gideon's voice broke through the tension, quiet and clipped. "Oliver, track fissure shifts. Liri, shimmer coverage and forward support. Barrett, left-side pressure. Cassara, sweep right. Keep moving."

Cassara gave a tight nod. The obsidian platform beneath her feet trembled again, a reminder that the ground here didn't care who stood atop it. It would swallow anyone if given the chance.

The match began with no fanfare. No signal flare, no call from the sidelines. Just the shift of magic beneath their boots, the unmistakable hum of the beacons activating, and the first pulse of searing heat as the arena came alive.

Auric Vow moved fast, formation clean despite the tension.

Gideon led the charge down the center path, Lockstep already braced and angled to deflect molten debris. Vangal soared overhead, wings slicing air as it cast long shadows over the cracked terrain. Every movement was deliberate—cover, assess, advance.

Cassara peeled right, Spireglass gleaming at her back. Flicker kept low beside her, paws light on glassy stone, his tail twitching every time the ground gave a warning tremor. The air around them shimmered with heat. She scanned the fissures, some wide enough to swallow a beast whole, some narrow but steaming like they'd burst open at any second.

"Three unstable ridgelines on the west quadrant," Oliver reported over comms. "Fissure flow increasing near the south platform, don't linger. I'm marking patterns."

He crouched by a jagged outcrop, Shadepiercer already loaded. Ilza clung to the wall behind him, her plating shifting shades to match the terrain, nearly invisible except for the shimmer of her eyes.

"Copy," Gideon said. "Barrett, stay on Cassara's diagonal. Maintain pressure and rotation intervals."

"Got it," Rett replied. He broke left for a short burst, clearing a loose arc before circling back to anchor her flank. Skelli moved like a coiled spring, low to the ground, spines flared in anticipation.

Liri kept behind the central line, Nym hovering above her head in slow, steady loops. The air glinted with petals of light from Nimbrush, the twin fans already deployed and spinning gently. Illusion shimmered faintly around them, just enough to make outlines blur and footing uncertain.

Across the arena, Dawnpierce barely moved. They didn't need to. They waited, positioned like a loaded trap, letting Auric Vow come to them.

Julian remained still, one hand resting lightly on Ceravolt's hilt. His wyvern waited behind him, wings tucked, eyes narrowed. No action. Just watching.

Cassara's pulse ticked faster.

They weren't attacking yet. Which meant they were watching her.

She shifted her grip on Spireglass. Flicker glanced up at her, ears tilted back, and for a breath, they both hesitated.

Then the ground quivered again, deeper this time.

The game had begun.

It was subtle, a ripple beneath the soles, but enough. The ground cracked wider ahead of her, belching steam and ember. Cassara pivoted left, fast and clean, thinking she'd gained a moment of control.

She was wrong.

Julian dropped from above with the force of a falling star.

The weight of his moonlit wyvern struck the ledge behind him as he landed, kicking up a wall of smoke and fire. His blade gleamed, Ceravolt mid-transformation, humming with volatile charge. She only had time to bring Spireglass halfway up.

Steel clashed, loud, jarring, and too close to her ear.

Cassara gritted her teeth and staggered backward. He'd come in high, forcing her to meet the blow off-balance. The impact rattled her from her elbow straight through to her shoulder. Flicker shrieked behind her, wings flaring, but Julian was already closing again.

He didn't fight like a teammate. He fought like someone who'd memorized her footwork. Who knew the tilt of her guard before she even raised it.

"You're slipping," he said, sounding pleased. "Didn't think you'd make it easy, but I should've known. You always leave your right side open when you're angry."

Cassara lunged forward, slicing with the mirrored arc of Spireglass. He knew she would. He twisted, caught it with Ceravolt's spine, and pivoted into a brutal counter-strike that slammed her hard in the ribs. The force didn't break anything, but it would bruise.

Her ACS sync dipped—orange, she realized distantly. She was pushing too hard. Flicker's pulse flared hot and anxious against her mind.

She tried to pull back, to reset, he followed.

Another blow, her shoulder this time. Not enough to break her guard, but enough to force her into a stagger.

"I warned you," Julian said as he pressed the assault, breath steady. "Told you what would happen if you kept pretending you belonged here."

She didn't respond. Spireglass swung up just in time to deflect another low cut. He was aiming for her leg, trying to drop her. She met his gaze through the heat shimmer, vision blurred by sweat and smoke. His eyes burned with cruel intentions.

And gods, he was strong.

Stronger than she remembered.

Her foot slipped on a patch of slag, and that hesitation cost her. Ceravolt cracked hard against her outer thigh, and pain screamed up through the muscle. Her leg buckled. She dropped to one knee.

Flicker roared, tiny but furious. A Flicker-shield burst between them at the last second, enough to buy her a breath.

Gideon's voice roared behind her. "Cassara!"

She twisted, just in time to see him breaking through the outer flank, but Jonas stepped in to intercept, his behemoth slamming the ground causing a seismic shock to ripple outward. Dust clouded the gap as a wall of stone rose to stand between her and help.

Julian didn't even look.

He drove her back again with a high cut that forced her to roll. Her hands shook as she got back to her feet, dragging Spireglass into position. Her ACS flickered red briefly before returning to orange.

Julian stepped in close, his movements holding the same grace she remembered from court dances—controlled, purposeful, inevitable. The volcanic heat distorted his features into something both familiar and monstrous.

"You were never going to last, Cass."

She swung wide, wild, reckless, Spireglass carving a desperate arc through sulfur-thick air. But he caught her wrist with ease.

She grimaced, his grip biting hard enough to grind bone, finding every tender spot from their earlier exchanges. His thumb pressed against her pulse point, feeling her racing heartbeat with the same intimacy he'd once used to comfort. But this wasn't comfort.

This was domination.

He shoved her back with casual violence, her boots skidding across obsidian glass. Ceravolt rose again, its edge catching volcanic light like blood on gold. His wyvern circled above, patient as an executioner.

Flicker darted in, streaking across Julian's line of sight, a living flashbang that painted wild shadows across the volcanic stone. Just enough distraction for Cassara to drop low, muscles screaming, and sweep Spireglass upward in a desperate parry.

The hit connected, finally, her blade glancing across his ACS rig with a shriek of metal on metal. Satisfaction flared for half a heartbeat before the cost became clear.

He punched her. Not with his weapon, not with any trained technique. Just a clean, hard fist driven into her ribs with all his considerable strength behind it.

The world whited out. She collapsed to one hand, knees hitting sharp volcanic stone hard enough to tear through reinforced fabric. Her lungs refused to work properly, each breath a ragged gasp that tasted of copper and sulfur. Her vision tunneled in and out, darkness creeping at the edges like the arena itself was swallowing her whole.

Flicker's voice brushed her mind again, fragmented and frightened, the bond flaring between them like a lifeline.

Cassara... please...

Blood dripped onto black stone, sizzling slightly in the ambient heat. Hers, she realized distantly. From her split lip, from her scraped palms, from a dozen other wounds she couldn't catalog.

She pushed up to her knees, arms shaking from the strain. Wiped the blood from her mouth with the back of one trembling hand. She blinked the sweat and worse from her eyes until the world steadied into cruel focus.

Julian stood above her, not even breathing hard, completely composed, and wearing that particular smirk she'd once found charming. The one that said he'd already won and was just enjoying the process of proving it.

"You should've taken the easy path," he said, Ceravolt's point drifting down to hover near her throat. Not quite touching, not yet. He wanted her to feel the threat of it first. "Marriage. Security. A life of comfort at my side. You should've stayed mine."

Her gaze burned up at him through tangled hair and blood and fury. Every breath was agony. Her ACS screamed warnings she couldn't process.

Despite the throbbing pain that made thinking difficult, the gasping breaths that barely brought the required oxygen needed to function,

She smiled.

Just a little. A bare curve of bloodied lips.

"I was never yours, Julian, and I never will be."

His smirk faltered, just for a second, a crack in his perfect composure that revealed an undeniable darkness underneath. His grip on Ceravolt tightened until his knuckles went white.

For a heartbeat, that silence between them held, thick, volatile, waiting to break.

And then it did.

A low groan split the air beneath her, the kind that vibrated up through bone. Her ears rang, not from a strike, but from the way the ground buckled under her feet. A tremor tore across the battlefield like something massive exhaling below the surface.

Cassara staggered to her feet, Spireglass shaking in her grip, as the obsidian ridge ahead of her split with a hiss of steam and light. It was too close and moving too fast. Her footing slipped on the freshly scorched stone, and she nearly lost her balance entirely.

A pulse through her ACS—stability compromised. She didn't need the readout to know. Her whole body already felt like it was vibrating apart.

"Ridge collapse, south side," Oliver's voice broke over the comms, crackling with static. "It's not holding,"

She couldn't even respond.

Heat bloomed behind her. She turned, too late, just in time to see a streak of gold carve a burning line across the arena. Pellia and her basilisk, its coils searing glowing scars through the terrain, had turned open ground into a no-man's-land of molten traps.

Behind you, don't stop, Flicker's voice pulsed into her mind, choppy with strain. The bond shimmered like stretched glass, too thin to hold for long.

She tried to cut left.

Jonas was there, his behemoth hammering down again, raising another jut of stone like a closing gate. Cassara caught a glimpse of Rett's silhouette, trapped on the far side of the barrier, mouth moving but she couldn't hear what he said.

They were splitting them. Herding them like prey.

Her lungs burned.

"Stay with me," she rasped, to Flicker, to herself, to whatever part of her was still upright.

I'm here.

"Cass, shift back, north line's thinning," Gideon's voice, but it was distant, barely cutting through the distortion.

She pivoted, staggered up a slope, only to be met by Vash's shimmer-threads coiling like vines across the open path. The threads pulsed through the haze, catching at her vision, distorting the heat. They weren't even attacking her anymore. They were controlling her and using her to control the rest.

They want to break you. Don't let them.

Another flare from the wyvern swept low across the field. The wind hit her first, dry, pressurized, tinged with ozone. Then the scream of air tore past her ears, forcing her to duck. Dust and ash exploded into her face. She coughed hard, one knee slamming into the ground.

Flicker pressed against her shoulder, whining low. His body was hot, too hot, and flickering again, his glow unstable and stuttering like a candle caught in a crosswind.

She reached for the bond, but her thoughts wouldn't focus.

They were scattered, just like her team.

Liri's illusions shimmered somewhere off to her right. Oliver's voice was gone. Rett hadn't come back into view. Everything was moving, fire, stone, noise, and she was stuck here, bruised and breathless, like the slowest link in a chain about to snap.

She tried to stand. Her thigh screamed. A warning flashed, sync instability—elevated stress response.

Cassara exhaled sharp through her teeth.

"I can still fight," she muttered. The words didn't come out steady. Didn't come out strong. But they came out.

No one answered.

She couldn't see Gideon through the smoke now, but she knew he was trying. He'd try, no matter how impossible the odds were. That's who he was.

But she'd made herself the weakness.

She'd let Julian get in her head. Let the heat and the weight and the words dig in like hooks.

She forced herself upright. Her knees threatened to give. Flicker's glow was frantic now, rippling in jittery pulses across his fur.

You're going too far, he whispered. *I'm here, but I can't reach you when you pull away.*

"Don't do that," she whispered. "Don't panic. I've got it."

She didn't and knew it.

And that made something in her twist, burning with shame and fury and something colder beneath it.

The thought rose before she could stop it—

If I push harder, if I just stop caring how this ends, maybe I can take him down with me.

Flicker flinched, his mental voice shrinking. *Please don't think that. Please.*

A tremor rocked the ledge beneath her again, and she gripped her glaive tighter.

The team was unraveling and it was her fault.

Another tremor. Bigger this time. The ledge beneath her cracked wide open.

Cassara barely jumped in time, Spireglass flashing downward to anchor herself on the next shelf, landing hard on her already-bruised thigh. Pain lanced through her side. She bit down on a cry, gasping, grinding her teeth against the taste of ash and blood.

She couldn't hear her team anymore. Their voices were lost in the cacophony of battle. The crackling of lava fissures opening like hungry mouths. The screech of Julian's wyvern wings cutting through sulfurous air.

The realization settled over her—she was alone.

And Julian was coming back.

His silhouette emerged through the smoke again, moving with that same predatory grace she'd once mistaken for elegance. Each step was measured, deliberate, a hunter who knew his prey was cornered. Ceravolt hummed in his grip, that deep resonance vibrating through the obsidian beneath their feet.

Cassara staggered upright, the world tilting dangerously before settling into a narrow tunnel of focus. Her ACS pulsed another warning against her wrist, orange bleeding into red again, the crystal heating enough to burn. The readings were clear—too high, unstable, approaching critical failure.

She didn't care.

Her breath hitched in her chest, short, painful gasps that never brought enough air. Still, she raised Spireglass with arms that trembled from more than exhaustion. Her grip was too tight, knuckles white beneath torn gloves. Her legs felt like water, muscles screaming from a dozen near-misses. The glaive's weight, usually perfect in her hands, now felt like she was trying to lift the world.

And still she stood.

Flicker darted forward, placing his small body between her and Julian's advance. His transformed state flickered like a dying flame, silver to gold to white and back again, fur rippling with unstable magic. Too much power channeling through too small a frame.

Stop. His voice brushed her mind, fragmented with desperation. *Please stop. You're breaking us.*

"I'm fine." The words came out cracked.

You're not. His mental voice was raw now, each word edged with pain that might have been hers or his or both. *You don't trust me. You still think you have to do this alone.*

The truth of it hit harder than Julian's blade ever could.

Because he was right. Even now, even bonded, even with Oliver's crystals creating perfect synchronization, she was still fighting like she always had. Alone. Carrying everything on breaking shoulders because trusting meant vulnerability and vulnerability meant—

Ceravolt arced through the air with deadly beauty. She brought Spireglass up just in time, but her body lagged a breath behind her intentions. The impact sent shockwaves through her arms. Sparks exploded across the mirrored surface in a shower of silver and gold. She staggered backward, boots sliding on stone made slick with her own sweat and blood.

Her heel caught on a ridge of cooled lava. The world tilted.

Cassara.

Flicker's voice rang in her head, not loud like his earlier pleas, not commanding like Gideon's orders. Just... there. Small, steady and certain.

I'm not enough when you shut me out. But I can be, if you let me.

Everything stopped. Just for a moment.

The world crystallized into perfect clarity. Julian raising his blade again, eyes cold with certainty. The volcanic arena with its rivers of fire and falling ash. Her team fighting their own battles in the distance, trusting her to hold her ground.

But she didn't look at any of it.

She looked at Flicker.

At the trembling creature who'd never once abandoned her. Who had asked to stay when she tried to push him away in those first bitter days. Who had chosen her, again and again, no matter how furious she'd been at his size, how afraid of their bond, how desperately she'd tried to close herself off from another disappointment.

Who was here now, small and fierce and undeniably hers, trying to shield her with a body that could barely cast a shadow.

And she realized.

He wasn't the weak one.

She was.

Cassara closed her eyes. The words rose from somewhere deeper than thought, deeper than strategy or pride or fear.

“I trust you,” she said.

CHAPTER FORTY TWO

It wasn't shouted across the battlefield like a war cry. It didn't need to be. The bond flared the moment the words left her lips, not just bright like before, but clean. Pure. Like every barrier she'd built between them simply... dissolved.

Flicker surged forward with a sound like cracking light, like dawn breaking, like every star igniting at once.

And then the heat changed.

The flare that erupted from his form wasn't the orange of common flame. It wasn't the gold of ordinary power.

It was white.

Blinding, searing, and beautiful.

Cassara stumbled backward, one arm thrown up to shield her eyes as her bond ignited with power that didn't rage or burn wild—it sang. The pulse in her ACS turned deep sapphire blue in an instant, stabilizing with a crystalline chime she'd never heard before. The readings didn't just settle, they soared past every limit she'd thought they had, into ranges that shouldn't exist for a C-rank bond.

Through the brilliance, she watched Flicker transform.

His body elongated, small form stretching into something elegant. Fire trailed from his limbs like feathers caught in an eternal wind, each one a perfect blend of silver mirror-light and white-hot flame. Wings unfurled from his back, not physical things but the impressions of wings, suggestions of flight made from pure energy.

His eyes opened, and they were molten gold, ancient and knowing. When he moved, his form shimmered with mirrored heat that turned the very air around him into a weapon.

Julian's forward momentum faltered, his perfect composure cracking as his wyvern banked hard to avoid the sudden wave of transformative heat.

Flicker flew.

Not the darting, desperate movements of before. Not the hovering uncertainty of partial transformation. He flew like he'd been born to it, arcing above her in a spiral of brilliant light. Where he passed, the air itself ignited, leaving contrails of flame that hung suspended like frozen fireworks. He landed beside her with perfect grace, and the sound that emerged from his throat wasn't the chirp of a small beast.

It was a low, rising note that sounded like crystal singing, like swords being drawn, like the universe acknowledging what they'd become together.

Cassara could hardly breathe—not from exhaustion, but from awe.

She raised Spireglass again, and the weapon responded instantly. The mirrored blade didn't just reflect light. It multiplied it, creating dozens of ghostly echoes that trailed her movements, syncing seamlessly with this new form. When she shifted her stance, the afterimages followed a heartbeat behind, each one perfectly synchronized, turning single movements into an army of possibilities.

When she moved, she didn't just step forward.

She glided.

Julian came for her again, because what else could he do? His perfect plan unraveling, his certain victory suddenly uncertain.

He lunged with every ounce of strength he possessed.

Cassara met him with something better than strength.

She met him with trust made manifest.

Their blades collided, Spireglass against Ceravolt, and this time, she didn't stagger. The mirrored surface of her weapon flared with trailing echoes, throwing off afterimages as she pivoted on the balls of her feet. Julian slashed downward in a clean arc—

—and hit nothing.

Her body flickered a half-step sideways, shifting into the opening he hadn't seen coming. Spireglass sliced upward in a vicious curve, catching his shoulder and biting through the outer plating.

He hissed and stumbled back, eyes narrowing.

"Cute trick," he spat.

Cassara didn't answer, Flicker was already in motion.

He tore across the field in his enhanced form, wings arcing wide. Every pass he made disrupted the Dawnpierce formation, his presence too fast and too unpredictable for them to track cleanly.

Dawnpierce's secondary support, Maurelle turned, shield raised, but Flicker's wing swept wide and sent a flashburst of mirrored fire across her line. Her cervidra reared back, antlers refracting the blast, but the illusionary doubles broke apart under the flare.

Cassara didn't waste the opportunity.

"Rett—now!"

Rett moved, Gravemaul flaring with synced power. Skelli, howled alongside him, and they surged forward, smashing into the disrupted line. Jonas attempted to intercept, but his behemoth was too slow. Rett's hammer struck first, causing a seismic shockwave.

It was a direct hit.

Stone cracked and pressure vented as the front line shuddered.

Above them, Gideon launched Vangal into a downward spiral, the griffin letting out a scream of thunder as he finally broke through Vash's interference field.

"Back in position," Gideon announced, dropping down beside Cassara.

"You took your time," she shot back, breath ragged but steady.

His mouth twitched, almost a smile.

They didn't need more words.

Oliver reappeared from cover near a slag outcrop, his crossbow Shadepiercer already loaded. The field was his now, the terrain, angles, movement patterns—he'd tracked them all.

"I've got two locking beacons," he called. "Northwest and inner ring. We take the center—Julian can't recover the spread."

Cassara nodded. "Flicker?"

Flicker answered with a shriek that sounded like her name. He shot upward in a flare of color and slammed into Julian's wyvern mid-dive, throwing it off trajectory.

Cassara sprinted forward. Her body moved in sync with the battlefield now, not the desperate scrambling of before, but something deeper. Each footfall found perfect purchase on cracked obsidian, every breath flowing into the next like she'd been born to this rhythm. The chaos of volcanic fury and clashing weapons became a symphony she finally knew how to conduct. When she raised Spireglass, the gesture wasn't defensive anymore, wasn't reactive.

It was command.

And her team responded.

They moved with her like extensions of a single will. Barrett broke through the worst of the debris field, Gravemaul creating controlled quakes that opened paths where none existed before. Skelli darted ahead, blade-spines catching light as he carved through enemy formations.

Liri floated in his wake, her injuries forgotten in the heat of synchronized purpose. Nym had grown in size, massive wings casting prismatic illusions that rippled across the battlefield—false paths, phantom fighters, mirages that made Oliver's carefully laid traps invisible until they snapped shut.

Oliver himself had become the battlefield's hidden architect. His crossbow sang its quiet song, bolts phasing through solid matter to mark targets, create openings, layer the volcanic stone with runes that would activate at precisely the wrong moment for their enemies. Ilza flickered at the edges of perception, there and gone, disrupting sight lines.

Gideon locked down the right flank like he'd been forged for it. Vangal dove again and again, predatory precision in every strike, forcing Pellia and her basilisk toward the dead zones Oliver had mapped. Each movement was calculated, brutal in its simplicity, denying space, controlling options, being inevitable.

And Cassara—

She reached the central beacon first.

The platform hung suspended over bubbling lava, accessible only by narrow stone bridges that creaked with every tremor. But she didn't hesitate. Flicker soared beside her, wings of white fire turning falling ash to glittering snow. Together they crossed the final gap in a leap that should have been impossible—but wasn't, not anymore.

She slammed her palm against the core glyph with enough force to crack stone.

The platform erupted in light beneath her boots. Runes raced outward in spiraling patterns, claiming the space with absolute authority.

Blue light. Crystal clear. The floating displays throughout the arena flashed with updated information:

Auric Vow—Dominant Control

A chime rang out across the battlefield.

Julian's boots hit charred ground hard as he broke through the smoke screen Oliver had laid. His perfect composure was gone now, replaced by something rawer. Ash clung to his formerly immaculate coat, spiraling around him like the ghost of his certainty. Blood ran from a cut above his eye. His breathing came harsh, angry.

"You think this changes anything?" His voice cracked on the last word, hoarse from smoke and fury, but the sneer somehow remained intact. His hand found Ceravolt's hilt again, knuckles white. "A few lucky hits and a glowing thing don't make you strong, Cassara. They make you desperate. They make you loud."

The old Cassara would have risen to the bait, would have spat words back like weapons. But she wasn't that girl anymore. Her hands were steady on Spireglass now, the trembling exhaustion replaced by something deeper than muscle memory.

The glaive shimmered, each subtle movement leaving afterimages that made it impossible to track exactly where the blade ended and the air began.

Julian began to circle, boots grinding against volcanic glass. His expression had hardened into something she'd never seen before, not the casual cruelty or possessive charm, but genuine fury at being denied.

"You only mattered when you stood beside me." The words came out like accusations, each one meant to cut. "Without that, you're just another noble daughter playing at strength. Another disappointment to a legacy you'll never—"

Her ACS glowed on her wrist, not the chaotic red of before, not even the standard blue of stability. It had shifted to something deeper, cooler, like looking at the ocean from impossible depths. Flicker's wings spread above them both, silent and patient as death, each feather a tongue of white flame that cast no shadows.

Cassara's eyes never left Julian's. When she spoke, her voice carried across the arena with perfect clarity.

"I mattered long before you... and I'll matter long after."

Something in Julian's face cracked like the volcanic stone beneath their feet. His carefully constructed superiority shattered into something ugly and desperate. The snarl that twisted his features belonged on a beast, not a man.

He leapt, weapon raised.

She moved to meet him, and this time there was no hesitation in it.

Their blades collided in an explosion of sparks that put the volcano's fury to shame. Ceravolt's brutal arc met Spireglass's flowing defense. He fought like he always had, fast strikes meant to overwhelm, punishing blows designed to break guards, relentless pressure that had won him dozens of matches. His training showed in every movement, years of the finest instructors money could buy teaching him to fight with aristocratic brutality.

He aimed high, trying to use his height advantage. When she deflected, he reversed into a low sweep meant to knock her off-balance. When she danced away, he pressed forward with strike after strike, trying to pin her against the platform's edge where the lava waited below.

But she didn't stumble. Not anymore.

Instead, she shifted her weight like water finding its course, letting his momentum pass through the space where she'd been. Her body twisted, Spireglass spinning in her grip. The world blurred for half a heartbeat as she slipped through space itself, emerging at his exposed flank.

Her strike was poetry. The glaive's edge traced a perfect line across the outer layer of his ACS chest plate.

He growled, an animal sound of pure frustration, and spun to face her.

"You don't belong out here." His next series of strikes came faster, wilder, technique crumbling into rage. "You never did. This was supposed to be—"

She didn't let him finish. Their weapons locked again, Ceravolt's lance form grinding against Spireglass's mirrored edge. The proximity brought them close enough that she could see the desperation in his eyes, smell the acrid mix of sweat and blood and smoke that clung to them both.

"Is this about the betrothal?" he hissed, leaning his weight into the lock, trying to overpower her through sheer force. "Still clinging to the pathetic fantasy that you get to choose? That you get to refuse what's already been decided?"

Her response was quiet, delivered with the same certainty she'd found in trusting Flicker.

"I already chose."

And she drove her knee into his gut with all the force her position allowed.

The air left Julian's lungs in a whoosh. His grip on Ceravolt faltered, strength failing as his diaphragm spasmed. Cassara twisted Spireglass with precise violence, using his own weapon's weight against him, and shoved. Hard.

He staggered backward, coughing, barely managing to keep his weapon up. But she was already moving, pressing the advantage. Each strike targeted a weakness, a gap in his guard here, an over-extension there. She wasn't fighting to survive anymore.

She was fighting to win.

"You were mine!" The words tore from his throat, raw and ugly. His final attacks were wild things, all training abandoned for desperate fury. Ceravolt whistled through the air in patterns that made no tactical sense, just trying to land something, anything.

Cassara didn't flinch.

"You can't own what you're too weak to hold."

One perfect parry sent him stumbling. A riposte opened another line across his armor. Step by step, strike by strike, she drove him back.

Her final blow came from above.

She jumped, not the desperate leap of a cornered animal, but something planned and perfect. Flicker surged upward with her, their bond singing between them. His wings caught her weight, adding lift and momentum that turned a simple attack into something transcendent. For a moment, she hung suspended above the battlefield, Spireglass raised high, the glaive's surface reflecting every tongue of flame in the arena until it seemed she held a star.

Julian raised Ceravolt to block—

He was too slow.

Cassara's blade came down like judgment itself. The impact was catastrophic. Ceravolt flew from nerveless fingers, the weapon's final cry lost in the sound of Julian hitting stone. She followed through, letting gravity and momentum drive him into the platform with enough force to crack the obsidian beneath him.

The crater smoked. Julian lay at its center, gasping, eyes wide with shock.

He didn't get up.

Ceravolt clattered across stone, coming to rest just out of reach of his trembling hand. Above them, every display in the arena flashed the same message—

Victory—Auric Vow

The match was over.

Cassara stood over him, chest heaving with exertion that felt clean now instead of desperate. Blood had dried on her knuckles, and a dozen other wounds made themselves known in the sudden stillness. But she was standing. Victorious.

As she looked down at Julian, he stared back up at her, meeting his stunned gaze with eyes that held no triumph, no gloating. Just a simmering rage she was certain she hadn't seen the last of.

She didn't need to say anything else. Didn't need to twist the knife of his defeat. The message was clear in every line of her body, in the way Flicker landed beside her with ethereal grace, in the blue glow of her perfectly synchronized ACS.

She'd already won everything that mattered.

So she turned her back on Julian, on everything he represented, every chain he'd tried to wrap around her future, and walked away.

The battle haze hadn't lifted. Her pulse still crashed like thunder, Spireglass still warm in her grip. She was searching for her team, eyes catching on Liri's silhouette ahead.

Liri spotted her and began rushing towards her.

"Cassara! We won—"

The ground cracked open with a sound like the sky collapsing.

"Liri!"

A cloud of ash and brimstone belched upward as the cliffside ruptured, sending molten rock and debris crashing down the incline.

Liri had been sprinting toward them.

Now she was gone.

"No—" Rett's scream tore through the smoke. "LIRI!"

He didn't hesitate. He charged, sprinting down the crumbling slope, ignoring the falling slag and shifting ground. "LIRI!" he bellowed again, dropping to his knees where the earth still groaned.

Cassara stumbled after him. "She was right here—"

"I saw her," Oliver said, breath catching as he caught up, yanking out his Codex. "I saw her run— she—she didn't make it past the edge."

"Help me dig!" Rett roared, his voice breaking. His hands were already bloodied from wrenching rocks aside. "She's under here—she has to be—!"

"I'm scanning—just—give me a second—" Oliver's voice trembled, fingers flying across the Codex interface. "Pulse is weak. One signature, dim, flickering. Nym is still active but fading-"

Cassara dropped beside them, hands clawing through heat and grit. Her gloves tore. She didn't stop. "Flicker please—!"

He swept low overhead, shrieking, then dove, fanning his wings wide in a flash of shimmering pressure. The blast blew loose dust and debris off the pile, revealing a jagged basin of collapsed stone.

Rett didn't wait. He tore at it with raw hands.

"Come on, come on," Cassara chanted under her breath. Her throat burned. "Liri, answer me."

Then she saw it.

A pulse, soft at first, but glowing brighter.

The air shivered with radiant energy, like a dropped lantern flickering to life, and from within the wreckage, light burst outward in a bloom of color. Warm golds and violets crackling around a small, contained shield of woven light.

The cocoon shattered outward like breaking glass.

Liri lay curled inside, her arm twisted unnaturally at the elbow, but breathing. Nym hovered over her chest, its wings tattered but glowing, thin streams of protective magic still trailing from its body like silk threads.

"Liri!" Cassara gasped, heart stuttering.

Rett got to her first and dropped to his knees, his hands cupping her dirt-streaked face. "Hey. Hey, it's me. You're okay. You're okay now."

Liri blinked up at him, dazed. "Ow."

A broken, breathless laugh escaped Rett. He leaned his forehead against hers. "Don't you ever do that again."

"I didn't try to get buried under a mountain." Her voice wobbled. "But… I think my bug got braver."

Oliver crouched beside them, stunned. "She cocooned you. Your sparkfly, she shielded you instinctively. That's… new. That's not recorded behavior."

Cassara exhaled shakily. "It saved her."

Liri smiled faintly, tears tracing through ash on her cheek. "Guess she finally leveled up."

CHAPTER FORTY THREE

It was late evening and the halls were quiet save for the distant chimes marking the quarter hour. It was the kind of hush that settled over the academy once training concluded and mess tables began to fill.

Cassara moved slowly, each step a careful negotiation with muscles that screamed in protest. The edge of her coat brushed her legs, heavy wool catching on the gauze bandage wrapped around her left knee. Every breath pulled at ribs that hadn't quite forgiven Julian's fist.

She hadn't planned to stay with Liri all day, but the girl's determined brightness, joking through obvious pain—insisting her broken arm gave her "character"—had kept her from tending to her own obligations. And truthfully, resting in that cushioned chair beside the hospital bed had been nicer than she'd ever admit.

The archway ahead opened toward the dining hall, warm light and voices spilling out like honey. The scent of roasted meat and fresh bread made her stomach clench with hunger she hadn't noticed until now. She angled to skirt past it, quiet, unnoticed, just another shadow in the evening routine.

"Cassara."

She didn't turn to see who had called to her, instead she kept walking. Maybe if she pretended not to hear he would get the point and leave her alone.

Wishful thinking at its finest.

The sound of Julian's bootsteps trailed after her, a second set joining a moment later. Heavier, which meant Jonas. Finally a third, lighter but no less purposeful. Vash, she assumed. After a few seconds the steps tapered off and she chanced a glance over her shoulder.

There was no sign of them, no sign of anyone actually, but that did little to quell the feeling of unease that settled over her.

Rounding the corner, she stopped short when she caught sight of Julian leaning against the stone with studied nonchalance. Jonas stood to his left, massive arms crossed over a chest that could stop a charging beast.

Where was Vash?

She didn't have to wonder long, sensing him as he came up behind her to block any chance of retreat.

"You're limping," Julian observed, pushing off from the wall and stepping towards her. "I came to check on you earlier, but you were nowhere to be found."

She refused to give him the satisfaction of an answer.

"We all went a little hard in the arena." He continued as if her silence was an invitation, his voice sliding into that careful lilt he used when trying to turn fault into flattery. "Emotions were high. The stakes... well, we both know what was riding on that match. I may have overreacted."

She tried to move past him but he stepped with her, a dance they'd performed too many times before. But where once she might have found it charming, the focused attention and the refusal to be ignored, now it just made her sick.

"I'm trying to be decent here," he added, and something harder crept into his tone. Like his generosity was a gift she was foolish to refuse. "I shouldn't have hit you that hard. It was beneath me."

Cassara's gaze flicked up, meeting his for the first time. In the magelight, his eyes looked like chips of winter sky—beautiful and absolutely empty of warmth.

"You hit me because you were losing."

Julian blinked, the mask cracking to show the danger underneath. "I was provoked."

"Right, my mistake, it's never your fault," she snorted and stepped to the side again. He followed, persistent as a shadow.

"I'm being reasonable," he said, and his voice had dropped to that dangerous register she knew too well. The tone that preceded broken things and bruised hearts. "More reasonable than you deserve, considering how you've been acting. You don't want to make this worse, Cass."

The nickname was deliberate. Possessive. A reminder of intimacies she'd rather forget.

He reached for her face, fingers gentle, like they hadn't once curled into fists against her ribs, like they hadn't gripped her wrist hard enough to leave marks. The gesture was so tender, so careful, it might have fooled someone who didn't know better.

Cassara slapped his hand away.

The sound cracked through the corridor like a whip. For a moment, the only sound was her heightened breathing and the distant clatter of dishes from the dining hall.

Julian's face went very still. Behind him, she caught Jonas shifting his weight, preparing.

For what, she wasn't sure.

"That," Julian said softly, "was a mistake."

Jonas and Vash moved fast—faster than men their size should manage. She'd half-turned to run when hands gripped her arms from behind, Jonas's massive paw engulfing her right bicep while Vash's fingers found pressure points with surgical precision. Not hard enough to bruise, not yet, but enough to make it clear that struggling would change that quickly.

Her heart spiked so hard she felt it in her throat. Flicker stirred beneath her skin, heat building, but she forced him down. Not here. Not yet. Not when they were three on one and she was already injured.

Julian stepped closer.

His smile was a brittle thing, all edges and no warmth.

"You think you're above me now?" he murmured, voice pitched for her ears alone. One hand came up, hovering near her face without quite touching. "Think that beast of yours makes you untouchable? That little display in the arena changed anything?"

She didn't answer. Her silence wasn't submission, it was the fuse burning short, the calm before lightning struck. She felt Flicker pacing, eager to show Julian exactly what her 'little beast' could do.

Julian leaned in closer, his breath warm against her cheek.

"You keep acting like this, like you're not mine anymore, and I'll remind you how quickly I can break what you care about." His lips curved in something too sharp to be a smile. "Starting with the little cute one. What's her name again?"

A pause. His eyes glittered with malicious delight.

"Liri, was it?"

Cassara's blood turned molten. Every injury, every ache, every careful breath disappeared beneath the roar of protective fury.

Julian's grin widened, sharp and gleaming as a blade. "Cute thing like her wouldn't last long if something unfortunate happened. A fall down the stairs. Complications from that broken arm. These healing potions can be so tricky... one wrong ingredient..." He shrugged, elegant and casual. "And no one would question it."

The threat hung between them like a physical thing. Not just words, but a promise. Julian had resources, connections, the kind of power that made accidents easy to arrange and they both knew it.

"At it again, Tremaine?"

Gideon's voice came from behind them, cool and measured.

Jonas and Vash froze first, trained instincts recognizing danger. Julian's grin didn't falter, but his jaw ticked, a tell she'd learned to read years ago. Slowly, deliberately, making it clear this was his choice, he turned.

Gideon stood just beyond the archway's curve. His stance was quiet command, feet planted and shoulders set, and his eyes—his eyes looked like slate about to crack.

"I'm starting to wonder if I'm just not hitting you hard enough," Gideon continued, stepping forward, "I suggest you take your hands off her."

For one breath, no one moved, all of them waiting to see which way the violence would tilt. Finally, Jonas let go. Just like that, the massive hand disappeared from her arm. Vash followed a heartbeat later, gaze flicking toward Julian for confirmation he didn't give.

Cowards without orders. Just like always.

Cassara exhaled and stepped back. Her arms ached where they'd gripped her, phantom pressure that would become bruises by morning.

Julian's eyes narrowed, but his smile remained. "Careful, Delvanir. You keep stepping in where you're not wanted. Playing hero doesn't suit you."

"I don't care what you want." Gideon came to stand between them, cutting a clean line through the tension. Not quite touching Cassara, but close enough that she felt the heat of him, the solid presence that made her bruised ribs ease their grip on her lungs. "You make another threat like that? Especially to someone on my team? And I'll make sure you never set foot in another ranked match again."

Julian laughed. "You think Headmistress Kalisandra would believe anything you say? A disgraced family's last son, spreading lies about—"

"She won't have to." Gideon's interruption was soft, which somehow made it worse. "You've been sloppy, Tremaine. Too many eyes. Too many ears. Even your allies are getting tired of you."

Julian's smile finally slipped.

"And if you ever lay hands on Cassara again," Gideon added, stepping closer, voice dropping so low Julian had to lean in to hear it, "I won't report you."

Julian looked confused.

"I'll handle it myself."

For once, Julian Tremaine, master manipulator, silver-tongued prince of the upper ranks, had nothing clever to say. His mouth opened, closed, opened again. Behind him, Jonas took another step back.

Gideon didn't wait for a response. He turned to Cassara, and the transformation was immediate. The ice in his eyes thawed to concern, gaze flicking over her in quick assessment, checking and confirming, all without a word.

"You alright?" he asked, softer now. Private. Just for her.

She nodded, not trusting her voice to adequately mask the emotions warring within her.

Behind them Julian was already walking away, but the silence he left in his wake wasn't victory. It was a warning.

Cassara met Gideon's gaze and straightened.

"You didn't have to do that," she said, the moment the hallway turned empty. Her heel twisted on the polished stone as she turned to face him, voice low but sharp, each word edged with something more complex than anger. "You didn't have to step in like that."

Gideon blinked, confusion replacing the protective fury that had carried him through the confrontation. A frown pulled at his mouth. "He had you cornered. Three on one, Cassara. Jonas had his hands on you. Was I supposed to just ignore it?"

"I had it under control."

His eyes searched hers looking for something she couldn't give him. "Did you?"

That was enough to light the fuse. All the frustration, the guilt, the impossible weight of wants she couldn't voice, it all ignited at once. She shoved past him, shoulder checking harder than necessary, voice rising despite the empty corridor.

"This is exactly the problem, Gideon. You get to swoop in. You get to make threats and stand tall and look good doing it." The words tumbled free without her consent, as though her heart had finally had enough. "You get to be the hero in broad daylight while—"

She cut off, chest heaving, hands clenched into fists at her sides. The rest of it stuck in her throat. *While Auren hides in the shadows, while he pushes me away because he can't give me this.*

"I'm the one who has to live in the fallout," she finished instead, voice cracking on the last word. "You have no idea what this costs me."

"You're right, I don't, but I'm not sorry I stopped him." Gideon's words were simple and direct.

"I know," she bit out, and gods help her, that was the worst part. "That's what makes it worse."

He stepped forward, carefully, deliberately, the way one might when approaching something wounded but dangerous.

"Is this still about the kiss?"

She flinched, just slightly, just a tightening around her eyes and a catch in her breath. But it was enough for him to see, enough for understanding to dawn in his expression.

He exhaled, long and slow, like he was releasing something he'd been holding. "Cassara, if that's what this is, if I made you feel like you didn't have a choice—"

"No," she interrupted quickly, desperate to stop him from apologizing for the one thing that had felt like a choice in weeks.

"I won't apologize for wanting you." His gaze didn't waver. If anything, it softened, which was infinitely worse. "But I will for how I acted. I shouldn't have done that, not then, not like that. Not when you were vulnerable."

There was no guile in his tone. No dramatics, no grand gestures. Just quiet regret and beneath it a steadiness she realized she craved.

Cassara's throat closed around her next breath. Because he meant it. Every word. And that made it so much worse.

She didn't want to be grateful for his restraint. Didn't want to notice how he kept exactly one step between them, close enough to show he wasn't running, far enough to give her space. She didn't want to feel safer near him than she ever had with—

No. She couldn't think about that. Couldn't compare them when one was here, solid and real and offering apologies she didn't ask for, while the other was smoke and secrets and promises made in darkness.

So she did the one thing she hadn't let herself do since that night. The thing that had haunted her through injured midnights and complicated mornings.

She stepped forward and kissed him.

Not out of gratitude but because she needed to know if it had been real. If the fire she'd felt had been winter magic and loneliness, or something far more dangerous.

The moment their mouths met, she had her answer.

It was fire all over again. The same heat that had consumed her by the hearth, the same ache that had followed her through weeks of careful distance. Not fumbled or uncertain but real in a way that made her bones ache.

His surprise lasted half a heartbeat before he responded, and oh, that was worse. The careful way he kissed her back, like she was something breakable. She felt his hand come up, fingers curling just behind her jaw, the touch tentative as if afraid she might vanish if he held too tight.

And maybe she would.

Because even as her body sang with the rightness of it, her mind screamed with all the reasons this was wrong. Auren's sad eyes. His noble rejection. His confidence that he couldn't give her what she deserved—daylight and certainty and a hand to hold without checking for witnesses first.

And here was Gideon, offering exactly that. Threatening Julian in public corridors. Standing between her and danger without thought for consequences. Kissing her like she was worth any consequence.

It was everything Auren swore he couldn't give.

It was exactly why Auren was pushing her away.

The thought left her breathless, and she broke the kiss with a gasp. Her hands were curled in his shirt—when had that happened? His eyes were dark, pupils blown wide, and his thumb traced the edge of her jaw with devastating gentleness.

For a moment, they just breathed together, foreheads almost touching, sharing air and heat and dangerous possibilities.

Then Cassara pulled away, heart jackknifing against her ribs, pulse ragged as any arena battle. Her voice was already forming the lie before she could stop it, the words automatic as breathing.

"That was a mistake."

She saw him flinch, but he didn't reach for her, didn't try to argue. Just watched with those dark eyes that saw too much as she backed away.

"Cassara—"

"I have to go." The words came out strangled. "I just—I have to go."

She didn't wait for his reply. Didn't look back as she turned and walked away when what she really wanted to do was run. Behind her, she felt the weight of his gaze, the questions she couldn't answer, the want she couldn't afford.

Her lips still tingled. Her jaw still felt the ghost of his fingers.

And somewhere in the academy, Auren was probably staring at reports and telling himself he was doing the right thing by letting her go.

She pressed her fingers to her mouth and walked faster.

The storm hadn't stopped in days. Rain drummed steadily against the arched windows of the common room, a dull, relentless rhythm that blurred one hour into the next. The sky outside had forgotten how to be anything but gray, its colorless weight pressing down on the academy.

Their shared space had long since become a battlefield of study scrolls and reference guides, with color-coded tabs sticking out at erratic angles like the horns of some wild creature mid-transformation.

Cassara sat curled on the floor beside the low table, her blouse slightly wrinkled, boots off, hair damp from an earlier sprint across campus. Her beast classification guide rested in her lap, but she'd read the same paragraph three times without absorbing a word.

"Wait, wait—so is the Virethorn technically reptilian or avian?" Liri asked, perched upside down on the couch, legs hooked over the back, curls brushing the floor. "Because I swear it lays eggs, but the tail scales were classified as dermal armor and—ugh, I'm losing it."

"You lost it when you decided to study while hanging upside down," Talia said dryly from her corner. Her braid was half-undone, a sharp contrast to the usually pristine edges of her uniform. "Also, it's reptilian. Avian-class beasts can't channel earth-aligned aether. We went over this."

"I know that!" Liri groaned and flopped fully onto the floor. Nym flitted overhead in lazy loops, occasionally flashing pulses of soft pink that indicated encouragement or pity. "It's the pressure. I don't test well under pressure."

"You test fine," Cassara said, not bothering to look up from her notes. "You just panic before."

"I like that you think there's a difference."

Cassara offered the ghost of a smile, but her mind still drifted, half tethered to the past week, to everything unspoken between her and Gideon. Studying helped and so did Liri's complaints. Even the ridiculous way the Nym was now trying to land on Liri's head like a glowing crown served as a temporary distraction.

Across from her, Talia flipped a page with the precision of someone raised to make very few mistakes. "We've got sixteen hours before finals, and Liri still can't tell the difference between a bronzeplume chimera and a banded razorshrike."

"They both have feathers," Liri muttered into the rug. "That's misleading."

"They also both have talons. Doesn't mean they'll both rip your spleen out the same way."

"I'd like to keep my spleen intact, thank you."

Cassara blinked, surprised by the short laugh that escaped her.

For a moment, the weight eased.

When the door to the general common room swung open with a wet thump Cassara looked up from her notes.

Oliver hesitated on the threshold, dripping from head to toe, his cloak soaked through and plastered to his arms. His hood clung lopsided to his temple like it had given up halfway across campus.

"Hey, Oliver," she called out.

Liri groaned, already collapsing sideways across her cushion. "If he's here to talk about spectral ratios or whatever again, I'm throwing his Codex into the soup cauldron."

Talia didn't look up from her rune sheet, but she snorted softly.

"The lab's warded against rain, not crosswinds," he muttered, brushing water off his sleeves in quick, useless swipes as he joined them. "And I didn't come to talk about ratios."

Cassara blinked at him, then silently pushed a spare towel across the table.

"Thanks," he said, accepting it without protest.

He didn't sit, just stood there a moment, catching his breath like he'd run the whole way, because knowing Oliver, he probably had. And judging by the intensity flickering behind his eyes, he wasn't here to chat.

His eyes skipped past her shoulder to the chaos behind her, taking in the scrolls, the moth, Liri's sprawled position, and the steaming mug someone had left too close to an open book.

"I won't stay long," he said, quietly. "But I ran another simulation on the energy profile from Flicker's transformation. I thought you should see this."

Liri scrambled into a seated position and waved a soggy note card like a white flag. "No equations, please. I beg of you. We're fragile."

Oliver ignored her entirely, already clearing space on the table and pulling out a series of projected glyph charts from his Codex. The shimmering aether script spun midair, elegant and meticulous, if entirely incomprehensible to anyone not obsessed with spell schematics.

Cassara leaned over his shoulder. "Is this the moment his form changed?"

"Right before." Oliver pointed to the spike, a steep climb in the power curve, sharper than any Cassara had seen in normal transformations. "The readings went wild once he absorbed the surrounding elemental energy. Fire. Wind. Even some ambient arcane charge from the arena barrier. It didn't just empower him—it triggered something deeper."

"So it wasn't just instinct," she murmured.

"No. It was opportunity. His magic hit a threshold. The gate opened, and he surged through." Oliver turned slightly toward her, more serious now. "But it didn't last. He burned through the reservoir too fast. And when it dropped? It dropped hard. That's why he's been so quiet."

Cassara glanced toward the corner where Flicker now lay curled on the cushioned bench, half-asleep, his glow a gentle thrum beneath his skin. He still hadn't spoken since that final strike in the arena.

"He hasn't shifted since," she said.

"Good. Don't force it. Not yet." Oliver tapped the bottom of the projection. "He needs stability. Control. If he flares like that again without preparation, the cost could be more than just temporary burnout. We're still figuring out what his core actually is. No other recorded creature has synced this way."

Liri groaned and pulled her blanket over her head. "You're syncing with an unstable elemental miracle and I can't even remember what a Glassen Howler eats."

Talia muttered, "Small rodents and ego."

Oliver blinked at the interruption, clearly confused. Cassara pressed her fingers to her eyes, half a laugh caught in her throat.

"Thanks, Oliver," she said, guiding him back toward the door before Liri summoned another rant about magical unfairness. "We'll be careful."

"You should also consider an energy redirect rune," he added as he headed towards the door. "I'll send you a draft schematic."

Of course he would.

The door clicked shut behind him, and Cassara turned back to the war zone of notes and half-memorized beast lore. Liri had gone still again, the sparkfly gently preening her damp curls.

"So," Liri said, voice muffled, "we're all screwed."

CHAPTER FORTY FOUR

Hours passed and the words on the page began to blur.

Cassara rubbed her forehead, blinking hard, but the sentence still refused to make sense. Some obscure detail about beast-line hybrids and migratory patterns. Useless. Or maybe just unreadable when her mind wouldn't stop pacing.

The magelight in the general common room flickered above their table, casting a tired yellow wash over open books, half-drunk mugs of tea, and Talia's growing tower of flashcards. Liri had given up entirely and was now dramatically draping herself across the bench, mumbling made-up beast names like "Fanged skyfish" and "Spine-tailed truffle weasel" between yawns.

Cassara set her pen down. "I left my field notes in the library," she said, trying to keep it casual.

Talia barely glanced up. "You brought three notebooks and two Codex tabs, how many notes do you need?"

"I need those."

She didn't wait for a retort. Grabbing her coat from the hook, she swept it around her shoulders and stepped out into the hall before either of them could press her further.

Truth was, the notes weren't essential, but the walls were closing in and her patience was hanging by a thread. The storm had been pressing on her temples all day, and the last thing she needed was to keep pretending everything was fine. Especially with Gideon's name etched into her thoughts like a bruise she couldn't rub out.

The corridors were dim, the academy quiet as most students were either buried in study dens or hiding from the storm.

She rounded a corner, heading for the stairwell down to the library, when movement in the rain-cast glass caught her eye.

There, outside.

A lone figure crossing the slick stones of the upper training yard. Tall. Broad-shouldered. Moving with that familiar restraint that always masked something more volatile beneath.

Auren.

He hadn't seen her, of course he hadn't. Hood down, hair soaked, shirt already clinging to his frame like he hadn't cared to stay dry. He moved with quiet purpose, not toward the dormitories, not toward the mess hall or the labs, but the training hall.

The one where they first...

Cassara's fingers curled around the door frame.

She knew she should turn back, get her notes and return to the common room. Instead, determination flared beneath her ribs. Not longing. Not hurt. Something sharper and far more defiant.

She eased the door open and stepped into the rain.

Cassara kept to the shadows along the upper walk and hesitated when she reached the edge of the path. The rain had already soaked through the thin parts of her coat causing her to shiver.

This was stupid. So stupid.

But the ache in her chest refused to subside. It wasn't just about him. It was everything she hadn't been allowed to say.

She moved again, faster this time.

When she finally reached the entrance to the training hall, the storm had picked up again. Thunder cracked across the floating isles above, their glow flickering like lanterns in the clouds. Her palm hovered over the door's handle for just a moment before she willed herself onward.

She pushed the door open and stepped inside.

The warmth hit her first, thick and cloying after the chill the storm had left behind. It carried the metallic tang of expended mana, the salt of exertion, the particular scent that haunted every combat space in the academy.

It didn't take her long to find him.

He stood half-turned away from the door, a towel in one hand, his bare torso still gleaming where sweat mixed with rainwater. The light caught on the planes of muscle she'd traced with her fingers, water dripped from his hair, trailing down the valley of his spine as he reached for a training wrap on the nearby bench.

She knew this room, knew that stance, his body ready to move even in rest. Knew the particular set of his shoulders when he was trying very hard not to feel anything at all.

He turned the second her boot scraped against stone.

And froze.

The recognition came in stages across his face. First the automatic assessment, threat or student, then the widening of his eyes as he placed her. Disbelief followed, chased quickly by a brief glimmer of hope before he crushed it ruthlessly down.

The frown started slow, carving deeper with each heartbeat of silence. She watched it etch itself into his features like she was watching him rebuild every wall between them, brick by careful brick. The distance she'd been trying to breach for weeks solidified in the space of a breath.

"What are you doing here?" His voice wasn't harsh, but it was low, each word careful, like he was afraid of what might spill out if he spoke too quickly.

"I was going to the library," she said, but the lie fell flat before it even left her mouth. They both knew the library was nowhere near this part of the academy. She was soaked to the skin and had clearly been outside in the storm.

A beat passed. Then another. Thunder rolled overhead, muffled by stone but still powerful enough to feel in her bones.

He stepped forward, the towel still in his hand, and she caught the moment his instructor's instincts overrode whatever distance he was trying to maintain. "You're going to get sick."

She stiffened, every muscle locking as he moved. The gesture was so achingly familiar. How many times had he wrapped her in warmth and been the shelter she'd run to?

He moved like he meant to offer her the towel, arm already extending—

"Don't," she said quickly. She backed up a step, chin lifted, using defiance as armor. "You don't get to do that."

His hand lowered slowly, confusion flickering across his features before he locked it away.

"Do what?" he asked, and gods, there was actual bewilderment in his voice. As if he didn't know. As if he couldn't see.

"Act like you still care." The words tumbled out. "Like you didn't throw everything away and walk off like it didn't matter. Like *I* didn't matter."

Auren exhaled, the kind of breath that spoke of exhaustion deeper than any physical training could cause. His shoulders dropped a fraction, and suddenly he looked older. Tired in a way that had nothing to do with the late hour or whatever drill he'd been running.

He moved to the bench and sank down onto its edge like his legs couldn't quite hold him anymore. The towel lay forgotten beside him, and he let his head drop forward, elbows bracing on his knees.

"I didn't walk away because it didn't matter, Cassara."

The quiet confession was more damning than any shout could have been.

"Then why?" Her voice cracked, sounding too loud in the quiet of the training room. "Why this? Why silence? Why pretend none of it happened?"

She watched his jaw clench and for the first time since she'd walked in, he looked away, not at the walls or the floor, but through them, past them, at something she couldn't see.

"Because I'm leaving."

Her world tilted, the warmth of the room suddenly felt suffocating, and she couldn't quite draw a full breath.

"What?"

"When the year ends," he said quietly. "I'm not coming back to Vallemont."

Auren sat there on that bench, a figure carved from shadow and regret, elbows digging into his knees as if he could anchor himself to this moment. His gaze fixed somewhere beyond the training room walls, maybe on a future she couldn't see, maybe on a past that haunted him.

"I'm being reassigned," he said at last, voice barely above a whisper. "Not officially, or publicly. But... it's happening."

Cassara's throat constricted, words fighting to escape. "Where?"

A shake of his head, small, final. "I can't tell you."

"Can't or won't?"

He finally looked at her then, and the answer was written in every line of his face. Not defiance, not the stubborn refusal to share she'd grown used to. Just resignation.

"I don't want this," he said, and for a moment his careful control cracked, showing the raw edge beneath. "But what I want doesn't matter."

She stared at him, stunned by how quiet his voice had become. How final. How thoroughly he'd accepted this fate he claimed not to want.

"But you belong here," she whispered, the words scraping past the tightness in her throat. "With your students. With the academy. With us. With..."

With me.

"My place isn't here, Cassara."

It was here.

"I'll wait." The words spilled out before she could second-guess them, before pride or fear or logic could intervene. "I don't care where you go. I don't care how long it takes. I'll wait."

Auren closed his eyes like she'd struck him. His hands clenched where they rested on his knees, knuckles white.

When his eyes opened again, there was a pain she couldn't fully comprehend. They were the eyes of a man that had seen too much, lost too much, learned too well the price of hope. Her words hadn't comforted him, they'd wounded him in ways she didn't understand.

"Don't," he said gently, and the tenderness in it was worse than anger would have been. "Don't do that to yourself."

"I'm not doing anything to myself," she snapped. She moved towards him, closing the distance he'd tried to maintain. "I'm making a choice. For once, my choice. Not my father's, not the academy's, not anyone else's. Mine."

His smile was a slow, terrible thing. Soft at the edges and unbearably sad, like watching the last ember of a fire finally surrender to the cold.

"You're brave," he said, voice rough with a mixture of admiration and grief. "And you're foolish. And I love that about you."

Her breath caught, like her lungs had forgotten their purpose. The word hung between them, casual and devastating. *Love*. Present tense. Not loved. Not used to love. Love.

"But don't wait for me, Cassara."

He stood then, rising from the bench with that deadly grace that had first caught her attention. He reached out, fingers extending toward her face in a gesture so familiar her skin ached for it. But he stopped just short of touching, hand hovering in the space between them like all the words they couldn't say.

"Don't build your future around a maybe. Don't put your life on hold for something that might never..." He swallowed, the movement visible in the strong column of his throat. "You deserve more than shadows and stolen moments. More than a memory."

Her lip trembled, like she was some lovesick child and not a tamer who'd faced down beasts and tribunals and her own father's fury. She bit it hard enough to taste copper and refused to cry. Not here. Not over this.

"You're not a memory," she said, fierce and low. "You're not past tense. You're here, right now, and you're real, and you're mine even if you're too stupid to see it."

He didn't agree, but he didn't deny it either.

Auren reached for her slowly. His hand trembled slightly as it found the edge of her jaw, knuckles brushing her rain-chilled skin. His thumb found the corner of her mouth, hesitated there like he was memorizing the shape of it.

"Thank you," he murmured. "For reminding me what it felt like to want something and to be wanted in return."

He leaned in, no hesitation this time, and when his mouth found hers, it carried none of the desperate hunger of their early encounters, none of the careful restraint of stolen moments. This was something else entirely.

This was goodbye.

The kiss was deep, searing, carved not in hope but in farewell. He kissed her like he was trying to pour everything he couldn't say into the contact, every apology, every regret, every moment they'd never have. His hands slid to her waist, fingers spreading wide as if he could hold more of her that way, anchoring them both to a moment neither wanted to end.

Her hands found his bare shoulders, still damp with sweat and rain, muscles tensing under her touch like he was fighting not to pull her closer.

She kissed him like she could undo time, rewrite the inevitability of morning. Like she could kiss him hard enough to change his mind, to make him stay, to make him choose her over whatever shadow called him away.

Her fingers curled against his skin, nails leaving crescents that would fade by dawn, marks that wouldn't last, just like them.

One hand slid up her spine, tangling in her wet hair, holding her steady as he deepened the kiss with something approaching desperation. She felt him shake and realized with stunning clarity that this was killing him too.

The storm outside was nothing compared to this and for a heartbeat, one perfect, terrible heartbeat, nothing existed but the pull of him. His warmth seeping through her soaked clothes. His strength, coiled and careful even now, even as control frayed at the edges while every breath shared between kisses grew more desperate as they both felt time slipping away.

But it ended.

It had to.

When they broke apart, it was reluctant, gradual, a series of smaller kisses, gentler, like neither could bear to be the one who stopped first. His lips brushed her mouth, her cheek, her temple, each touch a small goodbye.

He rested his forehead against hers, and she could feel him breathing, rough, ragged, like he'd run for miles. His eyes stayed closed, lashes dark against his cheeks, and she wondered if he was trying to hold onto this moment the way she was. Trying to burn it into memory before reality crashed back.

"I'll never forget this," he said, and his voice broke on the last word. Not much, just a hairline fracture, but enough to crack her heart along the same lines.

Her throat had closed around everything she wasn't ready to lose, arguments and pleas and declarations all trapped behind the salt-burn of tears she refused to shed. A part of her was terrified that if she spoke now, she'd beg. And if she begged, he'd stay. And if he stayed, whatever was hunting him would find them both.

So she kept silent, breathing his breath, existing in the space between his body and hers where anything still felt possible.

Until a sound, soft and innocuous, shattered the moment.

A clatter. Metal on stone. The practice room door bouncing gently off its frame as if someone had pushed it too fast and fled.

Cassara's head turned first, instinct faster than thought. Through the inch of open doorway, she caught a glimpse of a silhouette, one she recognized all too well, retreating into the corridor's dancing shadows.

Gideon.

Her heart didn't drop into her stomach, it ceased to exist entirely, leaving a hollow space that filled immediately with ice.

She saw the moment in perfect clarity—how long he'd stood there, what he'd witnessed, the kiss that had looked like a greeting when it was goodbye. He couldn't know, couldn't understand that this was ending, not beginning. All he'd seen was her in Auren's arms, kissing him like the world was ending.

Which it was. Just not the way he thought.

She stepped forward, mouth opening to call after him, to explain, to say something, anything, that might undo the damage. But no sound came. Her voice had fled with her heart, leaving only the echo of boots on wet stone growing fainter with each step.

He didn't look back. Didn't pause. Didn't give her the chance to see his face, to gauge the damage, to know if this had broken something irreparable. He was already halfway down the hall, his figure swallowed by the flickering mage-lights that made everything look like a dream turned nightmare.

The silence that followed was complete.

Even the storm seemed to pause, holding its breath.

She felt Auren's hand on her shoulder, gentle, understanding, useless.

"Cassara..."

"Don't." The word came out raw. "Just... don't."

Because there was nothing he could say. No comfort he could offer. He'd protected her from so many things, hidden dangers, political machinations, the weight of secrets she couldn't know.

But he couldn't protect her from this. From the look she hadn't seen on Gideon's face but knew had been there. From the words that would never be spoken now. From the careful trust she'd built with her captain, shattered in a single glimpse of something he couldn't understand.

And worse, hadn't tried to.

Because letting Gideon leave, letting him believe the worst, letting him carry that image away, that was protection too. The kind that built walls where bridges should be. The kind that kept her safe and alone.

Cassara ran.

Her boots thudded against slick stone, each impact jarring, water splashing up with every stride. Her focus was solely fixed on the figure ahead, straight-backed, steady-paced, inexorable as the storm itself.

She didn't know what she was going to say, what she even could say. *It's not what it looked like* was a lie. *It didn't mean anything* was worse. The kiss still burned on her lips like a brand, Auren's broken voice echoing with every step—*I'll never forget this.*

But it wasn't him she was chasing through the rain-lashed night. It wasn't goodbye she was running toward.

"Gideon!"

Her voice fought against the storm, raw and desperate. The sound tore from her throat, nearly swallowed by thunder, but somehow reaching him.

He stopped.

Not abruptly. Not like he was surprised she'd followed. He stopped like he'd been expecting it, like he'd been counting her footsteps behind him, measuring the exact moment she'd break and call his name.

Halfway down the path that led toward the main building, just beneath the overhang of an arched corridor where rain became a silver curtain, he turned.

Water streamed between them, not gentle rain but the kind of downpour that turned the world to water and shadow. His dark hair clung to his forehead in wet spikes, his collar soaked through, the fine fabric of his shirt transparent where it stuck to his shoulders.

When he met her eyes, it wasn't fury that looked back.

It was hurt.

Cassara slowed, her boots skidding slightly. Her chest heaved with each breath, lungs burning from the sprint. The wind pulled at her soaked coat, tried to push her back the way she'd come. Thunder rolled high above, nature's judgment on the mess she'd made.

"I..." she began, but the words collapsed before they could form. What could she say? I'm sorry? For what, for the kiss, for being seen, for not choosing him, for wanting to? The explanations tangled in her throat, each one more inadequate than the last.

"You told me you were with someone," he said. His voice wasn't harsh. If anything, it was soft, softer than she deserved, soft enough to cut straight through every defense she might have raised. He spoke like someone stating a simple fact, like someone who'd already accepted it, already made peace with a truth that was killing her to hear. "And I kissed you anyway."

The guilt in his voice was worse than anger would have been.

"It's not that simple," she said desperately.

"I know," he shook his head, as though he couldn't quite believe his own foolishness. "I'm not angry at you, Cassara." He paused, seeming to test the truth of his own words. "I'm angry at myself for hoping when you'd already given me an answer."

That cut deeper than a shout ever could.

Because he meant it. She could see it in the set of his shoulders, the quiet acceptance in his eyes. He wasn't trying to hurt her with kindness. He wasn't wielding understanding like a weapon. He was being honest.

"But I won't do this again," he said quietly, his voice nearly lost under the storm's symphony. "I won't hang around waiting for you to choose me. I won't chase someone who's already made it clear where I stand."

The words landed with devastating simplicity. No ultimatum. No demand. Just quiet truth delivered with the same steady resolve he brought to everything.

"I have more respect for myself than that. And more respect for you than to put you in that position."

Silence stretched between them, heavy with rain and heavier with everything they weren't saying. The space between them felt vast, unbridgeable despite how easily she could reach out and touch him.

But she didn't.

Because he wasn't accusing her. He wasn't demanding explanations, or justifications, or promises she couldn't keep. He wasn't asking her to explain what he'd seen.

He was letting go.

Without fight, without making her feel like the villain in their story, even though she'd given him every reason to cast her as one.

And it hurt more than she expected. More than it had any right to. The quiet dignity of his retreat, the careful way he held his pain where it wouldn't spill onto her, it was everything Auren thought he was protecting her from, and everything Julian would never understand.

Her pulse was a tangled mess beneath her skin, twisted by guilt and longing and the dawning awareness that something inside her had shifted. When had Gideon's steady presence become so necessary? When had his rare smiles started mattering more than grand gestures? When had she started running to him instead of away?

Gideon gave her a long look, not searching, not hoping, just seeing. Taking her in one last time, maybe. Memorizing this moment when everything hung suspended between what was and what might have been.

Then he turned again and stepped back into the rain.

She watched him walk away, no hesitation in his stride. The storm swallowed him gradually, first blurring his edges, then claiming his form entirely until he was just another shadow in the water-veiled night. He didn't look back, didn't pause, didn't give her any opening to call him back, to change her mind, to choose.

He simply vanished from view, taking with him all the uncomplicated things she'd never known she wanted.

Cassara didn't follow this time.

She stayed rooted there beneath the awning, water pooling around her boots, soaked to the bone and shaking, not from cold but from the unraveling truth that no one could make this choice for her.

Not Auren with his noble sacrifices and necessary distances.

Not Gideon with his steady presence and patient heart.

Only her.

She pressed her fingers to her lips where two different kisses still lingered, one that tasted like endings and the other like beginnings she'd been too scared to want. Her heart felt like a broken compass, spinning wildly between magnetic Norths that pulled in opposite directions.

And standing there in the storm's embrace, caught between the ghost of what was and the shadow of what if, she realized with crystalline clarity—

She didn't know what she wanted anymore.

Or worse, maybe she did, and just couldn't bear to choose.

CHAPTER FORTY FIVE

Water ran in steady streams from her hair, her coat had soaked through during her pursuit of Auren and now the heavy fabric clung to her frame with uncomfortable weight. The cold alone should have driven her inside. The rational part of her mind knew this, cataloged it alongside other facts that didn't seem to matter anymore.

But still, she couldn't make herself go back inside.

The argument played on repeat in her head. She'd expected fury. Had been prepared for it. But that quiet acceptance had torn through her defenses in ways rage never could.

She tilted her head back and closed her eyes. Rain traced paths down her cheeks, following the hollows of her face. The water was cold enough to numb, and she welcomed it.

She wasn't crying.

But gods, she wanted to scream. Wanted to rage at the sky until her throat went raw. Wanted to break something just to hear it shatter.

It was never supposed to be like this.

Without warning, a strong gust of wind slammed through the archway behind her, carrying the scent of ozone and something else. Something wrong. The temperature dropped another degree, raising goosebumps along her arms. She flinched at the cold but stayed where she was, rooted by exhaustion more than determination.

The silence that followed felt heavy. The usual sounds of the academy at night had vanished, leaving only the steady percussion of water hitting stone. Even that seemed muted.

Then the sky cracked.

Lightning tore overhead in a blinding arc of white-blue energy. Too close. Much too close. The flash left afterimages dancing across her vision followed by a scream.

It was unlike anything she had ever heard, bypassing her ears and driving straight into her bones. Sharp and piercing and impossibly vast, it filled every space, pressed against her from all sides.

Her knees buckled and she hit the ground hard, barely registering the impact through the overwhelming pressure in her skull. Her hands flew to her ears in futile defense, but the sound was already inside. Behind her eyes. In her teeth. Vibrating through every cell with a frequency that felt unmistakably wrong.

Around her the air itself warped, reality bending around the edges of that terrible cry.

Through tears she didn't remember shedding, she saw the academy's defenses respond. Ancient glyphs carved into the very sky flickered to life. Protective wards that had stood for centuries blazed in brilliant arcs of blue and gold. For one heartbeat, they held, magic flaring bright enough to turn night to day.

Then they fractured.

She watched in stunned horror as the wards split apart like ice under pressure. Each glyph splintered with sharp, crystalline cracks, blue flames racing along the breaking points. The protective weave that had kept Vallemont safe for generations failed in real time, unraveling in a way that spoke of power beyond comprehension.

Something had torn straight through them.

A second bolt of lightning split the clouds, and in its harsh illumination, she finally saw it.

A silhouette twisted through the storm clouds above. Massive beyond scale, moving in ways that hurt to track. The shape coiled and uncoiled, each movement wrong on a fundamental level. Where it passed, the air itself seemed to recoil.

A leviathan.

Cassara couldn't look away.

She'd studied them, of course. Every student at Vallemont learned about the great beasts that had driven humanity to the sky. But the diagrams in textbooks, the carefully rendered illustrations, the preserved specimens in the lower vaults... none of it had prepared her for this.

Far above, the leviathan moved through the clouds with terrible purpose. It didn't fly in any way she understood. Instead, it seemed to carve space around itself, reality bending to accommodate its passage. Its body twisted in impossible coils, each segment moving independently yet in perfect coordination.

The storm followed in its wake like an obedient pet.

Its form shifted with each glimpse, never quite solid, never quite there. Translucent scales that seemed to be made of frozen lightning covered its hide. They didn't reflect light so much as break it apart, creating prismatic halos. One moment it seemed crystalline, the next organic, the next something between states of matter that had no name.

She couldn't move, couldn't breathe, she could only stare upward as her mind tried and failed to process what she was seeing.

The creature tilted its massive head, and she caught sight of the crest that ran along its neck. Spines that vibrated at frequencies she could feel, each one fracturing into smaller spines that fractured into smaller still, an endless recursion of organic weaponry.

Vapor hissed from vents along its sides, but it wasn't steam. The gas hung in the air too long, moved against the wind, left trails of nothingness where it passed. Ghost smoke from a creature that seemed more spirit than flesh.

It had no wings.

It had no eyes.

Only that mouth, which she glimpsed as it turned. Wide and angular and utterly alien, built for purposes she didn't want to imagine. The geometry of it made her stomach turn, too many teeth in too many rows, some facing inward, some facing out, all of them wrong.

The leviathan paused in its passage, hanging impossibly in the air above the academy. For one terrible moment, she thought it might be looking at her. How it could look without eyes, she didn't know, but the weight of its attention pressed down on her like a physical thing.

Then it opened that impossible mouth again.

The second scream was worse. Not louder, but deeper. It resonated in frequencies human ears weren't meant to process, carrying meanings her mind couldn't comprehend. The sound of it made her vision blur and her bones ache. It made every instinct scream at her to run, hide, cease existing rather than endure another second of that attention.

Cassara stared up into the storm and felt something inside her break.

The certainty she'd carried since arriving at Vallemont shattered like the wards above. The bone-deep belief that within these walls, surrounded by the best beast tamers in the realm, nothing could truly touch her.

It was gone.

This wasn't an opponent to be fought. It wasn't a challenge to overcome. It wasn't even an enemy in any sense she understood.

This was a force, like the storm itself had been given form and purpose and hunger.

And, like a thief in the night, it had made it inside.

The leviathan's scream cut off abruptly, leaving a silence that rang louder than sound. In that terrible quiet she remained frozen in the courtyard, rain-soaked and shaking, staring up at the hole in their defenses where something impossible swam through the sky.

The war they'd been training for had arrived on their doorstep and they'd already lost the first exchange.

Without warning, the wind shifted.

For one breathless second, the storm paused—like the world inhaled.

And then Gideon was there.

He burst through the rain like he'd torn himself from the shadows, boots skidding on slick stone as his arms caught her without hesitation. His hands, solid and grounding, gripped her shoulders as she staggered upright.

"You're alright," he said, low and urgent, barely audible over the wind. "Cassara. You're alright. Stay with me."

Stay with me.

It wasn't the first time she'd heard those words.

She blinked, dazed. Her ears still rang from that otherworldly shriek, a sound that seemed to have carved itself into her skull. Her legs felt hollow, like the sound had shaken her bones loose from their sockets. The courtyard spun around her, rain and stone and flickering lamplight blurring together. But the grip on her shoulders steadied her, and when she focused, she could see the wild tension in his eyes. Rain coursed down his face, flattening his dark hair against his forehead, but his gaze stayed locked on hers, grounding her.

She tried to speak, to tell him she was fine, but her throat felt raw. The words wouldn't come.

Before she could try again, another figure broke through the haze—fast, focused, cutting through the storm like it didn't dare slow him.

"Inside. Now." Auren commanded, sharp enough to override the wind.

He didn't stop running, didn't wait for questions, just turned and sprinted toward the tower steps. Water streamed from his uniform, and Cassara caught the gleam of something in his hand—a communication crystal, already glowing with urgent signals. Gideon took Cassara's arm and followed, pulling her into motion before her mind caught up. They crossed the flooded entryway and ducked through an auxiliary door Cassara barely remembered being there.

Inside, the walls trembled with the pressure of the storm. The narrow corridor felt like being inside a drum, every thunderclap reverberating through stone and mortar. Damp stone, shivering magelight, and the sharp stink of dirt and decay filled her nostrils. Emergency runes along the walls pulsed in irregular patterns, their usual steady blue replaced by warning amber.

They emerged into a small control alcove behind the watch station—a command post normally manned by upper class techs during routine operations. Now it flickered with panicked sigils and half-scrambled reports. Three monitoring stations hummed with frantic activity, their crystal screens casting harsh white light across the faces of the technicians bent over them. Arcane maps of the campus flared with warning symbols: breach points marked in angry red, shattered barrier lines showing as jagged tears across the protective grid, failing sensory glyphs winking out one by one like dying stars.

Cassara's stomach twisted. She'd seen these maps during safety drills, but never lit up like a battlefield.

Auren snapped a switch on the wall, his voice barking through the comms: "We need a threat sweep. Full spectrum. Tuning high-range elemental sensors."

A nearby technician answered without looking up from her console. Sweat beaded on her forehead despite the cool air. "Already tried. It's not showing up."

"What do you mean it's not showing—"

"It's not on the map!" the tech snapped, frustration bleeding through her professional composure. "It didn't appear until the perimeter failed. No trace before that. No glyph fluctuation, no aether anomaly, no forecasted elemental surge. Nothing until it was already here."

How was that possible?

It hadn't tripped a single defense until it had entered Vallemont's supposedly impenetrable barriers. Cassara felt a chill sweep over her that had nothing to do with her soaked clothes. Every first-year learned about the academy's legendary defenses—layers of detection magic that could sense a hostile pigeon three miles out.

Cassara heard the door slam open again. This time it was Nareen, soaked and furious, stepping into the alcove with her coat clinging to her like a second skin. She froze at the sight of Cassara and Gideon, her eyes flicking between them with a question she didn't voice, but said nothing, turning instead to Auren.

"What the hell is going on?"

Auren kept his eyes on the readouts, but Cassara saw his knuckles whiten as he gripped the console edge. "Tempestrix. Mid A-class. Air elemental. It came in under the radar. The wards didn't catch it."

An A-class Leviathan. She'd only read about creatures of that magnitude in theoretical texts, creatures that required full tamer squads and military-grade containment protocols.

Nareen swore. "Half the seasoned tamers are in the field evaluating fourth years. They're not due back until morning."

Auren shook his head. "The nearest reserve unit is thirty minutes out. More for a full squad."

Nareen swore again.

Thirty minutes was too long.

Outside, the storm howled with renewed fury—and something deeper screamed with it. The building shuddered, and somewhere in the distance, Cassara heard the crack of splintering stone.

Auren didn't hesitate.

He turned from the readouts, eyes already scanning the hall like he could see through the stone itself, calculating distances and tactical positions. "We're out of time. Follow me."

Cassara and Gideon obeyed without a word, falling in step as he led them back into the storm. The door slammed open under his palm, and rain rushing in as thunder cracked overhead. The sky hadn't stopped breaking since the leviathan appeared.

Across the main courtyard, figures clustered at the base of the central stair—the sharp outlines of third-year tamers, half-geared, wide-eyed, waiting for instruction. Most hadn't even strapped on their aether shards yet. Their beasts huddled close, sensing the wrongness in the air. A drake's scales rippled with nervous energy. A wind sprite flickered in and out of visibility, too agitated to maintain solid form.

"Five minutes!" Auren's voice cut through the roar of the wind like a blade. "Gear up. Meet me in the south training yard. I want a full sync briefing before we engage."

Some moved immediately, years of training overriding their fear. Others hesitated, casting nervous glances skyward at the churning mass of clouds that seemed to pulse with its own malevolent life.

He didn't wait to see who listened. Cassara and Gideon followed him through the entry hall as he pushed the doors open again and pointed them toward the east corridor.

"You two—get back to the first-year commons. Keep everyone inside and calm until we call for evac."

Gideon nodded, but Cassara's mouth parted, a protest forming. The words built in her throat—she wasn't helpless, she could help, she had Flicker—

Auren cut her off with a look. Not cruel. Not dismissive. Just focused. The look of someone who had already calculated every variable and reached his conclusion.

"This isn't your fight, not yet," he said, firm but not unkind. "Your cohort needs you. Go."

He vanished back into the storm, his figure swallowed by sheets of rain within seconds.

Cassara stood frozen for a heartbeat longer, the wind tangling her hair and water stinging her skin like tiny needles. She didn't argue—but she wanted to.

Gideon caught her arm gently, already turning toward the commons and pulling her with him.

She didn't resist.

Not yet.

The common room was in an uproar when they arrived.

Students were shouting, crowding the windows, craning for a better look at what was happening in the storm beyond. The protective illumination that usually bathed the commons in steady blue now stuttered and dimmed, casting everything in sickly, uncertain shadows.

Cassara barely had time to catch her breath before a voice called her name.

"Cass!"

Liri shoved her way through the nearest knot of students, eyes wild with relief and fear in equal measure. Nym flitted restlessly around her head, wings pulsing in tight, agitated beats that scattered rainbow sparks. "Are you okay? We heard something scream—it wasn't a drill, was it?"

The hope in her voice made Cassara's chest tight. She opened her mouth, searching for words that might somehow soften the truth. No words came out.

Oliver arrived next, nearly slamming into them, his Codex bag dragging off his shoulder, books and components spilling across the floor. Ilza crawled in twitchy half-climbs along his arm, her usual graceful movements replaced by nervous scuttling. "Glyphs are collapsing. I was tracking the perimeter nodes—they're falling inward. That thing didn't strike from above. It snuck in."

His voice cracked on the last words, the implications hitting him even as he spoke them. If something could slip past Vallemont's legendary defenses undetected, what else might be out there?

Rett trailed after him, silent but tense, jaw tight with the kind of controlled fear that came from understanding exactly how bad things had become. Skelli's plated tail tapped nervously against the floor behind him, each strike creating tiny sparks against the stone.

Gideon raised his voice, cutting through the growing panic. "Everyone, off the windows. Stay clear. This is a level-red threat. If you don't have an assigned duty, hold position and wait for instructions."

That got some attention. The official terminology, the command in his voice—it made the situation real in a way that whispered rumors couldn't. Students began pulling back, reluctantly at first, but with growing urgency as the implications sank in. Someone had finally checked the Crestboard—which had just locked into full emergency mode, its usual cheerful announcements replaced by stark red warnings.

Talia appeared from deeper in the room, already half-geared despite the chaos, her dual pistols holstered at her hips and a determined gleam in her eyes that reminded Cassara why she'd made it this far at Vallemont. "What's happening? And don't tell me it's just a storm."

Cassara started to answer—

And the world exploded.

The shriek that followed wasn't from the sky. It was closer.

Much closer.

A concussive burst ripped through the wall behind them—not a direct hit, but something that sounded like a mountain had just slammed into the adjacent tower. The impact sent shock waves through the stone, the ground lurching beneath their feet. Stone screamed as wards buckled under pressure they were never designed to withstand, and the windows didn't just rattle—they cracked. Spiderweb lines of stress split across the glass in jagged veins, each fracture spreading with audible pops.

A second impact hit lower, closer to the foundation. The lights sputtered and died, plunging half the room into darkness before the emergency glyphs kicked in, bathing everything in harsh amber.

Students screamed.

"Get down!" Gideon shouted, dragging Cassara behind a reinforced support column as pieces of the outer frame buckled inward with a groaning roar that sounded like the building's death cry.

From outside came the unmistakable sound of something massive landing—wet and wrong and impossible. It didn't shake the ground like falling stone or crashing timber.

It bent the air.

Cassara's ears rang again. This time, not from noise but from pressure.

The kind of pressure that came from being too close to something that existed on a scale beyond human comprehension. Her vision blurred at the edges, and she tasted copper.

The Leviathan was here. Not coming. Not breaching.

It had arrived.

The walls groaned again, a sound of structural surrender that made her stomach drop. Somewhere above them, she heard the crash of falling masonry.

Smoke or dust—or maybe the lingering residue of disrupted glyphwork—began to spill from the far corridor, curling like ash around the windows. The air grew thick and acrid. Cassara coughed, the taste of aether static thick on her tongue, metallic and wrong.

She didn't remember standing. One second she was crouched behind the column, listening to the panicked breathing of her friends, and the next she was moving, weaving between half-panicked students as they scrambled for cover or tried to push toward the stairs. Her legs carried her forward without conscious thought.

She reached for him instinctively—and found nothing. The aether shard wasn't with her. Flicker wasn't with her. And yet the pull toward the window didn't fade.

"Cassara!" Liri's voice caught behind her, sharp with panic. She felt Liri's hand catch her sleeve and shook it off. "Where are you going?"

The question barely registered through the buzzing in her head, the pull that dragged her toward the windows.

The glass was nearly shattered. Lines of fracture cut through the rain-slick surface like veins in ice, distorting the view but not blocking it entirely. She pressed her palm against the cold surface, ignoring the way it flexed under the pressure.

She could still see it.

Out there, at the edge of the northern courtyard, the Leviathan moved.

It was so much larger now.

No longer a distant shimmer in the clouds—but real, terrifying, and impossibly close. Its serpentine body hovered above the cracked flagstones, coiled midair as if gravity had given up trying to claim it. The translucent plates that covered its hide refracted the failing magelight around it until it looked like it was made of broken sky and liquid lightning.

A ripple passed down its spine—storm-spines flaring like the fins of some impossible fish swimming through air instead of water.

Then its mouth opened.

No sound came.

Not at first.

The silence stretched, pregnant with potential energy, and Cassara felt her lungs seize. Even through the fractured glass, she could see into that maw—see the swirling vortex of compressed air and electrical discharge building in its throat.

And then—boom.

A rolling pulse of compressed air slammed against the building like an invisible wave, sending fresh cracks through the stone, through the windows, through the very air itself. The impact lifted Cassara off her feet for a heartbeat, suspended between earth and sky.

Cassara's balance wavered. She caught herself on the windowsill, breath shaking, her palm slick with sweat. Around her, students cried out as the wave hit them, some falling, others clutching at furniture or each other for stability.

Through the chaos, one thought cut clear—

They weren't going to hold it back.

Not from inside. Not with half the senior tamers gone. Not with students who'd barely learned to sync with their beasts.

Auren's voice echoed in her memory, steady and certain.

This isn't your fight, not yet.

But that was a lie, wasn't it?

The fight had already found her, had found all of them.

CHAPTER FORTY SIX

Across the room, Gideon shoved aside a table someone had overturned and turned toward her with a look of disbelief. "What are you doing?"

Cassara turned to him slowly, the words rising before she had time to make them sound strategic or reasonable or anything at all. Her voice came out steadier than she felt.

"If we don't fight it," she said, "we lose more than the wards."

He stared at her for a moment, something unreadable twisting behind his eyes. She could see him weighing her words, weighing the risks, weighing the cost of action against the cost of inaction.

Then he gave a single, sharp nod.

"Thought you'd never say it," Liri breathed as she slipped back into view, with Nym fluttering close. In one hand she held Spireglass and in the other an aether shard.

Cassara's aether shard.

Liri grinned, though it didn't quite hide the tension in her shoulders. "Thought you might want your angry sparkle fox and your murder glaive."

A shimmer burst beside her, soft and brilliant, and Flicker popped into view, glowing faintly, tail curling upward like a flame caught mid-flick. He chittered, nose nudging her wrist with urgent affection, and her ACS pinged a half-second later.

Sync established.

The familiar weight of their bond settled into place, steadying her racing heart. Whatever happened next, they would face it together.

"Hope you're ready," Cassara whispered.

Always.

Rett was already strapping his bracers tight, the leather worn smooth from countless training sessions. Skelli paced behind him like a caged predator, her plated form reflecting the storm light as she sensed blood in the air. "No one else is coming."

Oliver adjusted a strap across his chest, checking the placement of his support gear with practiced efficiency. Ilza clung to his shoulder, her camouflage plates already shifting and adapting against the dim stormlight. "And the leviathan won't wait."

Gideon slid his gauntlet into place with deliberate precision. The last lock snapped with a hiss of engaging mechanisms.

Auric Vow stood together, not perfect. Not even close to ready. But together.

Around them, other first-years watched with wide eyes, some still pressed against the fractured windows, others huddled in the corners where the emergency lighting cast the deepest shadows. A few looked like they wanted to join, hands drifting toward their own gear, but fear held them back.

Cassara understood. She was terrified too.

They made it as far as the archway before the doors burst inward again.

"You've got to be kidding me."

Julian strode towards them, his expression settling somewhere between outrage and disdain. His unit flanked him in perfect formation, Jonas with his beast already summoned, Vash loading arc-tethers into a containment pack with swift, efficient movements, the others sharp-eyed and silent.

Julian's gaze locked on Cassara, then snapped to Gideon. The look that passed between them carried months of rivalry and resentment.

"What are you doing, Julian?"

"You think we're going to let you play heroes while we watch from a window?" he demanded. "Think again."

Cassara frowned.

This wasn't about heroics, this was about survival.

She glanced at Gideon who simply nodded and moved toward the shattered wall.

The breach was wide enough for three people to pass through side-by-side, jagged stone and twisted metal framing the gap where the leviathan's attack had torn through. Cassara climbed over the rubble first, boots finding purchase on broken masonry. Rain immediately soaked through her training gear, cold and sharp.

Gideon followed, then the rest of Auric Vow, picking their way through the debris with weapons drawn. Julian's unit came after, moving with practiced coordination.

They'd barely cleared the common room when Talia appeared at the breach behind them, twin pistols holstered at her sides. Her braid whipped behind her like a battle banner, soaked and shining with rain.

Cassara stopped. "What are you doing here?"

"I want to help," Talia said, raising her voice to carry over the wind.

No one spoke. The wind answered instead, howling between the towers above. Lightning split the sky, illuminating the leviathan's form as it coiled through the air above the northern courtyard.

Liri looked to Cassara, then to Gideon. Her mouth twitched, almost a smile. "The more the merrier?"

Gideon didn't argue. He stepped aside, making room.

Talia crossed the distance and fell into formation like she'd always been there.

Two teams. Eleven students. Against something that had shattered Vallemont's legendary defenses.

The odds were terrible.

But they were all they had.

"We need a plan," Gideon said, water streaming down his face. "Something to keep it occupied without getting ourselves killed."

"Hit and move," Julian cut in before anyone else could speak. "Rotating strikes. My team takes the north approach, yours flanks from the east. We keep it turning, distracted."

"That puts us in its direct line of fire," Gideon said evenly. "Better to—"

"Better to what?" Julian's voice sharpened. "Wait for it to level another building? We don't have time for your overcautious—"

"What the hell do you think you're doing?"

The voice cut through the storm like a blade.

Auren crossed the courtyard, his coat plastered to him, strands of dark hair dripping over his brow. His expression was thunder—fury barely contained, every line of his body radiating authority and barely restrained anger.

Cassara's stomach dropped.

He was going to order them back inside. Going to pull rank and send them away and—

But Auren's gaze swept over them—over their weapons, their beasts, their formation—and the fury in his eyes sharpened into assessment.

They were already committed. Already outside the walls with steel in hand.

"Distraction is the priority," he said at last. "Hold it off. Keep it moving. The others are evacuating. Protect the dorms at all costs." A pause. "Reinforcements are en route. We just need to hold it off until they get here."

Their eyes met briefly and Cassara offered a curt nod.

Gideon was already calling for Vangal. The griffin answered with a screech, wings beating back the storm in rhythmic bursts. Lightning lit his feathers in sharp flashes, silver-gray, soaked and gleaming. Cassara ran, boots slipping once on the stones, before Gideon's hand caught hers and pulled her up in one clean motion.

The saddle was built for one. She didn't ask where to sit. She just hooked an arm around his torso and held on.

"You alright?" he called over his shoulder.

"No," she replied, tightening her grip. "Go anyway."

Vangal launched like a living storm.

They were airborne before she could adjust, slicing through sleet with terrifying speed. The wind ripped at her clothes, stole the breath from her lungs. Below them, the courtyard shrank, glimmers of fire and magelight scattered as the rest of the unit split.

Liri and Nym darted toward the west hall, casting light illusions that danced like false targets. Oliver knelt near the crumbled gate, hands pressed into the glyph lattice. Rett jogged alongside Skelli, their path angling toward the broken observatory.

And from the far side of the courtyard, Julian rose, his wyvern carving a graceful spiral into the clouds. His team followed behind in tight formation, glittering and perfect.

Cassara didn't watch long.

The real storm was ahead of them, and it was hungry.

Vangal banked left, cutting across the air with a bone-jarring lurch. Cassara clung to the saddle spine, breath locked in her throat, the world below vanishing into a churn of wind and vapor.

"There!" Gideon shouted, pointing.

The Tempestrix coiled just beyond the shattered watchtower, its crown of storm-spines flared outward in a vibrating arc, a signal of alert and rage.

Gideon leaned forward with a sharp whistle and a flick of the reins. Vangal responded instantly. The griffin let out a piercing shriek, wings tilting to catch the updraft as he twisted into a dive. Just before they passed the leviathan's flank, Vangal unleashed a sonic pulse of his own, a thunderous, echoing cry that split the air and shimmered with sync-born distortion.

The sound collided with the storm-spines flaring along Tempestrix's back, drawing its attention like a challenge hurled across the sky.

The creature turned and screamed, a pressure-blast of compressed sound rippled through the clouds, and Vangal shuddered midflight.

Another burst cut across the sky, a streak of radiant gold. Julian dove in from above on his wyvern, loosing an arc-bolt that cracked against Tempestrix's side. The impact lit up the rain like fireworks, and the leviathan hissed, turning its focus away from the dormitories and onto the skyborne threats now circling like insects.

"It's working," Gideon said, almost to himself.

Cassara's gaze locked on the leviathan's spiraling body, already rising through the upper cloud line, its form flickering with speed that defied its massive size. Each movement carved wind currents into invisible blades.

They looped for another pass.

And disaster struck.

Julian was the first to reengage, his wyvern diving low with another volley prepped, the beast's wings cutting through the rain with practiced precision. But the Tempestrix twisted faster than anything that large had a right to move. Its tail lashed out like a whip, cracking the sky apart with a sound like breaking glass. The strike clipped the wyvern's wing with a flash of kinetic backlash that sent sparks of displaced energy cascading through the air.

Julian's mount shrieked, a sound of pain and confusion that cut through the storm's roar. The wyvern dipped hard, its injured wing struggling to maintain lift, and veered straight into Vangal's path.

"Hold on!" Gideon barked, yanking the reins with desperate strength.

Vangal vaulted upward, wings wrenching into a vertical climb that defied aerodynamics. Cassara's fingers slipped on the slick leather of the harness. Her center of gravity pitched sideways as the world tilted around them.

She felt her grip slipping and then—she was falling.

There was no time to scream, but she did anyway.

The wind roared in her ears, rain blinded her, turning the world into a confusion of gray and silver. Cassara tumbled end over end, the storm swallowing every sound that tore from her throat. Flashes of lightning lit the clouds in stuttering bursts, brief glimpses of the academy grounds spinning far, far below like a child's toy set.

She braced for impact, for death.

But something else broke through the storm first.

A rush of air that felt different from the chaotic winds around her. A flicker of light that cut through the darkness.

And then, wings.

A powerful body collided with hers mid-fall. Arms of wind and feather wrapped around her, halting her descent with a force that knocked the breath clean from her lungs but held her safe. The impact should have been crushing, but instead it felt like being caught by a guardian made of starlight.

Mirrored feathers shimmered all around her, each one catching and reflecting the storm's fury in fractals of impossible beauty. They trailed streams of distorted light like the storm itself had birthed a guardian from its heart.

I won't let you fall.

The voice whispered, not through her ears, but through her body, her pulse, her very soul. The tether between them blazed with warmth and certainty.

She gasped, looking up into eyes that reflected the storm like liquid mercury. "Flicker?"

He was massive—no, not massive, but long. His body stretched in a sinuous, serpentine curve that undulated through the air with liquid grace, easily twelve feet from nose to tail-tip. His frame was sleek and covered in a stunning blend of silver-white fur and mirrored feathers that seemed to shift and exchange places as he moved, creating an ever-changing pattern across his hide. Four wings sprouted from his elongated body in symmetrical pairs, feathered and powerful, beating in perfect rhythm to keep them both aloft.

His face was still fox-like—the same large ears, the pointed muzzle, those too-knowing eyes—but refined, majestic, with features that seemed carved from wind and starlight. His legs had shortened, pulled close to his serpentine body, but ended in powerful taloned feet that gleamed like polished steel. And his tail—his tail had split into twin plumes that streamed behind them like ribbons of captured lightning, leaving trails of shimmer in the storm-torn air.

He looked like a myth given form. A storm guardian pulled from ancient tapestries.

And he was hers.

He didn't answer again in words, but the sync pulsed bright and steady and absolutely sure, as he climbed. His wings beat with power she'd never felt before, each stroke lifting them higher through the chaos.

They streaked past a shape in freefall, Gideon, still diving after her, Vangal's wings folded as they cut through the air. His wide eyes met hers for a breathless instant, shock and relief warring across his features before Flicker overtook him with impossible speed.

Higher still, they passed Julian and his wounded wyvern, both frozen mid-beat in a moment of pure astonishment. His mouth parted in shock as the creature he'd once dismissed as a mistake rose past him, carrying his rival to safety on wings that shouldn't exist.

The clouds broke. For one impossible second, there was no rain. No wind. No chaos. Only sky, vast and quiet, stained silver with moonlight and scattered stars that turned the world into something from a dream.

Cassara clutched the thick tufts at Flicker's neck, heart pounding against her ribs as they hovered above the world. The silence felt sacred, like they'd found the eye of not just the storm, but of fate itself.

Above it all, she flew.

Then—Flicker dove.

He became a silver arc slicing through the rain like a comet hurled by the sky itself, his transformed body cutting through the air with predatory grace. Cassara tightened her grip, wind tearing at her hair and clothes as clouds blurred around them in a dizzying rush of speed and purpose.

Below, the Tempestrix writhed, its translucent body coiling through vapor and storm like a living mirage born from nightmare. The spines along its back crackled with contained energy. Air distorted in ripples around it, space itself seeming to bend under the pressure of its gathering power. It was preparing something massive.

Cassara didn't wait.

"Now," she whispered, and her glaive snapped open in her hand, Spireglass no longer. Tempest Shear materialized, its twin blades hovering apart from their central shaft, glinting with refracted aether that seemed to drink in the storm's light. They shimmered with mirrored sync trails as Flicker's pulse aligned perfectly with hers, two hearts beating as one.

I see it. Flicker said, his voice resonating with newfound power.

She raised the glaive, angling toward a pressure swell just beneath the creature's right flank where the armor plates met in a vulnerable seam. "There."

A sharp intake of wind, and Flicker released a spray of compressed air shards that split mid-flight, each one refracting into smaller projectiles. The mirrored projectiles tore through the air in erratic arcs, confusing the Tempestrix's defenses with their unpredictable paths before one struck home in a brief, satisfying pulse of light. The creature recoiled with a sound like breaking thunder.

Cassara barely had time to cheer before a whip-tail lashed through the clouds. Too fast to dodge, too large to avoid.

"Left..."

Flicker vanished.

Not gone, shifted, blinking sideways in a snap of thunder and shimmer that left afterimages burning in the air. The tail sliced through empty space, striking only the ghostly echoes he'd left behind like shed light.

They reappeared behind the creature, reality solidifying around them with a pulse of displaced air. Flicker beat his wings once and a massive shockwave burst outward, the force of it visible as ripples in the rain. The wave struck the leviathan full-force, sending it reeling midair, its perfect coils thrashing in sudden disarray. The pressure disrupted its targeting glyphs; stray winds buckled and scattered like broken glass.

"Up, above it!"

Flicker surged skyward, twisting into position with dizzying speed that made Cassara's stomach lurch. His wings shimmered before blinking them through a cluster of storm currents in a maneuver that should have been impossible, and they came out right above the creature's crown where lightning gathered.

Cassara didn't hesitate.

"Spiral now!"

Their bond flared like a star being born.

They moved as one, Flicker's wings stretched wide, trailing mirrored motes that caught the lightning and threw it back. He and Cassara dove into a spiraling descent that turned them into a living drill of light and wind. The glaive shimmered, slicing through the clouds like a starborn helix. Light and wind converged, building into a cyclone of mirrored shards that tore through the Tempestrix's chest in a brilliant cascade of silver fire.

The leviathan screamed.

Its storm-crown flared with blinding intensity, pressure spinning around its body like a coalescing vortex that pulled at the very air in their lungs.

Cassara's breath caught as she recognized what was building.

It was preparing a shockburst. A massive one that would level everything within miles.

And this time, they weren't going to outrun it.

The Tempestrix's jaws opened wider, an impossible yawning maw of pressure and sound, stormlight spiraling inward toward a single devastating crescendo that would shatter stone and bone alike. Cassara braced, barely able to lift Tempest Shear against the rising force that tried to tear the weapon from her hands. Flicker strained beneath her, his transformed wings faltering mid-beat as the wind turned sharp enough to slice skin, the very air becoming hostile.

The gathering energy turned the storm around them into a weapon, and they were caught at its heart.

And then...

A bolt of fire tore down from the sky.

It wasn't lightning. It was aimed, blazing with purpose and fury.

A massive, armored griffin collided with the leviathan's side in a burst of flame and gold, sending the creature into a shocked, reeling spin. The impact rang across the sky like a bell of war. The attack staggered it mid-charge, its storm-crown flickering like a candle in wind, mouth snapping closed in a thunderless snarl that spoke of ancient rage suddenly checked.

Below, the earth pulsed with answering power.

Lines of glowing sigils snapped to life across the perimeter, ground-cast wards and reinforced barriers flaring into activation with military precision. The rain hissed against their edges like acid meeting metal, outlining the magical grid like veins of molten glass carved into the very foundations of the academy.

Figures emerged through the haze, dozens of them, tamers and hex mages. Clad in field-caster gear that gleamed with protective enchantments and elite taming gear that marked them as veterans of conflicts most students had only read about.

Battle glyphs already glowed across their arms in patterns too complex for academy learning, and beasts at their sides that radiated power. Some rose into the sky on wyverns and sky-serpents whose wings cut through the storm without effort. Others stood firm behind shield formations, anchoring spellwork with the practiced unity that came only from shared battles.

Cassara blinked into the wind, heart hammering against her ribs as recognition dawned.

"Reinforcements," she breathed, stunned by the sheer scale of the response.

The reserve units. The full military response. Everything Auren had said was thirty minutes out had arrived with perfect timing, their coordination speaking of emergency protocols she'd never seen activated.

The Tempestrix gave one last, spiraling shriek that seemed to contain all the fury of a storm denied its prey. Its crystal plates shimmered before it vanished upward, retreating into the broken stormline in a blur of vapor and flickering windlight.

Not defeated, but driven back.

The immediate threat was over.

Flicker dipped low through thinning clouds, his wings shivering with fatigue that she could feel echoing through their bond. The storm had softened to a steady mist, rain falling in thin veils across the shattered field below where crater marks and scorched earth told the story of their battle. His descent was slow, measured, less a landing than a quiet surrender to gravity after holding them both aloft through impossible odds.

Cassara didn't speak. She barely breathed, afraid that words might break whatever magic still held them together.

The moment Flicker's talons brushed wet earth, he folded his wings and dropped to a low crouch, letting her slide from his back with gentle care. She hit the ground harder than expected, knees bending to catch herself, legs shaking with spent adrenaline that made her muscles feel like water.

She looked up.

Liri stood frozen, wide-eyed, Nym fluttering beside her like even the moth couldn't process what she'd witnessed.

Oliver's mouth hung open, his usual stream of technical analysis temporarily short-circuited.

Rett whispered, "No way..." his voice carrying the awe of someone whose understanding of the possible had just been fundamentally rewritten.

Talia had gone completely still, her mind clearly racing to process what she'd just witnessed. Her hand rested unconsciously on one of her pistols, not in threat but in the instinctive gesture of someone realizing they'd just seen the entire game change.

They were all watching her. Or maybe not her, but *him*.

Flicker stood still as a statue carved from starlight. His form shimmered with fading windlight, feathers still trailing mirrored motes in the air like shed pieces of the sky itself. Every line of his body radiated presence that made the air around him feel heavier, more real.

This was what legends looked like in the moment of their making.

Then Gideon landed.

Vangal's hooves struck down hard behind her, wings flaring in a final, grounded burst of wind that sent droplets scattering. Gideon dismounted before his beast had fully settled and was at her side the next heartbeat, sweeping her into a fierce, crushing hug that drove the breath from her lungs.

"I thought I'd lost you," he said, voice raw and low against her temple, the words carrying all the terror of watching her fall and all the relief of having her back.

She didn't answer immediately. Her arms clung to him just long enough to steady herself, to remember what solid ground felt like, before he pulled back. His eyes flicked over her like a final check, cataloguing every detail to assure himself she was whole...

And froze.

His hand lifted slowly, fingertips barely grazing her cheek as he brushed strands of damp hair from her face. "Your eyes..."

Cassara blinked at him, confused by the wonder in his expression.

"They're glowing," Liri whispered, stepping forward with reverent steps. "Like, opal."

And they were. Faintly, but unmistakably. The irises shimmered in the shifting light, not a glow exactly, but deeper, a prismatic sheen that caught every movement like wind on water, like looking into depths that held their own light. The remnants of the sync still echoed in her, like the magic hadn't quite left her body yet, like some part of Flicker's transformation had left its mark on her soul.

Oliver let out a strangled gasp, his scientific mind finally catching up with what he was seeing. "Residual echo burn, visible ocular manifestation, I've never seen it stabilize post-sync, not even in top tier tamers, Cassara, this is..." His hands gestured wildly as he struggled to find words for the unprecedented. "This shouldn't be possible. The threshold requirements alone..."

"Later," she muttered, still breathless and overwhelmed by the intensity of everyone's stares.

Flicker let out a small chitter from beside her, his stormlight finally dimming like a sunset in reverse.

Well, that was unnecessarily dramatic, his voice whispered through their bond, tinged with exhaustion but unmistakably pleased with himself.

The transformation cracked, light fractured and folded inward with mathematical precision, and with a soft shimmer of wind that tasted of high altitudes and impossible speeds, Flicker collapsed gently into his small form. His fur was slicked dark with rain, ears twitching with exhaustion, his breathing shallow from the effort of maintaining a form that should have been beyond his reach. But his eyes held a spark of unmistakable smugness, like he'd just proven every doubter wrong in the most spectacular way possible.

"Synaptic overload doesn't even begin to explain it, he broke three known transformation laws, those patterns weren't just adaptive, they were signature-manipulated on the fly, and that Aether Spiral, I saw it, that's not theoretical anymore, that's documented, that's documented now..."

"Four," Talia confirmed, her voice carrying the authority of someone who'd actually studied advanced theory. "Possibly five, depending on how you classify the dimensional displacement."

Oliver blinked at her. "You saw the displacement vectors?" He turned back to Cassara. "You're aware you've just become the case study of a lifetime, right?"

Case study? Flicker's voice echoed dryly in her mind. *I prefer 'magnificent aerial predator of legend,' but I suppose that's acceptable.*

Liri crouched beside Cassara, her eyes wide with reverence and something deeper, the recognition that she'd just witnessed her best friend become something more than any of them had imagined possible. "You flew," she said softly, the words carrying the weight of dreams made real. "You really flew."

Cassara finally exhaled, the last of the adrenaline leaving her system as the full weight of what had happened began to settle. She reached out with fingers that still trembled slightly, brushing her hand along Flicker's damp fur. The familiar texture grounded her, reminded her that beneath all the impossible magic and legendary transformations, this was still her partner, still the small fox who'd chosen her when no one else would.

"I didn't fall," she murmured, the words carrying layers of meaning she was only beginning to understand.

Flicker made a pleased sound deep in his throat and tucked himself against her leg like he hadn't just become a living legend, like he was still just her companion who happened to defy the laws of magic when the situation called for it.

Next time, he added with a mental yawn, *let's skip the part where you plummet to your death. Bad for my hearts. All nine of them.*

Around them, the academy grounds slowly returned to life as the immediate danger passed, but Cassara knew nothing would ever be quite the same. They'd crossed a threshold tonight, stepped into a realm of possibility that most tamers never glimpsed.

And somehow, impossibly, they'd made it back.

Liri glanced over at Talia, hope creeping into her voice. "You don't think they'll still make us take our Beast Classification final in the morning, do you?"

Talia's mouth quirked into the faintest smile. "After tonight? I think Professor Marlowe might have some revisions to make to the curriculum."

CHAPTER FORTY SEVEN

Four days later and the main courtyard still smelled like scorched skyglass.

Cassara stepped over a broken tile, its jagged edge faintly pulsing where residual mana hadn't fully faded. The ward-line beneath her boots flickered once, dim but alive, slowly knitting itself back together like a wound starting to heal.

All around her, Vallemont was rebuilding.

Stone groaned and realigned overhead as floating scaffolding drifted past, carrying a pair of hex mages in reinforced harnesses. Their tools gleamed with protective charms, and sweat beaded on their faces despite the cool morning air.

One spoke incantations while the other traced repair glyphs along the shattered archway, his fingers leaving trails of silver light that sank into the stone. Above them, rune-wrought cranes hovered, lifting slabs of gray stone that should have required a dozen men.

Cassara pulled her coat tighter and kept walking, her boots crunching on fragments of crystal that caught the pale sunlight.

She paused near the edge of a collapsed terrace, its marble surface split clean through by the creature's passage. Someone had placed a string of tiny windchimes along the broken railing. They jingled faintly in the breeze, a soft, high sound that didn't quite match the destruction around them.

The contrast felt deliberate. Beautiful and broken, existing side by side.

Across the grounds, students moved in loose clusters, their voices carrying on the wind. Some walked in contemplative silence, others spoke in that tight, too-fast way that said they didn't know what to do with the quiet moments yet.

The attack had changed everyone differently. Some had withdrawn into themselves, others had thrown themselves into helping with repairs, and still others seemed determined to prove that nothing had changed at all.

Cassara spotted Liri near the garden beds, sleeves rolled past her elbows, knees caked in dark earth as she helped a small group of underclassmen reset toppled stone planters. Her usual bright chatter had been replaced by focused concentration, her hands gentle as she coaxed damaged roots back into soil. Nym hovered close, wings glowing faintly as it fluttered from one wilted sprig to another, spreading tiny motes of healing light over the struggling plants.

A few paces away, Oliver stood at the base of a weathered pillar, scribbling frantically in a wide leather-bound notebook while Ilza extended a delicate claw over the exposed runes etched into the stone base.

His beast traced the ancient symbols with care while Oliver muttered calculations under his breath. His hair was a windblown mess that said he'd forgotten about food and sleep and possibly his own name in favor of documenting every detail of the magical aftermath.

Rett wasn't in view, but she knew he was around. Likely volunteering for perimeter watch or assisting maintenance crews with anything that required raw strength and steady hands. That was his way. Practical, reliable, the kind of person who showed up when things needed doing and never asked for credit.

Cassara sighed.

Above, pale light filtered through a patchy cloudline, casting long shadows across the field that shifted with each passing cloud. The damage to the dormitory towers had already been repaired, their walls sealed and reinforced with fresh protective glyphs. Most of the academy's outer defenses were stable again, humming with renewed power. The groundskeepers had cleared away the worst of the debris, and new flowers had been planted where the old ones had been destroyed.

But nothing looked quite the same.

She could feel the change beneath her skin, in the way conversations paused when she passed, in how people's eyes lingered on the faint shimmer that still clung to her irises. There was a weight to everything now, a heightened awareness that made ordinary moments feel significant.

Students paid attention to things they'd taken for granted before—the strength of the wards, the location of emergency exits, the importance of staying close to their teams.

She ran a hand along the courtyard railing, fingertips brushing stone still warm with restoration magic. The surface felt different under her touch, denser somehow, as if the repair spells had added layers of protection that went deeper than the original construction. Her own reflection caught for a moment in a shard of shattered glass that someone had missed in the cleanup, just long enough to see the faint prismatic gleam still lingering in her eyes.

Echo burn, Oliver called it. A side effect of magical overload, when a person channeled more power than their system was designed to handle. Temporary, hopefully. Most cases faded within a week.

But hers hadn't dimmed yet.

And neither had the memories.

She could still hear the wind screaming in her ears as they'd flown through the storm. The way the world had narrowed to pure light and instinct, everything else falling away except the connection between her and Flicker and the desperate need to survive. The moment he had transformed into something magnificent and impossible, carrying her through the sky when she should have fallen.

The moment when she'd discovered what the two of them together were truly capable of.

Cassara lowered her hand and stepped back, her gaze sweeping across the courtyard one more time.

The academy wasn't whole. Not yet. Cracks still showed in the older stonework, and some of the protective spells flickered with instability that would take weeks to fully resolve. But in its brokenness, something new had taken root. The bonds forged during the attack hadn't vanished in the aftermath. If anything, they had deepened, creating connections between students who might never have spoken before that night.

And maybe that was the point.

Not to emerge from chaos untouched and unchanged.

But to survive it with the people who mattered.

Together.

Cassara turned back towards the garden where Liri still knelt in the dark earth. She held a small silver trowel in one hand and a bedraggled shrub in the other, her tongue poking out slightly in concentration as she worked to coax the damaged plant back to health.

Her hair had mostly come free of its pale blue ribbon, copper strands catching the afternoon light as they framed her dirt-smudged face. Her sleeves were a disaster of soil smudges and grass stains, and her academy skirt bore the evidence of an entire morning spent crawling between flower beds.

"Almost," Liri muttered to the plant as if it were a skittish creature that might bolt if startled. Her voice carried that particular tone she used with nervous animals and homesick first-years. "You just need a little lift, a little encouragement. There we go."

Cassara didn't move from her spot by the broken terrace. Not yet. The sight of Liri working with such focused determination, bright and ridiculous and utterly unchanged despite everything they'd all been through, settled the restlessness that had taken root in her chest. Not because Liri wasn't affected by what had happened. She was. They all were. But because she refused to let the darkness dim her natural radiance.

After a long moment, Cassara stepped closer, her boots crunching softly on the gravel path that wound between the garden beds.

"You do realize final assembly starts in an hour, right?"

Liri glanced up from her work, eyes going wide with sudden panic. Dirt streaked her left cheek, and a smudge of something green decorated her chin.

"What? No, that can't be right. Wait, are you serious?" She looked down at herself as if seeing her appearance for the first time, taking in the mud caked under her fingernails and the streak of decomposed leaf matter on her skirt.

"Oh no. Oh no, no, no. I was supposed to be helping with the east hedgerow repairs, and then someone mentioned that the west bed was completely lopsided after the attack, and I thought I could just fix this one little section, and..." She trailed off, gesturing helplessly at her disheveled state. "Ugh, I can't show up to the assembly looking like I wrestled a tree."

Cassara tilted her head, her expression perfectly deadpan. "The tree in this scenario definitely won."

Before Liri could formulate a properly indignant response, Oliver's voice cut in from a few paces away, carrying that particular tone he used when explaining something he found genuinely fascinating.

"Technically speaking, the trees didn't wrestle anyone, but the residual flux in the east quadrant glyphs did spike enough to displace structural balance. Which is fascinating. Especially considering how the leviathan's impact disrupted directional aether flow."

He appeared beside them, his nose buried in his Codex as if this conversation had been going on for hours rather than seconds.

Liri groaned, a sound of pure exasperation. "Oliver. Assembly. One hour. Me covered in mud. Do you see the problem here?"

Oliver blinked, finally looking up from his research to take in her appearance. "Right. Yes. Assembly. The final ranking ceremony." He adjusted his glasses, considering. "I still think it's rather absurd to attempt to quantify individual worth using inconsistent combat performance metrics and completely arbitrary numerical ranking systems. But sure. Ceremony it is."

Cassara gave him a look that suggested his philosophical objections to the academy's evaluation methods were not currently helpful. "Arbitrary or not, it's happening in exactly fifty-seven minutes. Don't be late."

He nodded absently, already drifting away with his attention returning to whatever calculations occupied his mind. "Mana elasticity coefficients," he muttered to himself as he wandered off. "Layered ward failure patterns. The correlation between impact vectors and magical dispersion rates..."

Liri shook her head with a fond smile, watching Oliver disappear around the corner with Ilza trailing faithfully behind him. "Sometimes I wonder how he remembers to breathe." She scrambled to her feet, brushing ineffectively at the dirt on her clothes. "Okay, okay. I'm going. Emergency cleaning protocols engaged."

"Don't forget to scrub under your nails!" Cassara called after her as Liri hurried toward the dormitory halls, Nym spiraling around her head in glittering loops.

Alone again, Cassara turned toward the stone path that led to the Great Hall. The wind had picked up again, crisp and clean, carrying the kind of fresh clarity that always followed a storm. Students filtered across the academy lawns in small groups, dressed in the slightly more formal variations of their uniforms reserved for important ceremonies. A few instructors watched from the covered balconies above, their expressions carefully neutral as they observed the pre-assembly gathering.

Cassara adjusted the silver clasp on her collar and stepped through the arched entrance into the marble corridor that led to the Great Hall. The walls here bore fresh repair work, seamless patches where the stone had been mended and reinforced.

Her pace slowed just as she reached the threshold of the Great Hall, and there he was.

Gideon.

He stood near one of the outer pillars, his posture perfect, his hands clasped behind his back in the formal stance they'd all been taught during deportment classes. His dark uniform was immaculate, every button polished, every crease sharp. His expression held that carefully controlled neutrality that always made her stomach twist with uncertainty, giving nothing away of his thoughts or feelings.

He glanced over as if he'd sensed her arrival rather than seen her approach, some invisible thread drawing his attention. For a long moment, their eyes held across the space between them, neither moving nor speaking.

Neither of them had brought up the conversation they'd shared that night, just before the leviathan attack. Not about the kiss. Not about the things that had been said in the quiet darkness of the training hall.

It should have been awkward, but when she stepped forward into the hall, he fell into stride beside her without hesitation. No careful distance maintained. No fumbling for the right words.

For the first time in days, his presence didn't feel like something fragile and tentative trying desperately to hold its shape against the wind.

It felt like something finally settling into place.

As Cassara stepped through the wide arched entry with Gideon at her side, her eyes automatically scanned the familiar space.

The maintenance crews had done excellent work, but traces of the recent damage remained for those who knew where to look. Someone had polished the floor tiles until they gleamed, but no amount of shine could hide the spiderweb of fractures running beneath them where the leviathan's energy had cracked the ancient stone.

Evie and Talia waved from their seats at a long table near the front of the hall, their faces bright with anticipation. Cassara spotted Liri rushing in from the east corridor, her copper hair still damp from what had obviously been a very quick wash, still hopping into one boot, her uniform hastily straightened. Rett followed at his usual measured pace, quiet and steady as always, while Oliver trailed behind with his Codex clutched in one hand and his eyes scanning the repaired walls as if he expected the protective glyphs to start sparking again at any moment.

He hadn't combed his hair.

Cassara took a seat between Evie and Gideon, settling into the polished wooden chair as conversations swirled around them. She offered Liri a quick visual assessment as her friend hurried to join them.

"You cleaned up surprisingly well."

Liri grinned and flopped into the chair beside Talia with her characteristic lack of ceremony. "Don't get too close. I still smell like mulch."

Talia, as if to test the claim, leaned in and took a sniff.

Her nose wrinkled slightly and she scooted closer to Oliver.

Before anyone else could speak, Headmistress Kalisandra rose from her position at the elevated stage at the front of the hall. She moved with the precise grace that marked all her public appearances, her dark robes flowing around her as she approached the ornate podium. The crowd stilled instantly, hundreds of voices falling into complete silence in the span of a single breath.

"This year," she began, her voice carrying easily through the vast space with the kind of projection that came from decades of addressing large gatherings, "we have seen remarkable perseverance, impressive adaptability, and, yes, unexpected chaos."

A quiet ripple of uneasy laughter moved through the assembled students at the last words, a shared acknowledgment of the events that had shaken the academy to its foundations.

She continued, her gaze sweeping across the sea of faces before her. "While it is not our policy to reward recklessness or to encourage students to place themselves in unnecessary danger, we recognize the extraordinary bravery and unity shown by many of you during recent events. Vallemont was founded on the pursuit of excellence, but it survives and thrives through integrity, courage, and the bonds forged between partners."

Cassara's spine stiffened involuntarily, her hands tightening on the edge of the table as she sensed the weight of what was coming.

"And so, with the term drawing to a close and summer break approaching, we now announce the final rankings for our first-year tamers, both individual performance and unit standings."

The hall fell into absolute silence, every student holding their breath as they waited to see where they stood among their peers.

"Top ranking," the headmistress announced, "Gideon Delvanir."

A swell of applause echoed across the hall, not deafening but firm and sustained. The sound carried genuine respect rather than mere politeness, acknowledgment of achievement that had been clearly earned through skill and dedication.

Cassara didn't look at him sitting beside her. She didn't need to. She could feel the subtle tension in his posture, the way he barely reacted to the announcement beyond a slight straightening of his shoulders. As if the recognition was already behind him, filed away and dismissed as unimportant compared to whatever challenges lay ahead.

"Second place," the headmistress continued, pausing for just a moment to let the suspense build, "Cassara Allencourt."

The applause that followed was sharper now, more surprised. Several heads turned in her direction, and she caught glimpses of impressed nods and a few envious glances from students who had clearly expected different results.

Cassara exhaled slowly, but her stomach dropped with the weight of the announcement. Second place was impressive by any reasonable standard, but reasonable standards didn't govern the expectations placed on her shoulders. It wasn't first.

One more mistake, and I will send for the carriage myself.

Her father's words echoed in her memory, and her hands curled into fists on the polished edge of the table.

The next few names blurred past in a wash of sound and motion. Julian claiming third place with his usual swagger. Talia accepting fourth with gracious composure. Liri looking pleasantly surprised at fifth.

Then came the team rankings, and the energy in the hall shifted again.

"Top Unit Performance," the headmistress announced, her voice carrying a note of thinly veiled approval, "Auric Vow."

The hall erupted in a cacophony of responses. Some students clapped enthusiastically, others groaned in disappointment, and the sound mixed into a chaotic blend of cheers, good-natured complaints, and quiet nods of acknowledgment.

Cassara glanced at her teammates, catching the look that passed between them like a shared secret. Liri beamed with unrestrained joy, her earlier panic about her appearance completely forgotten. Rett gave one of his rare, crooked smiles, the expression transforming his usually serious face. Even Oliver, for once, didn't offer any cynical commentary about the arbitrariness of ranking systems.

They'd made it.

Despite everything that had happened, despite the chaos and the fear and the moments when it had seemed like they might not survive the term at all, they had claimed the top spot among all first-year units.

But even as the accomplishment settled over her, Cassara's gaze drifted almost against her will toward the long table where the faculty sat in their formal attire. Most were present, their expressions maintaining the carefully neutral composure that came from years of practiced professional detachment. But one seat remained conspicuously empty.

Auren's chair sat unclaimed and undisturbed, a stark reminder of the absence that had shaped the final week of the term.

The victory she should have been savoring turned bitter in her mouth.

The rest of the assembly passed in a blur of formal announcements and ceremonial traditions.

Applause rose and fell in predictable waves. More names were called for various honors and recognitions, a few tearful speeches were delivered by upper-year students whose time at Vallemont had finally come to an end. The headmistress offered the traditional closing remarks about growth, responsibility, and the bonds forged through shared struggle.

But Cassara barely registered the words. Her thoughts drifted like smoke, spooling back through recent memories of lightning and chaos, the wind screaming in her ears during their desperate flight, the sharp echo of a voice that would never get the chance to say a proper goodbye.

She sat perfectly still in her chair, hands folded carefully in her lap, eyes fixed on some point in the distance that she couldn't quite identify or describe.

It wasn't until the headmistress's voice rang out again, clipped and final with administrative efficiency, that Cassara stirred from her reverie. The announcement echoed across the Great Hall with practiced authority—students were to have their trunks packed and ready for transport by first light. The airships would depart promptly at noon, carrying them back to their families and whatever awaited them during the summer months.

Cassara stood with the rest of her unit as the formal dismissal was given, her legs carrying her automatically as the crowd began to file out of the hall. The movement flowed like a slow current, students clustering in groups as they made their way toward the exits, their voices rising in a mixture of excited chatter about summer plans and melancholy farewells.

She followed the stream of bodies, moving in silence among her chattering classmates. Not lost, exactly, but not entirely present either.

Which is why she wasn't sure how she ended up outside the training annex.

One minute she was walking across the outer corridor past the north wing—her boots echoing against stone worn smooth by centuries of academy students, her mind deliberately blank as she focused on the simple rhythm of her steps. The next, she was standing in front of the door to Auren's training room.

No. Not Auren's anymore.

The brass plaque still gleamed beneath its spell-polished runes—Advanced Combat Theory - Instructor A. Veth. Someone would come to change it soon, she supposed. Replace his name with another, as if switching out plaques could fill the space he'd left behind.

The chamber beyond was dark.

Cassara reached for the handle. The metal was cold beneath her palm, colder than it should have been. She pushed the door open.

Silence greeted her.

The room was bigger than she remembered. The practice dummies had been cleared away, leaving pale marks on the floor where they'd stood for years. The sparring circles had been wiped clean, their intricate geometries reduced to faint chalk ghosts. His desk sat bare in the corner—no scattered reports annotated in his precise script, no half-filled mugs of tea growing cold while he demonstrated a particularly complex maneuver, no trace of the man who once filled this place.

She could still see him there, standing in the center circle with that particular stillness he had—like a blade at rest, ready to move at any moment. Could still hear his voice, low and measured. Could still feel his hands on her waist, his mouth against her lips, burning with want.

He told her he was leaving. She hadn't wanted to believe it. A part of her hated him for it, for the growing ache in her chest, for the emptiness, the hurt. Maybe that was for the best because hating him would cost less than loving him.

She told him she understood. But standing here, in the absence he left behind, she realized she hadn't understood at all.

It hurt. Gods, it hurt.

The pain caught her off guard with its intensity—a physical thing, sharp and immediate, as if someone had reached into her chest, grabbed her heart, and twisted.

She bit down on the emotion swelling in her chest, the pressure building behind her eyes. She didn't cry.

You'll lose more important things in life. Better get used to it.

She hated that her father had been right about so many things.

Cassara's fingers curled at her sides, knuckles tight enough to ache. She sucked in a breath, shaky and thin, tasting dust and old magic on her tongue. Still not crying. Not yet. She was stronger than this. She had to be.

But the room seemed to press in on her, all that empty space where life used to be. Her eyes burned. She blinked hard, fast, refusing to let the tears fall. She was alone here. She could allow herself this moment of weakness, then pack it away with all the other things she didn't let herself feel. Tomorrow she'd be fine. Tomorrow she'd—

The air shifted. A whisper of warmth against the chill. A quiet presence behind her that she recognized before he spoke.

She turned.

Gideon stood a few paces away, framed by the doorway she'd left open. He must have followed her here. He always seemed to know when she needed him, even when she didn't know it herself.

He didn't speak, the silence stretching between them, full of all the words she couldn't bring herself to say.

I'm not okay.

I don't know how to do this.

I'm so tired of being strong.

And something inside her cracked.

The sound that escaped her throat was small, broken. A child's sound from a woman who'd forgotten how to be anything but composed. She saw his expression shift, surprise, maybe, or concern, before her vision blurred.

She closed the distance without conscious thought, walking straight into him, not caring how she must look, how vulnerable, how broken, how utterly unlike the Cassara everyone expected her to be. His arms came around her without hesitation, solid and sure, wrapping her in a quiet embrace that didn't ask anything of her.

He felt familiar. Safe. *Real* in a way that nothing else felt right now.

She pressed her face to his chest, fingers clutching at the fine fabric of his coat, and the tears came. Silent at first, and then in soft, shaking waves that seemed to pull from somewhere deep inside her. Years of unshed grief, maybe. Years of loss packed away and ignored, demanding their due at last.

His hand came up to cradle the back of her head, fingers gentle in her hair. The other arm curled around her, holding her steady as tremors ran through her. She could feel the solid beat of his heart against her cheek, steady as a drum, anchoring her to the moment.

He didn't flinch at her tears soaking through his shirt. Didn't stiffen at this unprecedented display of weakness from someone who'd faced down a leviathan just days before.

He just held her.

She didn't know how long they stood there. Long enough for the tears to run their course and for the crushing weight in her chest to ease, just a little.

When she finally pulled back, just far enough to look up at him, his eyes were soft with an understanding, a gentleness, that made her chest tighten in an entirely different way.

"Thank you," she whispered, voice raw.

He brushed a tear from her cheek with careful fingers. "Always," he said simply.

And she believed him.

CHAPTER FORTY EIGHT

The door clicked shut behind her with a soft finality that seemed to echo in the sudden quiet.

Cassara leaned against the smooth wood for a long moment, letting the familiarity of the dormitory wrap around her like an old, comfortable blanket.

The air held traces of everything that had made this space home over the past year—the warm glow of old magelight fixtures that had illuminated countless late-night study sessions, the clean smell of laundered cloth and carefully maintained linens, the faint herbal tang that drifted perpetually from Liri's ever-replenishing tea stash tucked away in the corner cabinet. It should have been comforting, this return to the sanctuary they'd all shared.

It wasn't.

The room felt hollow. Empty in a way that went deeper than the half-packed trunks and the general disarray of impending departure.

The space was quiet, lacking the usual chatter and bustle that filled their shared quarters. Everyone else was still out in the corridors and courtyards, finishing their final goodbyes, dragging heavy trunks down narrow staircases, clinging desperately to the last few precious hours of something that already felt fundamentally changed.

The term was ending whether they were ready or not.

Cassara pushed herself away from the door and stepped forward into the room, her boots silent on the worn wooden floorboards. She'd made it perhaps three steps when she noticed something that shouldn't have been there.

A folded square of parchment lay on the floor, its edges crisp and perfectly aligned. The paper was cream-colored, expensive, the kind used for official correspondence. It practically glowed against the dark wood beneath it.

Her name was written on the front in handwriting she recognized instantly, the letters formed with the same precise care that had marked every training report and tactical assessment she'd ever received.

She knelt slowly to pick it up, her fingers trembling slightly as they closed around the smooth paper. Academy letterhead, she noticed as she turned it over. There was no wax seal, no formal closure. Just her name and whatever message waited inside.

Cassara opened it carefully, revealing lines of text written in the same steady hand.

Cassara,

There are moments in life that shape us, some chosen, some thrust upon us without warning. You've had more than your share of both. Don't let them cage you.

Experience everything this world offers. Don't wait. Not for anyone.

If the time is right and our paths cross again, who knows what adventures await?

Until then, fly high.

– A

She held her breath as she read the words. It was exactly his voice, captured perfectly in ink, calm and unhurried, firm in its convictions.

She read it again, forcing herself to go slower the second time, letting each word settle properly before moving to the next. The message sank deeper that way, embedding itself in her memory where she could examine it later, when the immediate sting of parting had faded enough to let her think clearly.

Crossing the room to her bed, she sank onto the edge of the mattress that had been her refuge through so many difficult nights. She pulled open the bottom drawer of her traveling trunk, revealing the carefully organized contents within. Tucked away in the corner, wrapped in soft cloth for protection, lay her mother's journal.

She lifted it from its resting place and opened the book with the kind of care reserved for sacred things. The pages fell open to sections filled with her mother's flowing script, accounts of adventures and observations that had shaped Cassara's understanding of what it meant to be a tamer. But she turned past the familiar entries, seeking blank space near the back of the book.

She found an empty page that felt right and paused, holding Auren's letter above it.

Carefully, she folded the note again, making the creases sharper and more precise this time, ensuring it would lie flat and undisturbed. Then she slid it gently between the journal pages, nestling it among her mother's words like a flower pressed for preservation.

She closed the journal slowly and rested her hand on the worn leather cover, feeling the subtle warmth that seemed to emanate from within. The weight of two important presences now, two voices that would travel with her wherever she went.

It wasn't goodbye. Not really.

But an ending, all the same.

An ending that cleared space for whatever came next.

The airship's lift crystal thrummed beneath her boots as Cassara stood on the passenger deck, the familiar vibration sending tremors through the metal hull that she could feel in her bones.

She paused at the railing for a moment, looking back at Vallemont as it spread out below them like a painting come to life. The academy's towers caught the afternoon sunlight, their restored walls gleaming with fresh protective wards that sparkled like embedded jewels. From this height, she could see the careful patches where the leviathan's attack had been mended, new stone slightly lighter than the ancient foundations.

It was beautiful.

It was home.

And she was leaving it behind.

"You know, staring won't make the summer go faster."

Liri's voice broke through her thoughts, warm with affection and tinged with the particular kind of gentle teasing that could only come from someone who understood exactly what she was feeling.

Cassara turned to find her friend bouncing on her toes beside her, half-wrapped in a thick woolen blanket she'd clearly smuggled from her dormitory. Her copper curls were already mussed from the wind that swept across the departure platform, and her eyes sparkled with excitement despite the early hour.

Oliver followed close behind, his nose buried in a thin leather journal as he scribbled notes with single-minded focus. Even now, with Vallemont falling away beneath them, he was muttering about stabilizer enchantments and ward recalibration techniques, his mind already working on theoretical problems that wouldn't let him rest.

Gideon brought up the rear, his dark eyes taking in their small group with satisfaction. His usual silence seemed less guarded than it used to be and his presence felt like a tether, solid and reassuring in ways she was only beginning to understand.

They passed the stairs that would bring her to the legacy lounge, its polished railing gleaming, the plush carpet pristine.

She didn't even slow her pace.

Instead, she veered decisively toward the central cabin, where rows of reinforced benches faced wide, curved windows that offered unobstructed views of the world below. The common passenger area. No frills, no ceremony, no artificial barriers between her and the people who mattered.

Just them.

Rett and Talia had already claimed a section near the largest window, their gear stacked on the benches to save seats. Talia glanced up as they approached. She offered a wave before she returned her attention to the straps she had been adjusting on her travel pack. Rett lifted his chin in silent acknowledgment, his quiet presence as solid and dependable as ever.

Liri flopped into one of the saved seats with characteristic enthusiasm and immediately started rearranging the standard-issue cushions to suit her preferences.

"Thanks for saving the good spots. I call a window seat." She turned to Cassara, eyes bright with mischief. "Unless you were planning to pull rank and claim it for yourself?"

"By all means," Cassara said, settling into the seat beside her with a genuine smile tugging at her lips. "I'm feeling generous today."

Flicker chirped and leapt gracefully from her shoulder to her lap. He chittered once, low and curious, settling into a comfortable curl against her.

"He's been extra glowy all morning," Liri said, reaching over to nudge Flicker lightly with one finger. The little fox-creature responded by releasing a brief shower of glittering motes that danced around her hand. "Even more than usual."

Flying is almost as good as running, Flicker said, his mental voice carrying notes of contentment. *And everyone smells happy. Nervous-happy, but still happy.*

"I think he's glad we're all in one place," Cassara said, interpreting his observations for the others. "I might be too."

Across from them, Oliver looked up from his notes with the slightly dazed expression he wore when transitioning from theoretical calculations to actual conversation. "Did you know the northern turret uses a completely different dual-axis suspension glyph system to stabilize the upper walkways during periods of severe wind distortion? It's entirely different from the southern tower design, much more efficient." He tapped his journal enthusiastically. "I managed to get detailed sketches of the mechanism while they were repairing the garden spire. The applications for mobile platforms could be revolutionary."

Liri blinked at him with exaggerated confusion. "That's... a lot of very specific turret talk."

He blinked back, completely deadpan. "You asked."

"No, I definitely didn't."

"I assumed you would eventually."

Talia gave a soft laugh. The tension she always seemed to carry had eased since they'd left the academy grounds, as if distance from the formal structure allowed her to relax in ways she couldn't while under official observation. Rett leaned closer to Liri, their shoulders brushing in casual contact that spoke of comfort and trust built over months of shared challenges.

He didn't say much, he never did, but his expression conveyed everything that mattered. There was safety here among this group. Familiarity that went deeper than mere friendship.

We're a pack, Flicker observed with satisfaction. *Good pack. Safe pack.*

Cassara glanced around the cabin and let the moment settle properly in her memory, imprinting the details so she could call them back during the lonely summer ahead.

Months ago, she would have sat alone in the luxury lounge without question, convinced that she didn't need anyone's company or support, believing that isolation was strength, that independence was virtue.

Now?

Now she couldn't imagine voluntarily returning to that version of herself. The girl who had boarded this same airship at the beginning of the term felt like a stranger compared to who she was now.

The engine pulsed steadily beneath them, a rhythmic thrum that she could feel through the soles of her boots. Outside the curved windows, the landscape blurred as clouds began to pass, white and gray wisps that caught the sunlight and threw it back in ever-changing patterns.

"So," Cassara said, settling more comfortably into her seat as the airship reached cruising altitude, "any exciting plans for the summer break?"

Liri raised one hand like she was about to swear a solemn oath. "I'm going to sleep for three solid days, eat my body weight in my grandmother's fried dumplings, and sunbathe until I physically cannot remember what homework even looks like."

Cassara laughed, the sound lighter than she'd felt in weeks. "That sounds like an absolutely flawless strategy."

Can we eat dumplings too? Flicker asked hopefully.

"I'll see what I can arrange," she promised him with a smile.

She felt Gideon's gaze before she turned to meet it, that prickle of awareness that came from growing attuned to someone's attention. He didn't speak, but the look he gave her was soft and unguarded. Content. Present in the moment in ways that made her heart ache in ways she wasn't quite ready to name.

They didn't need words for this.

Whatever it was.

Not yet.

Cassara closed her eyes, Flicker's warm weight comfortable against her thighs, the quiet murmur of her team's conversation filling the space around her like the most natural thing in the world.

It was peaceful and for the first time in longer than she could remember, she wasn't looking back over her shoulder at what she was leaving behind, she wasn't dwelling on mistakes or missed opportunities.

She was ready to see what came next.

The airship docked with a gentle lurch that sent vibrations through the metal deck plating, but the moment the passenger ramp lowered with its familiar mechanical whir, the calm that had settled over their group during the journey unraveled completely.

The docking platform buzzed with chaotic motion. Families crowded near the designated landing zones, waving colorful banners and shouting names in voices that carried over the general din.

Uniformed porters scrambled between the masses to unload heavy trunks and travel cases, their movements efficient despite the obstacles. Magitech carriages hovered in and out of position with the smooth precision of well-maintained enchantments, while traditional horse-drawn vehicles waited in designated areas for those who preferred more conventional transportation.

Cassara stood at the top of the ramp, one hand shading her eyes as she blinked against the midday sun that seemed impossibly bright after the filtered light of the airship's interior.

"You helped save all our lives, you know," Talia said quietly, her voice cutting through the noise with the kind of certainty that made arguments impossible. "Don't forget that when things get complicated."

Caught off guard by the unexpected sentiment, Cassara wasn't sure what to say. Talia wasn't given to emotional declarations or dramatic farewells, which made the words carry extra weight.

Before she could formulate any kind of response, Talia had already stepped back, offering a wave of farewell before she turned and walked toward the sleek carriage that waited to carry her home.

A few paces away, Rett stood beside his family's more modest wagon, its wooden sides worn smooth by years of practical use but well-maintained and sturdy. Skelli perched alertly beside him, her raptor form radiating the kind of predatory grace that never fully relaxed even in peaceful moments. The beast's tail twitched with barely contained energy as she surveyed the crowded platform.

When Flicker bounded close with his characteristic enthusiasm, Skelli lowered her magnificent head in a gesture of recognition and respect. The two creatures exchanged a low, rumbling nuzzle that managed to be both sharp-edged and surprisingly gentle, a farewell between partners who had shared danger and emerged stronger for it.

"See you next year," Rett murmured, his gaze flicking to Cassara only briefly before settling somewhere over her shoulder. Even his goodbyes were economical, carrying maximum meaning in minimum words.

She gave a small nod, surprised by how deeply she felt it. "You too."

The wagon rolled away slowly at first, then gained speed as it passed beneath the rising arch of glyph-bound wards that protected the transportation hub. Soon it was just another vehicle disappearing into the flow of afternoon traffic.

Beside her, Oliver adjusted his Codex carrying strap and performed one final check of Ilza's harness and equipment pouches. His mantis companion submitted to the inspection with patient dignity.

"I'll finish mapping the complete resonance schema once I get home," he said without looking directly at her, his mind already racing ahead to the research possibilities that awaited him at home. "If your sync training shows any unusual anomalies or develops unexpected patterns, write me immediately. I want to compare results with my theoretical models."

Cassara smirked, feeling genuine fondness for his single-minded dedication to understanding their magical connections. "I'll write you. About some things, anyway."

Liri, of course, did not believe in subtle or restrained gestures.

"I absolutely hate goodbyes," she wailed dramatically, flinging her arms around Cassara's neck as if they hadn't just spent the entire journey sitting side by side. "Weekly letters, or I swear I'll show up at your family estate and make the kind of scene that gets talked about for years."

"I'm counting on it," Cassara murmured, hugging her back with genuine warmth and allowing herself to sink into the comfort of unconditional friendship.

Nym zipped in lazy spirals above their heads, trailing glimmers of golden pollen-like powder that caught the breeze and scattered across the platform.

Cassara pulled away slowly, savoring the moment before reality reasserted itself. As she did, she caught a glimpse of movement that made her stomach clench with familiar tension.

Julian stood on the far side of the plaza, positioned where he could observe the entire terminal without being easily approached. He was flanked by a small retinue of servants dressed in the distinctive emerald and black livery of House Tremaine.

He hadn't approached her since the night of the leviathan attack. Not once during the final days at the academy, not even for the basic courtesies that their families' close friendship typically demanded.

But his eyes were on her now, tracking her movements with the patience of a predator that knew its prey couldn't escape forever.

When their gazes met across the crowded space, he smiled. The expression was cold, knowing in ways that made her stomach twist.

There was no fury left in that look. No heated anger or wounded pride. Just that slow, cruel calculation that always meant he was planning something that would hurt in ways she couldn't imagine.

Just wait until summer, that smile said with crystalline clarity. *When Gideon isn't around to play the hero. When you're alone and vulnerable and I have all the time in the world.*

She knew at that moment that he was done chasing her.

He was going to wait until she came to a stop, and then he'd strike.

Cassara didn't flinch or look away immediately. She met his stare with level composure, refusing to give him the satisfaction of seeing her intimidated.

But when she finally turned her head, breaking the silent confrontation, the chill of his attention lingered because she knew with absolute certainty that the game between them wasn't over.

Julian, however, was a problem for another time.

Waiting across the crowded platform in a space that had been carefully cleared of other passengers, stood Lord Allencourt. He wore a fitted coat of dark wool with silver trim that marked his governmental position, and he checked his pocket watch with all the warmth and personal interest of a banker tallying figures in a ledger.

No wave of greeting. No gesture of welcome or acknowledgment of her achievements.

Just expectation wrapped in expensive cloth and political necessity.

Cassara's steps slowed involuntarily as she took in the familiar sight of her father's studied indifference.

Why had he come to collect her?

"Cassara?"

She turned at the sound of her name, spoken in a voice that had become as familiar as her own heartbeat over the past months.

Gideon stood a few paces away, arms crossed lightly over his chest in a pose that managed to be both casual and alert. The wind tugged at a loose curl that had fallen across his brow, and he made no effort to smooth it back into place. He didn't speak immediately, just studied her with eyes that always seemed to see more than she was comfortable revealing.

"You going to be alright?"

The question hit harder than it should have, carrying layers of meaning that went far deeper than simple concern for her immediate welfare. Was he asking about Julian's obvious hostility? Her father's cold reception? The long summer months ahead filled with political maneuvering and family expectations?

All of it, probably.

She didn't answer right away. Instead, her gaze dropped to Flicker, who had abandoned all dignity and was now chasing a bright butterfly across the terminal's carefully maintained grass border. He circled and leapt and occasionally tripped over his own paws in giddy pursuit, completely absorbed in the simple joy of the moment.

So utterly unaware of anything beyond the immediate pleasure of play.

So perfectly, brilliantly free.

Cassara drew in a slow, steadying breath and felt some of his infectious contentment settle over her.

"I will be," she said softly, meaning it more than she'd expected.

Gideon nodded once, like he believed her completely and without reservation.

She gave him a parting smile that carried more confidence than she felt but was real nonetheless, then turned toward the waiting vehicle that would carry her back to everything she'd left behind.

Her chin stayed high as she walked, spine straight with the deportment that had been drilled into her since childhood.

She was Cassara Allencourt, after all. And that meant something, even when, especially when, the world tried to tell her otherwise.

"Cassara, wait."

Gideon's voice stopped her mid-step. She turned to find him approaching, something serious stealing over his face in a way that made her pulse quicken.

"I just… I wanted you to know that my feelings haven't changed," he said quietly, close enough now that his words wouldn't carry to the other students still milling about the dock. "I know that you need space, time to figure things out…"

Her heart skipped at the careful way he spoke, as if he was giving her permission to walk away without looking back.

"But," he added, and a crooked smile tugged at the edge of his mouth, "I lied about something."

Her brow furrowed. "What?"

"I said I wouldn't wait," he continued, reaching into his coat. "The truth is, I've been waiting for five years. What's a few more months?"

Cassara blinked, confusion threading through her. "Five years? What do you mean..."

The words died in her throat as Gideon withdrew something small and held it out to her—a decorative dagger, its silver blade tarnished but unmistakable.

"You dropped this," he said simply, pressing the familiar weight into her palm.

She stared down at the weapon, her mind grasping for something just out of reach. The ornate handle, the delicate engravings... she knew this blade, but from where? When?

"Gideon, what—"

But when she looked up, he was gone. Already walking away toward his own transport, leaving her standing there with her heart hammering and a thousand questions burning in her throat.

What was that about? Flicker asked, appearing at her feet with a butterfly wing caught on his whisker. *He smells like secrets.*

"I don't know," she whispered, closing her fingers around the dagger.

Five years. The words echoed in her mind, stubborn and inexplicable. What had happened five years ago that she couldn't remember? And why did this dagger feel like a key to a door she'd forgotten existed?

"Cassara."

Her father's voice cut through her spiraling thoughts, sharp with impatience. She looked up to find him approaching, his expression unreadable but clearly displeased with the delay she was causing.

"The car is waiting," he said, not sparing a glance for the weapon in her hand.

She slipped the dagger quickly into her coat pocket, its weight settling against her ribs like a secret that demanded answers. Later. When she was alone and could think clearly, she would figure out what Gideon had meant.

"Of course," she said, falling into step beside him with practiced composure.

But as their carriage pulled away from the platform, Cassara found herself touching the hidden blade through the fabric of her pocket.

Five years.

Whatever had happened, whatever she'd forgotten, the summer would give her time to remember.

She didn't know what was coming. But whatever it was, she had a feeling this was only the beginning.

CONTENT WARNINGS

- Explicit Sexual Content
- Attempted Sexual Assault
- Emotional abuse
- Slight Age Gap
- Power Imbalance
- Fantasy combat and battle scenes
- Physical danger and injury
- Parental emotional abuse and manipulation
- Public humiliation

Avelley Greer is a romance and fantasy author who firmly believes that the best stories happen when magic gets messy and love gets complicated.

Growing up devouring the works of Robin Hobb, Tad Williams, Madeleine L'Engle, and Philip Pullman, Avelley learned early that the most compelling tales live in the grey areas—where heroes make terrible decisions, villains have excellent points, and nobody's moral compass points quite north.

When not conjuring up new ways to torment beloved characters (before giving them their hard-won happily-ever-afters, of course), Avelley can be found:

- Ugly-crying over the latest K-drama plot twist
- Defending unpopular BTS theories with the passion of a thousand suns
- Playing survival horror games while all four cats—Oliver, Hobi, Rosie, and Nova—judge from various perches
- Watching horror movies through strategically placed fingers

Avelley writes for readers who appreciate their fantasy with sharp edges, their romance with real stakes, and their happy endings earned through blood, sweat, and maybe a few supernatural tears. She's particularly drawn to stories featuring morally grey characters, unconventional magic systems, and relationships that challenge everything we think we know about love.

Currently plotting her next novel while surrounded by too many notebooks, an unreasonable amount of purple pens, and at least one cat who's definitely plotting world domination.

SOCIALS

Follow Me!

Want to stay up to date on the upcoming releases, sneak peaks, and other bookish related content?

Mailing List – subscribepage.io/m96ZTx
Instagram – https://www.instagram.com/avelley_greer/
Tiktok – https://www.tiktok.com/@authoravelleygreer

Want More...?

A KISS SO CRUEL

Book One of the Fractured Crown Trilogy

A HUNT SO WILD

Book Two of the Fractured Crown Trilogy

RACING RUIN

A Dark Contemporary Romance

Available on Barnes & Noble, Amazon & Kindle Unlimited

www.ingramcontent.com/pod-product-compliance
Lightning Source LLC
LaVergne TN
LVHW100459110826
845146LV00002B/457

* 9 7 9 8 9 9 4 9 6 8 0 1 7 *